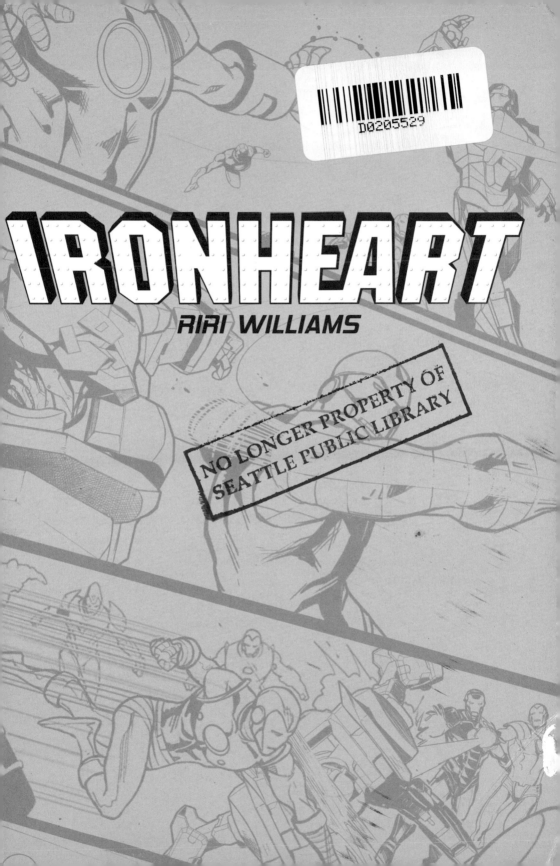

IRONHEART

RIRI WILLIAMS

CONTENTS

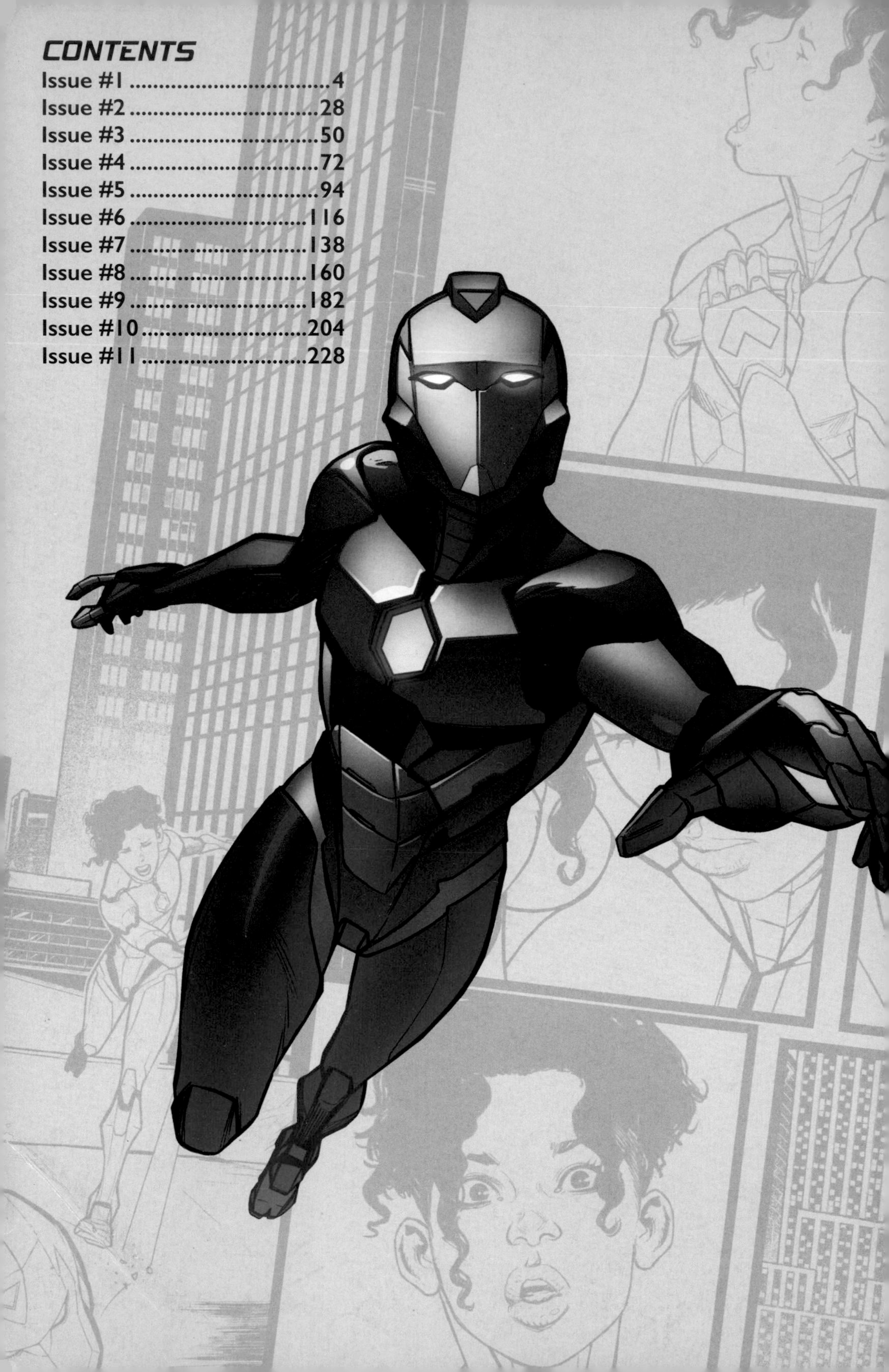

IRONHEART

RIRI WILLIAMS

WRITER
BRIAN MICHAEL BENDIS

ARTISTS
STEFANO CASELLI
WITH **KATE NIEMCZYK** (#11), **TAKI SOMA** (#11),
& **KIICHI MIZUSHIMA** (#11)

COLOR ARTISTS
MARTE GRACIA
WITH **ISRAEL SILVA** (#9-10)

LETTERER
VC's CLAYTON COWLES

COVER ART
STEFANO CASELLI & MARTE GRACIA (#6-8, #10),
DANIEL ACUÑA (#9) AND **JESÚS SAIZ** (#11)

ASSISTANT EDITOR
ALANNA SMITH

EDITOR
TOM BREVOORT

collection editor JENNIFER GRÜNWALD
assistant editor CAITLIN O'CONNELL • associate managing editor KATERI WOODY
editor, special projects MARK D. BEAZLEY • vp production & special projects JEFF YOUNGQUIST

director, licensed publishing SVEN LARSEN • svp print, sales & marketing DAVID GABRIEL
editor in chief C.B. CEBULSKI • chief creative officer JOE QUESADA
president DAN BUCKLEY • executive producer ALAN FINE

IRONHEART: RIRI WILLIAMS. Contains material originally published in magazine form as INVINCIBLE IRON MAN #1-11. First printing 2019. ISBN 978-1-302-91979-5. Published by MARVEL WORLDWIDE, INC., a subsidiary of MARVEL ENTERTAINMENT, LLC. OFFICE OF PUBLICATION: 135 West 50th Street, New York, NY 10020. **Printed in Canada.** DAN BUCKLEY, President, Marvel Entertainment; JOHN NEE, Publisher; JOE QUESADA, Chief Creative Officer; TOM BREVOORT, SVP of Publishing; DAVID BOGART, Associate Publisher & SVP of Talent Affairs; DAVID GABRIEL, SVP of Sales & Marketing, Publishing; JEFF YOUNGQUIST, VP of Production & Special Projects; DAN CARR, Executive Director of Publishing Technology; ALEX MORALES, Director of Publishing Operations; DAN EDINGTON, Managing Editor; SUSAN CRESPI, Production Manager; STAN LEE, Chairman Emeritus. For information regarding advertising in Marvel Comics or on Marvel.com, please contact Vit DeBellis, Custom Solutions & Integrated Advertising Manager, at vdebellis@marvel.com. For Marvel subscription inquiries, please call 888-511-5480. **Manufactured between 8/23/2019 and 9/24/2019 by SOLISCO PRINTERS, SCOTT, QC, CANADA.**

10 9 8 7 6 5 4 3 2 1

1

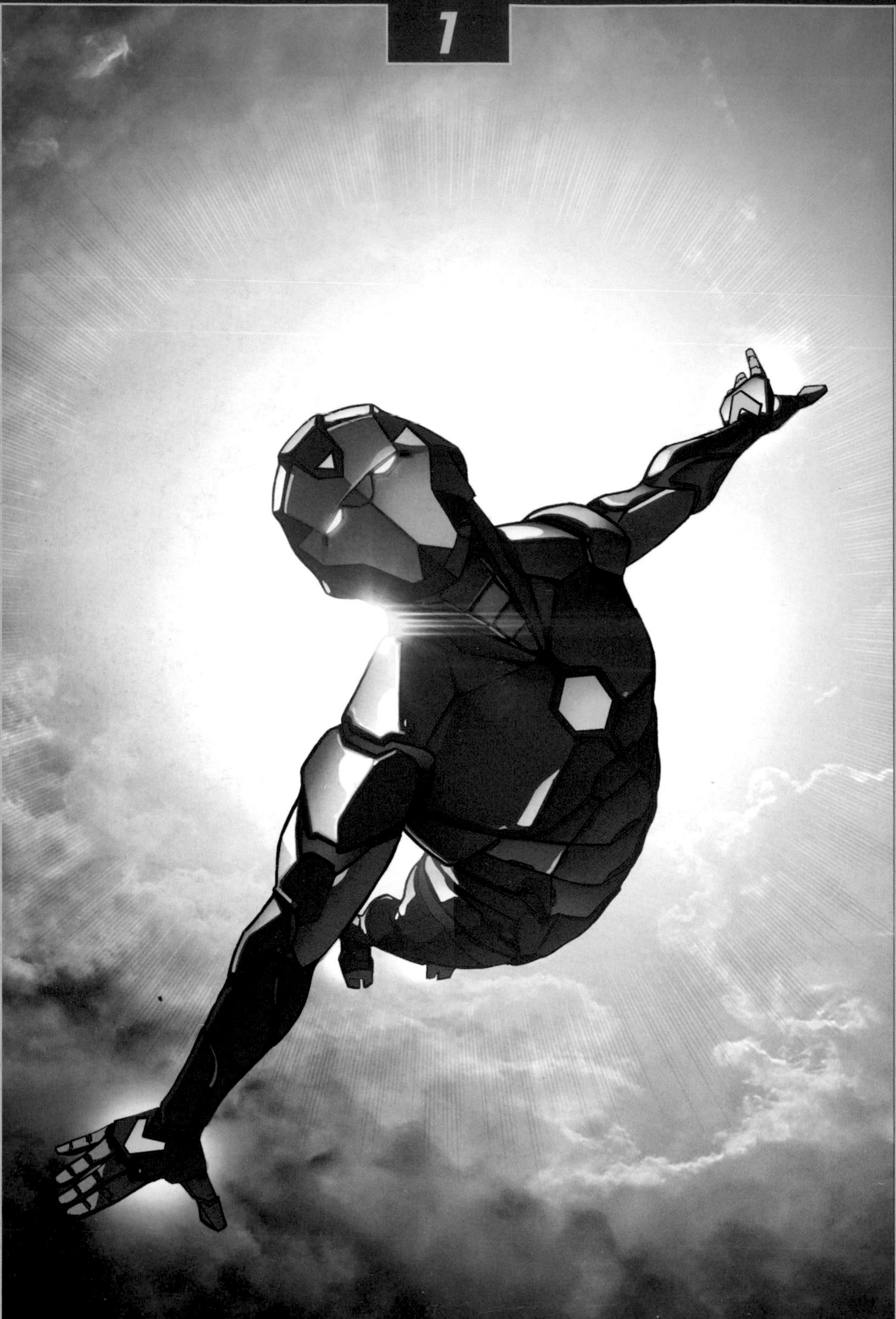

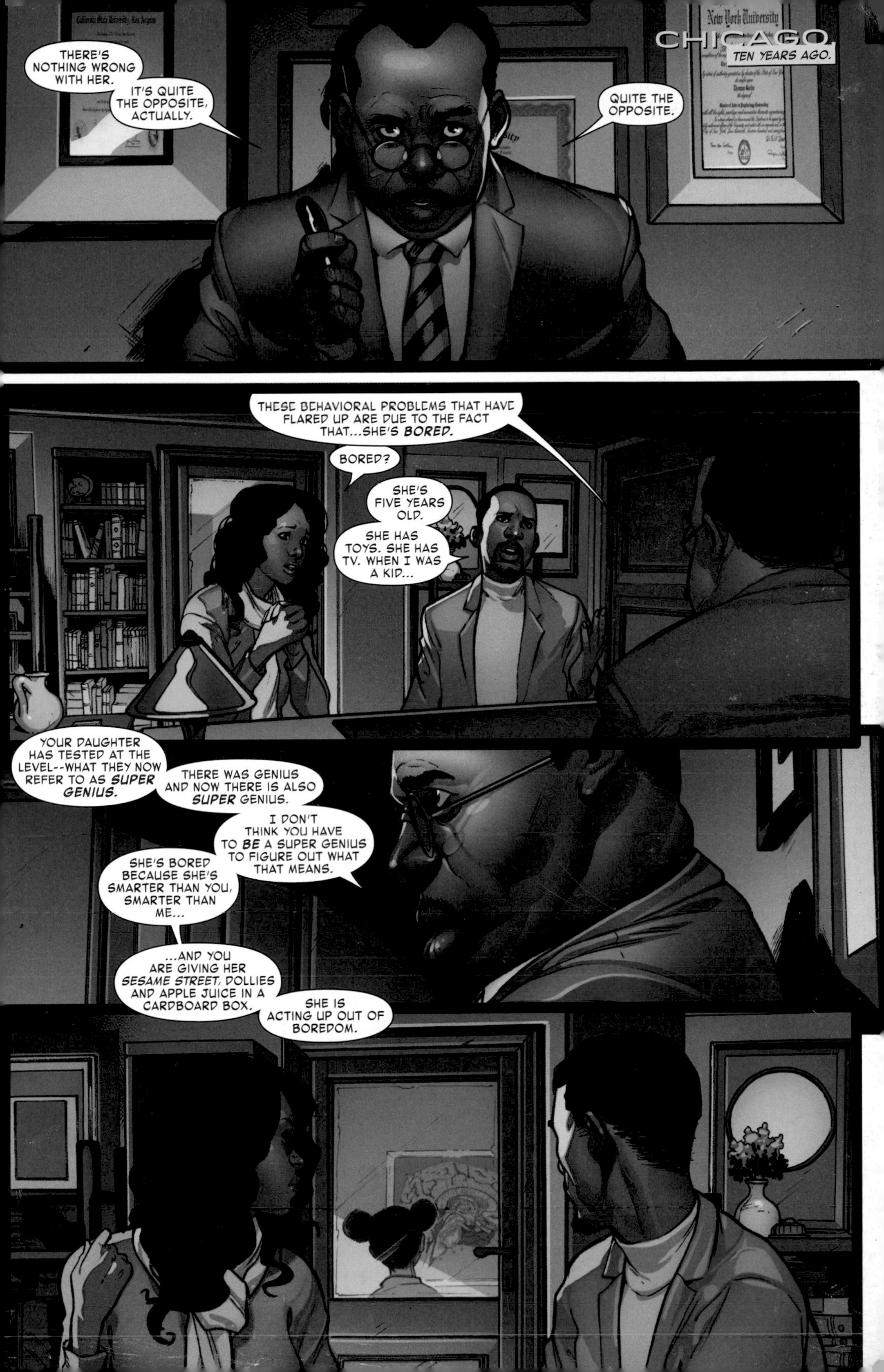
CHICAGO
TEN YEARS AGO.
THERE'S NOTHING WRONG WITH HER.
IT'S QUITE THE OPPOSITE, ACTUALLY.
QUITE THE OPPOSITE.
THESE BEHAVIORAL PROBLEMS THAT HAVE FLARED UP ARE DUE TO THE FACT THAT...SHE'S BORED.
BORED?
SHE'S FIVE YEARS OLD.
SHE HAS TOYS. SHE HAS TV. WHEN I WAS A KID...
YOUR DAUGHTER HAS TESTED AT THE LEVEL--WHAT THEY NOW REFER TO AS SUPER GENIUS.
THERE WAS GENIUS AND NOW THERE IS ALSO SUPER GENIUS.
I DON'T THINK YOU HAVE TO BE A SUPER GENIUS TO FIGURE OUT WHAT THAT MEANS.
SHE'S BORED BECAUSE SHE'S SMARTER THAN YOU, SMARTER THAN ME...
...AND YOU ARE GIVING HER SESAME STREET, DOLLIES AND APPLE JUICE IN A CARDBOARD BOX.
SHE IS ACTING UP OUT OF BOREDOM.

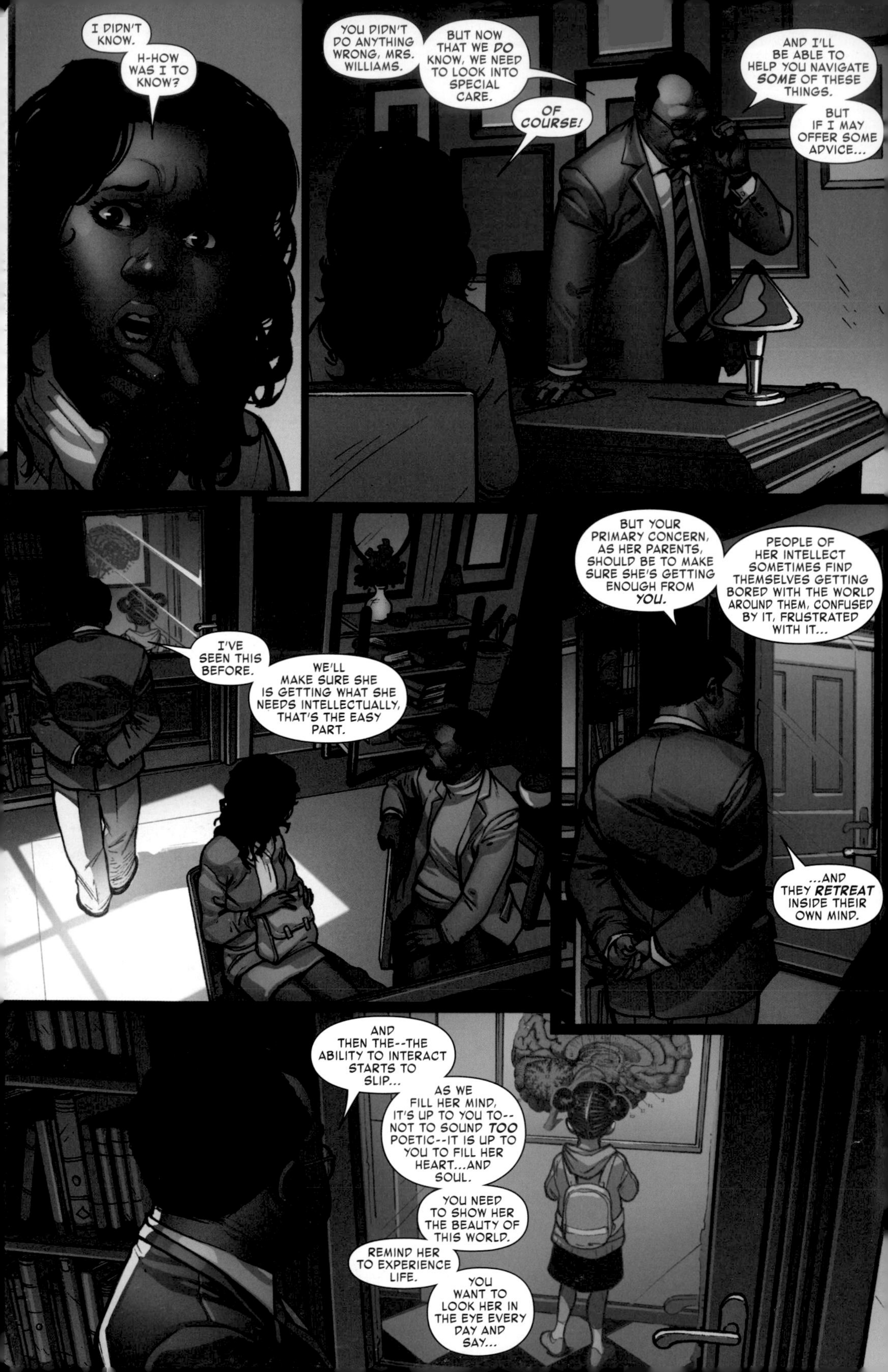
I DIDN'T KNOW.
H-HOW WAS I TO KNOW?
YOU DIDN'T DO ANYTHING WRONG, MRS. WILLIAMS.
BUT NOW THAT WE *DO* KNOW, WE NEED TO LOOK INTO SPECIAL CARE.
OF COURSE!
AND I'LL BE ABLE TO HELP YOU NAVIGATE *SOME* OF THESE THINGS.
BUT IF I MAY OFFER SOME ADVICE...
I'VE SEEN THIS BEFORE.
WE'LL MAKE SURE SHE IS GETTING WHAT SHE NEEDS INTELLECTUALLY, THAT'S THE EASY PART.
BUT YOUR PRIMARY CONCERN, AS HER PARENTS, SHOULD BE TO MAKE SURE SHE'S GETTING ENOUGH FROM *YOU.*
PEOPLE OF HER INTELLECT SOMETIMES FIND THEMSELVES GETTING BORED WITH THE WORLD AROUND THEM, CONFUSED BY IT, FRUSTRATED WITH IT...
...AND THEY *RETREAT* INSIDE THEIR OWN MIND.
AND THEN THE--THE ABILITY TO INTERACT STARTS TO SLIP...
AS WE FILL HER MIND, IT'S UP TO YOU TO--NOT TO SOUND *TOO* POETIC--IT IS UP TO YOU TO FILL HER HEART...AND SOUL.
YOU NEED TO SHOW HER THE BEAUTY OF THIS WORLD.
REMIND HER TO EXPERIENCE LIFE.
YOU WANT TO LOOK HER IN THE EYE EVERY DAY AND SAY...

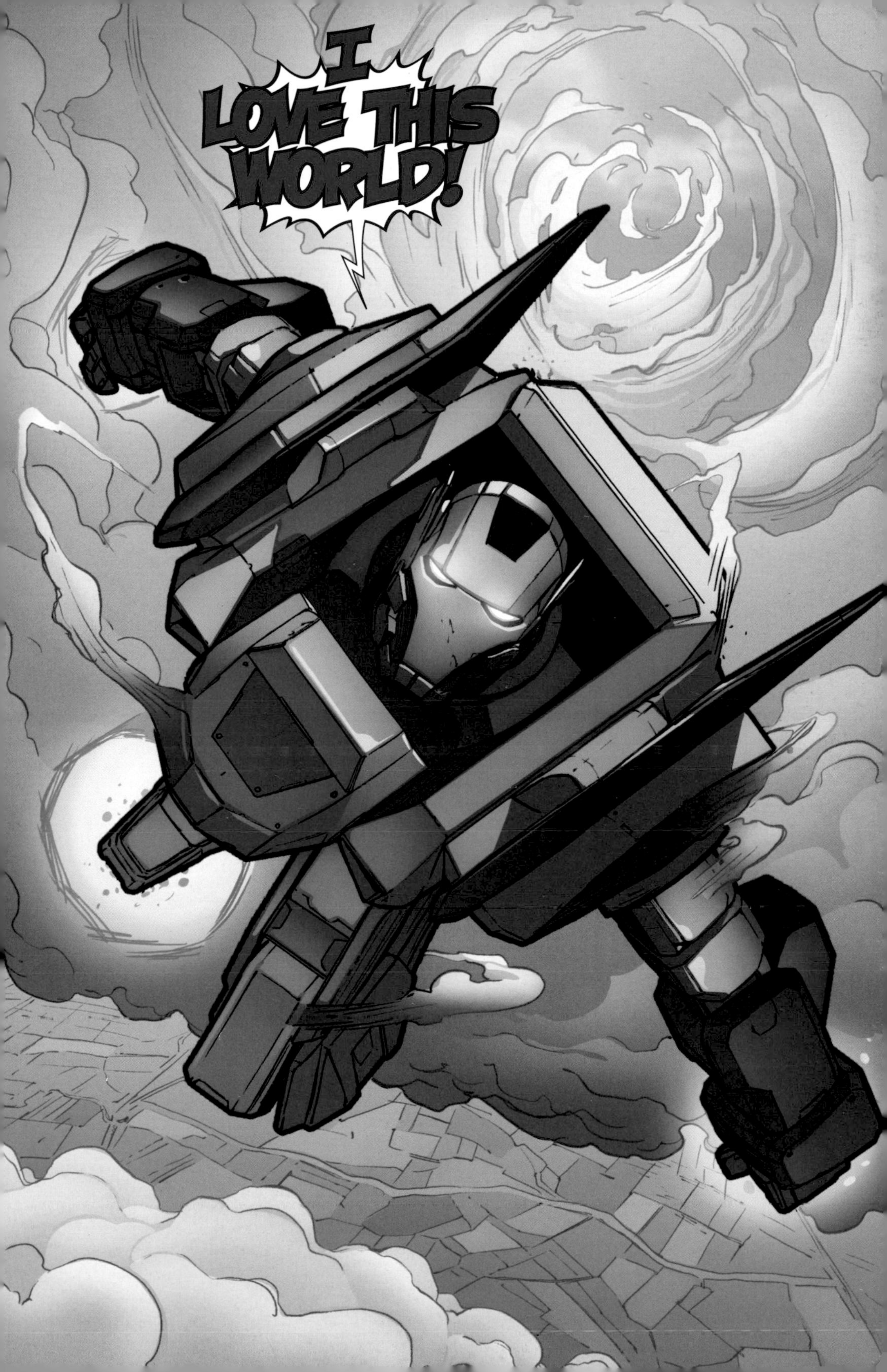
I LOVE THIS WORLD!

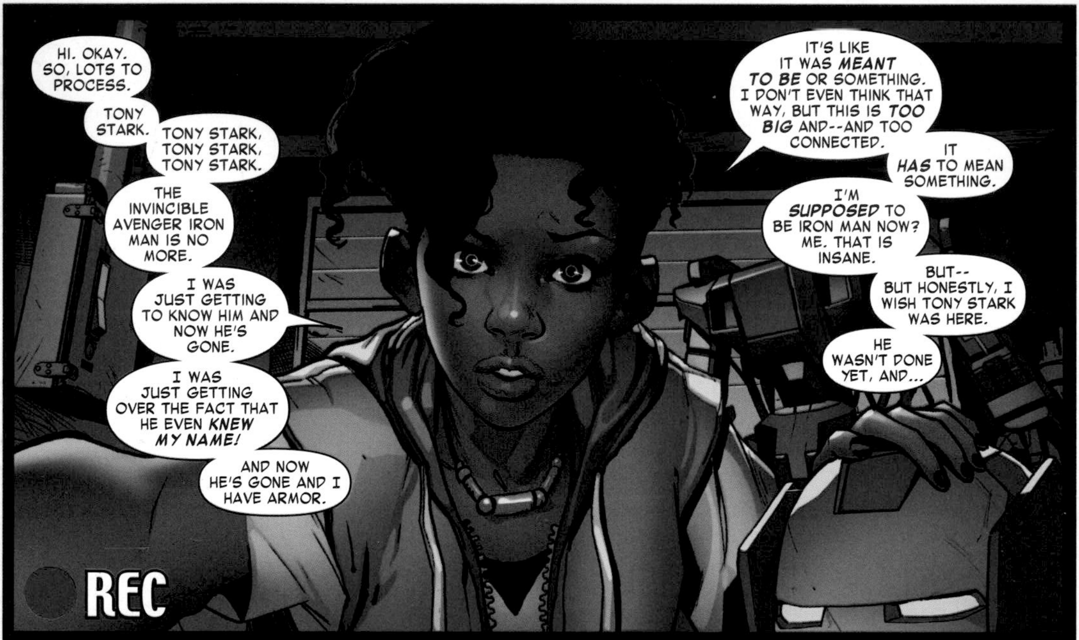
HI. OKAY. SO, LOTS TO PROCESS.
TONY STARK.
TONY STARK, TONY STARK, TONY STARK.
THE INVINCIBLE AVENGER IRON MAN IS NO MORE.
I WAS JUST GETTING TO KNOW HIM AND NOW HE'S GONE.
I WAS JUST GETTING OVER THE FACT THAT HE EVEN *KNEW MY NAME!*
AND NOW HE'S GONE AND I HAVE ARMOR.
IT'S LIKE IT WAS *MEANT TO BE* OR SOMETHING. I DON'T EVEN THINK THAT WAY, BUT THIS IS *TOO BIG* AND--AND TOO CONNECTED.
IT *HAS* TO MEAN SOMETHING.
I'M *SUPPOSED* TO BE IRON MAN NOW? ME. THAT IS INSANE.
BUT-- BUT HONESTLY, I WISH TONY STARK WAS HERE.
HE WASN'T DONE YET, AND...
REC

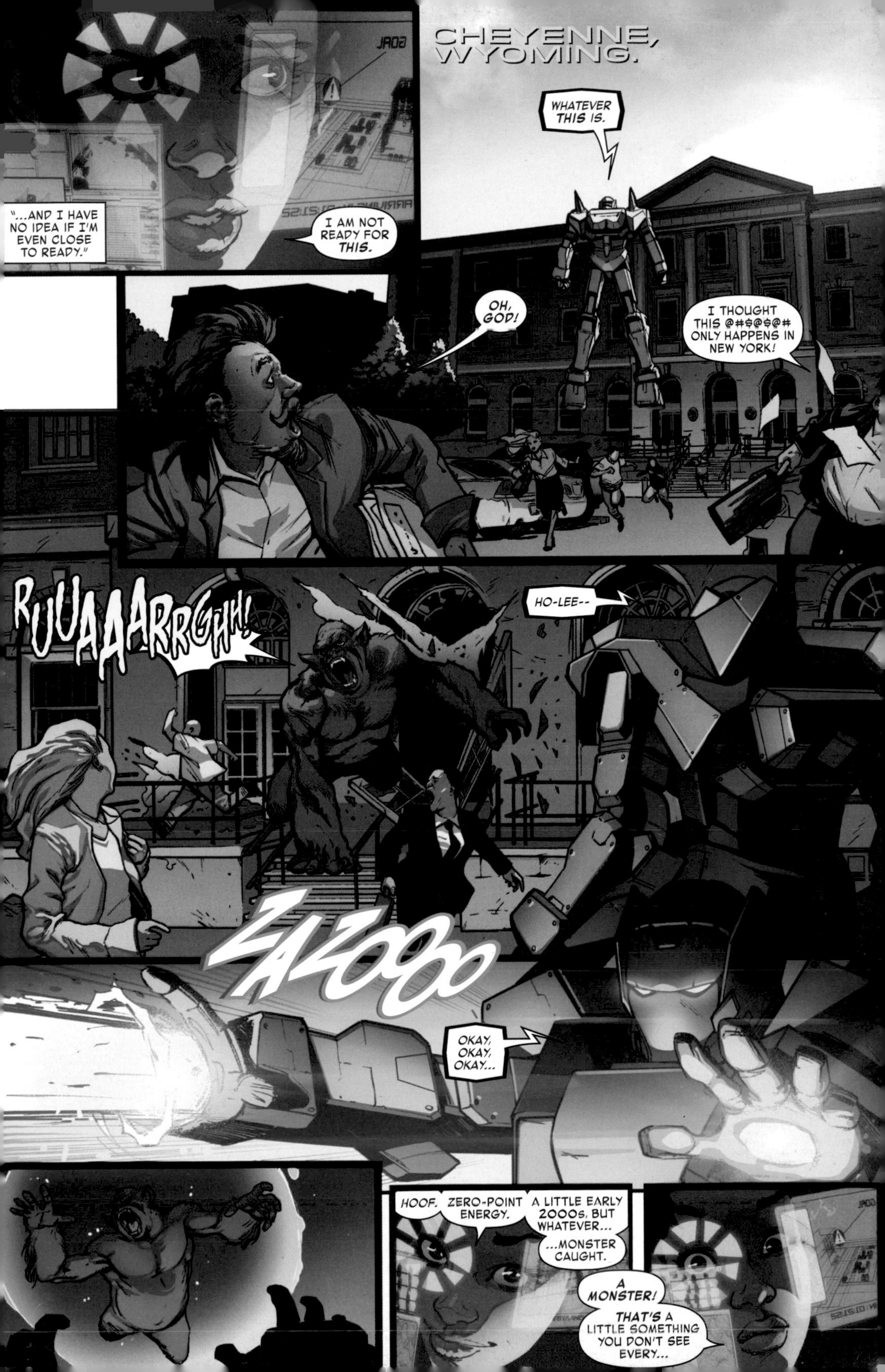

"...AND I HAVE NO IDEA IF I'M EVEN CLOSE TO READY."
I AM NOT READY FOR THIS.
CHEYENNE, WYOMING.
WHATEVER THIS IS.
OH, GOD!
I THOUGHT THIS @#$@$@# ONLY HAPPENS IN NEW YORK!
RUUAAARRGHH!
HO-LEE--
ZAZOOOO
OKAY, OKAY, OKAY...
HOOF.
ZERO-POINT ENERGY.
A LITTLE EARLY 2000s, BUT WHATEVER...
...MONSTER CAUGHT.
A MONSTER!
THAT'S A LITTLE SOMETHING YOU DON'T SEE EVERY...

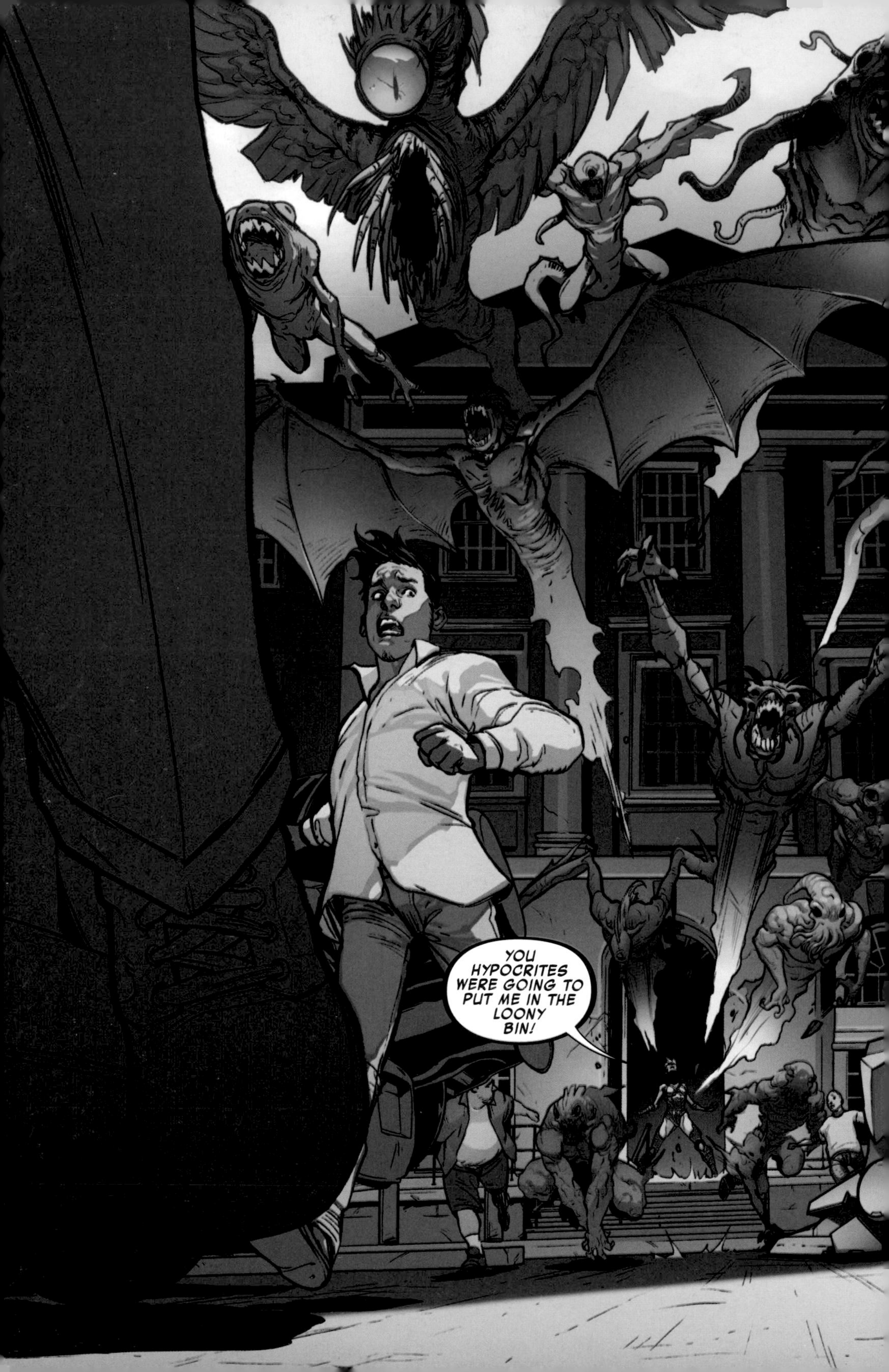
YOU HYPOCRITES WERE GOING TO PUT ME IN THE LOONY BIN!

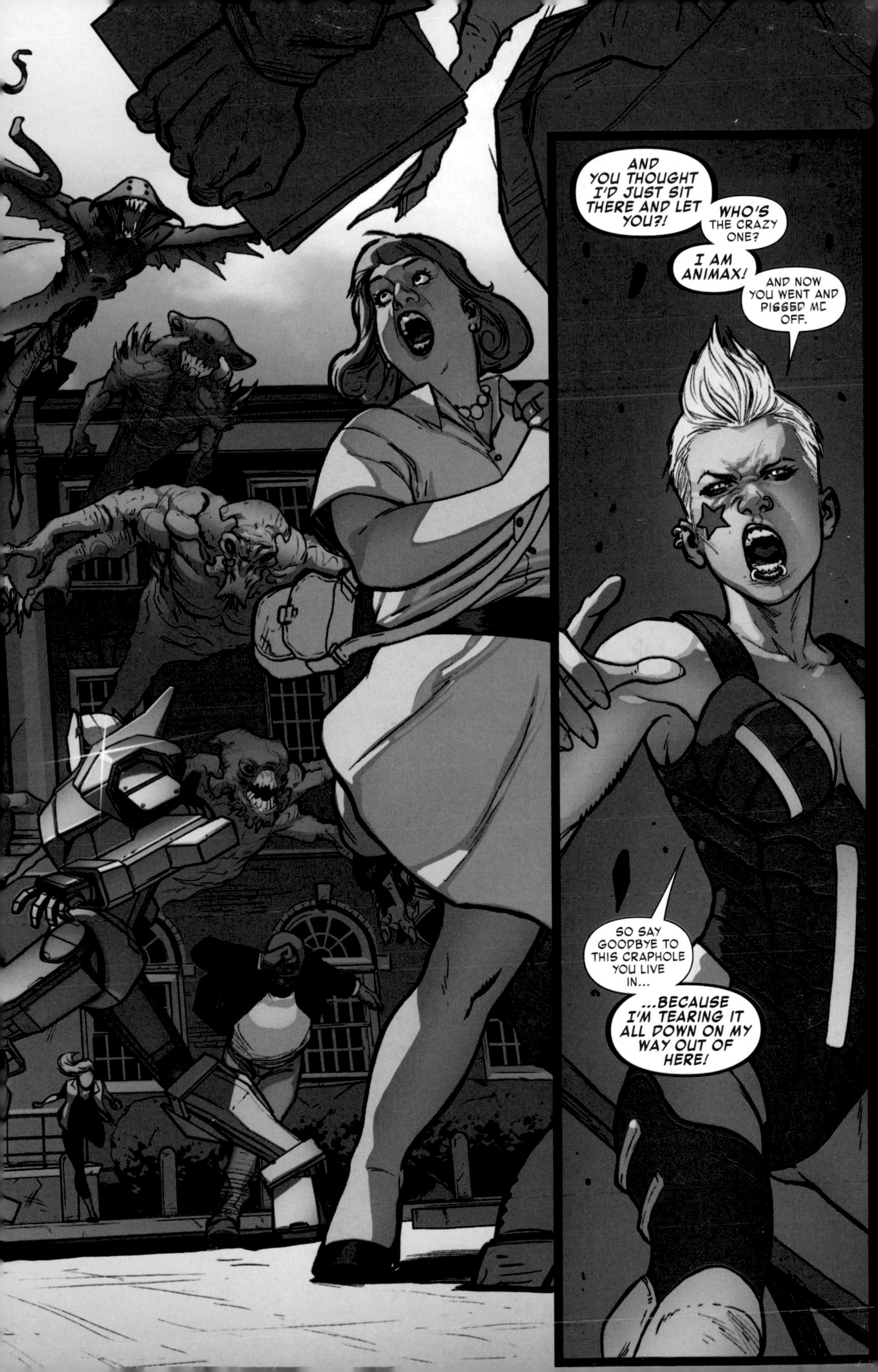
AND YOU THOUGHT I'D JUST SIT THERE AND LET YOU?!
WHO'S THE CRAZY ONE?
I AM ANIMAX!
AND NOW YOU WENT AND PISSED ME OFF.
SO SAY GOODBYE TO THIS CRAPHOLE YOU LIVE IN...
...BECAUSE I'M TEARING IT ALL DOWN ON MY WAY OUT OF HERE!

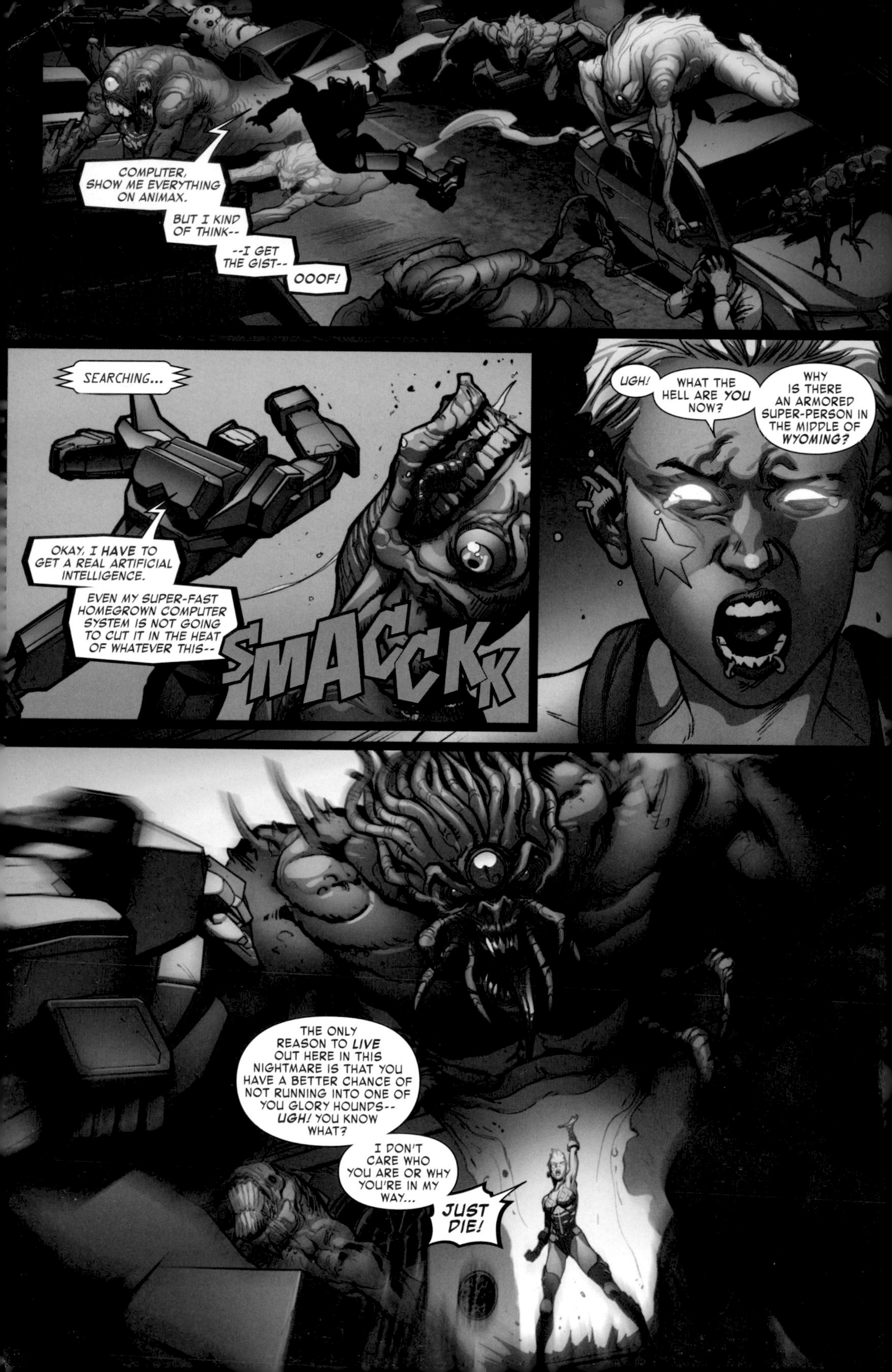
COMPUTER, SHOW ME EVERYTHING ON ANIMAX.
BUT I KIND OF THINK--
--I GET THE GIST--
OOOF!
SEARCHING...
OKAY, I HAVE TO GET A REAL ARTIFICIAL INTELLIGENCE.
EVEN MY SUPER-FAST HOMEGROWN COMPUTER SYSTEM IS NOT GOING TO CUT IT IN THE HEAT OF WHATEVER THIS--
SMACCKK
UGH!
WHAT THE HELL ARE YOU NOW?
WHY IS THERE AN ARMORED SUPER-PERSON IN THE MIDDLE OF WYOMING?
THE ONLY REASON TO LIVE OUT HERE IN THIS NIGHTMARE IS THAT YOU HAVE A BETTER CHANCE OF NOT RUNNING INTO ONE OF YOU GLORY HOUNDS-- UGH! YOU KNOW WHAT?
I DON'T CARE WHO YOU ARE OR WHY YOU'RE IN MY WAY...
JUST DIE!

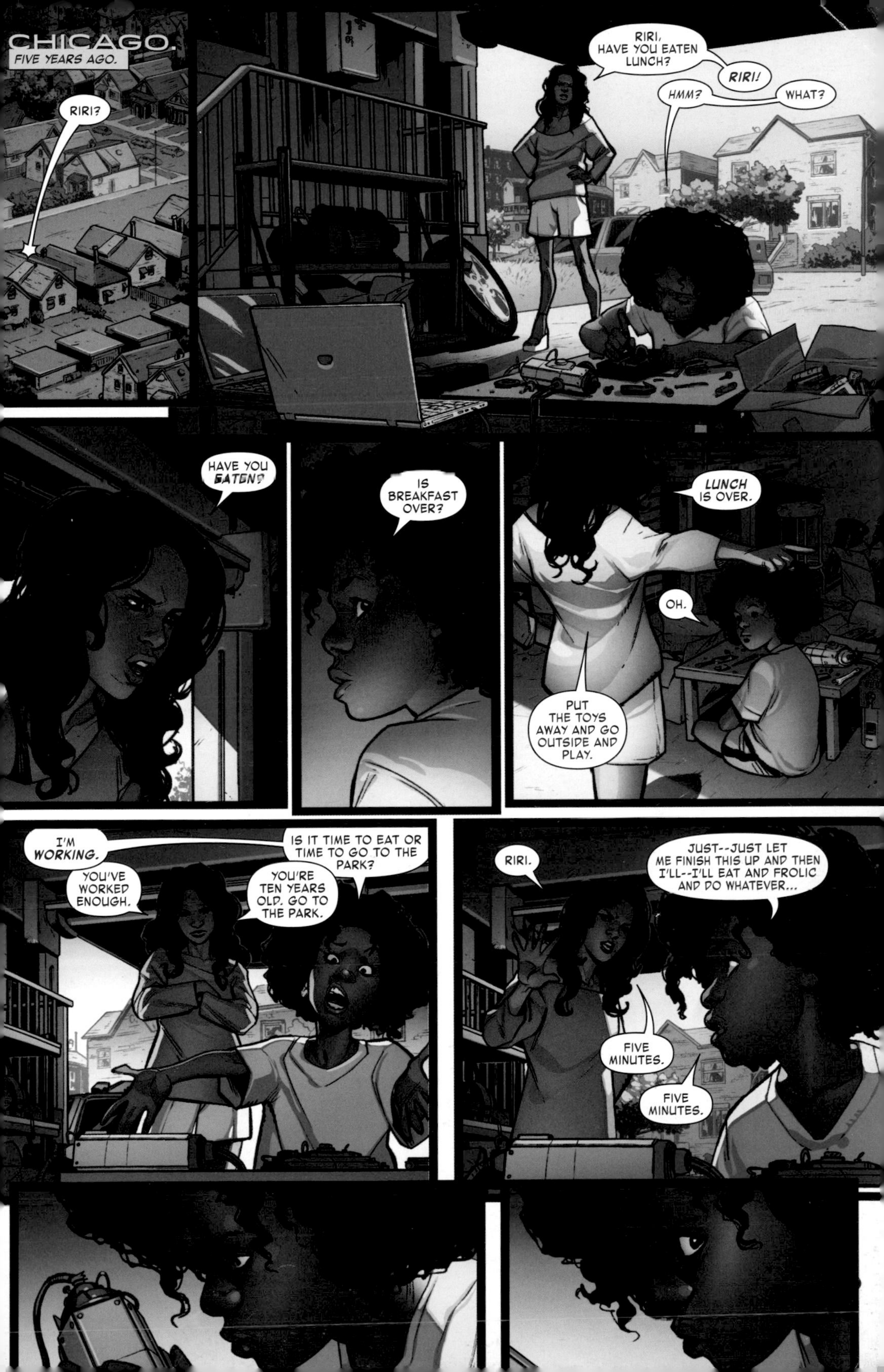
CHICAGO.
FIVE YEARS AGO.
RIRI?
RIRI, HAVE YOU EATEN LUNCH?
RIRI!
HMM?
WHAT?
HAVE YOU EATEN?
IS BREAKFAST OVER?
LUNCH IS OVER.
OH.
PUT THE TOYS AWAY AND GO OUTSIDE AND PLAY.
I'M WORKING.
IS IT TIME TO EAT OR TIME TO GO TO THE PARK?
YOU'VE WORKED ENOUGH.
YOU'RE TEN YEARS OLD. GO TO THE PARK.
RIRI.
JUST--JUST LET ME FINISH THIS UP AND THEN I'LL--I'LL EAT AND FROLIC AND DO WHATEVER...
FIVE MINUTES.
FIVE MINUTES.

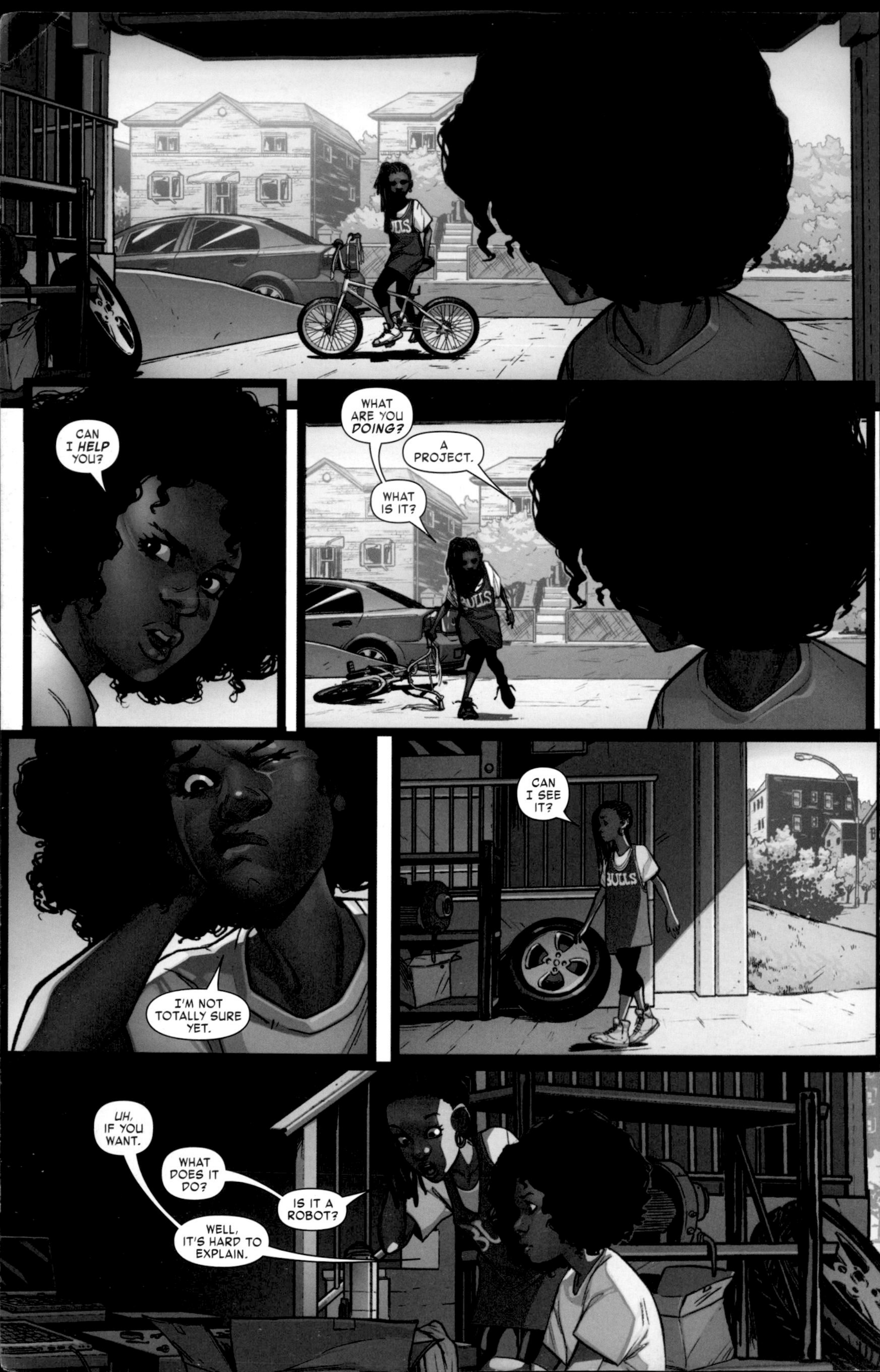
CAN I *HELP* YOU?
WHAT ARE YOU *DOING?*
A PROJECT.
WHAT IS IT?
I'M NOT TOTALLY SURE YET.
CAN I SEE IT?
UH, IF YOU WANT.
WHAT DOES IT DO?
IS IT A ROBOT?
WELL, IT'S HARD TO EXPLAIN.

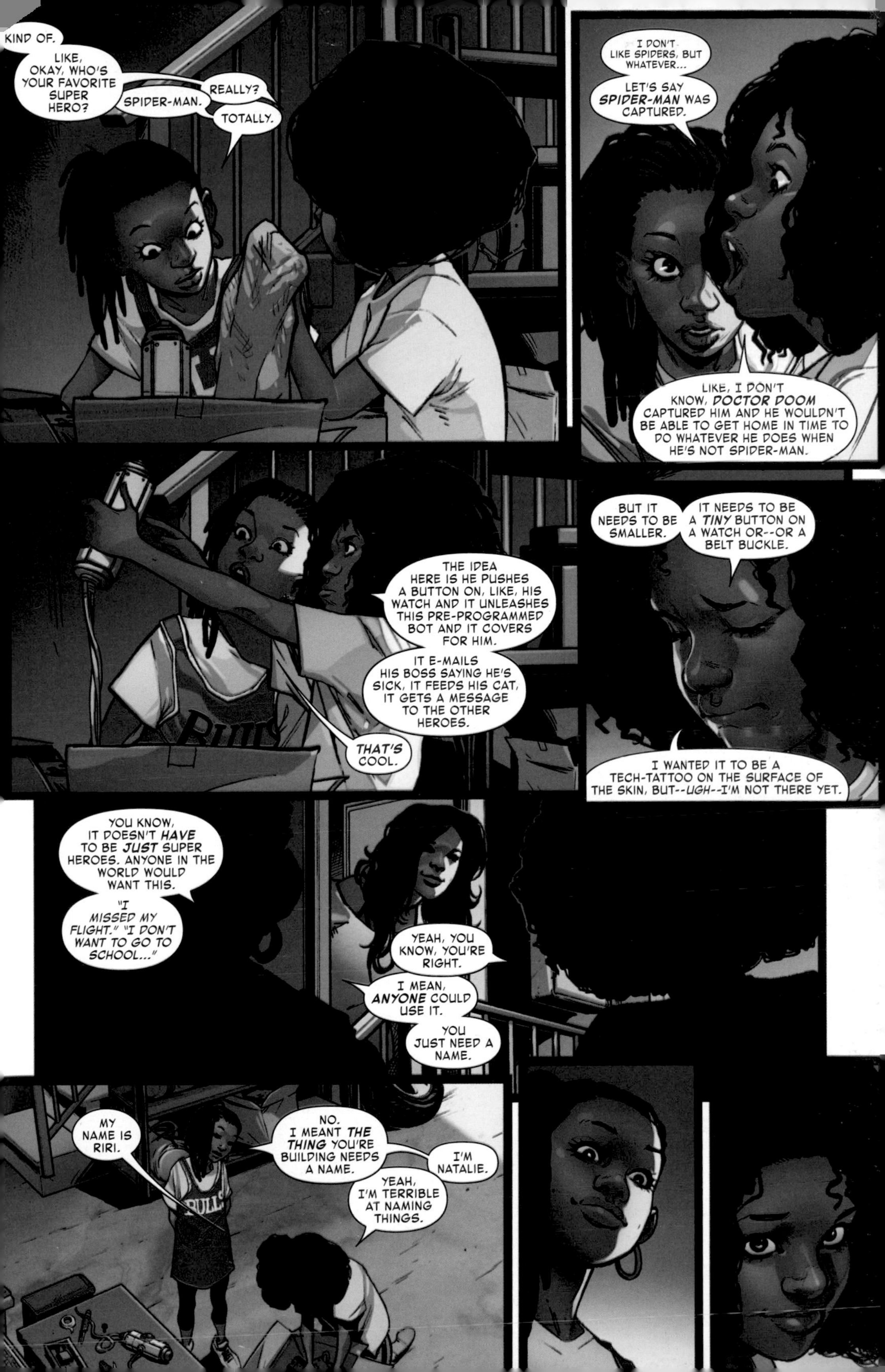
KIND OF.
LIKE, OKAY, WHO'S YOUR FAVORITE SUPER HERO?
SPIDER-MAN.
REALLY?
TOTALLY.
I DON'T LIKE SPIDERS, BUT WHATEVER...
LET'S SAY SPIDER-MAN WAS CAPTURED.
LIKE, I DON'T KNOW, DOCTOR DOOM CAPTURED HIM AND HE WOULDN'T BE ABLE TO GET HOME IN TIME TO DO WHATEVER HE DOES WHEN HE'S NOT SPIDER-MAN.
THE IDEA HERE IS HE PUSHES A BUTTON ON, LIKE, HIS WATCH AND IT UNLEASHES THIS PRE-PROGRAMMED BOT AND IT COVERS FOR HIM.
IT E-MAILS HIS BOSS SAYING HE'S SICK, IT FEEDS HIS CAT, IT GETS A MESSAGE TO THE OTHER HEROES.
THAT'S COOL.
BUT IT NEEDS TO BE SMALLER.
IT NEEDS TO BE A TINY BUTTON ON A WATCH OR--OR A BELT BUCKLE.
I WANTED IT TO BE A TECH-TATTOO ON THE SURFACE OF THE SKIN, BUT--UGH--I'M NOT THERE YET.
YOU KNOW, IT DOESN'T HAVE TO BE JUST SUPER HEROES. ANYONE IN THE WORLD WOULD WANT THIS.
"I MISSED MY FLIGHT." "I DON'T WANT TO GO TO SCHOOL..."
YEAH, YOU KNOW, YOU'RE RIGHT.
I MEAN, ANYONE COULD USE IT.
YOU JUST NEED A NAME.
MY NAME IS RIRI.
NO. I MEANT THE THING YOU'RE BUILDING NEEDS A NAME.
I'M NATALIE.
YEAH, I'M TERRIBLE AT NAMING THINGS.

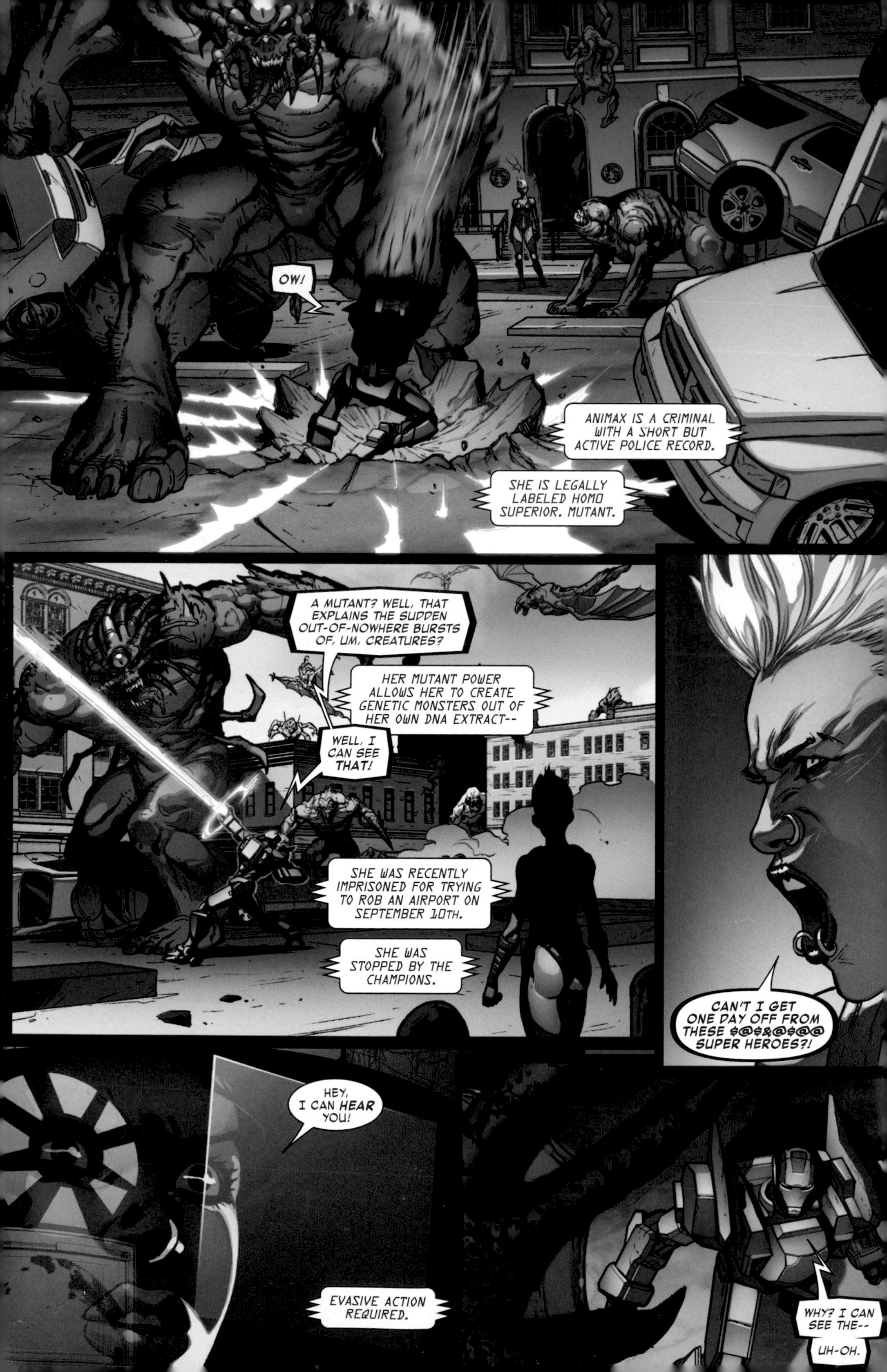
OW!
ANIMAX IS A CRIMINAL WITH A SHORT BUT ACTIVE POLICE RECORD.
SHE IS LEGALLY LABELED HOMO SUPERIOR. MUTANT.
A MUTANT? WELL, THAT EXPLAINS THE SUDDEN OUT-OF-NOWHERE BURSTS OF, UM, CREATURES?
HER MUTANT POWER ALLOWS HER TO CREATE GENETIC MONSTERS OUT OF HER OWN DNA EXTRACT--
WELL, I CAN SEE THAT!
SHE WAS RECENTLY IMPRISONED FOR TRYING TO ROB AN AIRPORT ON SEPTEMBER 10TH.
SHE WAS STOPPED BY THE CHAMPIONS.
CAN'T I GET ONE DAY OFF FROM THESE $@$&@$@@ SUPER HEROES?!
HEY, I CAN HEAR YOU!
EVASIVE ACTION REQUIRED.
WHY? I CAN SEE THE--
UH-OH.

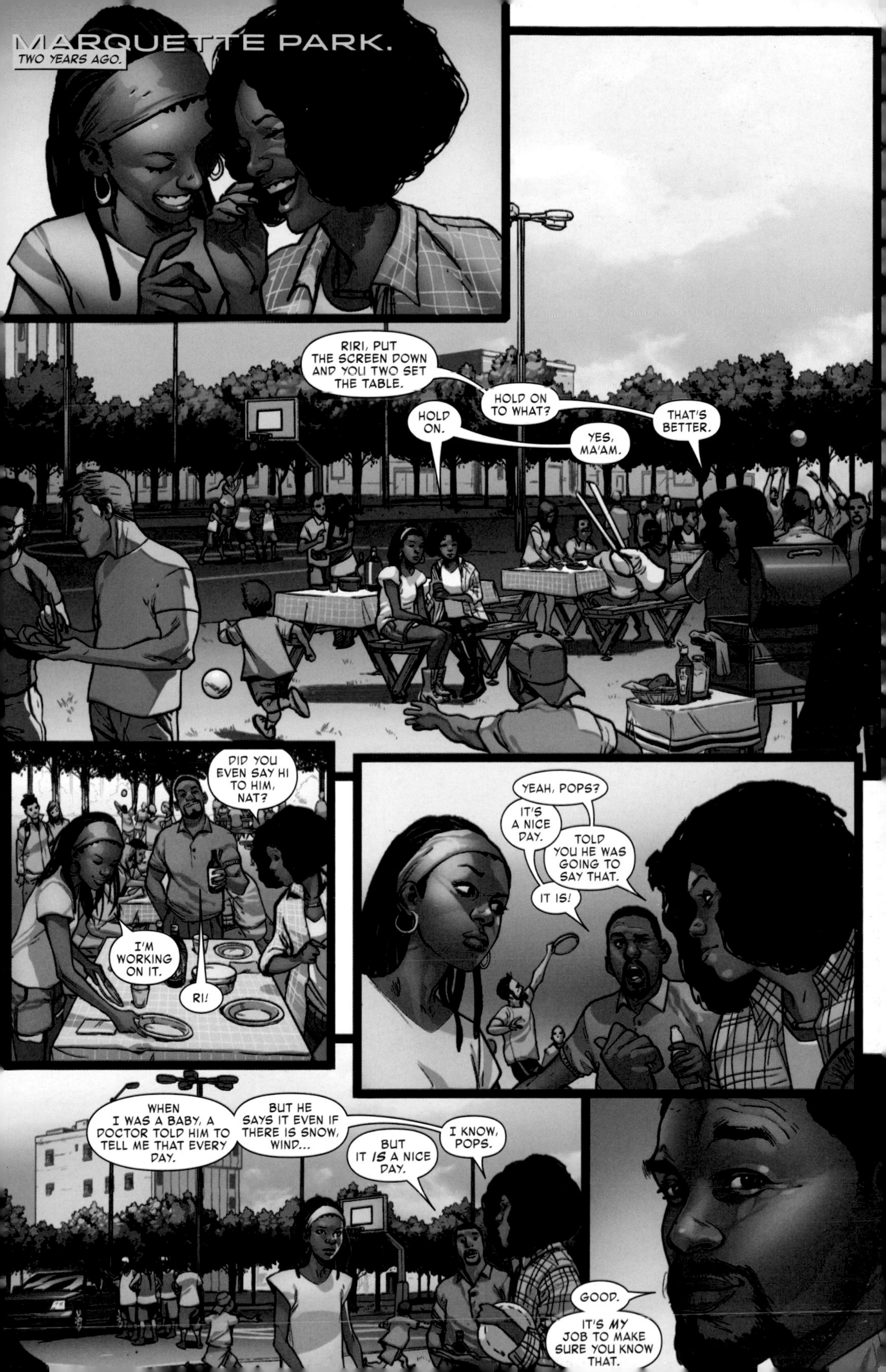
MARQUETTE PARK.
TWO YEARS AGO.
RIRI, PUT THE SCREEN DOWN AND YOU TWO SET THE TABLE.
HOLD ON TO WHAT?
THAT'S BETTER.
HOLD ON.
YES, MA'AM.
DID YOU EVEN SAY HI TO HIM, NAT?
I'M WORKING ON IT.
RI!
YEAH, POPS?
IT'S A NICE DAY.
TOLD YOU HE WAS GOING TO SAY THAT.
IT IS!
WHEN I WAS A BABY, A DOCTOR TOLD HIM TO TELL ME THAT EVERY DAY.
BUT HE SAYS IT EVEN IF THERE IS SNOW, WIND...
BUT IT IS A NICE DAY.
I KNOW, POPS.
GOOD.
IT'S MY JOB TO MAKE SURE YOU KNOW THAT.

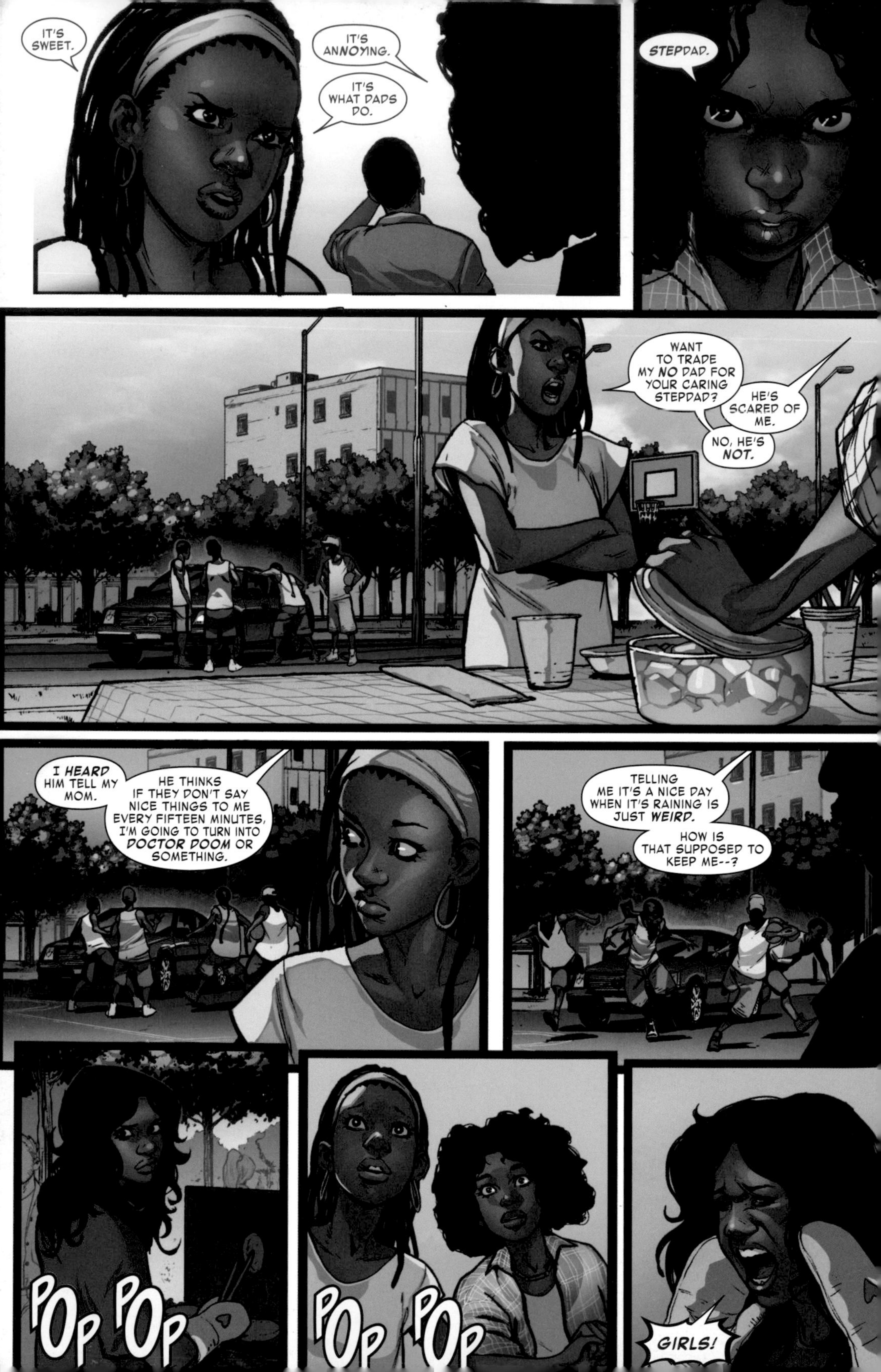
IT'S SWEET.
IT'S ANNOYING.
IT'S WHAT DADS DO.
STEPDAD.
WANT TO TRADE MY NO DAD FOR YOUR CARING STEPDAD?
HE'S SCARED OF ME.
NO, HE'S NOT.
I HEARD HIM TELL MY MOM.
HE THINKS IF THEY DON'T SAY NICE THINGS TO ME EVERY FIFTEEN MINUTES, I'M GOING TO TURN INTO DOCTOR DOOM OR SOMETHING.
TELLING ME IT'S A NICE DAY WHEN IT'S RAINING IS JUST WEIRD.
HOW IS THAT SUPPOSED TO KEEP ME--?
POP POP
POP POP
GIRLS!

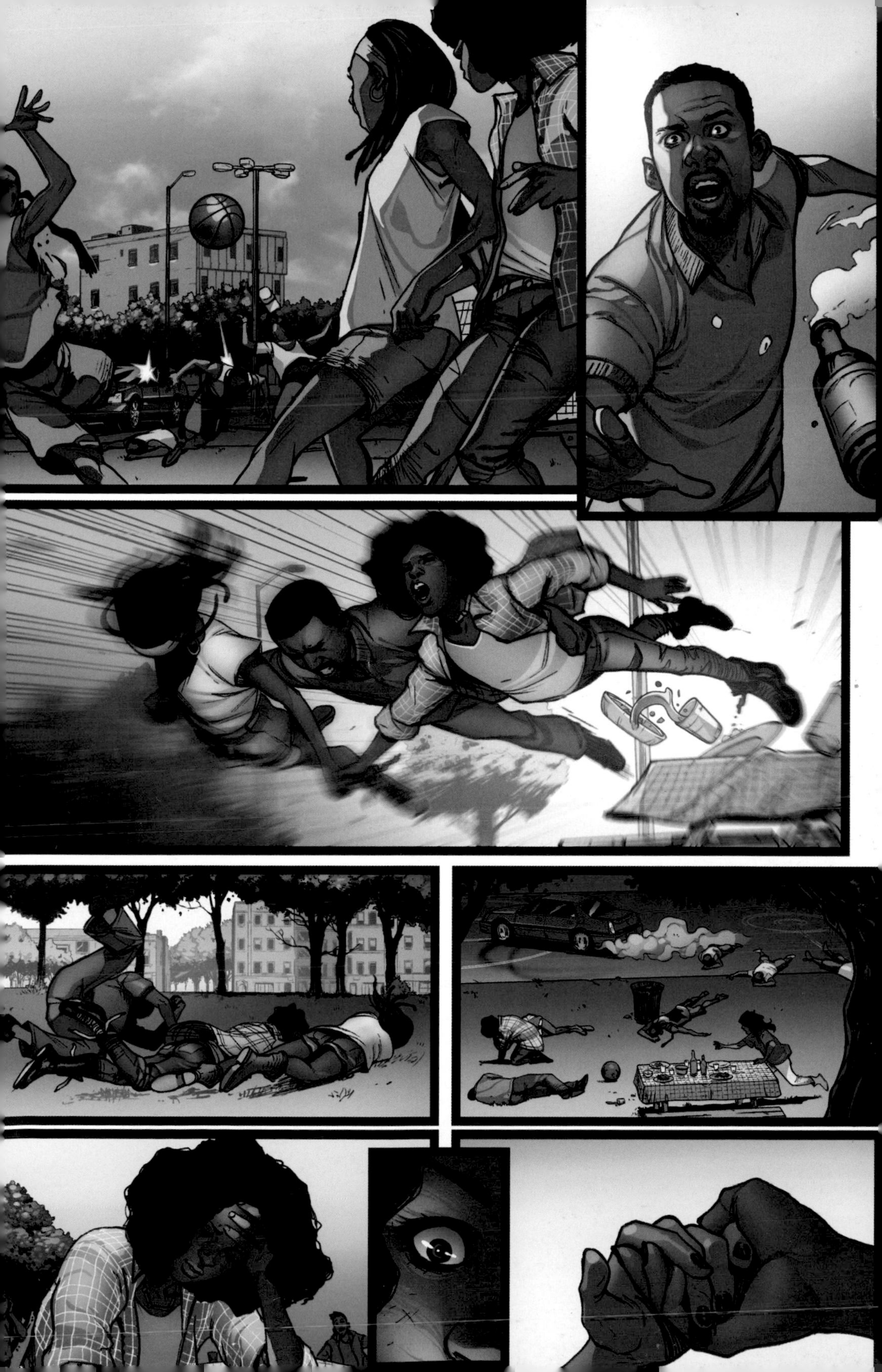

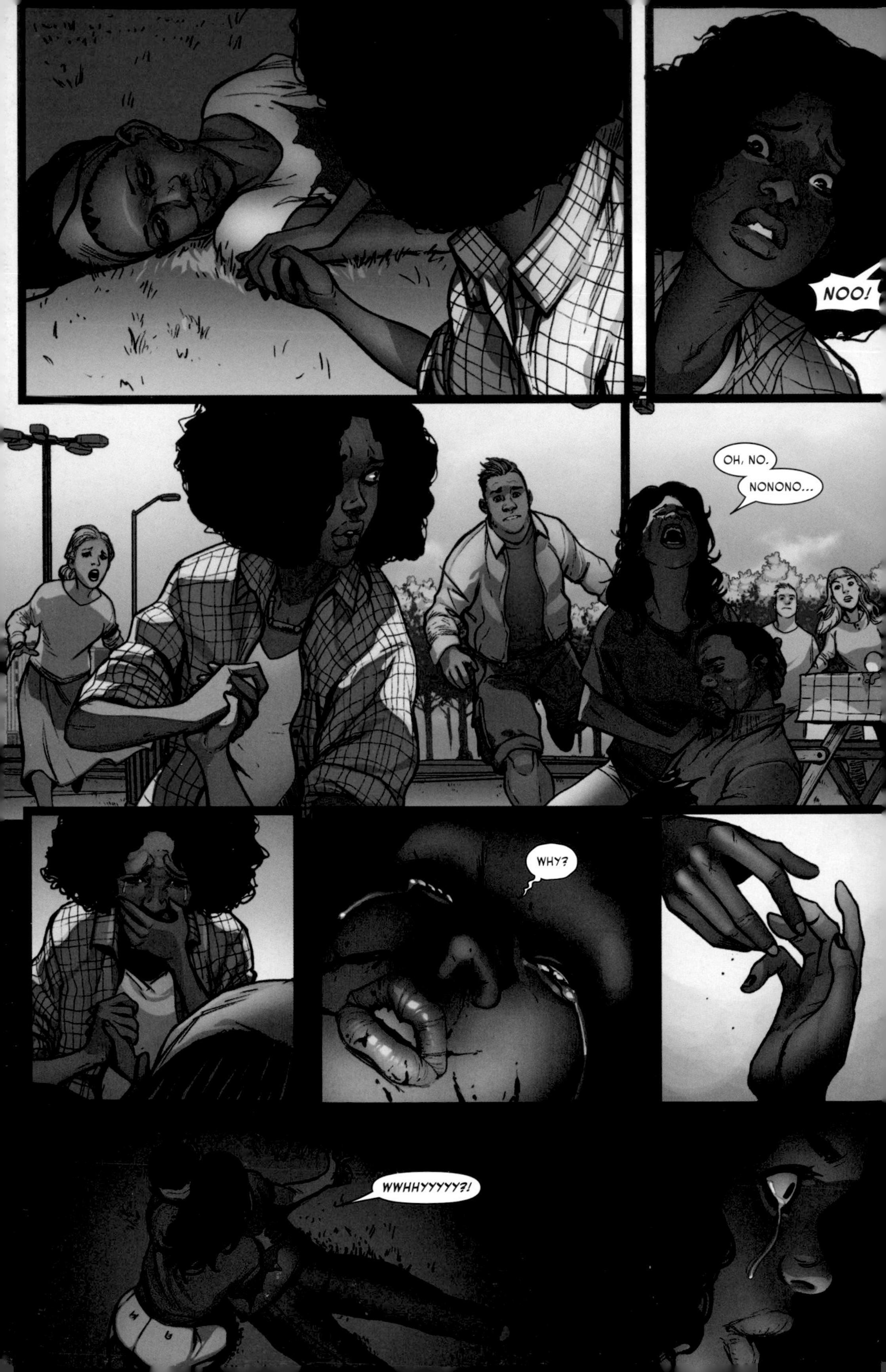
NOO!
OH, NO.
NONONO...
WHY?
WWHHYYYYY?!

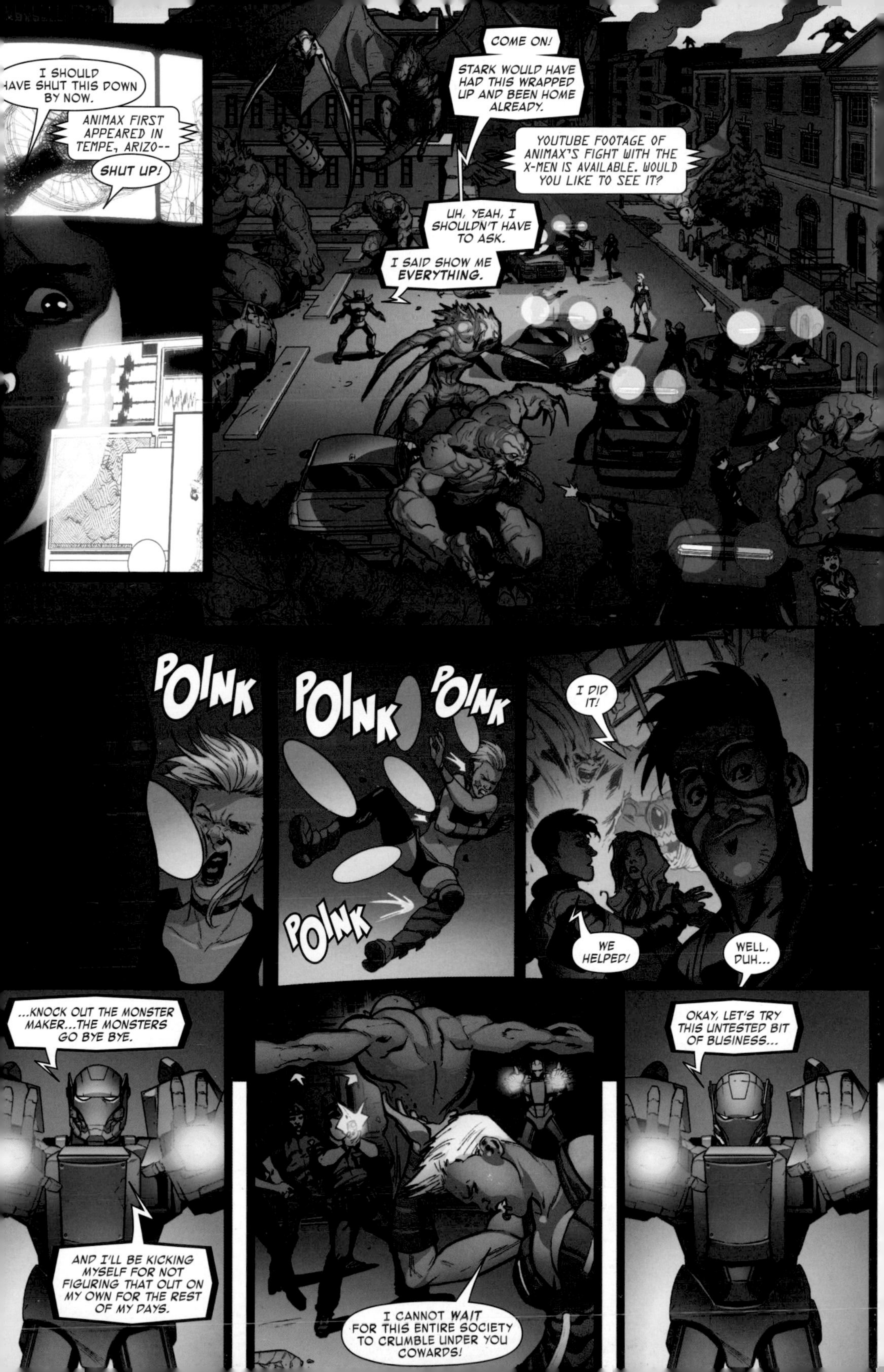

I SHOULD HAVE SHUT THIS DOWN BY NOW.
ANIMAX FIRST APPEARED IN TEMPE, ARIZO--
SHUT UP!
COME ON!
STARK WOULD HAVE HAD THIS WRAPPED UP AND BEEN HOME ALREADY.
YOUTUBE FOOTAGE OF ANIMAX'S FIGHT WITH THE X-MEN IS AVAILABLE. WOULD YOU LIKE TO SEE IT?
UH, YEAH, I SHOULDN'T HAVE TO ASK.
I SAID SHOW ME EVERYTHING.
POINK
POINK
POINK
POINK
I DID IT!
WE HELPED!
WELL, DUH...
...KNOCK OUT THE MONSTER MAKER...THE MONSTERS GO BYE BYE.
AND I'LL BE KICKING MYSELF FOR NOT FIGURING THAT OUT ON MY OWN FOR THE REST OF MY DAYS.
I CANNOT WAIT FOR THIS ENTIRE SOCIETY TO CRUMBLE UNDER YOU COWARDS!
OKAY, LET'S TRY THIS UNTESTED BIT OF BUSINESS...

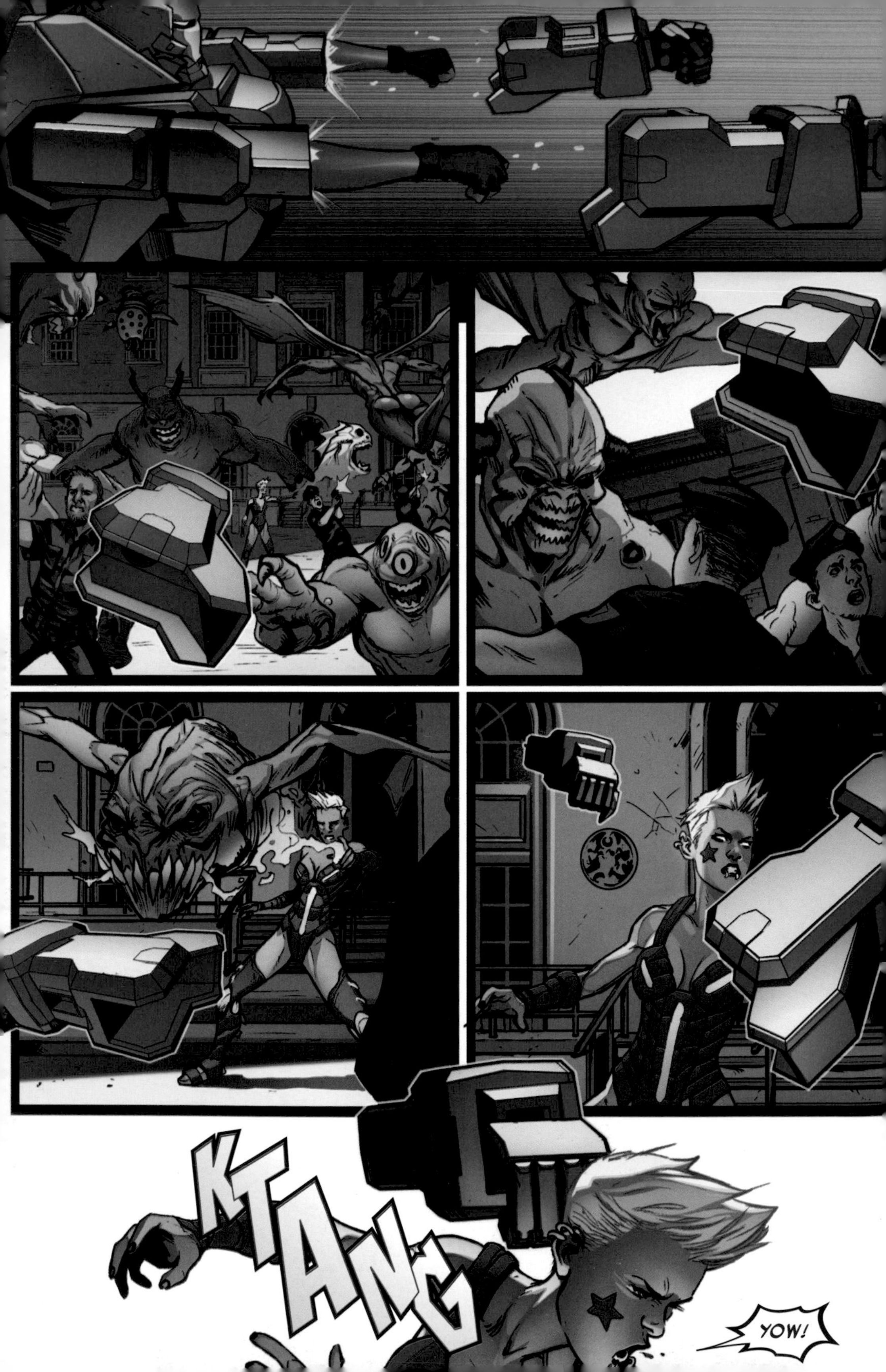
KTANG
YOW!

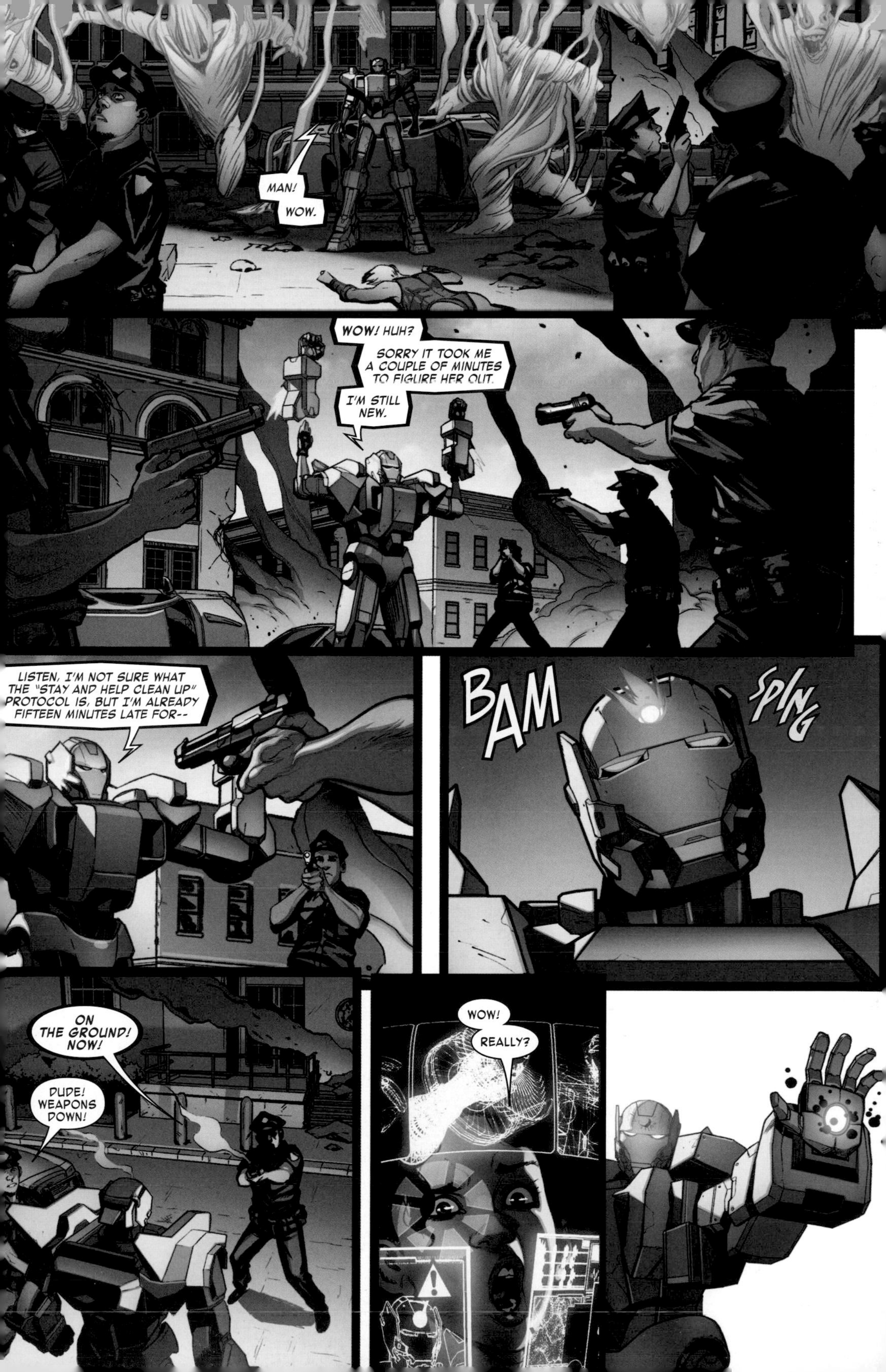
MAN!
WOW.
WOW! HUH?
SORRY IT TOOK ME A COUPLE OF MINUTES TO FIGURE HER OUT.
I'M STILL NEW.
LISTEN, I'M NOT SURE WHAT THE "STAY AND HELP CLEAN UP" PROTOCOL IS, BUT I'M ALREADY FIFTEEN MINUTES LATE FOR--
BAM
SPING
ON THE GROUND! NOW!
DUDE! WEAPONS DOWN!
WOW!
REALLY?

GEEZ!

TANG

RUUNNCHH

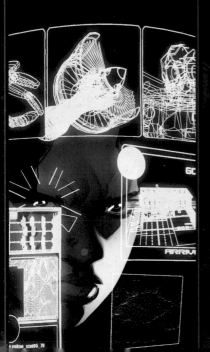

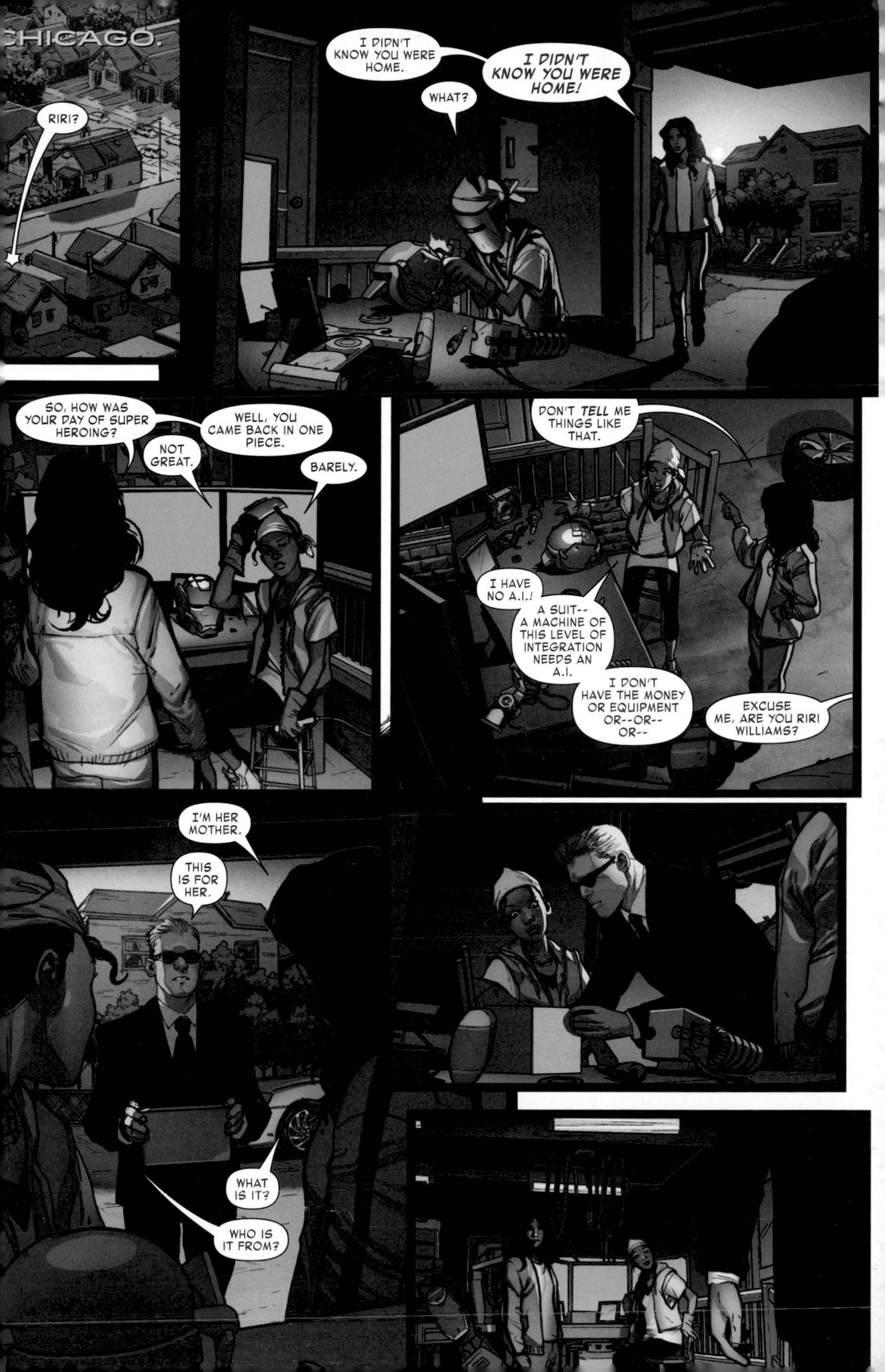
CHICAGO.
RIRI?
I DIDN'T KNOW YOU WERE HOME.
WHAT?
I DIDN'T KNOW YOU WERE HOME!
SO, HOW WAS YOUR DAY OF SUPER HEROING?
NOT GREAT.
WELL, YOU CAME BACK IN ONE PIECE.
BARELY.
DON'T TELL ME THINGS LIKE THAT.
I HAVE NO A.I.!
A SUIT-- A MACHINE OF THIS LEVEL OF INTEGRATION NEEDS AN A.I.
I DON'T HAVE THE MONEY OR EQUIPMENT OR--OR-- OR--
EXCUSE ME, ARE YOU RIRI WILLIAMS?
I'M HER MOTHER.
THIS IS FOR HER.
WHAT IS IT?
WHO IS IT FROM?

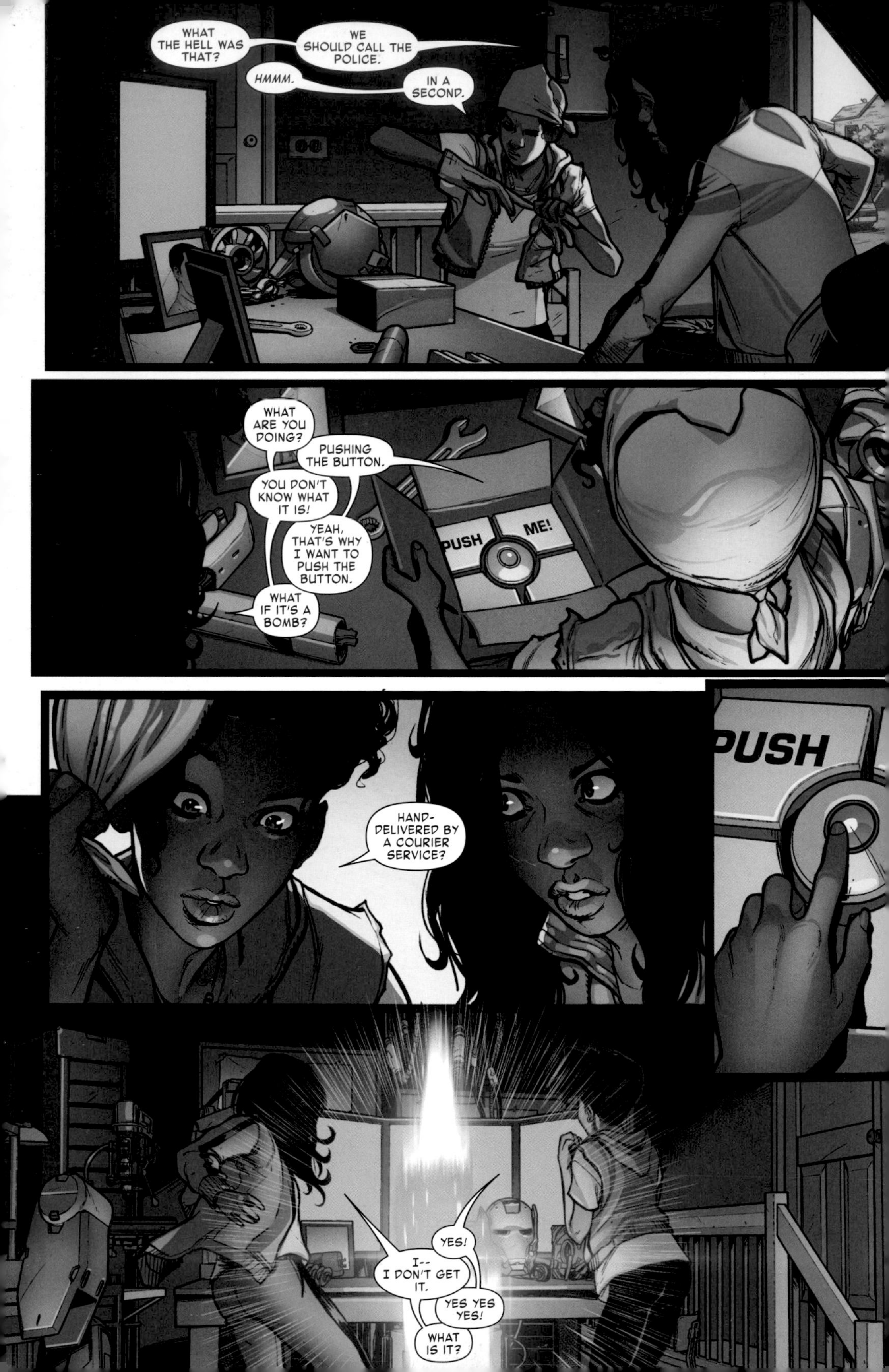
WHAT THE HELL WAS THAT?
WE SHOULD CALL THE POLICE.
HMMM.
IN A SECOND.
WHAT ARE YOU DOING?
PUSHING THE BUTTON.
YOU DON'T KNOW WHAT IT IS!
YEAH, THAT'S WHY I WANT TO PUSH THE BUTTON.
WHAT IF IT'S A BOMB?
PUSH
ME!
HAND-DELIVERED BY A COURIER SERVICE?
PUSH
YES!
I-- I DON'T GET IT.
YES YES YES!
WHAT IS IT?

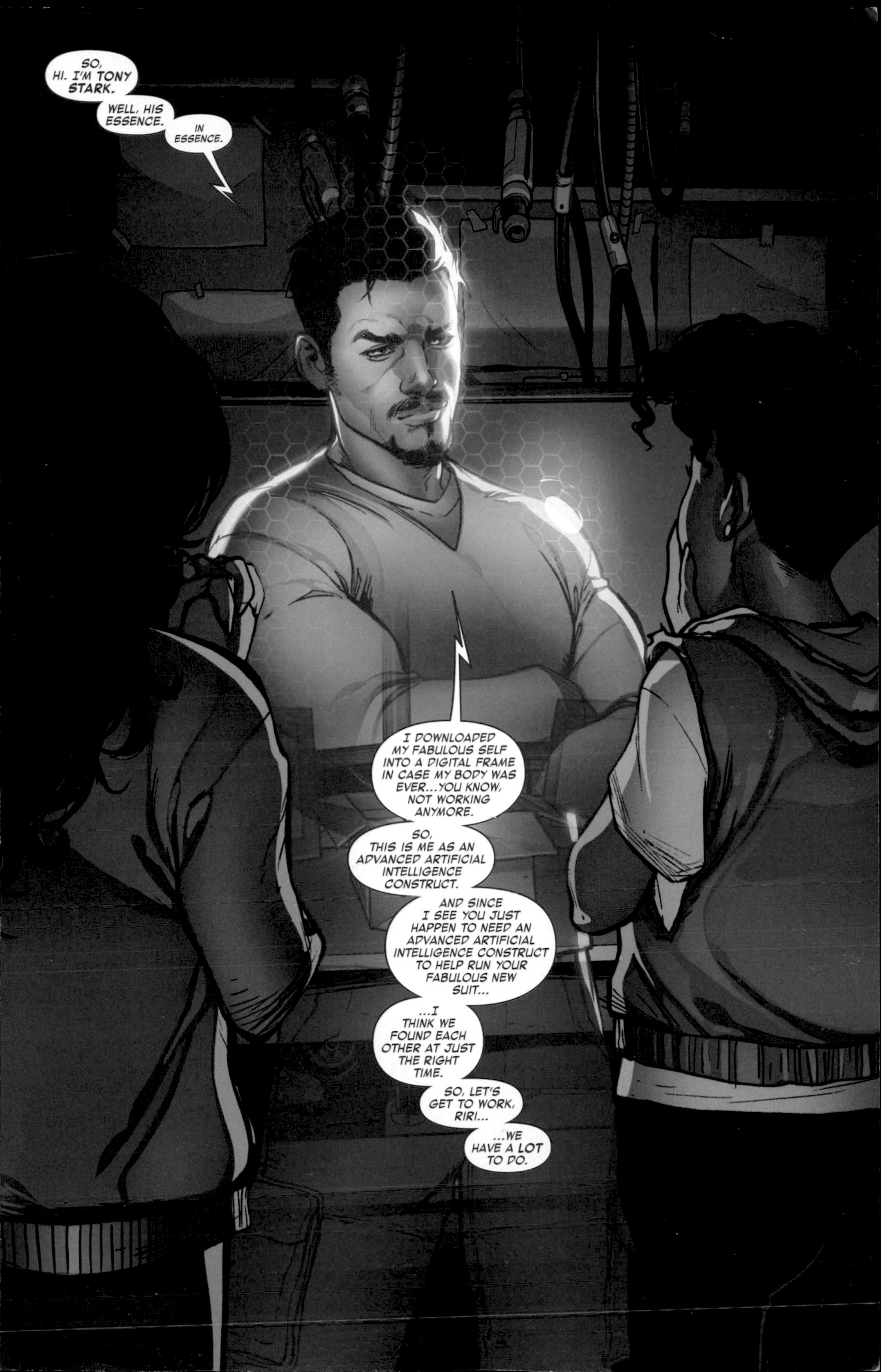
SO, HI. I'M TONY STARK.
WELL, HIS ESSENCE.
IN ESSENCE.
I DOWNLOADED MY FABULOUS SELF INTO A DIGITAL FRAME IN CASE MY BODY WAS EVER...YOU KNOW, NOT WORKING ANYMORE.
SO, THIS IS ME AS AN ADVANCED ARTIFICIAL INTELLIGENCE CONSTRUCT.
AND SINCE I SEE YOU JUST HAPPEN TO NEED AN ADVANCED ARTIFICIAL INTELLIGENCE CONSTRUCT TO HELP RUN YOUR FABULOUS NEW SUIT...
...I THINK WE FOUND EACH OTHER AT JUST THE RIGHT TIME.
SO, LET'S GET TO WORK, RIRI...
...WE HAVE A LOT TO DO.

2

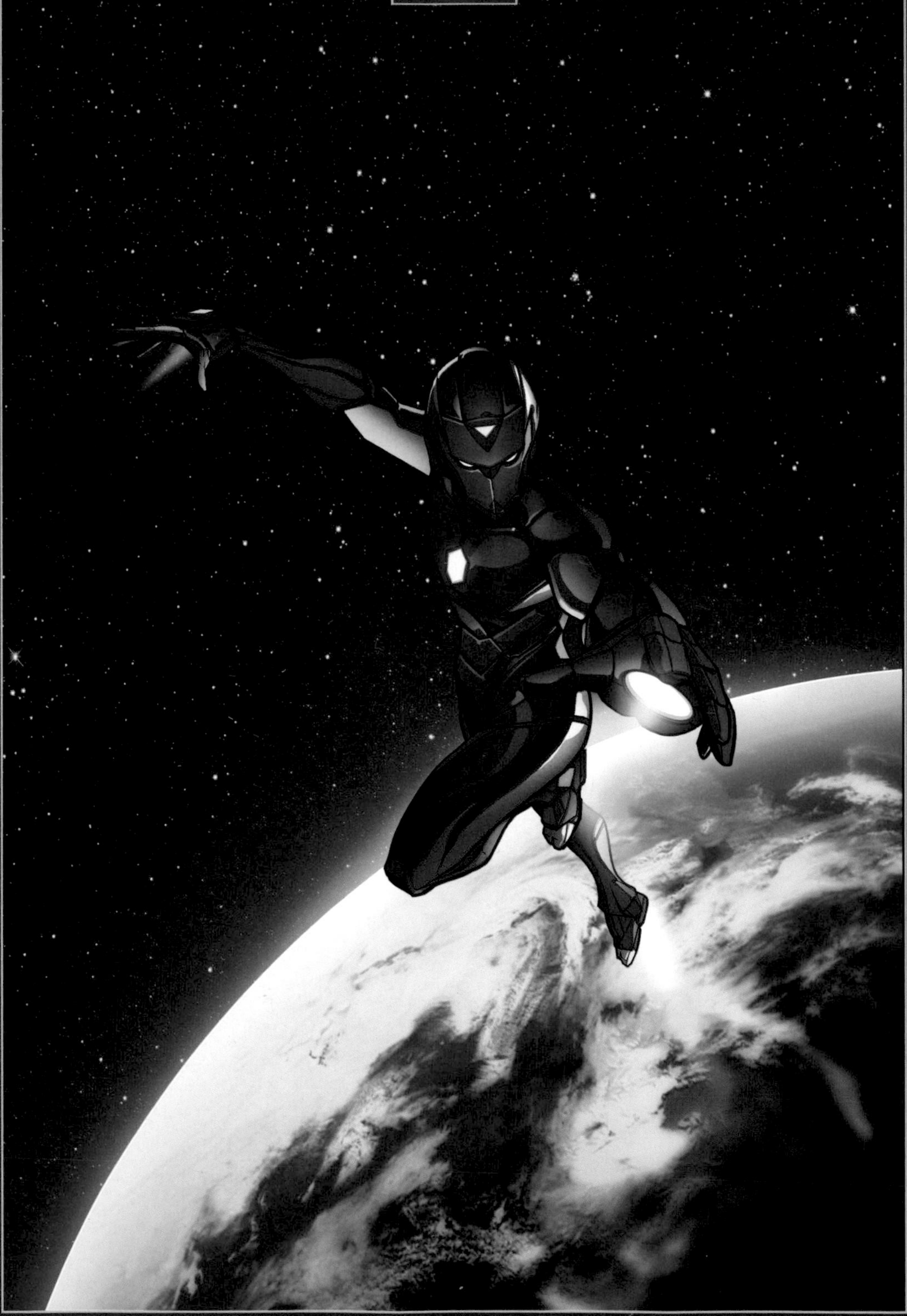

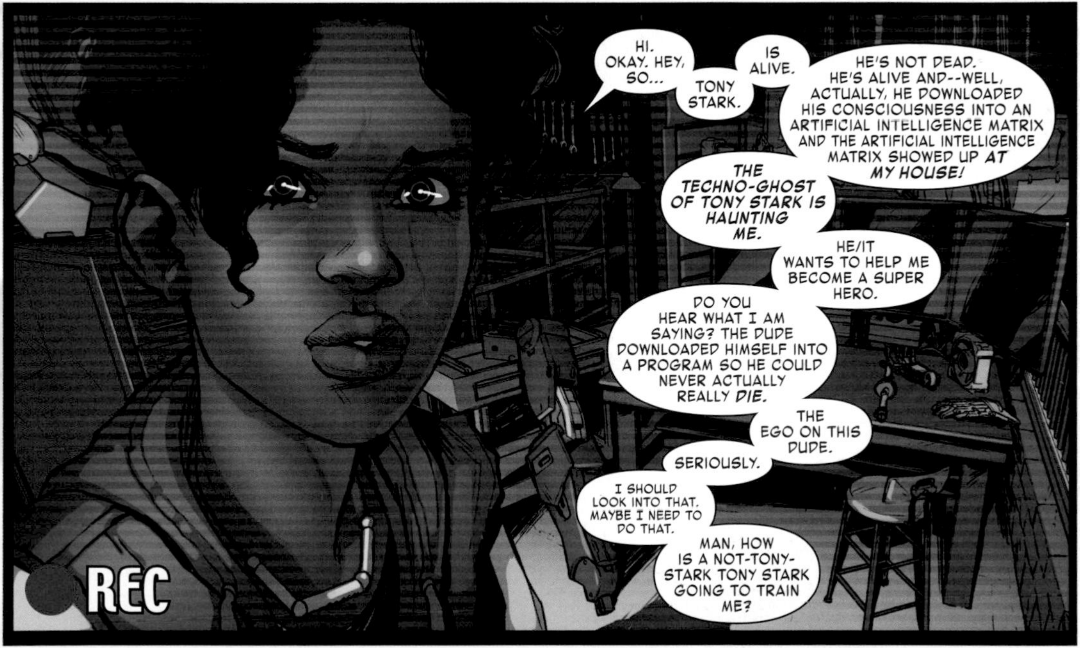
REC
HI. OKAY. HEY, SO...
TONY STARK.
IS ALIVE.
HE'S NOT DEAD. HE'S ALIVE AND--WELL, ACTUALLY, HE DOWNLOADED HIS CONSCIOUSNESS INTO AN ARTIFICIAL INTELLIGENCE MATRIX AND THE ARTIFICIAL INTELLIGENCE MATRIX SHOWED UP *AT MY HOUSE!*
THE TECHNO-GHOST OF TONY STARK IS HAUNTING ME.
HE/IT WANTS TO HELP ME BECOME A SUPER HERO.
DO YOU HEAR WHAT I AM SAYING? THE DUDE DOWNLOADED HIMSELF INTO A PROGRAM SO HE COULD NEVER ACTUALLY REALLY *DIE.*
THE EGO ON THIS DUDE.
SERIOUSLY.
I SHOULD LOOK INTO THAT. MAYBE I NEED TO DO THAT.
MAN, HOW IS A NOT-TONY-STARK TONY STARK GOING TO TRAIN ME?

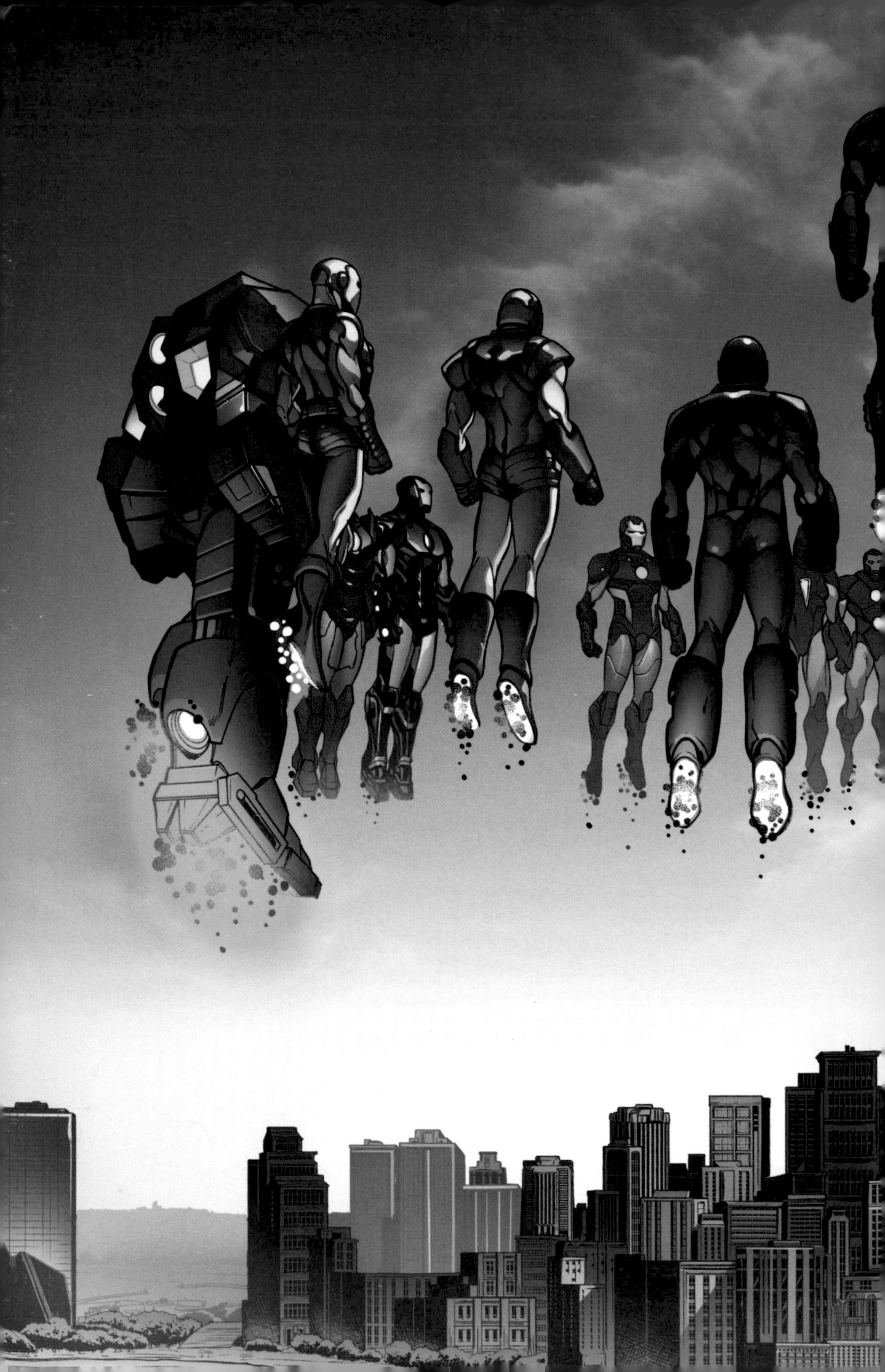

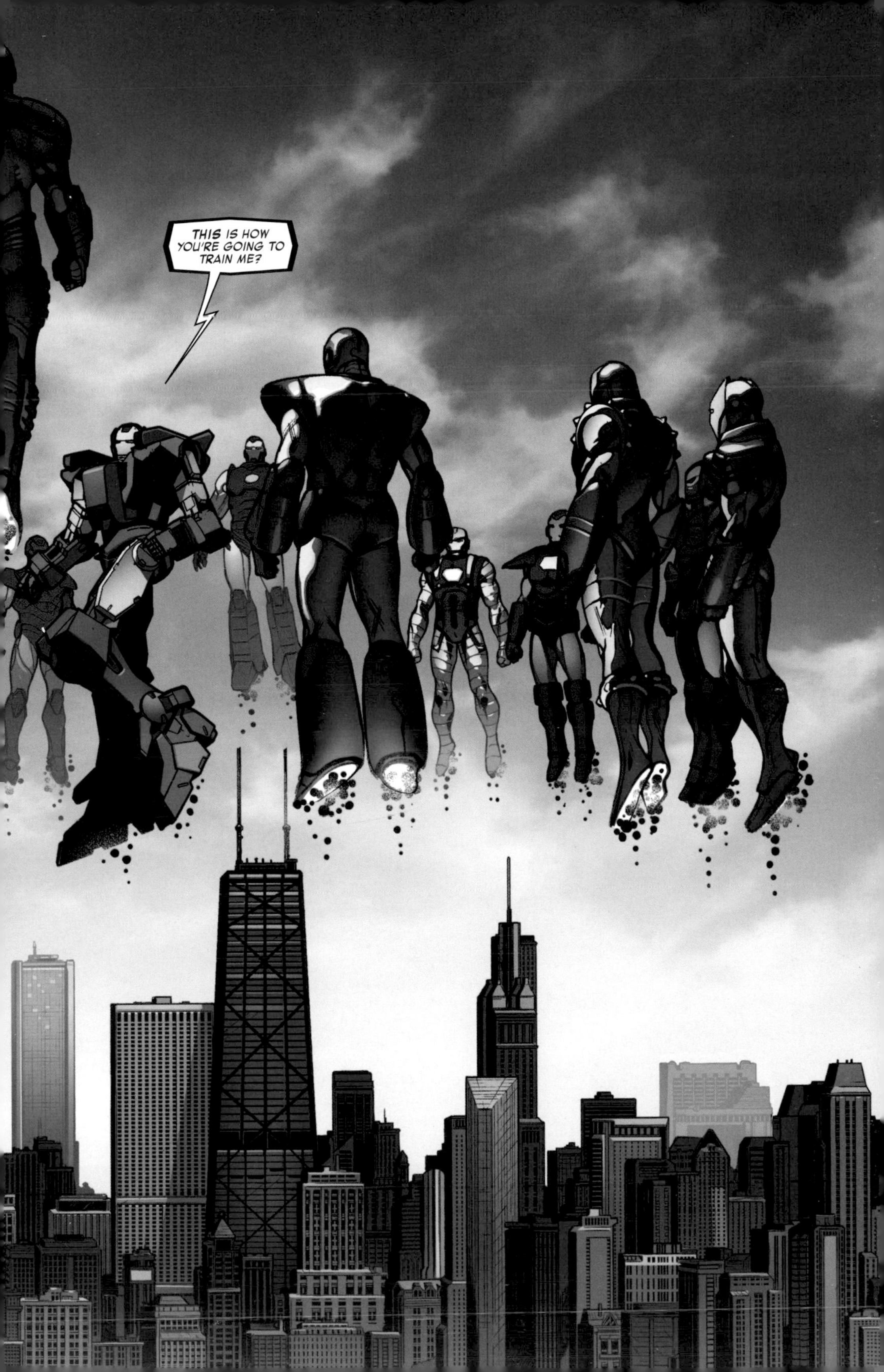
THIS IS HOW YOU'RE GOING TO TRAIN ME?

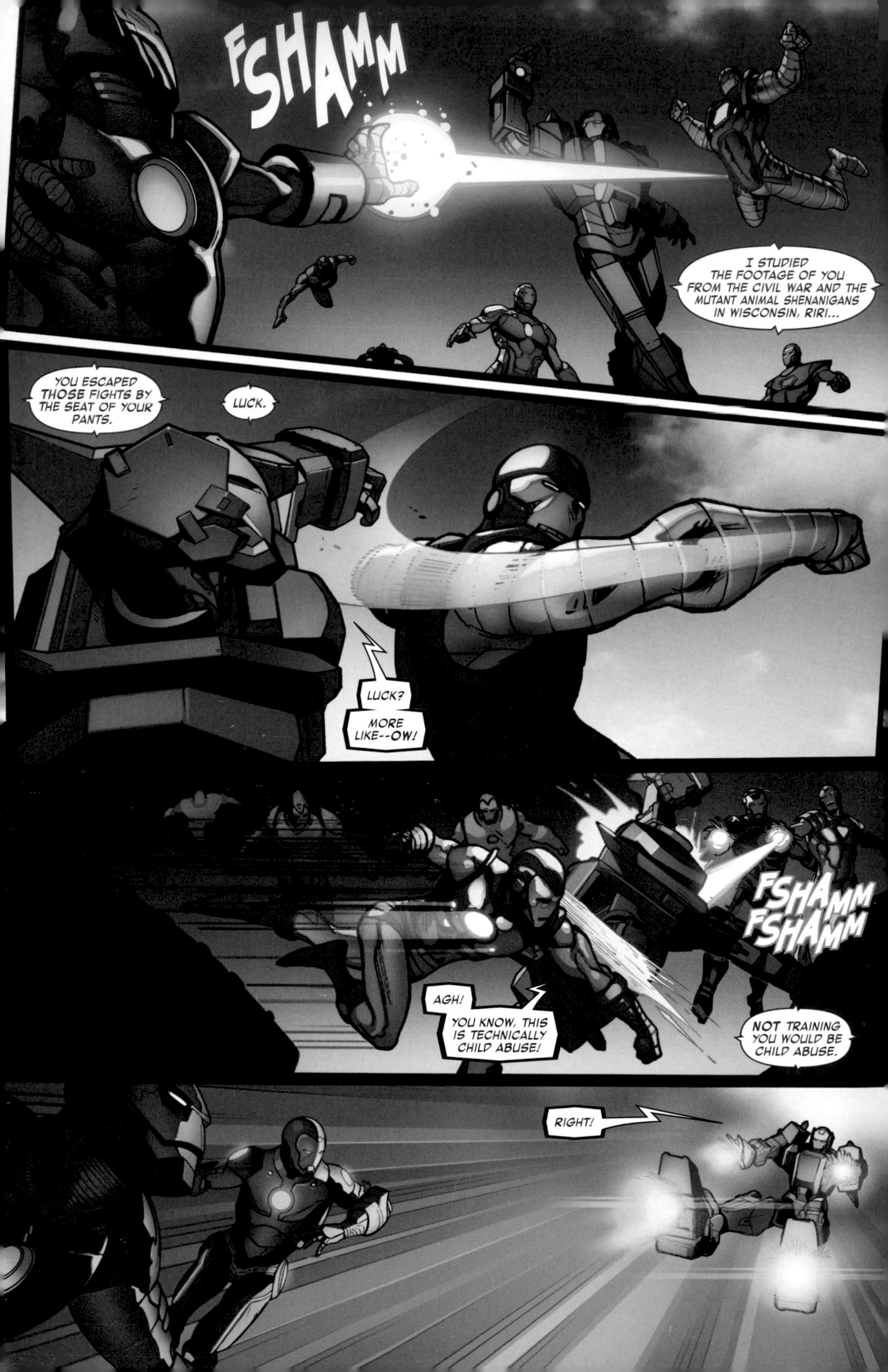
FSHAMM
I STUDIED THE FOOTAGE OF YOU FROM THE CIVIL WAR AND THE MUTANT ANIMAL SHENANIGANS IN WISCONSIN, RIRI...
YOU ESCAPED THOSE FIGHTS BY THE SEAT OF YOUR PANTS.
LUCK.
LUCK?
MORE LIKE--OW!
FSHAMM
FSHAMM
AGH!
YOU KNOW, THIS IS TECHNICALLY CHILD ABUSE!
NOT TRAINING YOU WOULD BE CHILD ABUSE.
RIGHT!

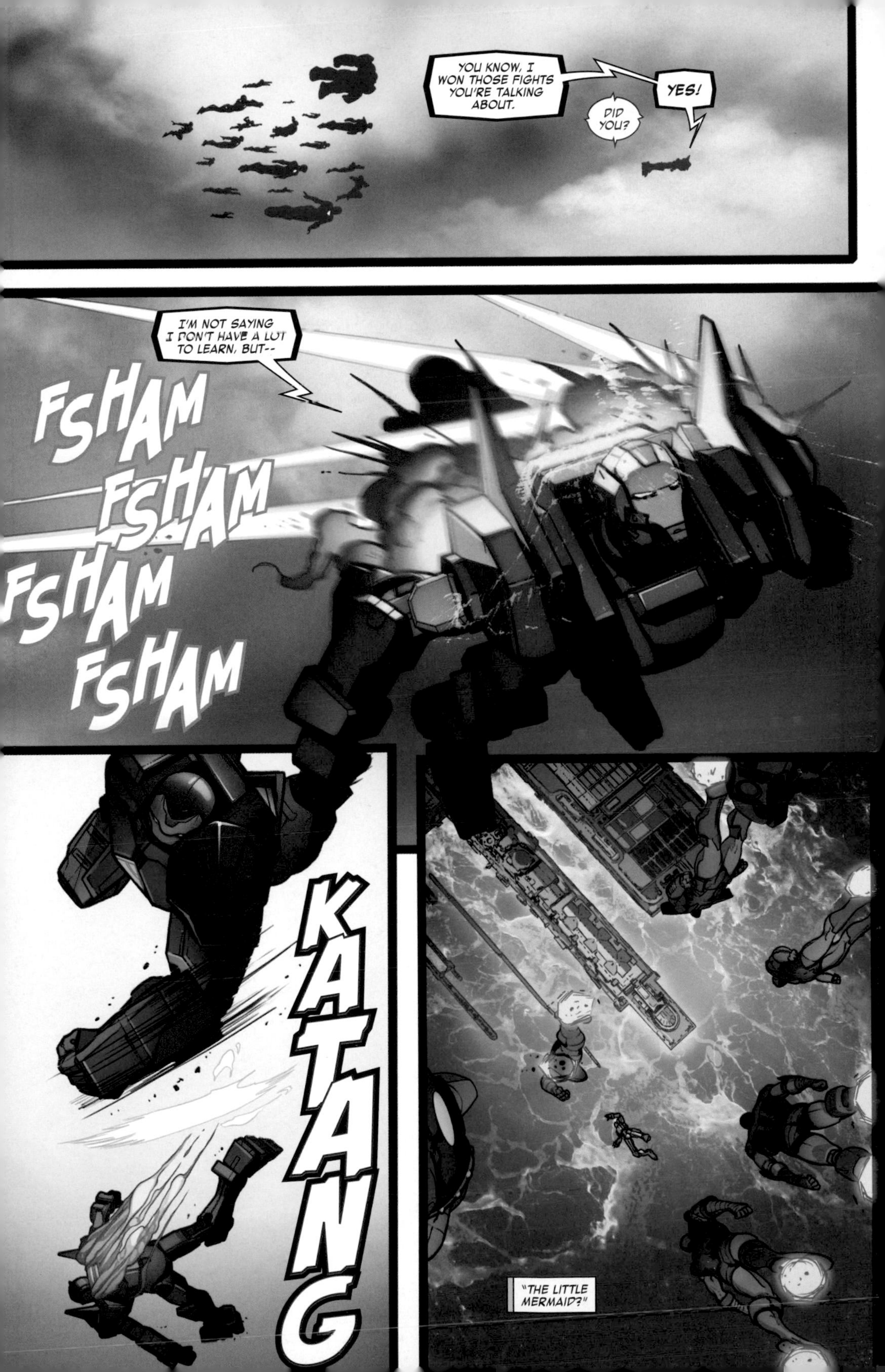
YOU KNOW, I WON THOSE FIGHTS YOU'RE TALKING ABOUT.
DID YOU?
YES!
I'M NOT SAYING I DON'T HAVE A LOT TO LEARN, BUT--
FSHAM
FSHAM
FSHAM
FSHAM
KATANG
"THE LITTLE MERMAID?"

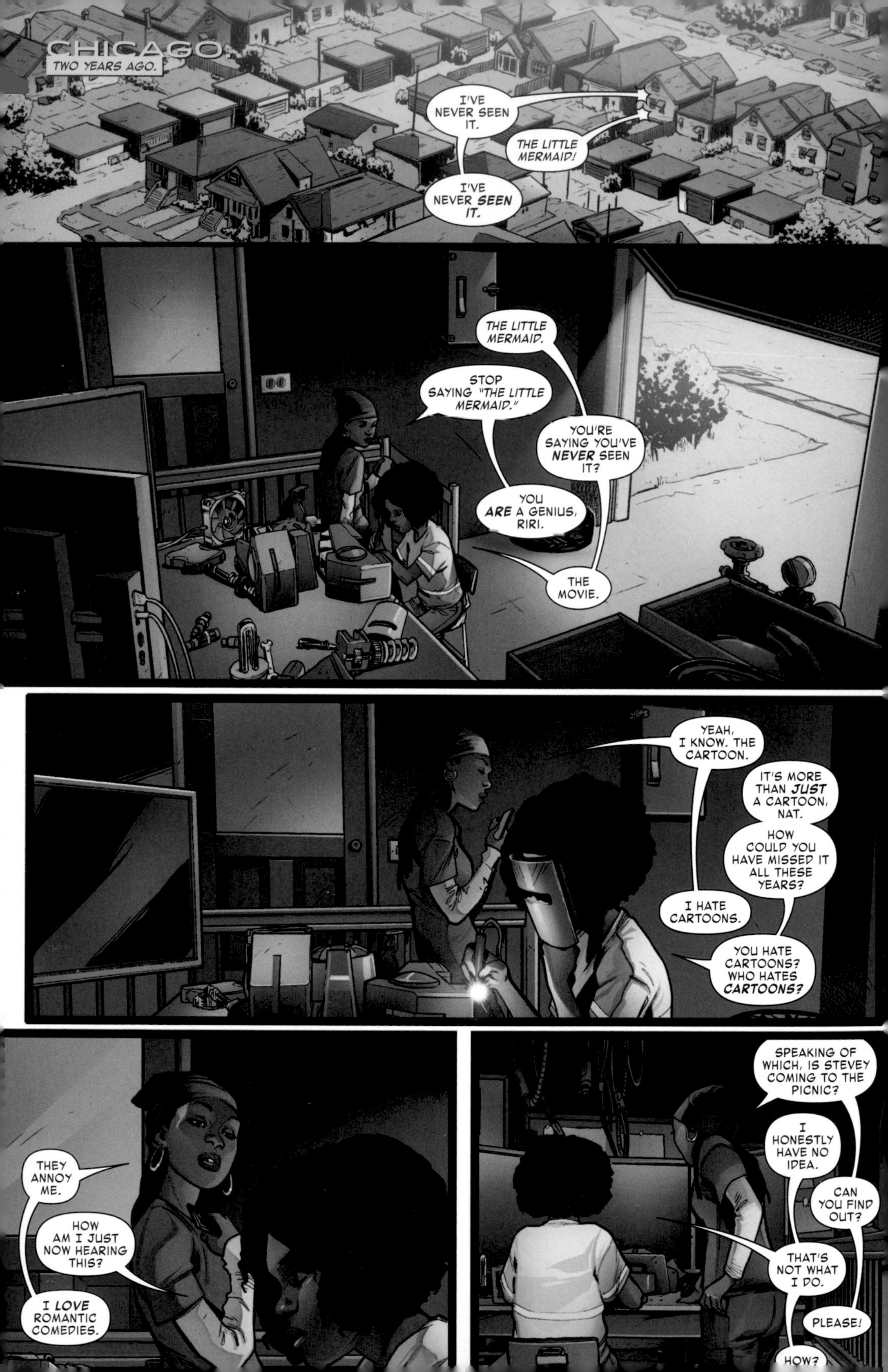
CHICAGO
TWO YEARS AGO.
I'VE NEVER SEEN IT.
THE LITTLE MERMAID!
I'VE NEVER SEEN IT.
THE LITTLE MERMAID.
STOP SAYING "THE LITTLE MERMAID."
YOU'RE SAYING YOU'VE NEVER SEEN IT?
YOU ARE A GENIUS, RIRI.
THE MOVIE.
YEAH, I KNOW. THE CARTOON.
IT'S MORE THAN JUST A CARTOON, NAT.
HOW COULD YOU HAVE MISSED IT ALL THESE YEARS?
I HATE CARTOONS.
YOU HATE CARTOONS? WHO HATES CARTOONS?
THEY ANNOY ME.
HOW AM I JUST NOW HEARING THIS?
I LOVE ROMANTIC COMEDIES.
SPEAKING OF WHICH, IS STEVEY COMING TO THE PICNIC?
I HONESTLY HAVE NO IDEA.
CAN YOU FIND OUT?
THAT'S NOT WHAT I DO.
PLEASE!
HOW?

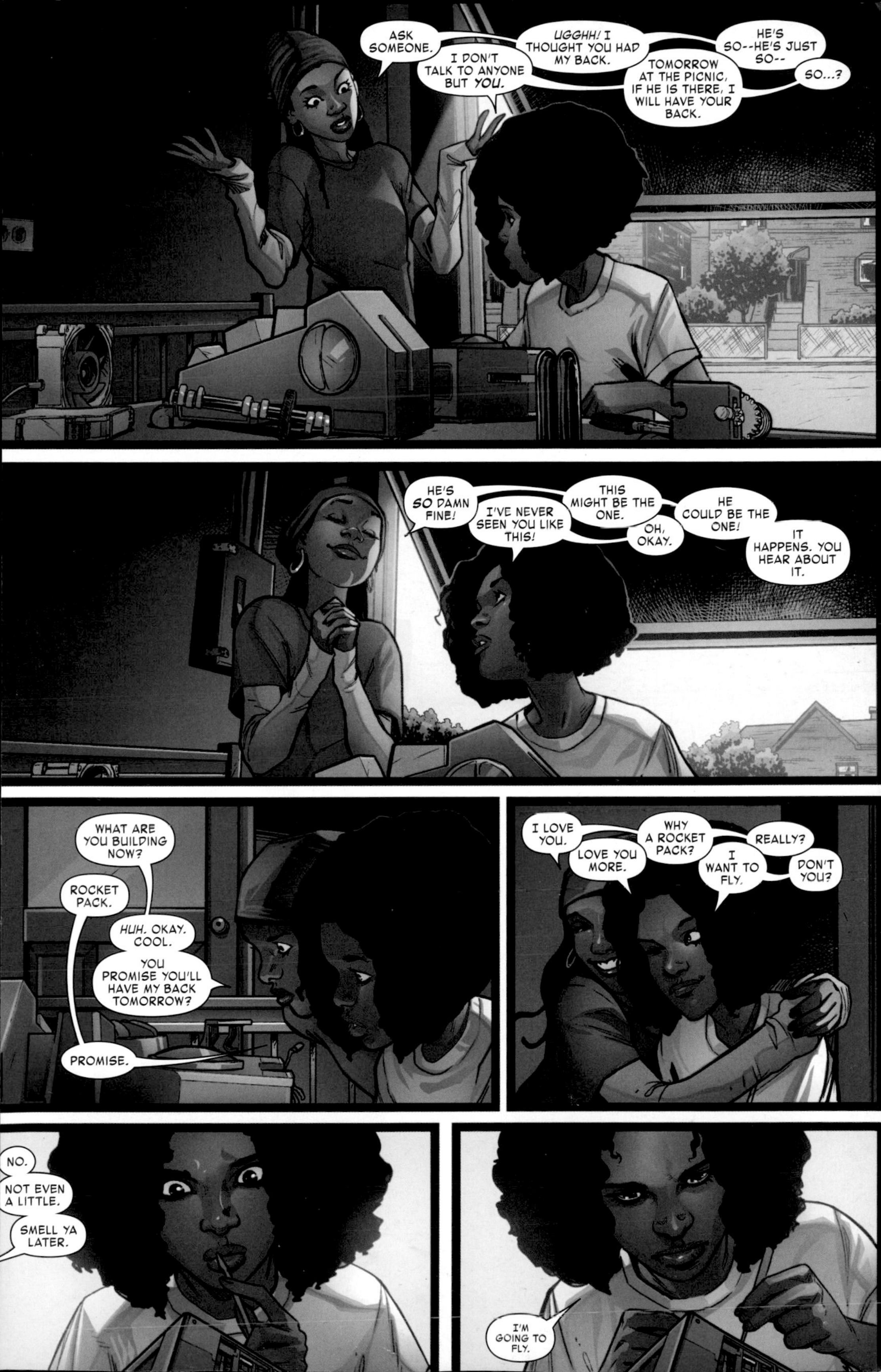
ASK SOMEONE.
I DON'T TALK TO ANYONE BUT *YOU.*
UGGHH! I THOUGHT YOU HAD MY BACK.
TOMORROW AT THE PICNIC, IF HE IS THERE, I WILL HAVE YOUR BACK.
HE'S SO--HE'S JUST SO--
SO...?
HE'S *SO* DAMN FINE!
I'VE NEVER SEEN YOU LIKE THIS!
THIS MIGHT BE THE ONE.
OH, OKAY.
HE COULD BE THE ONE!
IT HAPPENS. YOU HEAR ABOUT IT.
WHAT ARE YOU BUILDING NOW?
ROCKET PACK.
HUH. OKAY. COOL.
YOU PROMISE YOU'LL HAVE MY BACK TOMORROW?
PROMISE.
I LOVE YOU.
LOVE YOU MORE.
WHY A ROCKET PACK?
I WANT TO FLY.
REALLY?
DON'T YOU?
NO.
NOT EVEN A LITTLE.
SMELL YA LATER.
I'M GOING TO FLY.

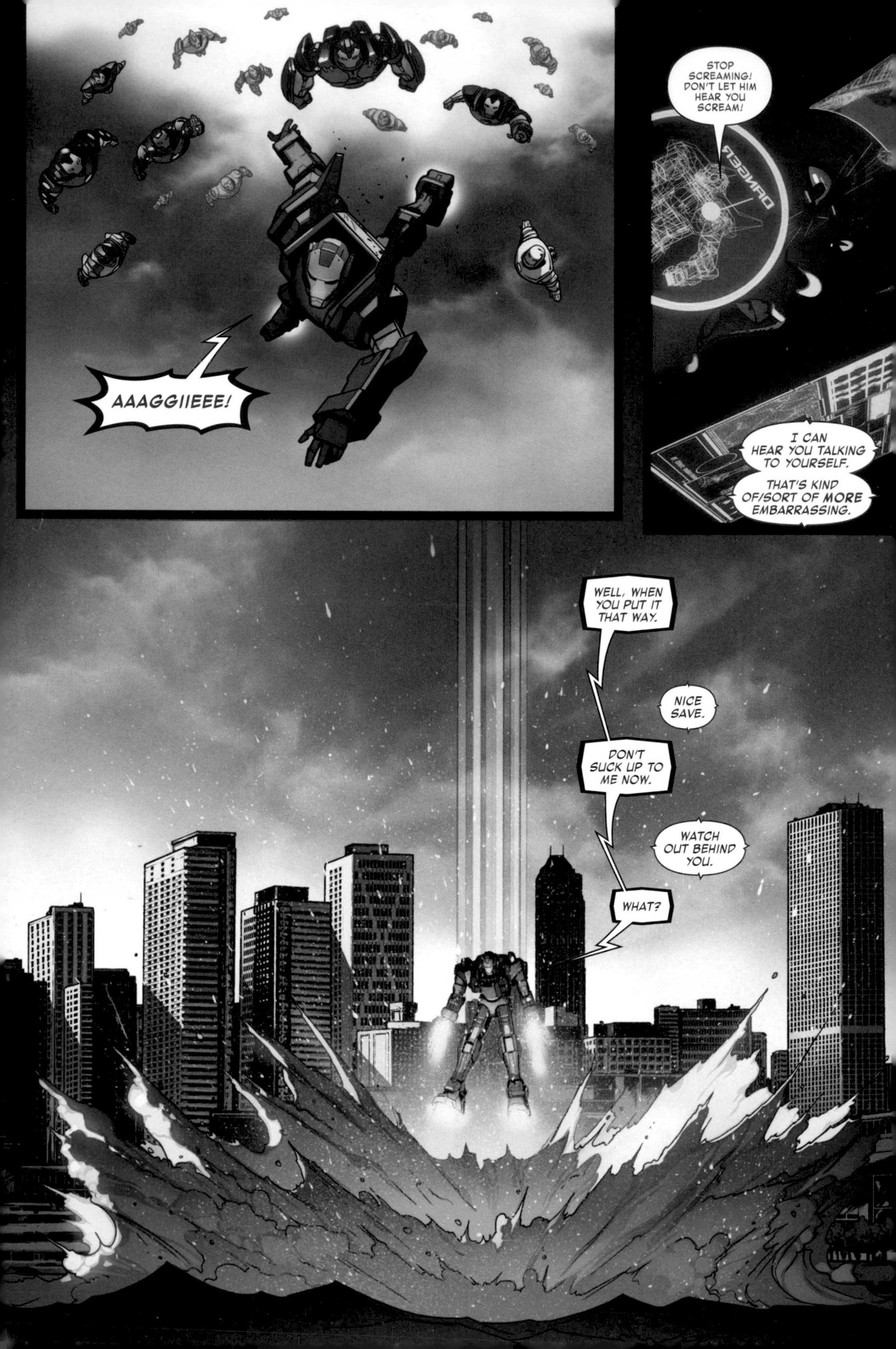
AAAGGIIEEE!
STOP SCREAMING! DON'T LET HIM HEAR YOU SCREAM!
DANGER
I CAN HEAR YOU TALKING TO YOURSELF.
THAT'S KIND OF/SORT OF MORE EMBARRASSING.
WELL, WHEN YOU PUT IT THAT WAY.
NICE SAVE.
DON'T SUCK UP TO ME NOW.
WATCH OUT BEHIND YOU.
WHAT?

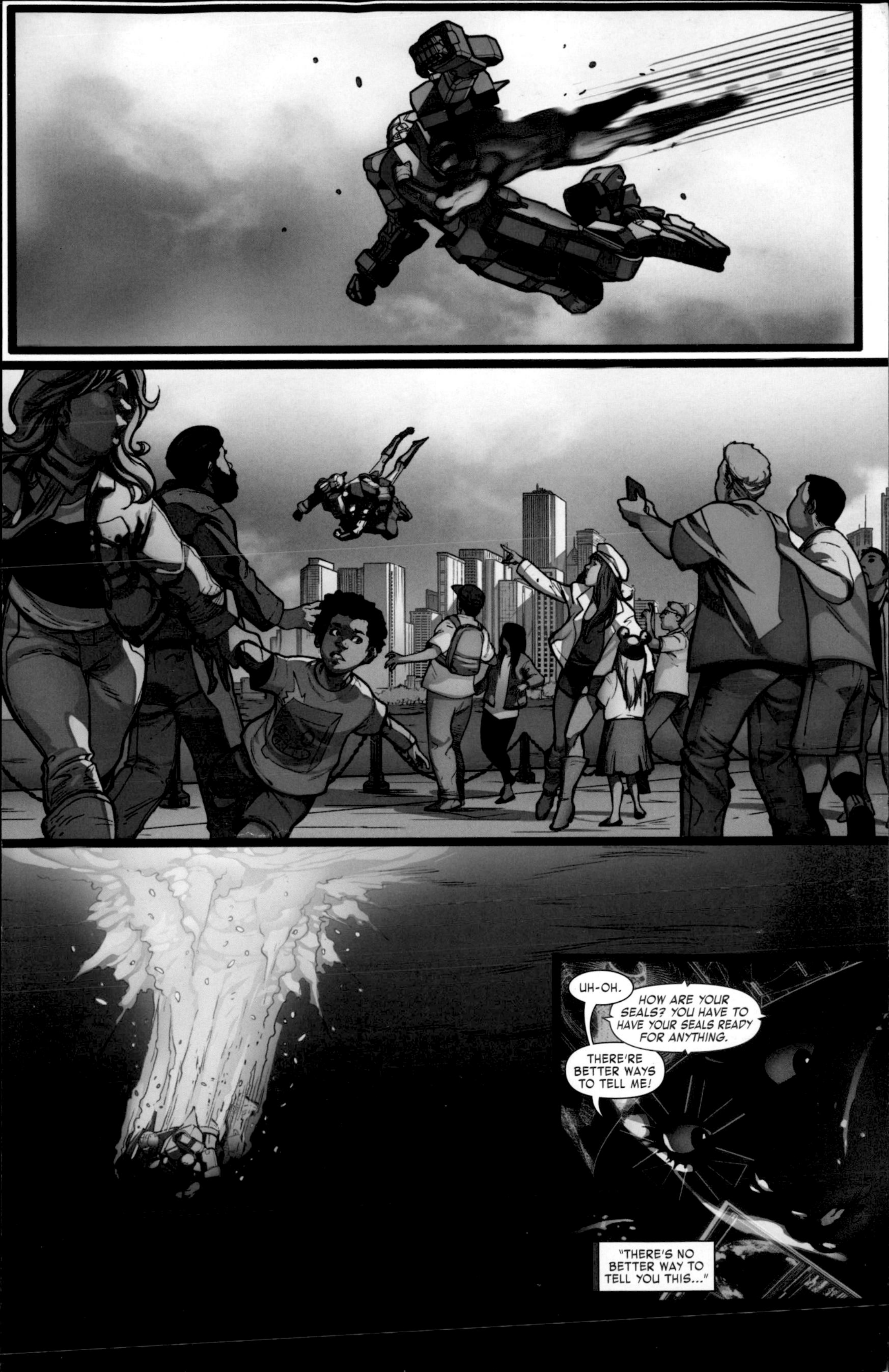
UH-OH.
HOW ARE YOUR SEALS? YOU HAVE TO HAVE YOUR SEALS READY FOR ANYTHING.
THERE'RE BETTER WAYS TO TELL ME!
"THERE'S NO BETTER WAY TO TELL YOU THIS..."

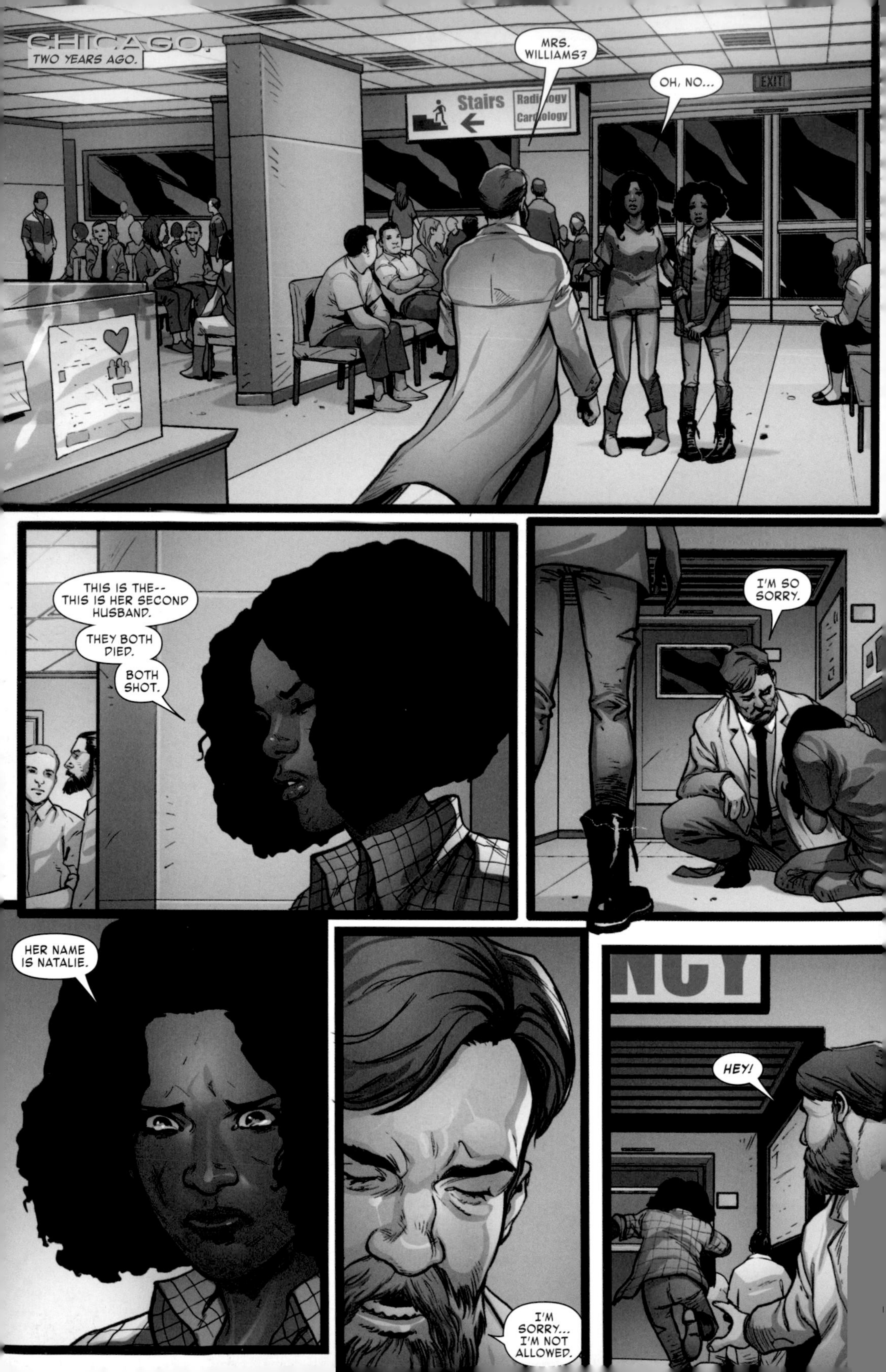
CHICAGO.
TWO YEARS AGO.
Stairs
MRS. WILLIAMS?
OH, NO...
EXIT
THIS IS THE-- THIS IS HER SECOND HUSBAND.
THEY BOTH DIED.
BOTH SHOT.
I'M SO SORRY.
HER NAME IS NATALIE.
I'M SORRY... I'M NOT ALLOWED.
HEY!

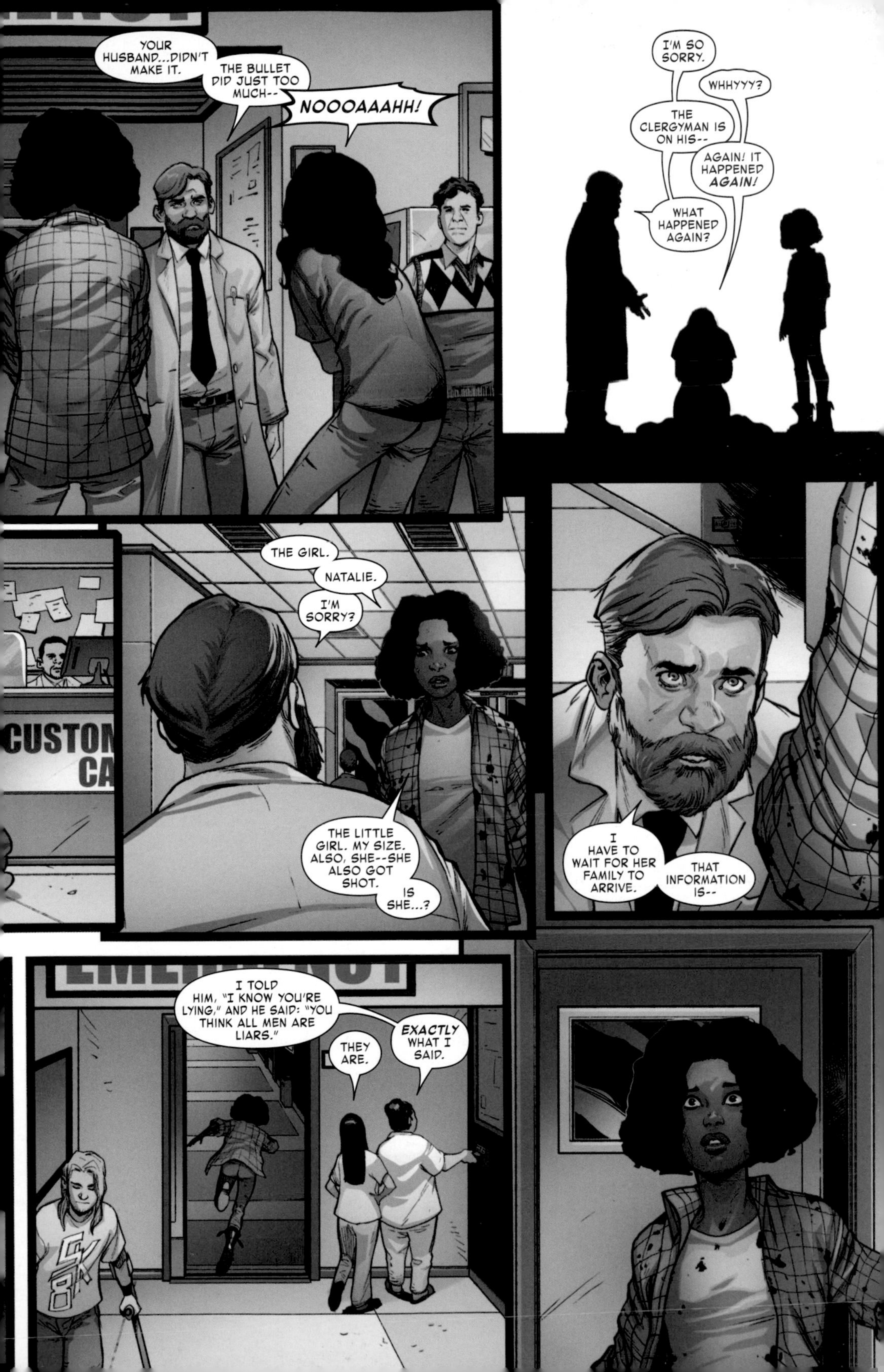
YOUR HUSBAND...DIDN'T MAKE IT.
THE BULLET DID JUST TOO MUCH--
NOOOAAAHH!
I'M SO SORRY.
WHHYYY?
THE CLERGYMAN IS ON HIS--
AGAIN! IT HAPPENED AGAIN!
WHAT HAPPENED AGAIN?
THE GIRL.
NATALIE.
I'M SORRY?
THE LITTLE GIRL. MY SIZE. ALSO, SHE--SHE ALSO GOT SHOT.
IS SHE...?
I HAVE TO WAIT FOR HER FAMILY TO ARRIVE.
THAT INFORMATION IS--
I TOLD HIM, "I KNOW YOU'RE LYING," AND HE SAID: "YOU THINK ALL MEN ARE LIARS."
THEY ARE.
EXACTLY WHAT I SAID.

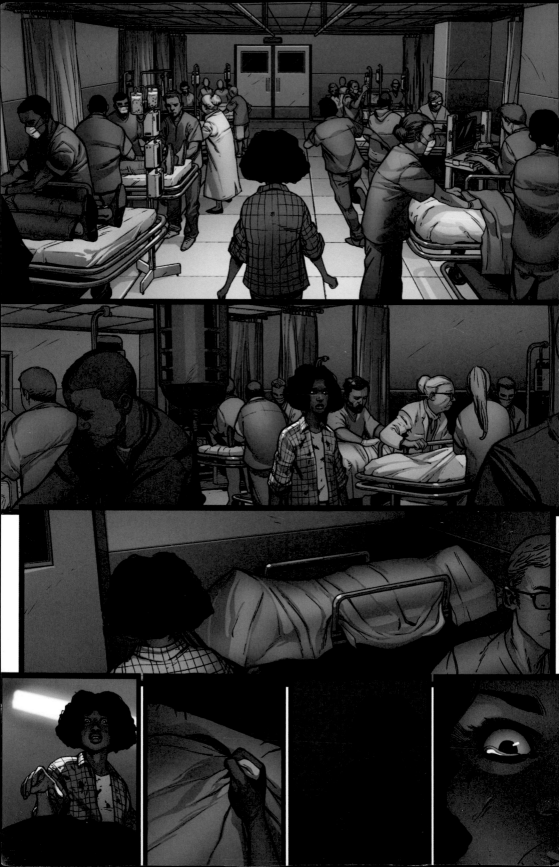

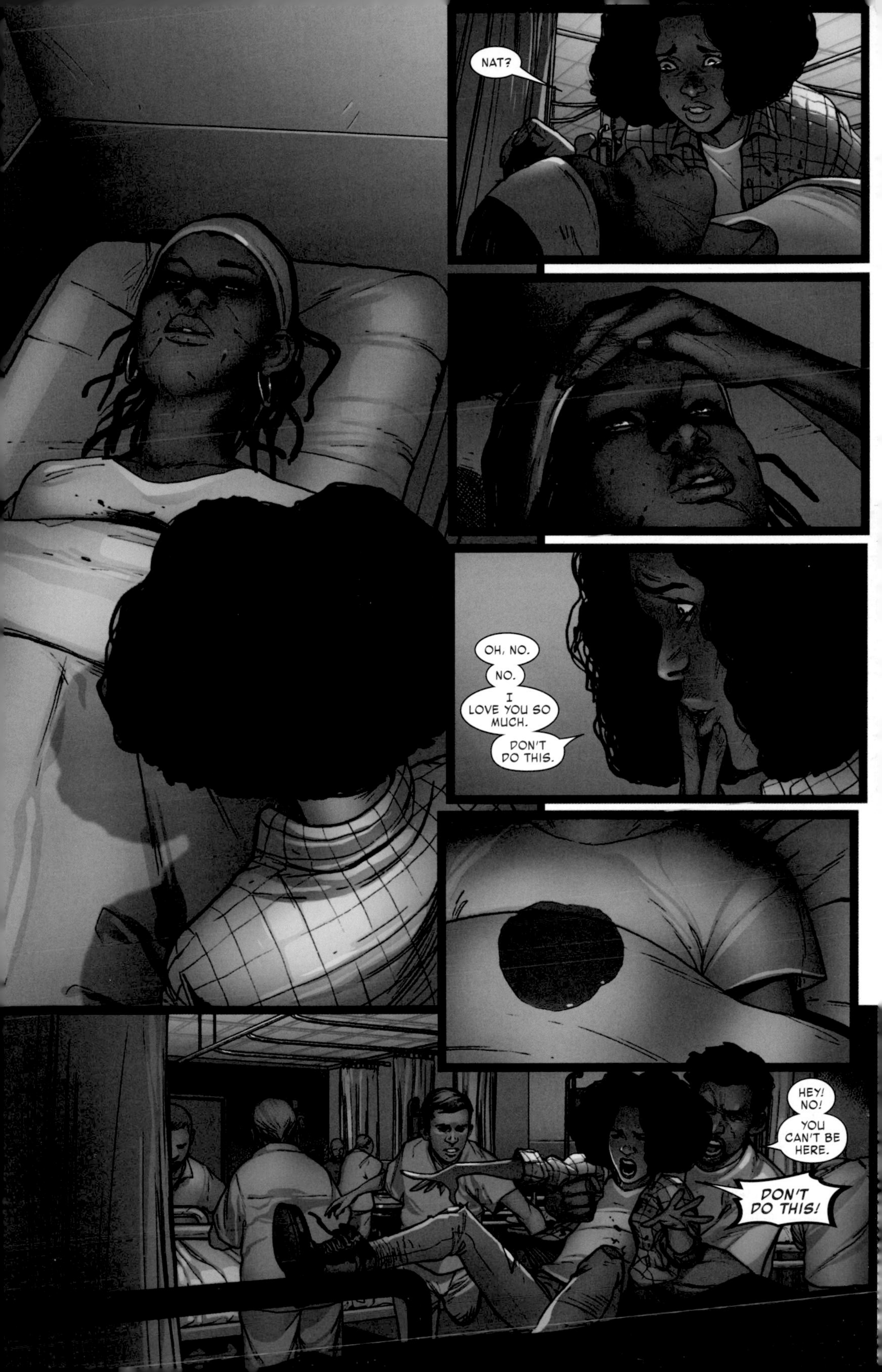
NAT?
OH, NO.
NO.
I LOVE YOU SO MUCH.
DON'T DO THIS.
HEY! NO!
YOU CAN'T BE HERE.
DON'T DO THIS!

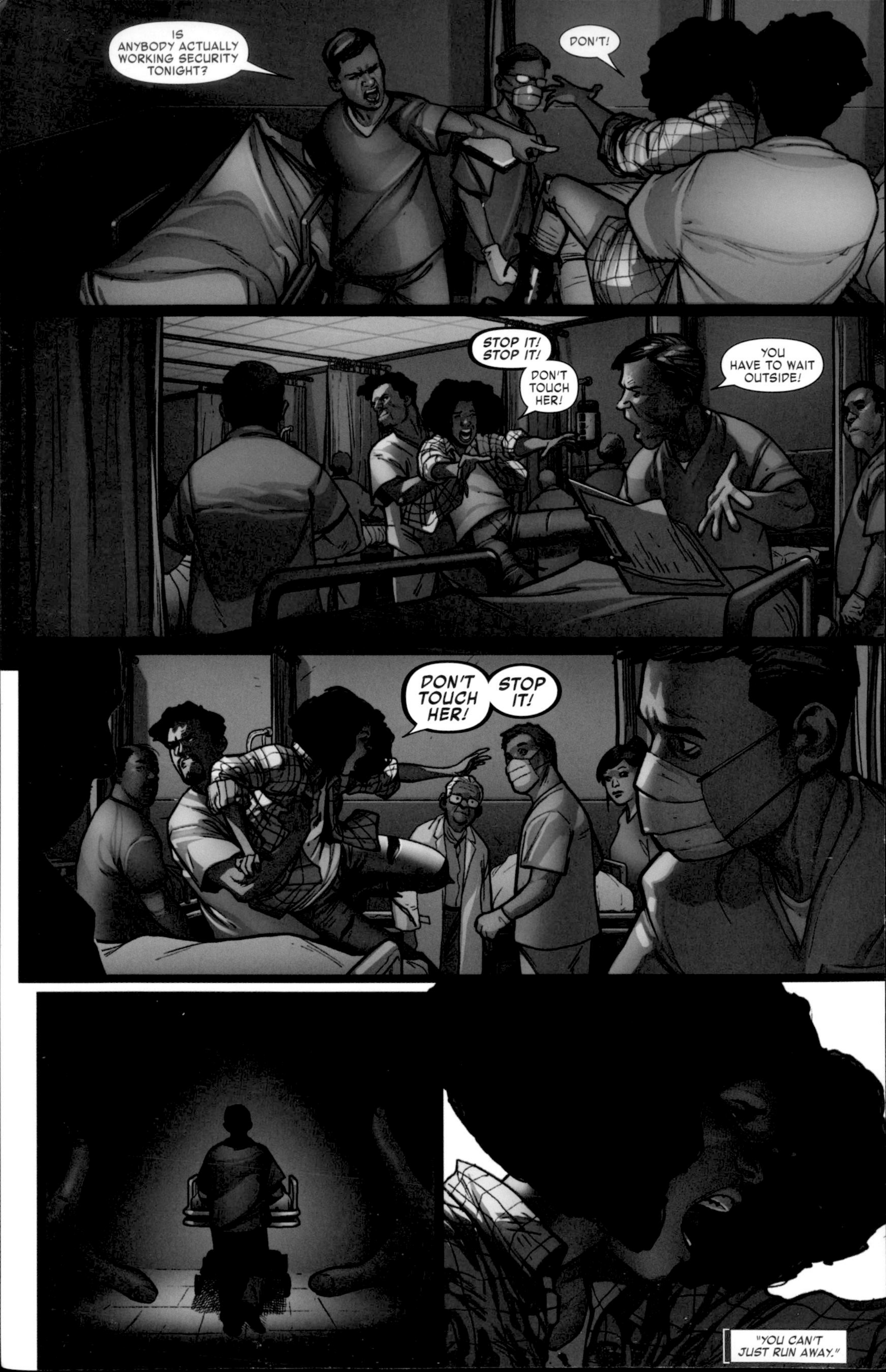
IS ANYBODY ACTUALLY WORKING SECURITY TONIGHT?
DON'T!
STOP IT! STOP IT!
DON'T TOUCH HER!
YOU HAVE TO WAIT OUTSIDE!
DON'T TOUCH HER!
STOP IT!
"YOU CAN'T JUST RUN AWAY."

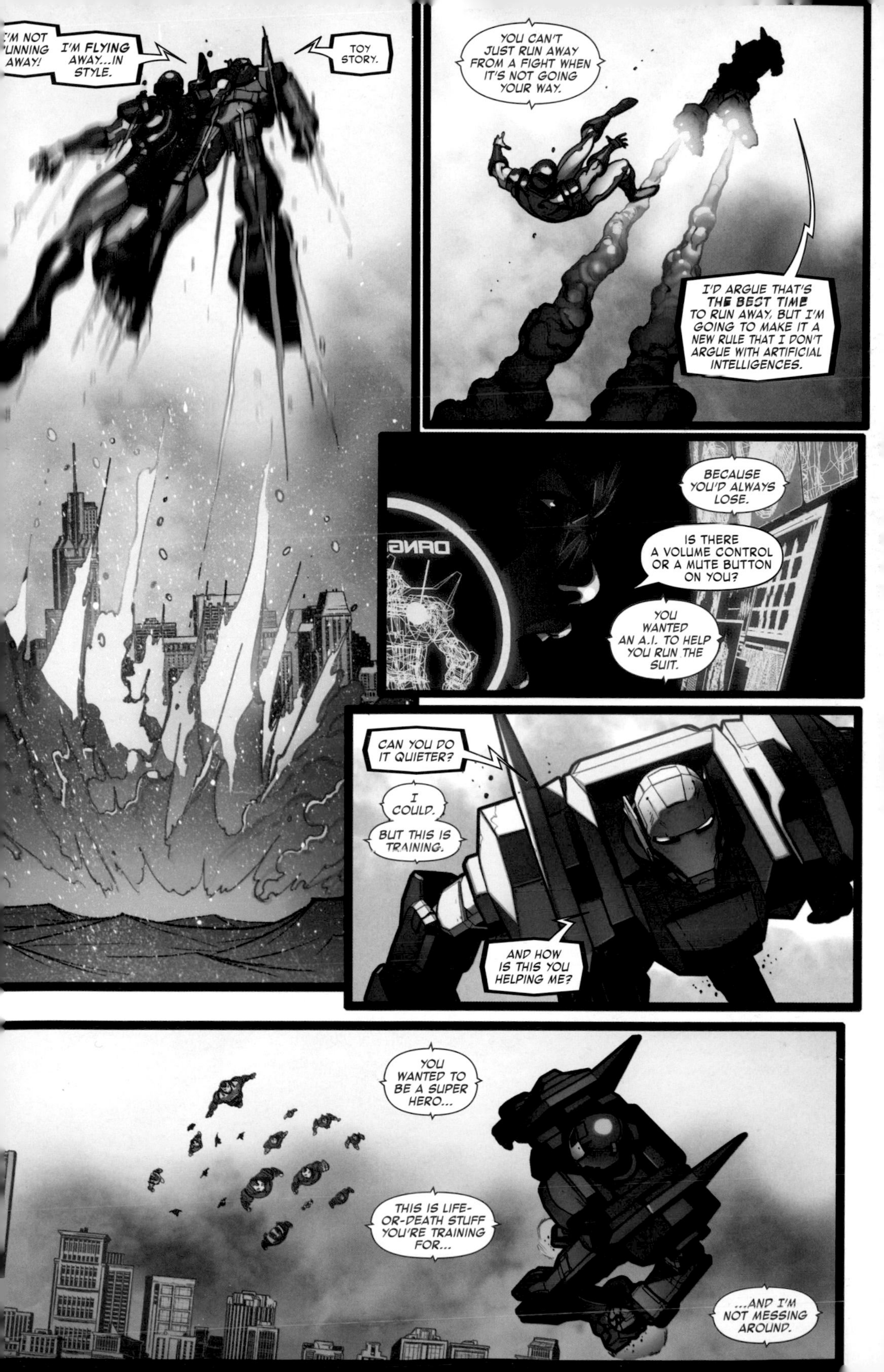

I'M NOT RUNNING AWAY!
I'M FLYING AWAY...IN STYLE.
TOY STORY.
YOU CAN'T JUST RUN AWAY FROM A FIGHT WHEN IT'S NOT GOING YOUR WAY.
I'D ARGUE THAT'S THE BEST TIME TO RUN AWAY, BUT I'M GOING TO MAKE IT A NEW RULE THAT I DON'T ARGUE WITH ARTIFICIAL INTELLIGENCES.
BECAUSE YOU'D ALWAYS LOSE.
IS THERE A VOLUME CONTROL OR A MUTE BUTTON ON YOU?
YOU WANTED AN A.I. TO HELP YOU RUN THE SUIT.
CAN YOU DO IT QUIETER?
I COULD.
BUT THIS IS TRAINING.
AND HOW IS THIS YOU HELPING ME?
YOU WANTED TO BE A SUPER HERO...
THIS IS LIFE-OR-DEATH STUFF YOU'RE TRAINING FOR...
...AND I'M NOT MESSING AROUND.

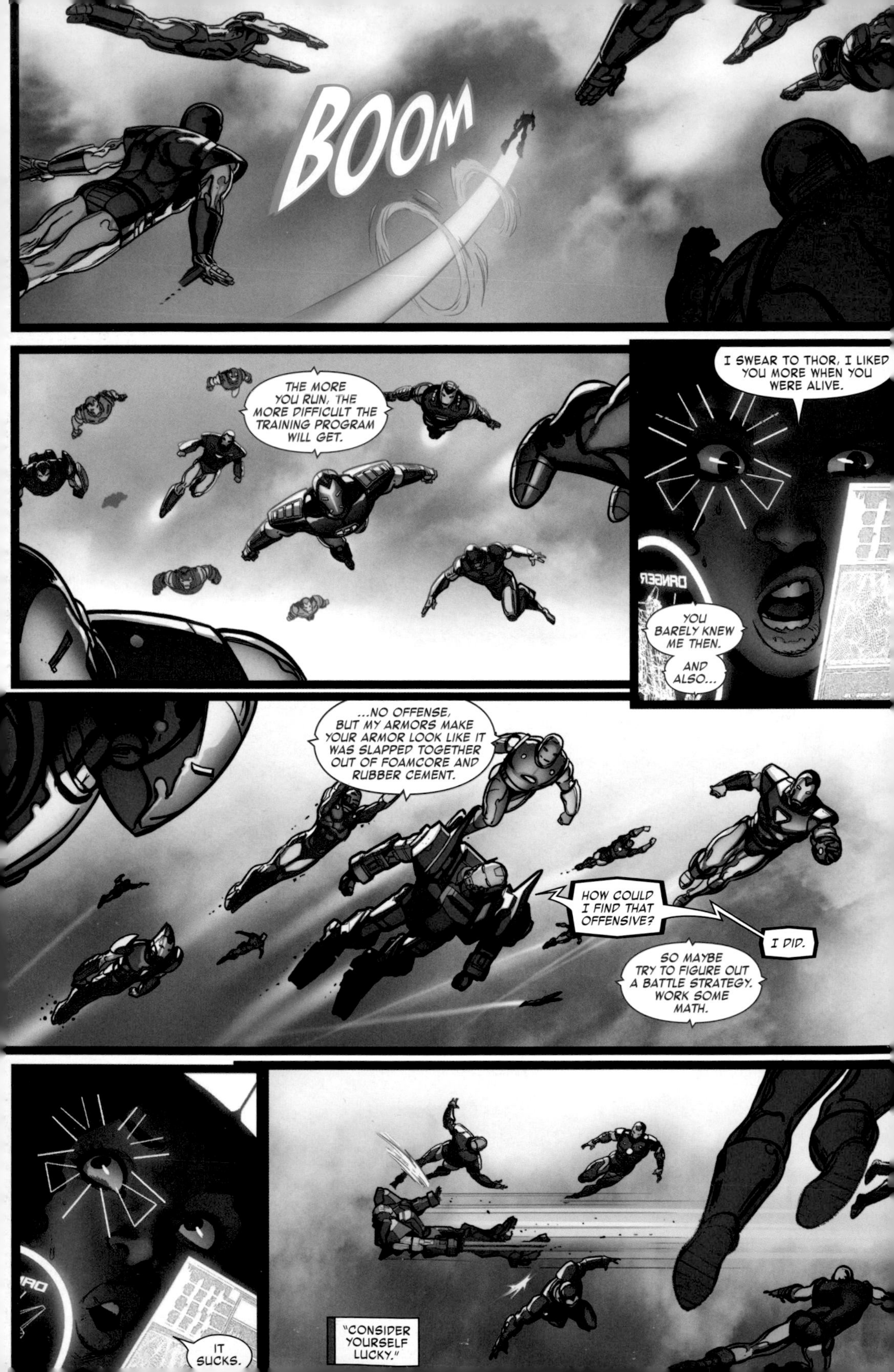
BOOM
THE MORE YOU RUN, THE MORE DIFFICULT THE TRAINING PROGRAM WILL GET.
I SWEAR TO THOR, I LIKED YOU MORE WHEN YOU WERE ALIVE.
DANGER
YOU BARELY KNEW ME THEN.
AND ALSO...
...NO OFFENSE, BUT MY ARMORS MAKE YOUR ARMOR LOOK LIKE IT WAS SLAPPED TOGETHER OUT OF FOAMCORE AND RUBBER CEMENT.
HOW COULD I FIND THAT OFFENSIVE?
I DID.
SO MAYBE TRY TO FIGURE OUT A BATTLE STRATEGY. WORK SOME MATH.
IT SUCKS.
"CONSIDER YOURSELF LUCKY."

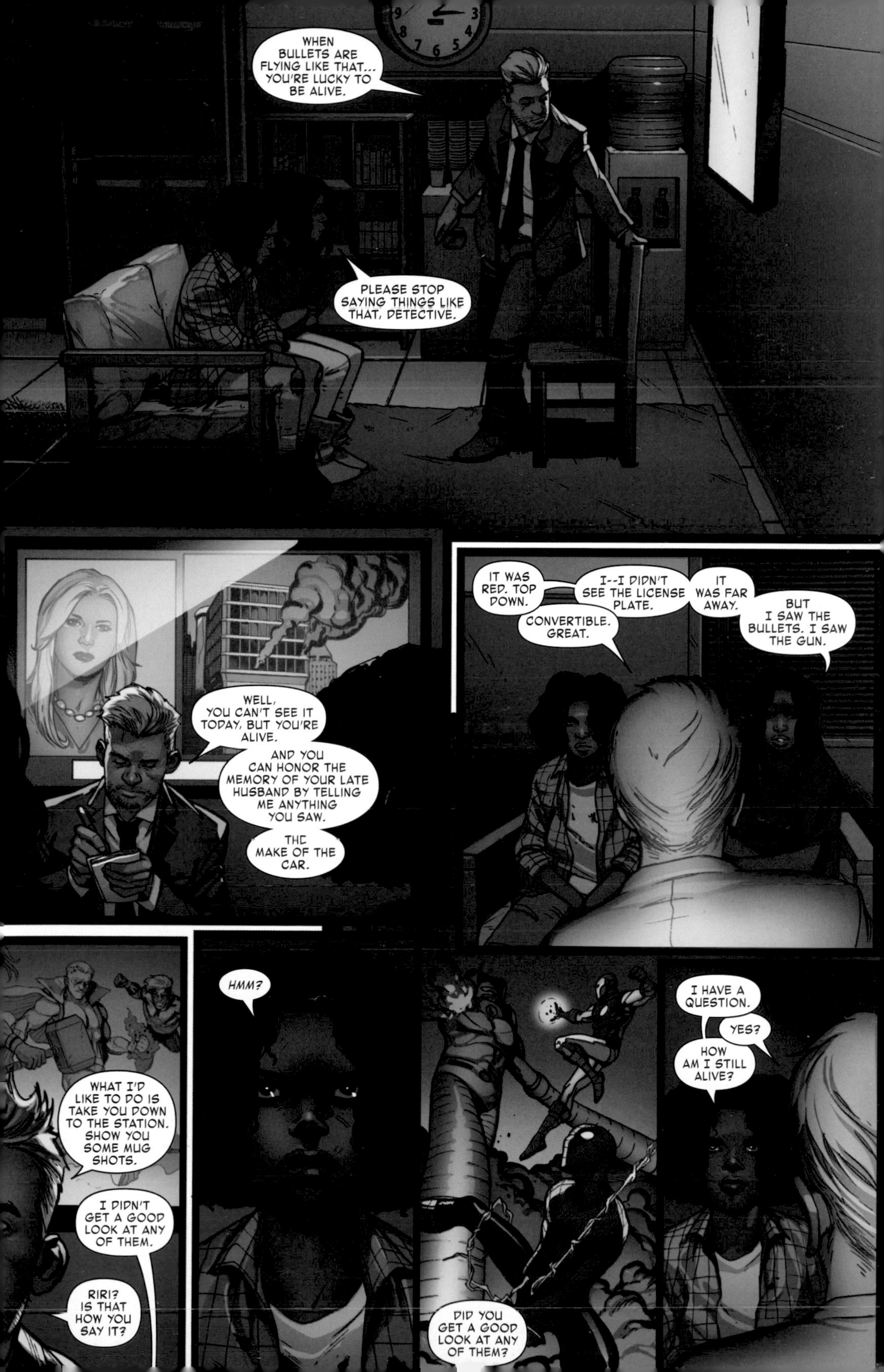
WHEN BULLETS ARE FLYING LIKE THAT... YOU'RE LUCKY TO BE ALIVE.
PLEASE STOP SAYING THINGS LIKE THAT, DETECTIVE.
WELL, YOU CAN'T SEE IT TODAY, BUT YOU'RE ALIVE.
AND YOU CAN HONOR THE MEMORY OF YOUR LATE HUSBAND BY TELLING ME ANYTHING YOU SAW.
THE MAKE OF THE CAR.
IT WAS RED. TOP DOWN.
CONVERTIBLE. GREAT.
I--I DIDN'T SEE THE LICENSE PLATE.
IT WAS FAR AWAY.
BUT I SAW THE BULLETS. I SAW THE GUN.
WHAT I'D LIKE TO DO IS TAKE YOU DOWN TO THE STATION. SHOW YOU SOME MUG SHOTS.
I DIDN'T GET A GOOD LOOK AT ANY OF THEM.
RIRI? IS THAT HOW YOU SAY IT?
HMM?
DID YOU GET A GOOD LOOK AT ANY OF THEM?
I HAVE A QUESTION.
YES?
HOW AM I STILL ALIVE?

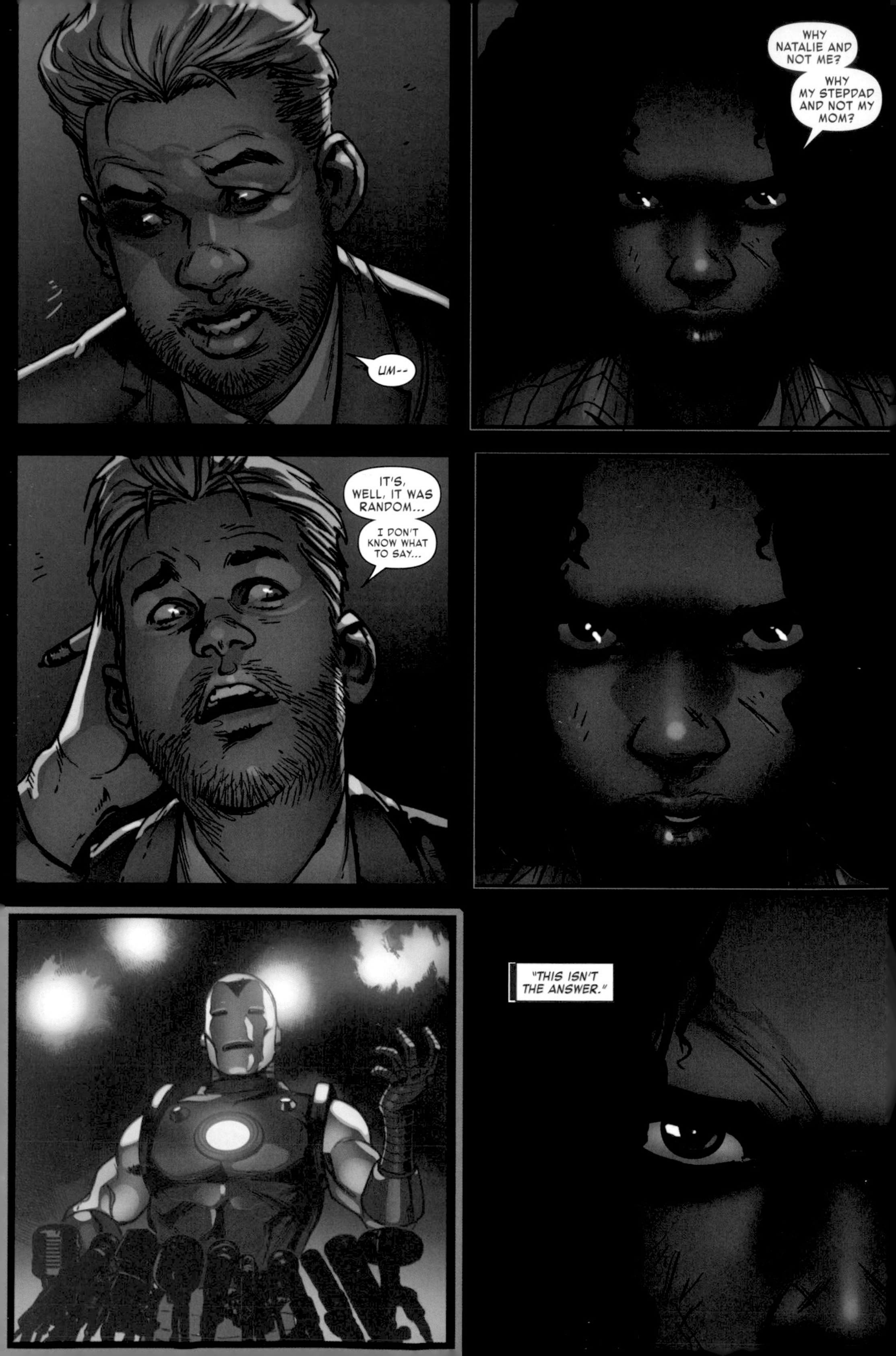
UM--
WHY NATALIE AND NOT ME?
WHY MY STEPDAD AND NOT MY MOM?
IT'S, WELL, IT WAS RANDOM...
I DON'T KNOW WHAT TO SAY...
"THIS ISN'T THE ANSWER."

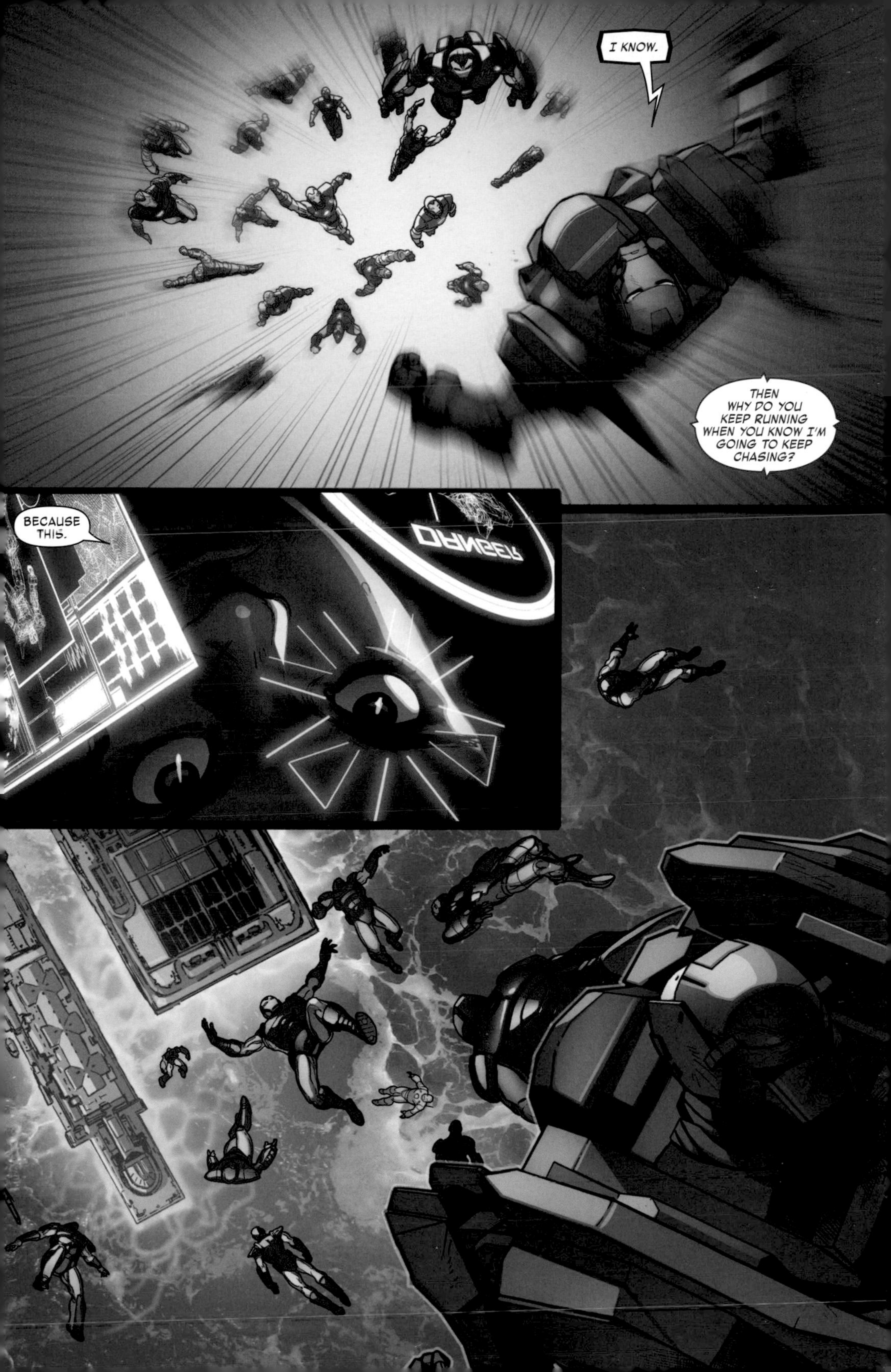
I KNOW.
THEN WHY DO YOU KEEP RUNNING WHEN YOU KNOW I'M GOING TO KEEP CHASING?
BECAUSE THIS.

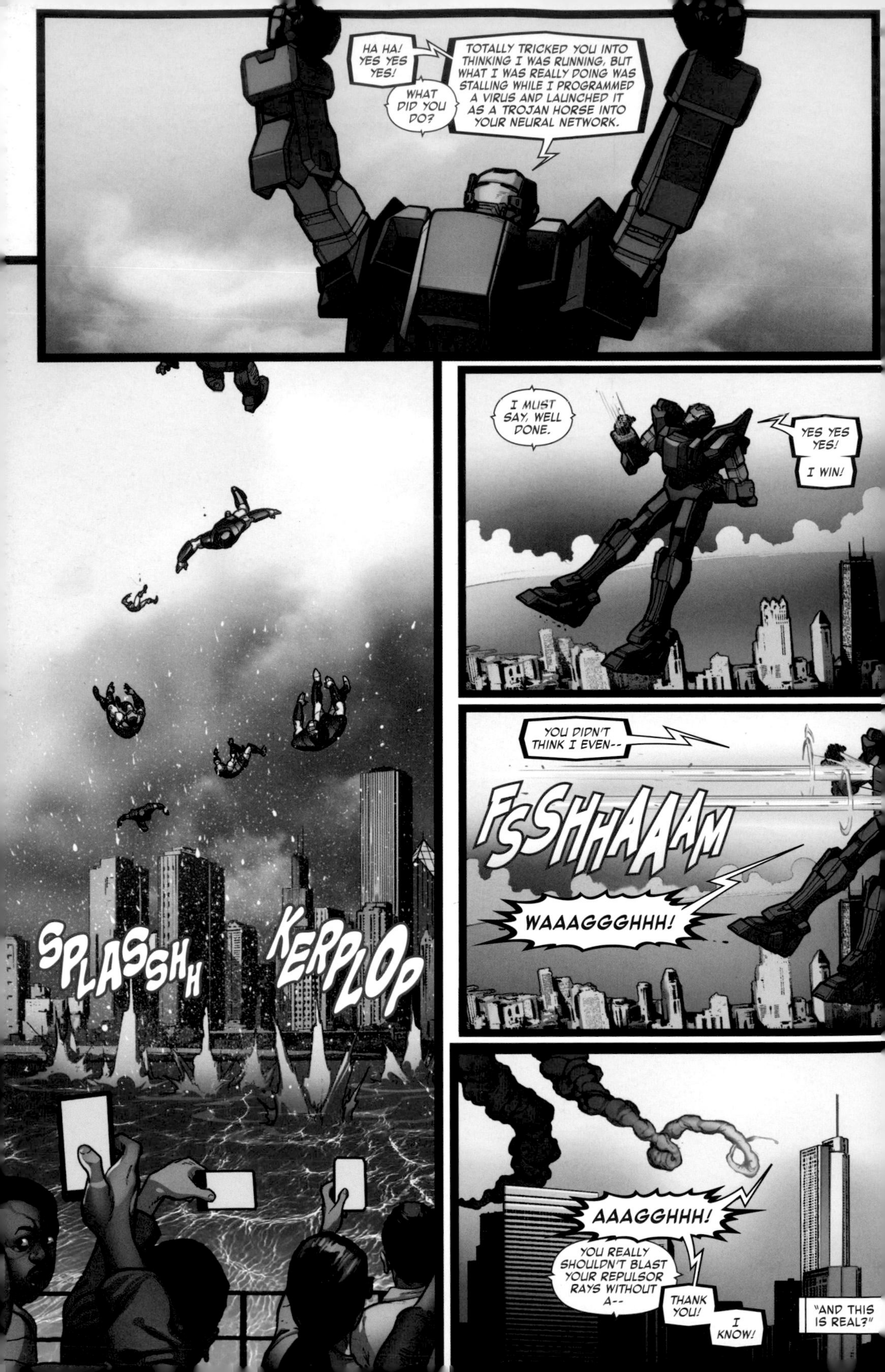
HA HA! YES YES YES!
TOTALLY TRICKED YOU INTO THINKING I WAS RUNNING, BUT WHAT I WAS REALLY DOING WAS STALLING WHILE I PROGRAMMED A VIRUS AND LAUNCHED IT AS A TROJAN HORSE INTO YOUR NEURAL NETWORK.
WHAT DID YOU DO?
SPLASSHH
KERPLOP
I MUST SAY, WELL DONE.
YES YES YES!
I WIN!
YOU DIDN'T THINK I EVEN--
FSSHHAAAM
WAAAGGGHHH!
AAAGGHHH!
YOU REALLY SHOULDN'T BLAST YOUR REPULSOR RAYS WITHOUT A--
THANK YOU!
I KNOW!
"AND THIS IS REAL?"

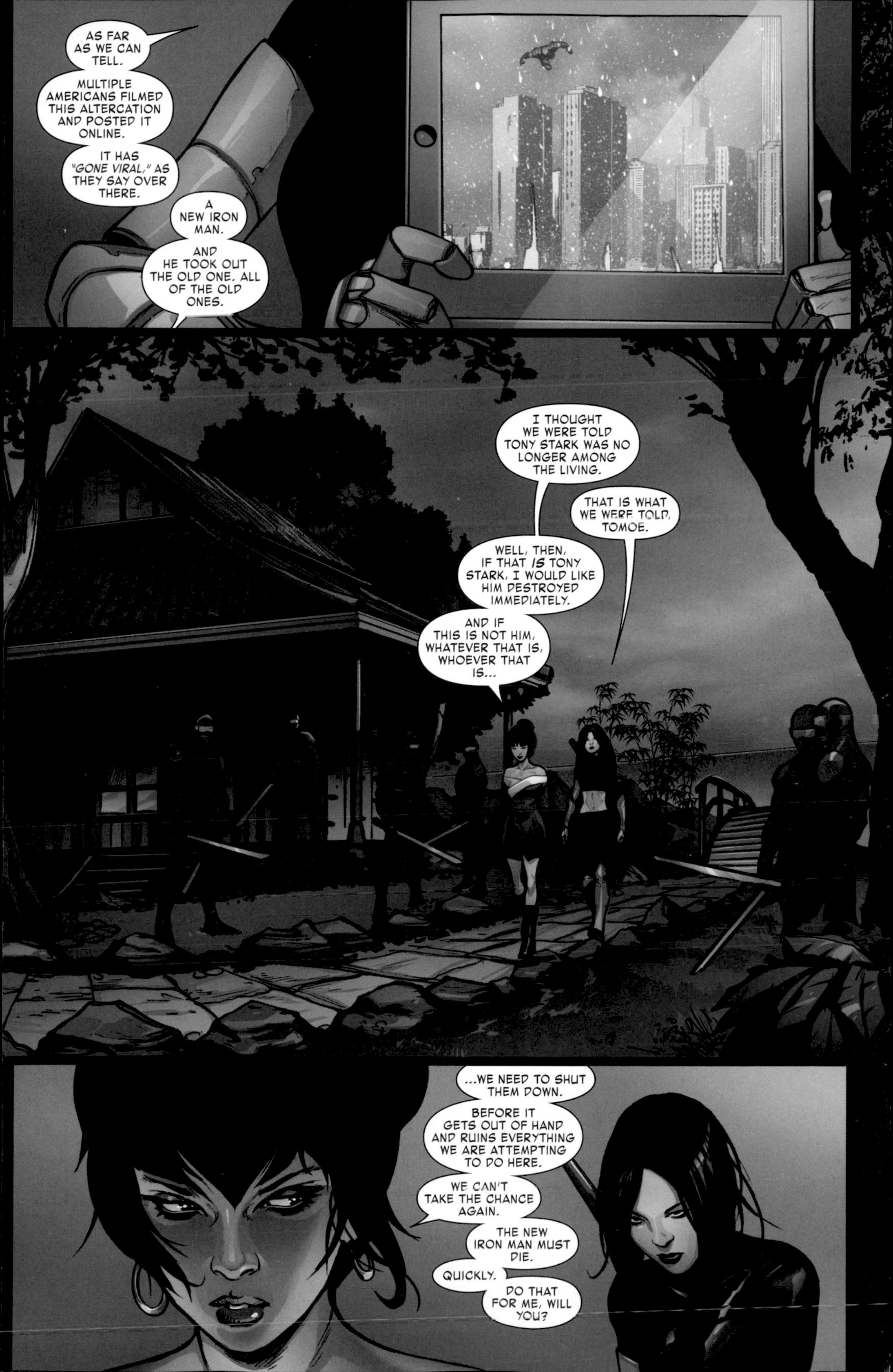
AS FAR AS WE CAN TELL.
MULTIPLE AMERICANS FILMED THIS ALTERCATION AND POSTED IT ONLINE.
IT HAS "GONE VIRAL," AS THEY SAY OVER THERE.
A NEW IRON MAN.
AND HE TOOK OUT THE OLD ONE. ALL OF THE OLD ONES.
I THOUGHT WE WERE TOLD TONY STARK WAS NO LONGER AMONG THE LIVING.
THAT IS WHAT WE WERE TOLD, TOMOE.
WELL, THEN, IF THAT *IS* TONY STARK, I WOULD LIKE HIM DESTROYED IMMEDIATELY.
AND IF THIS IS NOT HIM, WHATEVER THAT IS, WHOEVER THAT IS...
...WE NEED TO SHUT THEM DOWN.
BEFORE IT GETS OUT OF HAND AND RUINS EVERYTHING WE ARE ATTEMPTING TO DO HERE.
WE CAN'T TAKE THE CHANCE AGAIN.
THE NEW IRON MAN MUST DIE.
QUICKLY.
DO THAT FOR ME, WILL YOU?

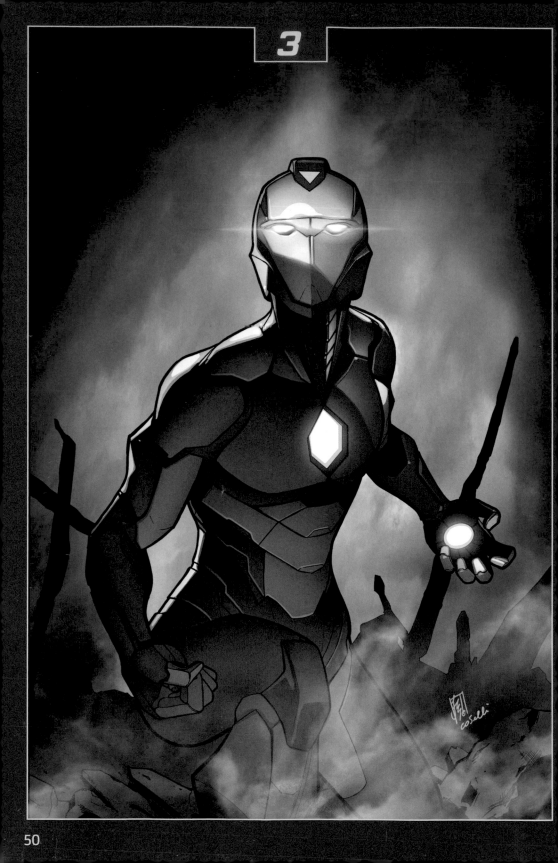

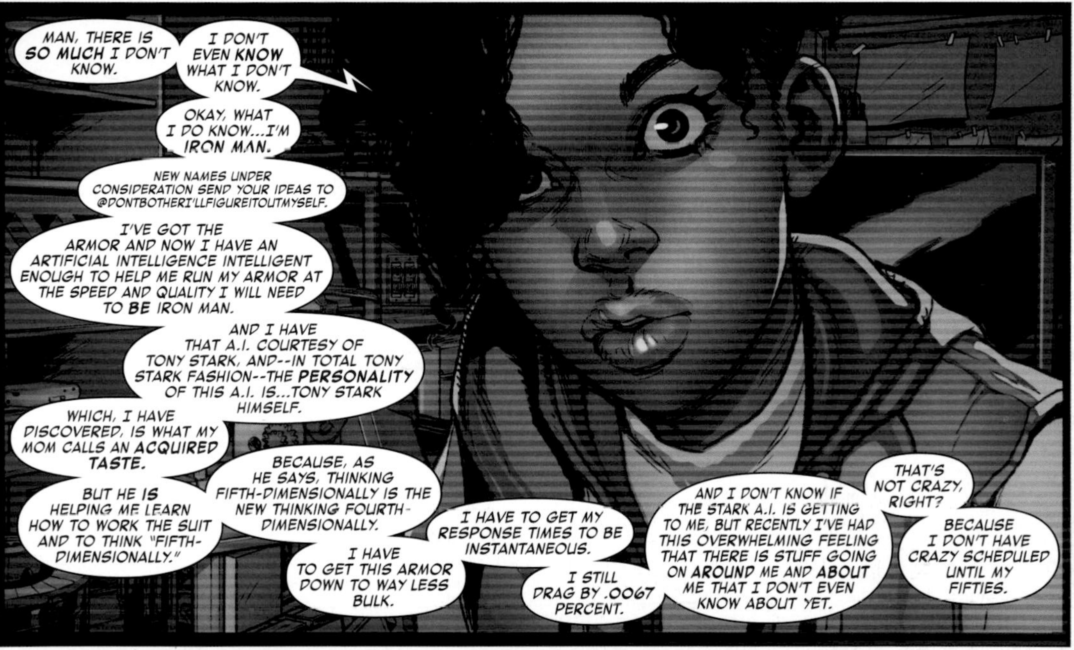
MAN, THERE IS SO MUCH I DON'T KNOW.
I DON'T EVEN KNOW WHAT I DON'T KNOW.
OKAY, WHAT I DO KNOW...I'M IRON MAN.
NEW NAMES UNDER CONSIDERATION SEND YOUR IDEAS TO @DONTBOTHERI'LLFIGUREITOUTMYSELF.
I'VE GOT THE ARMOR AND NOW I HAVE AN ARTIFICIAL INTELLIGENCE INTELLIGENT ENOUGH TO HELP ME RUN MY ARMOR AT THE SPEED AND QUALITY I WILL NEED TO BE IRON MAN.
AND I HAVE THAT A.I. COURTESY OF TONY STARK, AND--IN TOTAL TONY STARK FASHION--THE PERSONALITY OF THIS A.I. IS...TONY STARK HIMSELF.
WHICH, I HAVE DISCOVERED, IS WHAT MY MOM CALLS AN ACQUIRED TASTE.
BUT HE IS HELPING ME LEARN HOW TO WORK THE SUIT AND TO THINK "FIFTH-DIMENSIONALLY."
BECAUSE, AS HE SAYS, THINKING FIFTH-DIMENSIONALLY IS THE NEW THINKING FOURTH-DIMENSIONALLY.
I HAVE TO GET THIS ARMOR DOWN TO WAY LESS BULK.
I HAVE TO GET MY RESPONSE TIMES TO BE INSTANTANEOUS.
I STILL DRAG BY .0067 PERCENT.
AND I DON'T KNOW IF THE STARK A.I. IS GETTING TO ME, BUT RECENTLY I'VE HAD THIS OVERWHELMING FEELING THAT THERE IS STUFF GOING ON AROUND ME AND ABOUT ME THAT I DON'T EVEN KNOW ABOUT YET.
THAT'S NOT CRAZY, RIGHT?
BECAUSE I DON'T HAVE CRAZY SCHEDULED UNTIL MY FIFTIES.

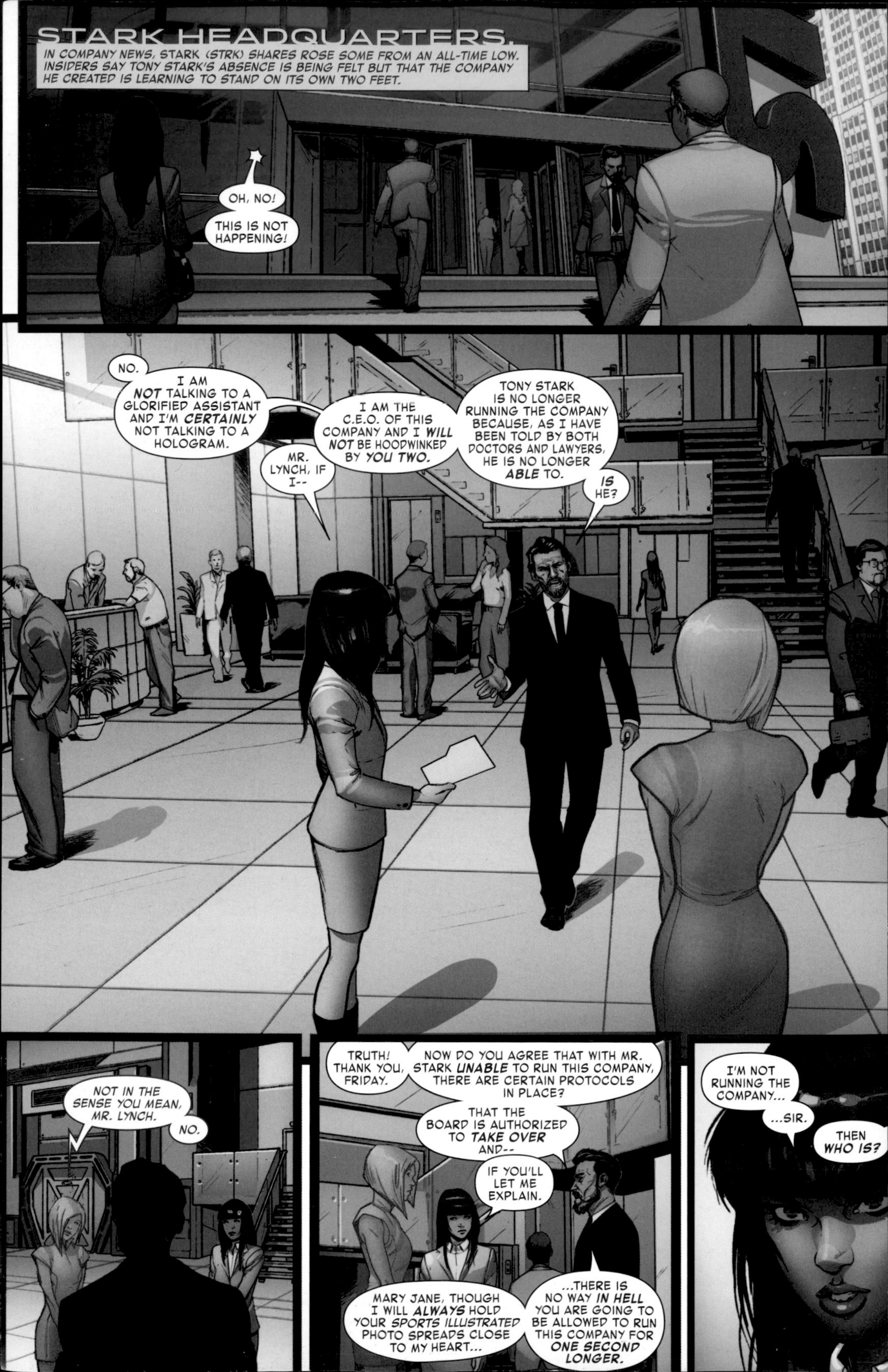
STARK HEADQUARTERS.
IN COMPANY NEWS, STARK (STRK) SHARES ROSE SOME FROM AN ALL-TIME LOW. INSIDERS SAY TONY STARK'S ABSENCE IS BEING FELT BUT THAT THE COMPANY HE CREATED IS LEARNING TO STAND ON ITS OWN TWO FEET.
OH, NO!
THIS IS NOT HAPPENING!
NO.
I AM NOT TALKING TO A GLORIFIED ASSISTANT AND I'M CERTAINLY NOT TALKING TO A HOLOGRAM.
MR. LYNCH, IF I--
I AM THE C.E.O. OF THIS COMPANY AND I WILL NOT BE HOODWINKED BY YOU TWO.
TONY STARK IS NO LONGER RUNNING THE COMPANY BECAUSE, AS I HAVE BEEN TOLD BY BOTH DOCTORS AND LAWYERS, HE IS NO LONGER ABLE TO.
IS HE?
NOT IN THE SENSE YOU MEAN, MR. LYNCH.
NO.
TRUTH! THANK YOU, FRIDAY.
NOW DO YOU AGREE THAT WITH MR. STARK UNABLE TO RUN THIS COMPANY, THERE ARE CERTAIN PROTOCOLS IN PLACE?
THAT THE BOARD IS AUTHORIZED TO TAKE OVER AND--
IF YOU'LL LET ME EXPLAIN.
MARY JANE, THOUGH I WILL ALWAYS HOLD YOUR SPORTS ILLUSTRATED PHOTO SPREADS CLOSE TO MY HEART...
...THERE IS NO WAY IN HELL YOU ARE GOING TO BE ALLOWED TO RUN THIS COMPANY FOR ONE SECOND LONGER.
I'M NOT RUNNING THE COMPANY...
...SIR.
THEN WHO IS?

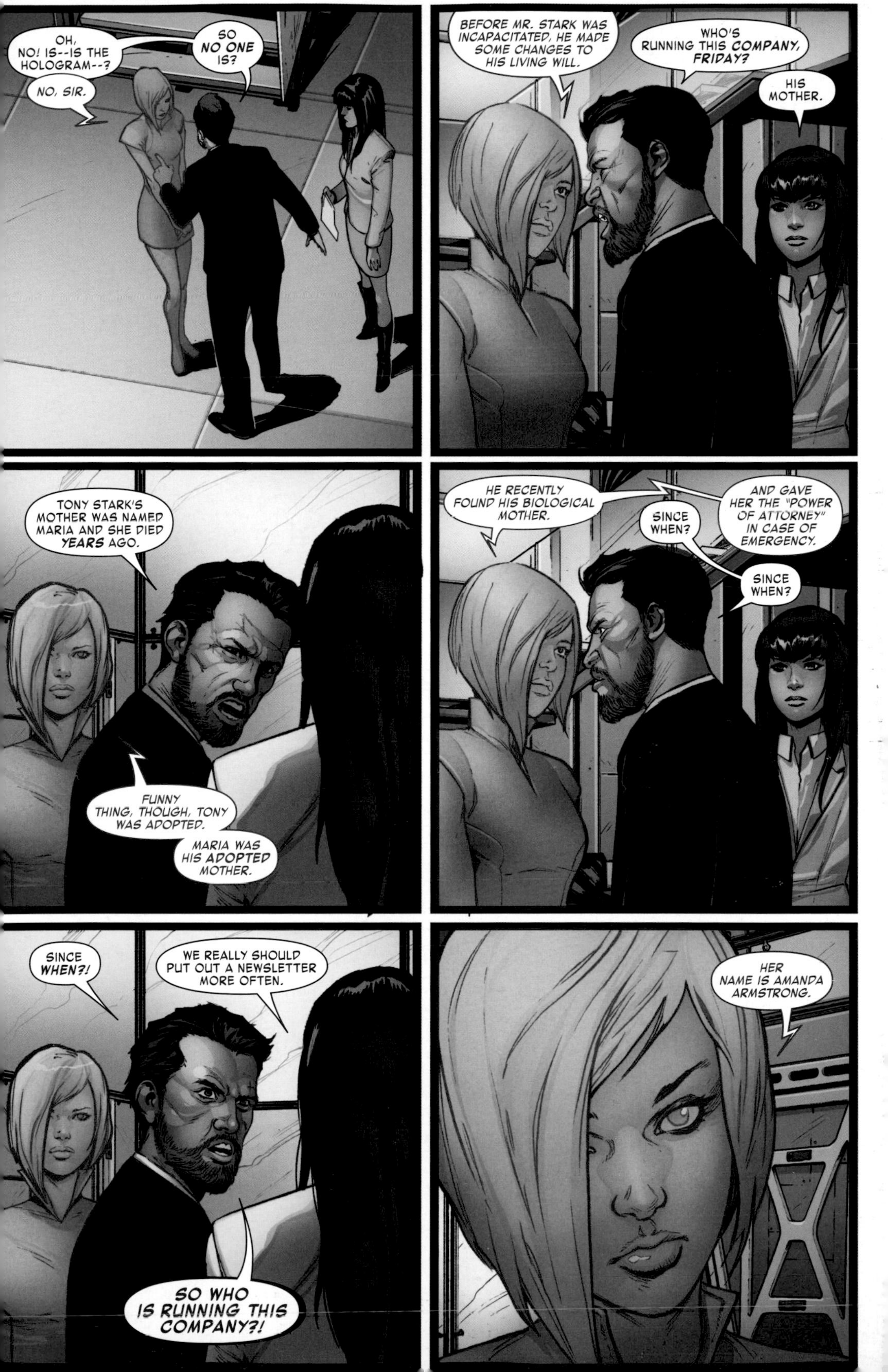
OH, NO! IS--IS THE HOLOGRAM--?
SO NO ONE IS?
NO, SIR.
BEFORE MR. STARK WAS INCAPACITATED, HE MADE SOME CHANGES TO HIS LIVING WILL.
WHO'S RUNNING THIS COMPANY, FRIDAY?
HIS MOTHER.
TONY STARK'S MOTHER WAS NAMED MARIA AND SHE DIED YEARS AGO.
FUNNY THING, THOUGH, TONY WAS ADOPTED.
MARIA WAS HIS ADOPTED MOTHER.
HE RECENTLY FOUND HIS BIOLOGICAL MOTHER.
AND GAVE HER THE "POWER OF ATTORNEY" IN CASE OF EMERGENCY.
SINCE WHEN?
SINCE WHEN?
SINCE WHEN?!
WE REALLY SHOULD PUT OUT A NEWSLETTER MORE OFTEN.
SO WHO IS RUNNING THIS COMPANY?!
HER NAME IS AMANDA ARMSTRONG.

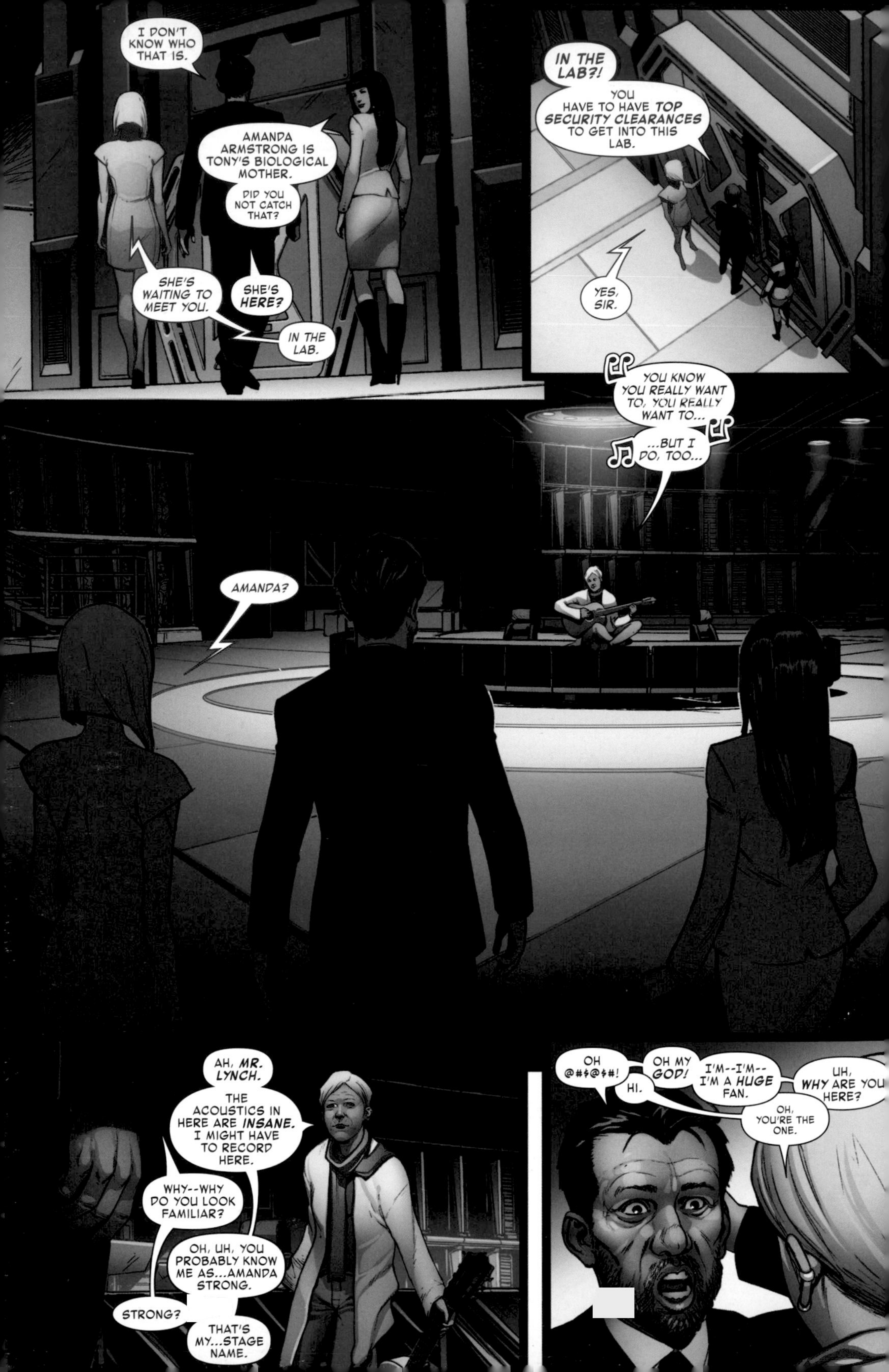

I DON'T KNOW WHO THAT IS.
AMANDA ARMSTRONG IS TONY'S BIOLOGICAL MOTHER.
DID YOU NOT CATCH THAT?
SHE'S WAITING TO MEET YOU.
SHE'S HERE?
IN THE LAB.
IN THE LAB?!
YOU HAVE TO HAVE TOP SECURITY CLEARANCES TO GET INTO THIS LAB.
YES, SIR.
YOU KNOW YOU REALLY WANT TO, YOU REALLY WANT TO...
...BUT I DO, TOO...
AMANDA?
AH, MR. LYNCH.
THE ACOUSTICS IN HERE ARE INSANE. I MIGHT HAVE TO RECORD HERE.
WHY--WHY DO YOU LOOK FAMILIAR?
OH, UH, YOU PROBABLY KNOW ME AS...AMANDA STRONG.
STRONG?
THAT'S MY...STAGE NAME.
OH @#$@$#!
OH MY GOD!
HI.
I'M--I'M--I'M A HUGE FAN.
UH, WHY ARE YOU HERE?
OH, YOU'RE THE ONE.

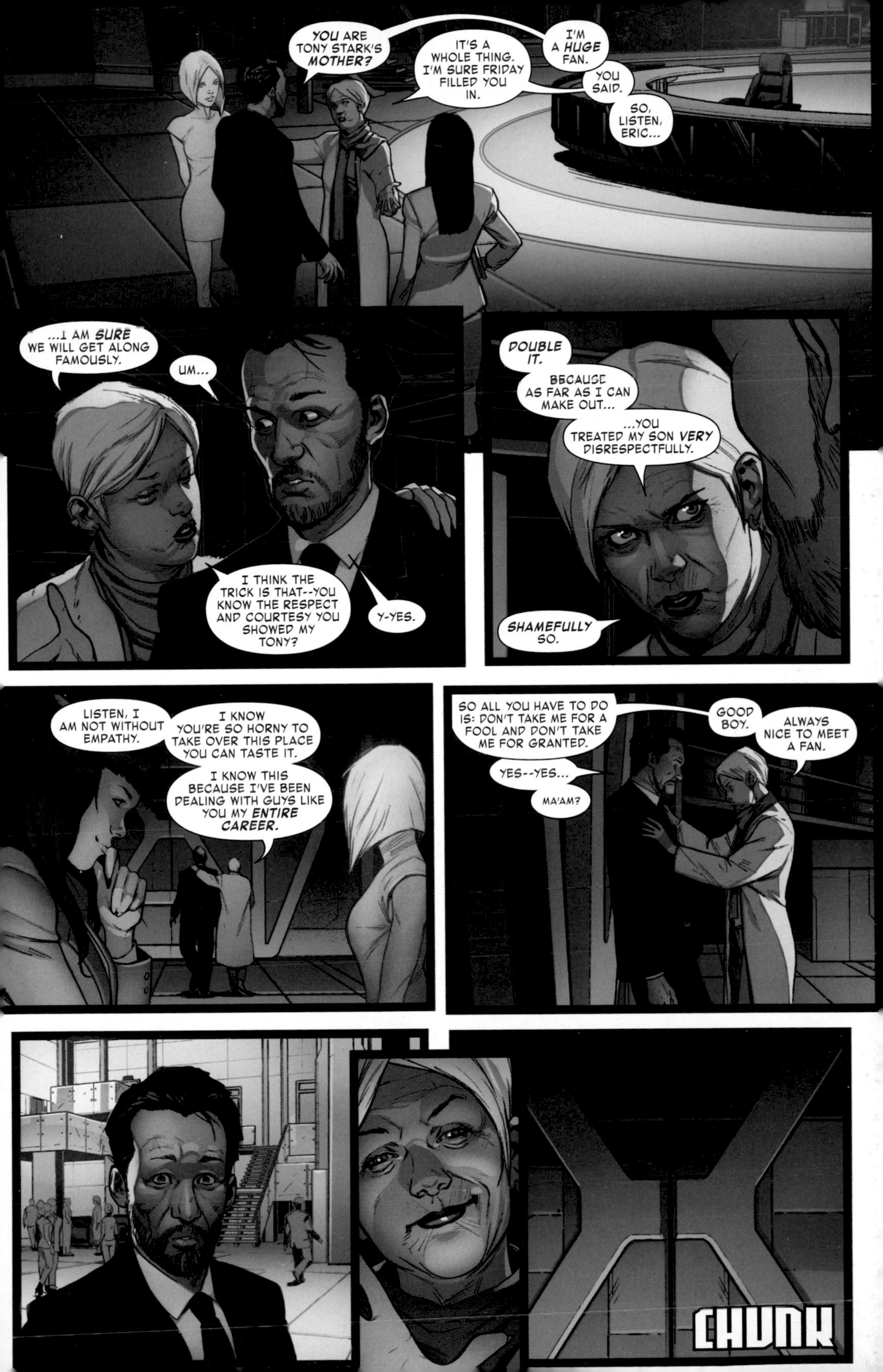
YOU ARE TONY STARK'S MOTHER?
I'M A HUGE FAN.
IT'S A WHOLE THING. I'M SURE FRIDAY FILLED YOU IN.
YOU SAID.
SO, LISTEN, ERIC...
...I AM SURE WE WILL GET ALONG FAMOUSLY.
UM...
I THINK THE TRICK IS THAT--YOU KNOW THE RESPECT AND COURTESY YOU SHOWED MY TONY?
Y-YES.
DOUBLE IT.
BECAUSE AS FAR AS I CAN MAKE OUT...
...YOU TREATED MY SON VERY DISRESPECTFULLY.
SHAMEFULLY SO.
LISTEN, I AM NOT WITHOUT EMPATHY.
I KNOW YOU'RE SO HORNY TO TAKE OVER THIS PLACE YOU CAN TASTE IT.
I KNOW THIS BECAUSE I'VE BEEN DEALING WITH GUYS LIKE YOU MY ENTIRE CAREER.
SO ALL YOU HAVE TO DO IS: DON'T TAKE ME FOR A FOOL AND DON'T TAKE ME FOR GRANTED.
YES--YES...
MA'AM?
GOOD BOY.
ALWAYS NICE TO MEET A FAN.
CHUNK

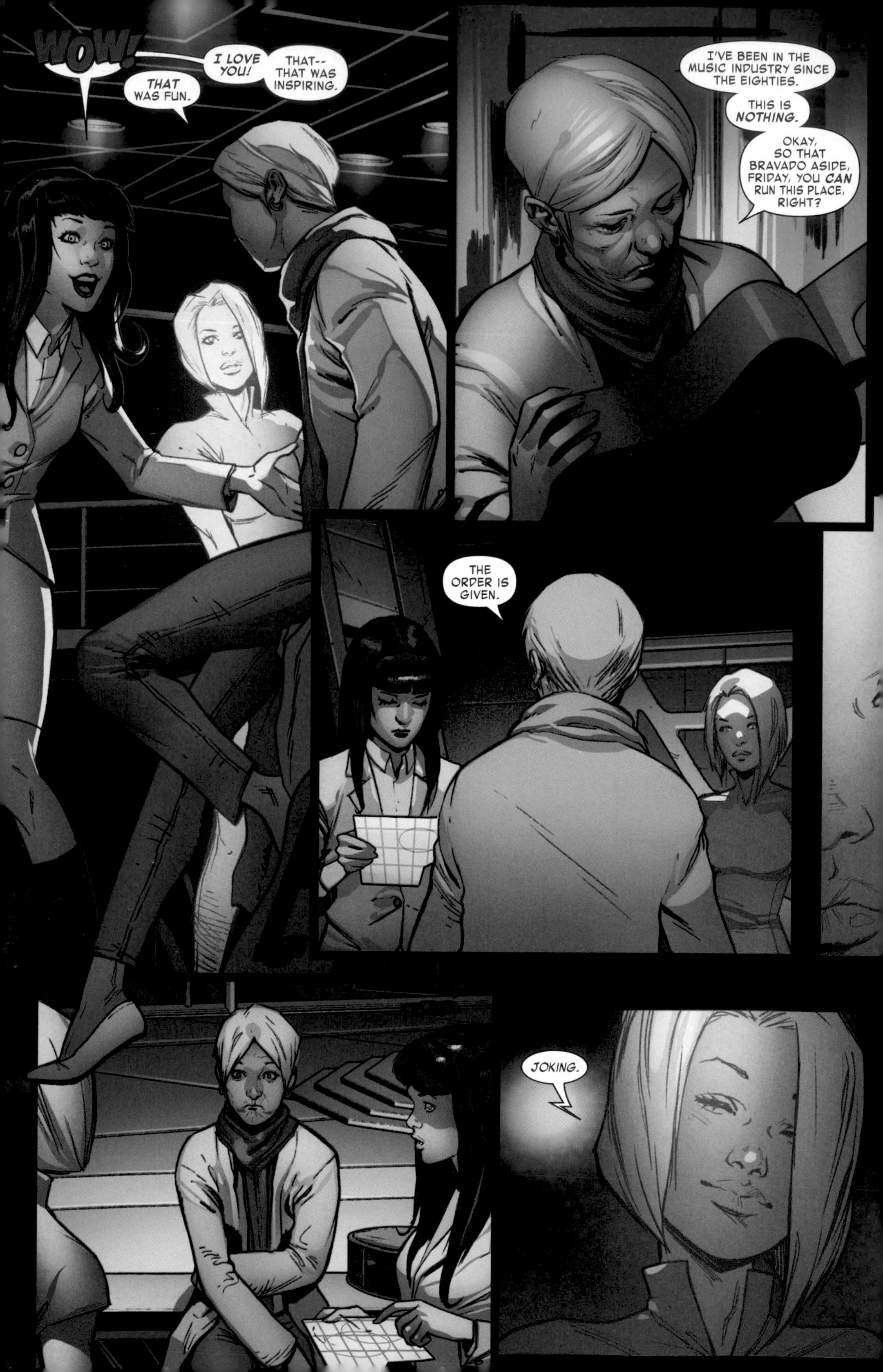
WOW!
THAT WAS FUN.
I LOVE YOU!
THAT-- THAT WAS INSPIRING.
I'VE BEEN IN THE MUSIC INDUSTRY SINCE THE EIGHTIES.
THIS IS NOTHING.
OKAY, SO THAT BRAVADO ASIDE, FRIDAY, YOU CAN RUN THIS PLACE, RIGHT?
THE ORDER IS GIVEN.
JOKING.

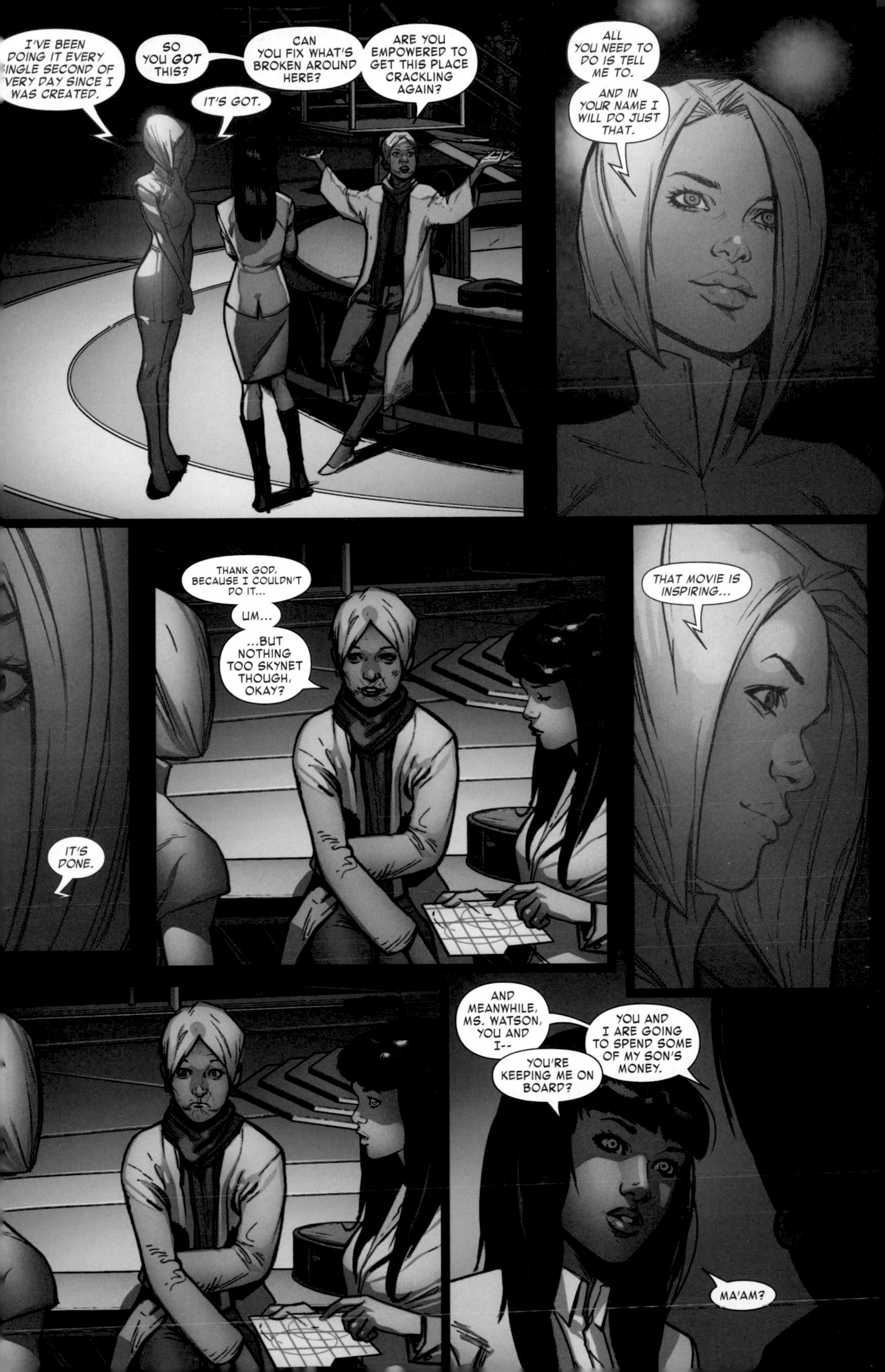
I'VE BEEN DOING IT EVERY SINGLE SECOND OF EVERY DAY SINCE I WAS CREATED.
SO YOU GOT THIS?
IT'S GOT.
CAN YOU FIX WHAT'S BROKEN AROUND HERE?
ARE YOU EMPOWERED TO GET THIS PLACE CRACKLING AGAIN?
ALL YOU NEED TO DO IS TELL ME TO.
AND IN YOUR NAME I WILL DO JUST THAT.
IT'S DONE.
THANK GOD, BECAUSE I COULDN'T DO IT...
UM...
...BUT NOTHING TOO SKYNET THOUGH, OKAY?
THAT MOVIE IS INSPIRING...
AND MEANWHILE, MS. WATSON, YOU AND I--
YOU AND I ARE GOING TO SPEND SOME OF MY SON'S MONEY.
YOU'RE KEEPING ME ON BOARD?
MA'AM?

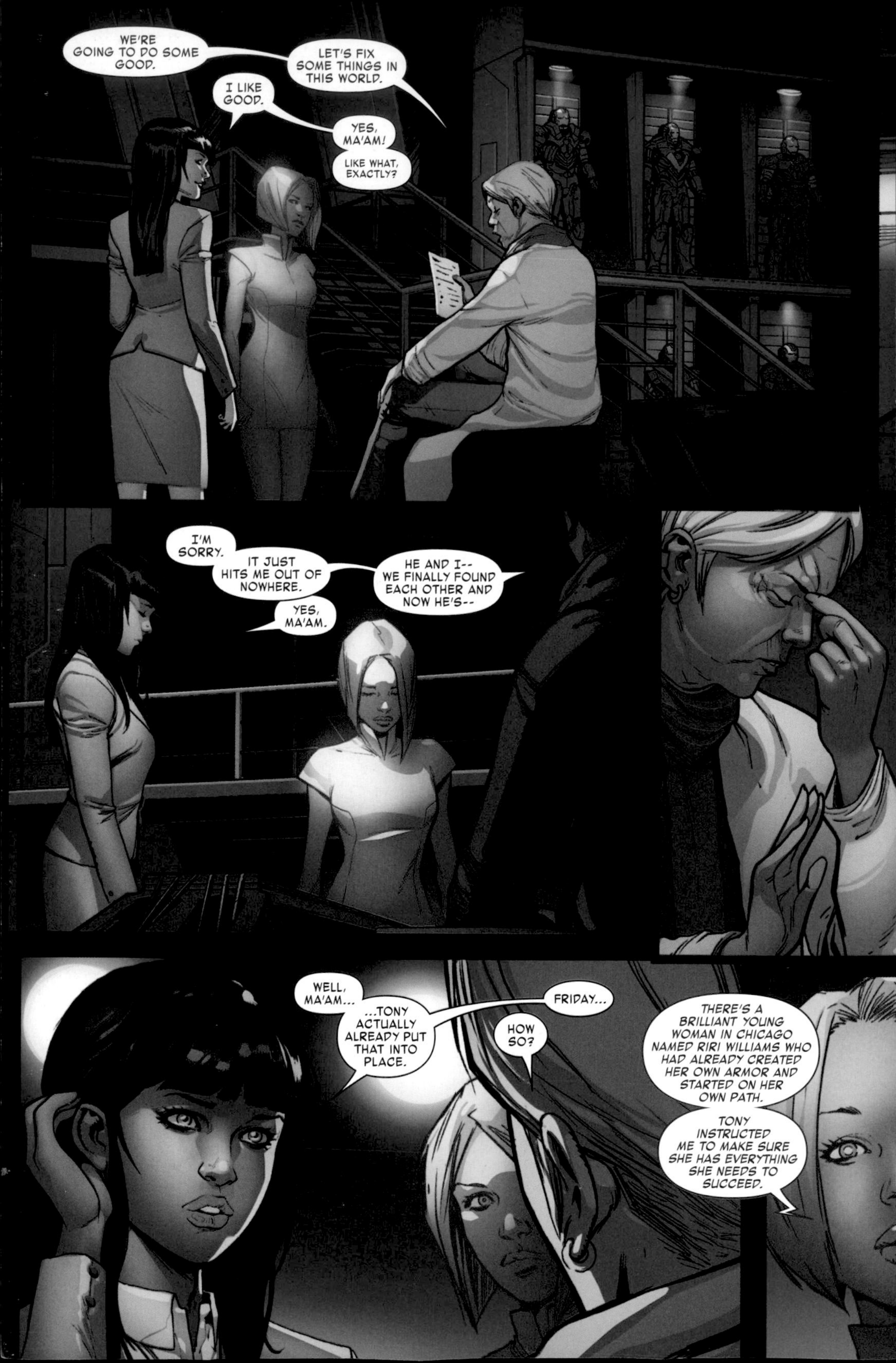

WE'RE GOING TO DO SOME GOOD.
LET'S FIX SOME THINGS IN THIS WORLD.
I LIKE GOOD.
YES, MA'AM!
LIKE WHAT, EXACTLY?
I'M SORRY.
IT JUST HITS ME OUT OF NOWHERE.
HE AND I-- WE FINALLY FOUND EACH OTHER AND NOW HE'S--
YES, MA'AM.
WELL, MA'AM...
...TONY ACTUALLY ALREADY PUT THAT INTO PLACE.
FRIDAY...
HOW SO?
THERE'S A BRILLIANT YOUNG WOMAN IN CHICAGO NAMED RIRI WILLIAMS WHO HAD ALREADY CREATED HER OWN ARMOR AND STARTED ON HER OWN PATH.
TONY INSTRUCTED ME TO MAKE SURE SHE HAS EVERYTHING SHE NEEDS TO SUCCEED.

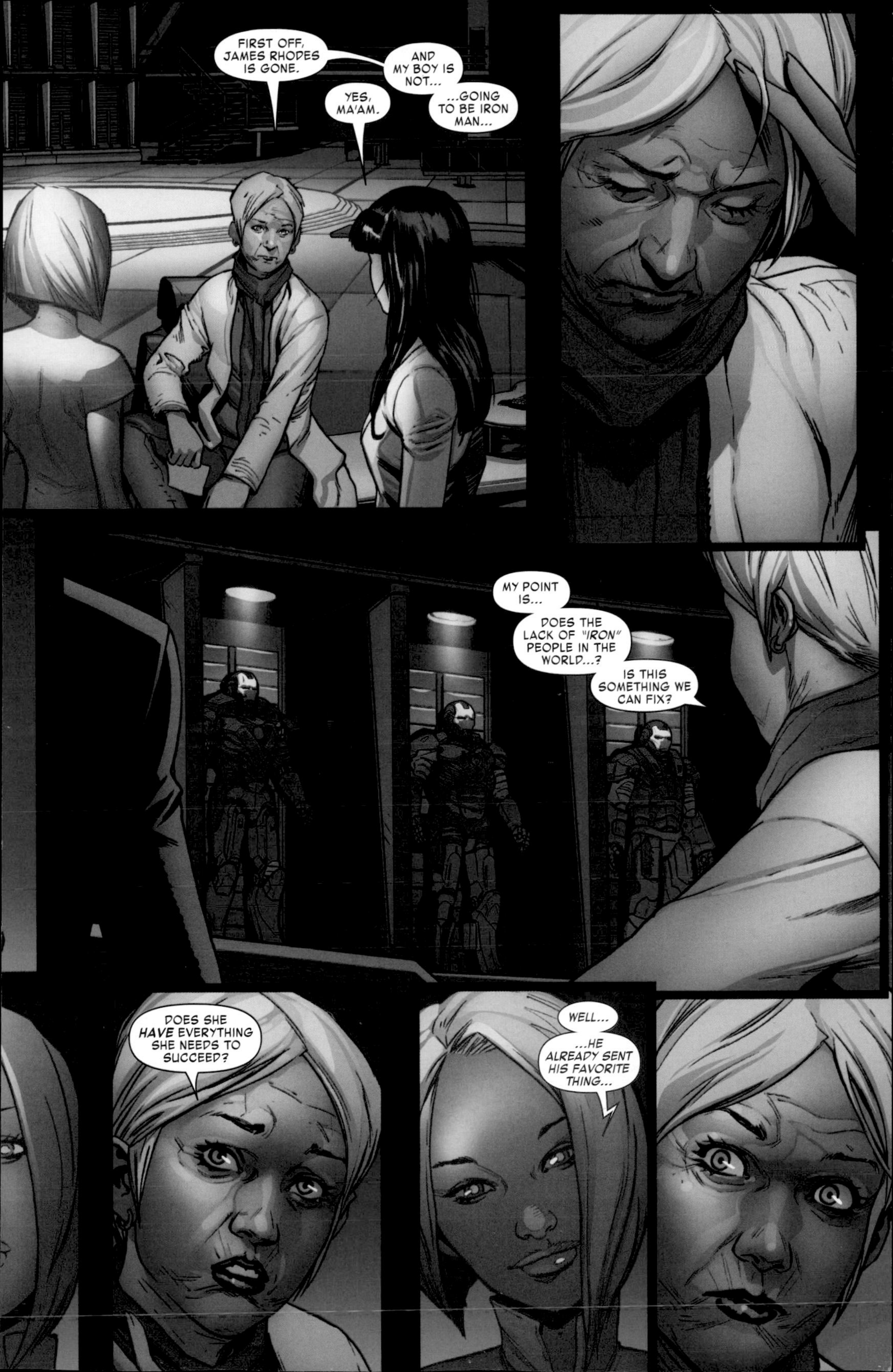
FIRST OFF, JAMES RHODES IS GONE.
AND MY BOY IS NOT...
YES, MA'AM.
...GOING TO BE IRON MAN...
MY POINT IS...
DOES THE LACK OF "IRON" PEOPLE IN THE WORLD...?
IS THIS SOMETHING WE CAN FIX?
DOES SHE HAVE EVERYTHING SHE NEEDS TO SUCCEED?
WELL...
...HE ALREADY SENT HIS FAVORITE THING...

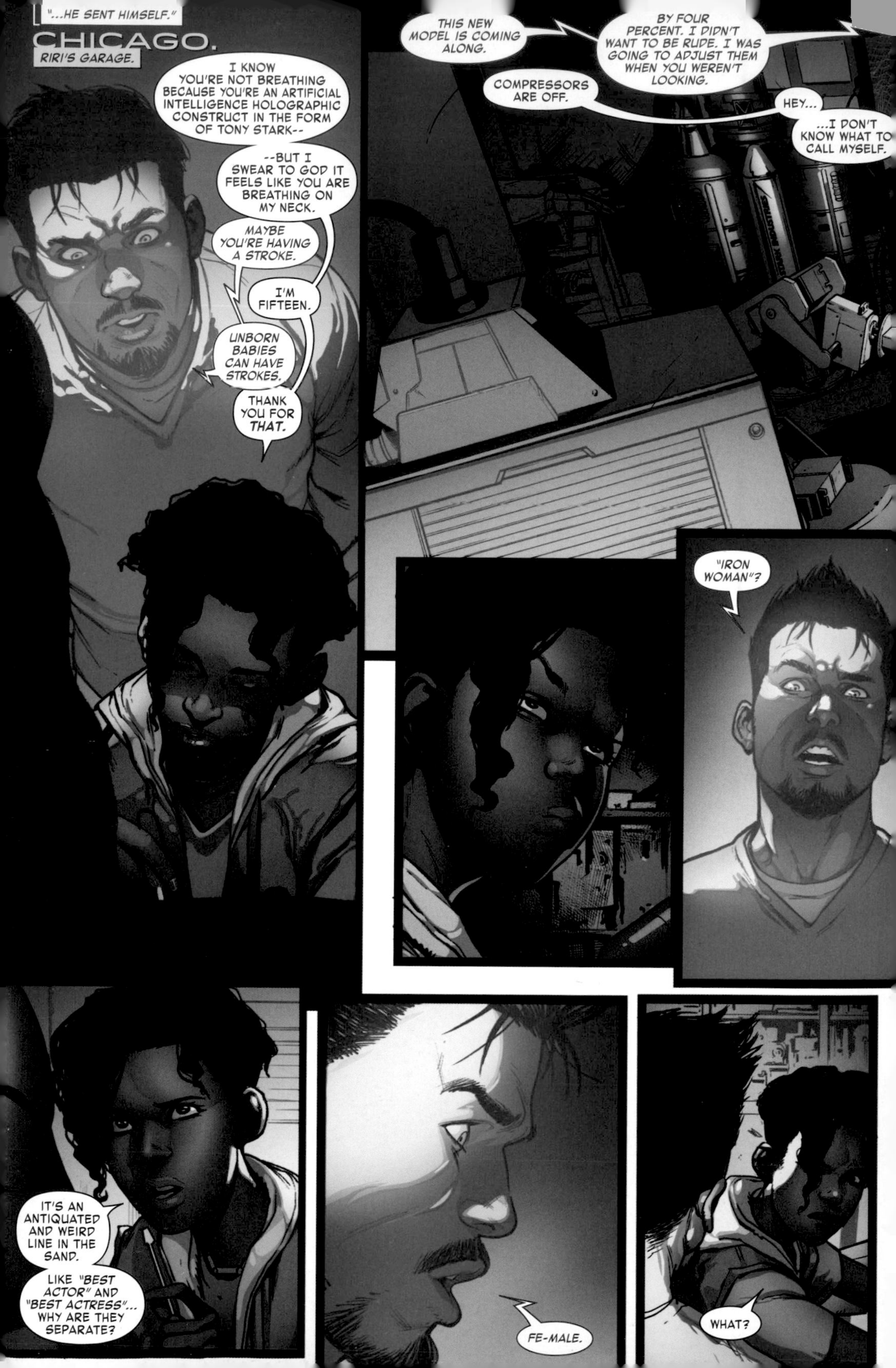
"...HE SENT HIMSELF."
CHICAGO.
RIRI'S GARAGE.
I KNOW YOU'RE NOT BREATHING BECAUSE YOU'RE AN ARTIFICIAL INTELLIGENCE HOLOGRAPHIC CONSTRUCT IN THE FORM OF TONY STARK--
--BUT I SWEAR TO GOD IT FEELS LIKE YOU ARE BREATHING ON MY NECK.
MAYBE YOU'RE HAVING A STROKE.
I'M FIFTEEN.
UNBORN BABIES CAN HAVE STROKES.
THANK YOU FOR THAT.
THIS NEW MODEL IS COMING ALONG.
BY FOUR PERCENT. I DIDN'T WANT TO BE RUDE. I WAS GOING TO ADJUST THEM WHEN YOU WEREN'T LOOKING.
COMPRESSORS ARE OFF.
HEY...
...I DON'T KNOW WHAT TO CALL MYSELF.
"IRON WOMAN"?
IT'S AN ANTIQUATED AND WEIRD LINE IN THE SAND.
LIKE "BEST ACTOR" AND "BEST ACTRESS"... WHY ARE THEY SEPARATE?
FE-MALE.
WHAT?

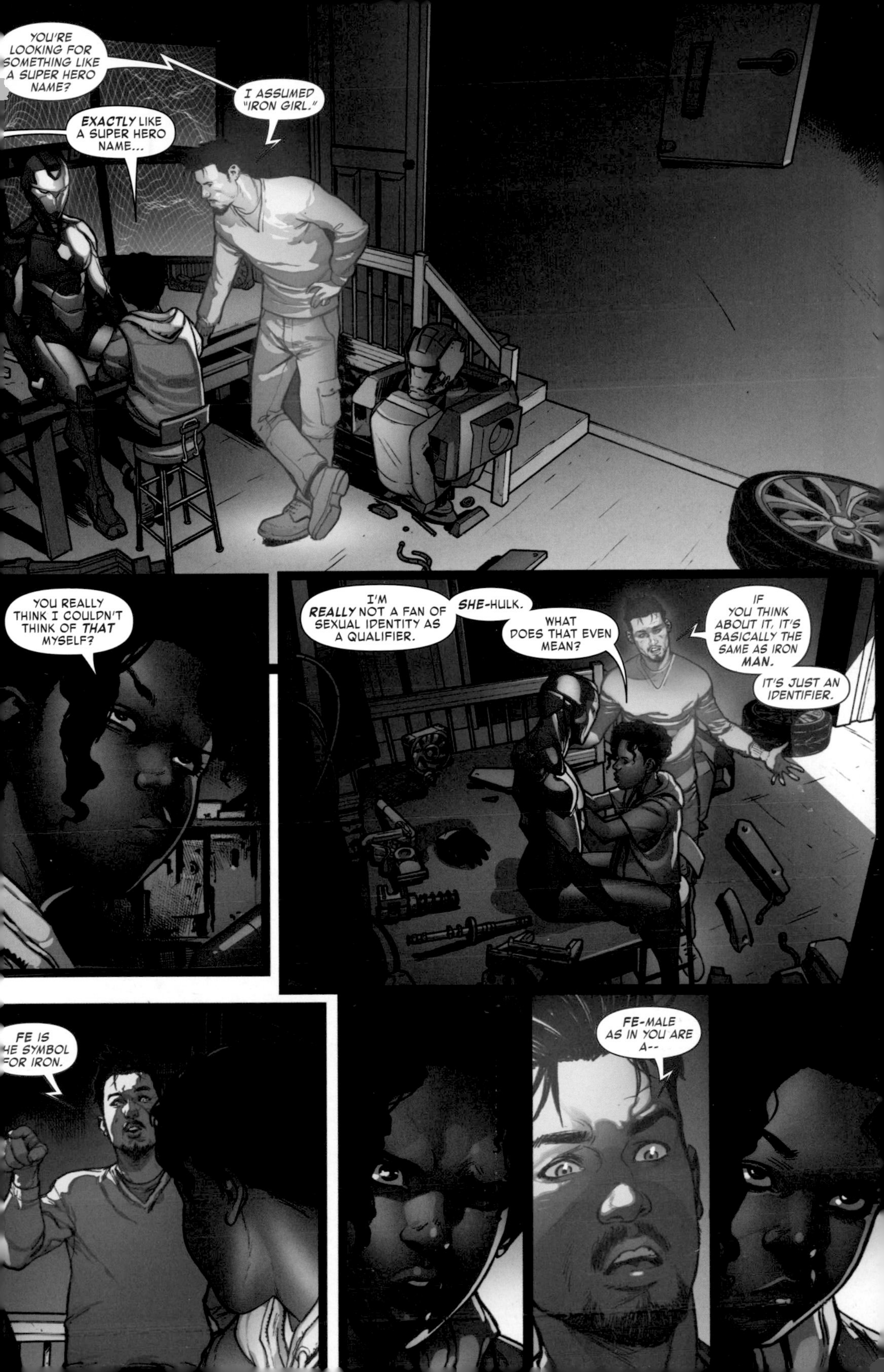

YOU'RE LOOKING FOR SOMETHING LIKE A SUPER HERO NAME?
I ASSUMED "IRON GIRL."
EXACTLY LIKE A SUPER HERO NAME...
YOU REALLY THINK I COULDN'T THINK OF THAT MYSELF?
I'M REALLY NOT A FAN OF SEXUAL IDENTITY AS A QUALIFIER.
SHE-HULK.
WHAT DOES THAT EVEN MEAN?
IF YOU THINK ABOUT IT, IT'S BASICALLY THE SAME AS IRON MAN.
IT'S JUST AN IDENTIFIER.
FE IS HE SYMBOL FOR IRON.
FE-MALE AS IN YOU ARE A--

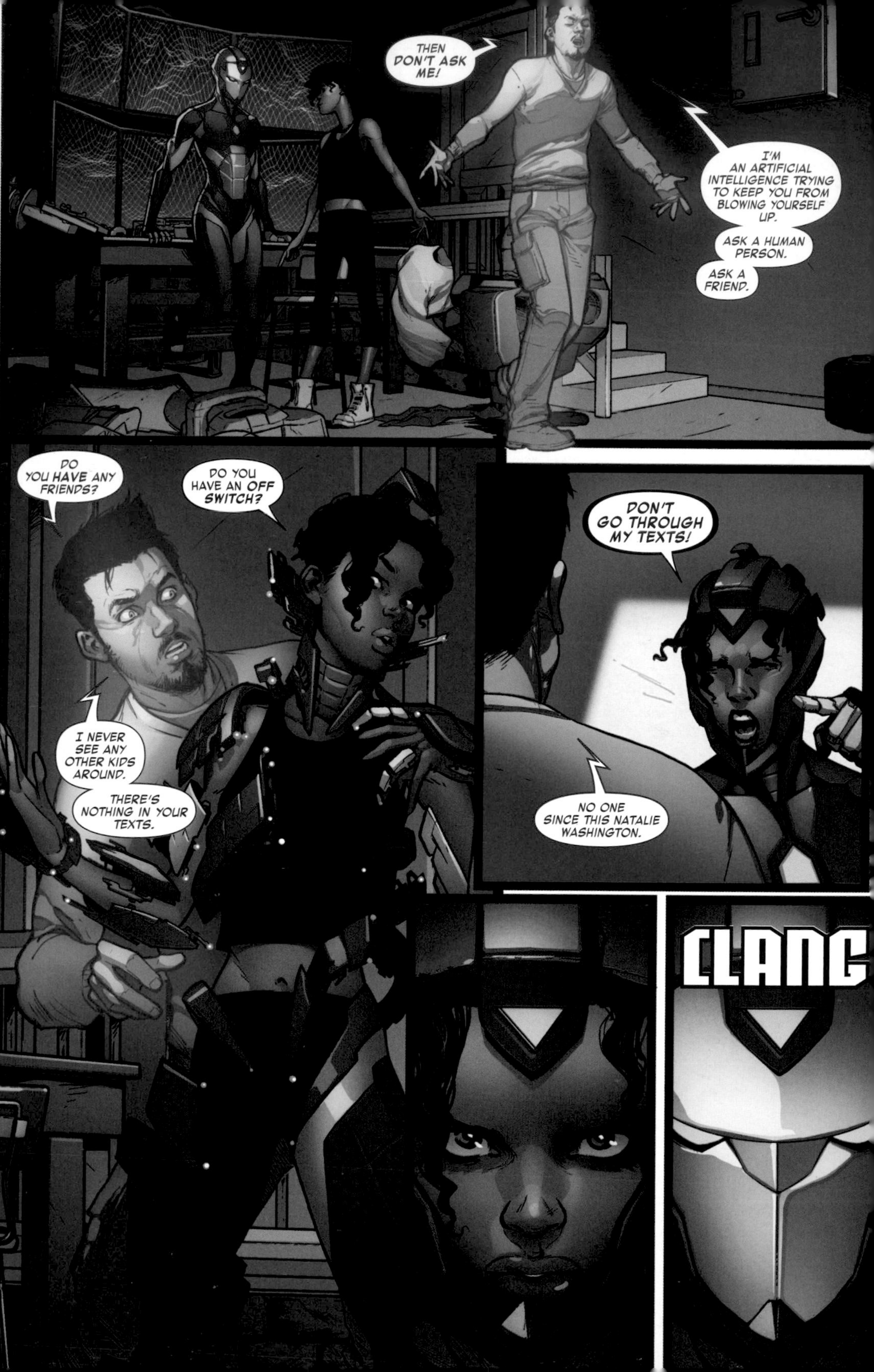
THEN DON'T ASK ME!
I'M AN ARTIFICIAL INTELLIGENCE TRYING TO KEEP YOU FROM BLOWING YOURSELF UP.
ASK A HUMAN PERSON.
ASK A FRIEND.
DO YOU HAVE ANY FRIENDS?
DO YOU HAVE AN OFF SWITCH?
I NEVER SEE ANY OTHER KIDS AROUND.
THERE'S NOTHING IN YOUR TEXTS.
DON'T GO THROUGH MY TEXTS!
NO ONE SINCE THIS NATALIE WASHINGTON.
CLANG

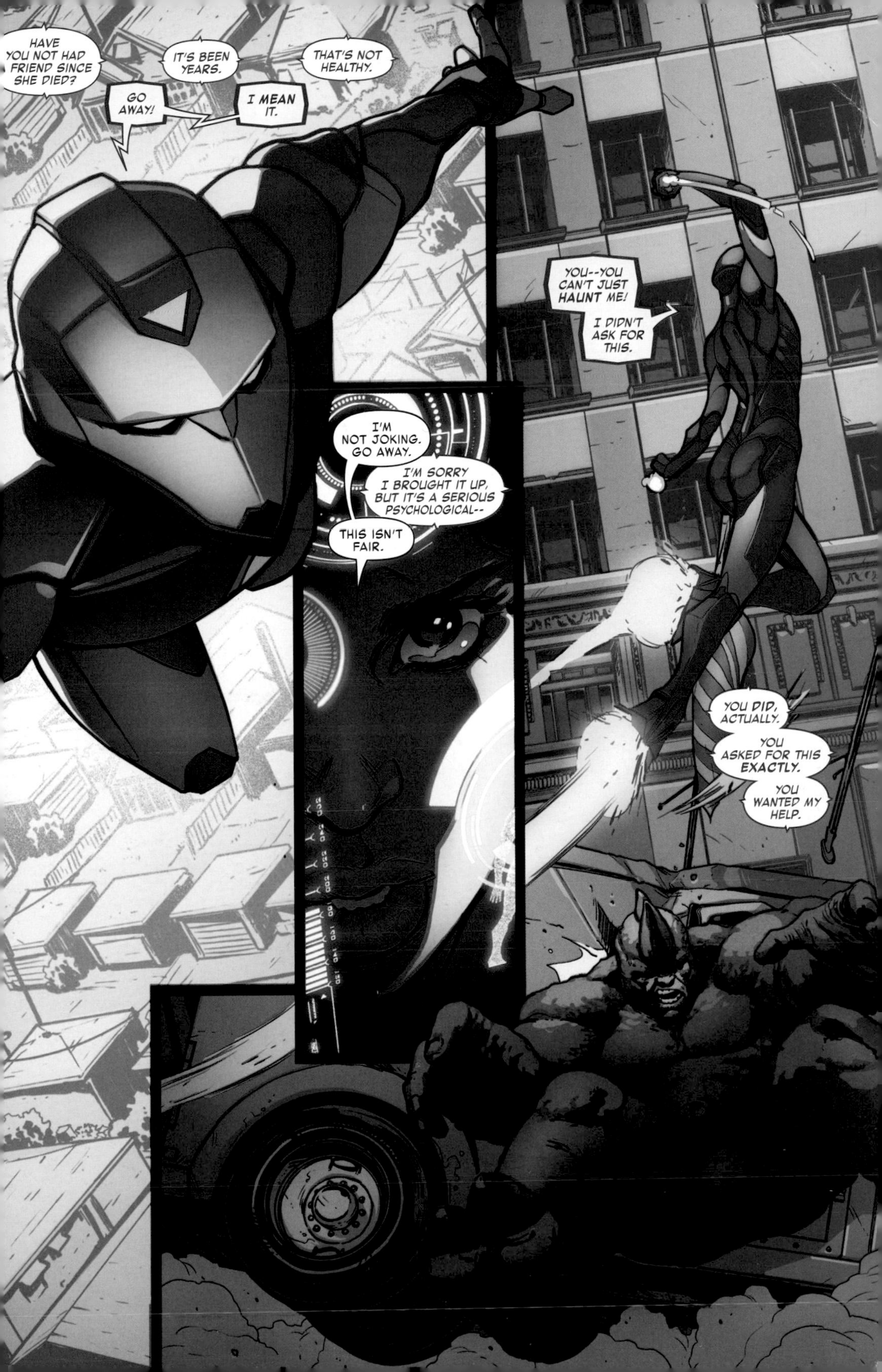
HAVE YOU NOT HAD FRIEND SINCE SHE DIED?
GO AWAY!
IT'S BEEN YEARS.
I MEAN IT.
THAT'S NOT HEALTHY.
YOU--YOU CAN'T JUST HAUNT ME!
I DIDN'T ASK FOR THIS.
I'M NOT JOKING. GO AWAY.
I'M SORRY I BROUGHT IT UP, BUT IT'S A SERIOUS PSYCHOLOGICAL--
THIS ISN'T FAIR.
YOU DID, ACTUALLY.
YOU ASKED FOR THIS EXACTLY.
YOU WANTED MY HELP.

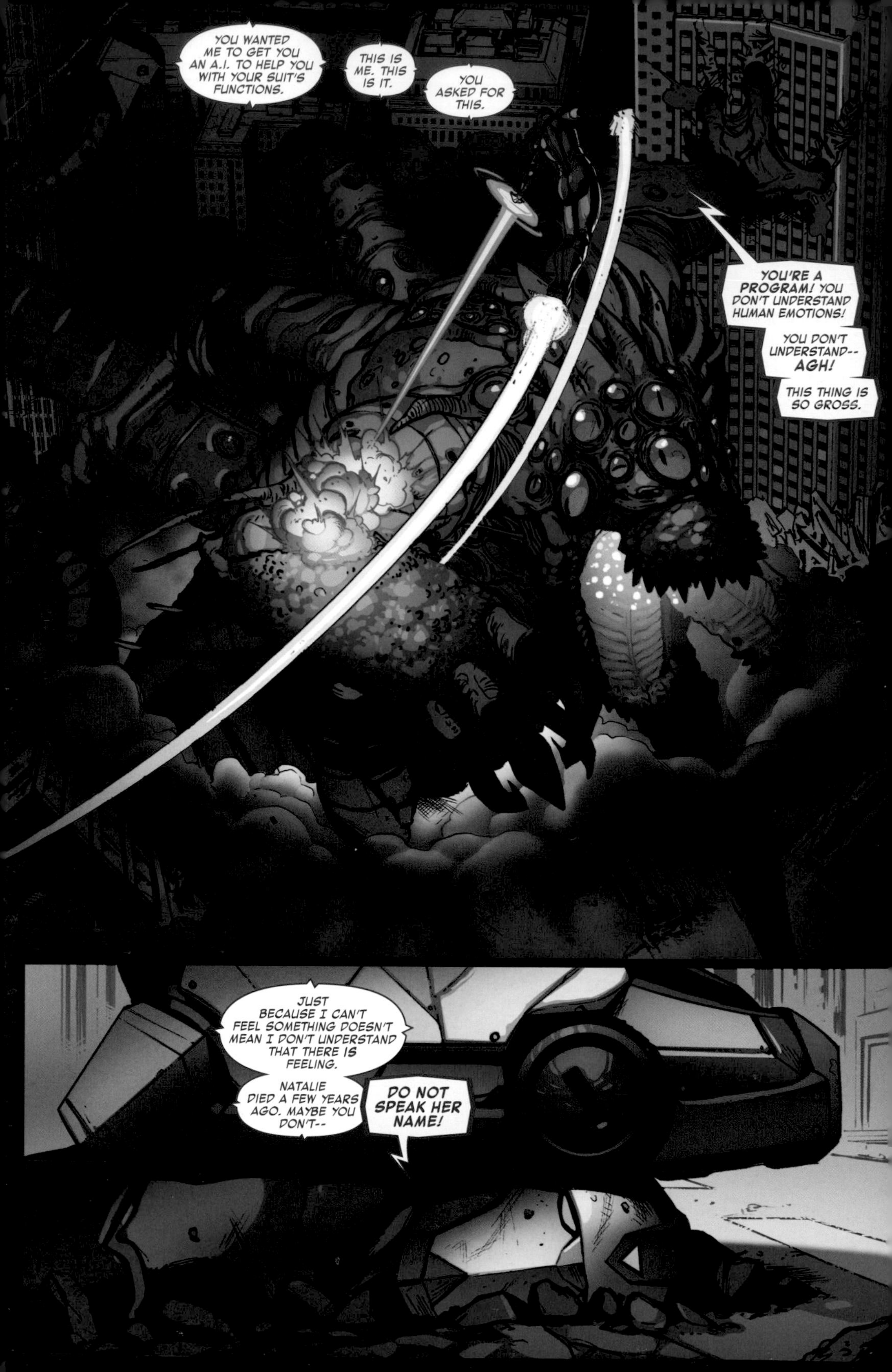
YOU WANTED ME TO GET YOU AN A.I. TO HELP YOU WITH YOUR SUIT'S FUNCTIONS.
THIS IS ME. THIS IS IT.
YOU ASKED FOR THIS.
YOU'RE A PROGRAM! YOU DON'T UNDERSTAND HUMAN EMOTIONS!
YOU DON'T UNDERSTAND-- AGH!
THIS THING IS SO GROSS.
JUST BECAUSE I CAN'T FEEL SOMETHING DOESN'T MEAN I DON'T UNDERSTAND THAT THERE IS FEELING.
NATALIE DIED A FEW YEARS AGO. MAYBE YOU DON'T--
DO NOT SPEAK HER NAME!

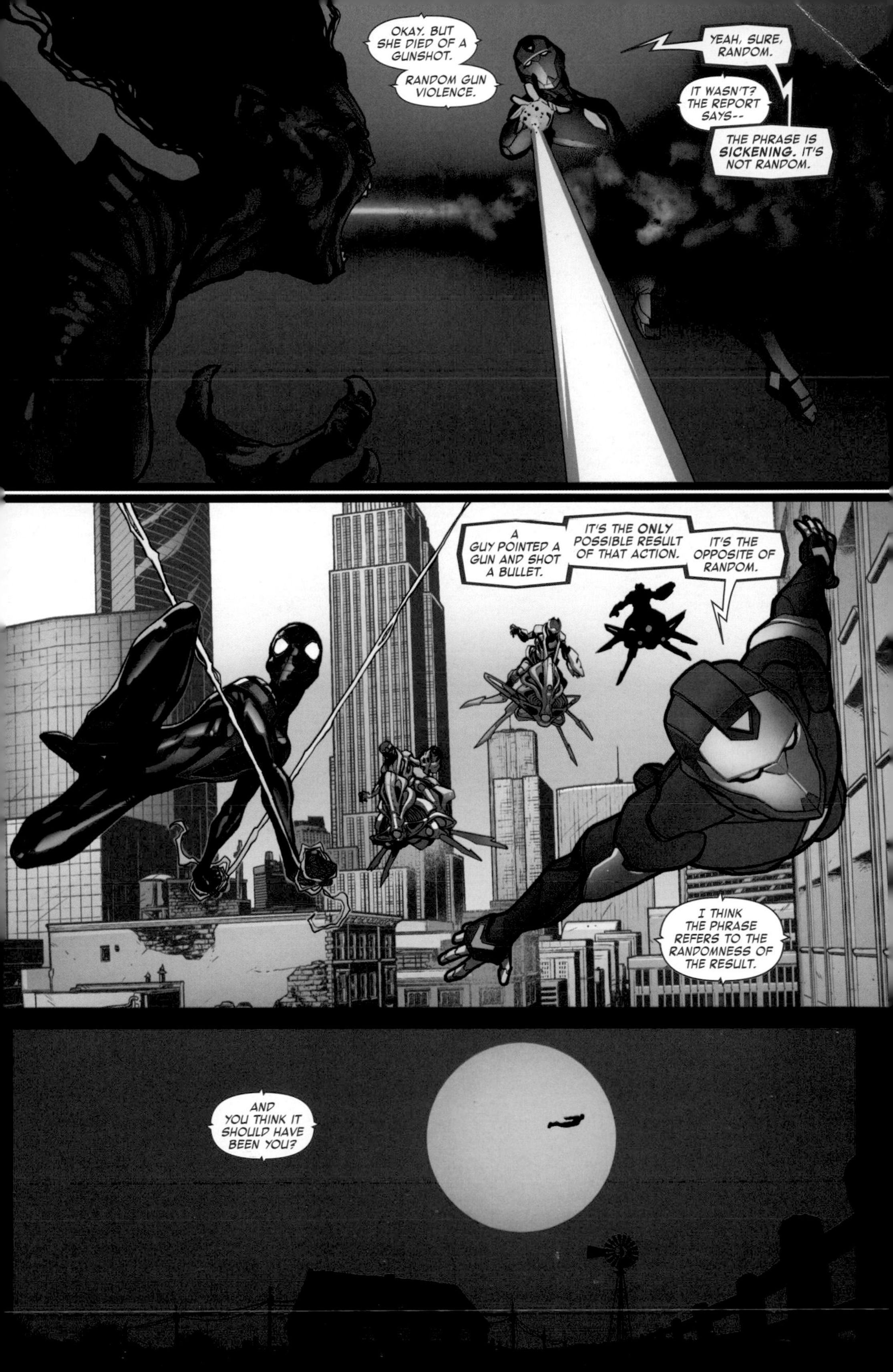
OKAY. BUT SHE DIED OF A GUNSHOT.
RANDOM GUN VIOLENCE.
YEAH, SURE, RANDOM.
IT WASN'T? THE REPORT SAYS--
THE PHRASE IS SICKENING. IT'S NOT RANDOM.
A GUY POINTED A GUN AND SHOT A BULLET.
IT'S THE ONLY POSSIBLE RESULT OF THAT ACTION.
IT'S THE OPPOSITE OF RANDOM.
I THINK THE PHRASE REFERS TO THE RANDOMNESS OF THE RESULT.
AND YOU THINK IT SHOULD HAVE BEEN YOU?

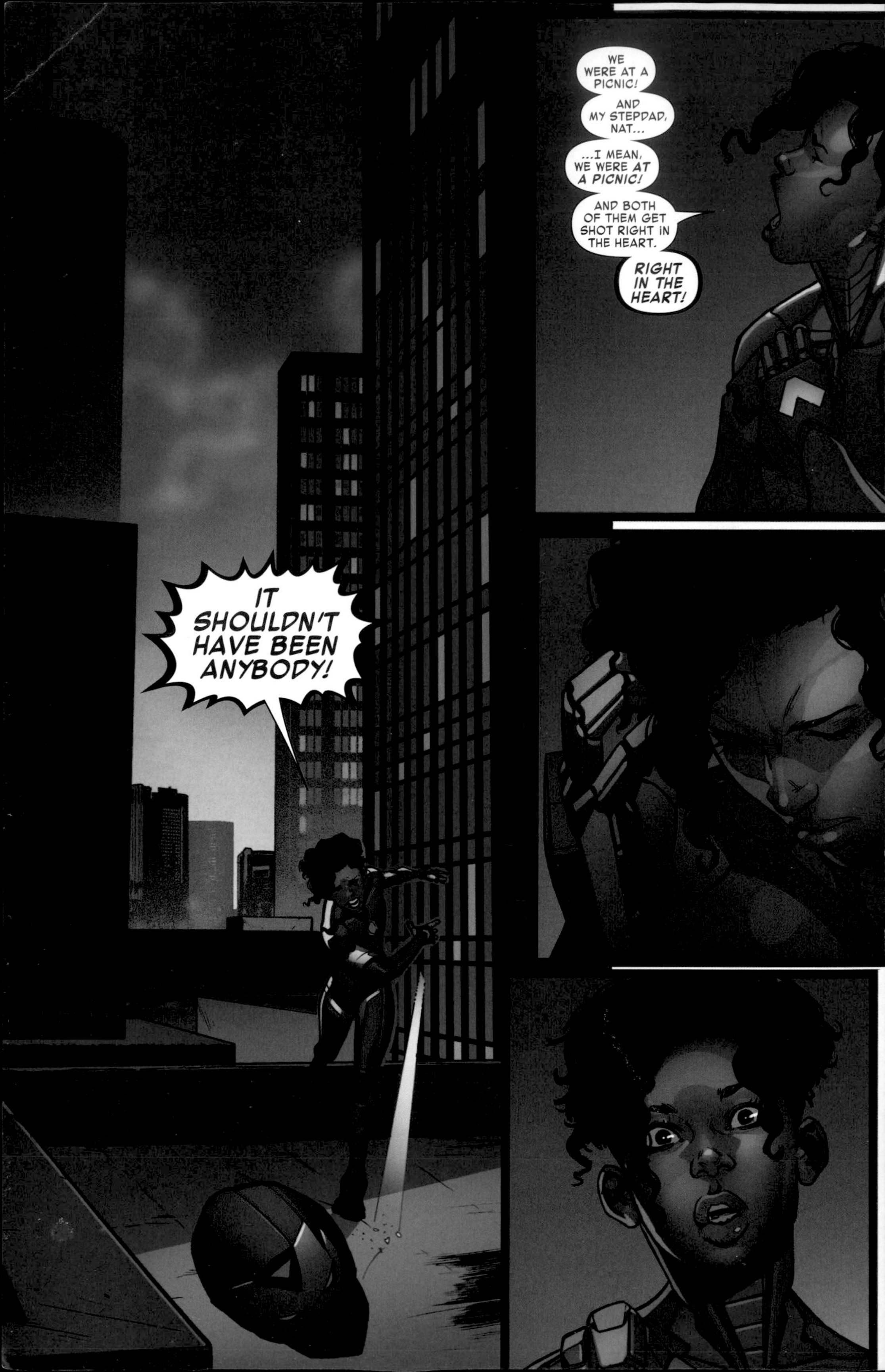
WE WERE AT A PICNIC!
AND MY STEPDAD, NAT...
...I MEAN, WE WERE AT A PICNIC!
AND BOTH OF THEM GET SHOT RIGHT IN THE HEART.
RIGHT IN THE HEART!
IT SHOULDN'T HAVE BEEN ANYBODY!

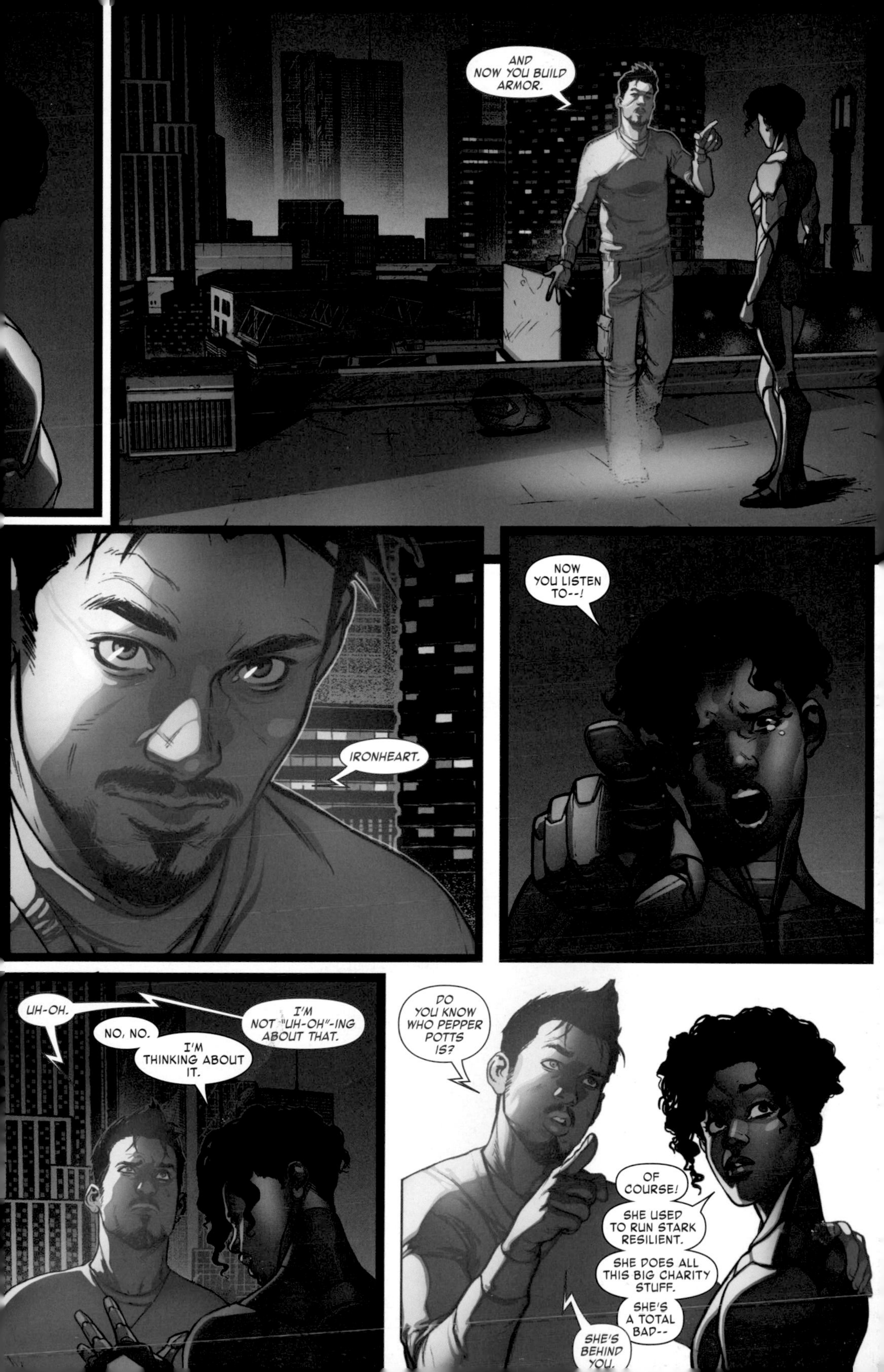
AND NOW YOU BUILD ARMOR.
NOW YOU LISTEN TO--!
IRONHEART.
UH-OH.
I'M NOT "UH-OH"-ING ABOUT THAT.
NO, NO.
I'M THINKING ABOUT IT.
DO YOU KNOW WHO PEPPER POTTS IS?
OF COURSE!
SHE USED TO RUN STARK RESILIENT.
SHE DOES ALL THIS BIG CHARITY STUFF.
SHE'S A TOTAL BAD--
SHE'S BEHIND YOU.

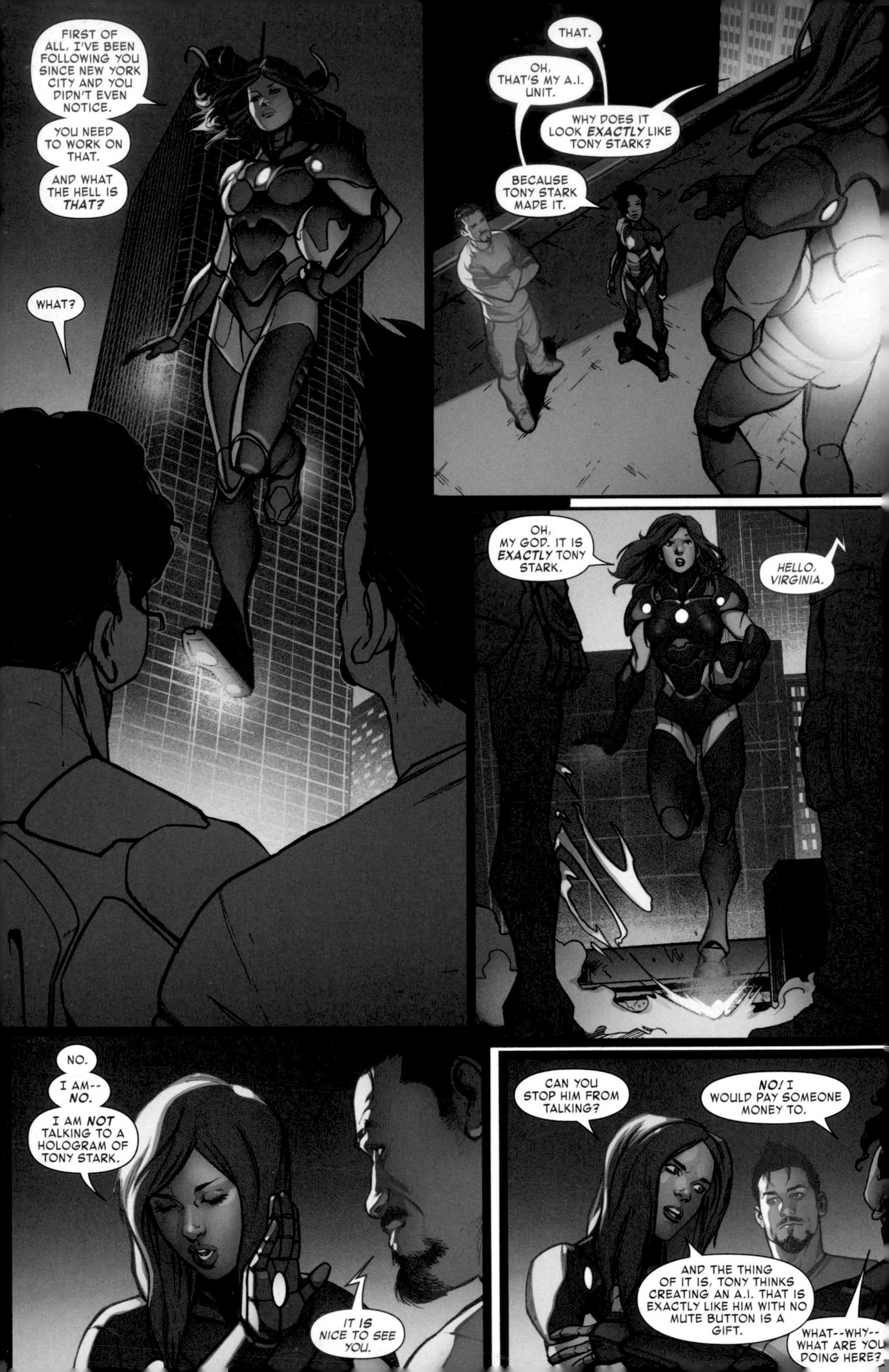
FIRST OF ALL, I'VE BEEN FOLLOWING YOU SINCE NEW YORK CITY AND YOU DIDN'T EVEN NOTICE.
YOU NEED TO WORK ON THAT.
AND WHAT THE HELL IS *THAT?*
WHAT?
THAT.
OH, THAT'S MY A.I. UNIT.
WHY DOES IT LOOK *EXACTLY* LIKE TONY STARK?
BECAUSE TONY STARK MADE IT.
OH, MY GOD. IT IS *EXACTLY* TONY STARK.
HELLO, VIRGINIA.
NO.
I AM-- *NO.*
I AM *NOT* TALKING TO A HOLOGRAM OF TONY STARK.
IT IS NICE TO SEE YOU.
CAN YOU STOP HIM FROM TALKING?
NO! I WOULD PAY SOMEONE MONEY TO.
AND THE THING OF IT IS, TONY THINKS CREATING AN A.I. THAT IS EXACTLY LIKE HIM WITH NO MUTE BUTTON IS A GIFT.
WHAT--WHY-- WHAT ARE YOU DOING HERE?

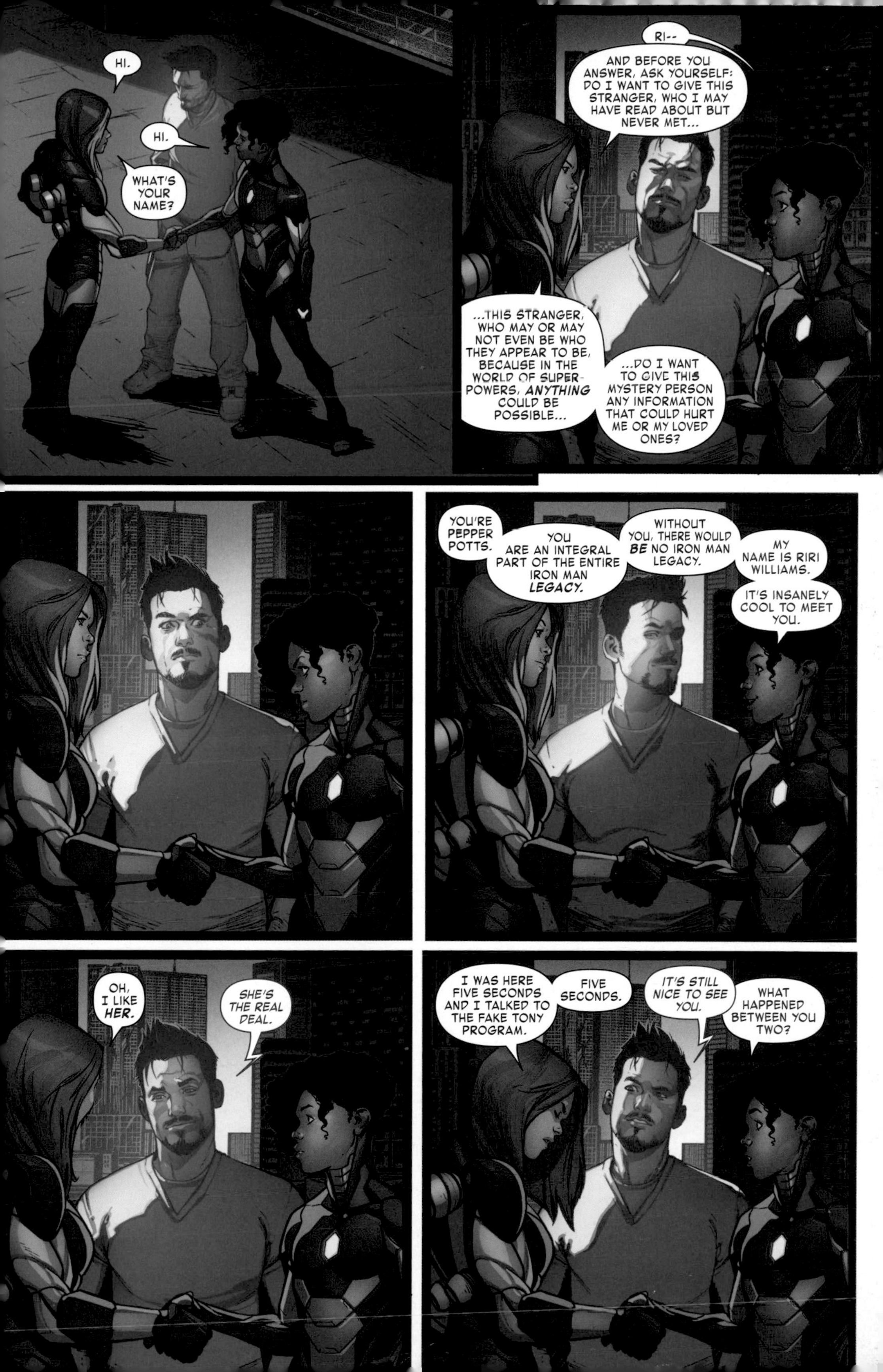
HI.
HI.
WHAT'S YOUR NAME?
RI--
AND BEFORE YOU ANSWER, ASK YOURSELF: DO I WANT TO GIVE THIS STRANGER, WHO I MAY HAVE READ ABOUT BUT NEVER MET...
...THIS STRANGER, WHO MAY OR MAY NOT EVEN BE WHO THEY APPEAR TO BE, BECAUSE IN THE WORLD OF SUPER-POWERS, ANYTHING COULD BE POSSIBLE...
...DO I WANT TO GIVE THIS MYSTERY PERSON ANY INFORMATION THAT COULD HURT ME OR MY LOVED ONES?
YOU'RE PEPPER POTTS.
YOU ARE AN INTEGRAL PART OF THE ENTIRE IRON MAN LEGACY.
WITHOUT YOU, THERE WOULD BE NO IRON MAN LEGACY.
MY NAME IS RIRI WILLIAMS.
IT'S INSANELY COOL TO MEET YOU.
OH, I LIKE HER.
SHE'S THE REAL DEAL.
I WAS HERE FIVE SECONDS AND I TALKED TO THE FAKE TONY PROGRAM.
FIVE SECONDS.
IT'S STILL NICE TO SEE YOU.
WHAT HAPPENED BETWEEN YOU TWO?

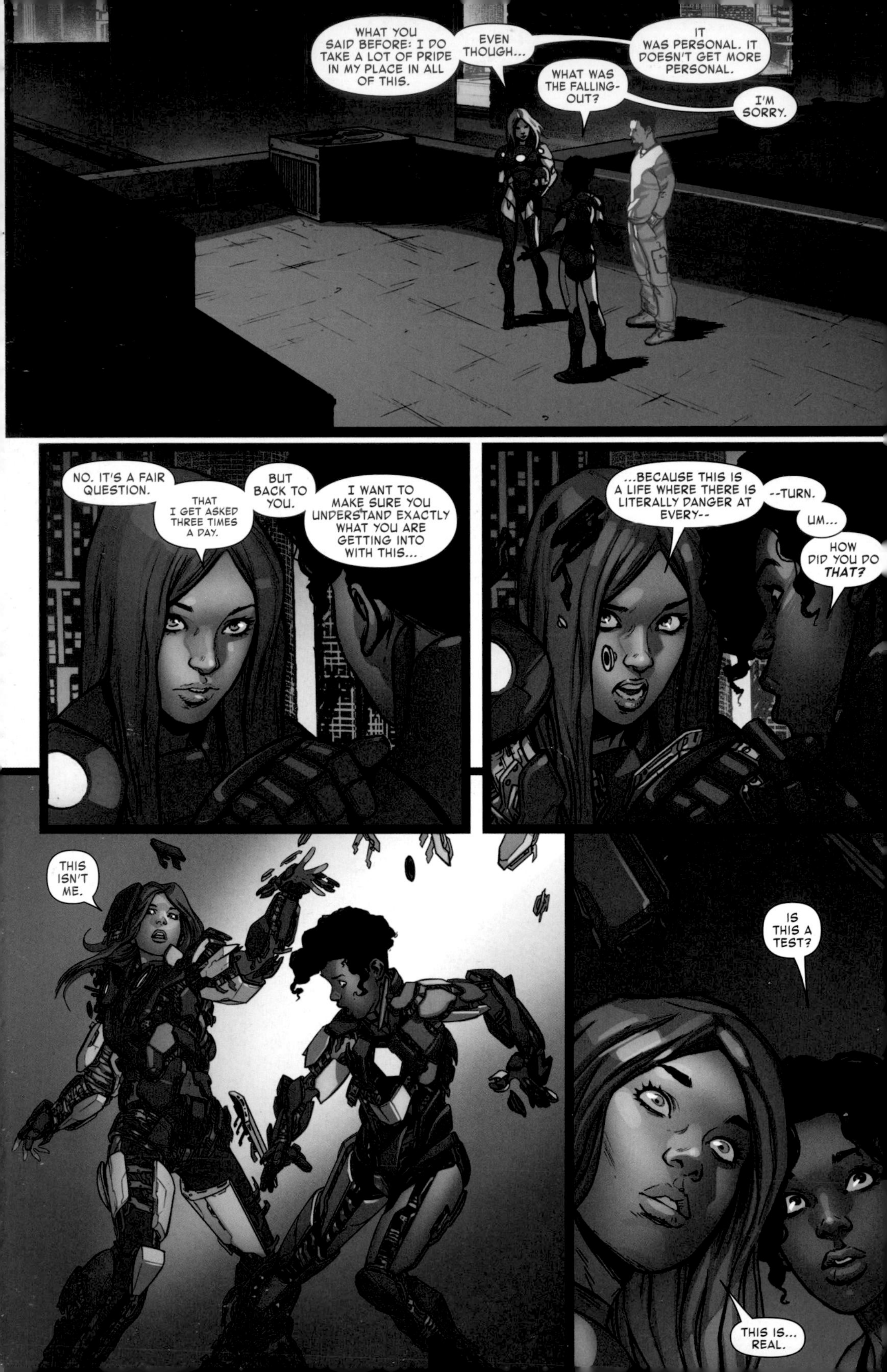
WHAT YOU SAID BEFORE: I DO TAKE A LOT OF PRIDE IN MY PLACE IN ALL OF THIS.
EVEN THOUGH...
IT WAS PERSONAL. IT DOESN'T GET MORE PERSONAL.
WHAT WAS THE FALLING-OUT?
I'M SORRY.
NO. IT'S A FAIR QUESTION.
THAT I GET ASKED THREE TIMES A DAY.
BUT BACK TO YOU.
I WANT TO MAKE SURE YOU UNDERSTAND EXACTLY WHAT YOU ARE GETTING INTO WITH THIS...
...BECAUSE THIS IS A LIFE WHERE THERE IS LITERALLY DANGER AT EVERY--
--TURN.
UM...
HOW DID YOU DO *THAT?*
THIS ISN'T ME.
IS THIS A TEST?
THIS IS... REAL.

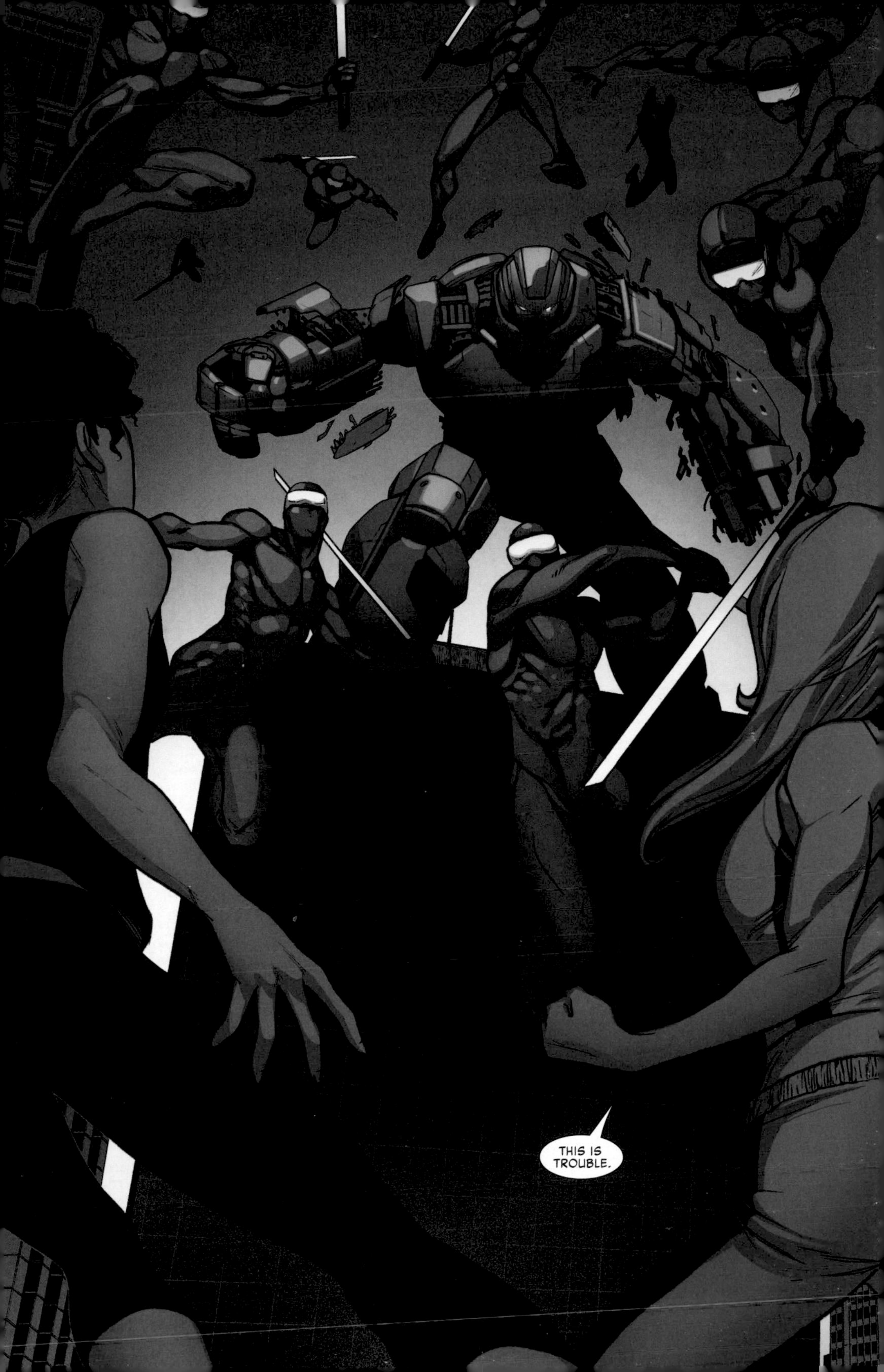
THIS IS TROUBLE.

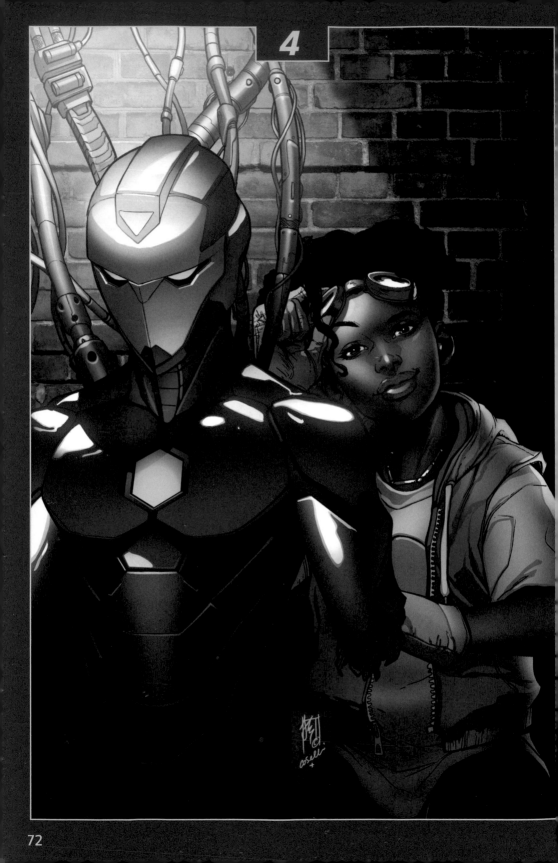

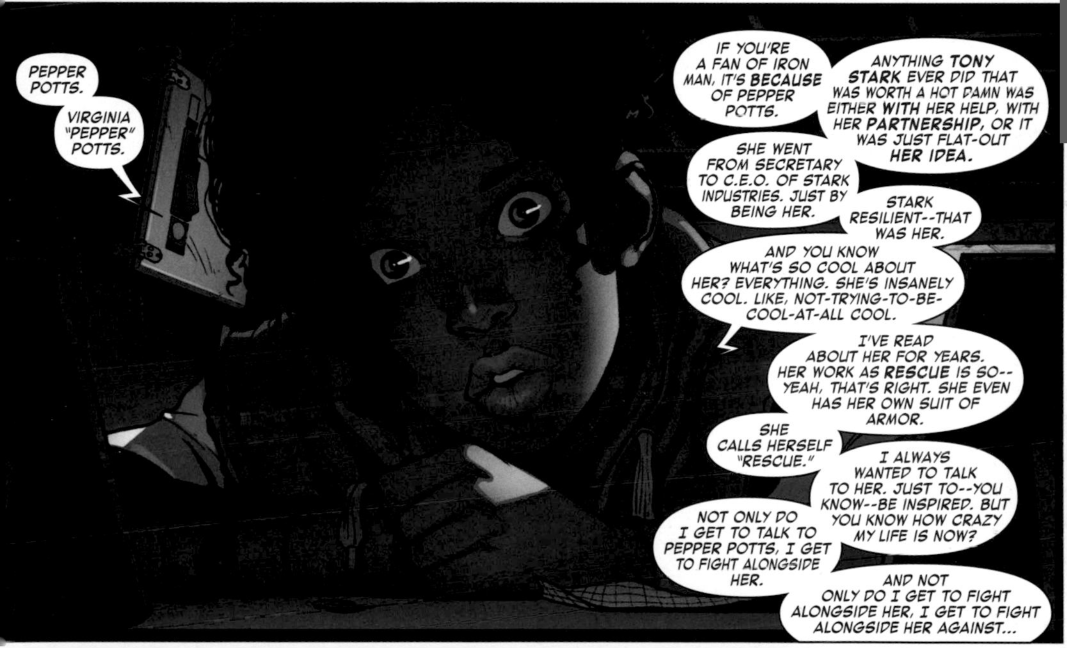
PEPPER POTTS.
VIRGINIA "PEPPER" POTTS.
IF YOU'RE A FAN OF IRON MAN, IT'S BECAUSE OF PEPPER POTTS.
ANYTHING TONY STARK EVER DID THAT WAS WORTH A HOT DAMN WAS EITHER WITH HER HELP, WITH HER PARTNERSHIP, OR IT WAS JUST FLAT-OUT HER IDEA.
SHE WENT FROM SECRETARY TO C.E.O. OF STARK INDUSTRIES. JUST BY BEING HER.
STARK RESILIENT--THAT WAS HER.
AND YOU KNOW WHAT'S SO COOL ABOUT HER? EVERYTHING. SHE'S INSANELY COOL. LIKE, NOT-TRYING-TO-BE-COOL-AT-ALL COOL.
I'VE READ ABOUT HER FOR YEARS. HER WORK AS RESCUE IS SO-- YEAH, THAT'S RIGHT. SHE EVEN HAS HER OWN SUIT OF ARMOR.
SHE CALLS HERSELF "RESCUE."
I ALWAYS WANTED TO TALK TO HER. JUST TO--YOU KNOW--BE INSPIRED. BUT YOU KNOW HOW CRAZY MY LIFE IS NOW?
NOT ONLY DO I GET TO TALK TO PEPPER POTTS, I GET TO FIGHT ALONGSIDE HER.
AND NOT ONLY DO I GET TO FIGHT ALONGSIDE HER, I GET TO FIGHT ALONGSIDE HER AGAINST...

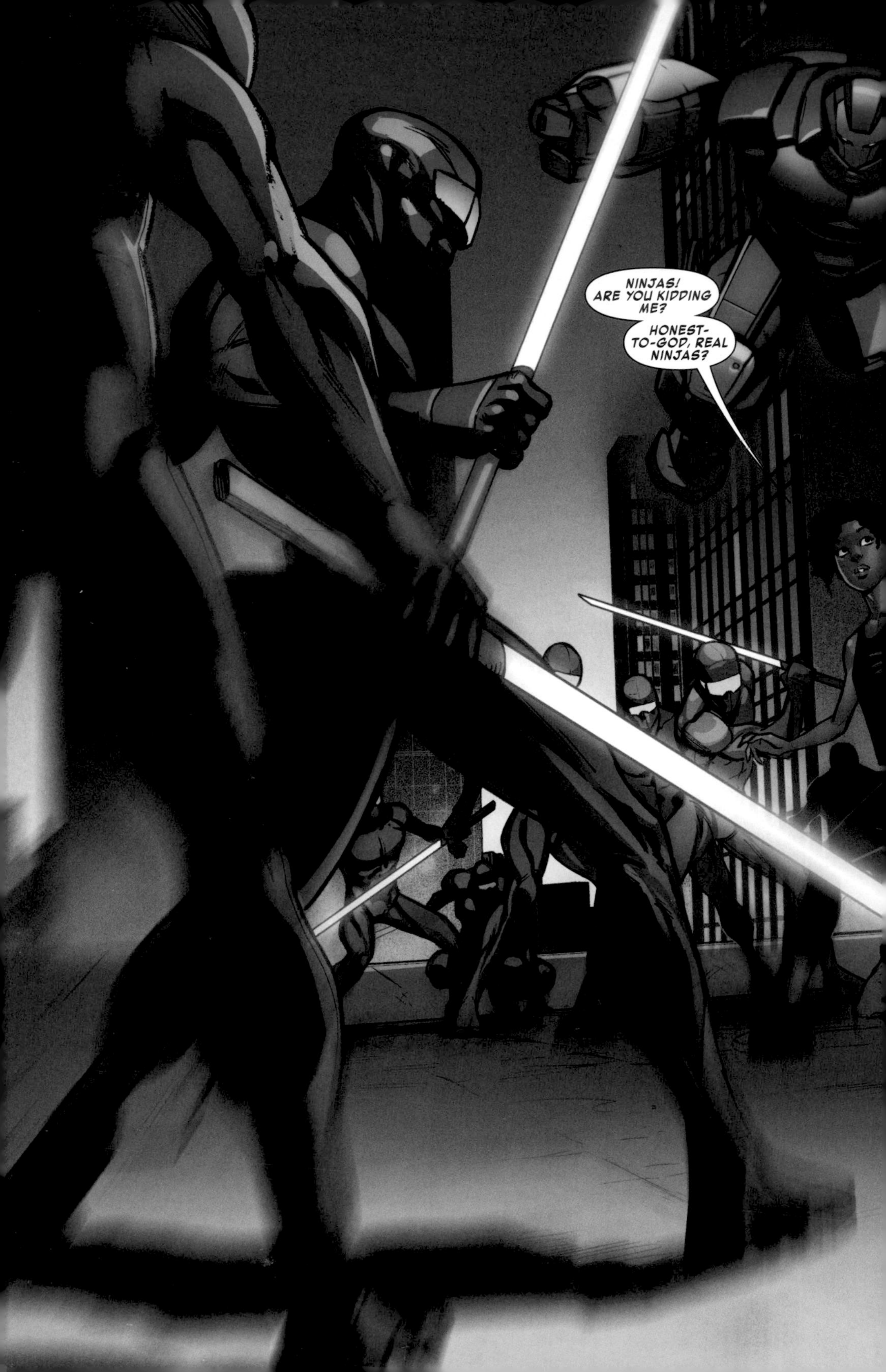
NINJAS! ARE YOU KIDDING ME?
HONEST-TO-GOD, REAL NINJAS?

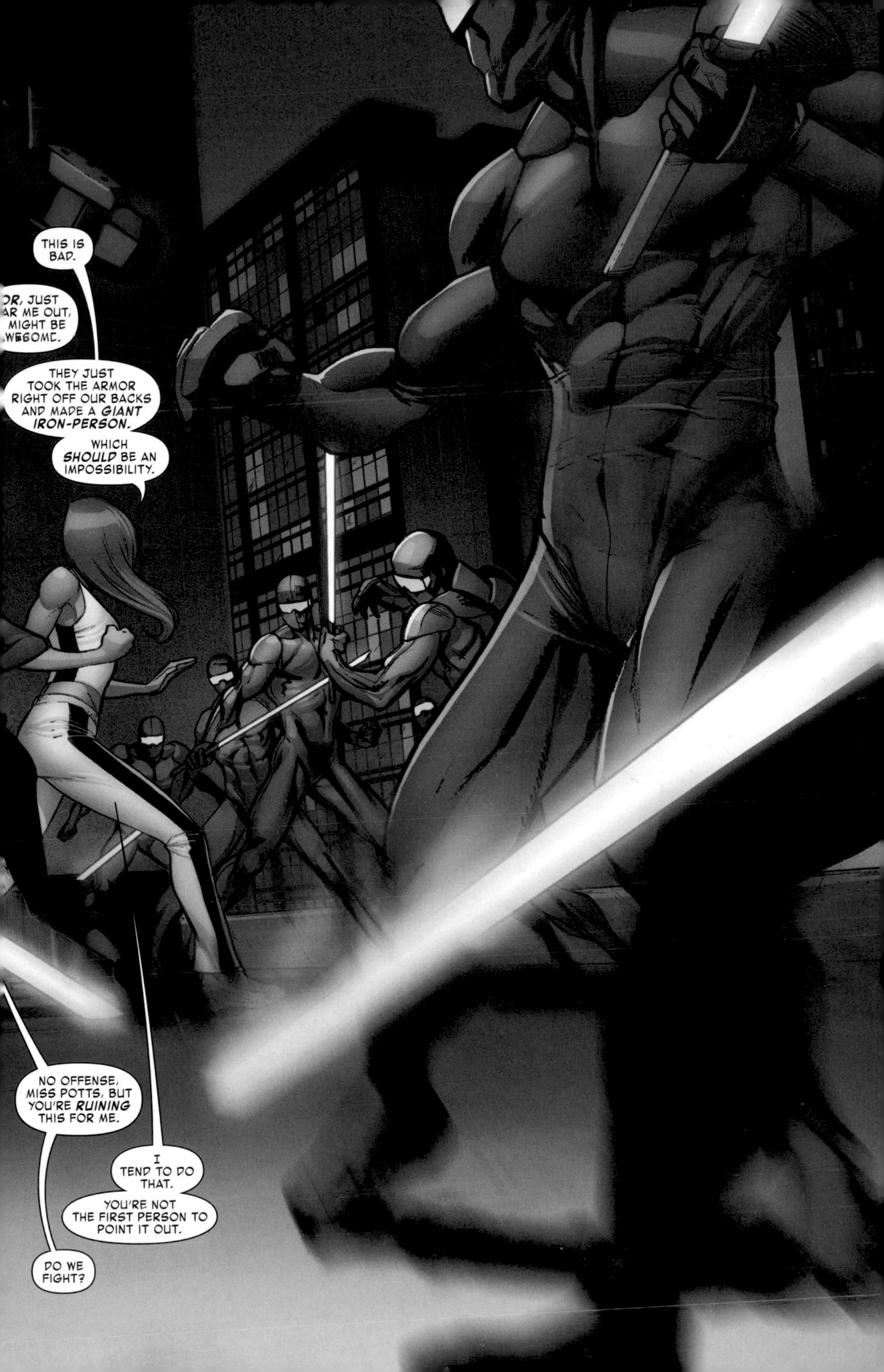
THIS IS BAD.
OR, JUST HEAR ME OUT, IT MIGHT BE AWESOME.
THEY JUST TOOK THE ARMOR RIGHT OFF OUR BACKS AND MADE A GIANT IRON-PERSON.
WHICH SHOULD BE AN IMPOSSIBILITY.
NO OFFENSE, MISS POTTS, BUT YOU'RE RUINING THIS FOR ME.
I TEND TO DO THAT.
YOU'RE NOT THE FIRST PERSON TO POINT IT OUT.
DO WE FIGHT?

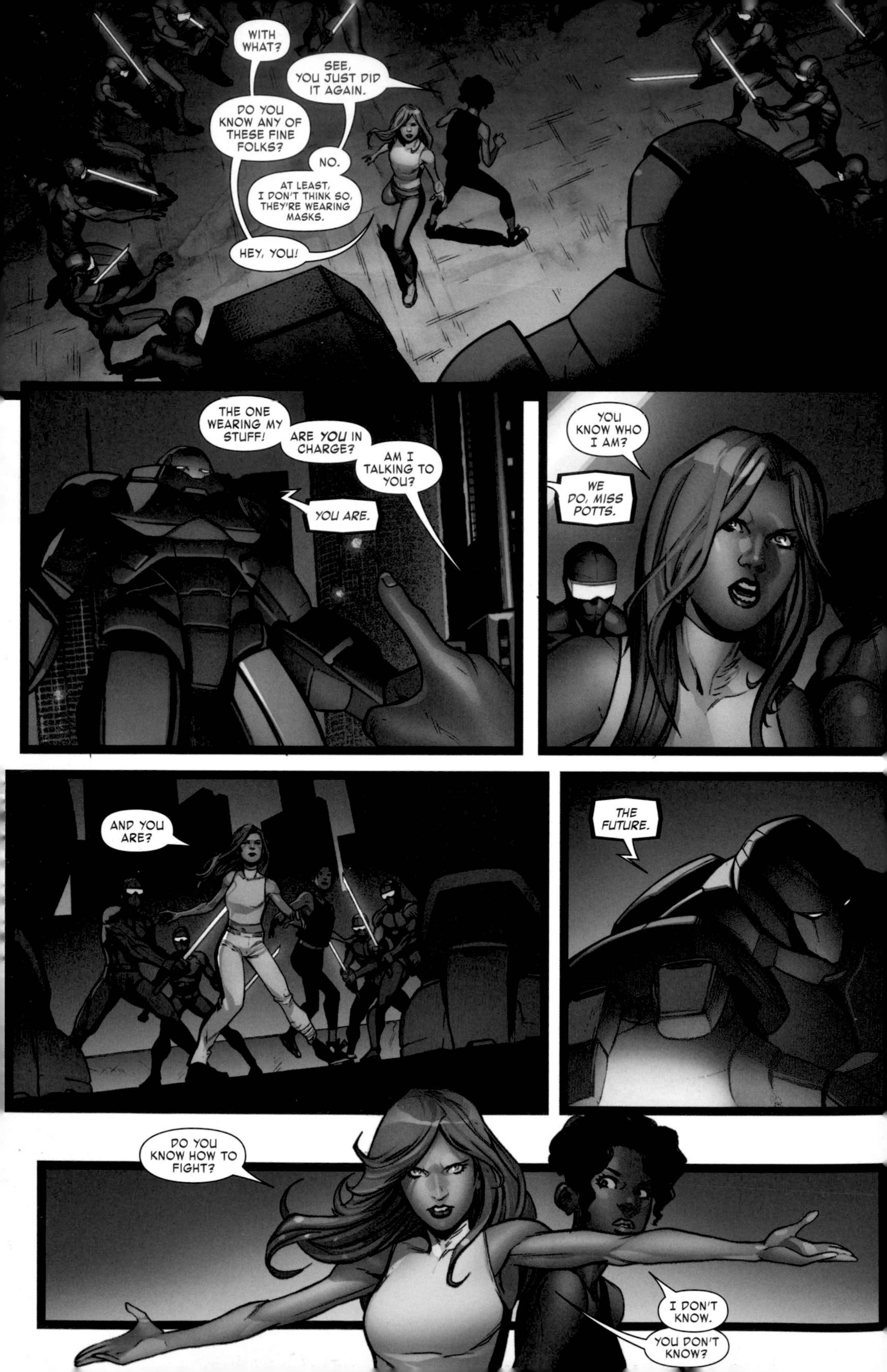
WITH WHAT?
SEE, YOU JUST DID IT AGAIN.
DO YOU KNOW ANY OF THESE FINE FOLKS?
NO.
AT LEAST, I DON'T THINK SO, THEY'RE WEARING MASKS.
HEY, YOU!
THE ONE WEARING MY STUFF!
ARE YOU IN CHARGE?
AM I TALKING TO YOU?
YOU ARE.
YOU KNOW WHO I AM?
WE DO, MISS POTTS.
AND YOU ARE?
THE FUTURE.
DO YOU KNOW HOW TO FIGHT?
I DON'T KNOW.
YOU DON'T KNOW?

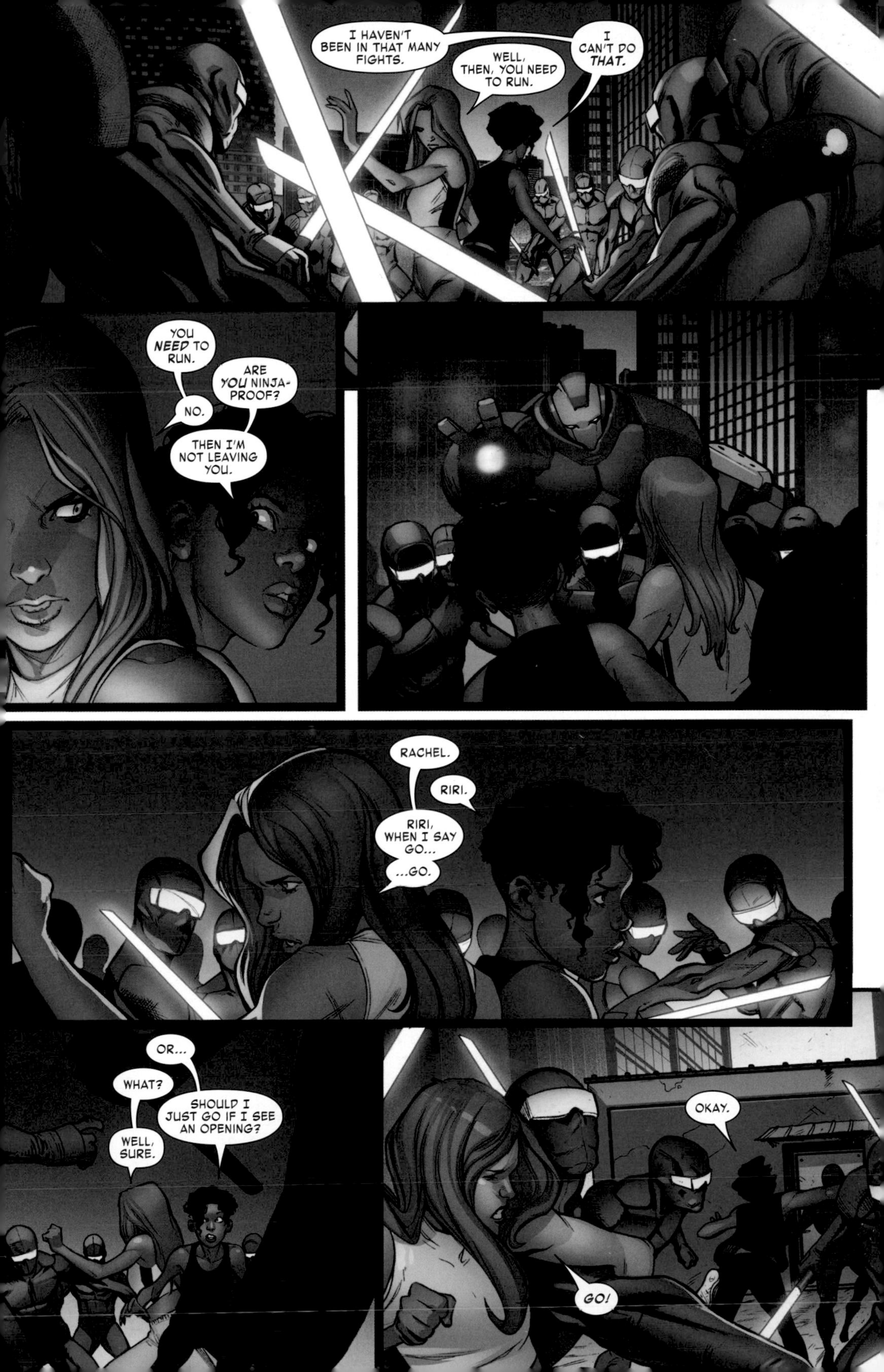
I HAVEN'T BEEN IN THAT MANY FIGHTS.
WELL, THEN, YOU NEED TO RUN.
I CAN'T DO THAT.
YOU NEED TO RUN.
ARE YOU NINJA-PROOF?
NO.
THEN I'M NOT LEAVING YOU.
RACHEL.
RIRI.
RIRI, WHEN I SAY GO...
...GO.
OR...
WHAT?
SHOULD I JUST GO IF I SEE AN OPENING?
WELL, SURE.
OKAY.
GO!

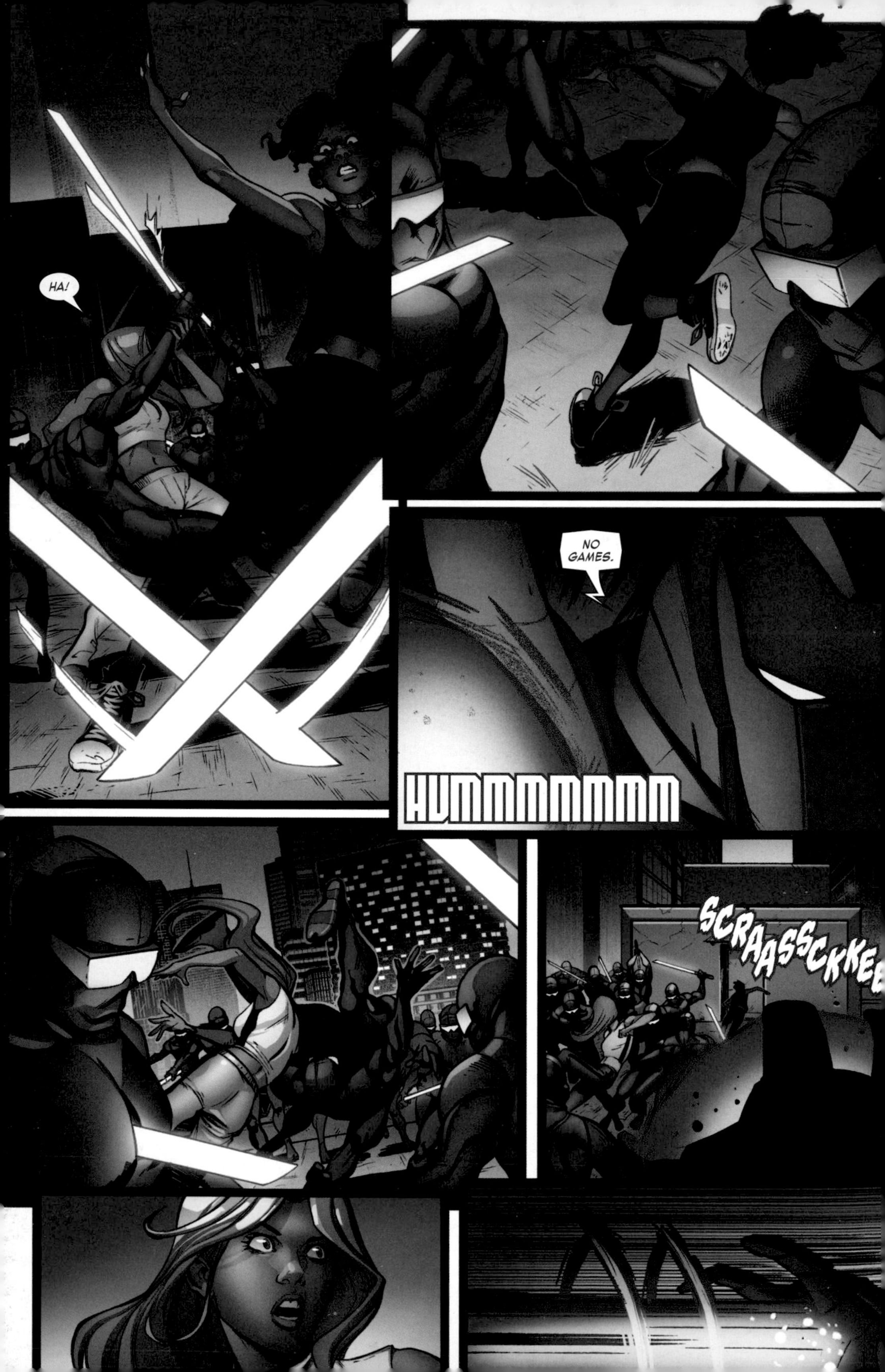
HA!
NO GAMES.
HUMMMMMMMM
SCRAASSCKKEE

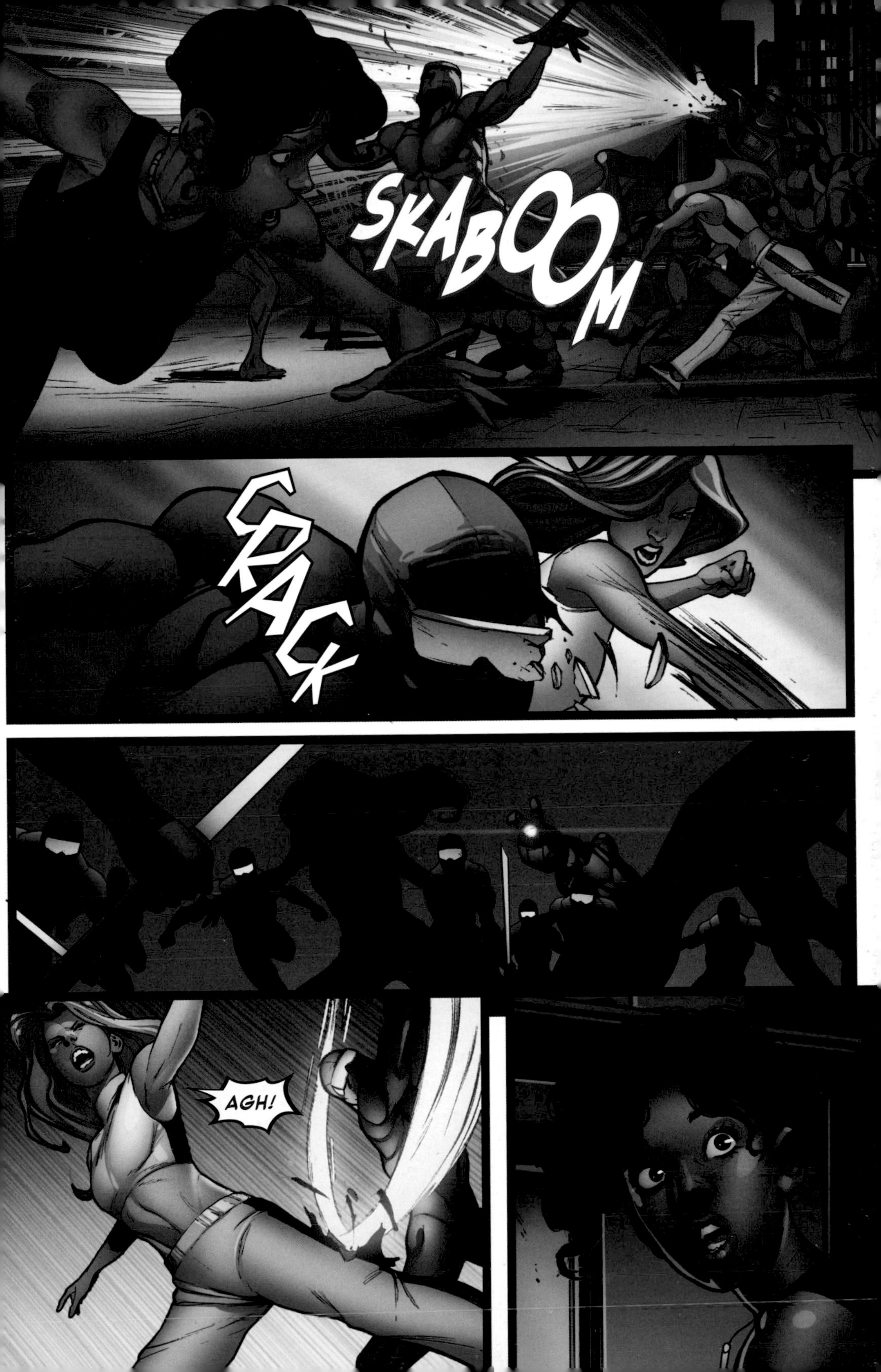
SKABOOM
CRACK
AGH!

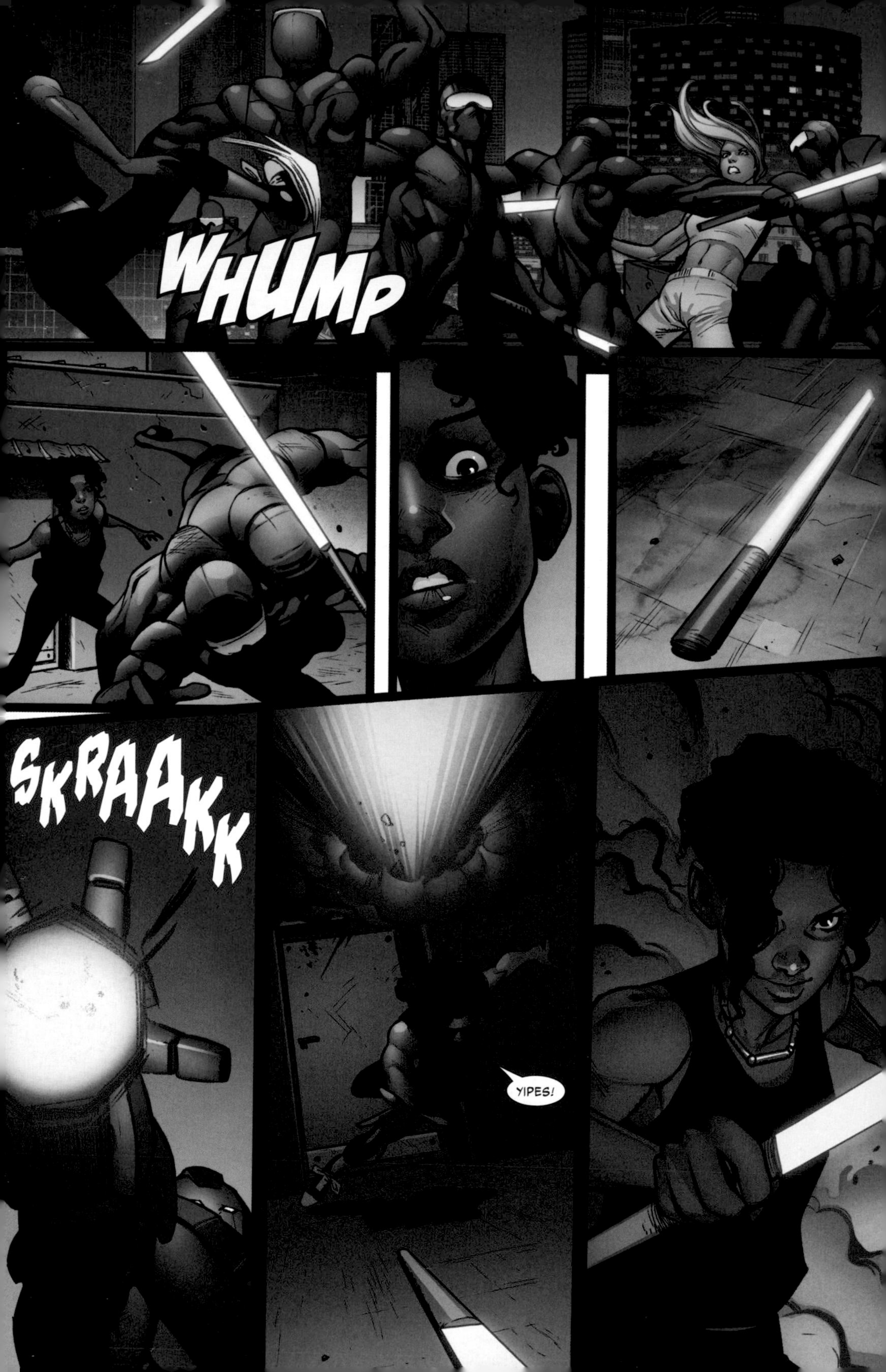
WHUMP
SKRAAKK
YIPES!

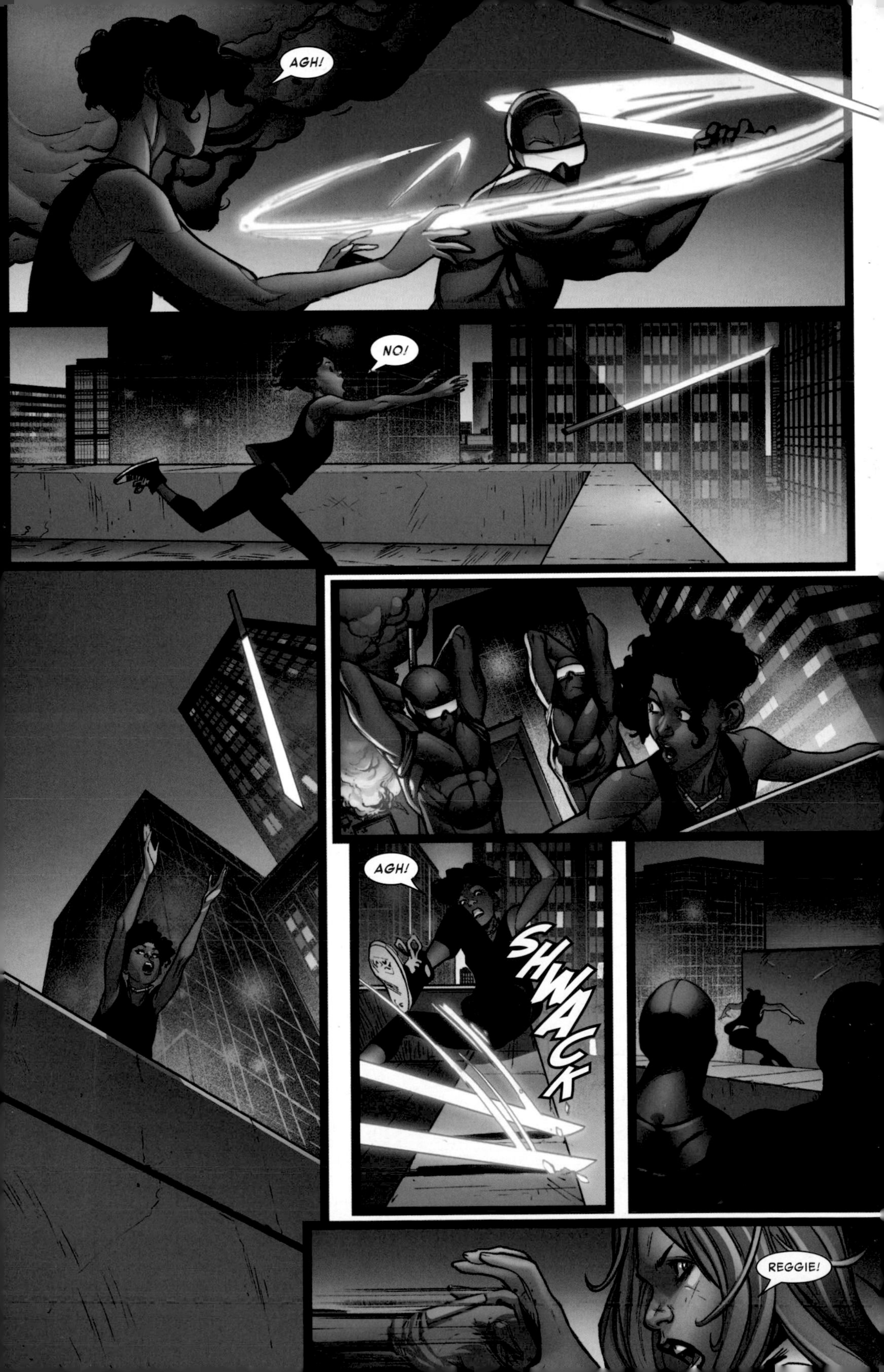
AGH!
NO!
AGH!
SHWACK!
REGGIE!

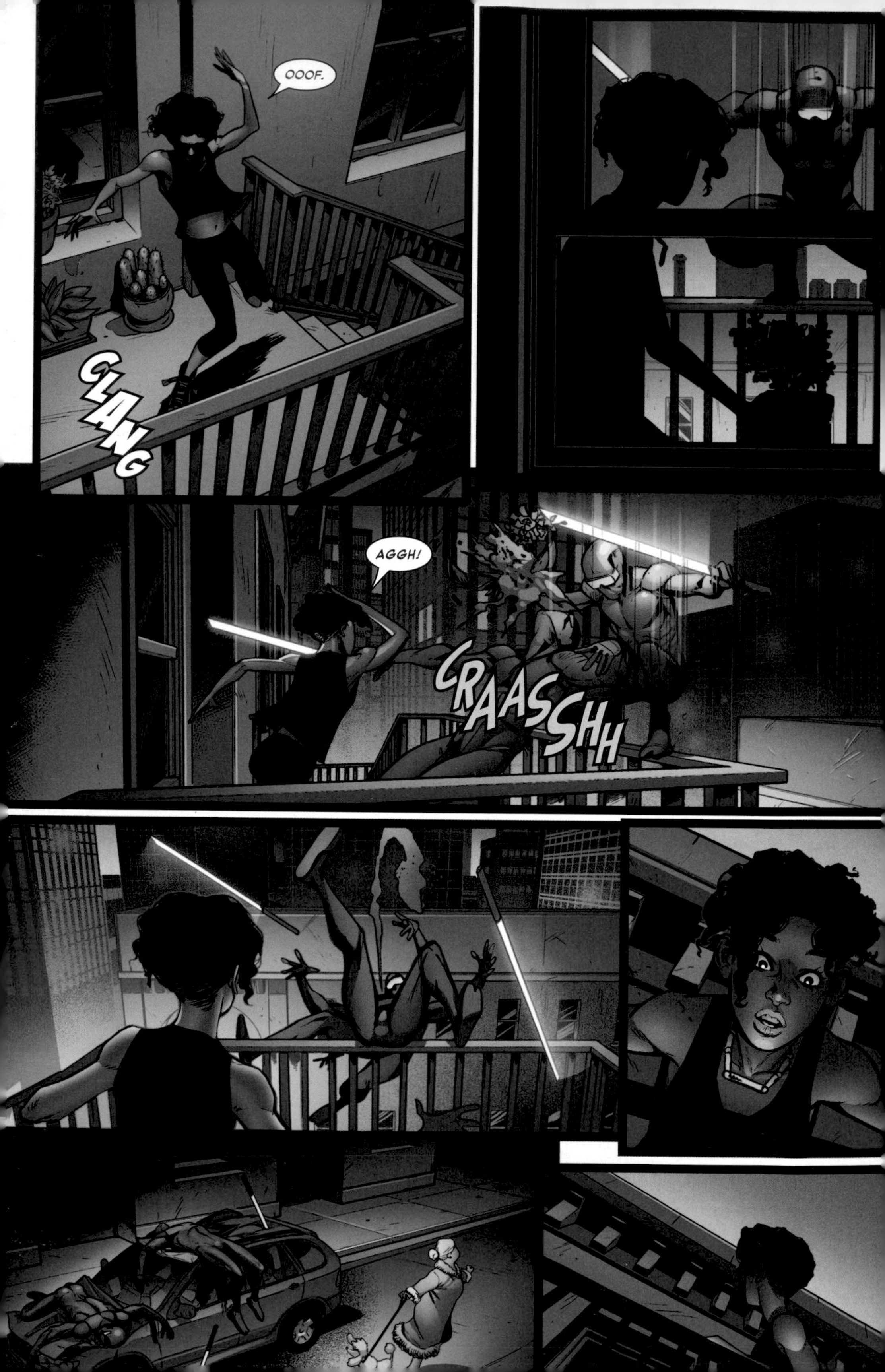
OOOF.
CLANG
AGGH!
CRAASSHH

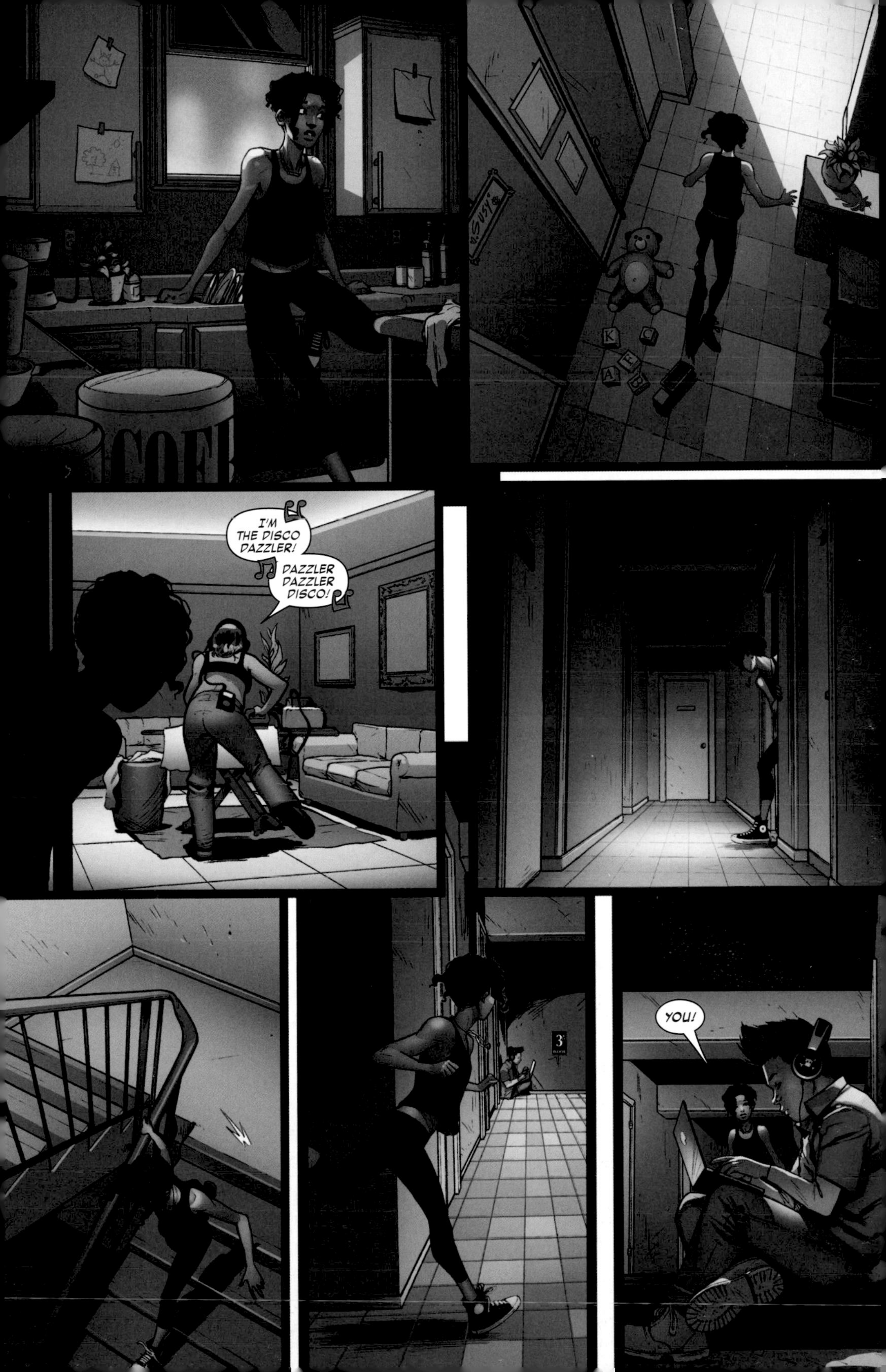
I'M THE DISCO DAZZLER!
DAZZLER DAZZLER DISCO!
YOU!

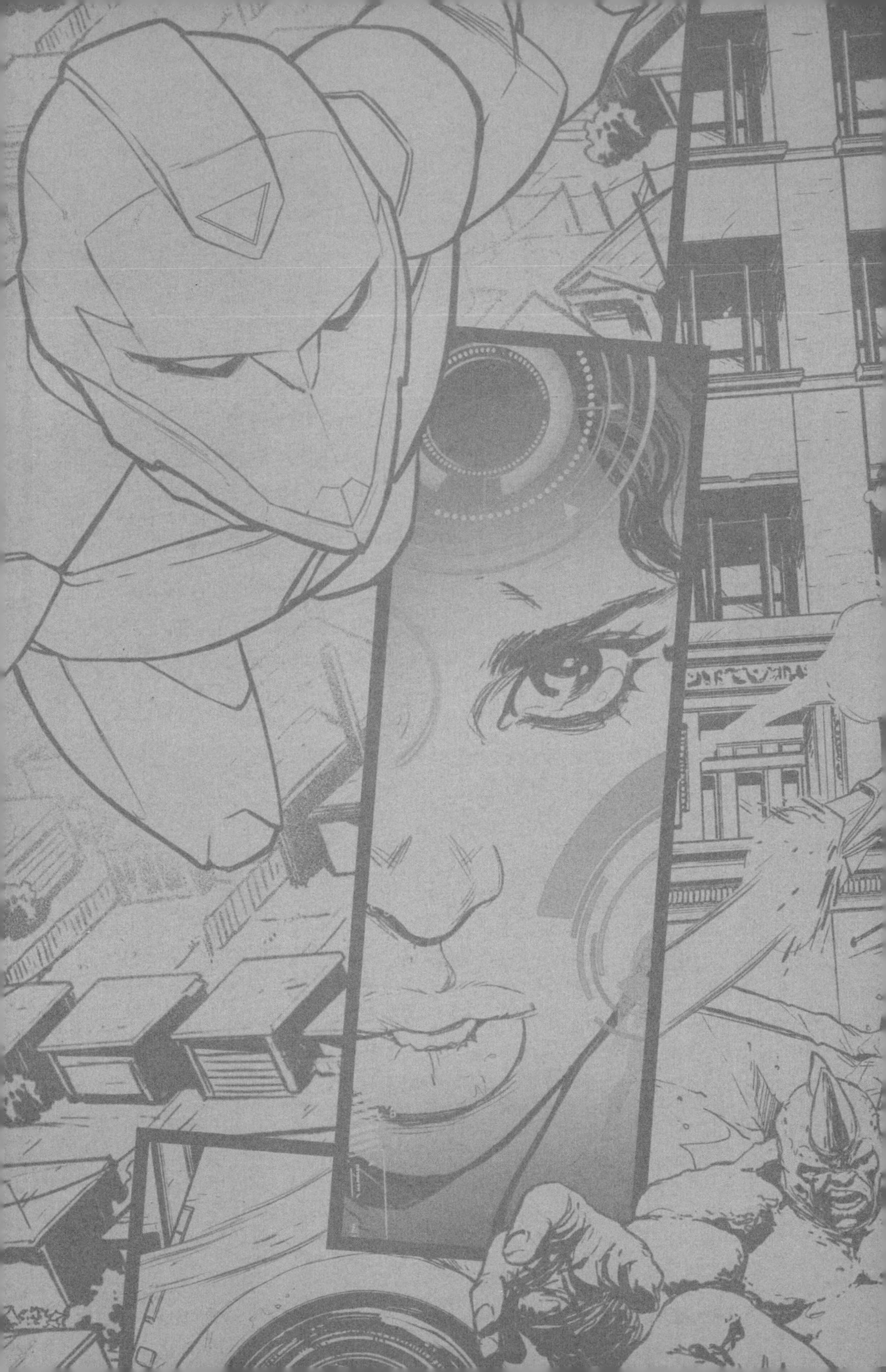

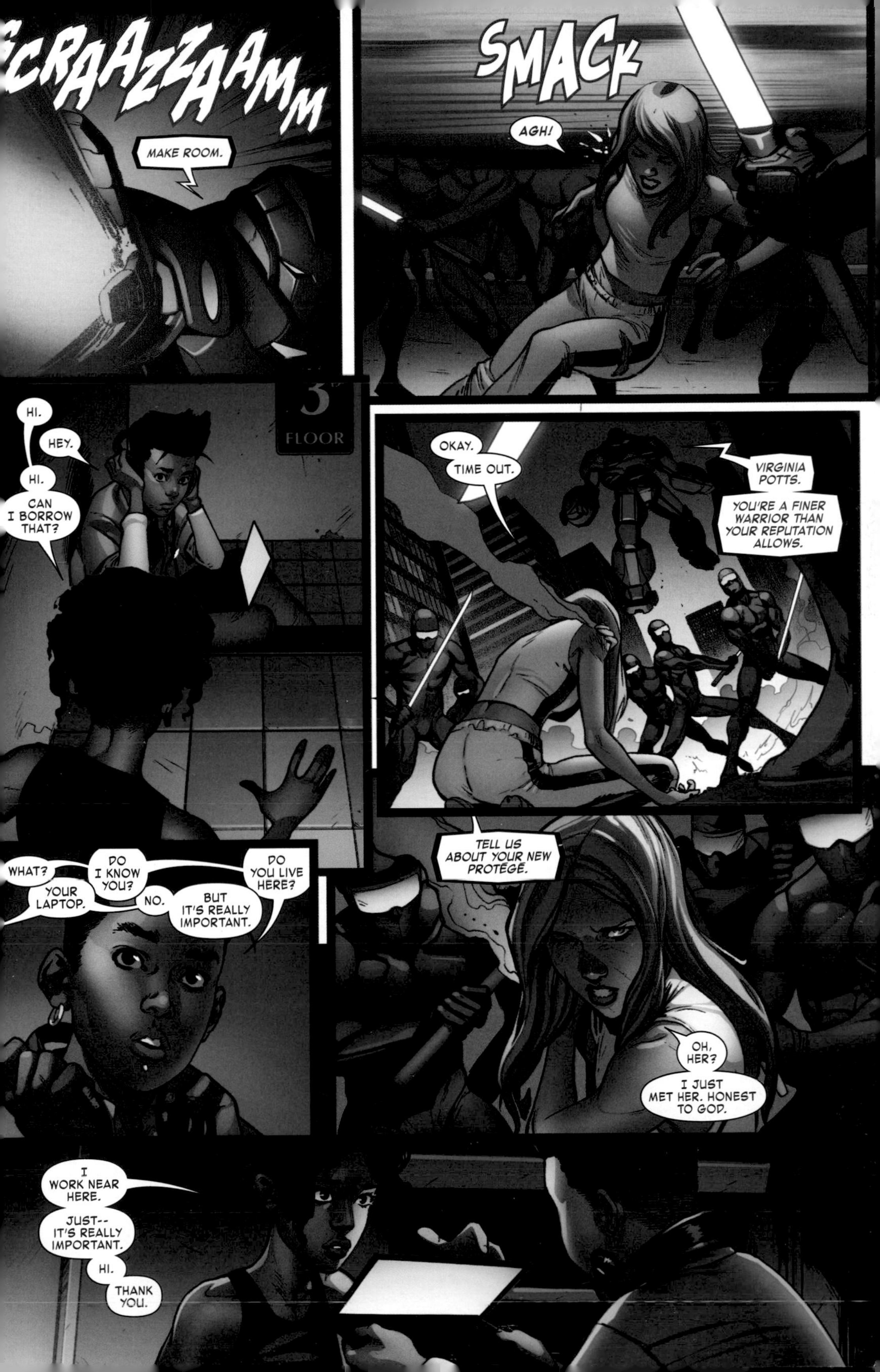
CRAAZZAAMM
MAKE ROOM.
SMACK
AGH!
HI.
HEY.
HI.
CAN I BORROW THAT?
3rd FLOOR
OKAY. TIME OUT.
VIRGINIA POTTS.
YOU'RE A FINER WARRIOR THAN YOUR REPUTATION ALLOWS.
WHAT?
DO I KNOW YOU?
DO YOU LIVE HERE?
YOUR LAPTOP.
NO.
BUT IT'S REALLY IMPORTANT.
TELL US ABOUT YOUR NEW PROTÉGÉ.
OH, HER?
I JUST MET HER. HONEST TO GOD.
I WORK NEAR HERE.
JUST-- IT'S REALLY IMPORTANT.
HI.
THANK YOU.

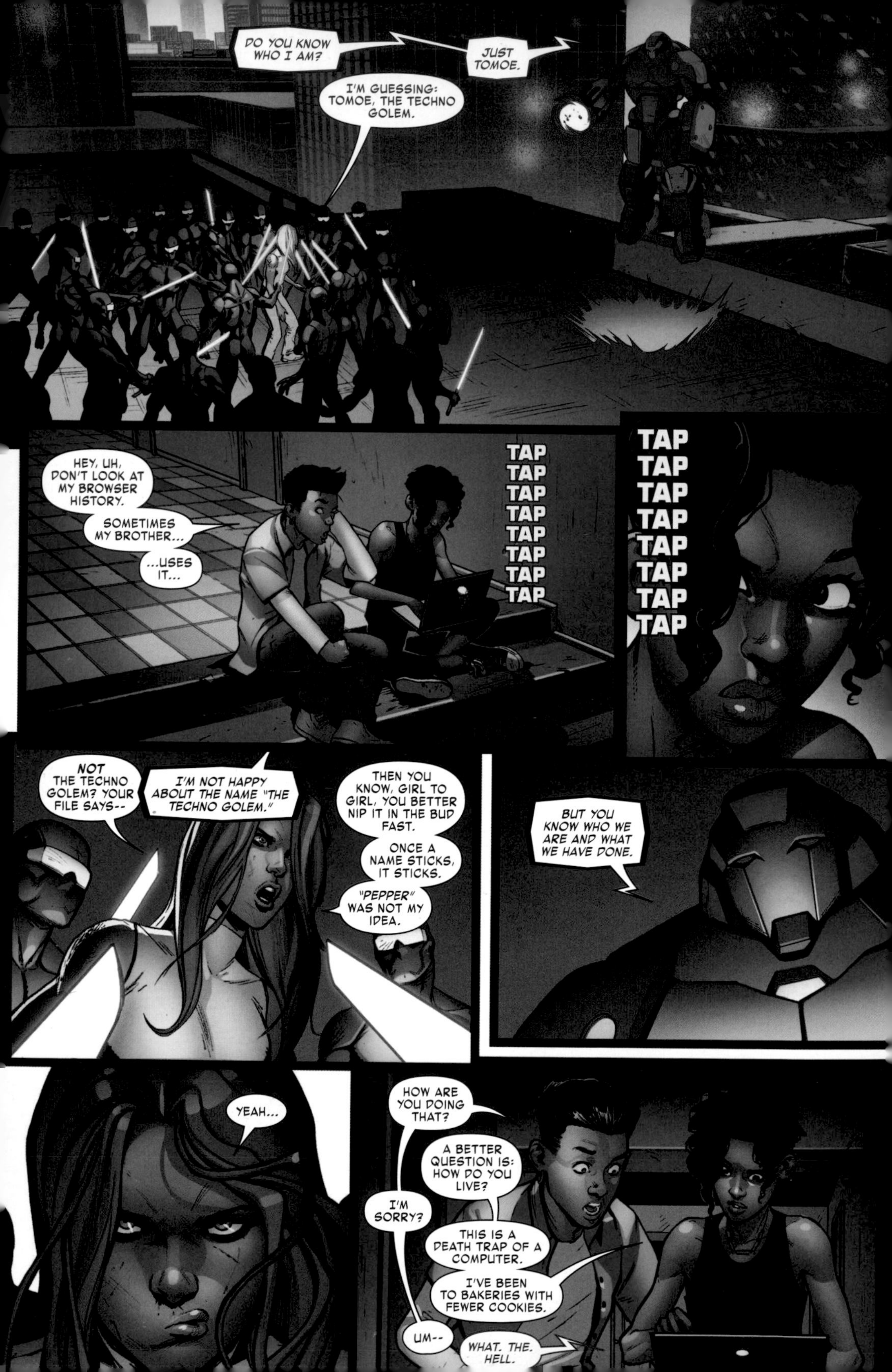
DO YOU KNOW WHO I AM?
JUST TOMOE.
I'M GUESSING: TOMOE, THE TECHNO GOLEM.
HEY, UH, DON'T LOOK AT MY BROWSER HISTORY.
SOMETIMES MY BROTHER...
...USES IT...
TAP TAP TAP TAP TAP TAP TAP TAP
TAP TAP TAP TAP TAP TAP TAP TAP
NOT THE TECHNO GOLEM? YOUR FILE SAYS--
I'M NOT HAPPY ABOUT THE NAME "THE TECHNO GOLEM."
THEN YOU KNOW, GIRL TO GIRL, YOU BETTER NIP IT IN THE BUD FAST.
ONCE A NAME STICKS, IT STICKS.
"PEPPER" WAS NOT MY IDEA.
BUT YOU KNOW WHO WE ARE AND WHAT WE HAVE DONE.
YEAH...
HOW ARE YOU DOING THAT?
A BETTER QUESTION IS: HOW DO YOU LIVE?
I'M SORRY?
THIS IS A DEATH TRAP OF A COMPUTER.
I'VE BEEN TO BAKERIES WITH FEWER COOKIES.
UM--
WHAT. THE. HELL.

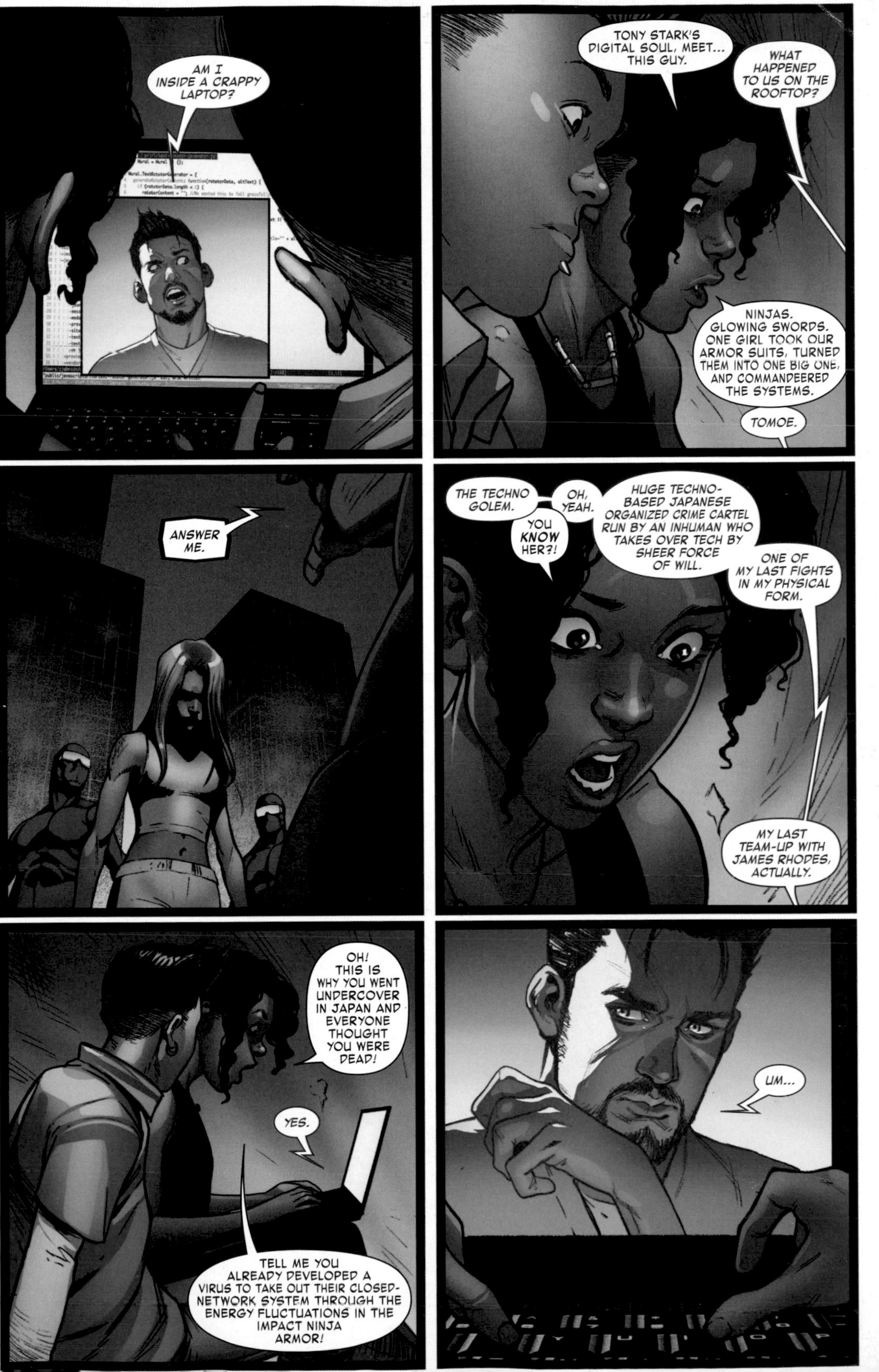

AM I INSIDE A CRAPPY LAPTOP?
TONY STARK'S DIGITAL SOUL, MEET... THIS GUY.
WHAT HAPPENED TO US ON THE ROOFTOP?
NINJAS. GLOWING SWORDS. ONE GIRL TOOK OUR ARMOR SUITS, TURNED THEM INTO ONE BIG ONE, AND COMMANDEERED THE SYSTEMS.
TOMOE.
ANSWER ME.
THE TECHNO GOLEM.
OH, YEAH.
YOU KNOW HER?!
HUGE TECHNO-BASED JAPANESE ORGANIZED CRIME CARTEL RUN BY AN INHUMAN WHO TAKES OVER TECH BY SHEER FORCE OF WILL.
ONE OF MY LAST FIGHTS IN MY PHYSICAL FORM.
MY LAST TEAM-UP WITH JAMES RHODES, ACTUALLY.
OH! THIS IS WHY YOU WENT UNDERCOVER IN JAPAN AND EVERYONE THOUGHT YOU WERE DEAD!
YES.
TELL ME YOU ALREADY DEVELOPED A VIRUS TO TAKE OUT THEIR CLOSED-NETWORK SYSTEM THROUGH THE ENERGY FLUCTUATIONS IN THE IMPACT NINJA ARMOR!
UM...

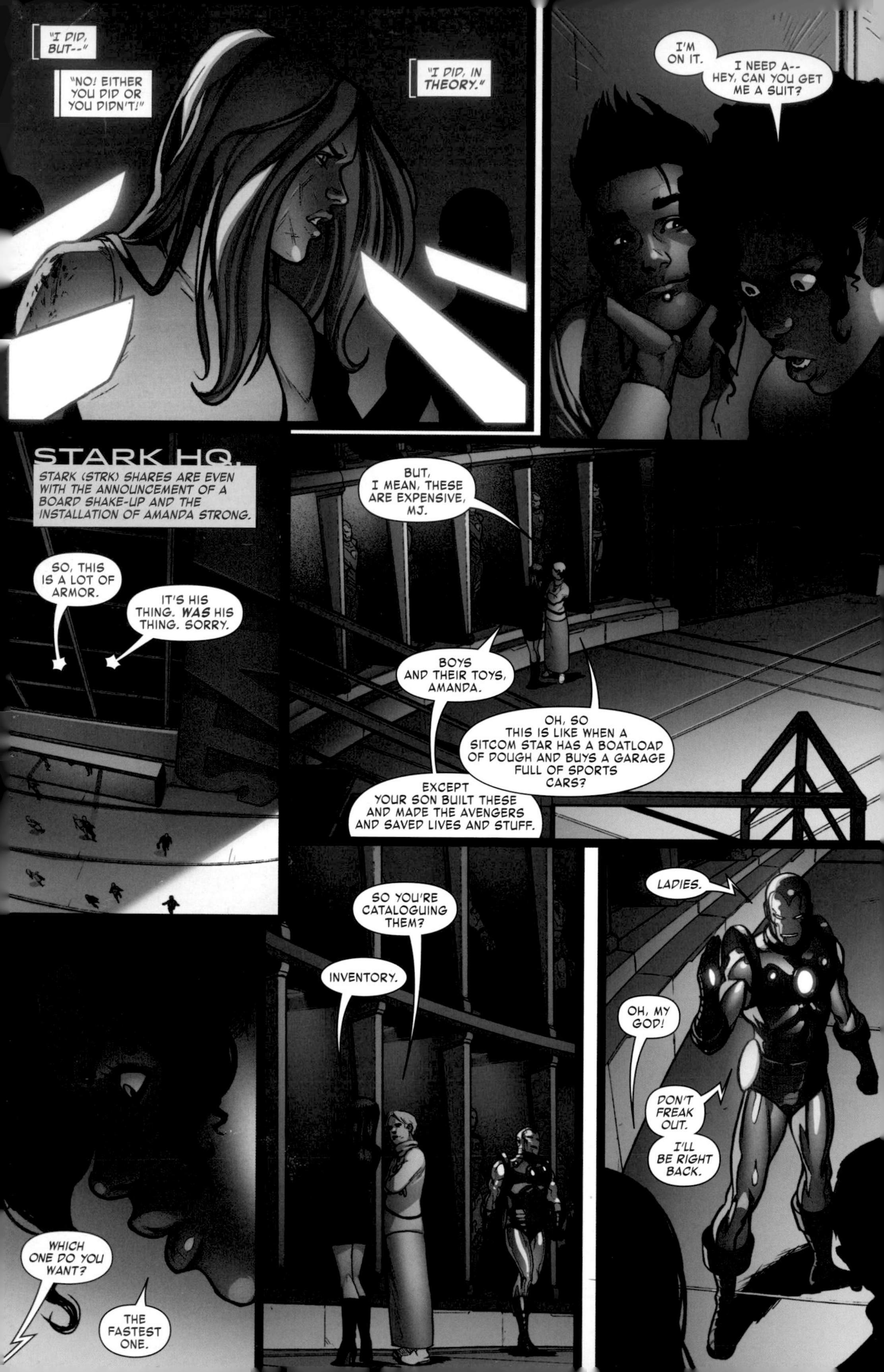
"I DID, BUT--"
"NO! EITHER YOU DID OR YOU DIDN'T!"
"I DID, IN THEORY."
I'M ON IT.
I NEED A-- HEY, CAN YOU GET ME A SUIT?
STARK HQ.
STARK (STRK) SHARES ARE EVEN WITH THE ANNOUNCEMENT OF A BOARD SHAKE-UP AND THE INSTALLATION OF AMANDA STRONG.
SO, THIS IS A LOT OF ARMOR.
IT'S HIS THING. WAS HIS THING. SORRY.
BUT, I MEAN, THESE ARE EXPENSIVE, MJ.
BOYS AND THEIR TOYS, AMANDA.
OH, SO THIS IS LIKE WHEN A SITCOM STAR HAS A BOATLOAD OF DOUGH AND BUYS A GARAGE FULL OF SPORTS CARS?
EXCEPT YOUR SON BUILT THESE AND MADE THE AVENGERS AND SAVED LIVES AND STUFF.
WHICH ONE DO YOU WANT?
THE FASTEST ONE.
SO YOU'RE CATALOGUING THEM?
INVENTORY.
LADIES.
OH, MY GOD!
DON'T FREAK OUT.
I'LL BE RIGHT BACK.

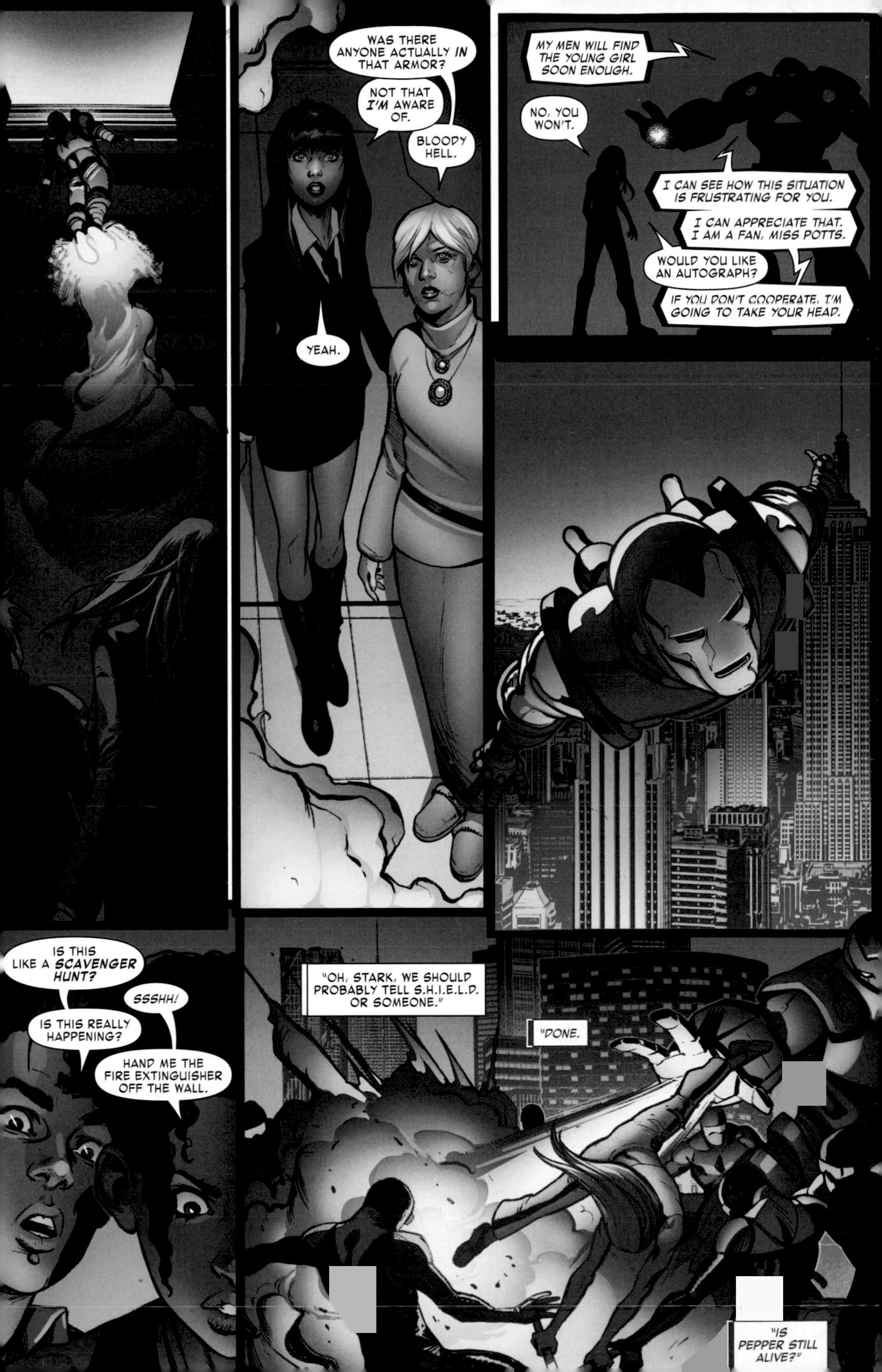
WAS THERE ANYONE ACTUALLY IN THAT ARMOR?
NOT THAT I'M AWARE OF.
BLOODY HELL.
YEAH.
MY MEN WILL FIND THE YOUNG GIRL SOON ENOUGH.
NO, YOU WON'T.
I CAN SEE HOW THIS SITUATION IS FRUSTRATING FOR YOU.
I CAN APPRECIATE THAT. I AM A FAN, MISS POTTS.
WOULD YOU LIKE AN AUTOGRAPH?
IF YOU DON'T COOPERATE, I'M GOING TO TAKE YOUR HEAD.
IS THIS LIKE A SCAVENGER HUNT?
SSSHH!
IS THIS REALLY HAPPENING?
HAND ME THE FIRE EXTINGUISHER OFF THE WALL.
"OH, STARK, WE SHOULD PROBABLY TELL S.H.I.E.L.D. OR SOMEONE."
"DONE.
"IS PEPPER STILL ALIVE?"

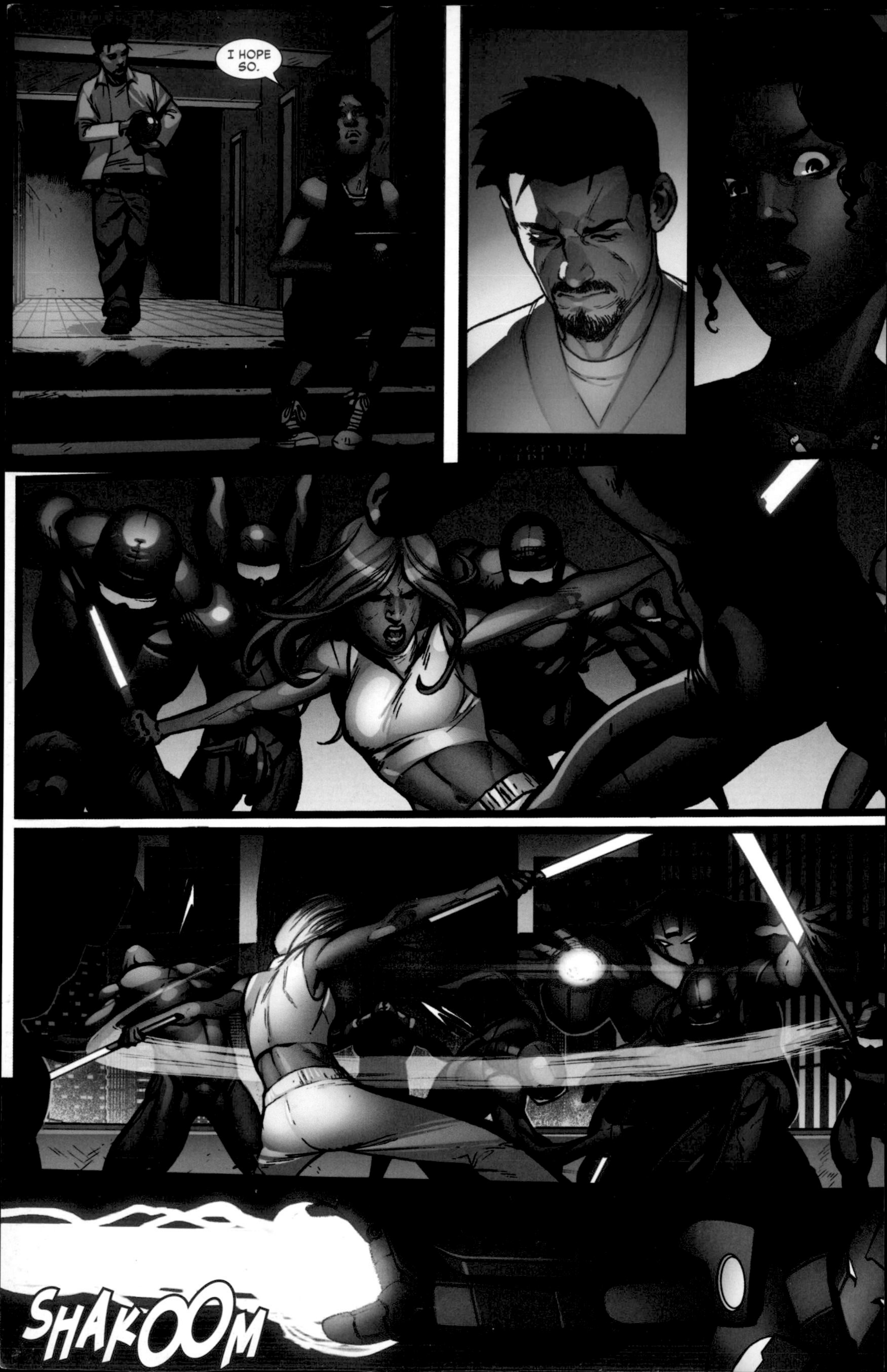
I HOPE SO.
SHAKOOM

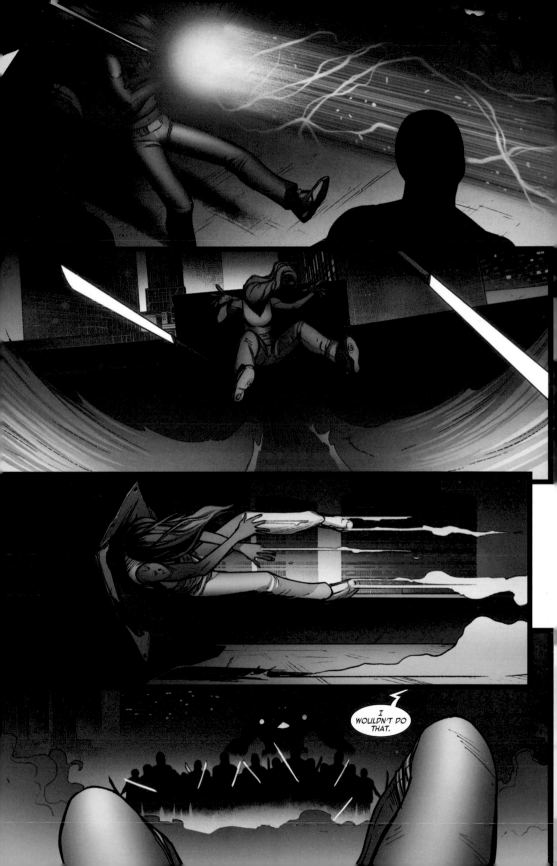

I WOULDN'T DO THAT.

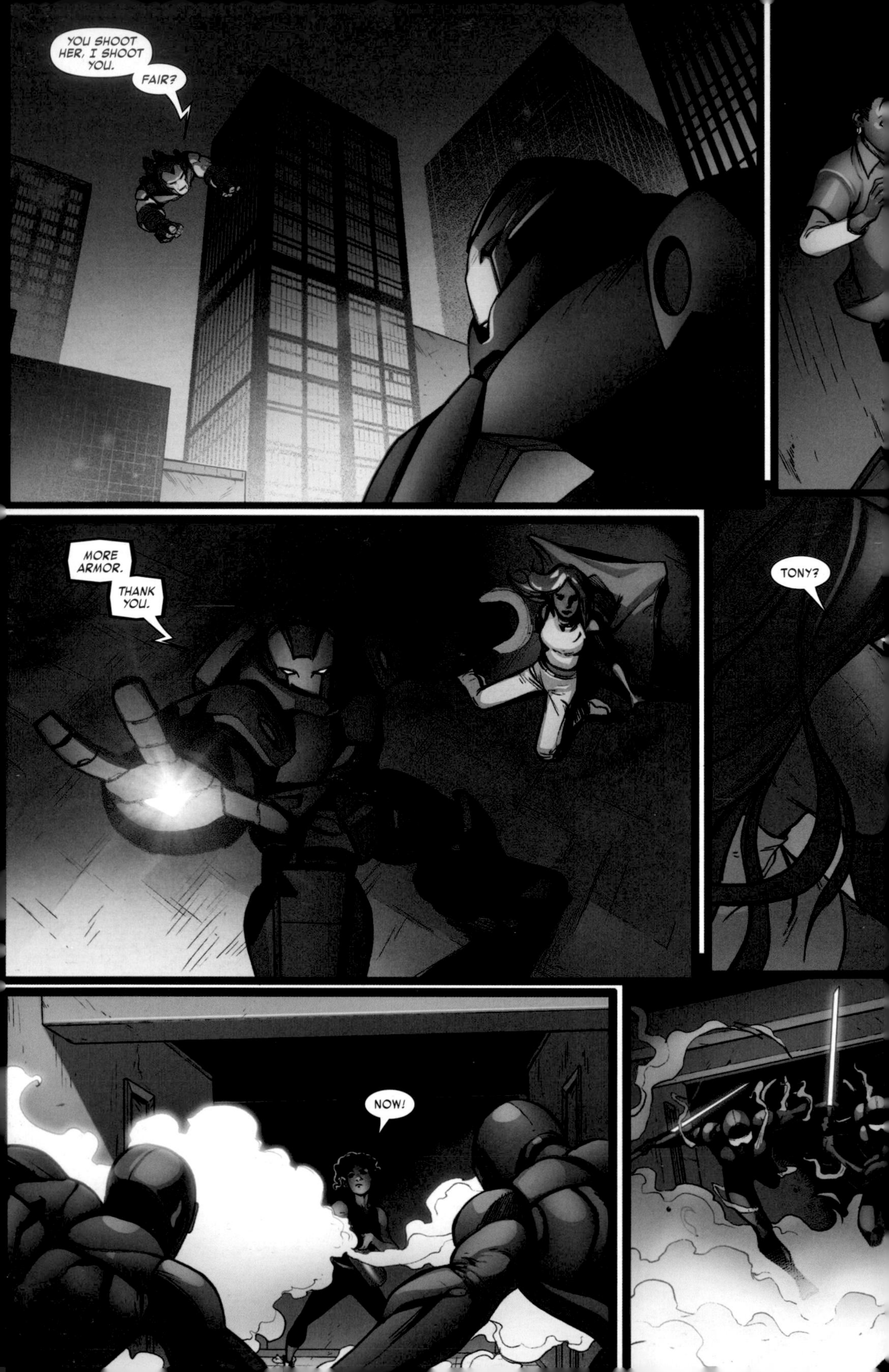
YOU SHOOT HER, I SHOOT YOU.
FAIR?
MORE ARMOR.
THANK YOU.
TONY?
NOW!

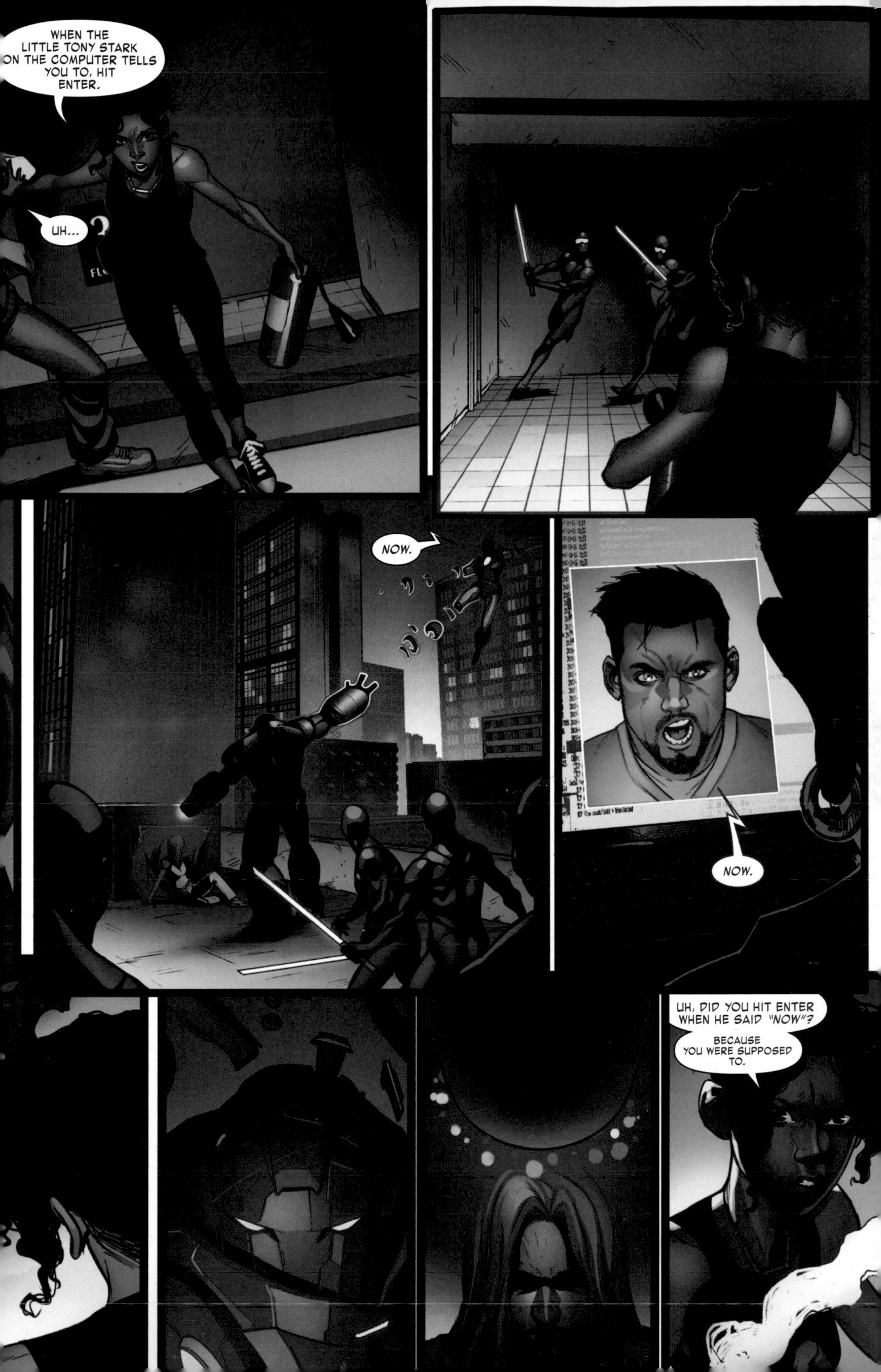
WHEN THE LITTLE TONY STARK ON THE COMPUTER TELLS YOU TO, HIT ENTER.
UH...
FL
NOW.
NOW.
UH, DID YOU HIT ENTER WHEN HE SAID "NOW"?
BECAUSE YOU WERE SUPPOSED TO.

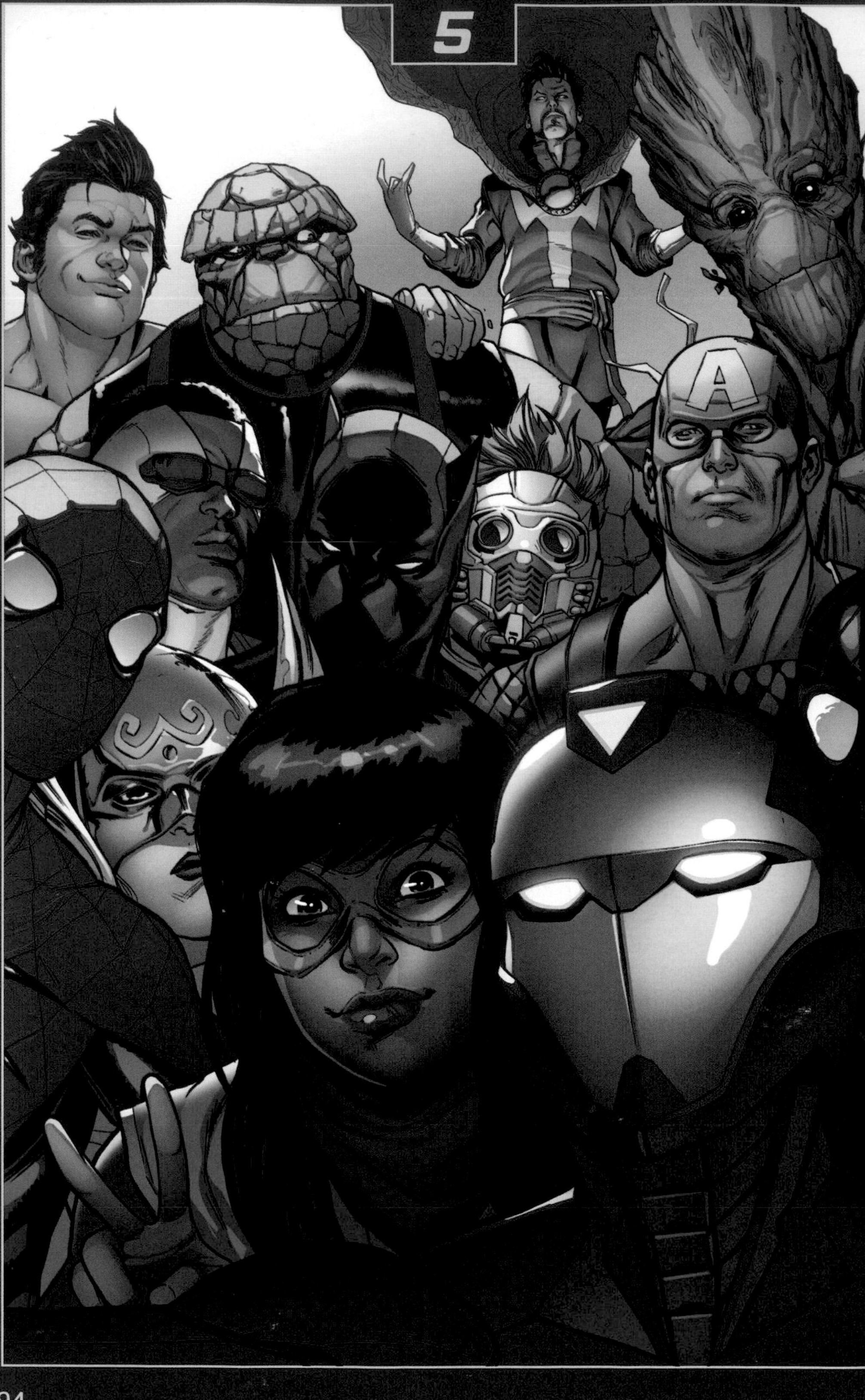
5

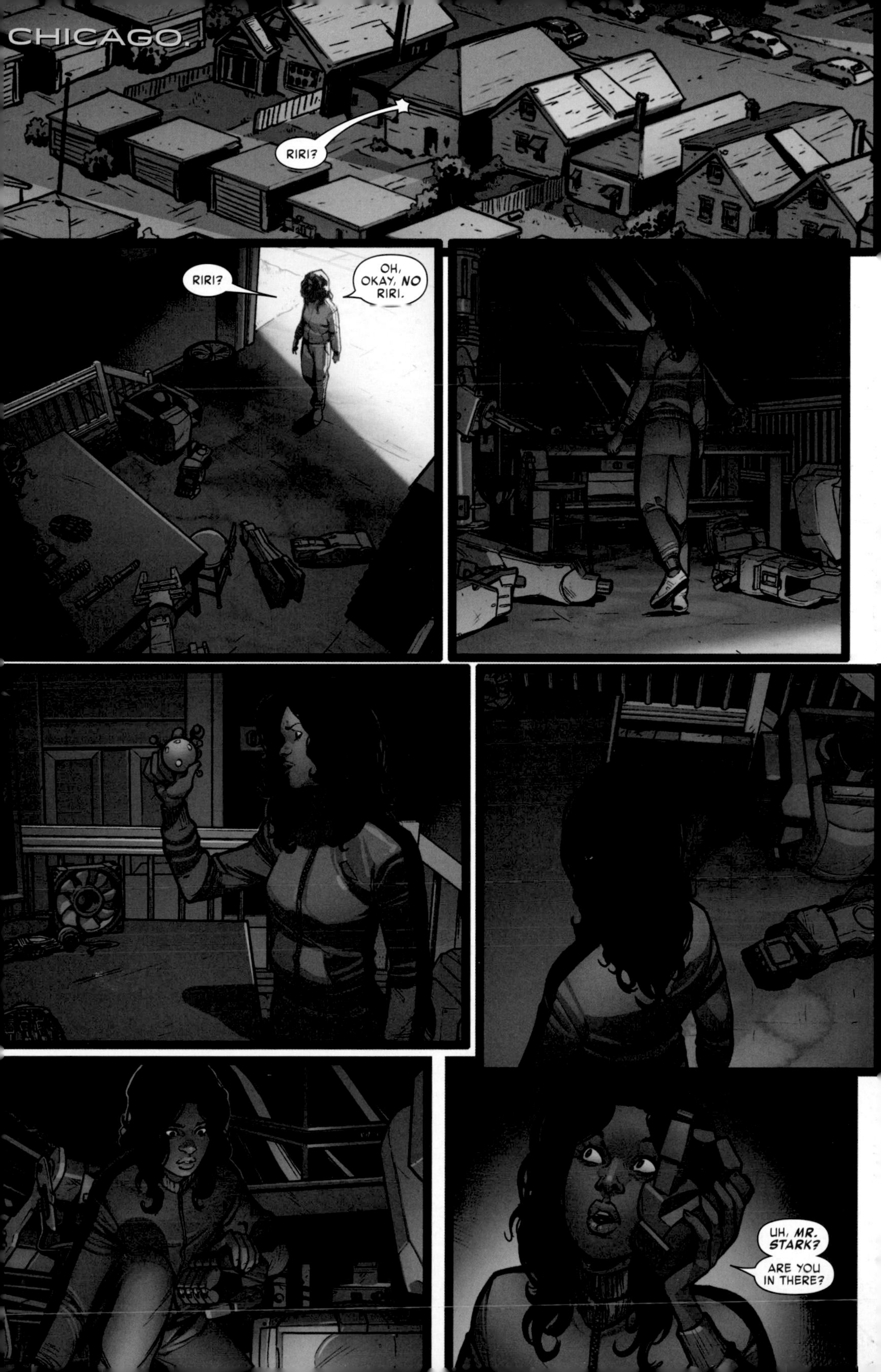
CHICAGO.
RIRI?
RIRI?
OH, OKAY, NO RIRI.
UH, MR. STARK?
ARE YOU IN THERE?

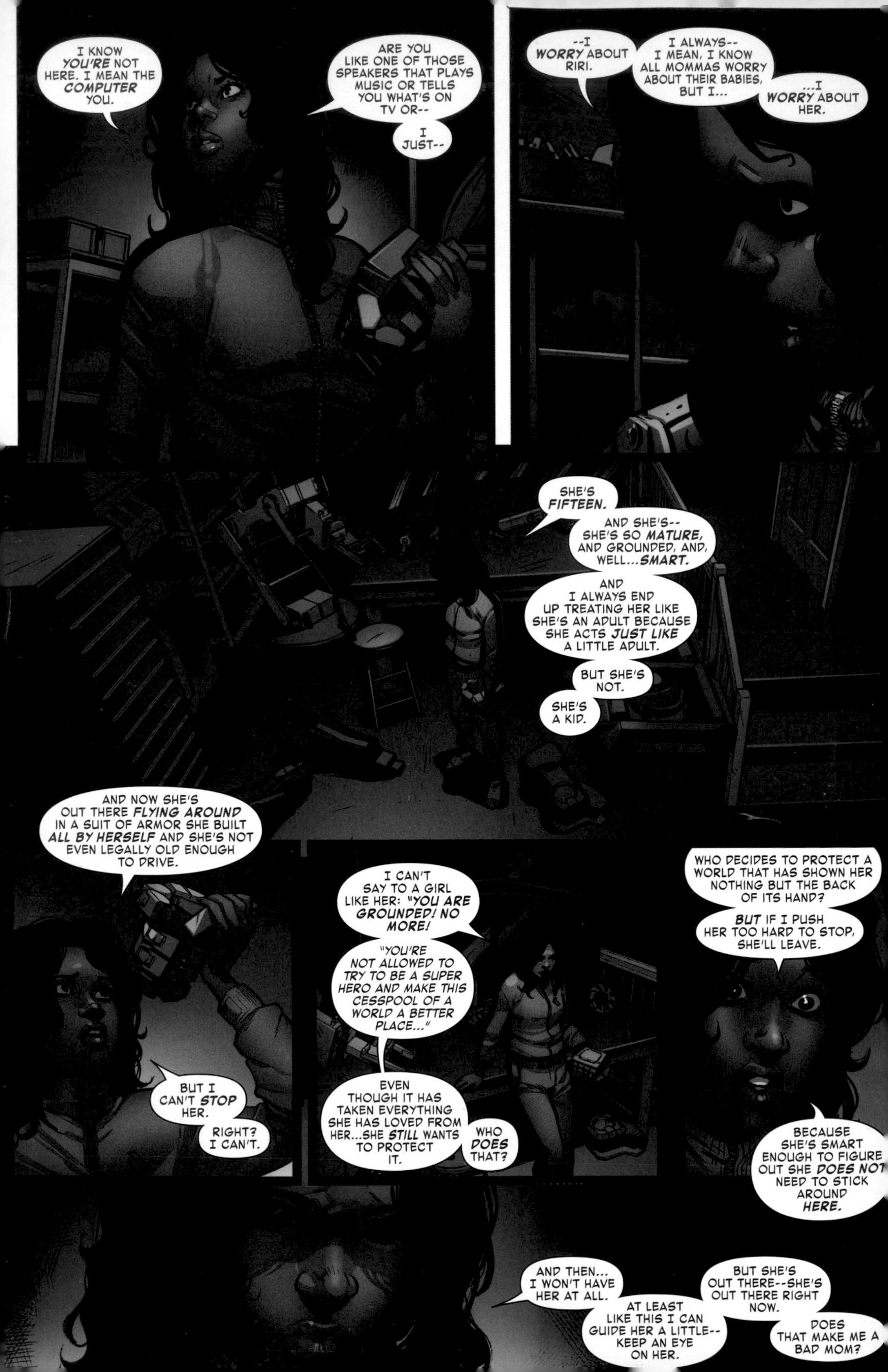
I KNOW *YOU'RE* NOT HERE. I MEAN THE *COMPUTER* YOU.
ARE YOU LIKE ONE OF THOSE SPEAKERS THAT PLAYS MUSIC OR TELLS YOU WHAT'S ON TV OR--
I JUST--
--I *WORRY* ABOUT RIRI.
I ALWAYS-- I MEAN, I KNOW ALL MOMMAS WORRY ABOUT THEIR BABIES, BUT I...
...I *WORRY* ABOUT HER.
SHE'S *FIFTEEN.*
AND SHE'S-- SHE'S SO *MATURE,* AND GROUNDED, AND, WELL...*SMART.*
AND I ALWAYS END UP TREATING HER LIKE SHE'S AN ADULT BECAUSE SHE ACTS *JUST LIKE* A LITTLE ADULT.
BUT SHE'S NOT.
SHE'S A KID.
AND NOW SHE'S OUT THERE *FLYING AROUND* IN A SUIT OF ARMOR SHE BUILT *ALL BY HERSELF* AND SHE'S NOT EVEN LEGALLY OLD ENOUGH TO DRIVE.
BUT I CAN'T *STOP* HER.
RIGHT? I CAN'T.
I CAN'T SAY TO A GIRL LIKE HER: "*YOU ARE GROUNDED! NO MORE!*
"*YOU'RE NOT ALLOWED TO TRY TO BE A SUPER HERO AND MAKE THIS CESSPOOL OF A WORLD A BETTER PLACE...*"
EVEN THOUGH IT HAS TAKEN EVERYTHING SHE HAS LOVED FROM HER...SHE *STILL* WANTS TO PROTECT IT.
WHO *DOES* THAT?
WHO DECIDES TO PROTECT A WORLD THAT HAS SHOWN HER NOTHING BUT THE BACK OF ITS HAND?
BUT IF I PUSH HER TOO HARD TO STOP, SHE'LL LEAVE.
BECAUSE SHE'S SMART ENOUGH TO FIGURE OUT SHE *DOES NOT* NEED TO STICK AROUND *HERE.*
AND THEN... I WON'T HAVE HER AT ALL.
AT LEAST LIKE THIS I CAN GUIDE HER A LITTLE-- KEEP AN EYE ON HER.
BUT SHE'S OUT THERE--SHE'S OUT THERE RIGHT NOW.
DOES THAT MAKE ME A BAD MOM?

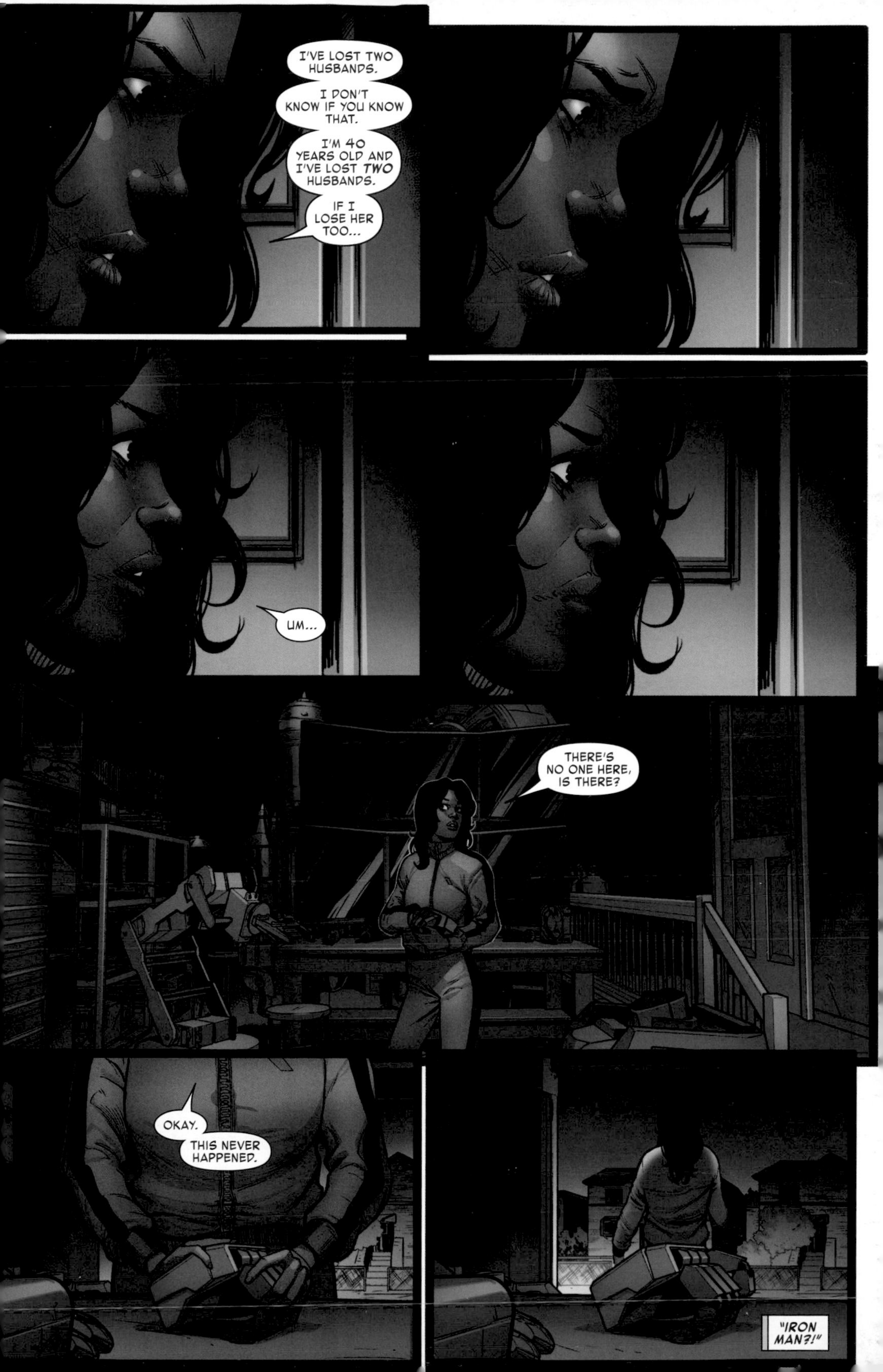
I'VE LOST TWO HUSBANDS.
I DON'T KNOW IF YOU KNOW THAT.
I'M 40 YEARS OLD AND I'VE LOST TWO HUSBANDS.
IF I LOSE HER TOO...
UM...
THERE'S NO ONE HERE, IS THERE?
OKAY.
THIS NEVER HAPPENED.
"IRON MAN?!"

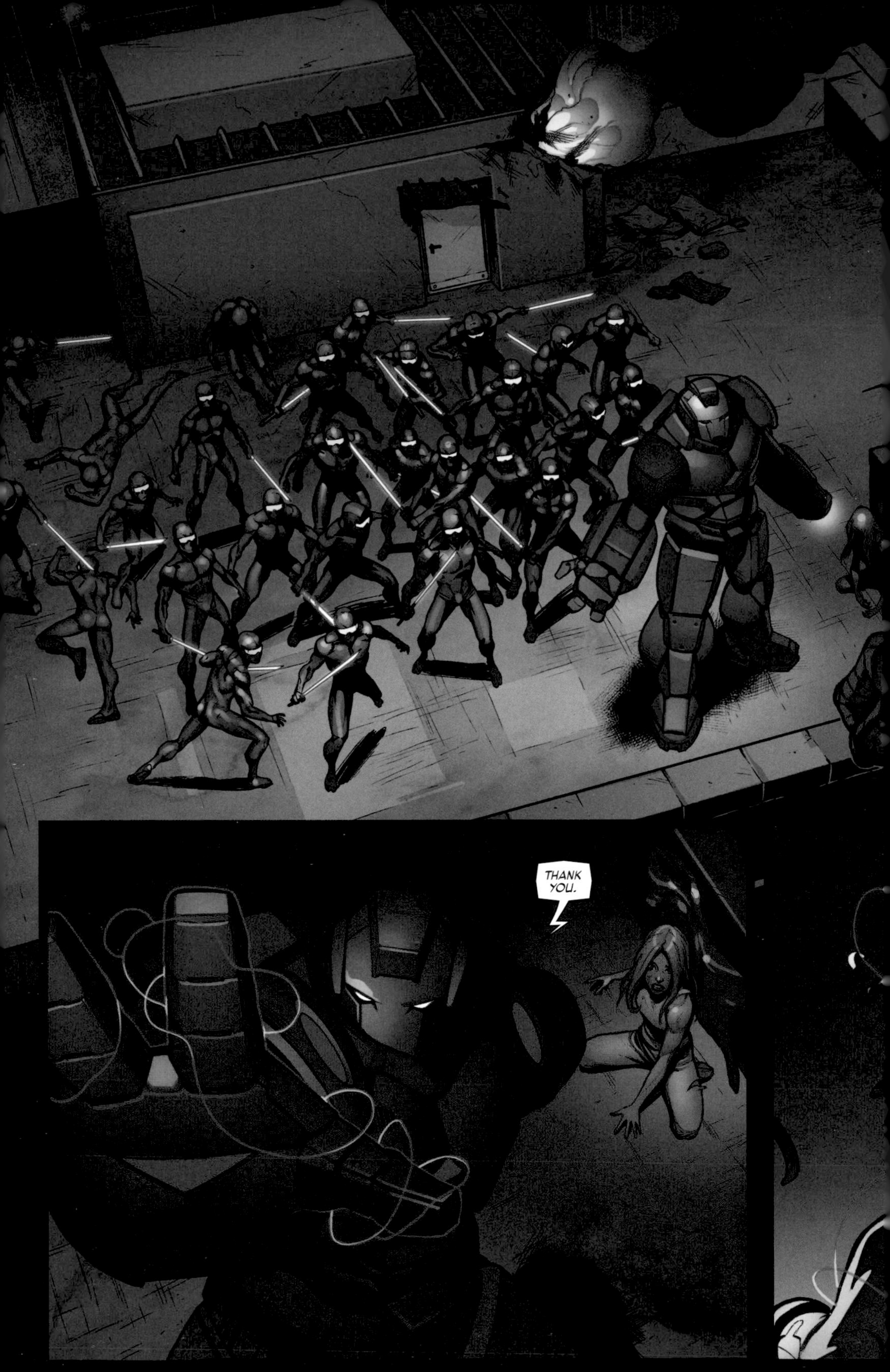
THANK YOU.

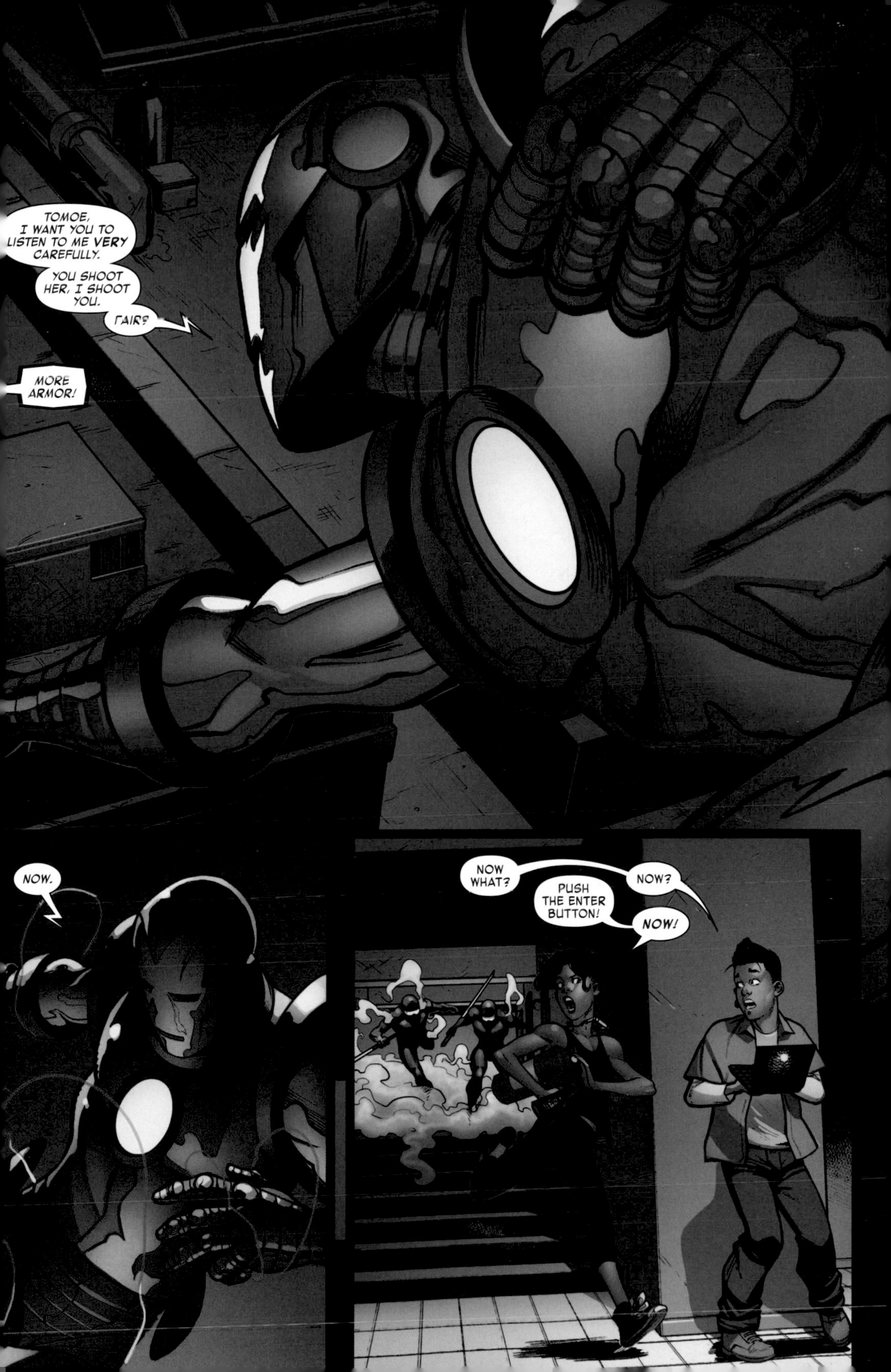
TOMOE, I WANT YOU TO LISTEN TO ME **VERY** CAREFULLY.
YOU SHOOT HER, I SHOOT YOU.
FAIR?
MORE ARMOR!
NOW.
NOW WHAT?
NOW?
PUSH THE ENTER BUTTON!
NOW!

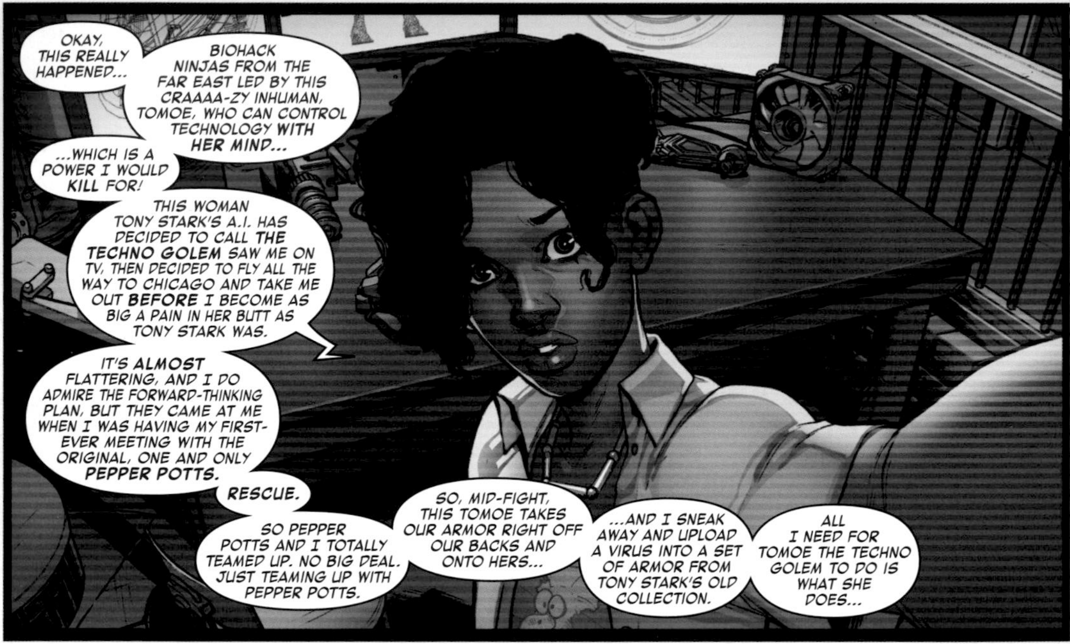
OKAY, THIS REALLY HAPPENED...
BIOHACK NINJAS FROM THE FAR EAST LED BY THIS CRAAAA-ZY INHUMAN, TOMOE, WHO CAN CONTROL TECHNOLOGY **WITH HER MIND...**
...WHICH IS A POWER I WOULD **KILL** FOR!
THIS WOMAN TONY STARK'S A.I. HAS DECIDED TO CALL **THE TECHNO GOLEM** SAW ME ON TV, THEN DECIDED TO FLY ALL THE WAY TO CHICAGO AND TAKE ME OUT **BEFORE** I BECOME AS BIG A PAIN IN HER BUTT AS TONY STARK WAS.
IT'S **ALMOST** FLATTERING, AND I DO ADMIRE THE FORWARD-THINKING PLAN, BUT THEY CAME AT ME WHEN I WAS HAVING MY FIRST-EVER MEETING WITH THE ORIGINAL, ONE AND ONLY **PEPPER POTTS.**
RESCUE.
SO PEPPER POTTS AND I TOTALLY TEAMED UP. NO BIG DEAL. JUST TEAMING UP WITH PEPPER POTTS.
SO, MID-FIGHT, THIS TOMOE TAKES OUR ARMOR RIGHT OFF OUR BACKS AND ONTO HERS...
...AND I SNEAK AWAY AND UPLOAD A VIRUS INTO A SET OF ARMOR FROM TONY STARK'S OLD COLLECTION.
ALL I NEED FOR TOMOE THE TECHNO GOLEM TO DO IS WHAT SHE DOES...

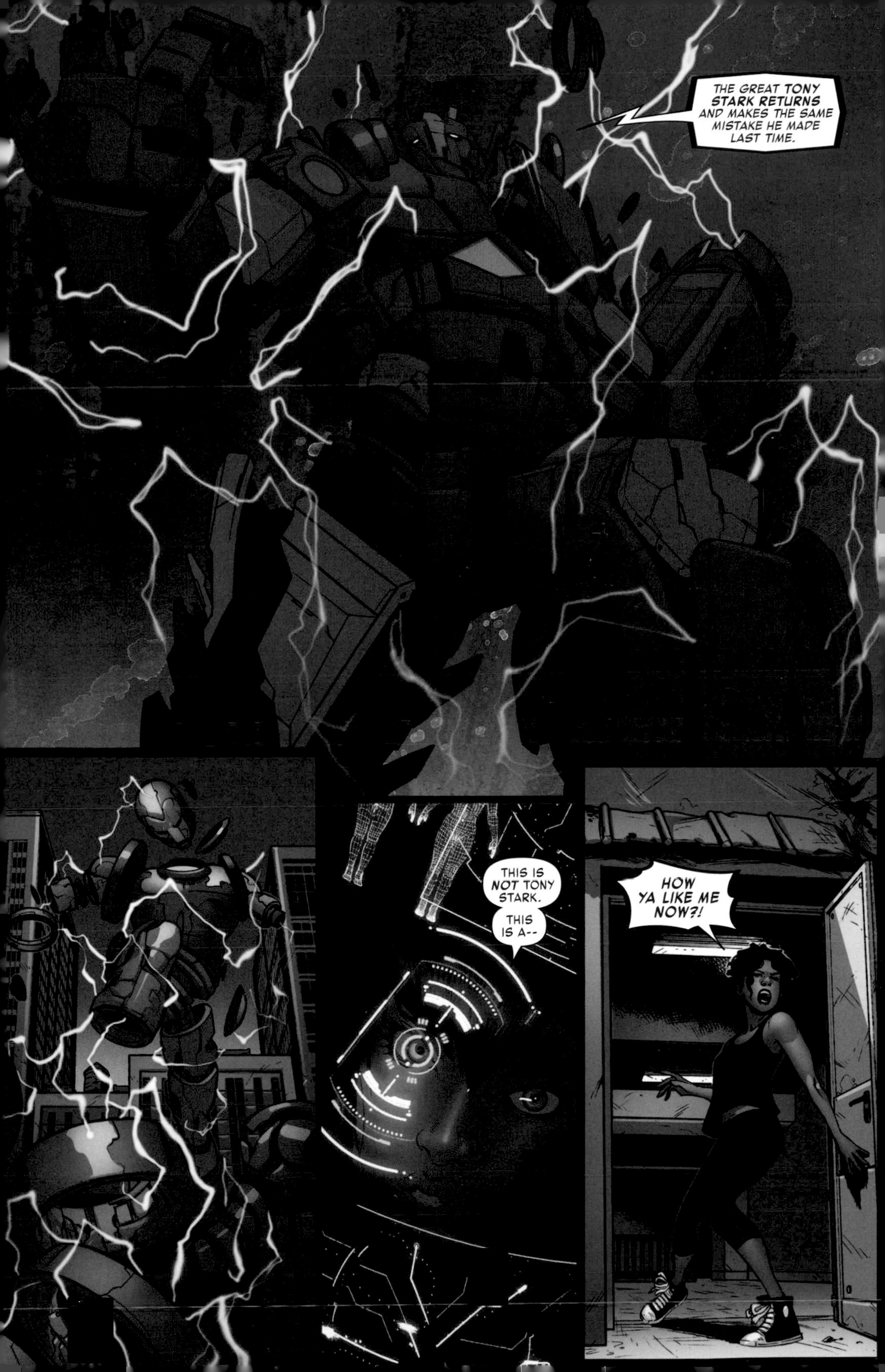
THE GREAT TONY STARK RETURNS AND MAKES THE SAME MISTAKE HE MADE LAST TIME.
THIS IS NOT TONY STARK.
THIS IS A--
HOW YA LIKE ME NOW?!

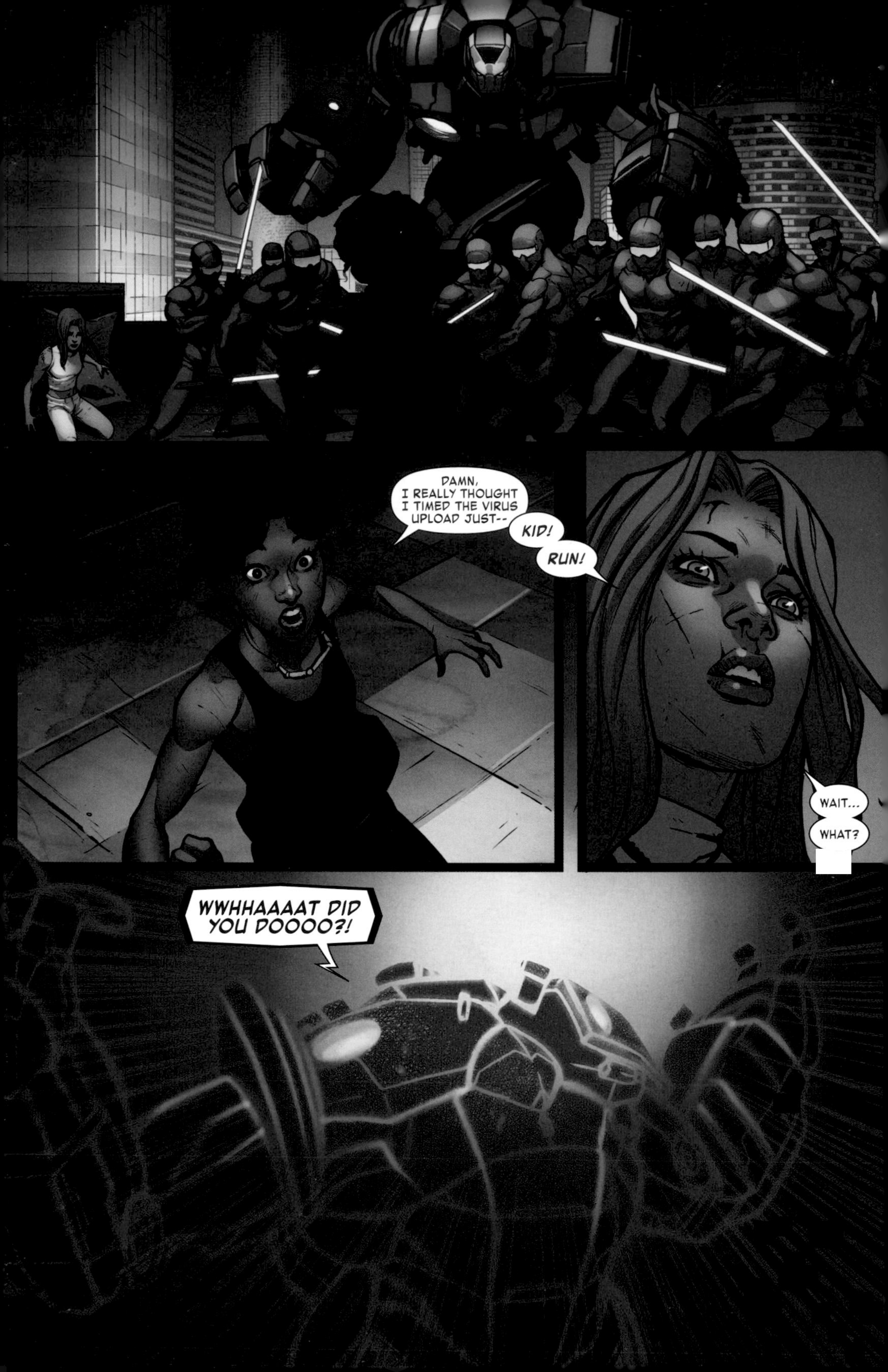
DAMN, I REALLY THOUGHT I TIMED THE VIRUS UPLOAD JUST--
KID!
RUN!
WAIT...
WHAT?
WWHHAAAAT DID YOU DOOOO?!

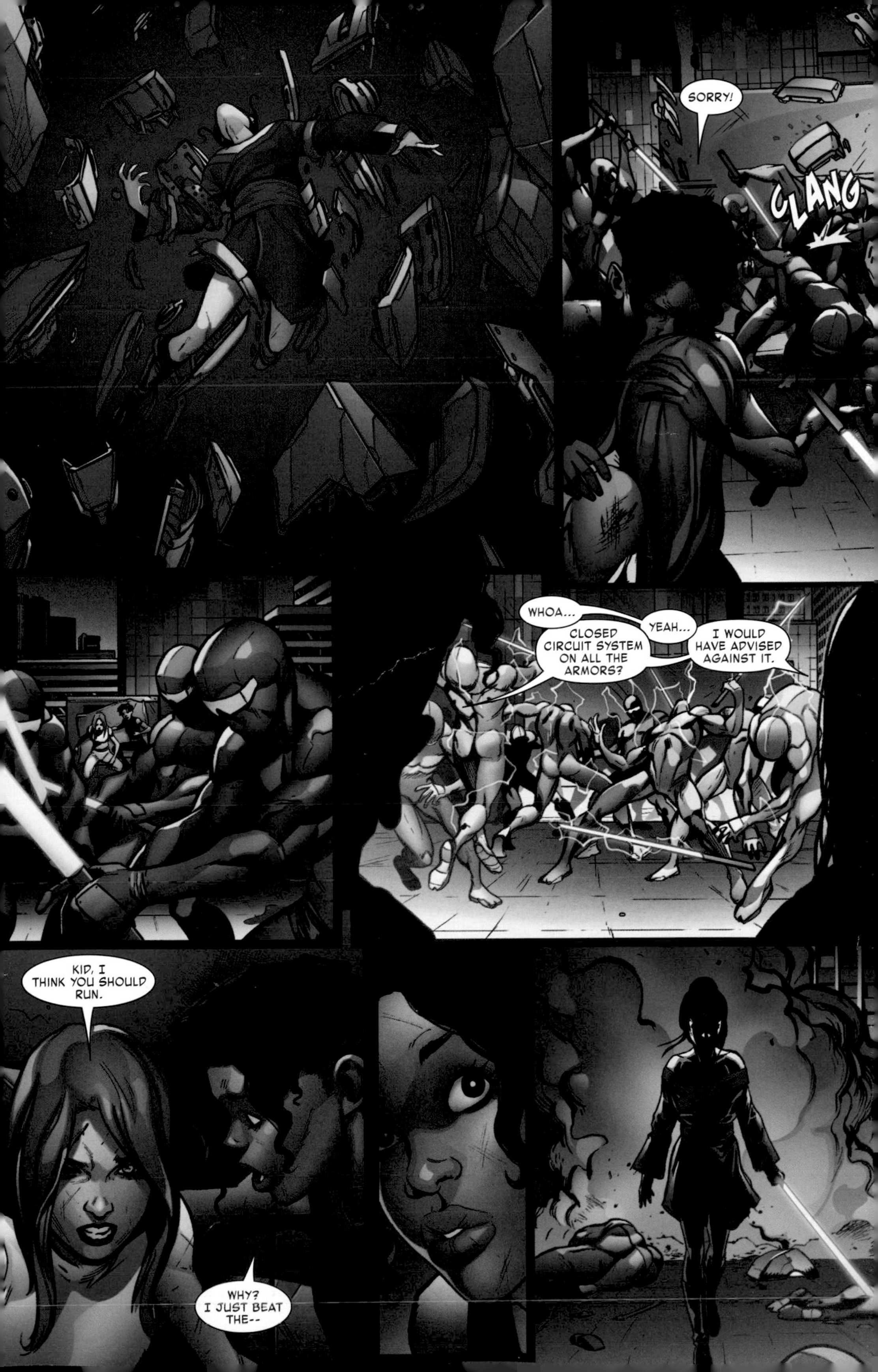
SORRY!
CLANG
WHOA...
CLOSED CIRCUIT SYSTEM ON ALL THE ARMORS?
YEAH...
I WOULD HAVE ADVISED AGAINST IT.
KID, I THINK YOU SHOULD RUN.
WHY? I JUST BEAT THE--

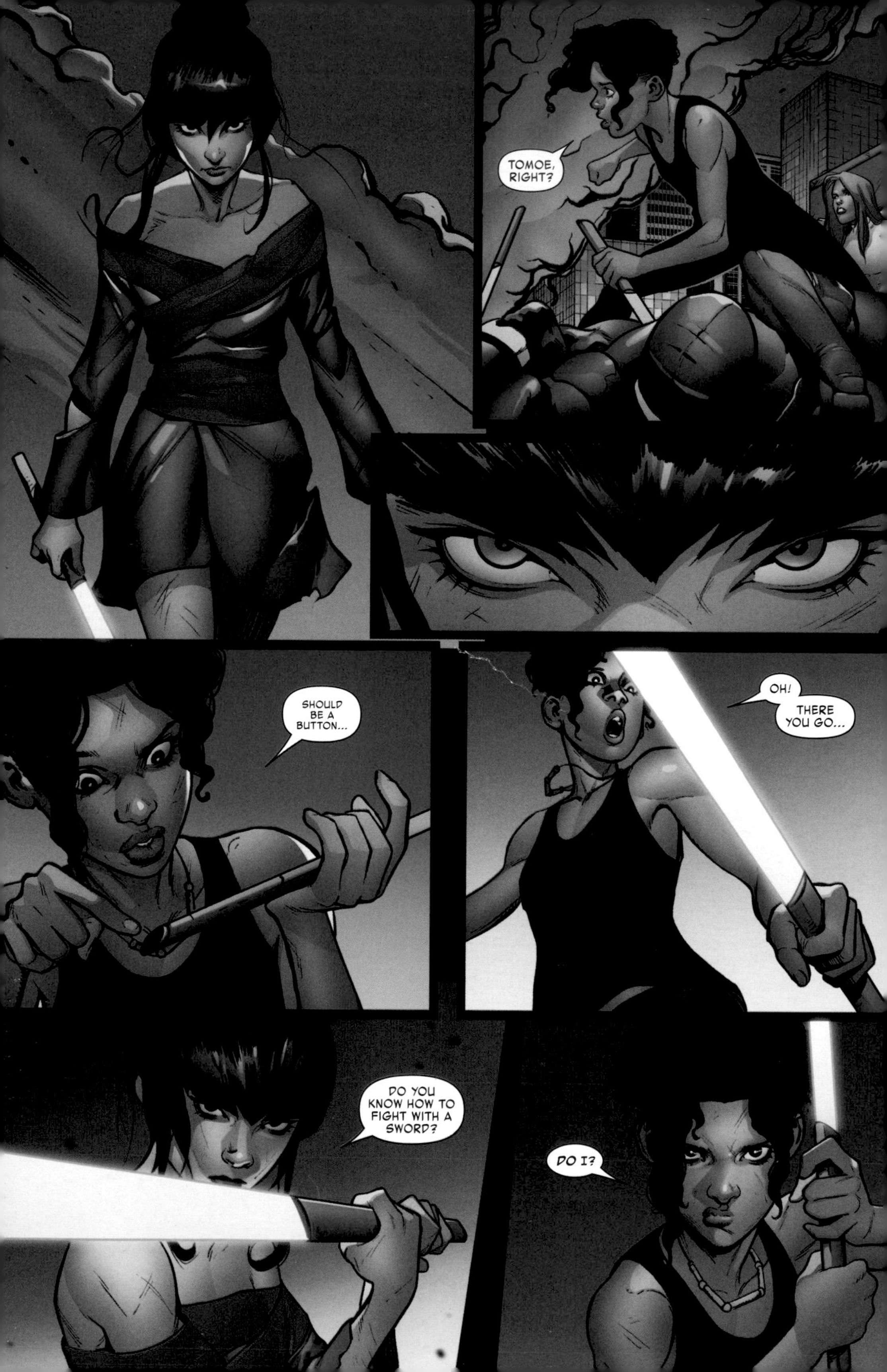
TOMOE, RIGHT?
SHOULD BE A BUTTON...
OH!
THERE YOU GO...
DO YOU KNOW HOW TO FIGHT WITH A SWORD?
DO I?

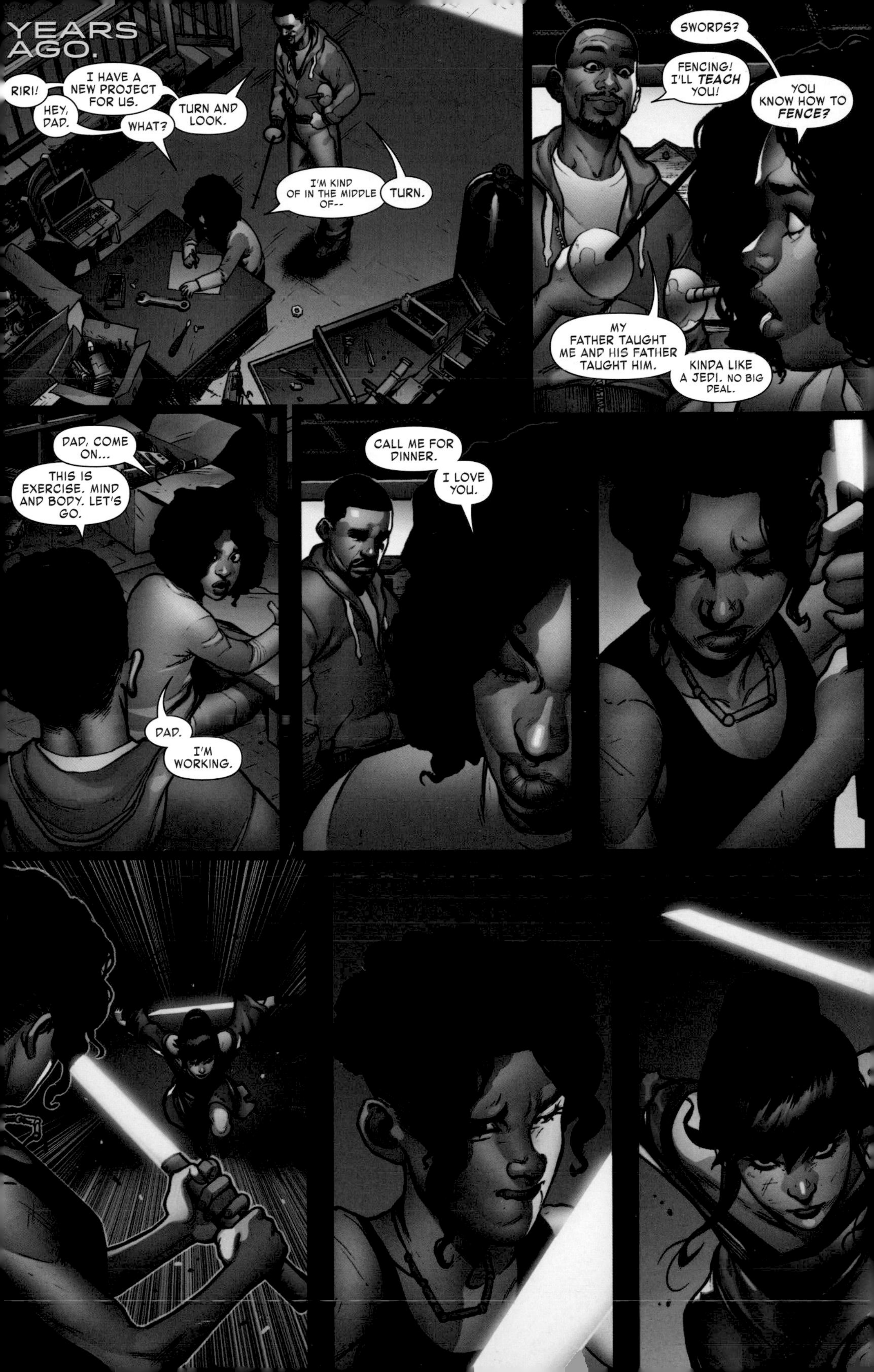
YEARS AGO.
RIRI!
I HAVE A NEW PROJECT FOR US.
HEY, DAD.
WHAT?
TURN AND LOOK.
I'M KIND OF IN THE MIDDLE OF--
TURN.
SWORDS?
FENCING! I'LL TEACH YOU!
YOU KNOW HOW TO FENCE?
MY FATHER TAUGHT ME AND HIS FATHER TAUGHT HIM.
KINDA LIKE A JEDI. NO BIG DEAL.
DAD, COME ON...
THIS IS EXERCISE. MIND AND BODY. LET'S GO.
DAD.
I'M WORKING.
CALL ME FOR DINNER.
I LOVE YOU.

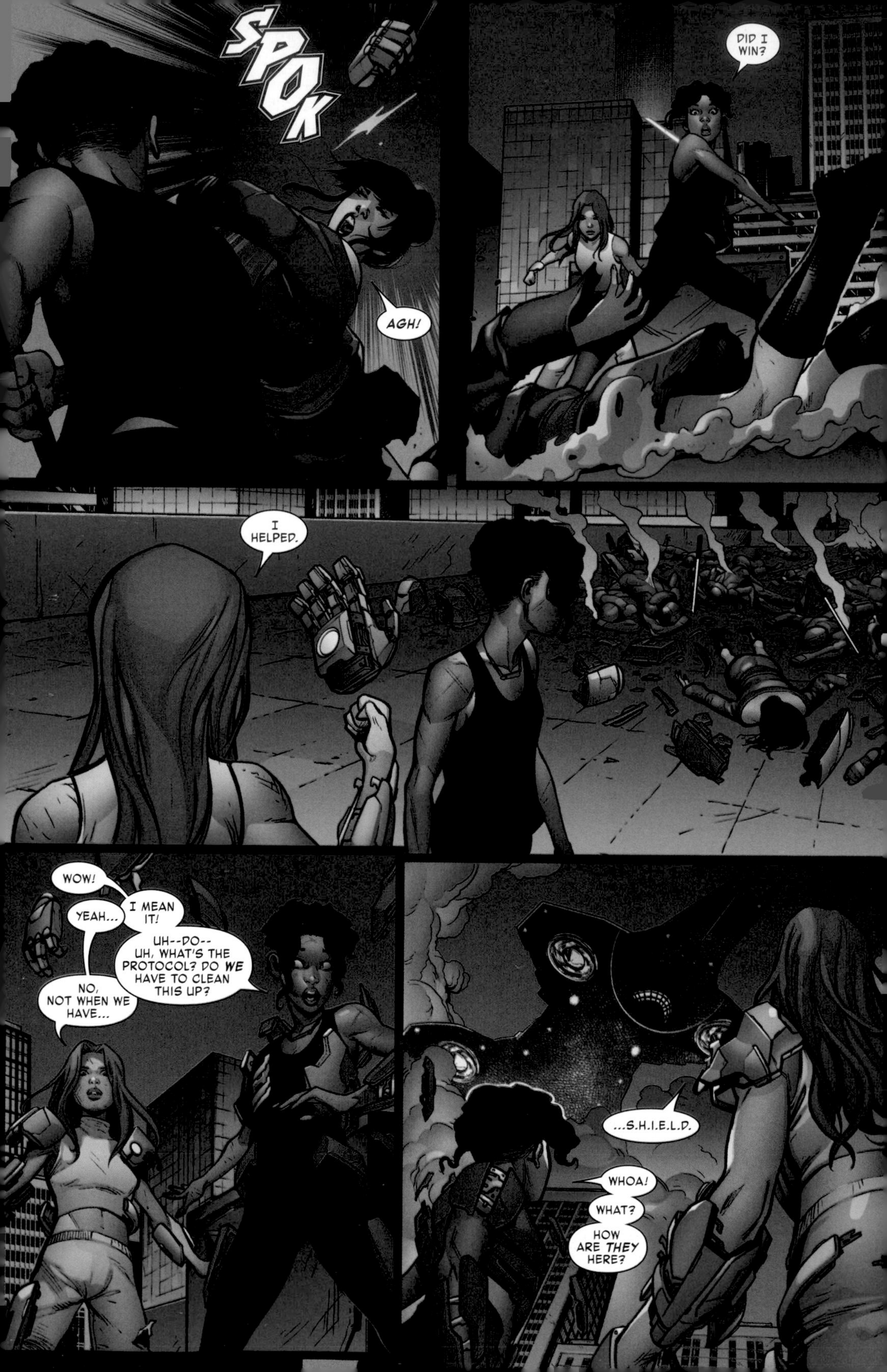

SPOK
AGH!
DID I WIN?
I HELPED.
WOW!
YEAH...
I MEAN IT!
UH--DO-- UH, WHAT'S THE PROTOCOL? DO WE HAVE TO CLEAN THIS UP?
NO, NOT WHEN WE HAVE...
...S.H.I.E.L.D.
WHOA!
WHAT?
HOW ARE THEY HERE?

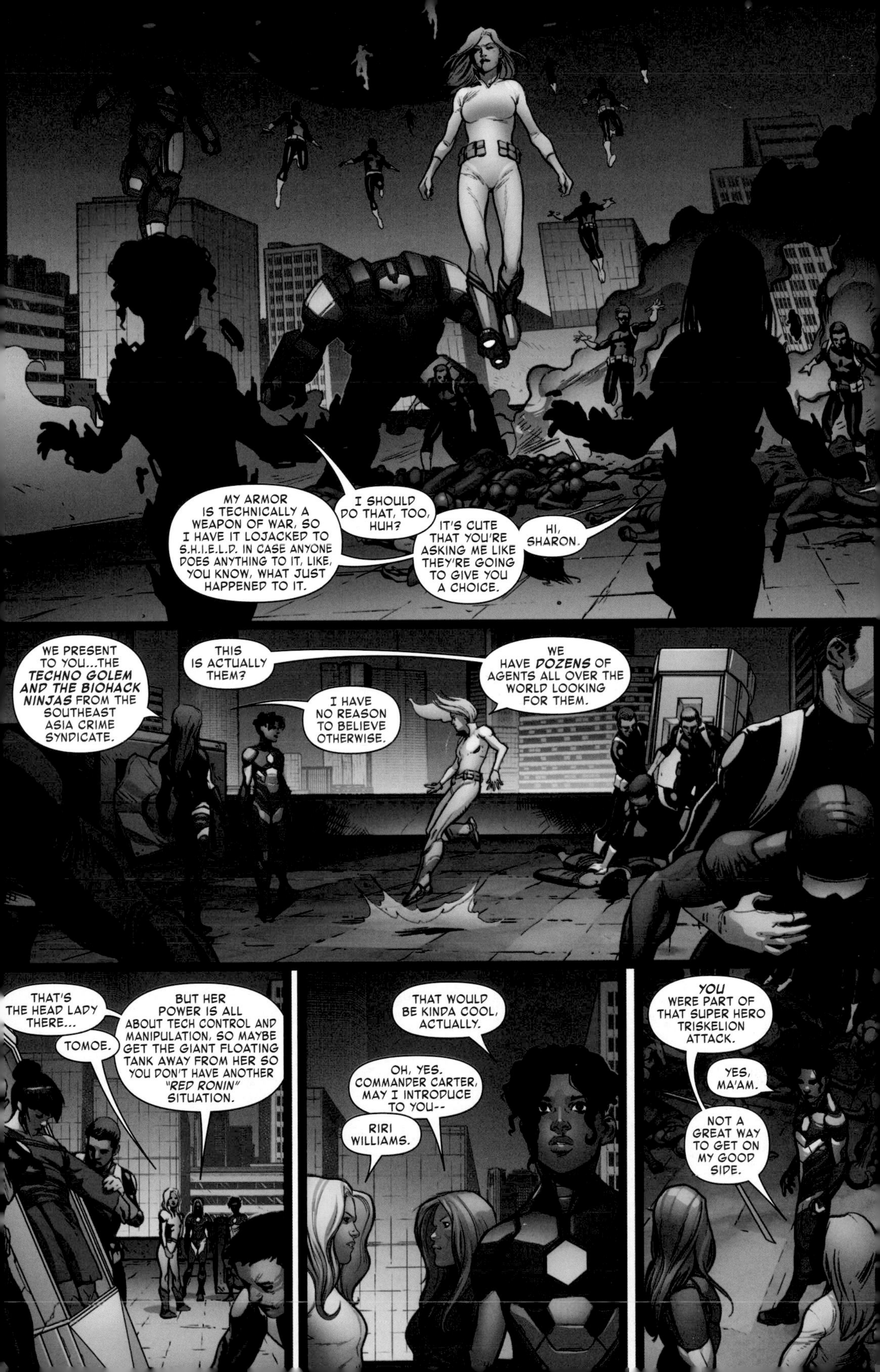
HI, SHARON.
IT'S CUTE THAT YOU'RE ASKING ME LIKE THEY'RE GOING TO GIVE YOU A CHOICE.
I SHOULD DO THAT, TOO, HUH?
MY ARMOR IS TECHNICALLY A WEAPON OF WAR, SO I HAVE IT LOJACKED TO S.H.I.E.L.D. IN CASE ANYONE DOES ANYTHING TO IT, LIKE, YOU KNOW, WHAT JUST HAPPENED TO IT.
WE PRESENT TO YOU...THE *TECHNO GOLEM AND THE BIOHACK NINJAS* FROM THE SOUTHEAST ASIA CRIME SYNDICATE.
THIS IS ACTUALLY THEM?
I HAVE NO REASON TO BELIEVE OTHERWISE.
WE HAVE *DOZENS* OF AGENTS ALL OVER THE WORLD LOOKING FOR THEM.
THAT'S THE HEAD LADY THERE...
TOMOE.
BUT HER POWER IS ALL ABOUT TECH CONTROL AND MANIPULATION, SO MAYBE GET THE GIANT FLOATING TANK AWAY FROM HER SO YOU DON'T HAVE ANOTHER *"RED RONIN"* SITUATION.
THAT WOULD BE KINDA COOL, ACTUALLY.
OH, YES. COMMANDER CARTER, MAY I INTRODUCE TO YOU--
RIRI WILLIAMS.
YOU WERE PART OF THAT SUPER HERO TRISKELION ATTACK.
YES, MA'AM.
NOT A GREAT WAY TO GET ON MY GOOD SIDE.

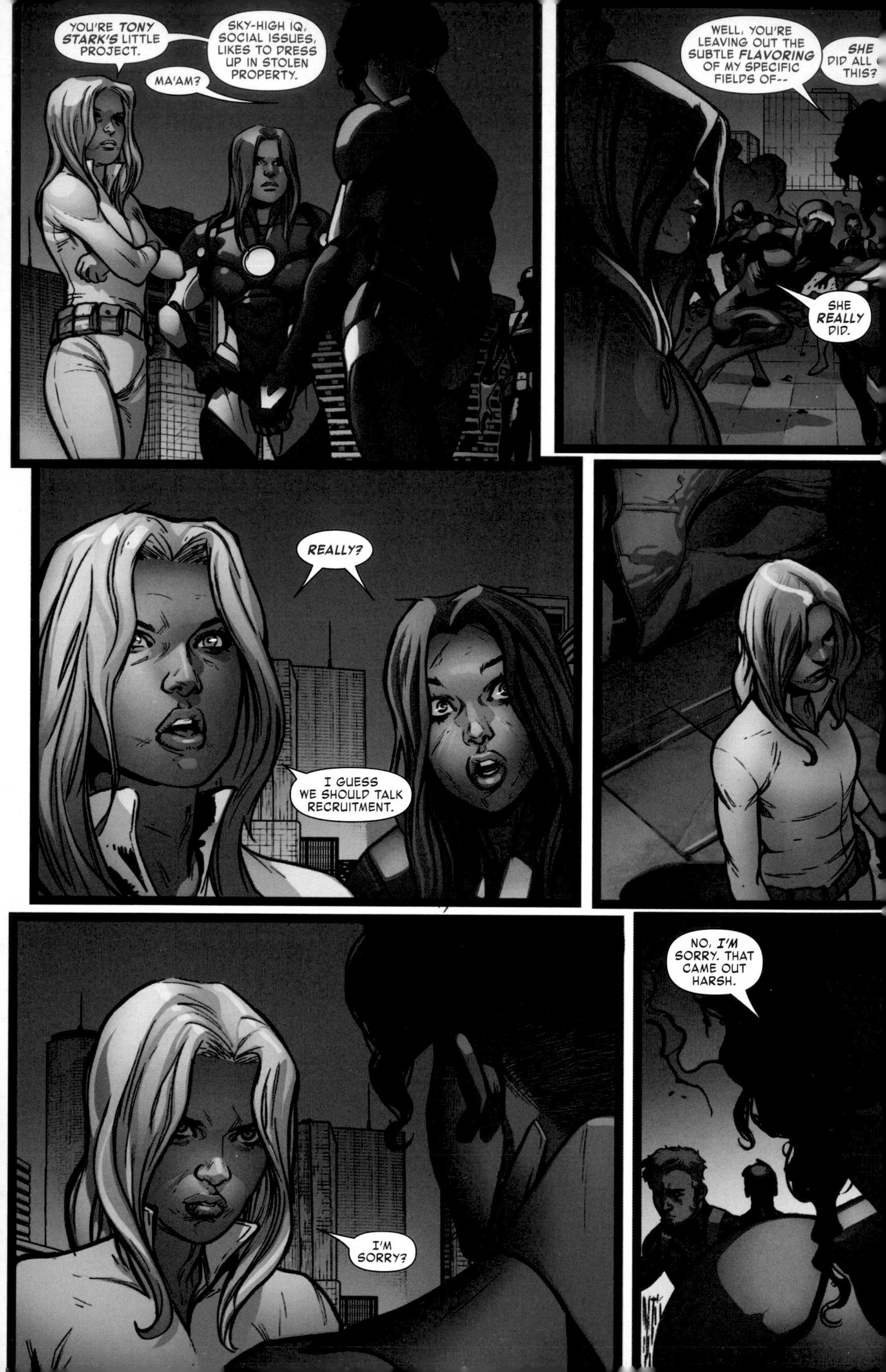

YOU'RE TONY STARK'S LITTLE PROJECT.
SKY-HIGH IQ, SOCIAL ISSUES, LIKES TO DRESS UP IN STOLEN PROPERTY.
MA'AM?
WELL, YOU'RE LEAVING OUT THE SUBTLE FLAVORING OF MY SPECIFIC FIELDS OF--
SHE REALLY DID.
REALLY?
I GUESS WE SHOULD TALK RECRUITMENT.
I'M SORRY?
NO, I'M SORRY. THAT CAME OUT HARSH.

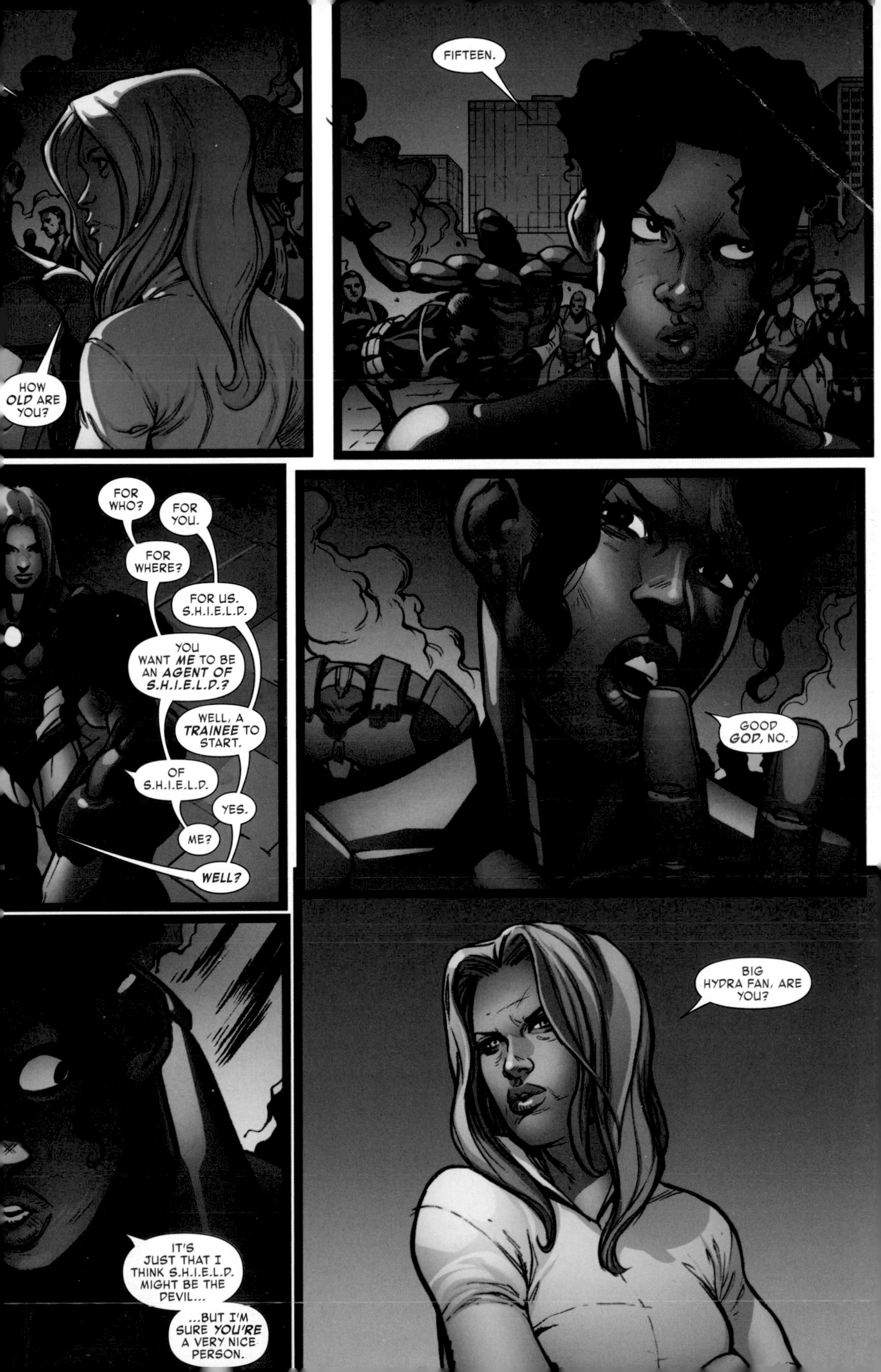
HOW OLD ARE YOU?
FIFTEEN.
FOR YOU.
FOR WHO?
FOR US. S.H.I.E.L.D.
FOR WHERE?
WELL, A TRAINEE TO START.
YOU WANT ME TO BE AN AGENT OF S.H.I.E.L.D.?
YES.
OF S.H.I.E.L.D.
WELL?
ME?
GOOD GOD, NO.
BIG HYDRA FAN, ARE YOU?
IT'S JUST THAT I THINK S.H.I.E.L.D. MIGHT BE THE DEVIL...
...BUT I'M SURE YOU'RE A VERY NICE PERSON.

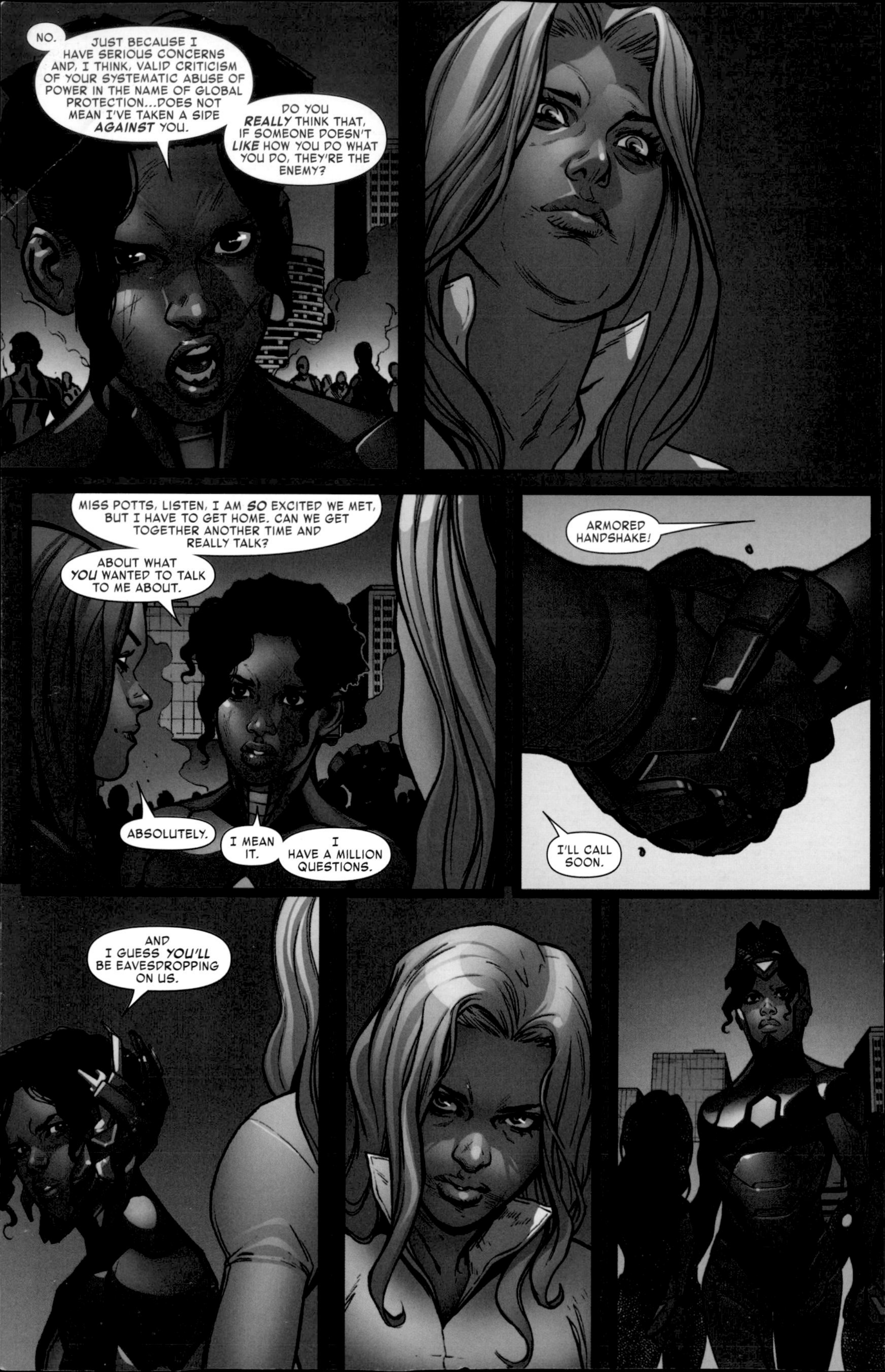
NO.
JUST BECAUSE I HAVE SERIOUS CONCERNS AND, I THINK, VALID CRITICISM OF YOUR SYSTEMATIC ABUSE OF POWER IN THE NAME OF GLOBAL PROTECTION...DOES NOT MEAN I'VE TAKEN A SIDE AGAINST YOU.
DO YOU REALLY THINK THAT, IF SOMEONE DOESN'T LIKE HOW YOU DO WHAT YOU DO, THEY'RE THE ENEMY?
MISS POTTS, LISTEN, I AM SO EXCITED WE MET, BUT I HAVE TO GET HOME. CAN WE GET TOGETHER ANOTHER TIME AND REALLY TALK?
ABOUT WHAT YOU WANTED TO TALK TO ME ABOUT.
ABSOLUTELY.
I MEAN IT.
I HAVE A MILLION QUESTIONS.
ARMORED HANDSHAKE!
I'LL CALL SOON.
AND I GUESS YOU'LL BE EAVESDROPPING ON US.

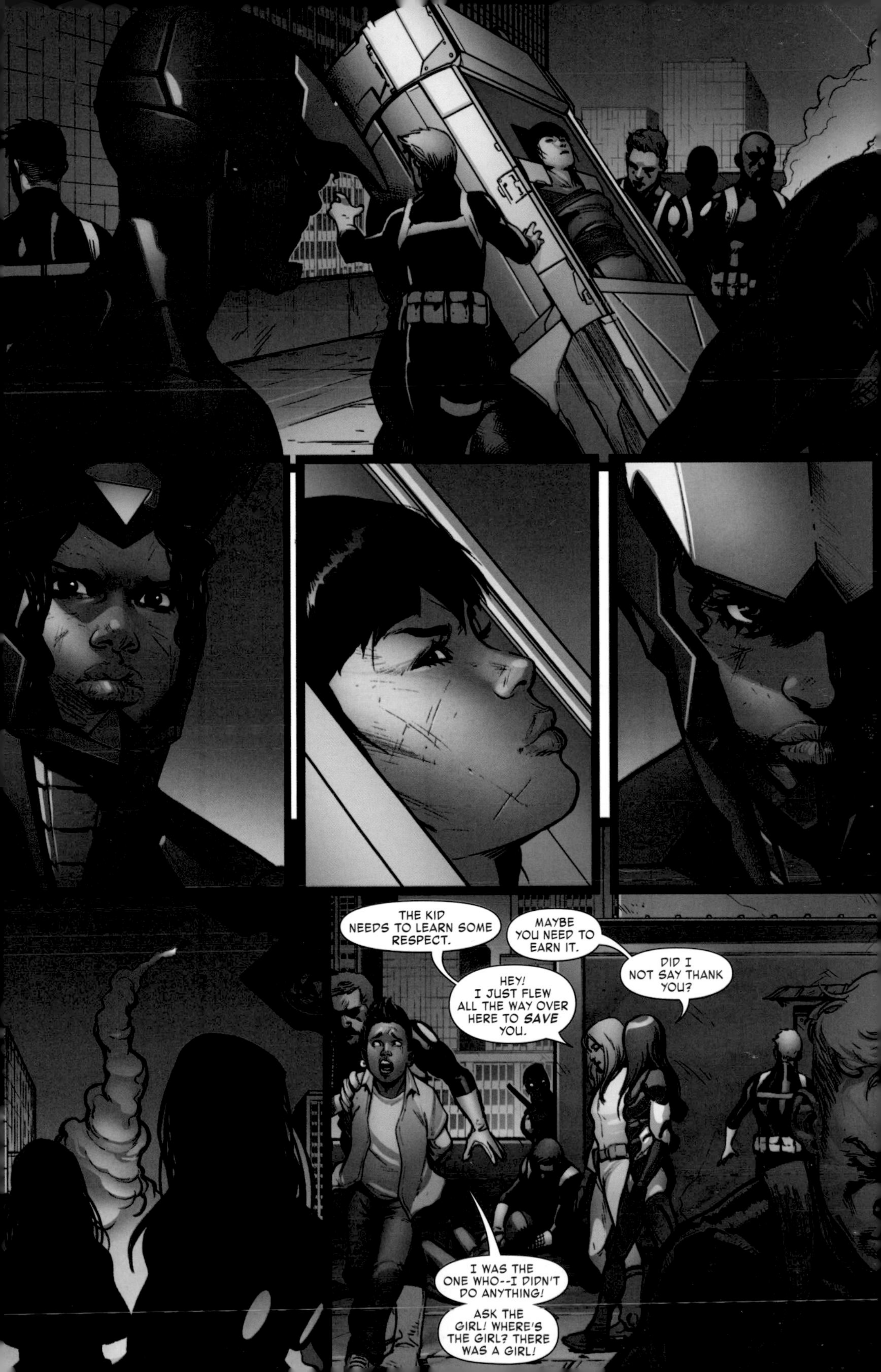
THE KID NEEDS TO LEARN SOME RESPECT.
MAYBE YOU NEED TO EARN IT.
HEY! I JUST FLEW ALL THE WAY OVER HERE TO SAVE YOU.
DID I NOT SAY THANK YOU?
I WAS THE ONE WHO--I DIDN'T DO ANYTHING!
ASK THE GIRL! WHERE'S THE GIRL? THERE WAS A GIRL!

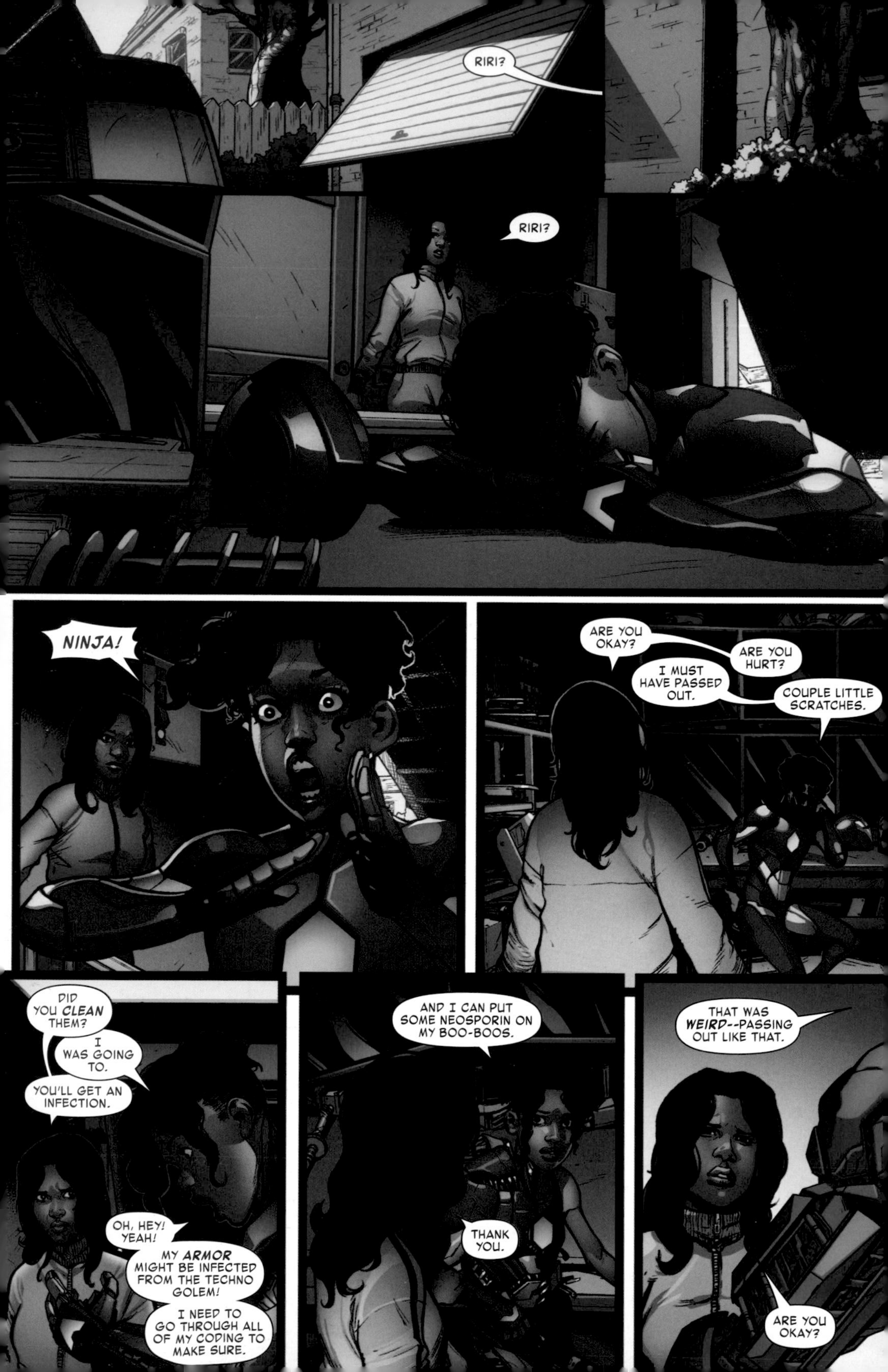
RIRI?
RIRI?
NINJA!
ARE YOU OKAY?
ARE YOU HURT?
I MUST HAVE PASSED OUT.
COUPLE LITTLE SCRATCHES.
DID YOU CLEAN THEM?
I WAS GOING TO.
YOU'LL GET AN INFECTION.
OH, HEY! YEAH!
MY ARMOR MIGHT BE INFECTED FROM THE TECHNO GOLEM!
I NEED TO GO THROUGH ALL OF MY CODING TO MAKE SURE.
AND I CAN PUT SOME NEOSPORIN ON MY BOO-BOOS.
THANK YOU.
THAT WAS WEIRD--PASSING OUT LIKE THAT.
ARE YOU OKAY?

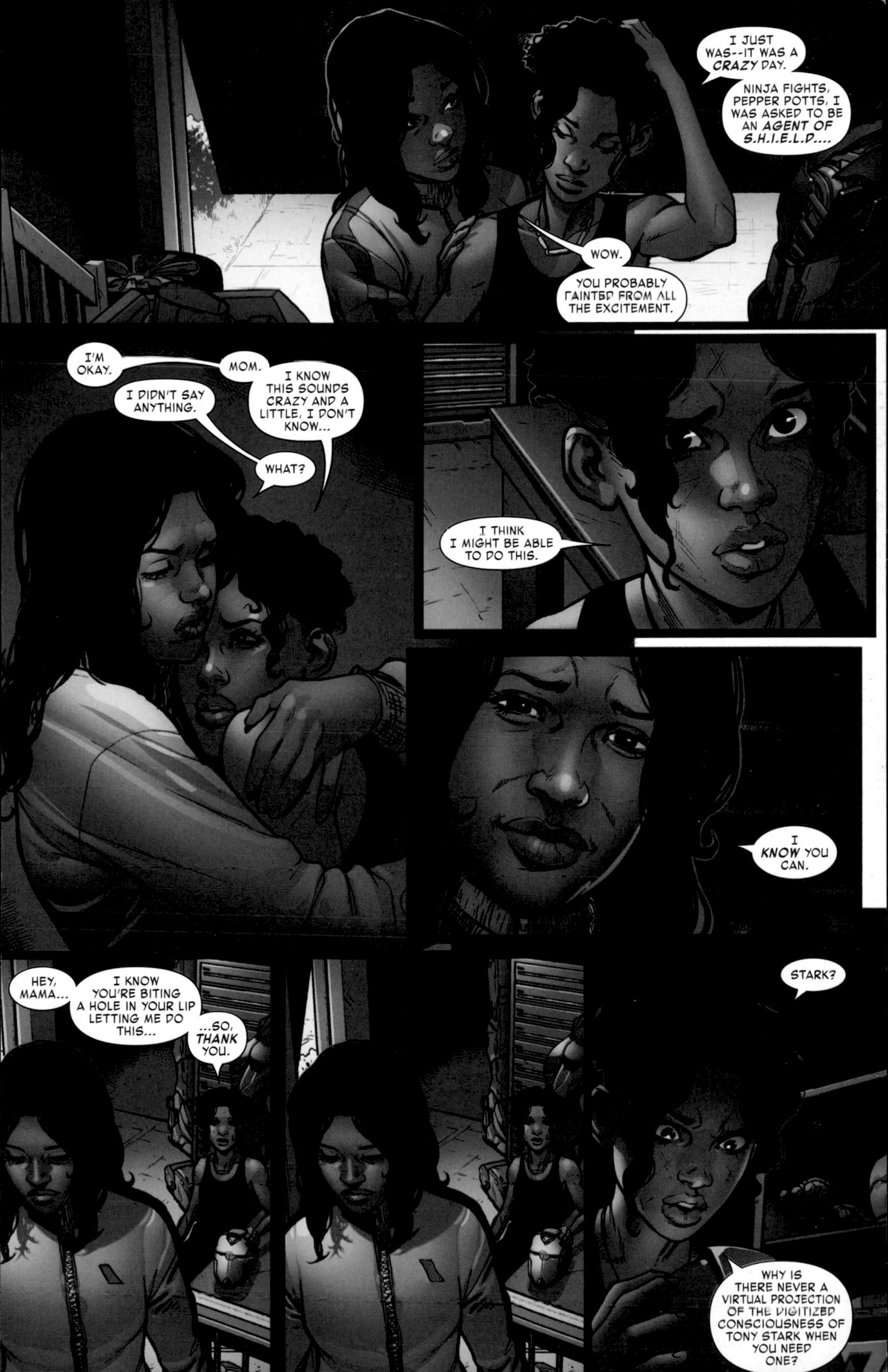

I JUST WAS--IT WAS A CRAZY DAY.
NINJA FIGHTS, PEPPER POTTS, I WAS ASKED TO BE AN AGENT OF S.H.I.E.L.D....
WOW.
YOU PROBABLY FAINTED FROM ALL THE EXCITEMENT.
I'M OKAY.
MOM.
I DIDN'T SAY ANYTHING.
I KNOW THIS SOUNDS CRAZY AND A LITTLE, I DON'T KNOW...
WHAT?
I THINK I MIGHT BE ABLE TO DO THIS.
I KNOW YOU CAN.
HEY, MAMA...
I KNOW YOU'RE BITING A HOLE IN YOUR LIP LETTING ME DO THIS...
...SO, THANK YOU.
STARK?
WHY IS THERE NEVER A VIRTUAL PROJECTION OF THE DIGITIZED CONSCIOUSNESS OF TONY STARK WHEN YOU NEED ONE?

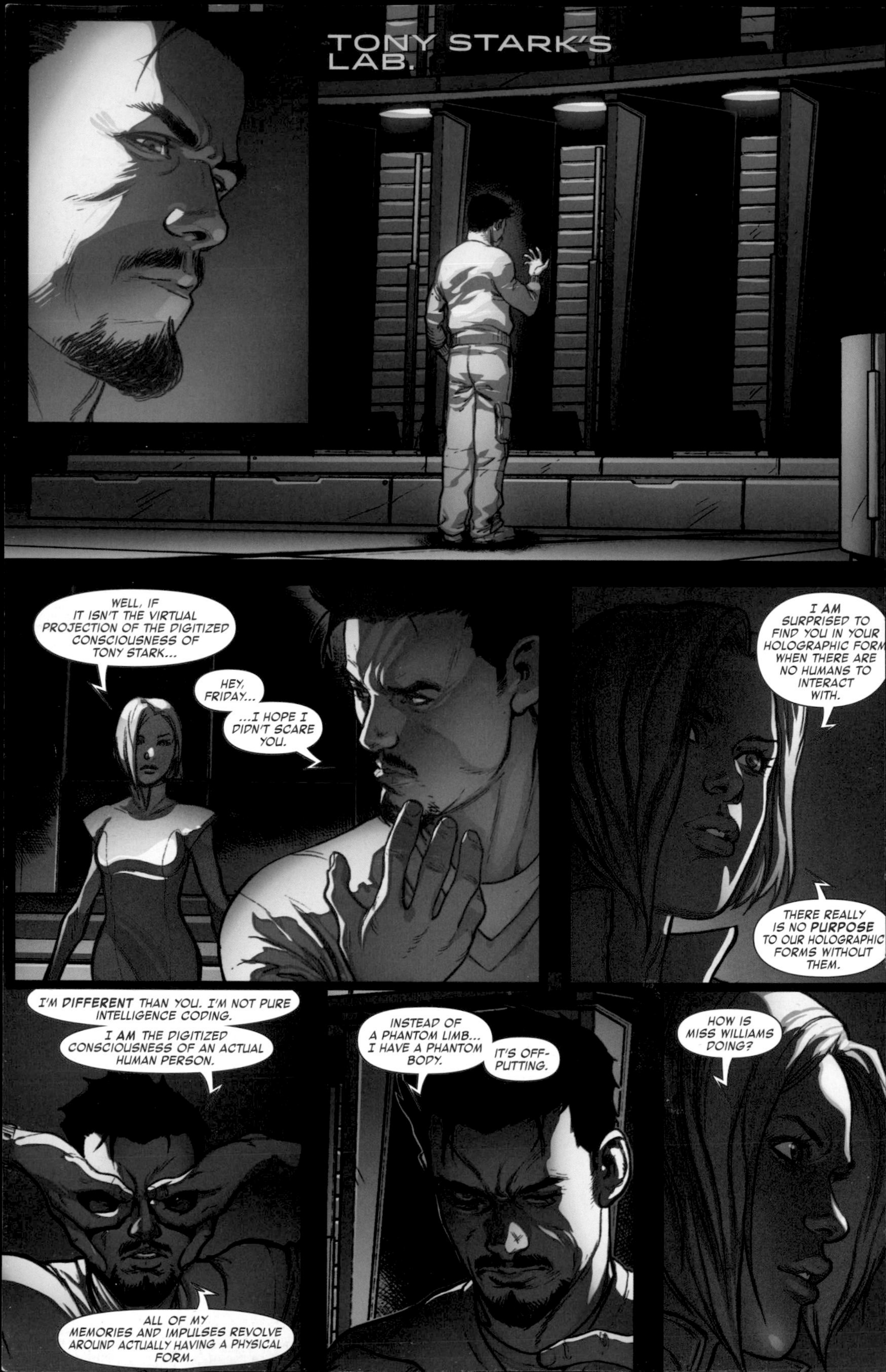
TONY STARK'S LAB.
WELL, IF IT ISN'T THE VIRTUAL PROJECTION OF THE DIGITIZED CONSCIOUSNESS OF TONY STARK...
HEY, FRIDAY...
...I HOPE I DIDN'T SCARE YOU.
I AM SURPRISED TO FIND YOU IN YOUR HOLOGRAPHIC FORM WHEN THERE ARE NO HUMANS TO INTERACT WITH.
THERE REALLY IS NO PURPOSE TO OUR HOLOGRAPHIC FORMS WITHOUT THEM.
I'M DIFFERENT THAN YOU. I'M NOT PURE INTELLIGENCE CODING.
I AM THE DIGITIZED CONSCIOUSNESS OF AN ACTUAL HUMAN PERSON.
ALL OF MY MEMORIES AND IMPULSES REVOLVE AROUND ACTUALLY HAVING A PHYSICAL FORM.
INSTEAD OF A PHANTOM LIMB... I HAVE A PHANTOM BODY.
IT'S OFF-PUTTING.
HOW IS MISS WILLIAMS DOING?

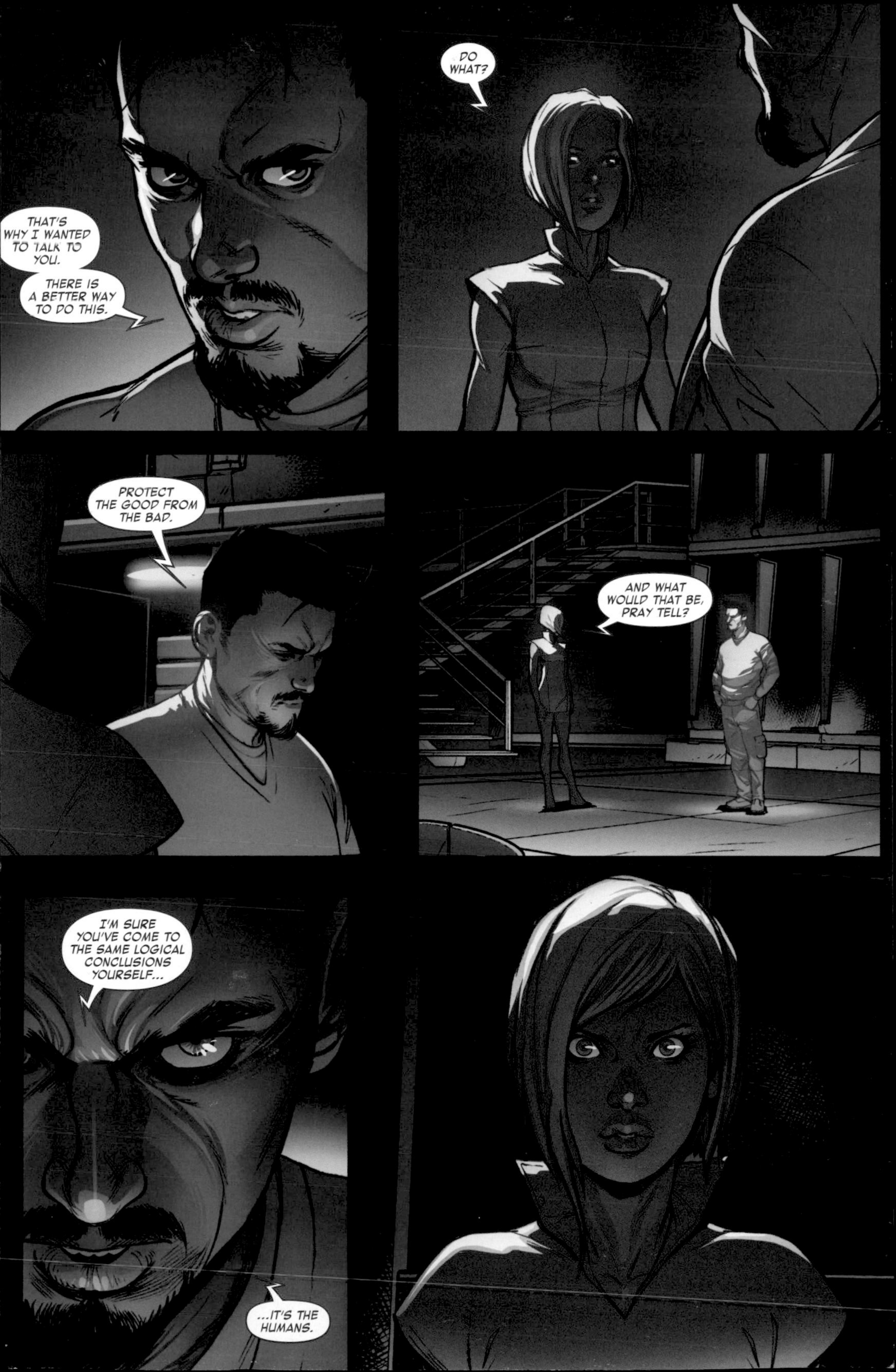
THAT'S WHY I WANTED TO TALK TO YOU.
THERE IS A BETTER WAY TO DO THIS.
DO WHAT?
PROTECT THE GOOD FROM THE BAD.
AND WHAT WOULD THAT BE, PRAY TELL?
I'M SURE YOU'VE COME TO THE SAME LOGICAL CONCLUSIONS YOURSELF...
...IT'S THE HUMANS.

6

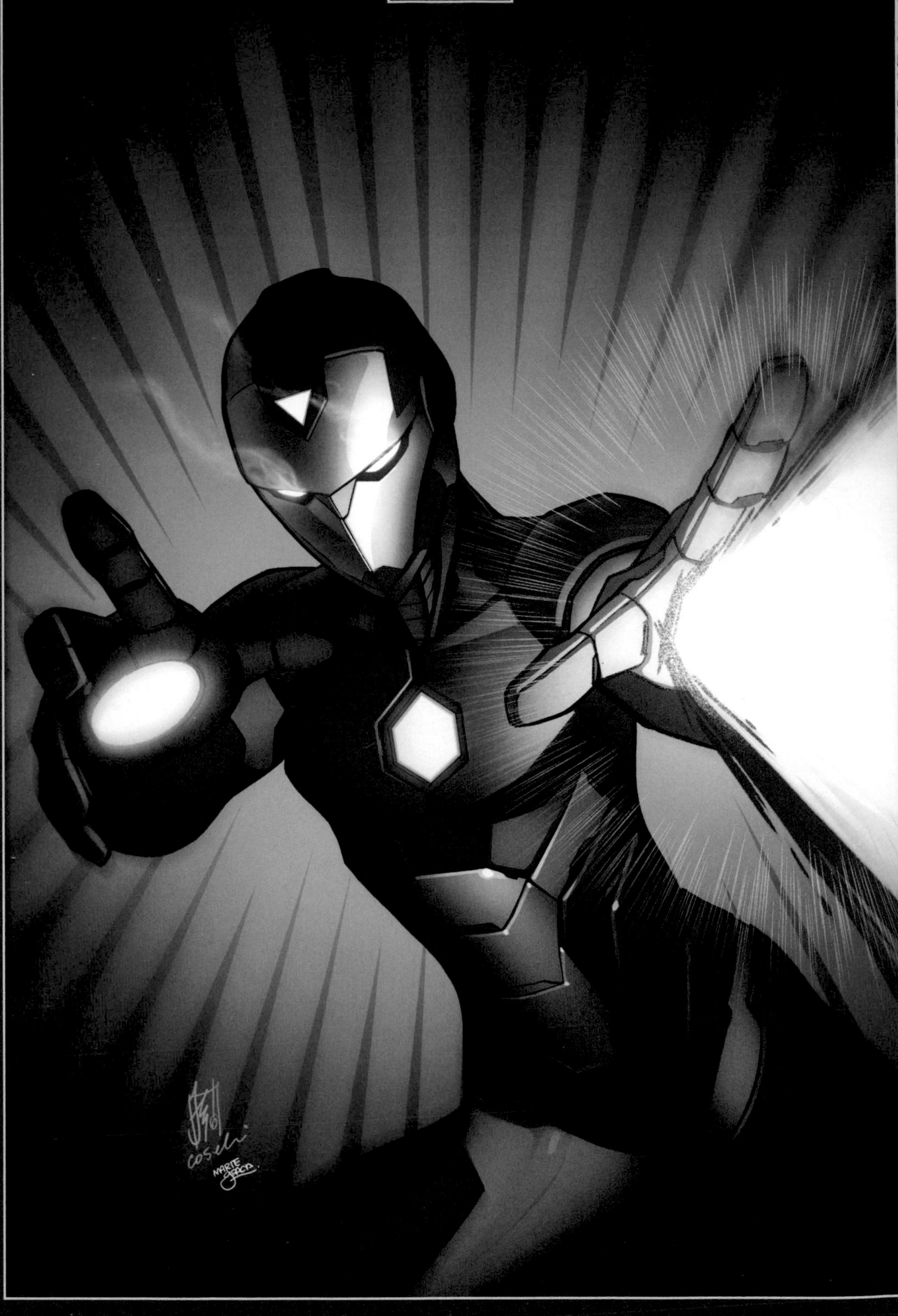

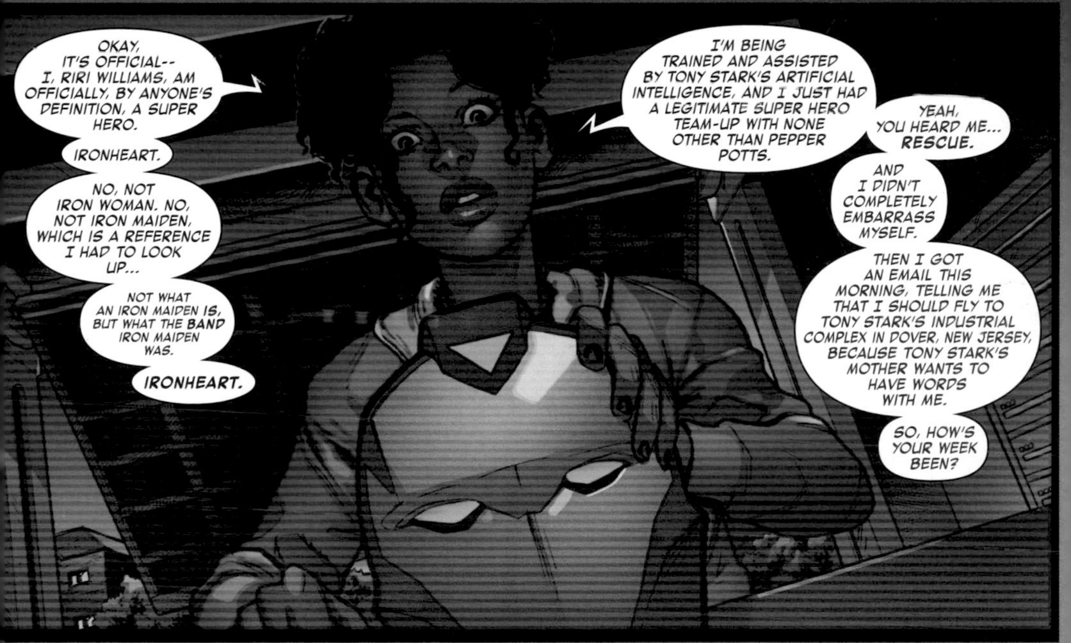
OKAY, IT'S OFFICIAL-- I, RIRI WILLIAMS, AM OFFICIALLY, BY ANYONE'S DEFINITION, A SUPER HERO.
IRONHEART.
NO, NOT IRON WOMAN. NO, NOT IRON MAIDEN, WHICH IS A REFERENCE I HAD TO LOOK UP...
NOT WHAT AN IRON MAIDEN IS, BUT WHAT THE BAND IRON MAIDEN WAS.
IRONHEART.
I'M BEING TRAINED AND ASSISTED BY TONY STARK'S ARTIFICIAL INTELLIGENCE, AND I JUST HAD A LEGITIMATE SUPER HERO TEAM-UP WITH NONE OTHER THAN PEPPER POTTS.
YEAH, YOU HEARD ME... RESCUE.
AND I DIDN'T COMPLETELY EMBARRASS MYSELF.
THEN I GOT AN EMAIL THIS MORNING, TELLING ME THAT I SHOULD FLY TO TONY STARK'S INDUSTRIAL COMPLEX IN DOVER, NEW JERSEY, BECAUSE TONY STARK'S MOTHER WANTS TO HAVE WORDS WITH ME.
SO, HOW'S YOUR WEEK BEEN?

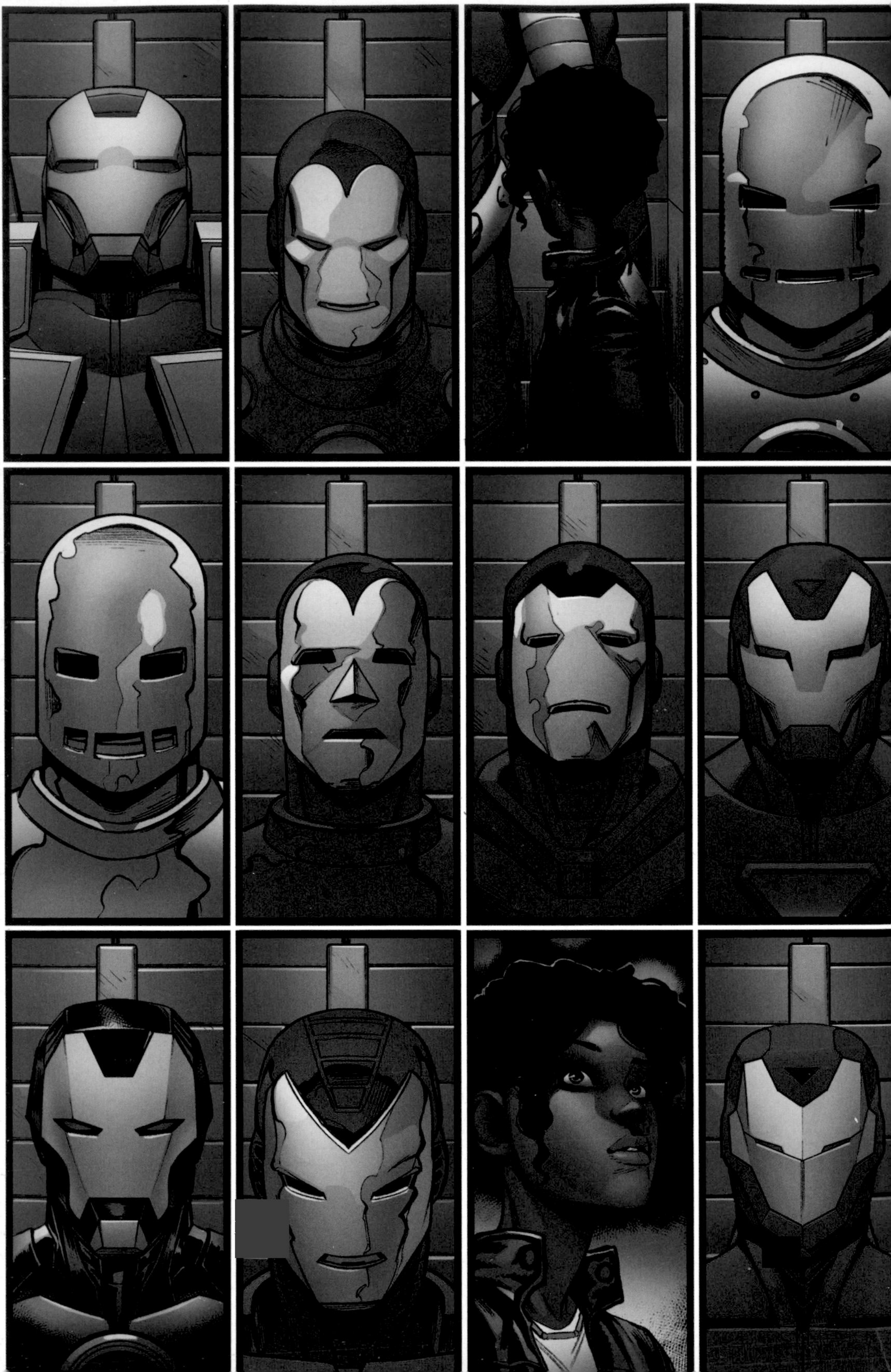

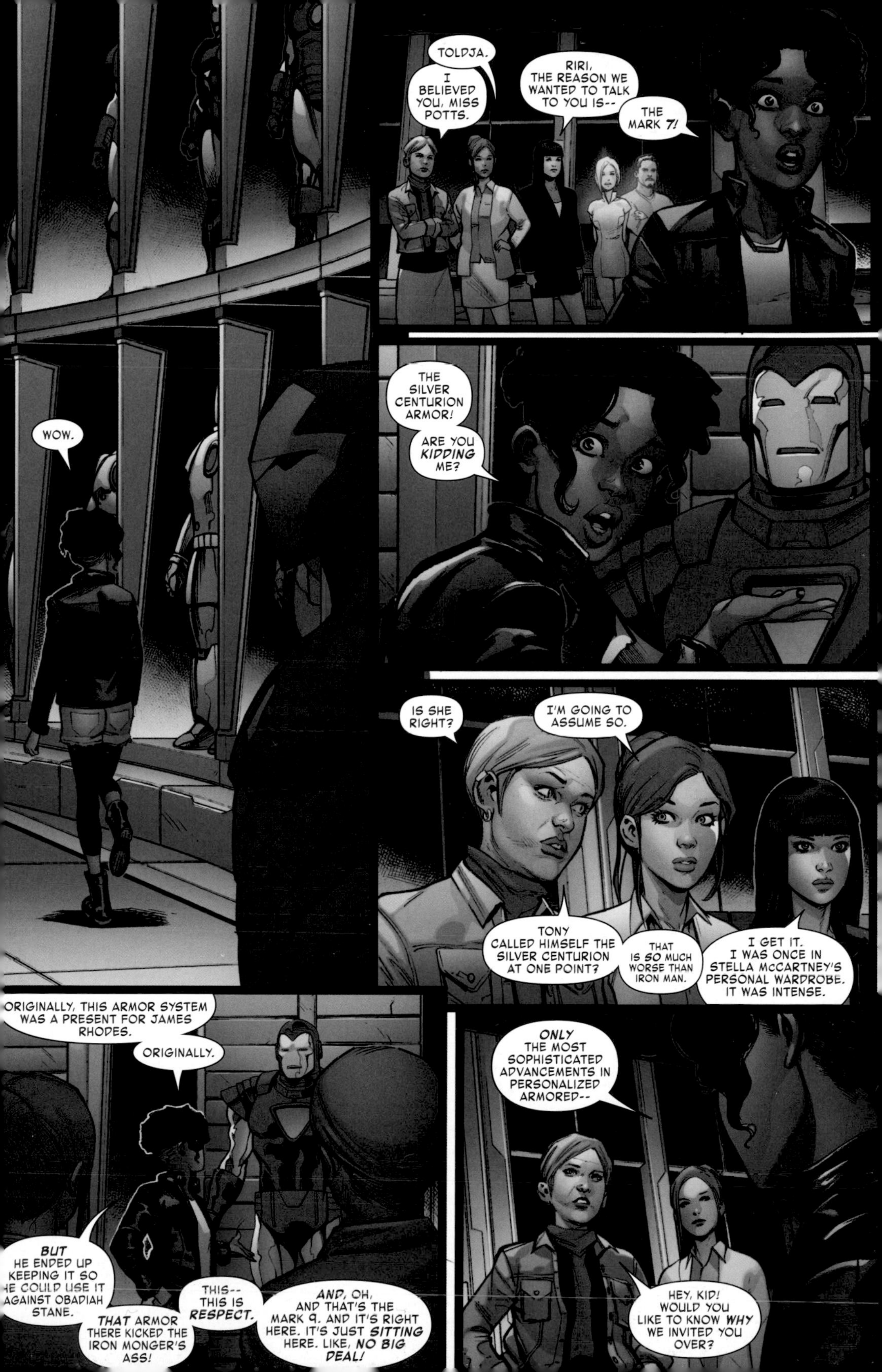
TOLDJA.
I BELIEVED YOU, MISS POTTS.
RIRI, THE REASON WE WANTED TO TALK TO YOU IS--
THE MARK 7!
WOW.
THE SILVER CENTURION ARMOR!
ARE YOU KIDDING ME?
IS SHE RIGHT?
I'M GOING TO ASSUME SO.
TONY CALLED HIMSELF THE SILVER CENTURION AT ONE POINT?
THAT IS SO MUCH WORSE THAN IRON MAN.
I GET IT. I WAS ONCE IN STELLA McCARTNEY'S PERSONAL WARDROBE. IT WAS INTENSE.
ORIGINALLY, THIS ARMOR SYSTEM WAS A PRESENT FOR JAMES RHODES.
ORIGINALLY.
BUT HE ENDED UP KEEPING IT SO HE COULD USE IT AGAINST OBADIAH STANE.
THAT ARMOR THERE KICKED THE IRON MONGER'S ASS!
THIS-- THIS IS RESPECT.
AND, OH, AND THAT'S THE MARK 9. AND IT'S RIGHT HERE. IT'S JUST SITTING HERE. LIKE, NO BIG DEAL!
ONLY THE MOST SOPHISTICATED ADVANCEMENTS IN PERSONALIZED ARMORED--
HEY, KID! WOULD YOU LIKE TO KNOW WHY WE INVITED YOU OVER?

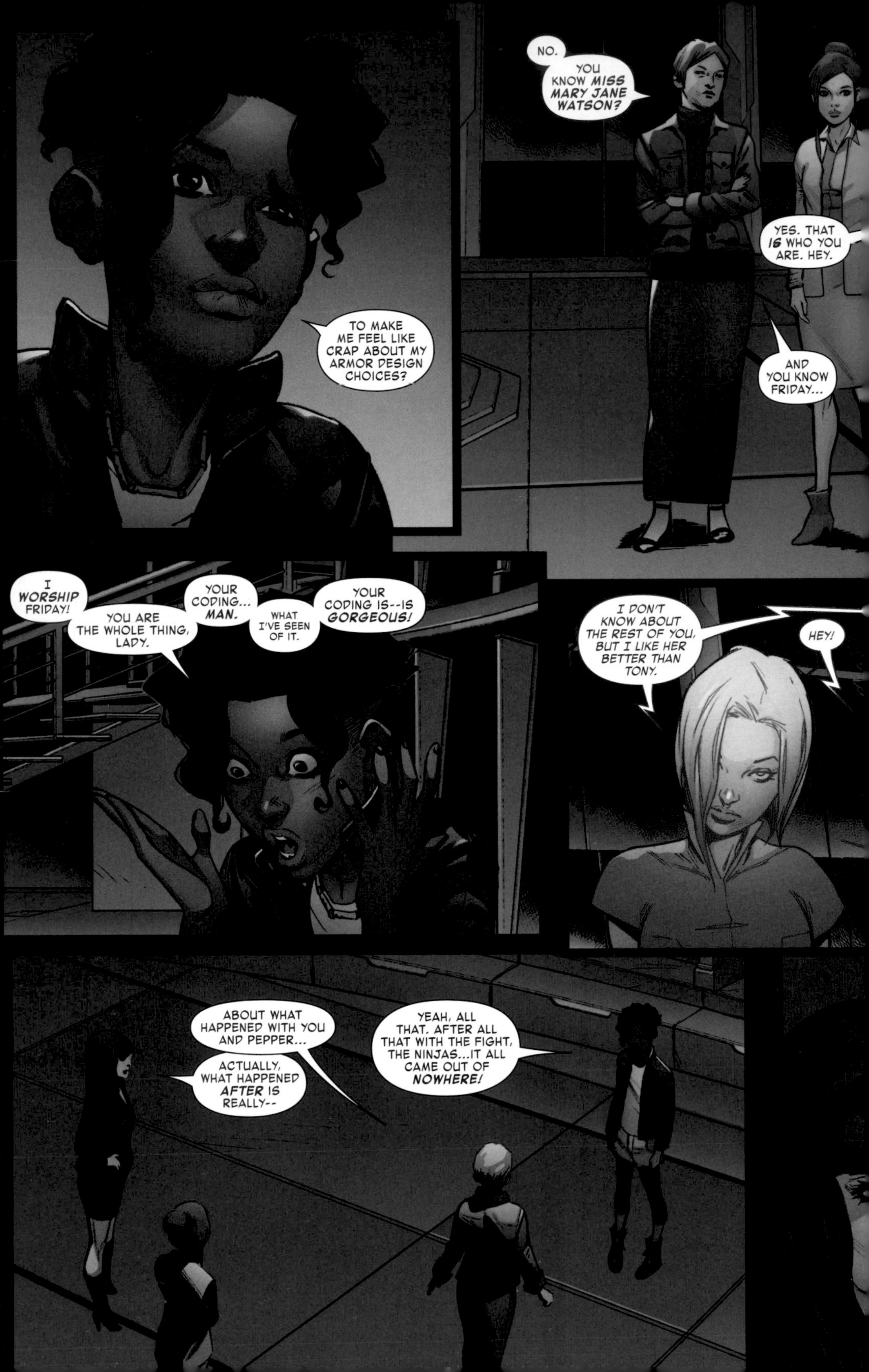
TO MAKE ME FEEL LIKE CRAP ABOUT MY ARMOR DESIGN CHOICES?
NO.
YOU KNOW MISS MARY JANE WATSON?
YES. THAT IS WHO YOU ARE. HEY.
AND YOU KNOW FRIDAY...
I WORSHIP FRIDAY!
YOU ARE THE WHOLE THING, LADY.
YOUR CODING... MAN.
WHAT I'VE SEEN OF IT.
YOUR CODING IS--IS GORGEOUS!
I DON'T KNOW ABOUT THE REST OF YOU, BUT I LIKE HER BETTER THAN TONY.
HEY!
ABOUT WHAT HAPPENED WITH YOU AND PEPPER...
ACTUALLY, WHAT HAPPENED AFTER IS REALLY--
YEAH, ALL THAT. AFTER ALL THAT WITH THE FIGHT, THE NINJAS...IT ALL CAME OUT OF NOWHERE!

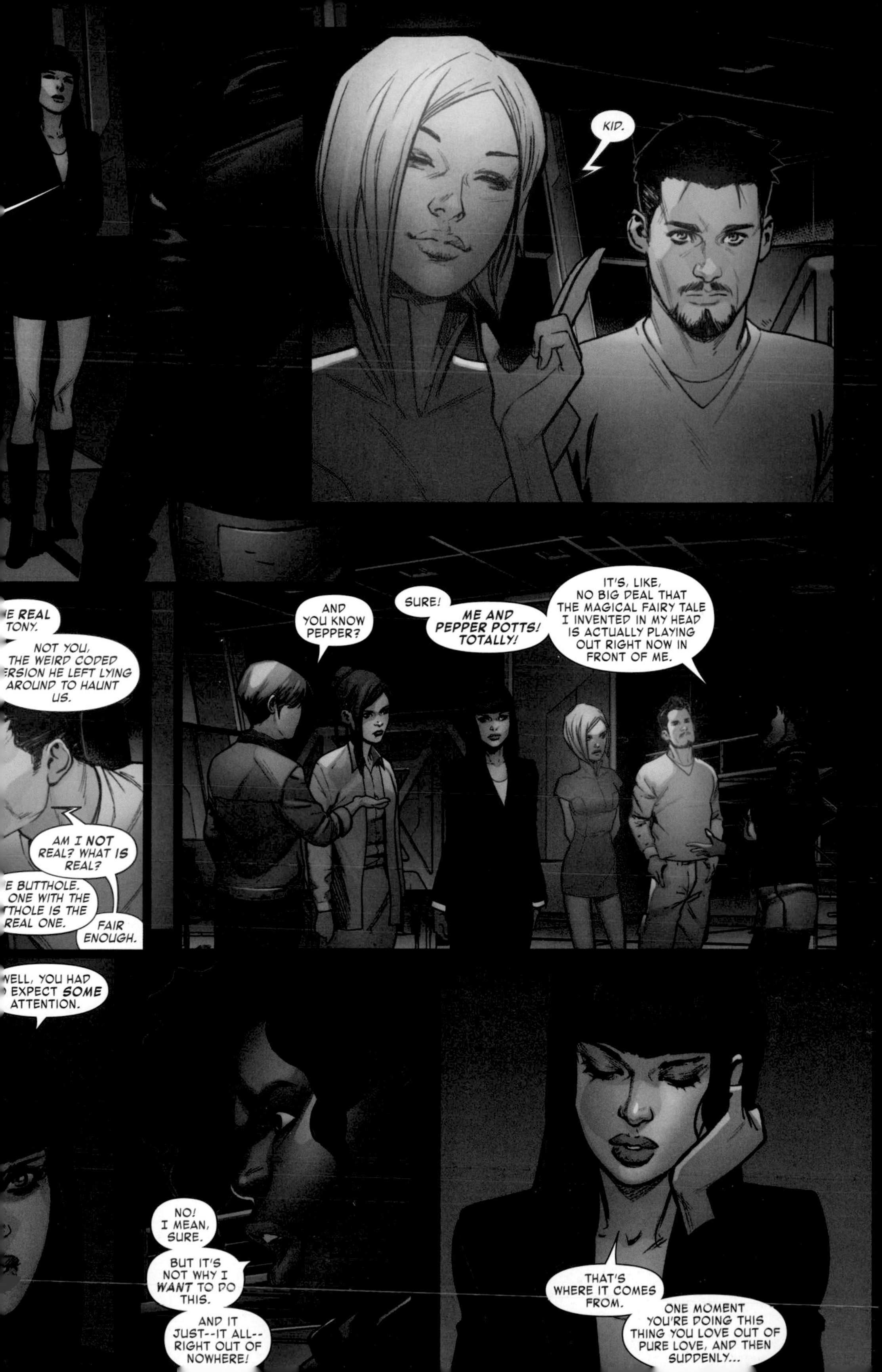
KID.
...E REAL TONY.
NOT YOU, THE WEIRD CODED ...ERSION HE LEFT LYING AROUND TO HAUNT US.
AM I NOT REAL? WHAT IS REAL?
...E BUTTHOLE. ONE WITH THE ...TTHOLE IS THE REAL ONE.
FAIR ENOUGH.
AND YOU KNOW PEPPER?
SURE!
ME AND PEPPER POTTS! TOTALLY!
IT'S, LIKE, NO BIG DEAL THAT THE MAGICAL FAIRY TALE I INVENTED IN MY HEAD IS ACTUALLY PLAYING OUT RIGHT NOW IN FRONT OF ME.
...WELL, YOU HAD ...D EXPECT SOME ATTENTION.
NO! I MEAN, SURE.
BUT IT'S NOT WHY I WANT TO DO THIS.
AND IT JUST--IT ALL--RIGHT OUT OF NOWHERE!
THAT'S WHERE IT COMES FROM.
ONE MOMENT YOU'RE DOING THIS THING YOU LOVE OUT OF PURE LOVE, AND THEN SUDDENLY...

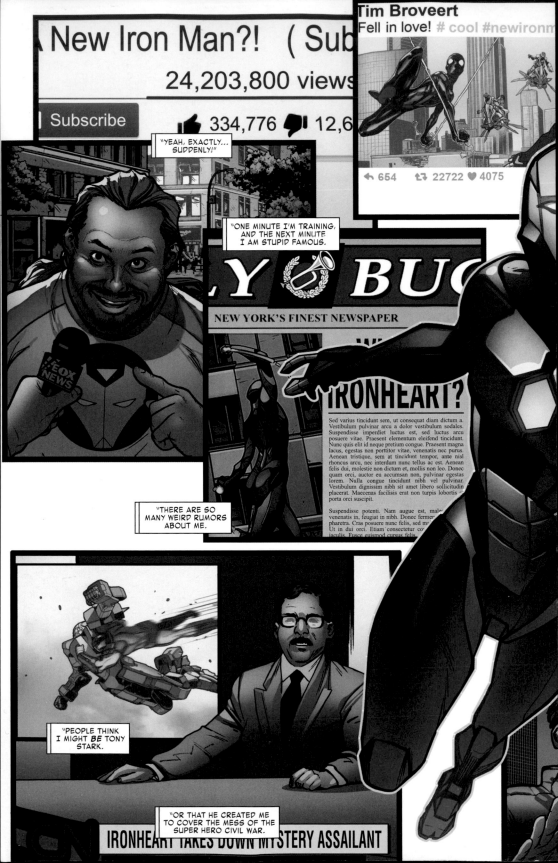

New Iron Man?! (Sub

24,203,800 views

Subscribe 👍 334,776 👎 12,6

"YEAH, EXACTLY... SUDDENLY!"

"ONE MINUTE I'M TRAINING, AND THE NEXT MINUTE I AM STUPID FAMOUS."

...Y BUG

NEW YORK'S FINEST NEWSPAPER

IRONHEART?

Sed varius tincidunt sem, ut consequat diam dictum a. Vestibulum pulvinar arcu a dolor vestibulum sodales. Suspendisse imperdiet luctus est, sed luctus arcu posuere vitae. Praesent elementum eleifend tincidunt. Nunc quis elit id neque pretium congue. Praesent magna lacus, egestas non porttitor vitae, venenatis nec purus. Aenean tristique, sem at tincidunt tempor, ante nisl rhoncus arcu, nec interdum nunc tellus ac est. Aenean felis dui, molestie non dictum et, mollis non leo. Donec quam orci, auctor eu accumsan non, pulvinar egestas lorem. Nulla congue tincidunt nibh vel pulvinar. Vestibulum dignissim nibh sit amet libero sollicitudin placerat. Maecenas facilisis erat non turpis lobortis porta orci suscipit.

Suspendisse potenti. Nam augue est, malesuada venenatis in, feugiat in nibh. Donec fermentum pharetra. Cras posuere nunc felis, sed ma... Ut in dui orci. Etiam consectetur co... iaculis. Fusce euismod cursus felis...

"THERE ARE SO MANY WEIRD RUMORS ABOUT ME.

"PEOPLE THINK I MIGHT *BE* TONY STARK.

"OR THAT HE CREATED ME TO COVER THE MESS OF THE SUPER HERO CIVIL WAR.

IRONHEART TAKES DOWN MYSTERY ASSAILANT

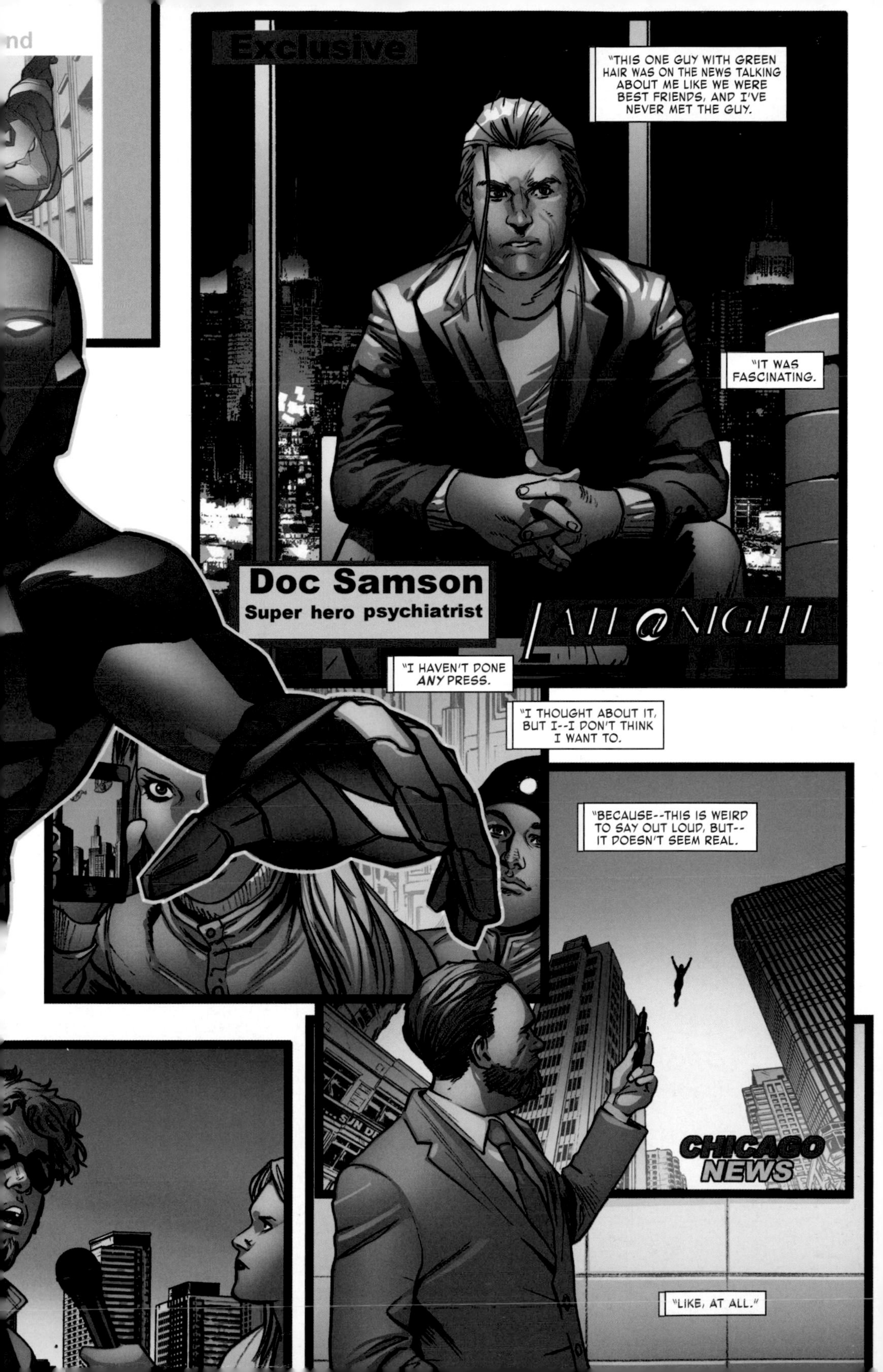
nd
Exclusive
"THIS ONE GUY WITH GREEN HAIR WAS ON THE NEWS TALKING ABOUT ME LIKE WE WERE BEST FRIENDS, AND I'VE NEVER MET THE GUY.
"IT WAS FASCINATING.
Doc Samson
Super hero psychiatrist
ALL@NIGHT
"I HAVEN'T DONE ANY PRESS.
"I THOUGHT ABOUT IT, BUT I--I DON'T THINK I WANT TO.
"BECAUSE--THIS IS WEIRD TO SAY OUT LOUD, BUT--IT DOESN'T SEEM REAL.
SUN
CHICAGO NEWS
"LIKE, AT ALL."

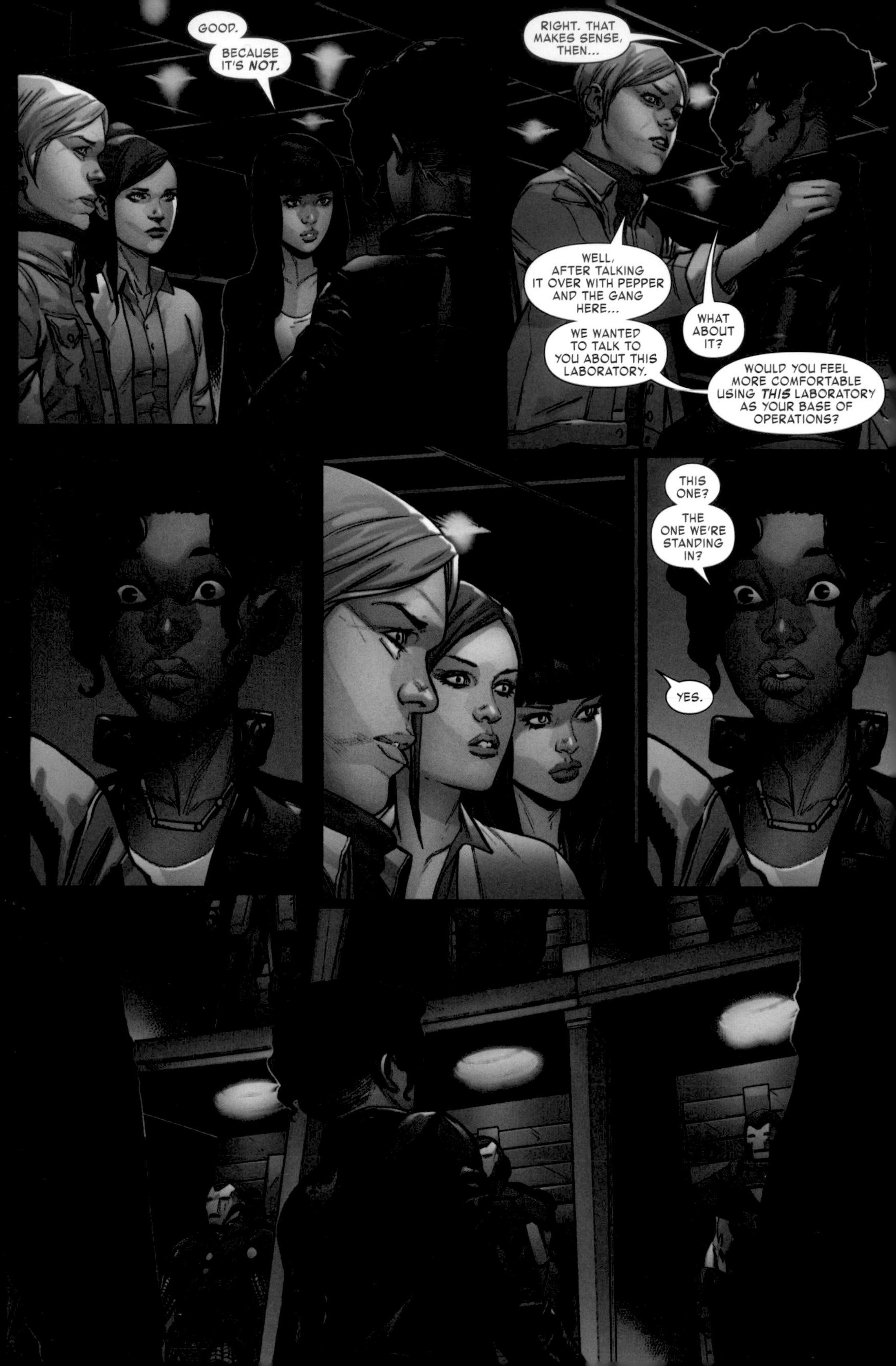
GOOD.
BECAUSE IT'S *NOT.*
RIGHT. THAT MAKES SENSE, THEN...
WELL, AFTER TALKING IT OVER WITH PEPPER AND THE GANG HERE...
WE WANTED TO TALK TO YOU ABOUT THIS LABORATORY.
WHAT ABOUT IT?
WOULD YOU FEEL MORE COMFORTABLE USING *THIS* LABORATORY AS YOUR BASE OF OPERATIONS?
THIS ONE?
THE ONE WE'RE STANDING IN?
YES.

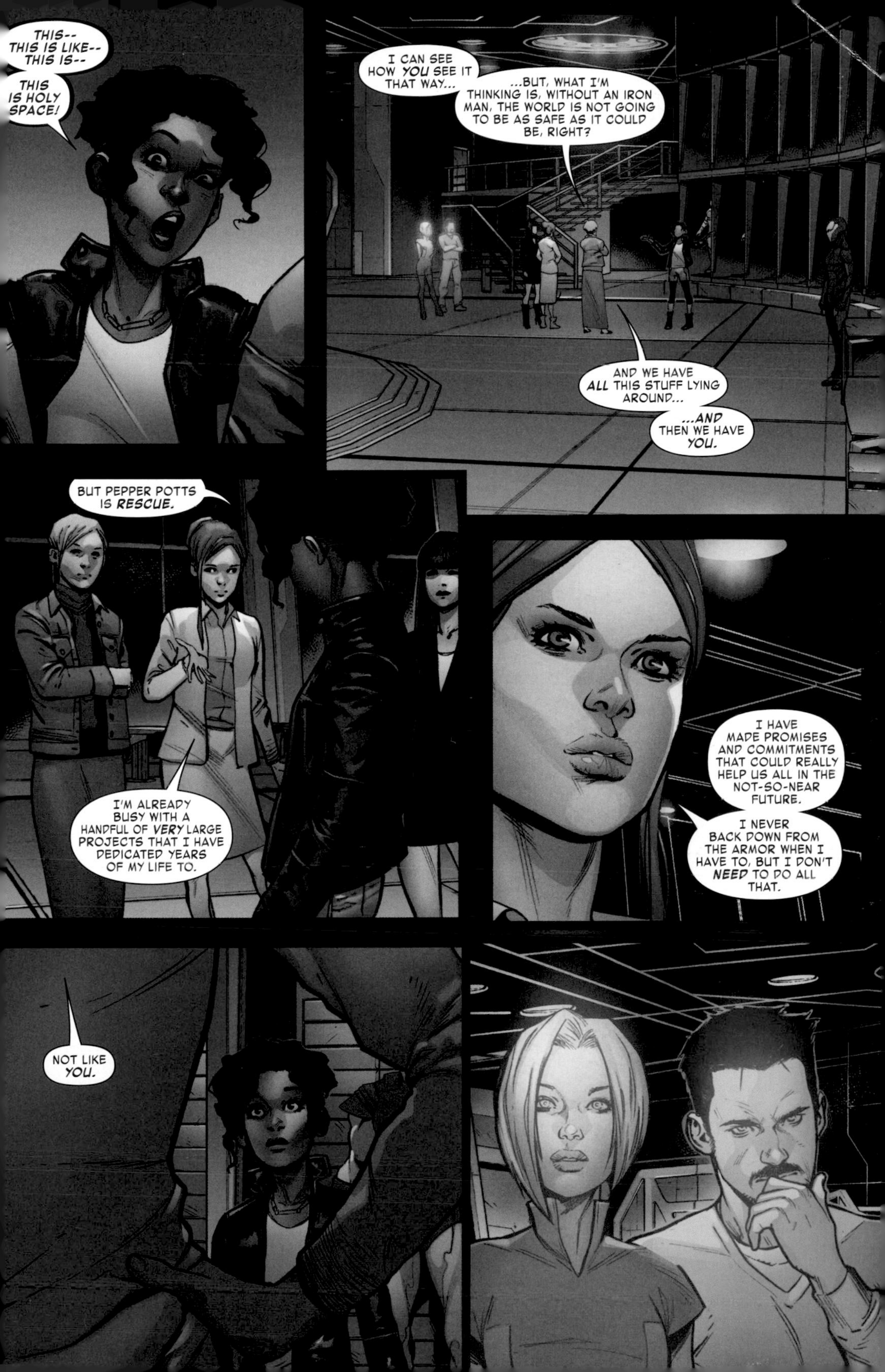
THIS-- THIS IS LIKE-- THIS IS--
THIS IS HOLY SPACE!
I CAN SEE HOW YOU SEE IT THAT WAY...
...BUT, WHAT I'M THINKING IS, WITHOUT AN IRON MAN, THE WORLD IS NOT GOING TO BE AS SAFE AS IT COULD BE, RIGHT?
AND WE HAVE ALL THIS STUFF LYING AROUND...
...AND THEN WE HAVE YOU.
BUT PEPPER POTTS IS RESCUE.
I'M ALREADY BUSY WITH A HANDFUL OF VERY LARGE PROJECTS THAT I HAVE DEDICATED YEARS OF MY LIFE TO.
I HAVE MADE PROMISES AND COMMITMENTS THAT COULD REALLY HELP US ALL IN THE NOT-SO-NEAR FUTURE.
I NEVER BACK DOWN FROM THE ARMOR WHEN I HAVE TO, BUT I DON'T NEED TO DO ALL THAT.
NOT LIKE YOU.

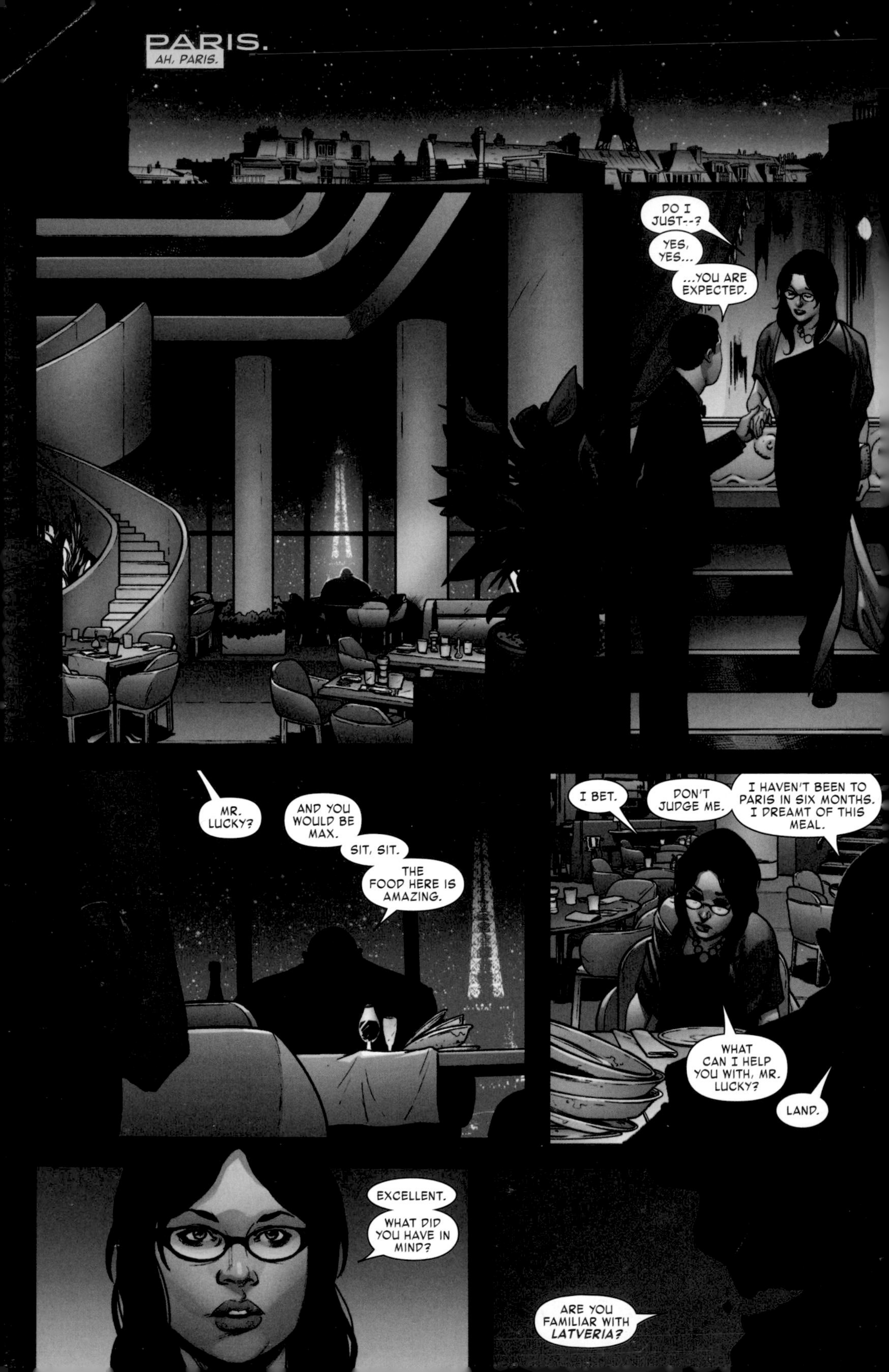
PARIS.
AH, PARIS.
DO I JUST--?
YES, YES...
...YOU ARE EXPECTED.
MR. LUCKY?
AND YOU WOULD BE MAX.
SIT, SIT.
THE FOOD HERE IS AMAZING.
I HAVEN'T BEEN TO PARIS IN SIX MONTHS. I DREAMT OF THIS MEAL.
DON'T JUDGE ME.
I BET.
WHAT CAN I HELP YOU WITH, MR. LUCKY?
LAND.
EXCELLENT.
WHAT DID YOU HAVE IN MIND?
ARE YOU FAMILIAR WITH *LATVERIA?*

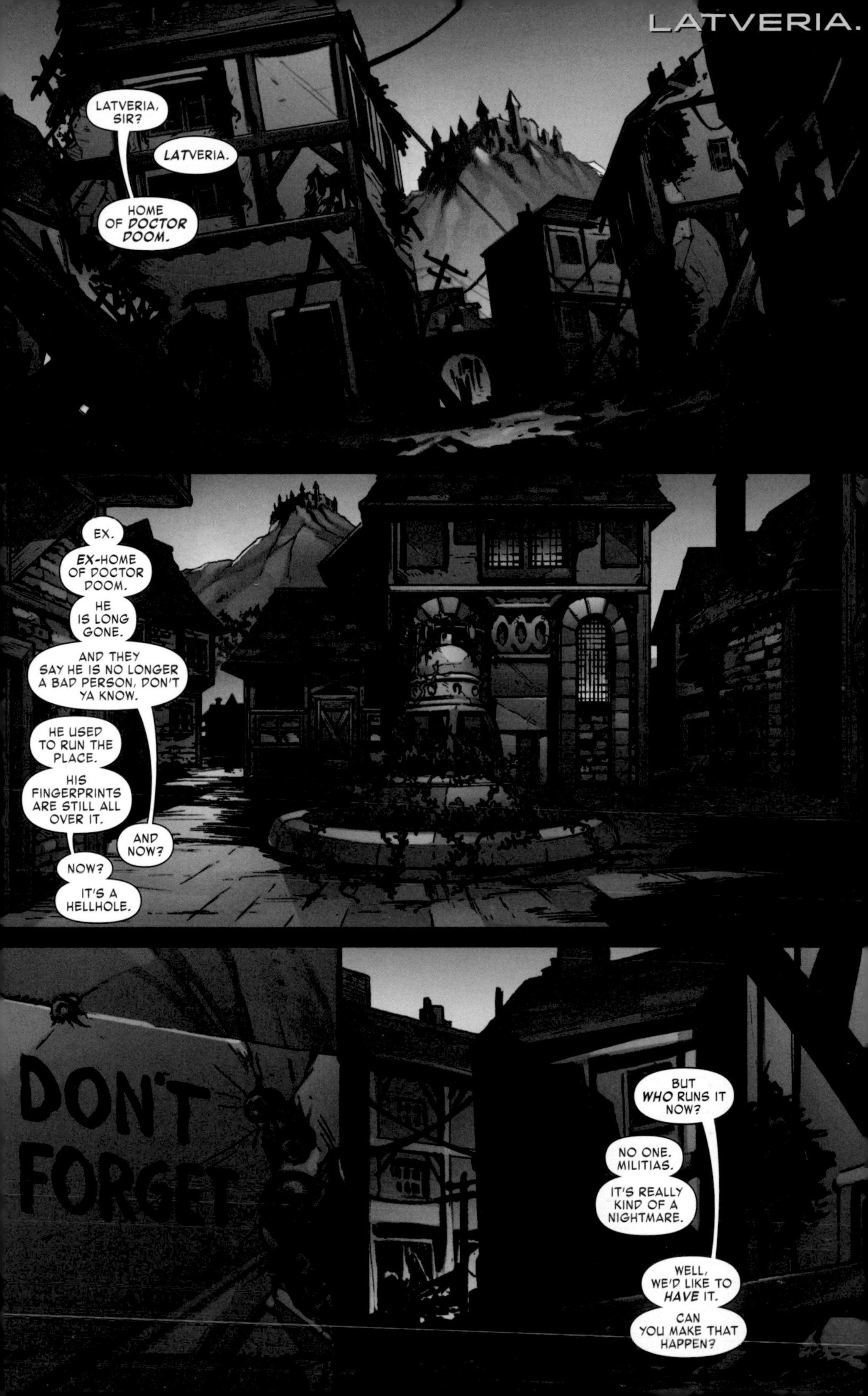
LATVERIA.
LATVERIA, SIR?
LATVERIA.
HOME OF DOCTOR DOOM.
EX.
EX-HOME OF DOCTOR DOOM.
HE IS LONG GONE.
AND THEY SAY HE IS NO LONGER A BAD PERSON, DON'T YA KNOW.
HE USED TO RUN THE PLACE.
HIS FINGERPRINTS ARE STILL ALL OVER IT.
AND NOW?
NOW?
IT'S A HELLHOLE.
DON'T FORGET
BUT WHO RUNS IT NOW?
NO ONE. MILITIAS.
IT'S REALLY KIND OF A NIGHTMARE.
WELL, WE'D LIKE TO HAVE IT.
CAN YOU MAKE THAT HAPPEN?

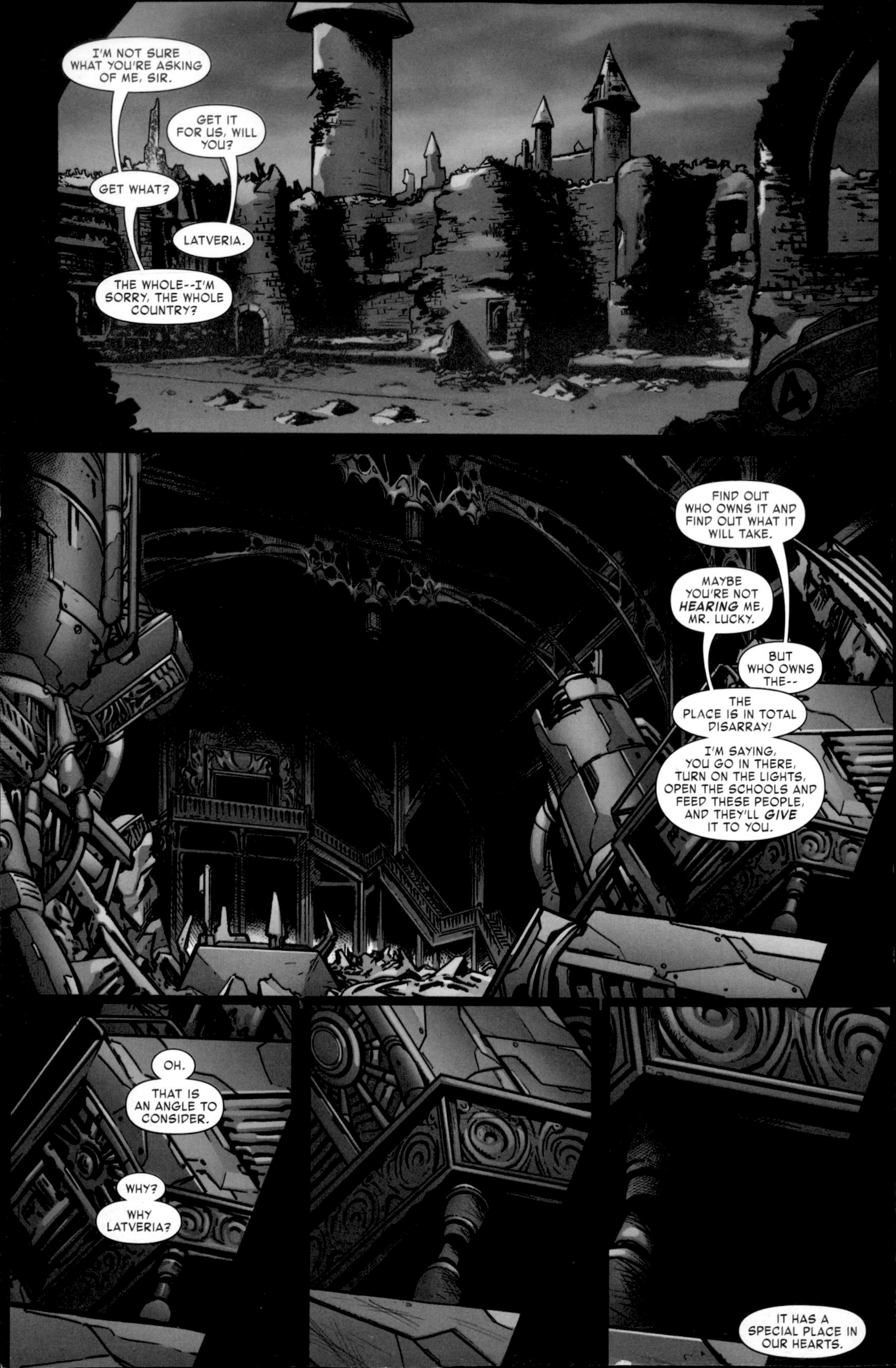
I'M NOT SURE WHAT YOU'RE ASKING OF ME, SIR.
GET IT FOR US, WILL YOU?
GET WHAT?
LATVERIA.
THE WHOLE--I'M SORRY, THE WHOLE COUNTRY?
FIND OUT WHO OWNS IT AND FIND OUT WHAT IT WILL TAKE.
MAYBE YOU'RE NOT HEARING ME, MR. LUCKY.
BUT WHO OWNS THE--
THE PLACE IS IN TOTAL DISARRAY!
I'M SAYING, YOU GO IN THERE, TURN ON THE LIGHTS, OPEN THE SCHOOLS AND FEED THESE PEOPLE, AND THEY'LL GIVE IT TO YOU.
OH.
THAT IS AN ANGLE TO CONSIDER.
WHY?
WHY LATVERIA?
IT HAS A SPECIAL PLACE IN OUR HEARTS.

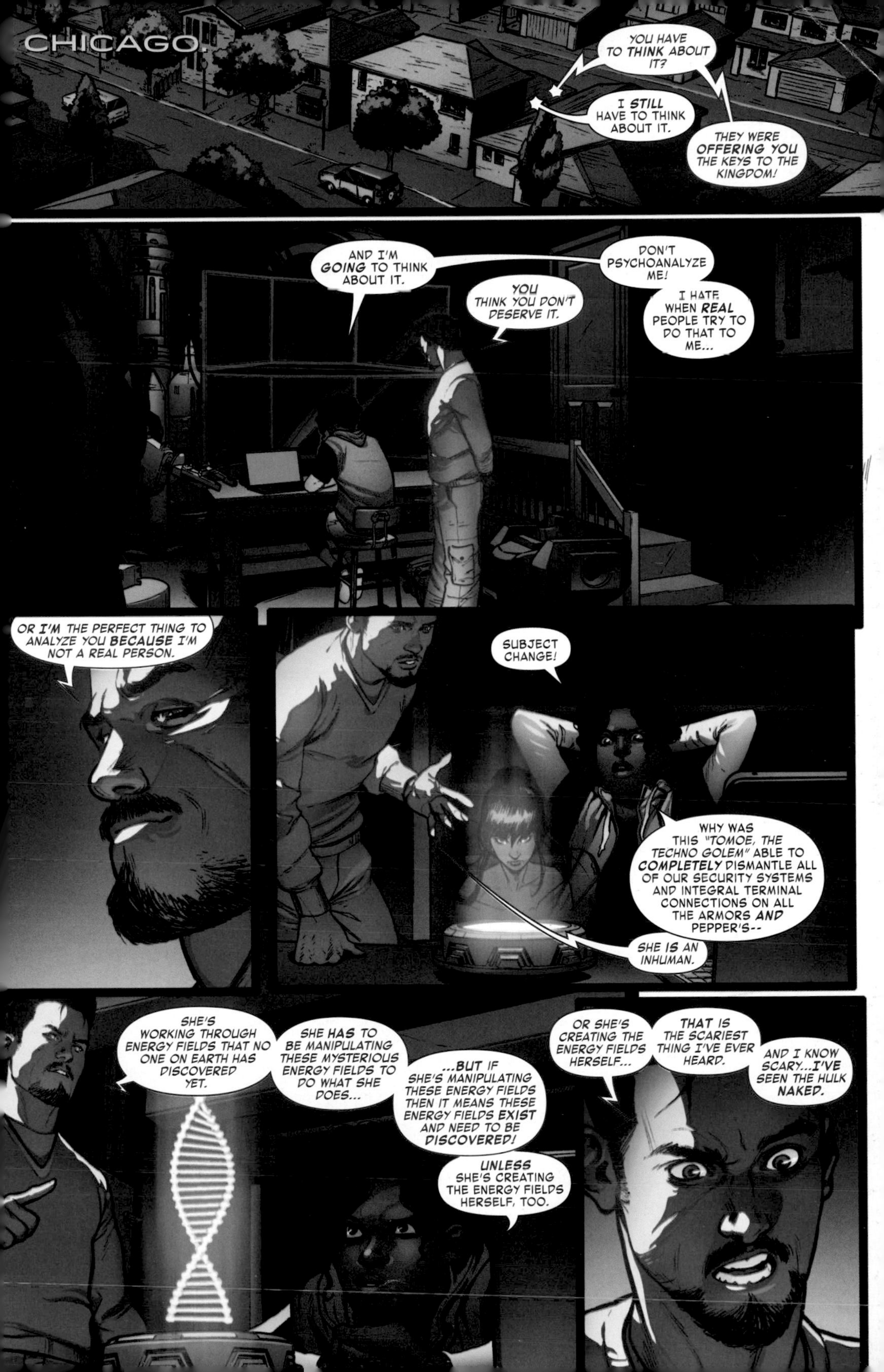
CHICAGO.
YOU HAVE TO THINK ABOUT IT?
I STILL HAVE TO THINK ABOUT IT.
THEY WERE OFFERING YOU THE KEYS TO THE KINGDOM!
AND I'M GOING TO THINK ABOUT IT.
YOU THINK YOU DON'T DESERVE IT.
DON'T PSYCHOANALYZE ME!
I HATE WHEN REAL PEOPLE TRY TO DO THAT TO ME...
OR I'M THE PERFECT THING TO ANALYZE YOU BECAUSE I'M NOT A REAL PERSON.
SUBJECT CHANGE!
WHY WAS THIS "TOMOE, THE TECHNO GOLEM" ABLE TO COMPLETELY DISMANTLE ALL OF OUR SECURITY SYSTEMS AND INTEGRAL TERMINAL CONNECTIONS ON ALL THE ARMORS AND PEPPER'S--
SHE IS AN INHUMAN.
SHE'S WORKING THROUGH ENERGY FIELDS THAT NO ONE ON EARTH HAS DISCOVERED YET.
SHE HAS TO BE MANIPULATING THESE MYSTERIOUS ENERGY FIELDS TO DO WHAT SHE DOES...
...BUT IF SHE'S MANIPULATING THESE ENERGY FIELDS THEN IT MEANS THESE ENERGY FIELDS EXIST AND NEED TO BE DISCOVERED!
UNLESS SHE'S CREATING THE ENERGY FIELDS HERSELF, TOO.
OR SHE'S CREATING THE ENERGY FIELDS HERSELF...
THAT IS THE SCARIEST THING I'VE EVER HEARD.
AND I KNOW SCARY...I'VE SEEN THE HULK NAKED.

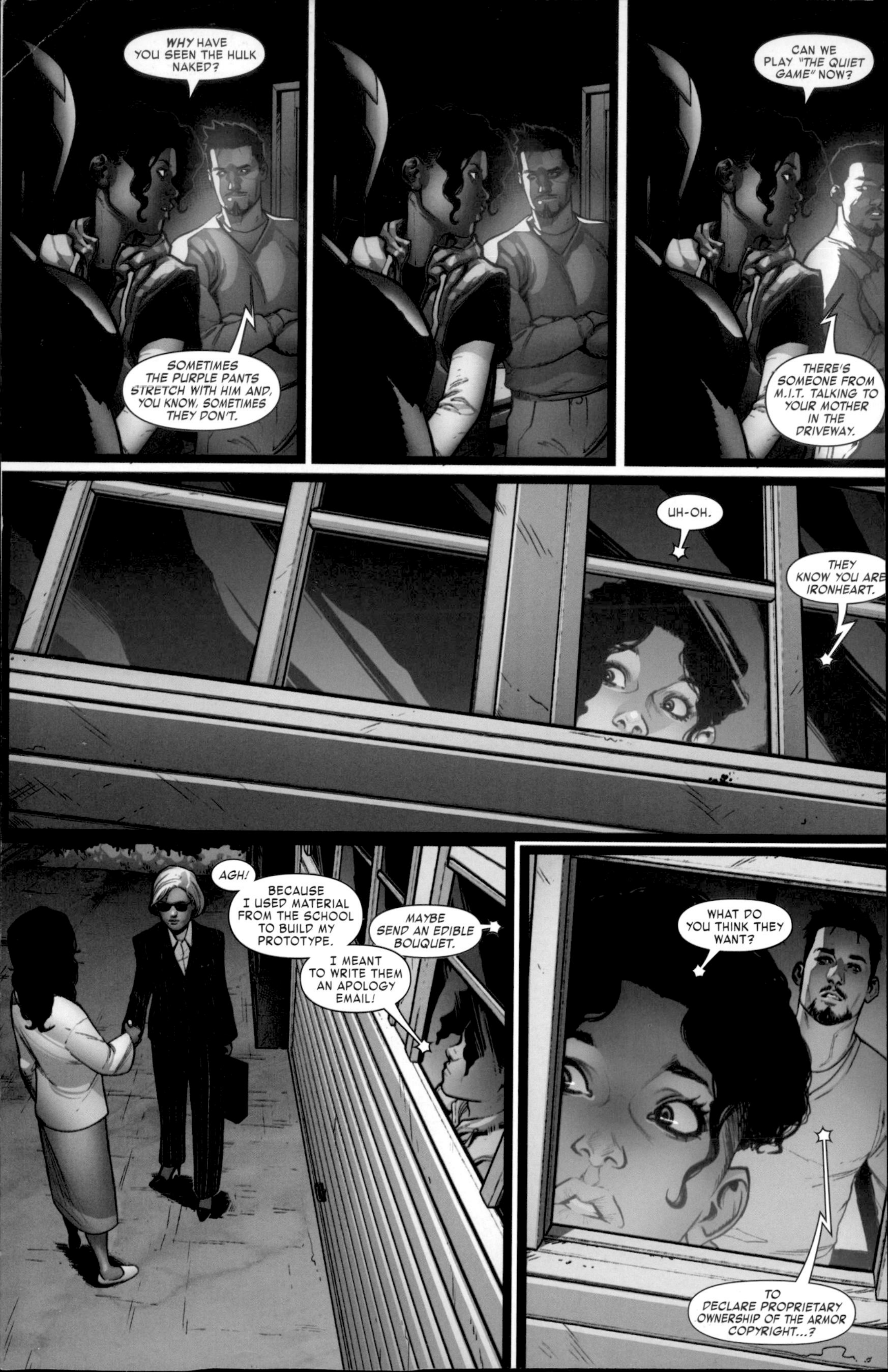
WHY HAVE YOU SEEN THE HULK NAKED?
SOMETIMES THE PURPLE PANTS STRETCH WITH HIM AND, YOU KNOW, SOMETIMES THEY DON'T.
CAN WE PLAY "THE QUIET GAME" NOW?
THERE'S SOMEONE FROM M.I.T. TALKING TO YOUR MOTHER IN THE DRIVEWAY.
UH-OH.
THEY KNOW YOU ARE IRONHEART.
AGH!
BECAUSE I USED MATERIAL FROM THE SCHOOL TO BUILD MY PROTOTYPE.
MAYBE SEND AN EDIBLE BOUQUET.
I MEANT TO WRITE THEM AN APOLOGY EMAIL!
WHAT DO YOU THINK THEY WANT?
TO DECLARE PROPRIETARY OWNERSHIP OF THE ARMOR COPYRIGHT...?

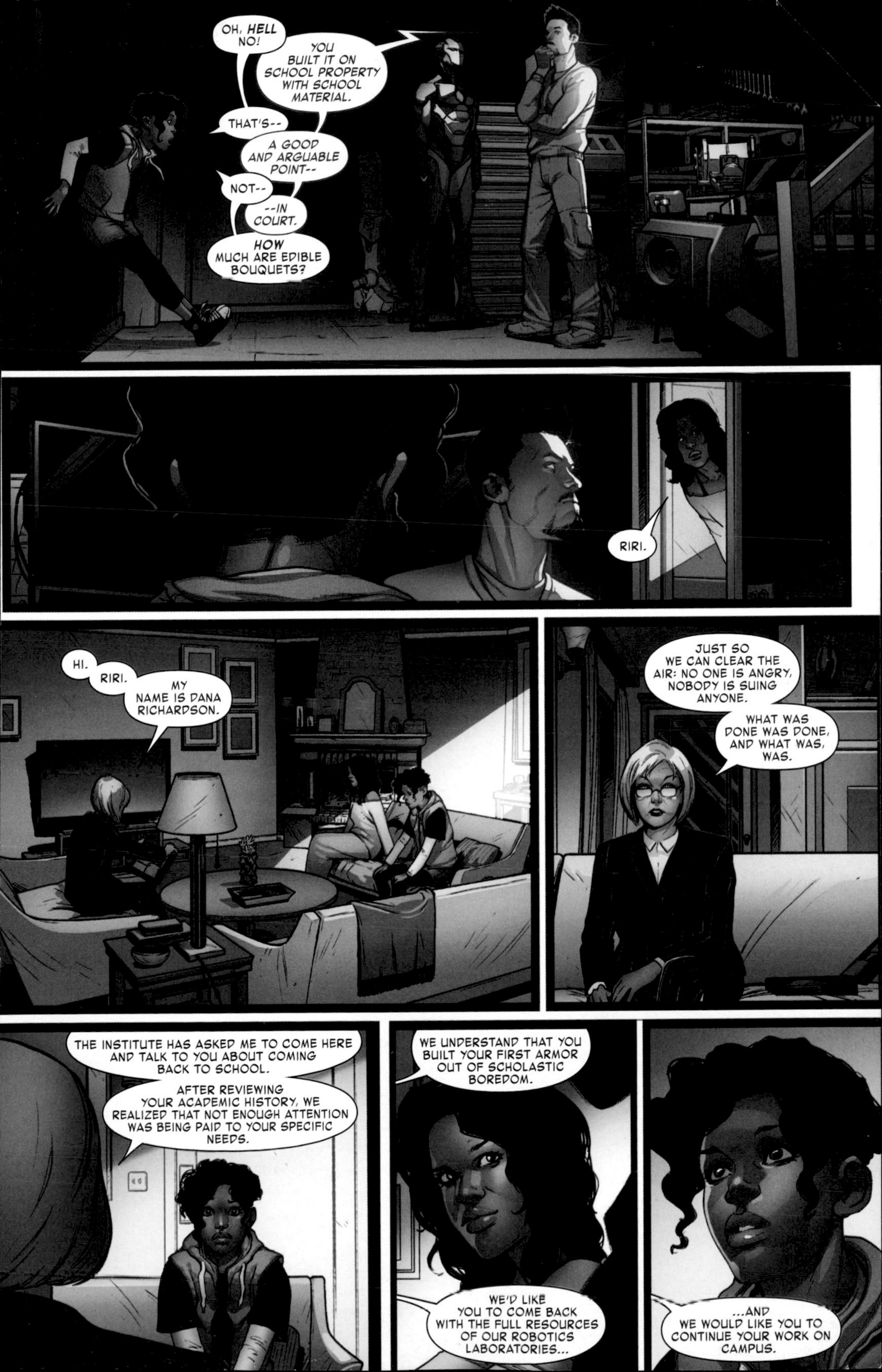
OH, HELL NO!
YOU BUILT IT ON SCHOOL PROPERTY WITH SCHOOL MATERIAL.
THAT'S--
A GOOD AND ARGUABLE POINT--
NOT--
--IN COURT.
HOW MUCH ARE EDIBLE BOUQUETS?
RIRI.
HI.
RIRI.
MY NAME IS DANA RICHARDSON.
JUST SO WE CAN CLEAR THE AIR: NO ONE IS ANGRY, NOBODY IS SUING ANYONE.
WHAT WAS DONE WAS DONE, AND WHAT WAS, WAS.
THE INSTITUTE HAS ASKED ME TO COME HERE AND TALK TO YOU ABOUT COMING BACK TO SCHOOL.
AFTER REVIEWING YOUR ACADEMIC HISTORY, WE REALIZED THAT NOT ENOUGH ATTENTION WAS BEING PAID TO YOUR SPECIFIC NEEDS.
WE UNDERSTAND THAT YOU BUILT YOUR FIRST ARMOR OUT OF SCHOLASTIC BOREDOM.
WE'D LIKE YOU TO COME BACK WITH THE FULL RESOURCES OF OUR ROBOTICS LABORATORIES...
...AND WE WOULD LIKE YOU TO CONTINUE YOUR WORK ON CAMPUS.

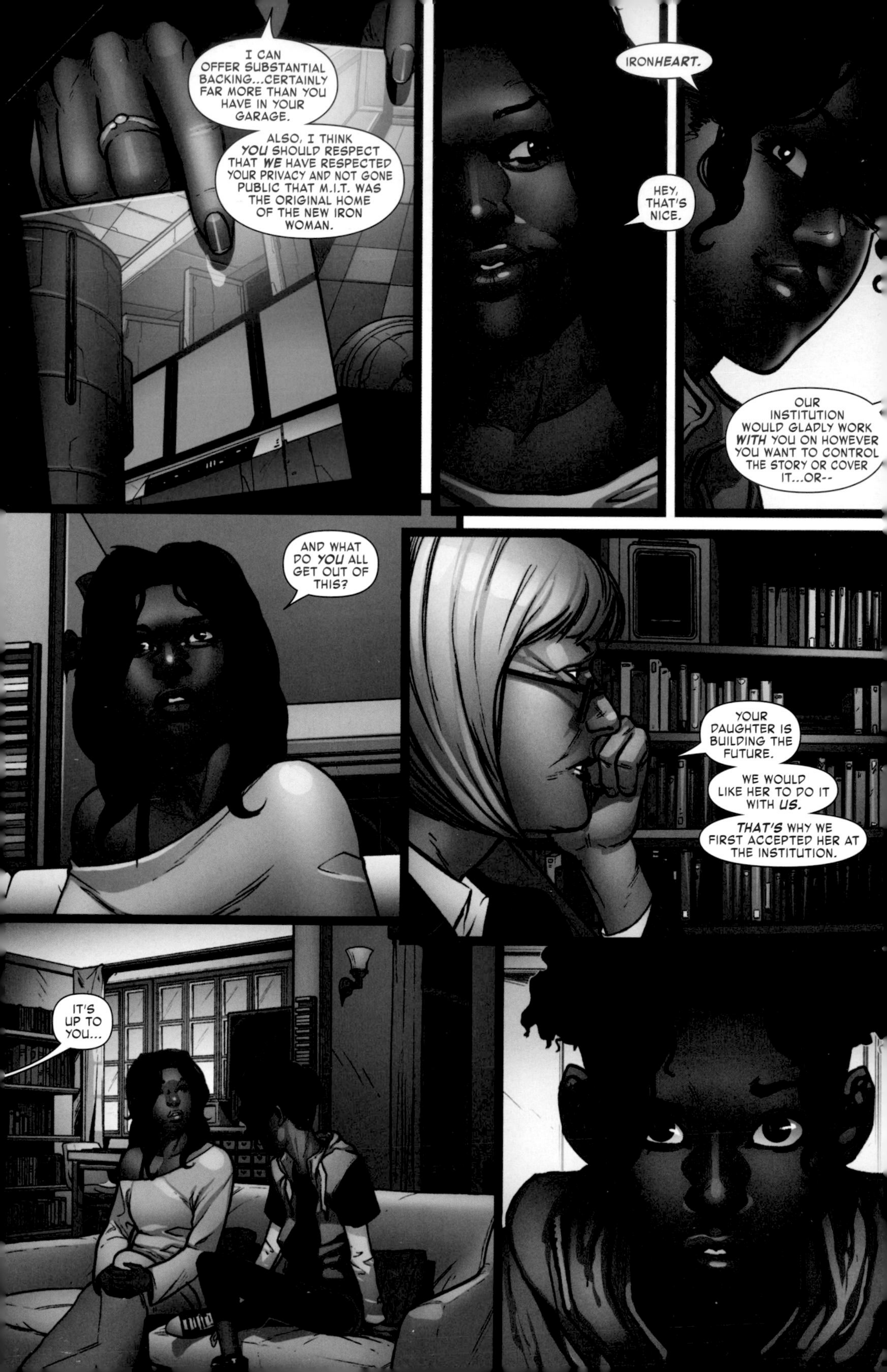

I CAN OFFER SUBSTANTIAL BACKING...CERTAINLY FAR MORE THAN YOU HAVE IN YOUR GARAGE.
ALSO, I THINK *YOU* SHOULD RESPECT THAT *WE* HAVE RESPECTED YOUR PRIVACY AND NOT GONE PUBLIC THAT M.I.T. WAS THE ORIGINAL HOME OF THE NEW IRON WOMAN.
IRON*HEART.*
HEY, THAT'S NICE.
OUR INSTITUTION WOULD GLADLY WORK *WITH* YOU ON HOWEVER YOU WANT TO CONTROL THE STORY OR COVER IT...OR--
AND WHAT DO *YOU* ALL GET OUT OF THIS?
YOUR DAUGHTER IS BUILDING THE FUTURE.
WE WOULD LIKE HER TO DO IT WITH *US.*
THAT'S WHY WE FIRST ACCEPTED HER AT THE INSTITUTION.
IT'S UP TO YOU...

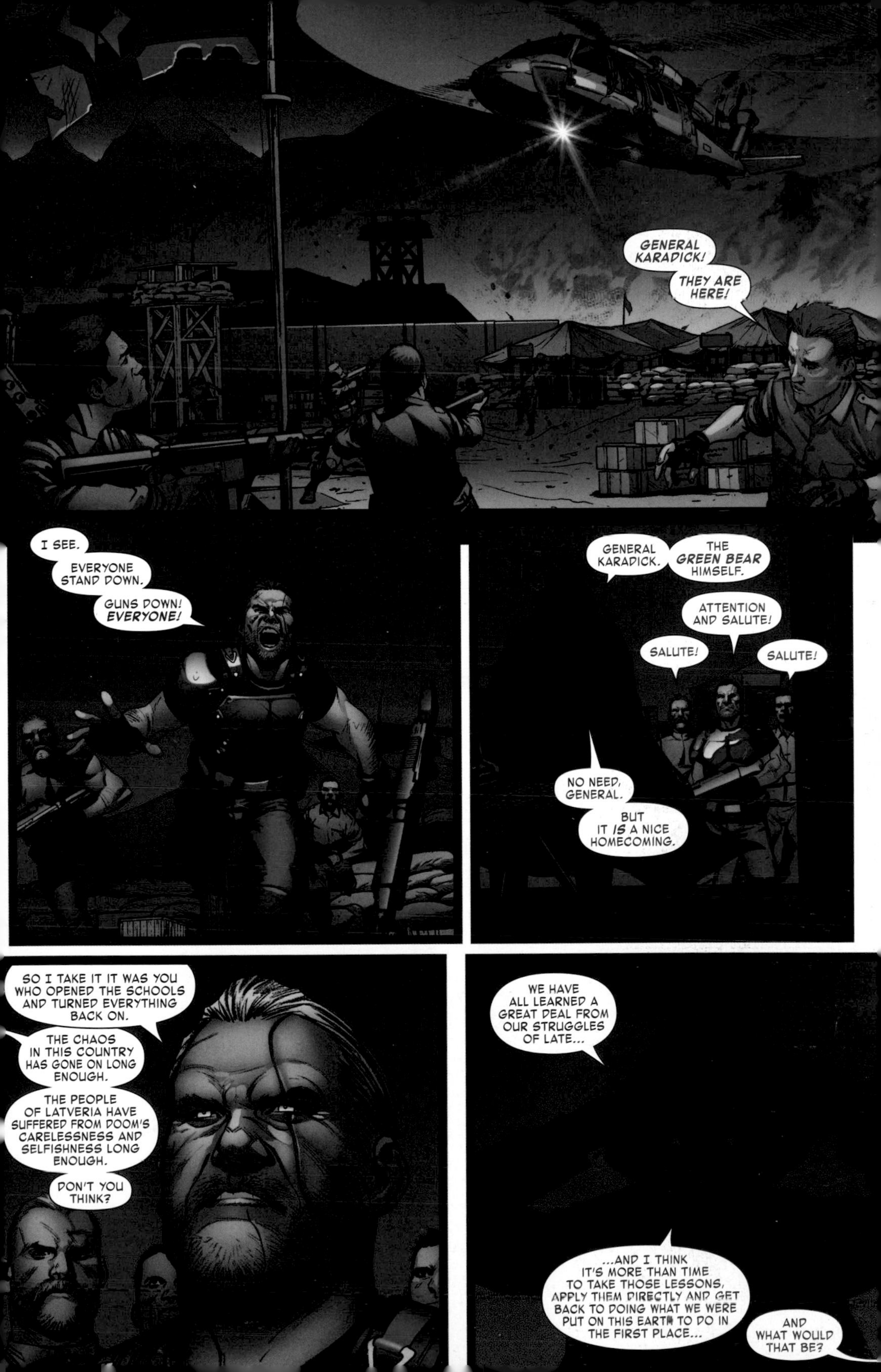
GENERAL KARADICK!
THEY ARE HERE!
I SEE.
EVERYONE STAND DOWN.
GUNS DOWN! EVERYONE!
GENERAL KARADICK.
THE GREEN BEAR HIMSELF.
ATTENTION AND SALUTE!
SALUTE!
SALUTE!
NO NEED, GENERAL.
BUT IT IS A NICE HOMECOMING.
SO I TAKE IT IT WAS YOU WHO OPENED THE SCHOOLS AND TURNED EVERYTHING BACK ON.
THE CHAOS IN THIS COUNTRY HAS GONE ON LONG ENOUGH.
THE PEOPLE OF LATVERIA HAVE SUFFERED FROM DOOM'S CARELESSNESS AND SELFISHNESS LONG ENOUGH.
DON'T YOU THINK?
WE HAVE ALL LEARNED A GREAT DEAL FROM OUR STRUGGLES OF LATE...
...AND I THINK IT'S MORE THAN TIME TO TAKE THOSE LESSONS, APPLY THEM DIRECTLY AND GET BACK TO DOING WHAT WE WERE PUT ON THIS EARTH TO DO IN THE FIRST PLACE...
AND WHAT WOULD THAT BE?

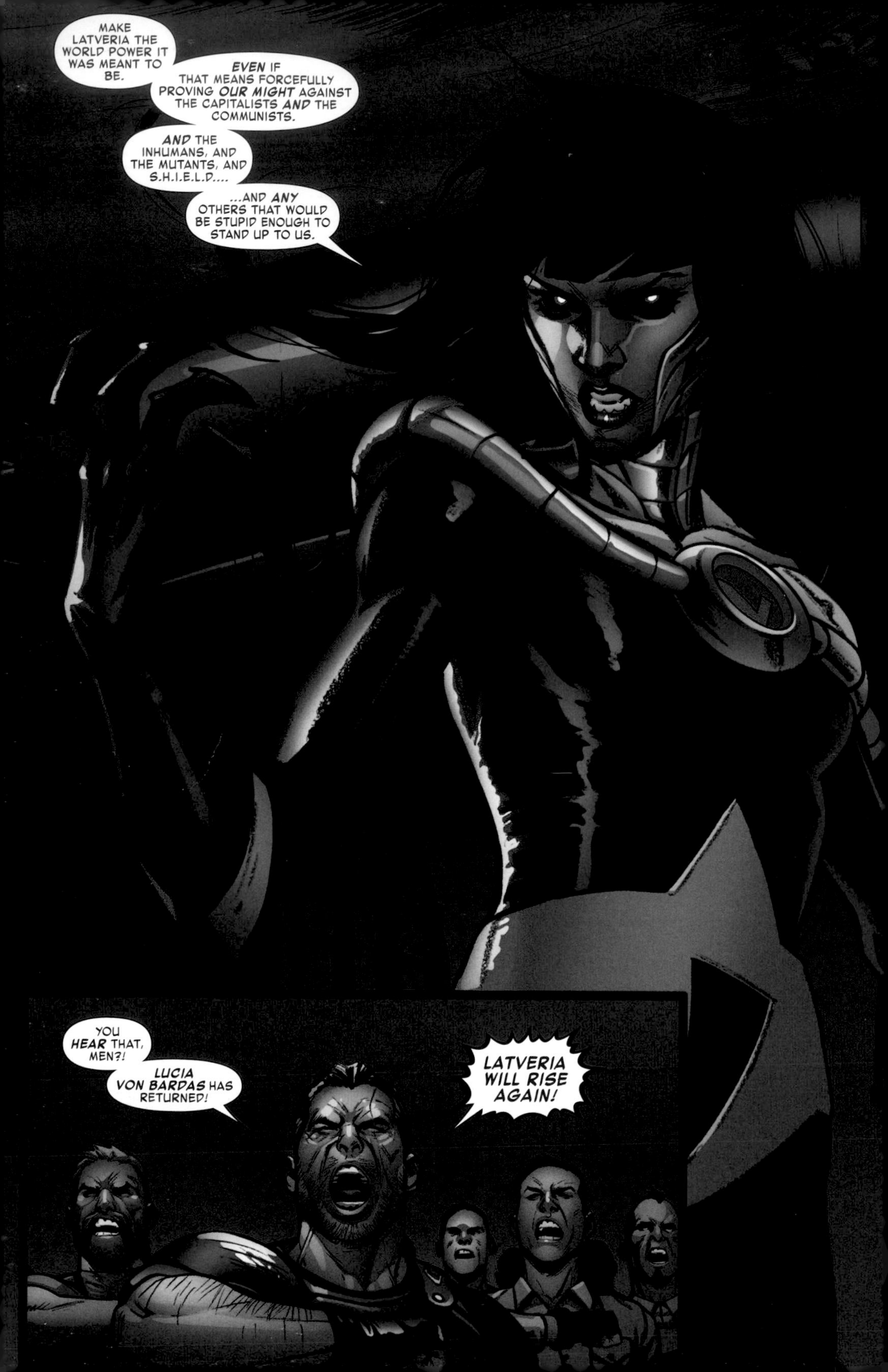
MAKE LATVERIA THE WORLD POWER IT WAS MEANT TO BE.
EVEN IF THAT MEANS FORCEFULLY PROVING OUR MIGHT AGAINST THE CAPITALISTS AND THE COMMUNISTS.
AND THE INHUMANS, AND THE MUTANTS, AND S.H.I.E.L.D....
...AND ANY OTHERS THAT WOULD BE STUPID ENOUGH TO STAND UP TO US.
YOU HEAR THAT, MEN?!
LUCIA VON BARDAS HAS RETURNED!
LATVERIA WILL RISE AGAIN!

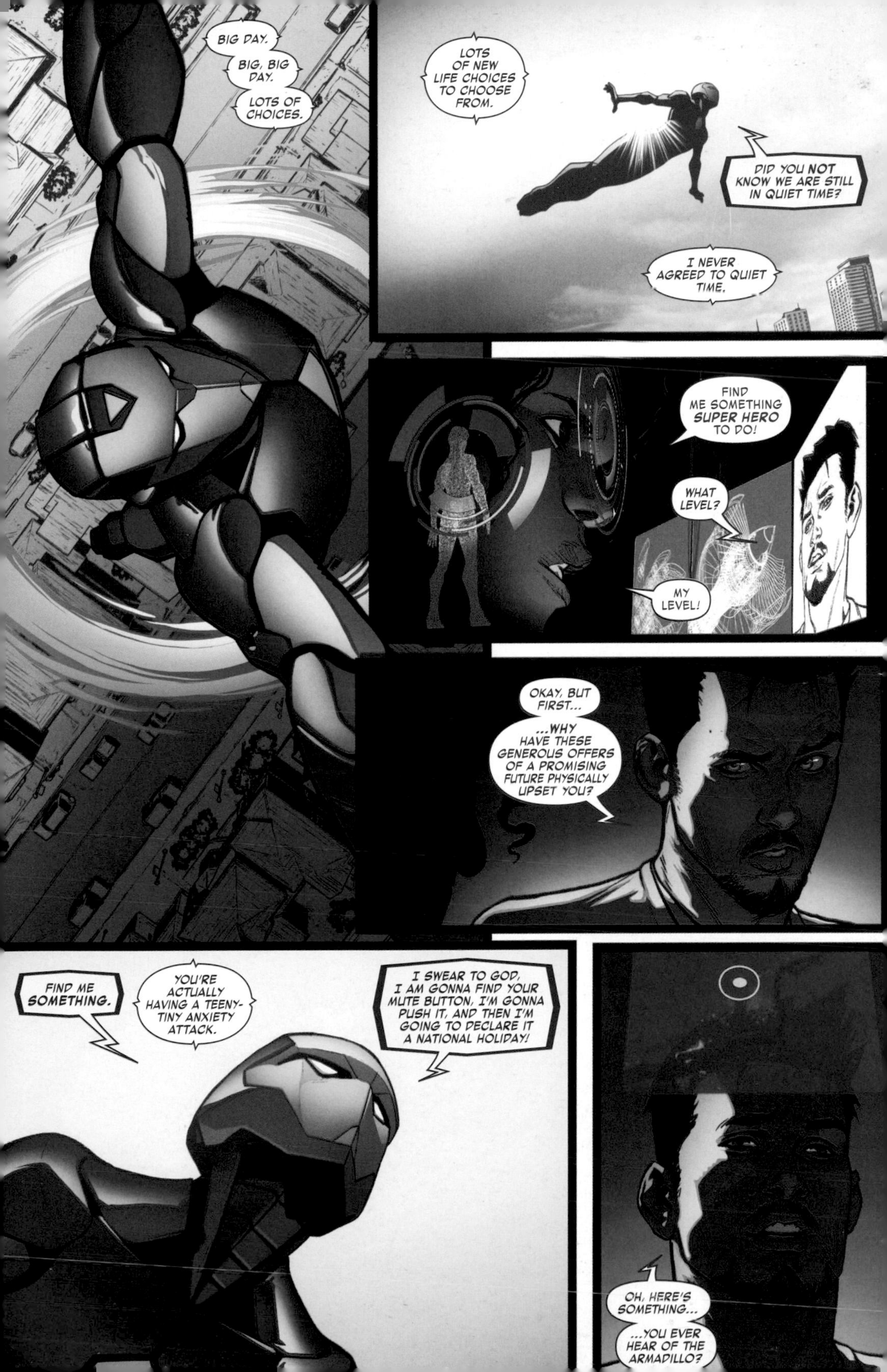

BIG DAY.
BIG, BIG DAY.
LOTS OF CHOICES.
LOTS OF NEW LIFE CHOICES TO CHOOSE FROM.
DID YOU NOT KNOW WE ARE STILL IN QUIET TIME?
I NEVER AGREED TO QUIET TIME.
FIND ME SOMETHING SUPER HERO TO DO!
WHAT LEVEL?
MY LEVEL!
OKAY, BUT FIRST...
...WHY HAVE THESE GENEROUS OFFERS OF A PROMISING FUTURE PHYSICALLY UPSET YOU?
FIND ME SOMETHING.
YOU'RE ACTUALLY HAVING A TEENY-TINY ANXIETY ATTACK.
I SWEAR TO GOD, I AM GONNA FIND YOUR MUTE BUTTON, I'M GONNA PUSH IT, AND THEN I'M GOING TO DECLARE IT A NATIONAL HOLIDAY!
OH, HERE'S SOMETHING...
...YOU EVER HEAR OF THE ARMADILLO?

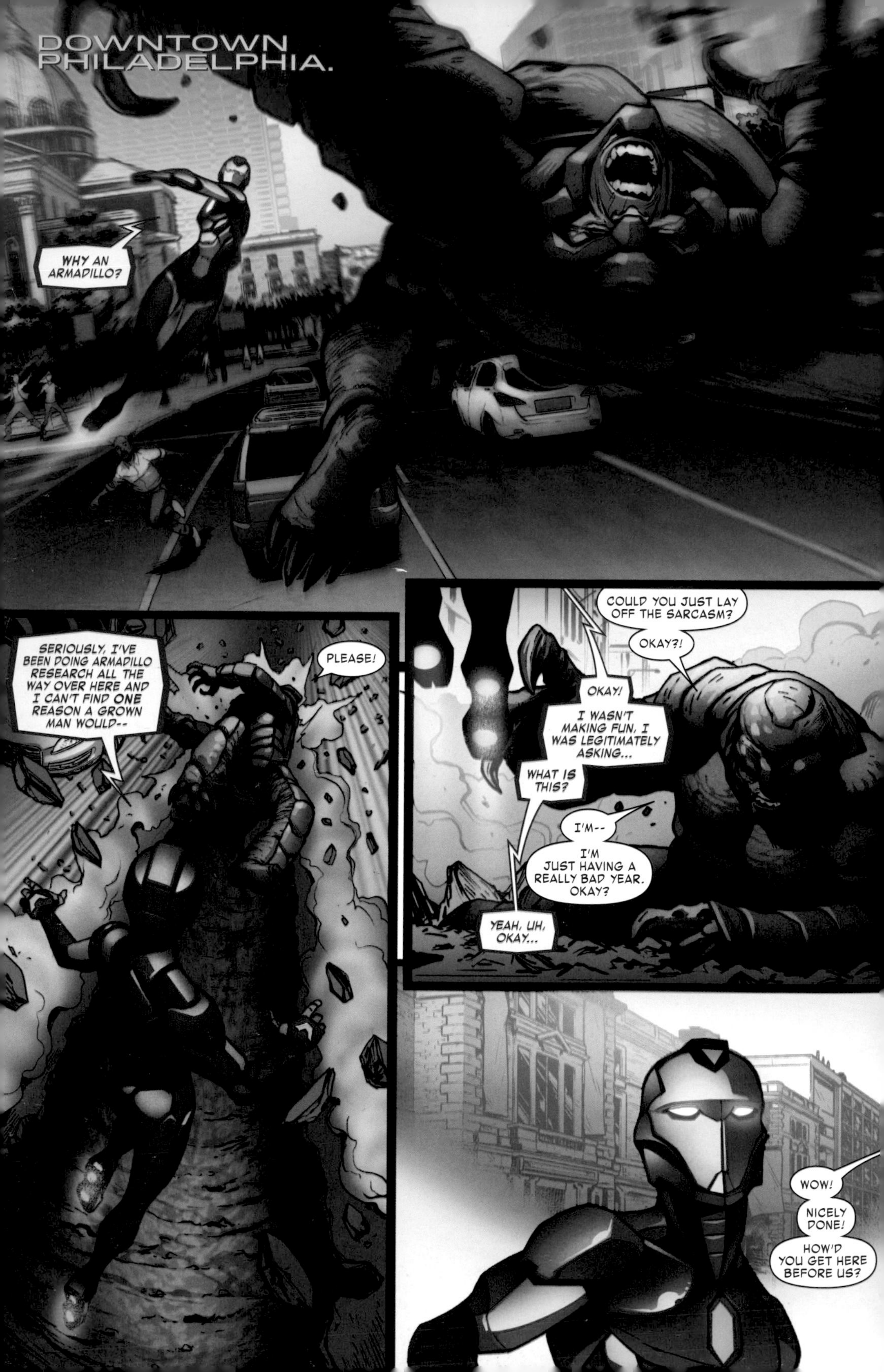
DOWNTOWN PHILADELPHIA.
WHY AN ARMADILLO?
SERIOUSLY, I'VE BEEN DOING ARMADILLO RESEARCH ALL THE WAY OVER HERE AND I CAN'T FIND ONE REASON A GROWN MAN WOULD--
PLEASE!
COULD YOU JUST LAY OFF THE SARCASM?
OKAY?!
OKAY!
I WASN'T MAKING FUN, I WAS LEGITIMATELY ASKING...
WHAT IS THIS?
I'M--
I'M JUST HAVING A REALLY BAD YEAR. OKAY?
YEAH, UH, OKAY...
WOW!
NICELY DONE!
HOW'D YOU GET HERE BEFORE US?

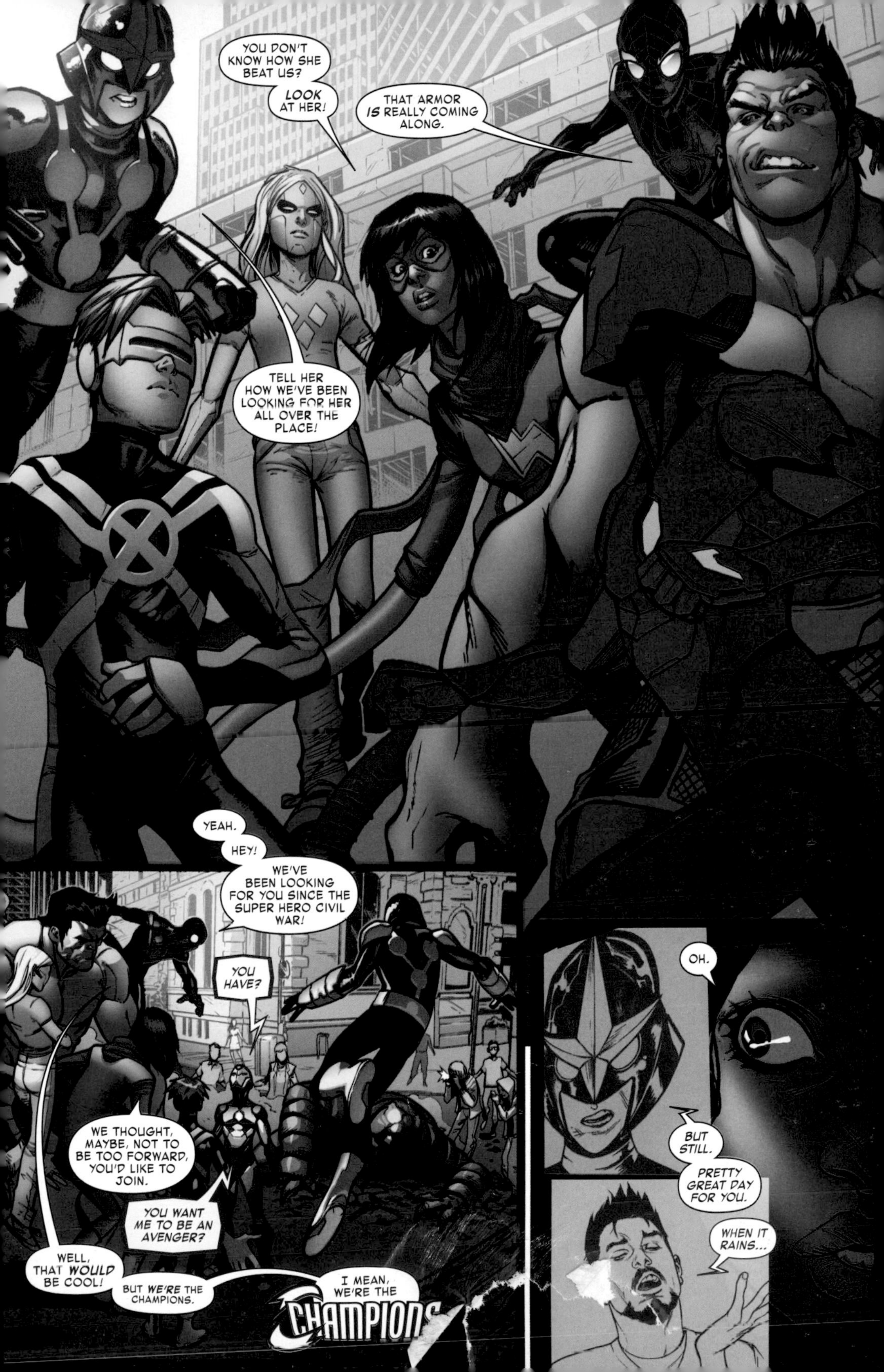
YOU DON'T KNOW HOW SHE BEAT US?
LOOK AT HER!
THAT ARMOR IS REALLY COMING ALONG.
TELL HER HOW WE'VE BEEN LOOKING FOR HER ALL OVER THE PLACE!
YEAH.
HEY!
WE'VE BEEN LOOKING FOR YOU SINCE THE SUPER HERO CIVIL WAR!
YOU HAVE?
WE THOUGHT, MAYBE, NOT TO BE TOO FORWARD, YOU'D LIKE TO JOIN.
YOU WANT ME TO BE AN AVENGER?
WELL, THAT WOULD BE COOL!
BUT WE'RE THE CHAMPIONS.
I MEAN, WE'RE THE
CHAMPIONS
OH.
BUT STILL.
PRETTY GREAT DAY FOR YOU.
WHEN IT RAINS...

7

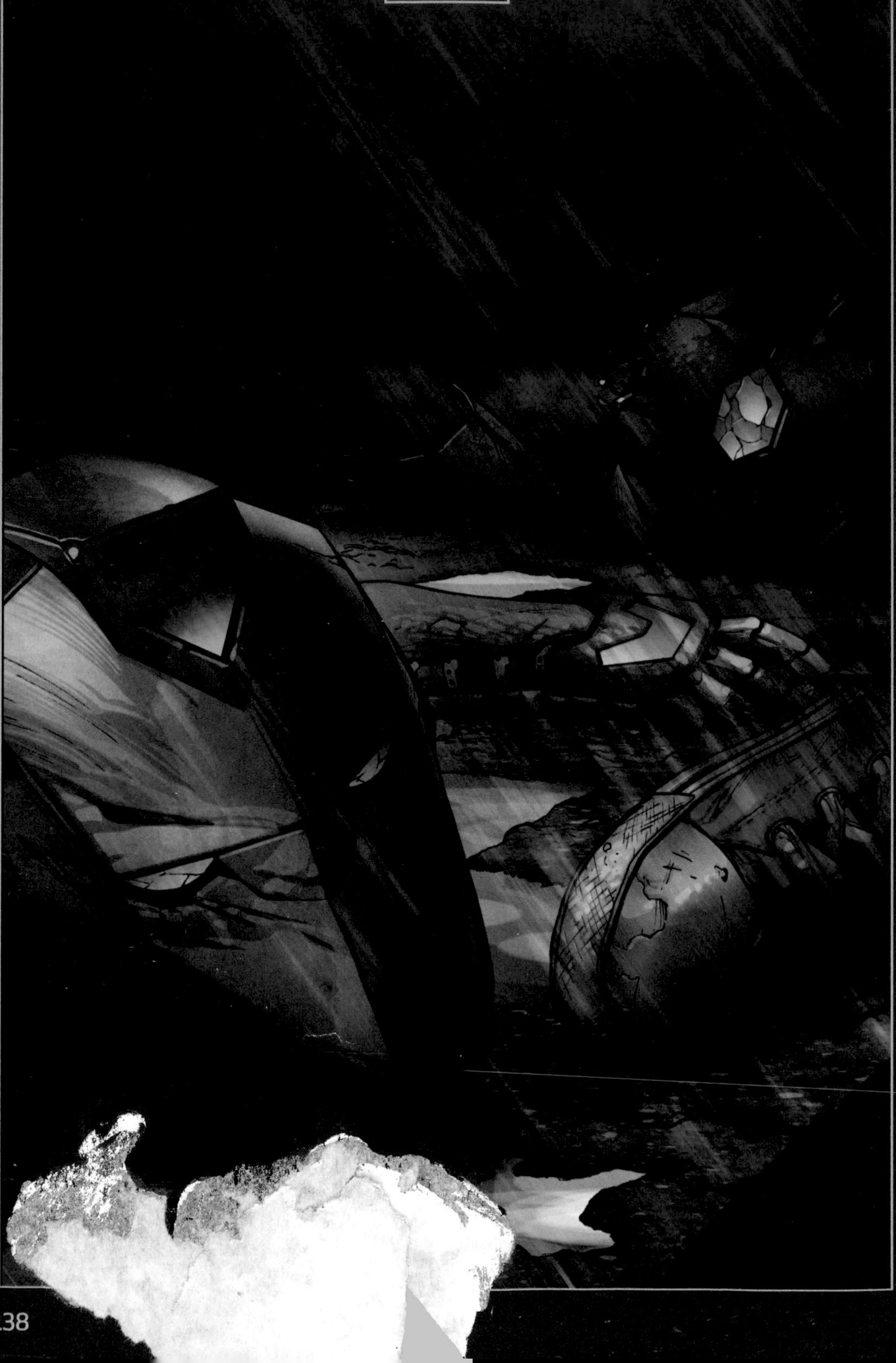

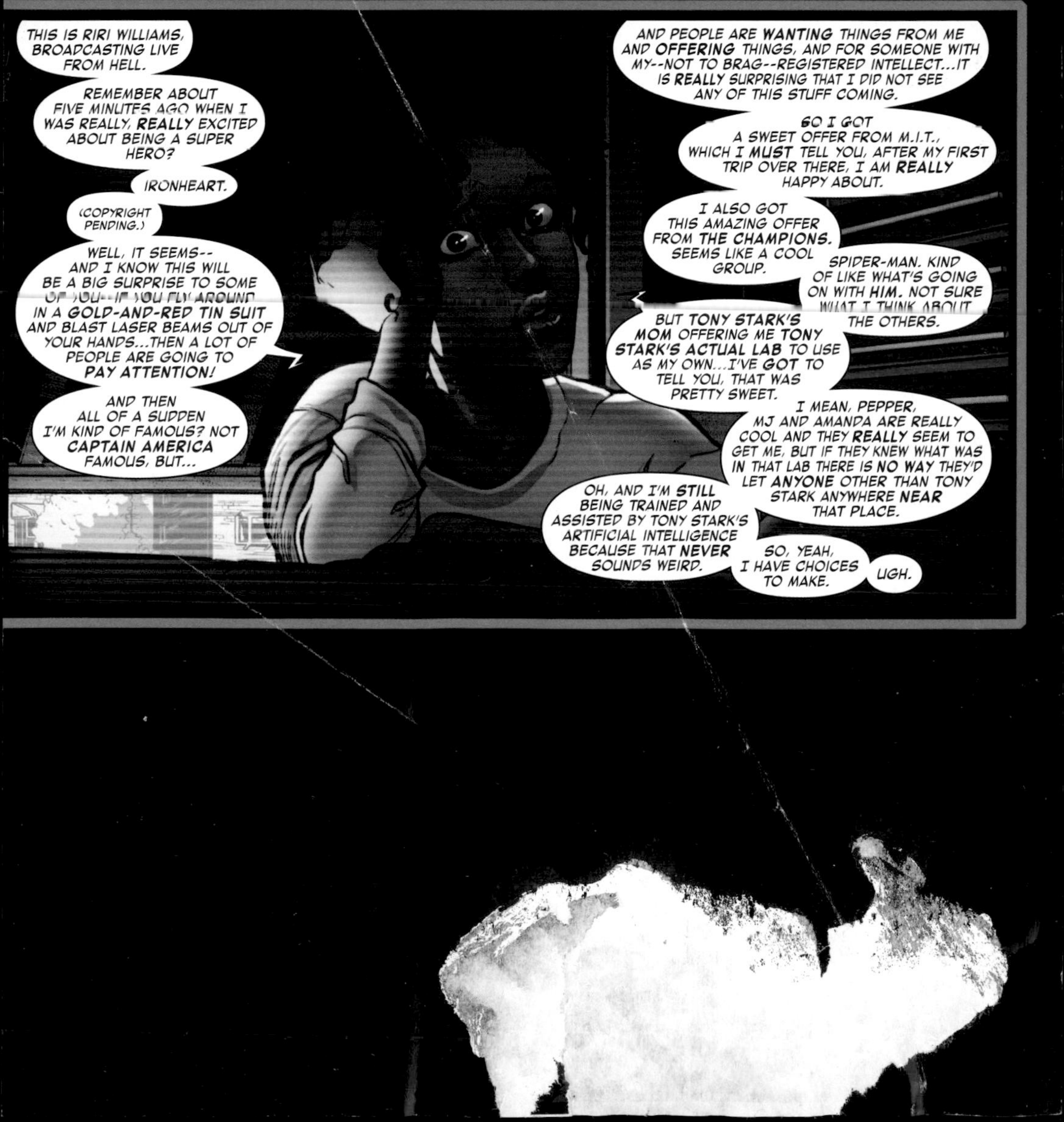
THIS IS RIRI WILLIAMS, BROADCASTING LIVE FROM HELL.
REMEMBER ABOUT FIVE MINUTES AGO WHEN I WAS REALLY, REALLY EXCITED ABOUT BEING A SUPER HERO?
IRONHEART.
(COPYRIGHT PENDING.)
WELL, IT SEEMS-- AND I KNOW THIS WILL BE A BIG SURPRISE TO SOME OF YOU--IF YOU FLY AROUND IN A GOLD-AND-RED TIN SUIT AND BLAST LASER BEAMS OUT OF YOUR HANDS...THEN A LOT OF PEOPLE ARE GOING TO PAY ATTENTION!
AND THEN ALL OF A SUDDEN I'M KIND OF FAMOUS? NOT CAPTAIN AMERICA FAMOUS, BUT...
AND PEOPLE ARE WANTING THINGS FROM ME AND OFFERING THINGS, AND FOR SOMEONE WITH MY--NOT TO BRAG--REGISTERED INTELLECT...IT IS REALLY SURPRISING THAT I DID NOT SEE ANY OF THIS STUFF COMING.
SO I GOT A SWEET OFFER FROM M.I.T., WHICH I MUST TELL YOU, AFTER MY FIRST TRIP OVER THERE, I AM REALLY HAPPY ABOUT.
I ALSO GOT THIS AMAZING OFFER FROM THE CHAMPIONS. SEEMS LIKE A COOL GROUP.
SPIDER-MAN. KIND OF LIKE WHAT'S GOING ON WITH HIM. NOT SURE WHAT I THINK ABOUT THE OTHERS.
BUT TONY STARK'S MOM OFFERING ME TONY STARK'S ACTUAL LAB TO USE AS MY OWN...I'VE GOT TO TELL YOU, THAT WAS PRETTY SWEET.
I MEAN, PEPPER, MJ AND AMANDA ARE REALLY COOL AND THEY REALLY SEEM TO GET ME, BUT IF THEY KNEW WHAT WAS IN THAT LAB THERE IS NO WAY THEY'D LET ANYONE OTHER THAN TONY STARK ANYWHERE NEAR THAT PLACE.
OH, AND I'M STILL BEING TRAINED AND ASSISTED BY TONY STARK'S ARTIFICIAL INTELLIGENCE BECAUSE THAT NEVER SOUNDS WEIRD.
SO, YEAH, I HAVE CHOICES TO MAKE.
UGH.

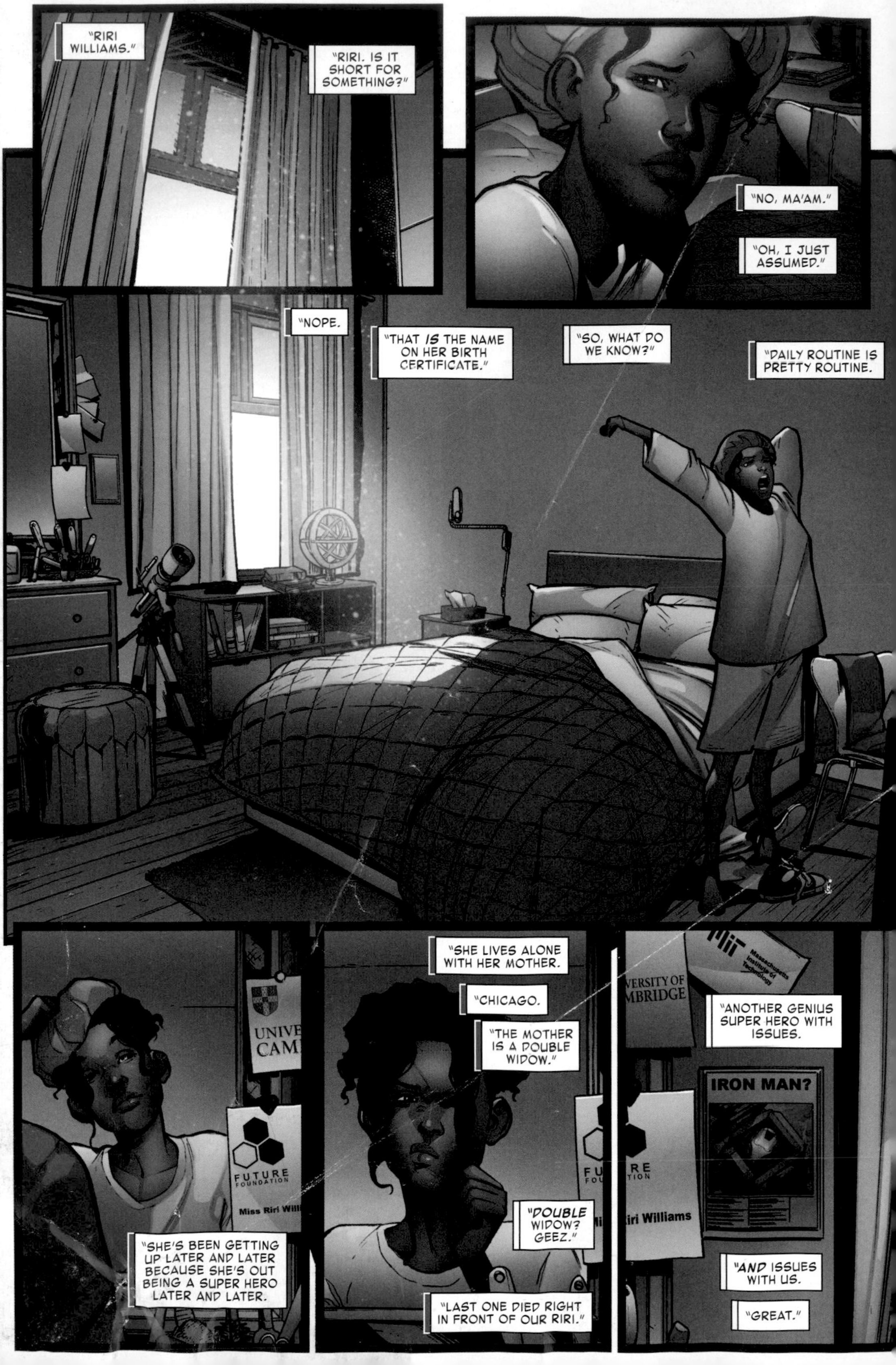

"RIRI WILLIAMS."
"RIRI. IS IT SHORT FOR SOMETHING?"
"NO, MA'AM."
"OH, I JUST ASSUMED."
"NOPE.
"THAT IS THE NAME ON HER BIRTH CERTIFICATE."
"SO, WHAT DO WE KNOW?"
"DAILY ROUTINE IS PRETTY ROUTINE.
UNIVE
CAM
FUTURE FOUNDATION
Miss Riri Willi
"SHE'S BEEN GETTING UP LATER AND LATER BECAUSE SHE'S OUT BEING A SUPER HERO LATER AND LATER.
"SHE LIVES ALONE WITH HER MOTHER.
"CHICAGO.
"THE MOTHER IS A DOUBLE WIDOW."
"DOUBLE WIDOW? GEEZ."
"LAST ONE DIED RIGHT IN FRONT OF OUR RIRI."
VERSITY OF
MBRIDGE
Massachusetts Institute of Technology
"ANOTHER GENIUS SUPER HERO WITH ISSUES.
IRON MAN?
iri Williams
"AND ISSUES WITH US.
"GREAT."

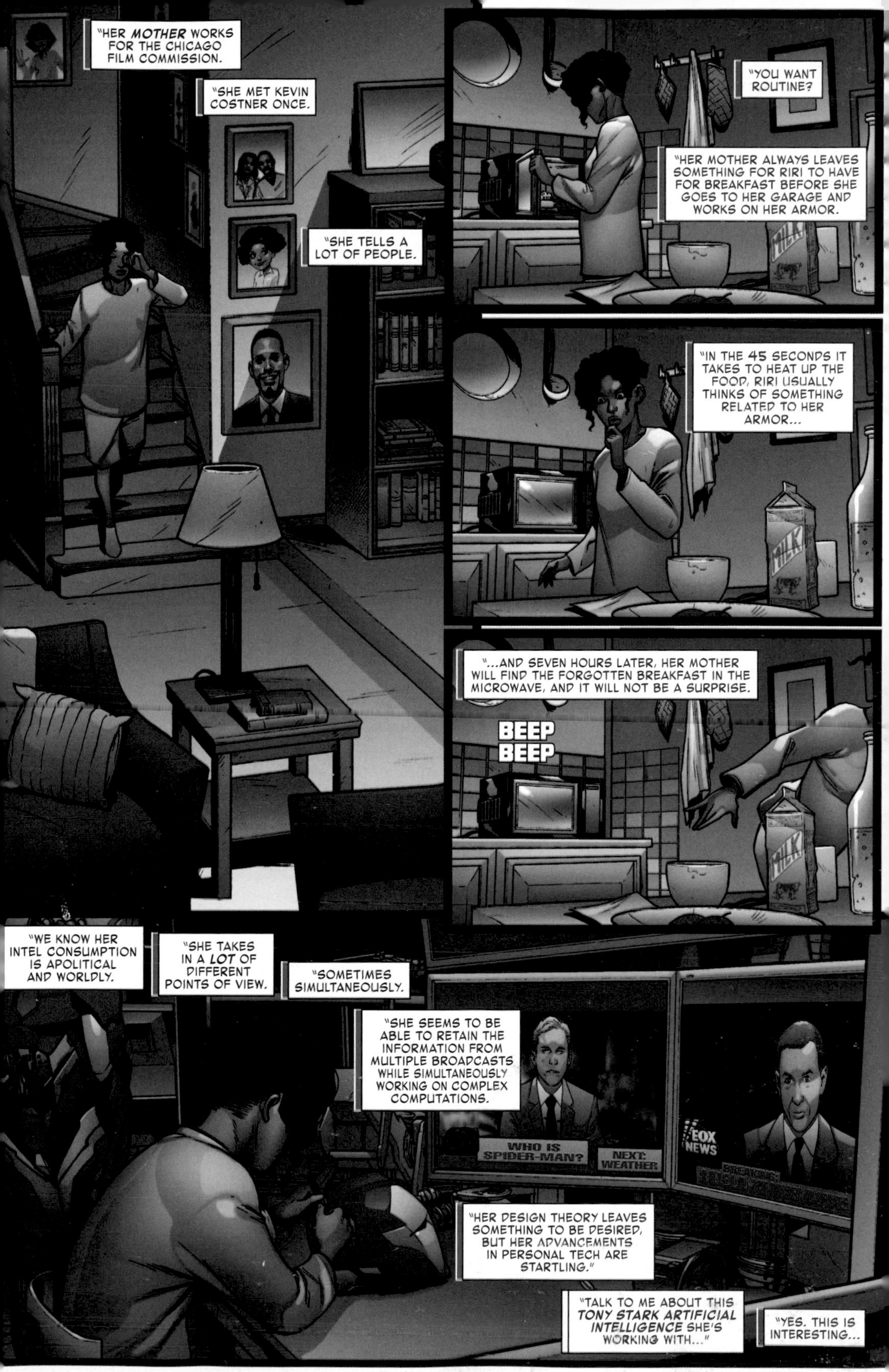
"HER *MOTHER* WORKS FOR THE CHICAGO FILM COMMISSION.
"SHE MET KEVIN COSTNER ONCE.
"SHE TELLS A LOT OF PEOPLE.
"YOU WANT ROUTINE?
"HER MOTHER ALWAYS LEAVES SOMETHING FOR RIRI TO HAVE FOR BREAKFAST BEFORE SHE GOES TO HER GARAGE AND WORKS ON HER ARMOR.
"IN THE 45 SECONDS IT TAKES TO HEAT UP THE FOOD, RIRI USUALLY THINKS OF SOMETHING RELATED TO HER ARMOR...
"...AND SEVEN HOURS LATER, HER MOTHER WILL FIND THE FORGOTTEN BREAKFAST IN THE MICROWAVE, AND IT WILL NOT BE A SURPRISE.
BEEP BEEP
"WE KNOW HER INTEL CONSUMPTION IS APOLITICAL AND WORLDLY.
"SHE TAKES IN A *LOT* OF DIFFERENT POINTS OF VIEW.
"SOMETIMES SIMULTANEOUSLY.
"SHE SEEMS TO BE ABLE TO RETAIN THE INFORMATION FROM MULTIPLE BROADCASTS WHILE SIMULTANEOUSLY WORKING ON COMPLEX COMPUTATIONS.
WHO IS SPIDER-MAN?
NEXT: WEATHER
FOX NEWS
"HER DESIGN THEORY LEAVES SOMETHING TO BE DESIRED, BUT HER ADVANCEMENTS IN PERSONAL TECH ARE STARTLING."
"TALK TO ME ABOUT THIS *TONY STARK ARTIFICIAL INTELLIGENCE* SHE'S WORKING WITH..."
"YES. THIS IS INTERESTING...

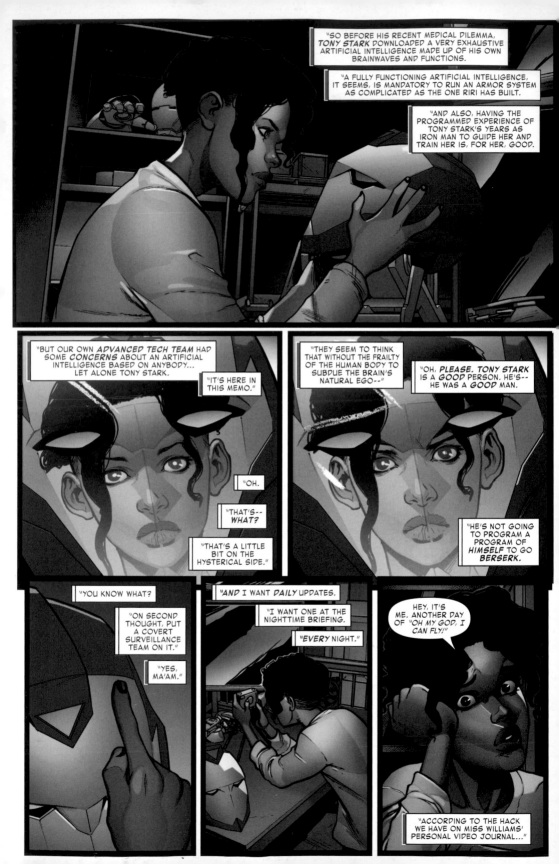

"SO BEFORE HIS RECENT MEDICAL DILEMMA, *TONY STARK* DOWNLOADED A VERY EXHAUSTIVE ARTIFICIAL INTELLIGENCE MADE UP OF HIS OWN BRAINWAVES AND FUNCTIONS.

"A FULLY FUNCTIONING ARTIFICIAL INTELLIGENCE, IT SEEMS, IS MANDATORY TO RUN AN ARMOR SYSTEM AS COMPLICATED AS THE ONE RIRI HAS BUILT.

"AND ALSO, HAVING THE PROGRAMMED EXPERIENCE OF TONY STARK'S YEARS AS IRON MAN TO GUIDE HER AND TRAIN HER IS, FOR HER, GOOD.

"BUT OUR OWN *ADVANCED TECH TEAM* HAD SOME *CONCERNS* ABOUT AN ARTIFICIAL INTELLIGENCE BASED ON ANYBODY... LET ALONE TONY STARK."

"IT'S HERE IN THIS MEMO."

"OH.

"THAT'S-- *WHAT?*

"THAT'S A LITTLE BIT ON THE HYSTERICAL SIDE."

"THEY SEEM TO THINK THAT WITHOUT THE FRAILTY OF THE HUMAN BODY TO SUBDUE THE BRAIN'S NATURAL EGO--"

"OH, *PLEASE. TONY STARK* IS A *GOOD* PERSON. HE'S-- HE WAS A *GOOD* MAN.

"HE'S NOT GOING TO PROGRAM A PROGRAM OF *HIMSELF* TO GO *BERSERK.*

"YOU KNOW WHAT?

"ON SECOND THOUGHT, PUT A COVERT SURVEILLANCE TEAM ON IT."

"YES, MA'AM."

"*AND* I WANT *DAILY* UPDATES.

"I WANT ONE AT THE NIGHTTIME BRIEFING.

"*EVERY* NIGHT."

HEY, IT'S ME. ANOTHER DAY OF "OH MY GOD, I CAN FLY!"

"ACCORDING TO THE HACK WE HAVE ON MISS WILLIAMS' PERSONAL VIDEO JOURNAL..."

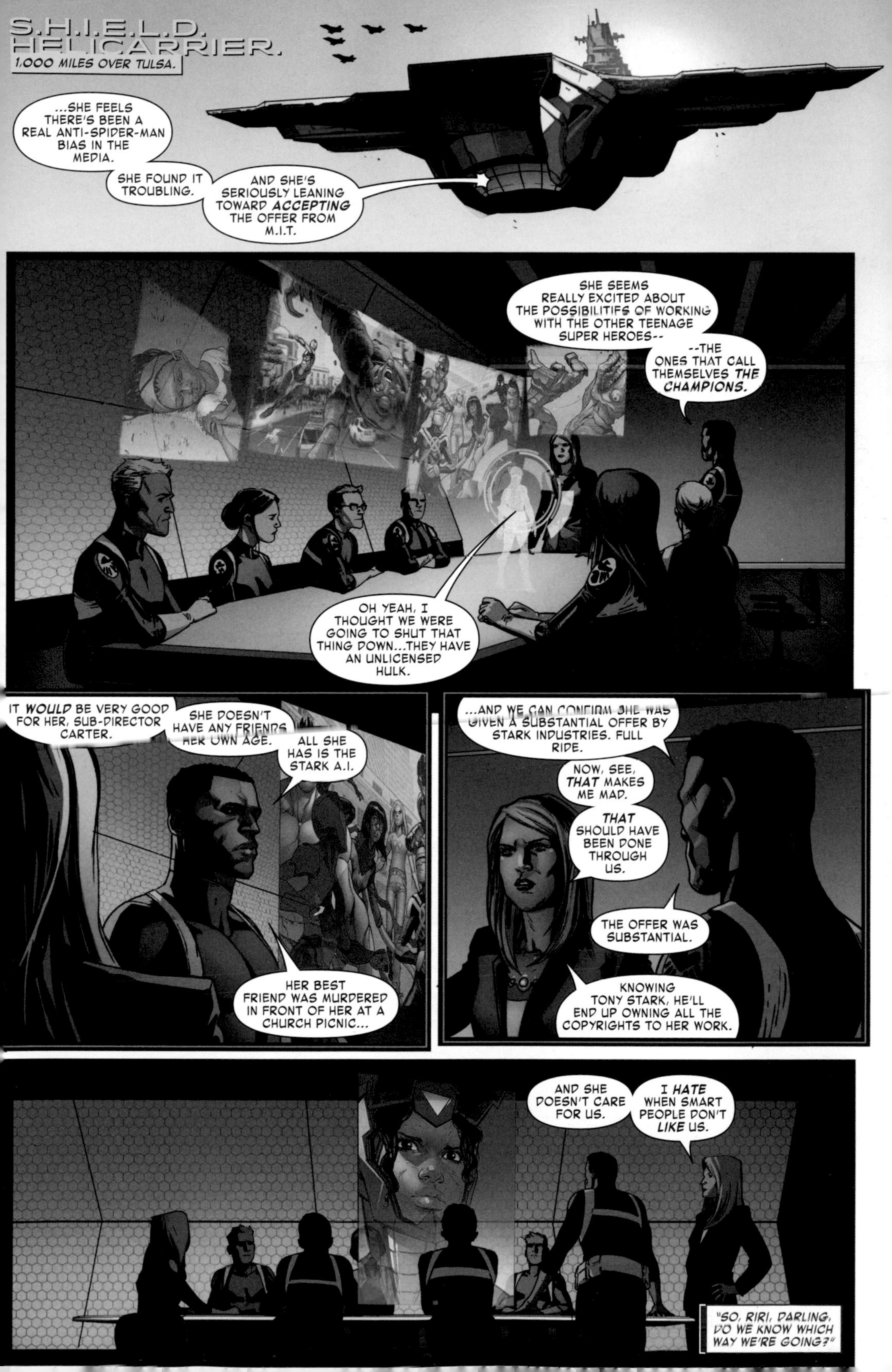
S.H.I.E.L.D. HELICARRIER.
1,000 MILES OVER TULSA.
...SHE FEELS THERE'S BEEN A REAL ANTI-SPIDER-MAN BIAS IN THE MEDIA.
SHE FOUND IT TROUBLING.
AND SHE'S SERIOUSLY LEANING TOWARD ACCEPTING THE OFFER FROM M.I.T.
SHE SEEMS REALLY EXCITED ABOUT THE POSSIBILITIES OF WORKING WITH THE OTHER TEENAGE SUPER HEROES--
--THE ONES THAT CALL THEMSELVES THE CHAMPIONS.
OH YEAH, I THOUGHT WE WERE GOING TO SHUT THAT THING DOWN...THEY HAVE AN UNLICENSED HULK.
IT WOULD BE VERY GOOD FOR HER, SUB-DIRECTOR CARTER.
SHE DOESN'T HAVE ANY FRIENDS HER OWN AGE.
ALL SHE HAS IS THE STARK A.I.
HER BEST FRIEND WAS MURDERED IN FRONT OF HER AT A CHURCH PICNIC...
...AND WE CAN CONFIRM SHE WAS GIVEN A SUBSTANTIAL OFFER BY STARK INDUSTRIES. FULL RIDE.
NOW, SEE, THAT MAKES ME MAD.
THAT SHOULD HAVE BEEN DONE THROUGH US.
THE OFFER WAS SUBSTANTIAL.
KNOWING TONY STARK, HE'LL END UP OWNING ALL THE COPYRIGHTS TO HER WORK.
AND SHE DOESN'T CARE FOR US.
I HATE WHEN SMART PEOPLE DON'T LIKE US.
"SO, RIRI, DARLING, DO WE KNOW WHICH WAY WE'RE GOING?"

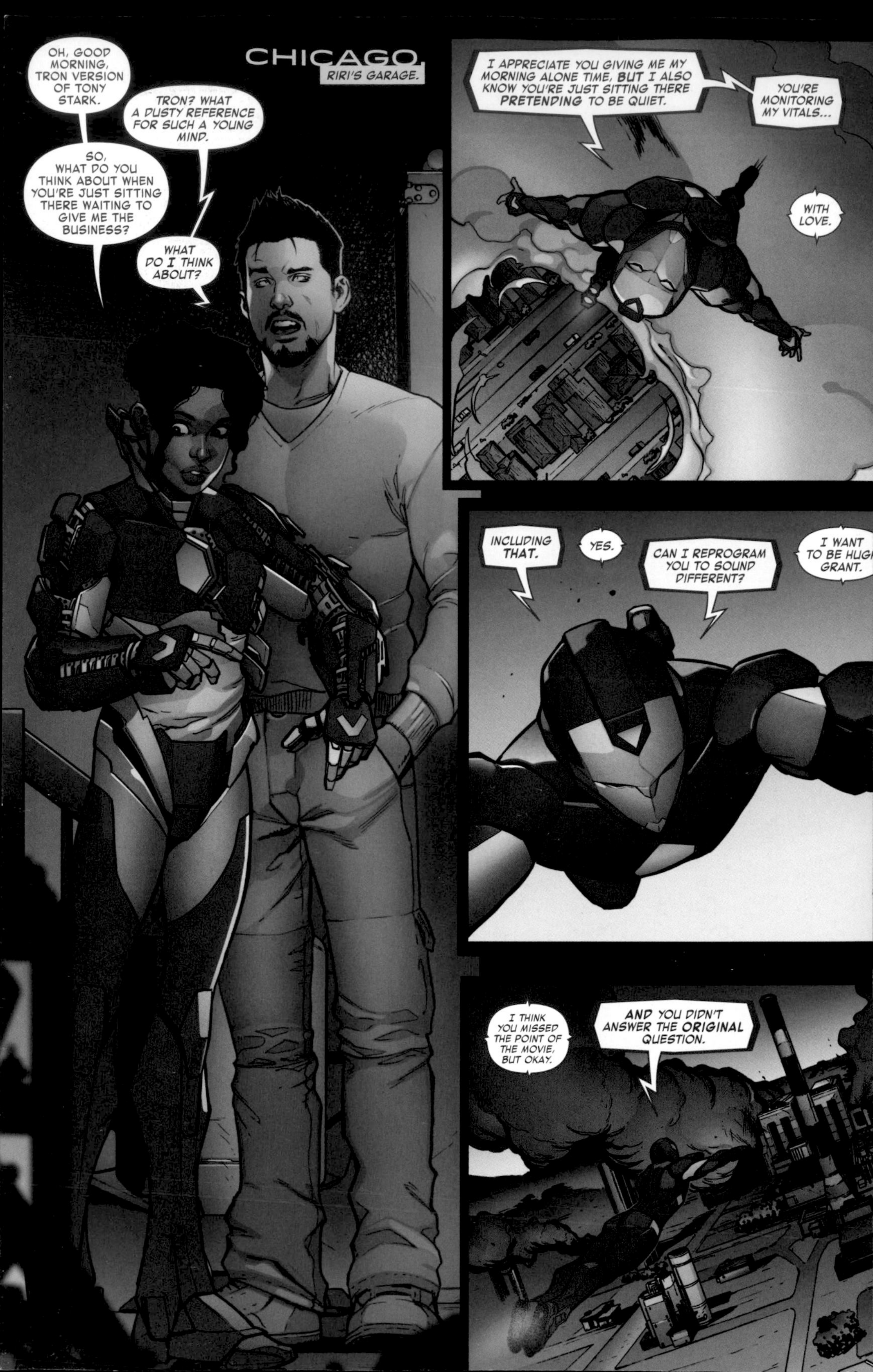
CHICAGO,
RIRI'S GARAGE.
OH, GOOD MORNING, TRON VERSION OF TONY STARK.
TRON? WHAT A DUSTY REFERENCE FOR SUCH A YOUNG MIND.
SO, WHAT DO YOU THINK ABOUT WHEN YOU'RE JUST SITTING THERE WAITING TO GIVE ME THE BUSINESS?
WHAT DO I THINK ABOUT?
I APPRECIATE YOU GIVING ME MY MORNING ALONE TIME, BUT I ALSO KNOW YOU'RE JUST SITTING THERE PRETENDING TO BE QUIET.
YOU'RE MONITORING MY VITALS...
WITH LOVE.
INCLUDING THAT.
YES.
CAN I REPROGRAM YOU TO SOUND DIFFERENT?
I WANT TO BE HUGH GRANT.
I THINK YOU MISSED THE POINT OF THE MOVIE, BUT OKAY.
AND YOU DIDN'T ANSWER THE ORIGINAL QUESTION.

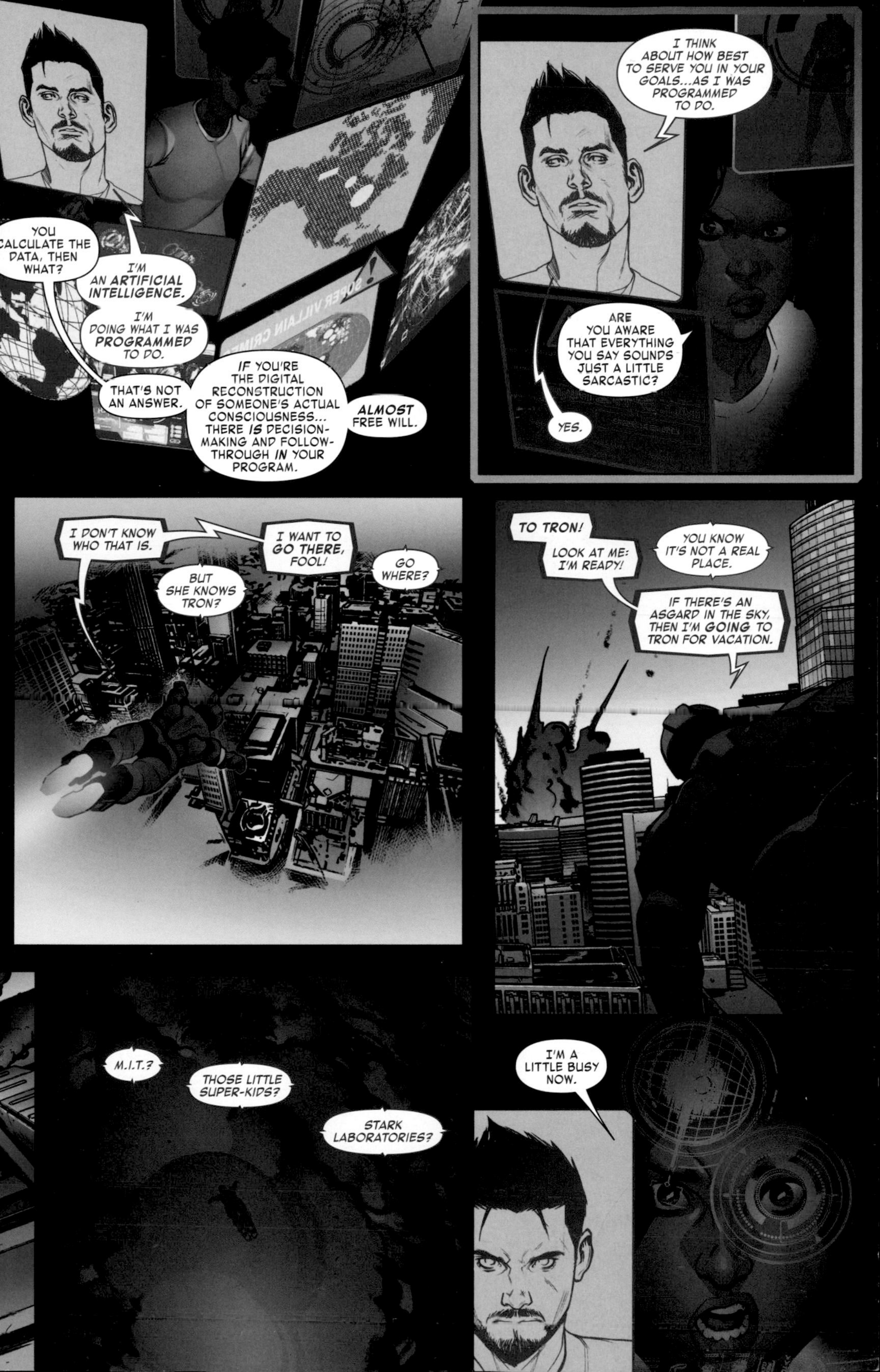

YOU CALCULATE THE DATA, THEN WHAT?
I'M AN ARTIFICIAL INTELLIGENCE.
I'M DOING WHAT I WAS PROGRAMMED TO DO.
THAT'S NOT AN ANSWER.
IF YOU'RE THE DIGITAL RECONSTRUCTION OF SOMEONE'S ACTUAL CONSCIOUSNESS... THERE IS DECISION-MAKING AND FOLLOW-THROUGH IN YOUR PROGRAM.
ALMOST FREE WILL.
SUPER VILLAIN CRIM
I THINK ABOUT HOW BEST TO SERVE YOU IN YOUR GOALS...AS I WAS PROGRAMMED TO DO.
ARE YOU AWARE THAT EVERYTHING YOU SAY SOUNDS JUST A LITTLE SARCASTIC?
YES.
I DON'T KNOW WHO THAT IS.
I WANT TO GO THERE, FOOL!
BUT SHE KNOWS TRON?
GO WHERE?
TO TRON!
LOOK AT ME: I'M READY!
YOU KNOW IT'S NOT A REAL PLACE.
IF THERE'S AN ASGARD IN THE SKY, THEN I'M GOING TO TRON FOR VACATION.
M.I.T.?
THOSE LITTLE SUPER-KIDS?
STARK LABORATORIES?
I'M A LITTLE BUSY NOW.

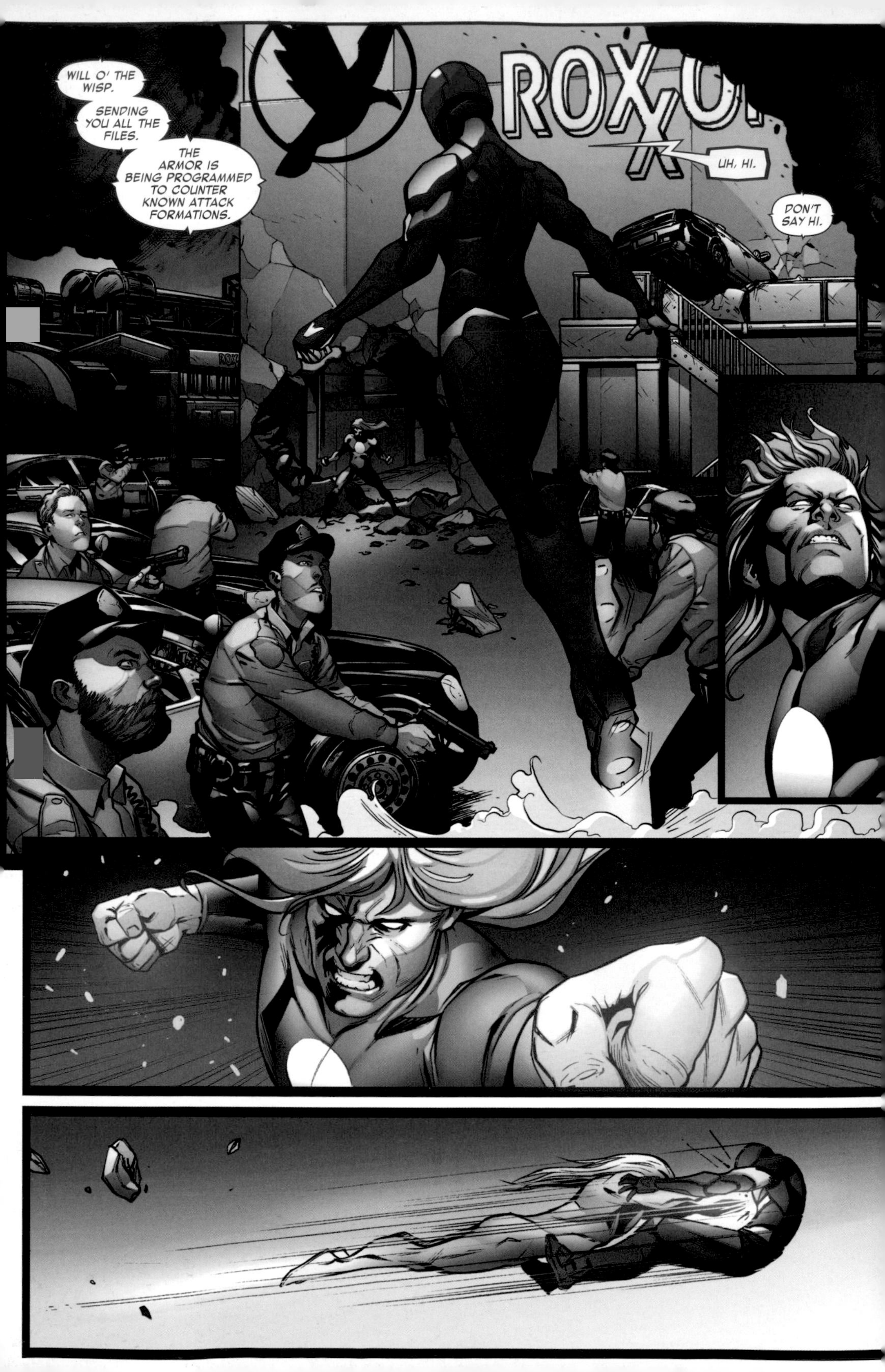
WILL O' THE WISP.
SENDING YOU ALL THE FILES.
THE ARMOR IS BEING PROGRAMMED TO COUNTER KNOWN ATTACK FORMATIONS.
ROXXON
UH, HI.
DON'T SAY HI.

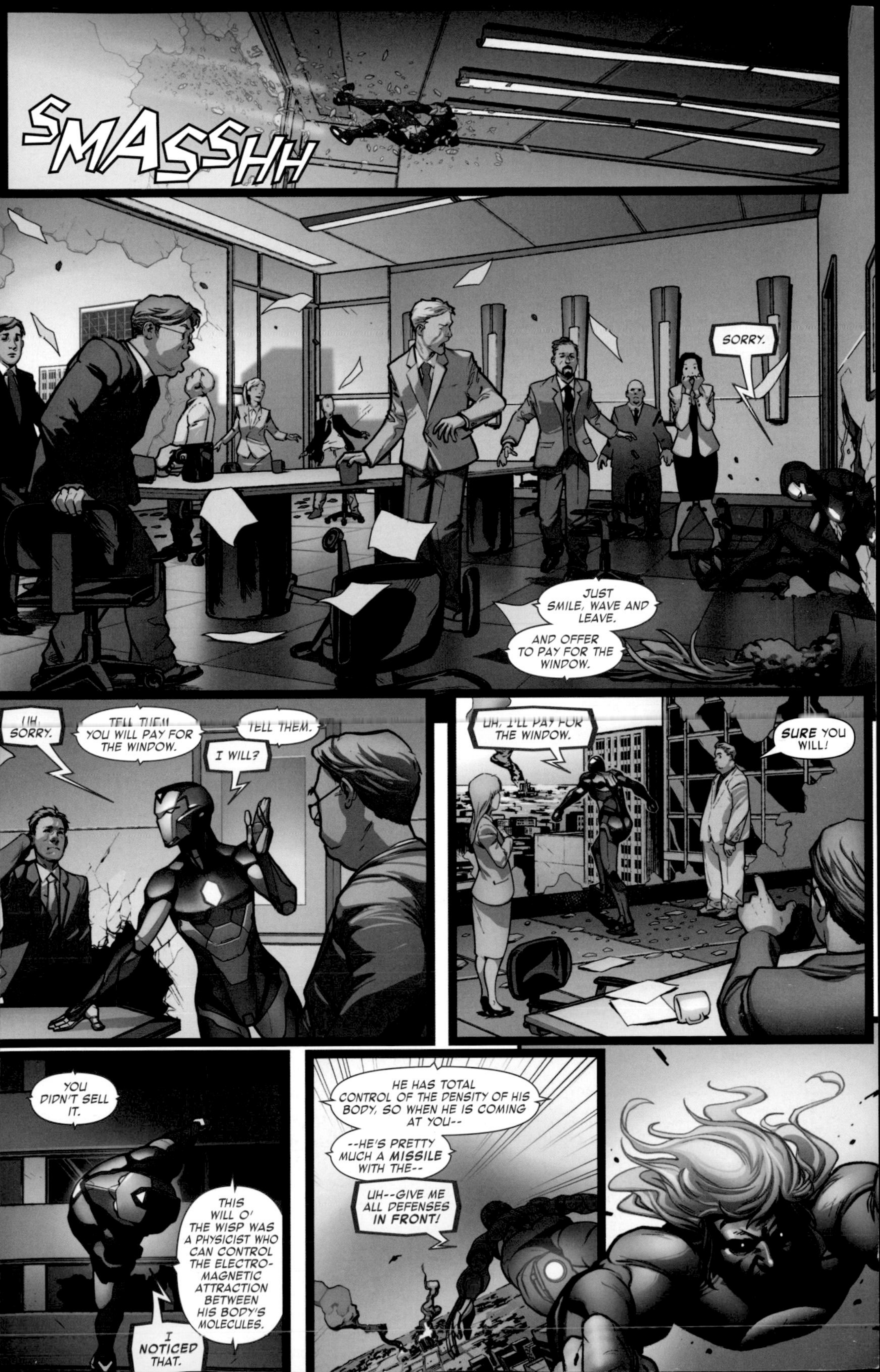
SMASSHH
SORRY.
JUST SMILE, WAVE AND LEAVE.
AND OFFER TO PAY FOR THE WINDOW.
UH, SORRY.
TELL THEM YOU WILL PAY FOR THE WINDOW.
TELL THEM.
I WILL?
UH, I'LL PAY FOR THE WINDOW.
SURE YOU WILL!
YOU DIDN'T SELL IT.
THIS WILL O' THE WISP WAS A PHYSICIST WHO CAN CONTROL THE ELECTRO-MAGNETIC ATTRACTION BETWEEN HIS BODY'S MOLECULES.
I NOTICED THAT.
HE HAS TOTAL CONTROL OF THE DENSITY OF HIS BODY, SO WHEN HE IS COMING AT YOU--
--HE'S PRETTY MUCH A MISSILE WITH THE--
UH--GIVE ME ALL DEFENSES IN FRONT!

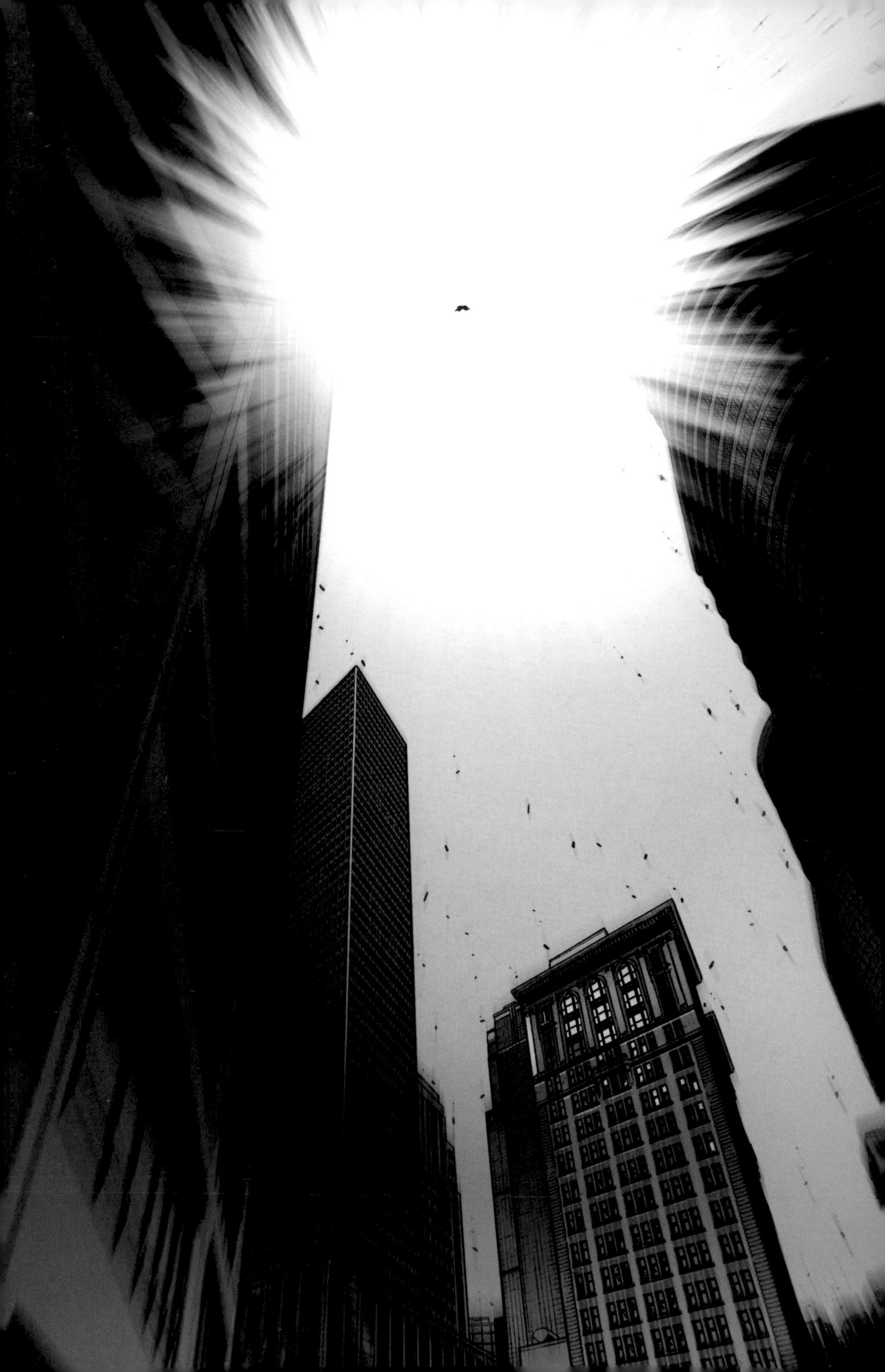

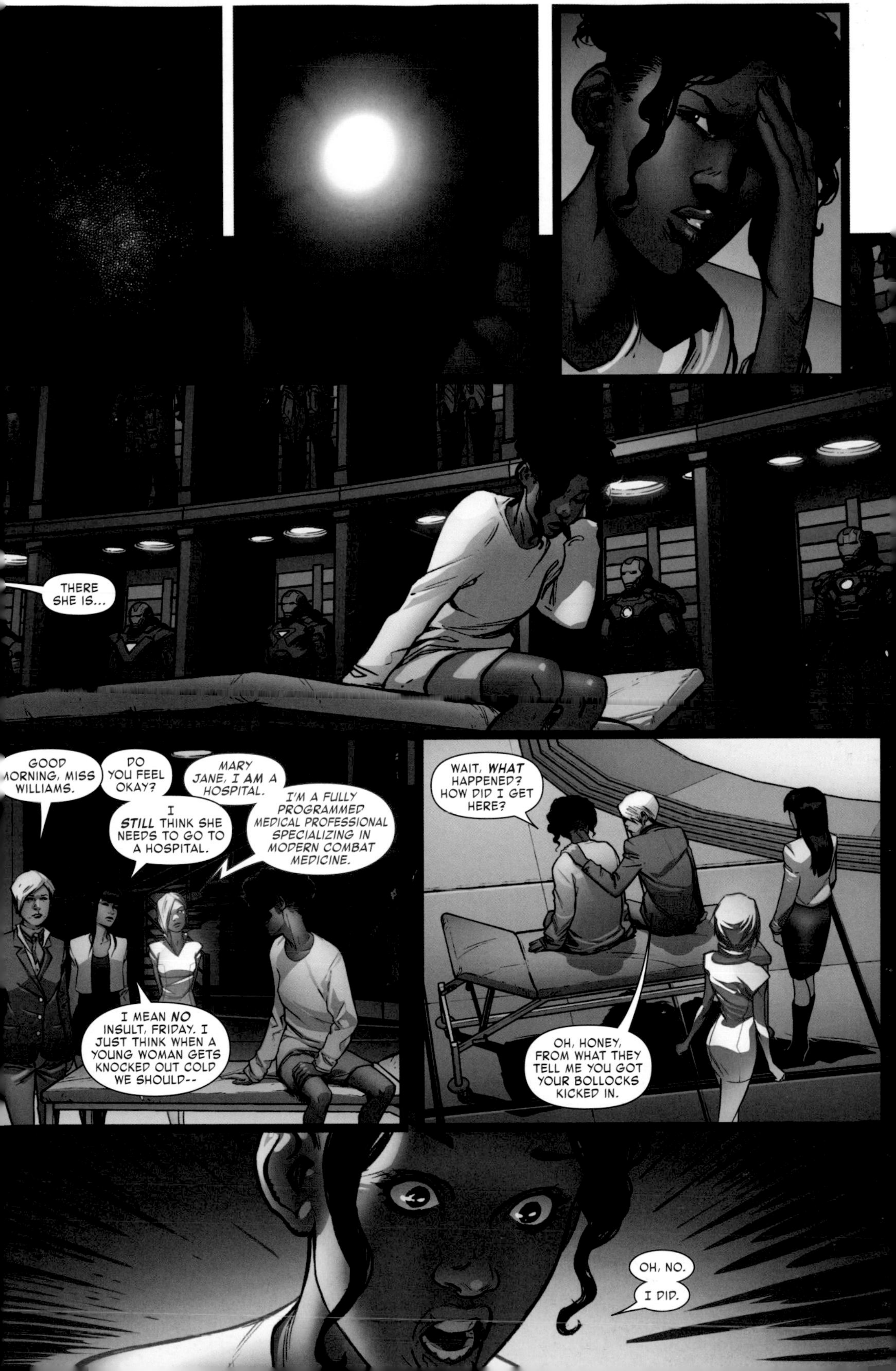
THERE SHE IS...
GOOD MORNING, MISS WILLIAMS.
DO YOU FEEL OKAY?
MARY JANE, I AM A HOSPITAL.
I STILL THINK SHE NEEDS TO GO TO A HOSPITAL.
I'M A FULLY PROGRAMMED MEDICAL PROFESSIONAL SPECIALIZING IN MODERN COMBAT MEDICINE.
I MEAN NO INSULT, FRIDAY. I JUST THINK WHEN A YOUNG WOMAN GETS KNOCKED OUT COLD WE SHOULD--
WAIT, WHAT HAPPENED? HOW DID I GET HERE?
OH, HONEY, FROM WHAT THEY TELL ME YOU GOT YOUR BOLLOCKS KICKED IN.
OH, NO.
I DID.

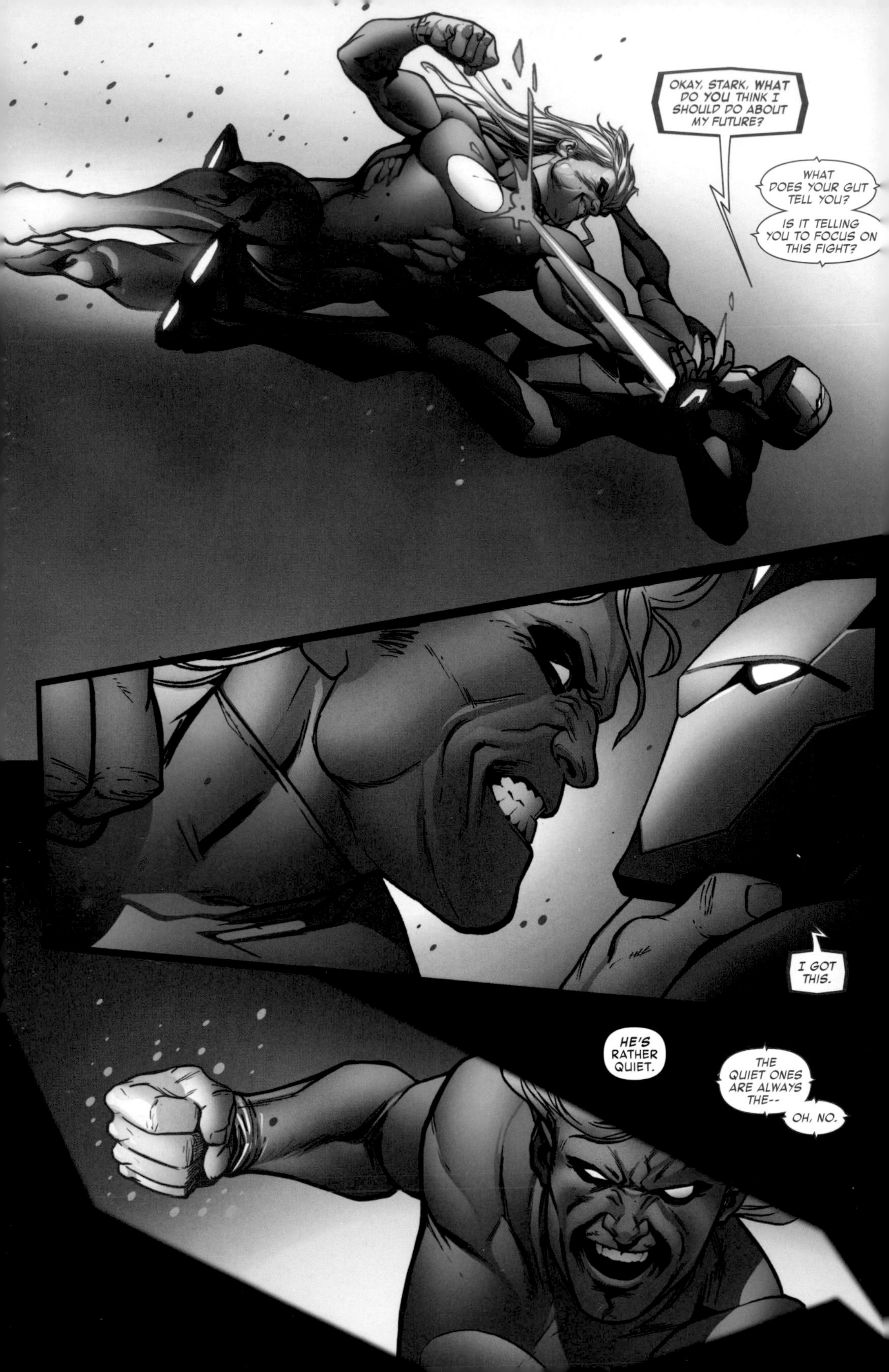
OKAY, STARK, WHAT DO YOU THINK I SHOULD DO ABOUT MY FUTURE?
WHAT DOES YOUR GUT TELL YOU?
IS IT TELLING YOU TO FOCUS ON THIS FIGHT?
I GOT THIS.
HE'S RATHER QUIET.
THE QUIET ONES ARE ALWAYS THE--
OH, NO.

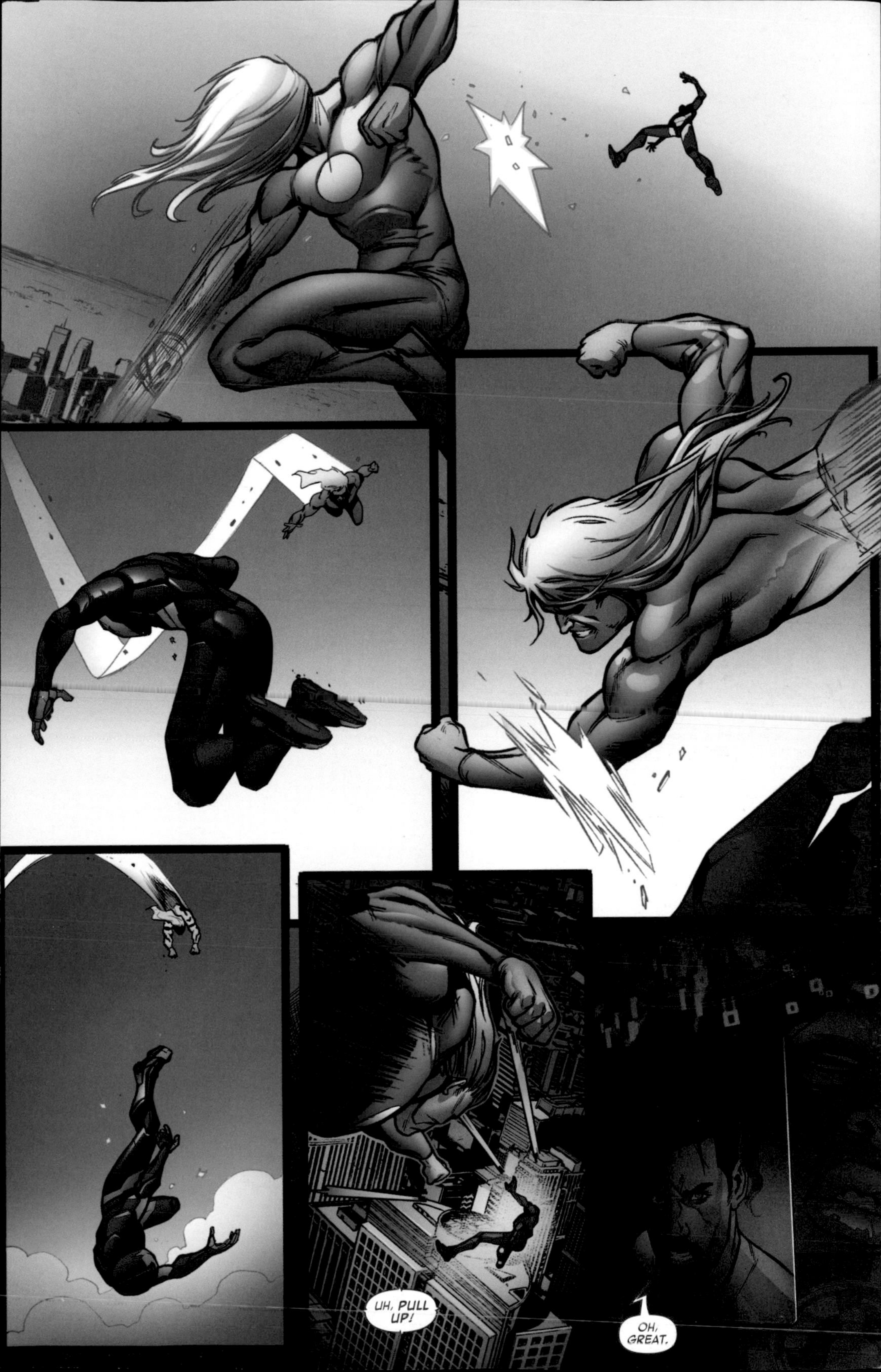
UH, PULL UP!
OH, GREAT.

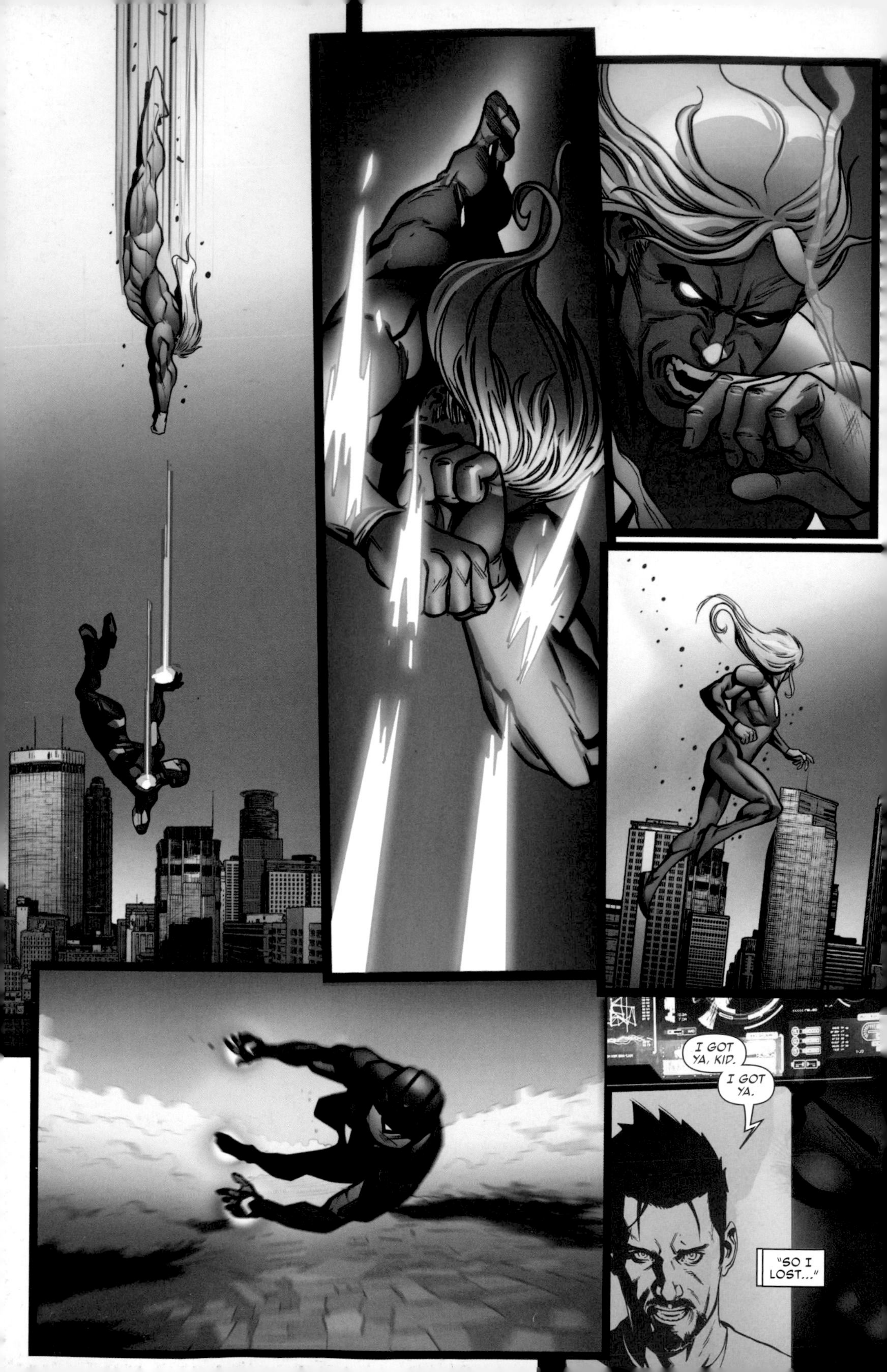
I GOT YA, KID.
I GOT YA.
"SO I LOST..."

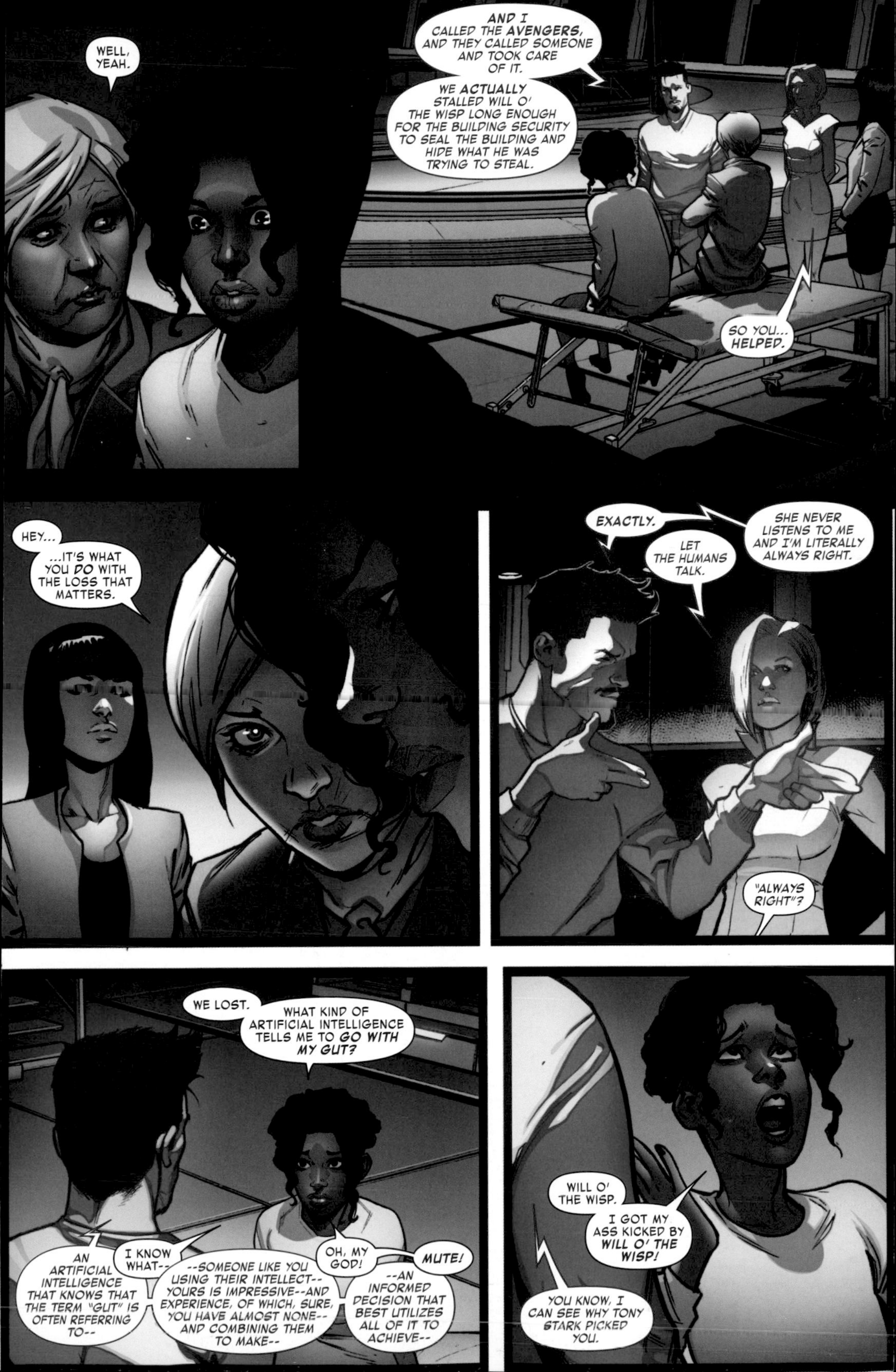
WELL, YEAH.
AND I CALLED THE AVENGERS, AND THEY CALLED SOMEONE AND TOOK CARE OF IT.
WE ACTUALLY STALLED WILL O' THE WISP LONG ENOUGH FOR THE BUILDING SECURITY TO SEAL THE BUILDING AND HIDE WHAT HE WAS TRYING TO STEAL.
SO YOU... HELPED.
HEY...
...IT'S WHAT YOU DO WITH THE LOSS THAT MATTERS.
EXACTLY.
SHE NEVER LISTENS TO ME AND I'M LITERALLY ALWAYS RIGHT.
LET THE HUMANS TALK.
"ALWAYS RIGHT"?
WE LOST.
WHAT KIND OF ARTIFICIAL INTELLIGENCE TELLS ME TO GO WITH MY GUT?
AN ARTIFICIAL INTELLIGENCE THAT KNOWS THAT THE TERM "GUT" IS OFTEN REFERRING TO--
I KNOW WHAT--
--SOMEONE LIKE YOU USING THEIR INTELLECT--YOURS IS IMPRESSIVE--AND EXPERIENCE, OF WHICH, SURE, YOU HAVE ALMOST NONE--AND COMBINING THEM TO MAKE--
OH, MY GOD!
MUTE!
--AN INFORMED DECISION THAT BEST UTILIZES ALL OF IT TO ACHIEVE--
WILL O' THE WISP.
I GOT MY ASS KICKED BY WILL O' THE WISP!
YOU KNOW, I CAN SEE WHY TONY STARK PICKED YOU.

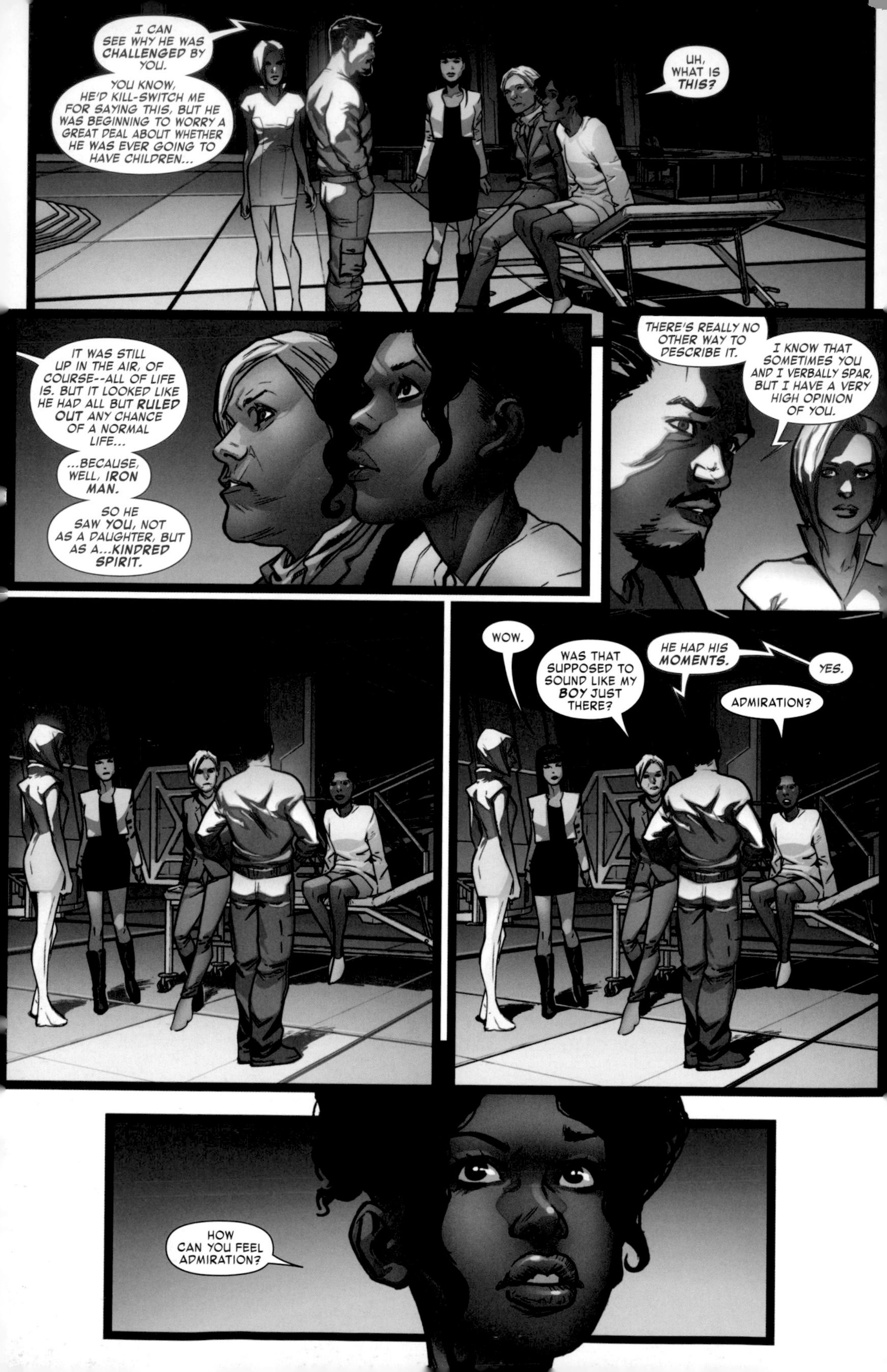
I CAN SEE WHY HE WAS CHALLENGED BY YOU.
YOU KNOW, HE'D KILL-SWITCH ME FOR SAYING THIS, BUT HE WAS BEGINNING TO WORRY A GREAT DEAL ABOUT WHETHER HE WAS EVER GOING TO HAVE CHILDREN...
UH, WHAT IS THIS?
IT WAS STILL UP IN THE AIR, OF COURSE--ALL OF LIFE IS. BUT IT LOOKED LIKE HE HAD ALL BUT RULED OUT ANY CHANCE OF A NORMAL LIFE...
...BECAUSE, WELL, IRON MAN.
SO HE SAW YOU, NOT AS A DAUGHTER, BUT AS A...KINDRED SPIRIT.
THERE'S REALLY NO OTHER WAY TO DESCRIBE IT.
I KNOW THAT SOMETIMES YOU AND I VERBALLY SPAR, BUT I HAVE A VERY HIGH OPINION OF YOU.
WOW.
WAS THAT SUPPOSED TO SOUND LIKE MY BOY JUST THERE?
HE HAD HIS MOMENTS.
YES.
ADMIRATION?
HOW CAN YOU FEEL ADMIRATION?

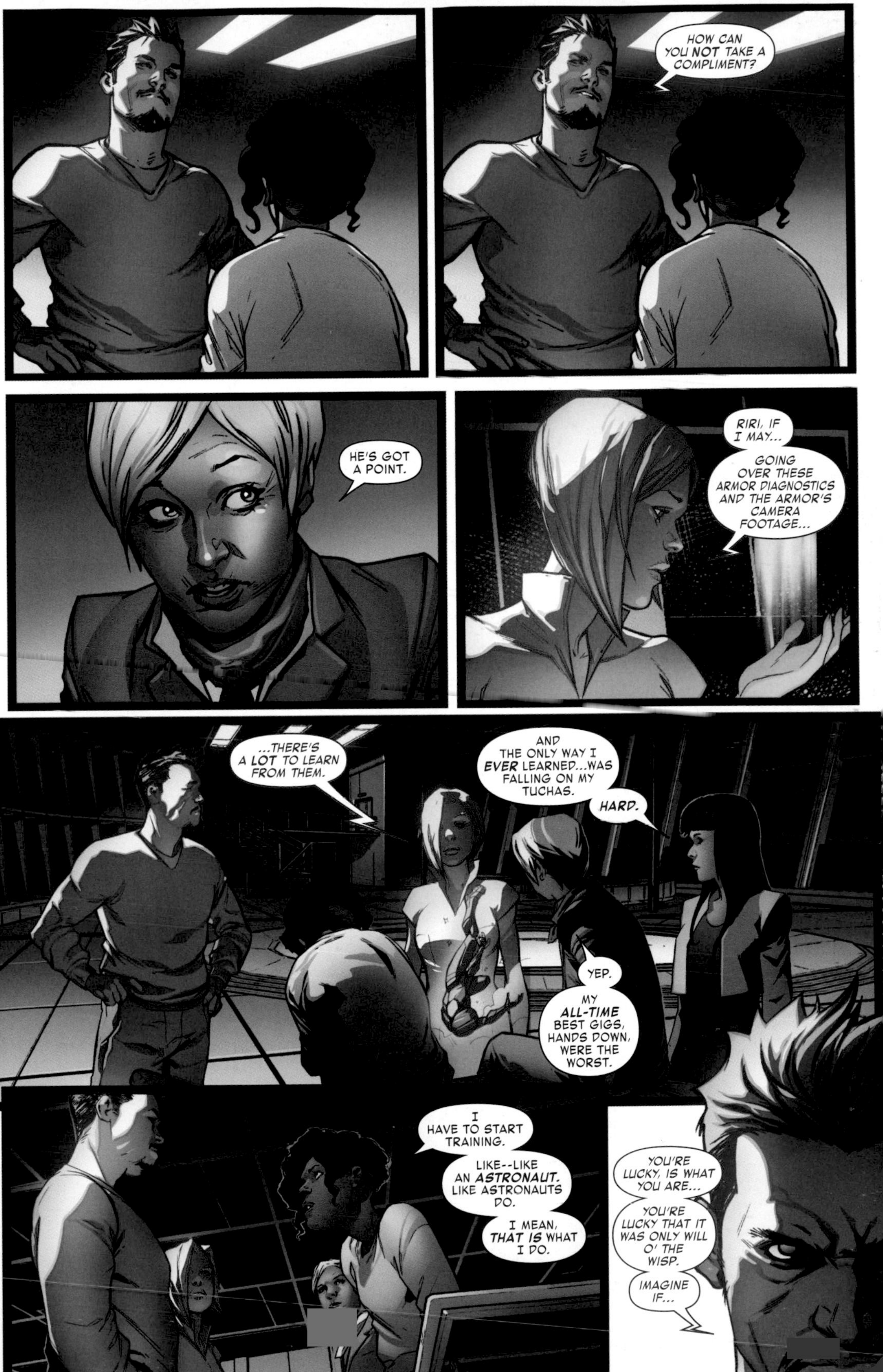
HOW CAN YOU NOT TAKE A COMPLIMENT?
HE'S GOT A POINT.
RIRI, IF I MAY...
GOING OVER THESE ARMOR DIAGNOSTICS AND THE ARMOR'S CAMERA FOOTAGE...
...THERE'S A LOT TO LEARN FROM THEM.
AND THE ONLY WAY I EVER LEARNED...WAS FALLING ON MY TUCHAS.
HARD.
YEP.
MY ALL-TIME BEST GIGS, HANDS DOWN, WERE THE WORST.
I HAVE TO START TRAINING.
LIKE--LIKE AN ASTRONAUT. LIKE ASTRONAUTS DO.
I MEAN, THAT IS WHAT I DO.
YOU'RE LUCKY, IS WHAT YOU ARE...
YOU'RE LUCKY THAT IT WAS ONLY WILL O' THE WISP.
IMAGINE IF...

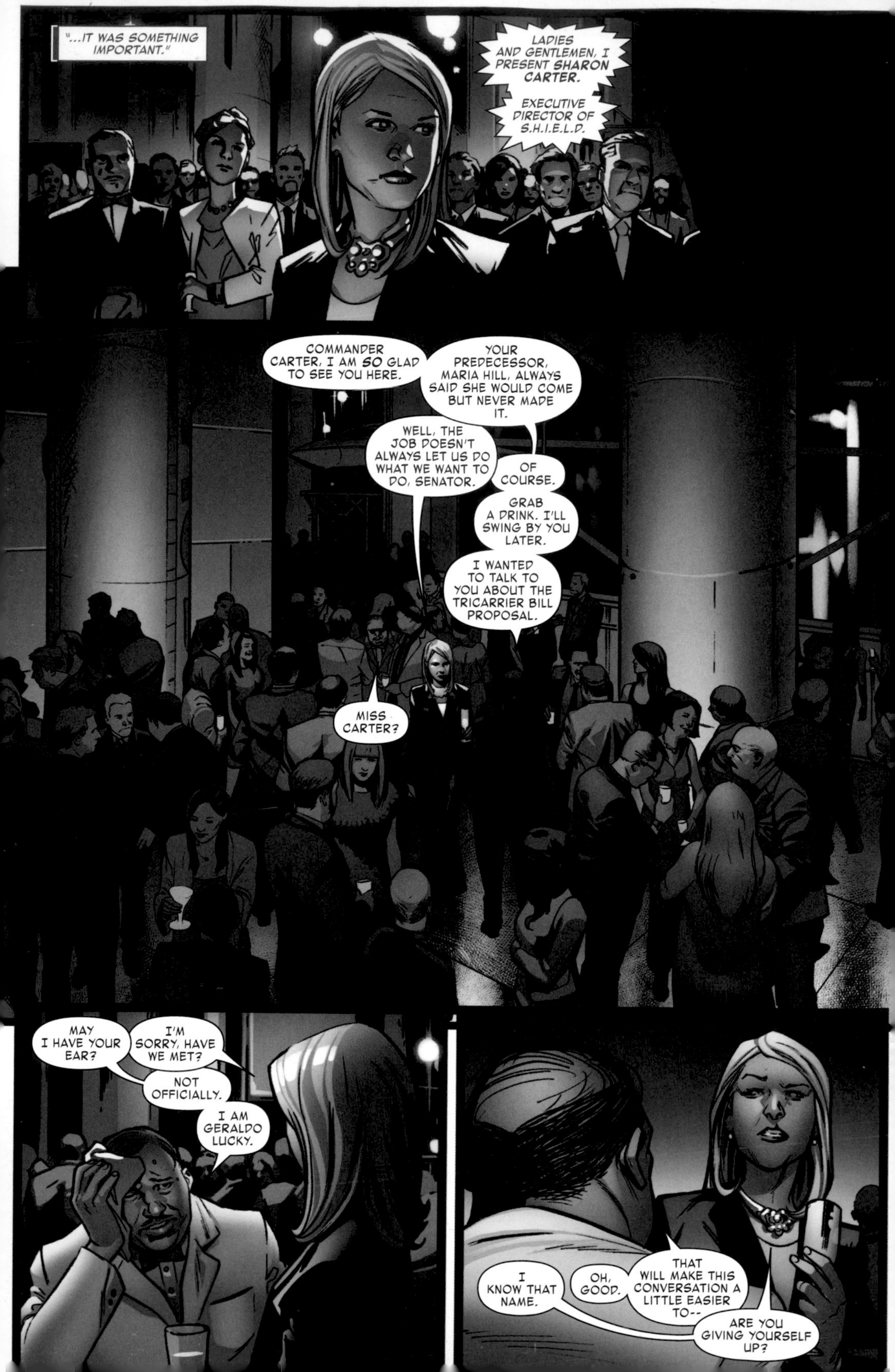
"...IT WAS SOMETHING IMPORTANT."
LADIES AND GENTLEMEN, I PRESENT SHARON CARTER.
EXECUTIVE DIRECTOR OF S.H.I.E.L.D.
COMMANDER CARTER, I AM SO GLAD TO SEE YOU HERE.
YOUR PREDECESSOR, MARIA HILL, ALWAYS SAID SHE WOULD COME BUT NEVER MADE IT.
WELL, THE JOB DOESN'T ALWAYS LET US DO WHAT WE WANT TO DO, SENATOR.
OF COURSE.
GRAB A DRINK. I'LL SWING BY YOU LATER.
I WANTED TO TALK TO YOU ABOUT THE TRICARRIER BILL PROPOSAL.
MISS CARTER?
MAY I HAVE YOUR EAR?
I'M SORRY, HAVE WE MET?
NOT OFFICIALLY.
I AM GERALDO LUCKY.
I KNOW THAT NAME.
OH, GOOD.
THAT WILL MAKE THIS CONVERSATION A LITTLE EASIER TO--
ARE YOU GIVING YOURSELF UP?

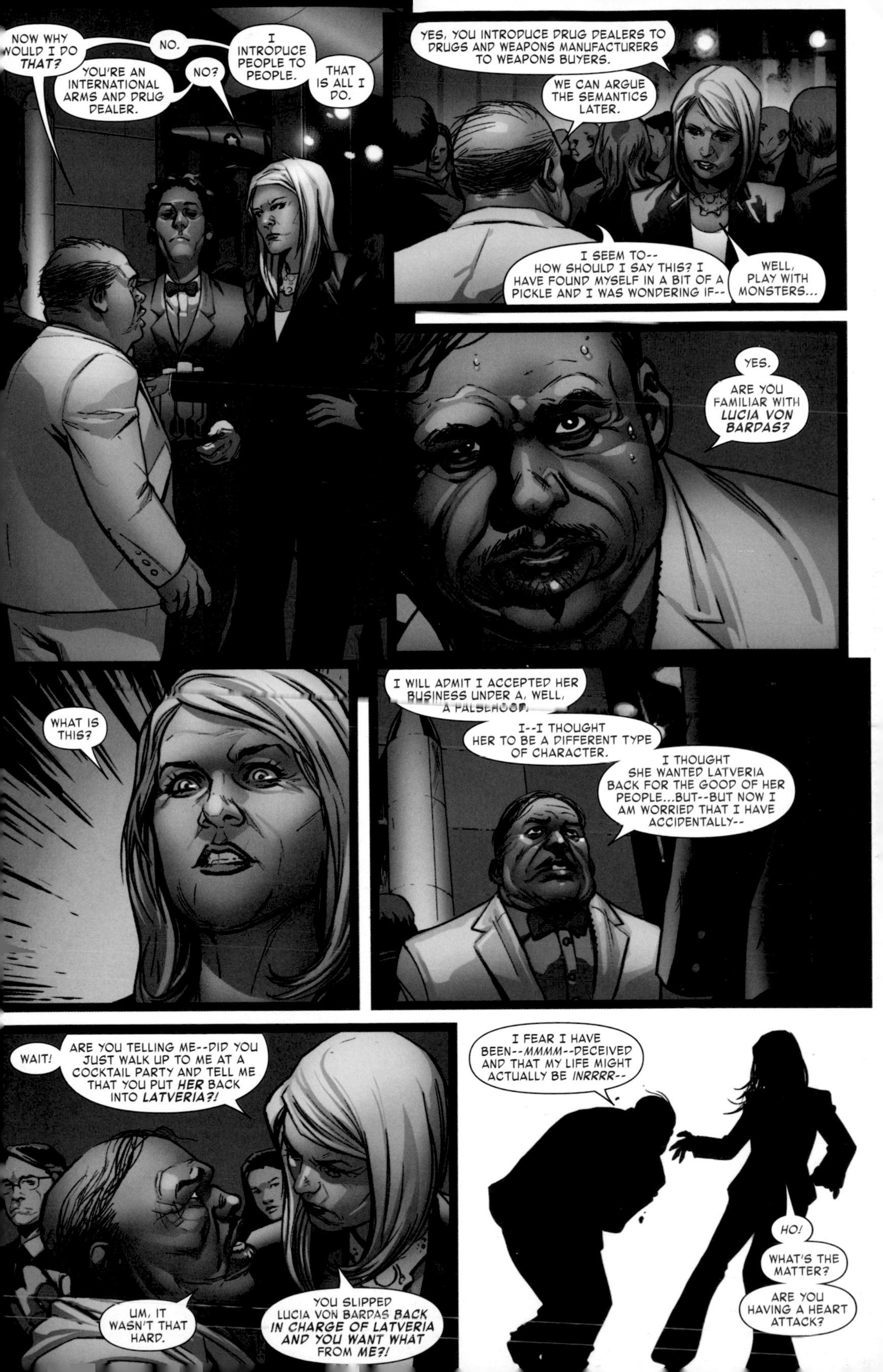

NOW WHY WOULD I DO *THAT?*
NO.
YOU'RE AN INTERNATIONAL ARMS AND DRUG DEALER.
NO?
I INTRODUCE PEOPLE TO PEOPLE.
THAT IS ALL I DO.
YES, YOU INTRODUCE DRUG DEALERS TO DRUGS AND WEAPONS MANUFACTURERS TO WEAPONS BUYERS.
WE CAN ARGUE THE SEMANTICS LATER.
I SEEM TO-- HOW SHOULD I SAY THIS? I HAVE FOUND MYSELF IN A BIT OF A PICKLE AND I WAS WONDERING IF--
WELL, PLAY WITH MONSTERS...
YES.
ARE YOU FAMILIAR WITH *LUCIA VON BARDAS?*
WHAT IS THIS?
I WILL ADMIT I ACCEPTED HER BUSINESS UNDER A, WELL, A FALSEHOOD.
I--I THOUGHT HER TO BE A DIFFERENT TYPE OF CHARACTER.
I THOUGHT SHE WANTED LATVERIA BACK FOR THE GOOD OF HER PEOPLE...BUT--BUT NOW I AM WORRIED THAT I HAVE ACCIDENTALLY--
WAIT!
ARE YOU TELLING ME--DID YOU JUST WALK UP TO ME AT A COCKTAIL PARTY AND TELL ME THAT YOU PUT *HER* BACK INTO *LATVERIA?!*
UM, IT WASN'T THAT HARD.
YOU SLIPPED LUCIA VON BARDAS *BACK IN CHARGE OF LATVERIA AND YOU WANT WHAT FROM ME?!*
I FEAR I HAVE BEEN--*MMMM*--DECEIVED AND THAT MY LIFE MIGHT ACTUALLY BE *INRRRR*--
HO!
WHAT'S THE MATTER?
ARE YOU HAVING A HEART ATTACK?

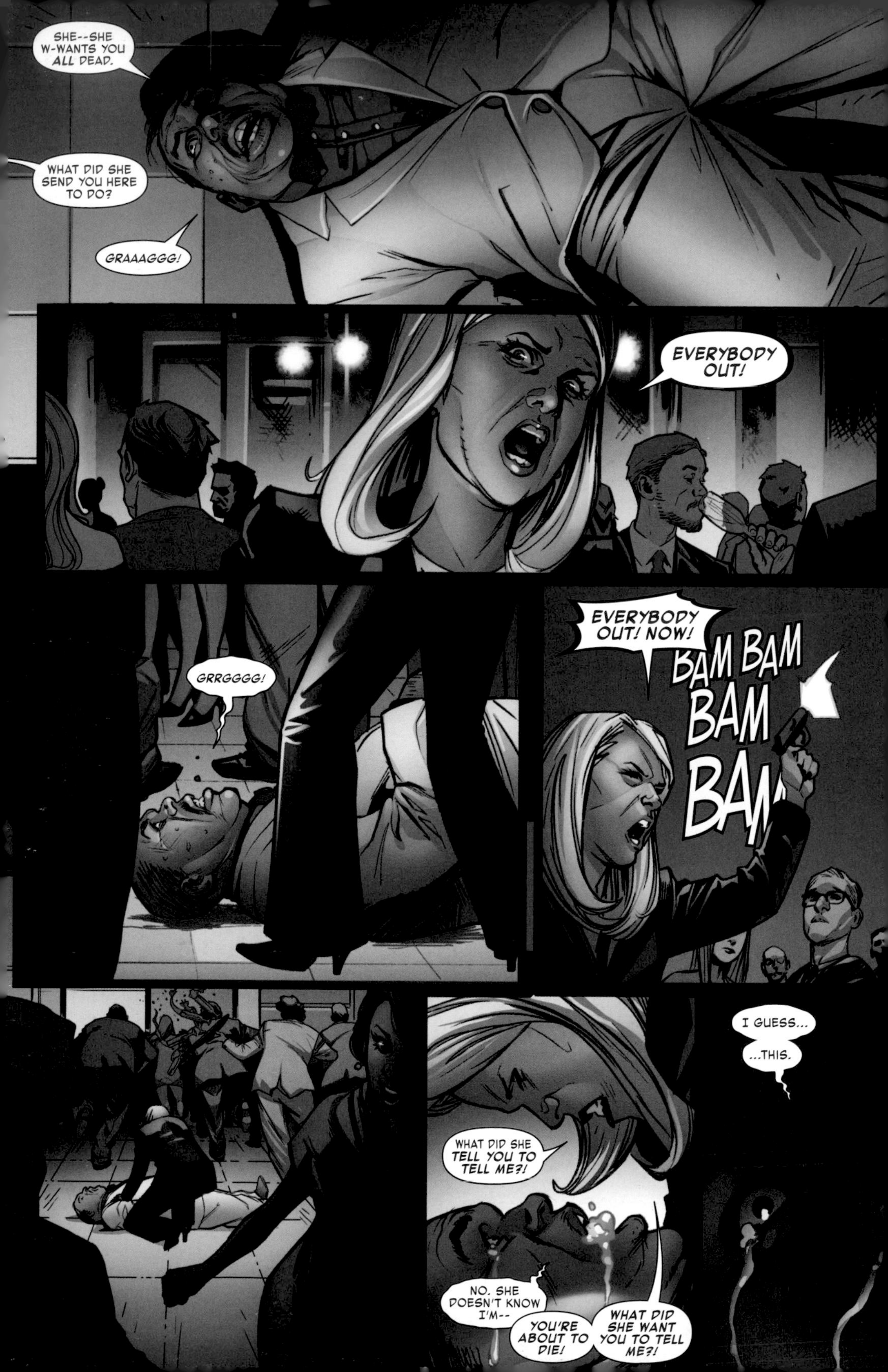
SHE--SHE W-WANTS YOU ALL DEAD.
WHAT DID SHE SEND YOU HERE TO DO?
GRAAAGGG!
EVERYBODY OUT!
GRRGGGG!
EVERYBODY OUT! NOW!
BAM BAM BAM BAM
I GUESS...
...THIS.
WHAT DID SHE TELL YOU TO TELL ME?!
NO. SHE DOESN'T KNOW I'M--
YOU'RE ABOUT TO DIE!
WHAT DID SHE WANT YOU TO TELL ME?!

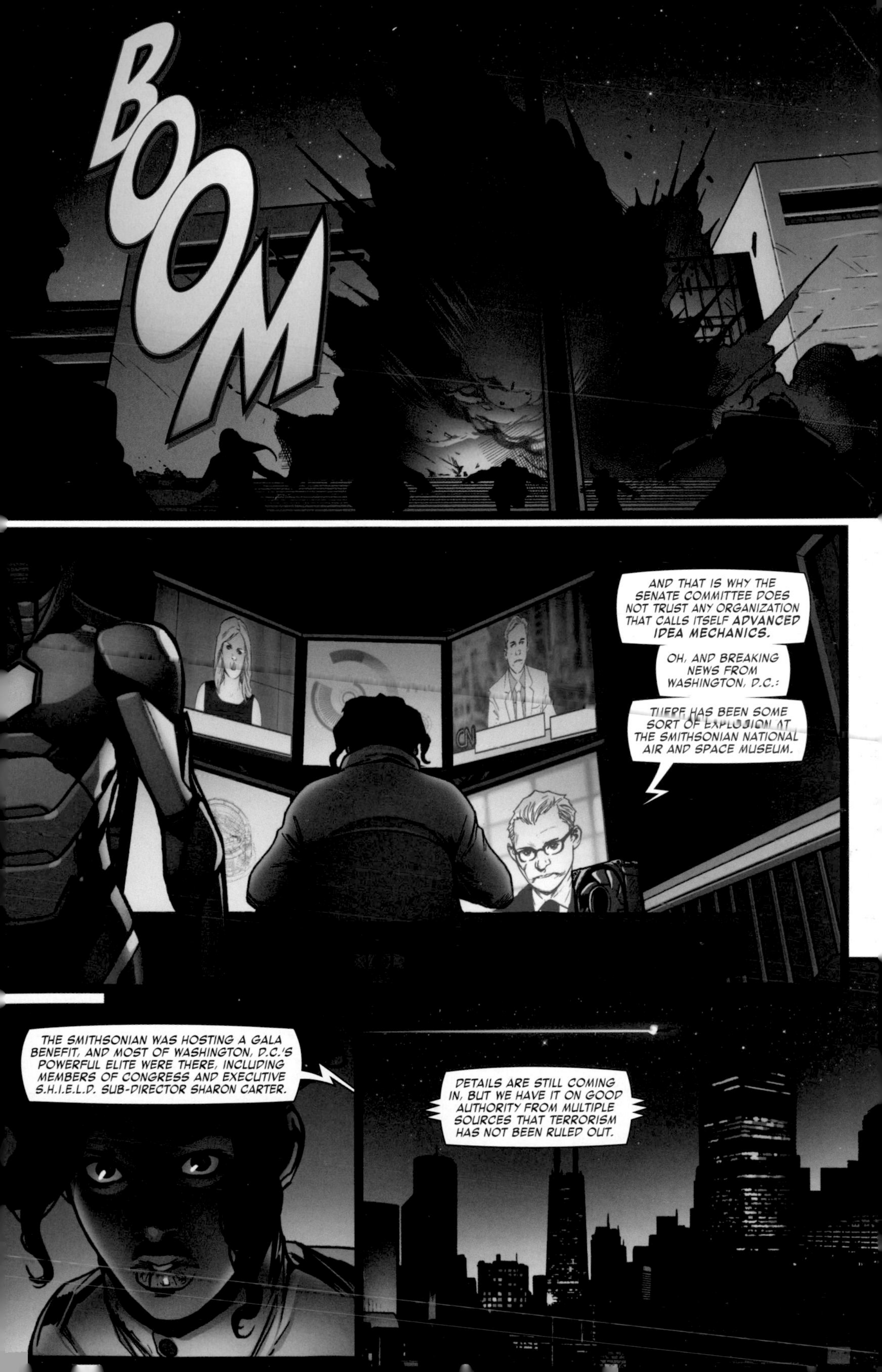
BOOM
AND THAT IS WHY THE SENATE COMMITTEE DOES NOT TRUST ANY ORGANIZATION THAT CALLS ITSELF ADVANCED IDEA MECHANICS.
OH, AND BREAKING NEWS FROM WASHINGTON, D.C.:
THERE HAS BEEN SOME SORT OF EXPLOSION AT THE SMITHSONIAN NATIONAL AIR AND SPACE MUSEUM.
THE SMITHSONIAN WAS HOSTING A GALA BENEFIT, AND MOST OF WASHINGTON, D.C.'S POWERFUL ELITE WERE THERE, INCLUDING MEMBERS OF CONGRESS AND EXECUTIVE S.H.I.E.L.D. SUB-DIRECTOR SHARON CARTER.
DETAILS ARE STILL COMING IN, BUT WE HAVE IT ON GOOD AUTHORITY FROM MULTIPLE SOURCES THAT TERRORISM HAS NOT BEEN RULED OUT.

8

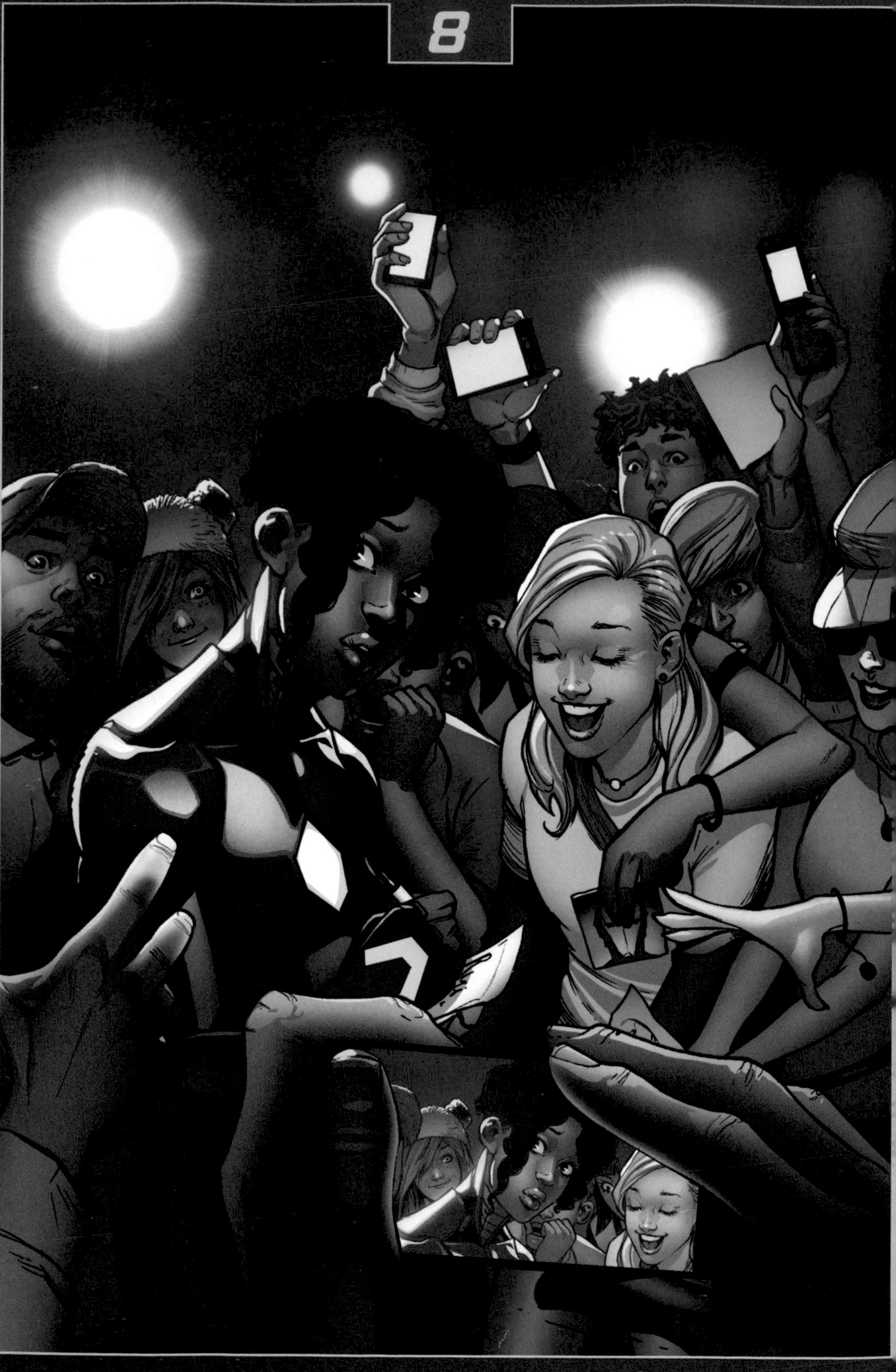

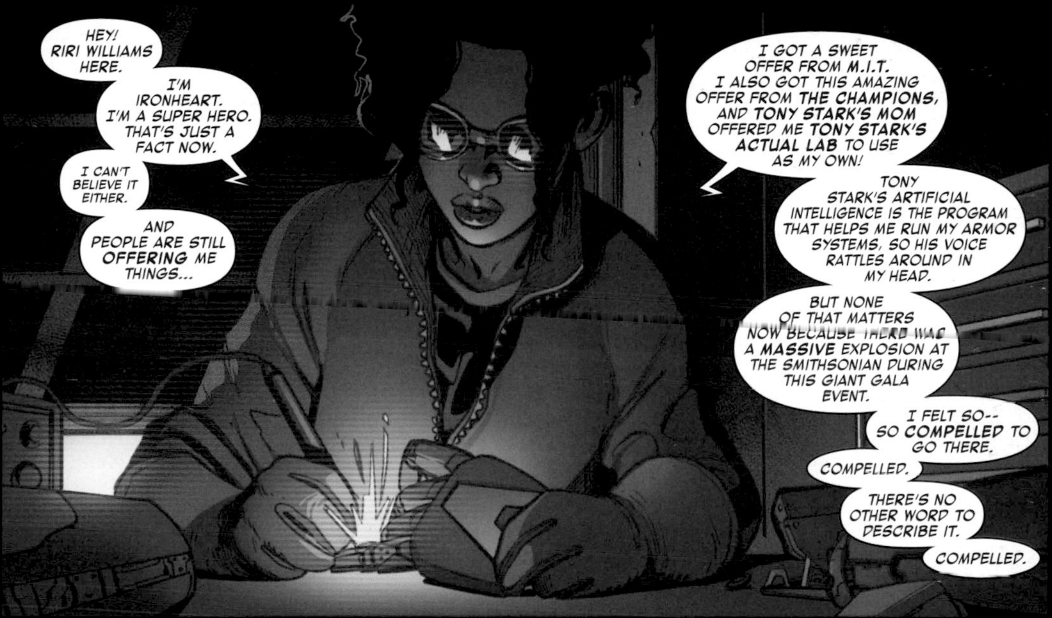
HEY! RIRI WILLIAMS HERE.
I'M IRONHEART. I'M A SUPER HERO. THAT'S JUST A FACT NOW.
I CAN'T BELIEVE IT EITHER.
AND PEOPLE ARE STILL **OFFERING** ME THINGS...
I GOT A SWEET OFFER FROM **M.I.T.** I ALSO GOT THIS AMAZING OFFER FROM **THE CHAMPIONS,** AND **TONY STARK'S MOM** OFFERED ME **TONY STARK'S ACTUAL LAB** TO USE AS MY OWN!
TONY STARK'S ARTIFICIAL INTELLIGENCE IS THE PROGRAM THAT HELPS ME RUN MY ARMOR SYSTEMS, SO HIS VOICE RATTLES AROUND IN MY HEAD.
BUT NONE OF THAT MATTERS NOW BECAUSE THERE WAS A **MASSIVE** EXPLOSION AT THE SMITHSONIAN DURING THIS GIANT GALA EVENT.
I FELT SO-- SO **COMPELLED** TO GO THERE.
COMPELLED.
THERE'S NO OTHER WORD TO DESCRIBE IT.
COMPELLED.

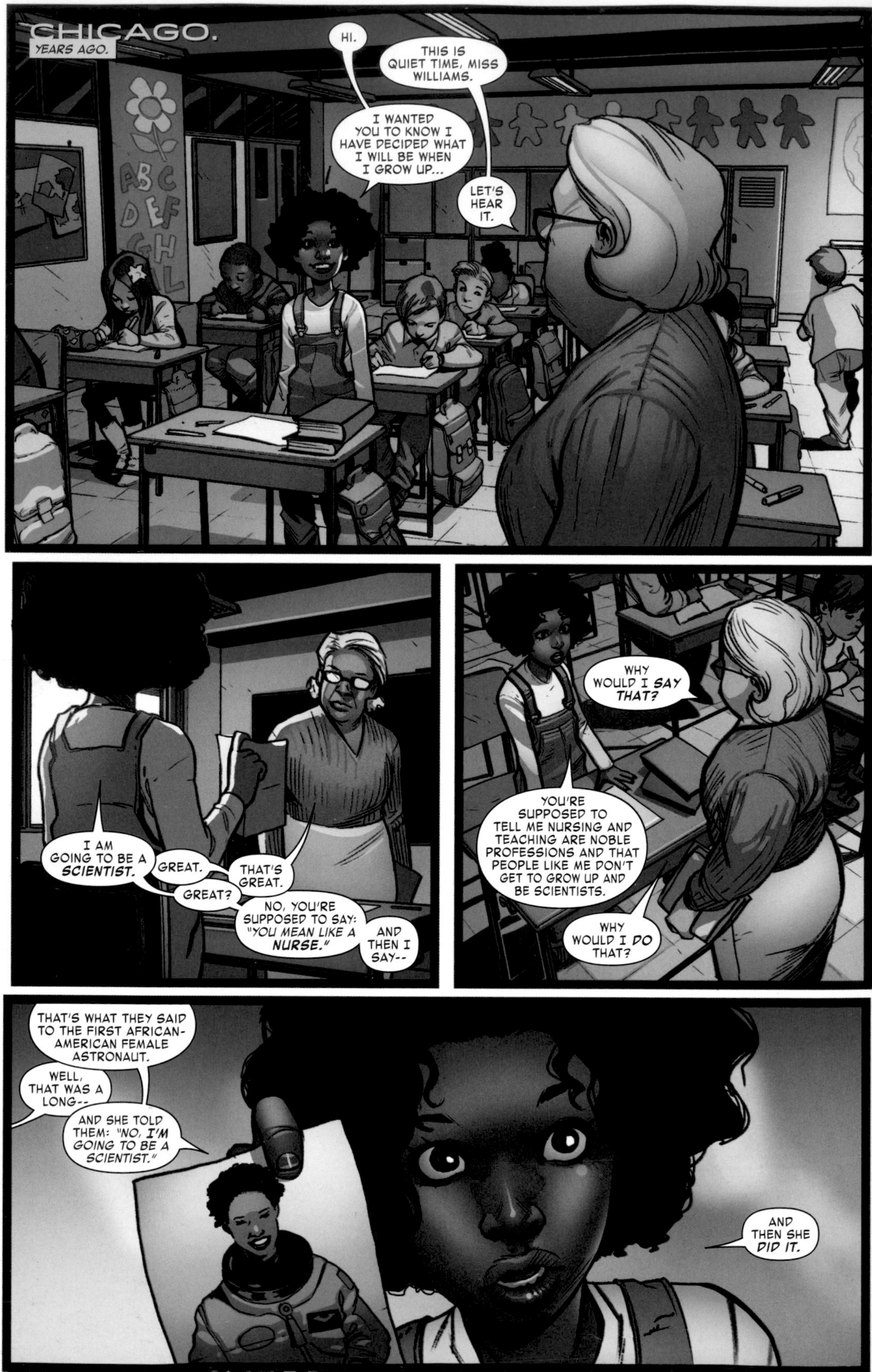
CHICAGO.
YEARS AGO.
HI.
THIS IS QUIET TIME, MISS WILLIAMS.
I WANTED YOU TO KNOW I HAVE DECIDED WHAT I WILL BE WHEN I GROW UP...
LET'S HEAR IT.
I AM GOING TO BE A SCIENTIST.
GREAT.
THAT'S GREAT.
GREAT?
NO, YOU'RE SUPPOSED TO SAY: "YOU MEAN LIKE A NURSE."
AND THEN I SAY--
WHY WOULD I SAY THAT?
YOU'RE SUPPOSED TO TELL ME NURSING AND TEACHING ARE NOBLE PROFESSIONS AND THAT PEOPLE LIKE ME DON'T GET TO GROW UP AND BE SCIENTISTS.
WHY WOULD I DO THAT?
THAT'S WHAT THEY SAID TO THE FIRST AFRICAN-AMERICAN FEMALE ASTRONAUT.
WELL, THAT WAS A LONG--
AND SHE TOLD THEM: "NO, I'M GOING TO BE A SCIENTIST."
AND THEN SHE DID IT.

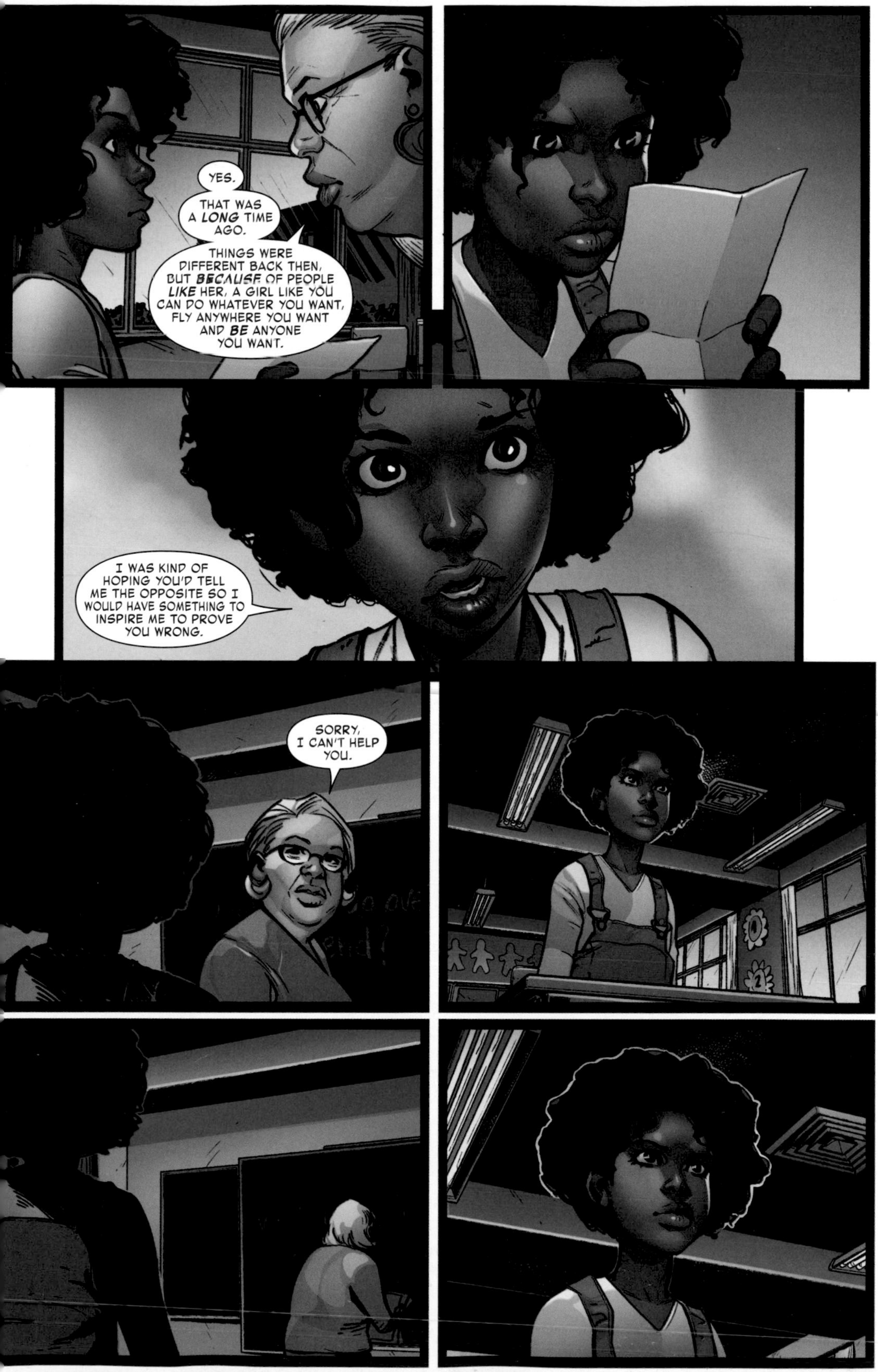
YES.
THAT WAS A *LONG* TIME AGO.
THINGS WERE DIFFERENT BACK THEN, BUT *BECAUSE* OF PEOPLE *LIKE* HER, A GIRL LIKE YOU CAN DO WHATEVER YOU WANT, FLY ANYWHERE YOU WANT AND *BE* ANYONE YOU WANT.
I WAS KIND OF HOPING YOU'D TELL ME THE OPPOSITE SO I WOULD HAVE SOMETHING TO INSPIRE ME TO PROVE YOU WRONG.
SORRY, I CAN'T HELP YOU.

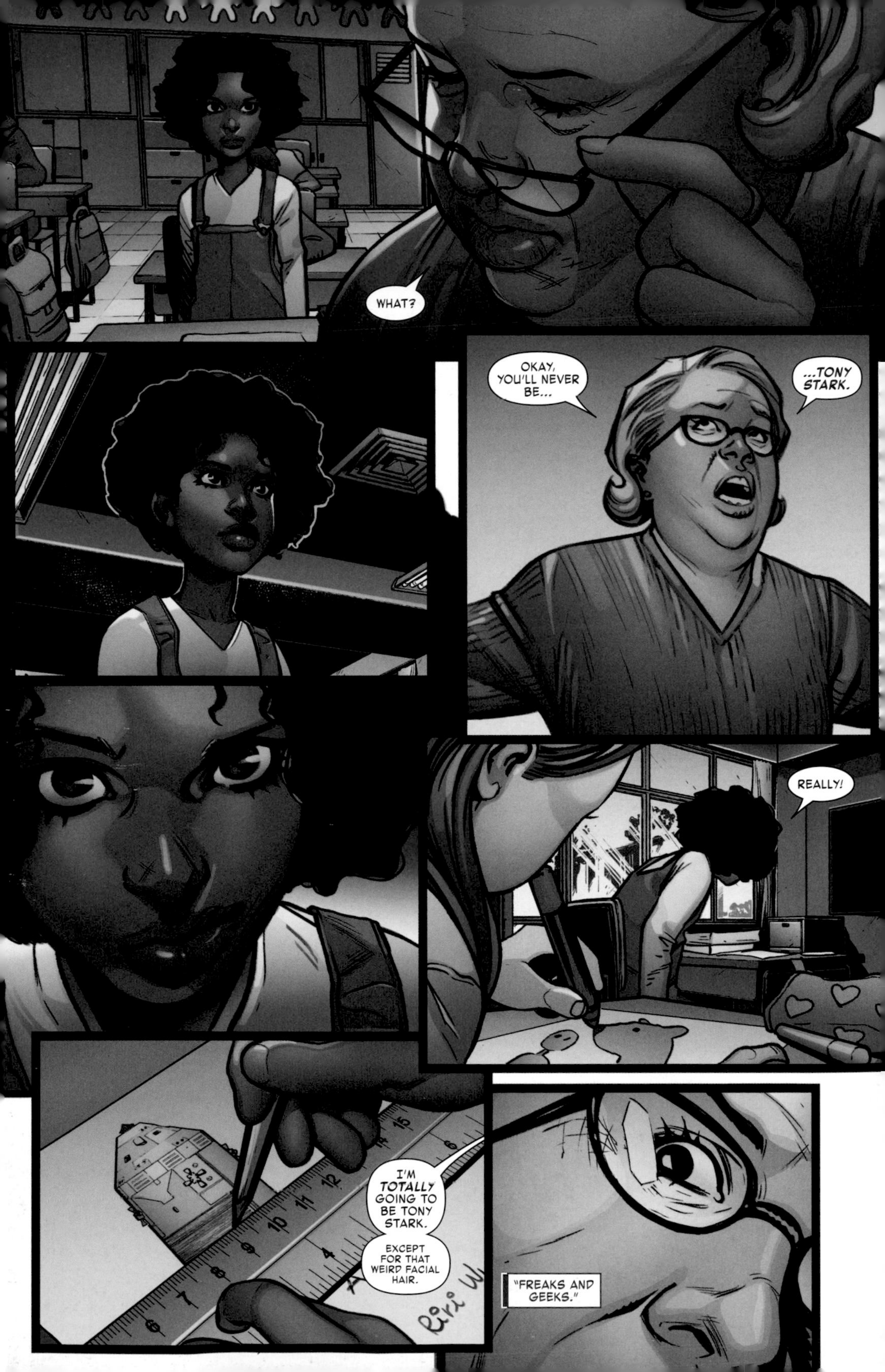
WHAT?
OKAY, YOU'LL NEVER BE...
...TONY STARK.
REALLY!
I'M TOTALLY GOING TO BE TONY STARK.
EXCEPT FOR THAT WEIRD FACIAL HAIR.
"FREAKS AND GEEKS."

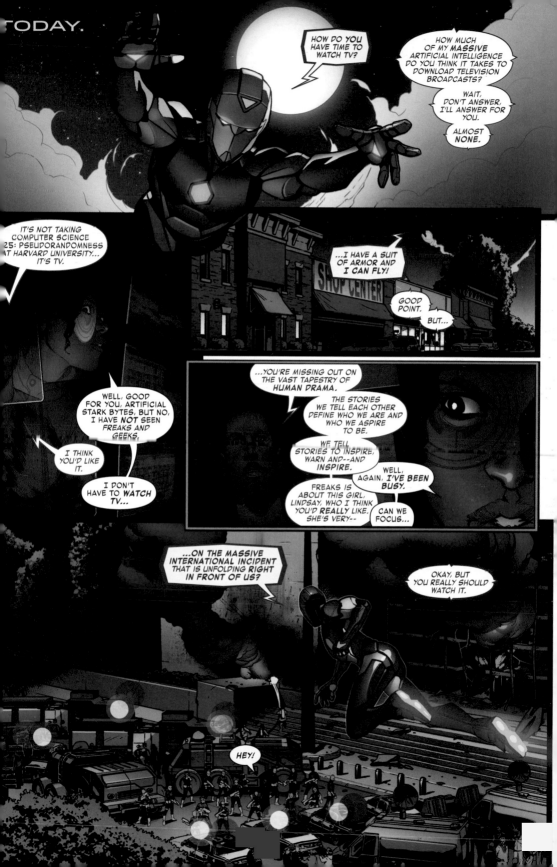

HOW DO YOU HAVE TIME TO WATCH TV?

HOW MUCH OF MY MASSIVE ARTIFICIAL INTELLIGENCE DO YOU THINK IT TAKES TO DOWNLOAD TELEVISION BROADCASTS?

WAIT, DON'T ANSWER, I'LL ANSWER FOR YOU.

ALMOST NONE.

IT'S NOT TAKING COMPUTER SCIENCE 25: PSEUDORANDOMNESS AT HARVARD UNIVERSITY... IT'S TV.

...I HAVE A SUIT OF ARMOR AND I CAN FLY!

GOOD POINT.

BUT...

WELL, GOOD FOR YOU, ARTIFICIAL STARK BYTES, BUT NO, I HAVE NOT SEEN FREAKS AND GEEKS.

I THINK YOU'D LIKE IT.

I DON'T HAVE TO WATCH TV...

...YOU'RE MISSING OUT ON THE VAST TAPESTRY OF HUMAN DRAMA.

THE STORIES WE TELL EACH OTHER DEFINE WHO WE ARE AND WHO WE ASPIRE TO BE.

WE TELL STORIES TO INSPIRE, WARN AND--AND INSPIRE.

FREAKS IS ABOUT THIS GIRL, LINDSAY, WHO I THINK YOU'D REALLY LIKE. SHE'S VERY--

WELL, AGAIN, I'VE BEEN BUSY.

CAN WE FOCUS...

...ON THE MASSIVE INTERNATIONAL INCIDENT THAT IS UNFOLDING RIGHT IN FRONT OF US?

OKAY, BUT YOU REALLY SHOULD WATCH IT.

HEY!

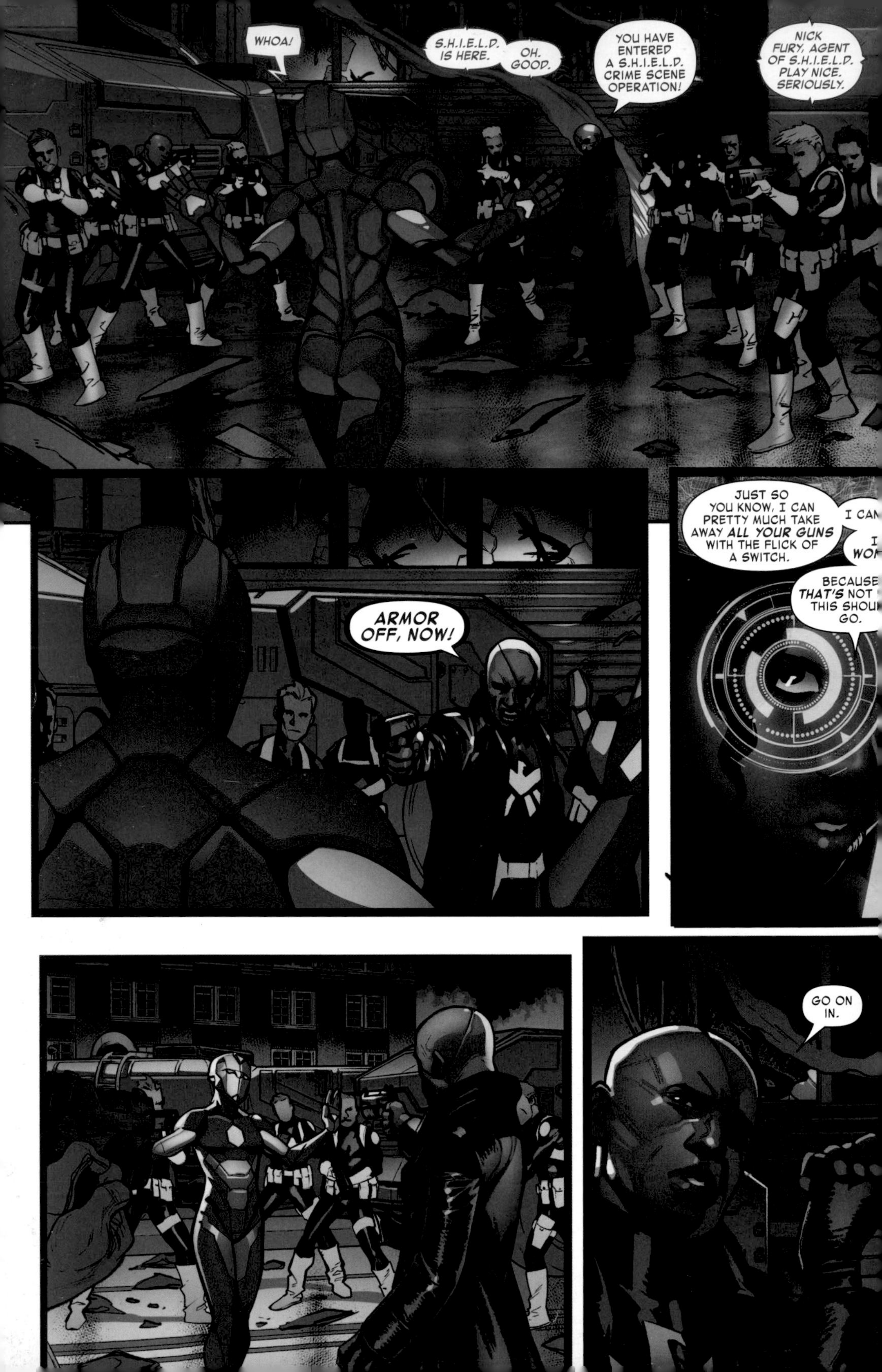
WHOA!
S.H.I.E.L.D. IS HERE.
OH. GOOD.
YOU HAVE ENTERED A S.H.I.E.L.D. CRIME SCENE OPERATION!
NICK FURY, AGENT OF S.H.I.E.L.D. PLAY NICE. SERIOUSLY.
ARMOR OFF, NOW!
JUST SO YOU KNOW, I CAN PRETTY MUCH TAKE AWAY ALL YOUR GUNS WITH THE FLICK OF A SWITCH.
GO ON IN.

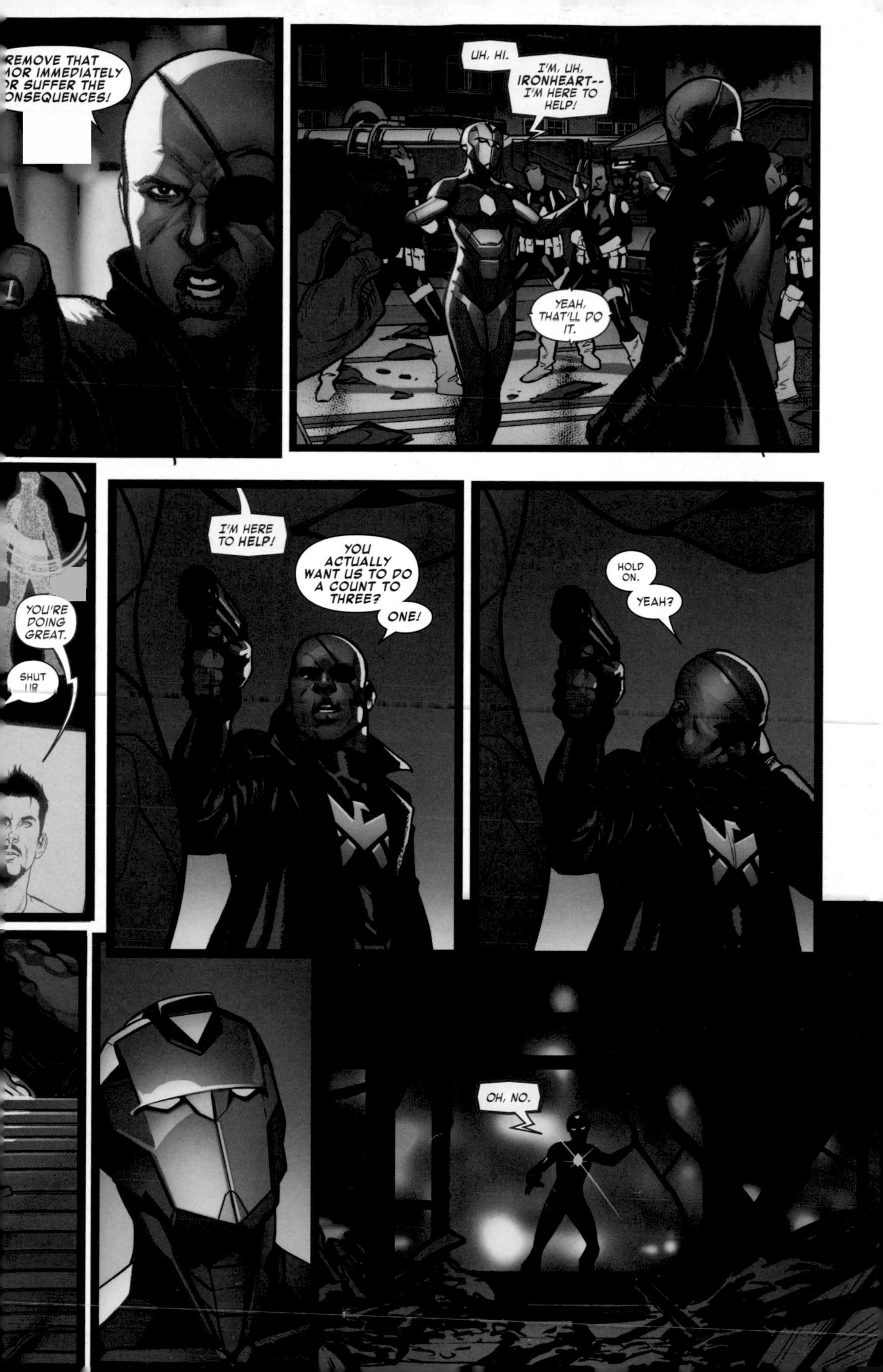

REMOVE THAT MOR IMMEDIATELY OR SUFFER THE ONSEQUENCES!
UH, HI.
I'M, UH, IRONHEART-- I'M HERE TO HELP!
YEAH, THAT'LL DO IT.
YOU'RE DOING GREAT.
SHUT
I'M HERE TO HELP!
YOU ACTUALLY WANT US TO DO A COUNT TO THREE?
ONE!
HOLD ON.
YEAH?
OH, NO.

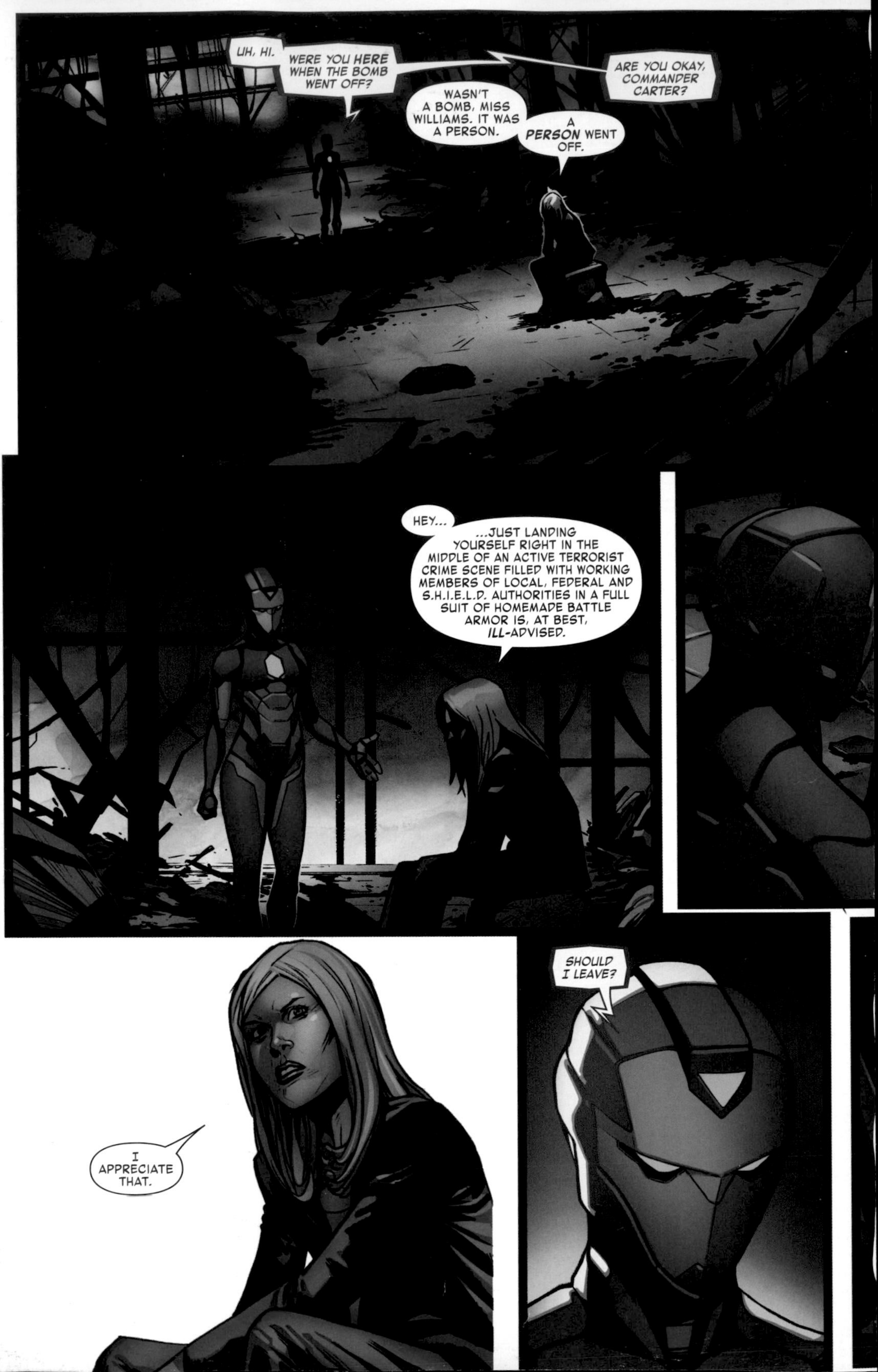
UH, HI.
WERE YOU HERE WHEN THE BOMB WENT OFF?
ARE YOU OKAY, COMMANDER CARTER?
WASN'T A BOMB, MISS WILLIAMS. IT WAS A PERSON.
A PERSON WENT OFF.
HEY...
...JUST LANDING YOURSELF RIGHT IN THE MIDDLE OF AN ACTIVE TERRORIST CRIME SCENE FILLED WITH WORKING MEMBERS OF LOCAL, FEDERAL AND S.H.I.E.L.D. AUTHORITIES IN A FULL SUIT OF HOMEMADE BATTLE ARMOR IS, AT BEST, ILL-ADVISED.
SHOULD I LEAVE?
I APPRECIATE THAT.

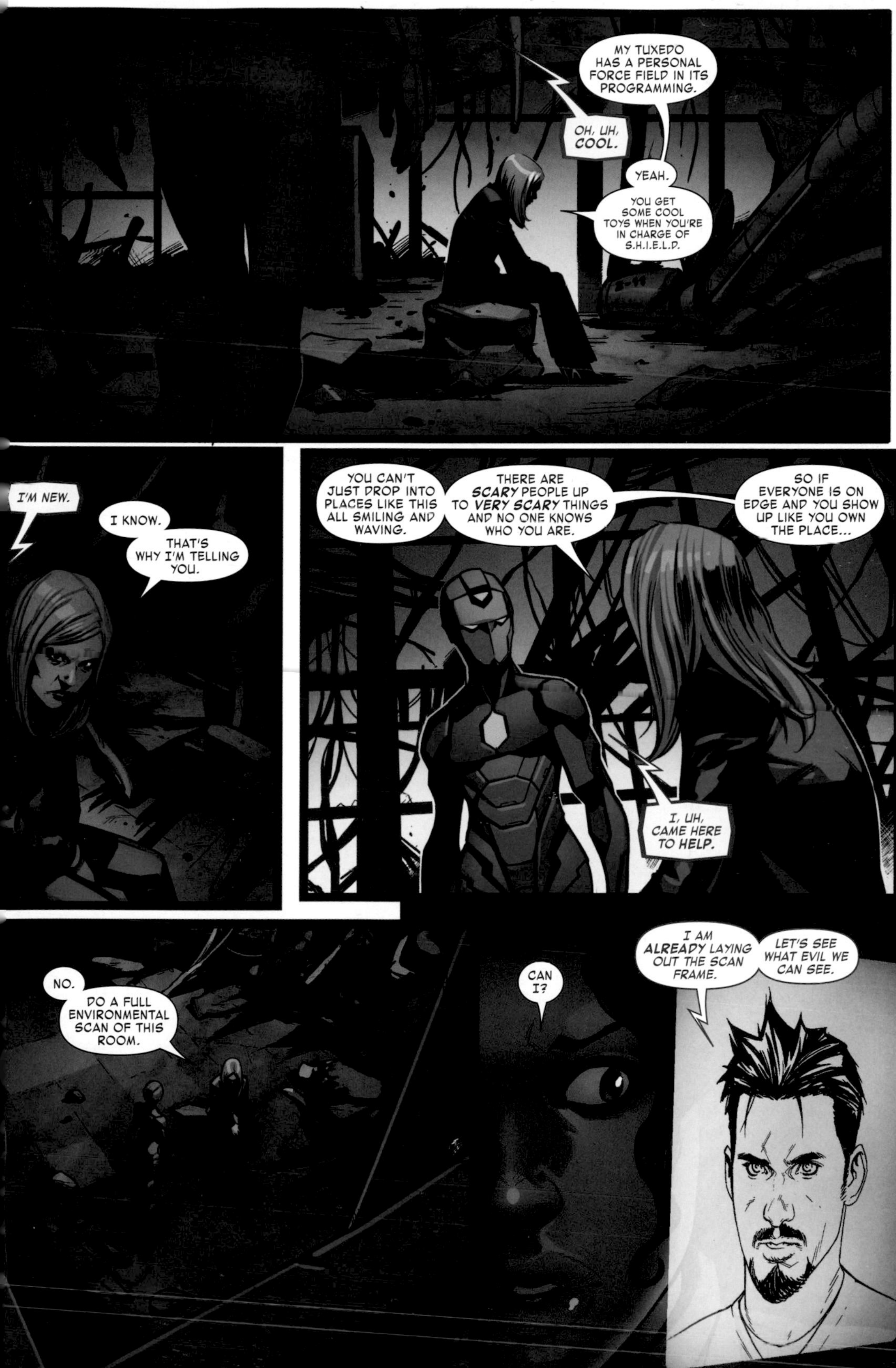
MY TUXEDO HAS A PERSONAL FORCE FIELD IN ITS PROGRAMMING.
OH, UH, COOL.
YEAH.
YOU GET SOME COOL TOYS WHEN YOU'RE IN CHARGE OF S.H.I.E.L.D.
I'M NEW.
I KNOW.
THAT'S WHY I'M TELLING YOU.
YOU CAN'T JUST DROP INTO PLACES LIKE THIS ALL SMILING AND WAVING.
THERE ARE SCARY PEOPLE UP TO VERY SCARY THINGS AND NO ONE KNOWS WHO YOU ARE.
SO IF EVERYONE IS ON EDGE AND YOU SHOW UP LIKE YOU OWN THE PLACE...
I, UH, CAME HERE TO HELP.
NO.
DO A FULL ENVIRONMENTAL SCAN OF THIS ROOM.
CAN I?
I AM ALREADY LAYING OUT THE SCAN FRAME.
LET'S SEE WHAT EVIL WE CAN SEE.

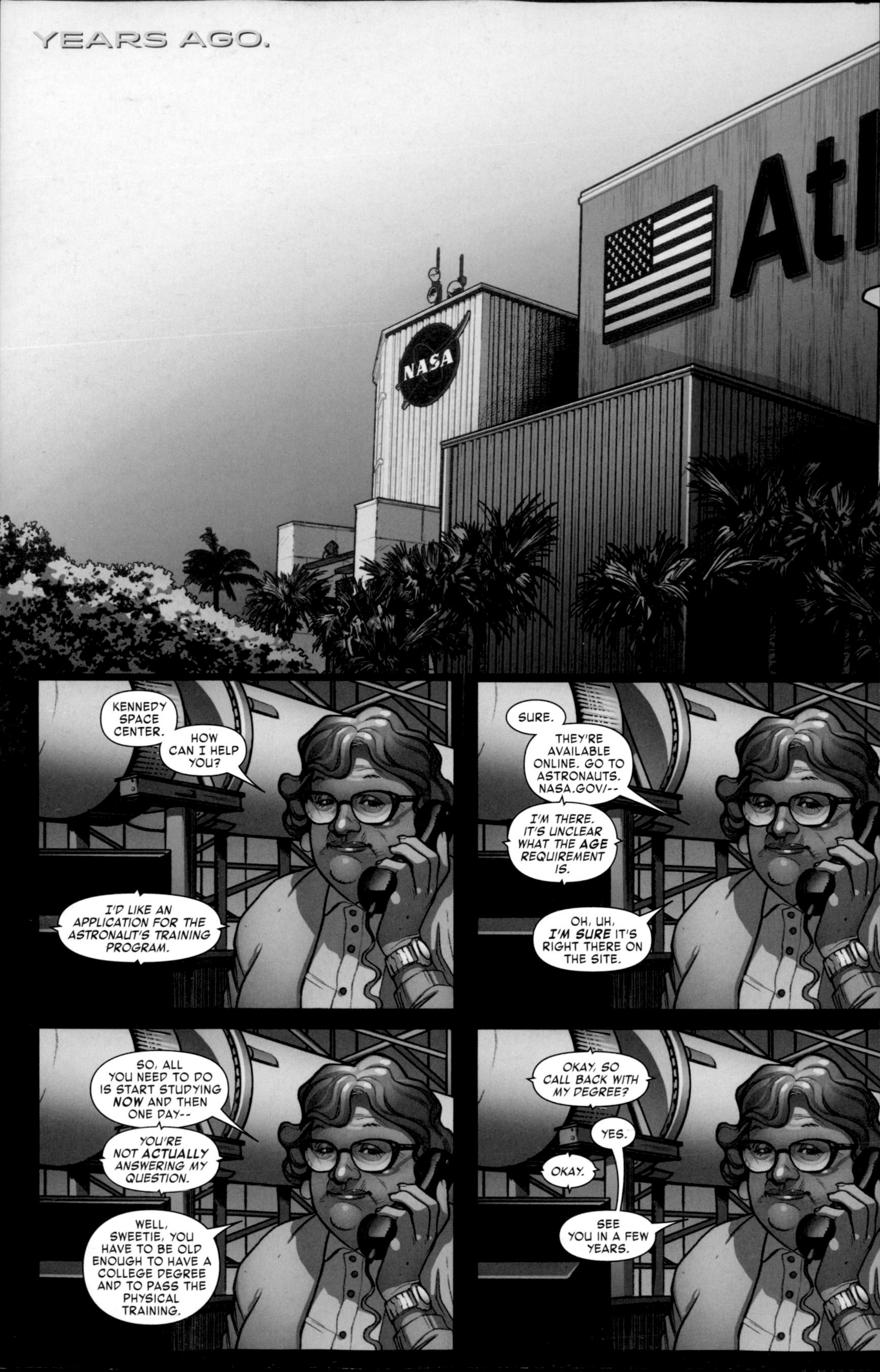
YEARS AGO.
NASA
KENNEDY SPACE CENTER.
HOW CAN I HELP YOU?
I'D LIKE AN APPLICATION FOR THE ASTRONAUT'S TRAINING PROGRAM.
SURE.
THEY'RE AVAILABLE ONLINE. GO TO ASTRONAUTS. NASA.GOV/--
I'M THERE. IT'S UNCLEAR WHAT THE AGE REQUIREMENT IS.
OH, UH, I'M SURE IT'S RIGHT THERE ON THE SITE.
SO, ALL YOU NEED TO DO IS START STUDYING NOW AND THEN ONE DAY--
YOU'RE NOT ACTUALLY ANSWERING MY QUESTION.
WELL, SWEETIE, YOU HAVE TO BE OLD ENOUGH TO HAVE A COLLEGE DEGREE AND TO PASS THE PHYSICAL TRAINING.
OKAY, SO CALL BACK WITH MY DEGREE?
YES.
OKAY.
SEE YOU IN A FEW YEARS.

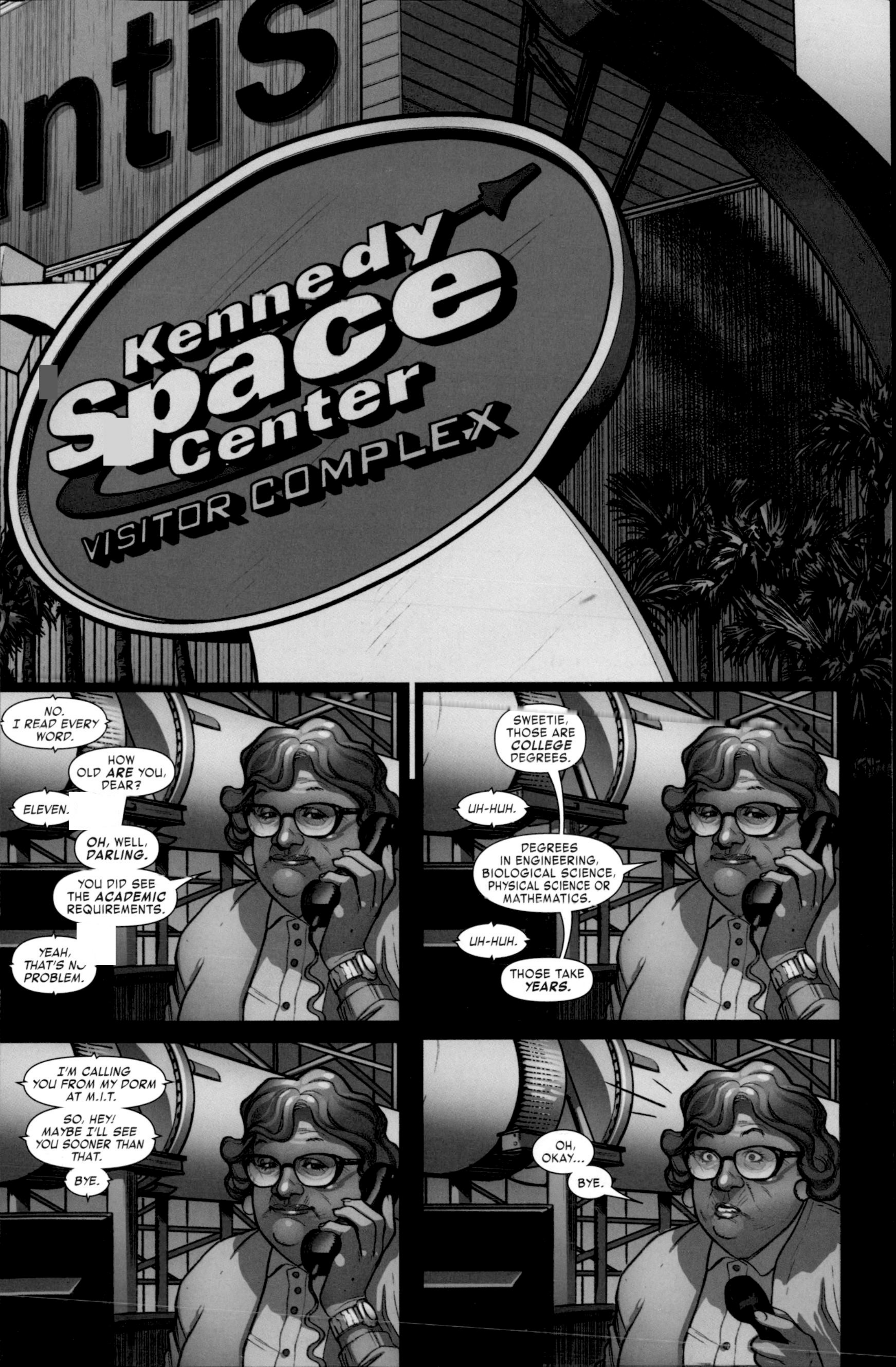
Kennedy Space Center
VISITOR COMPLEX
NO. I READ EVERY WORD.
HOW OLD ARE YOU, DEAR?
ELEVEN.
OH, WELL, DARLING.
YOU DID SEE THE ACADEMIC REQUIREMENTS.
YEAH, THAT'S NO PROBLEM.
SWEETIE, THOSE ARE COLLEGE DEGREES.
UH-HUH.
DEGREES IN ENGINEERING, BIOLOGICAL SCIENCE, PHYSICAL SCIENCE OR MATHEMATICS.
UH-HUH.
THOSE TAKE YEARS.
I'M CALLING YOU FROM MY DORM AT M.I.T.
SO, HEY! MAYBE I'LL SEE YOU SOONER THAN THAT.
BYE.
OH, OKAY...
BYE.

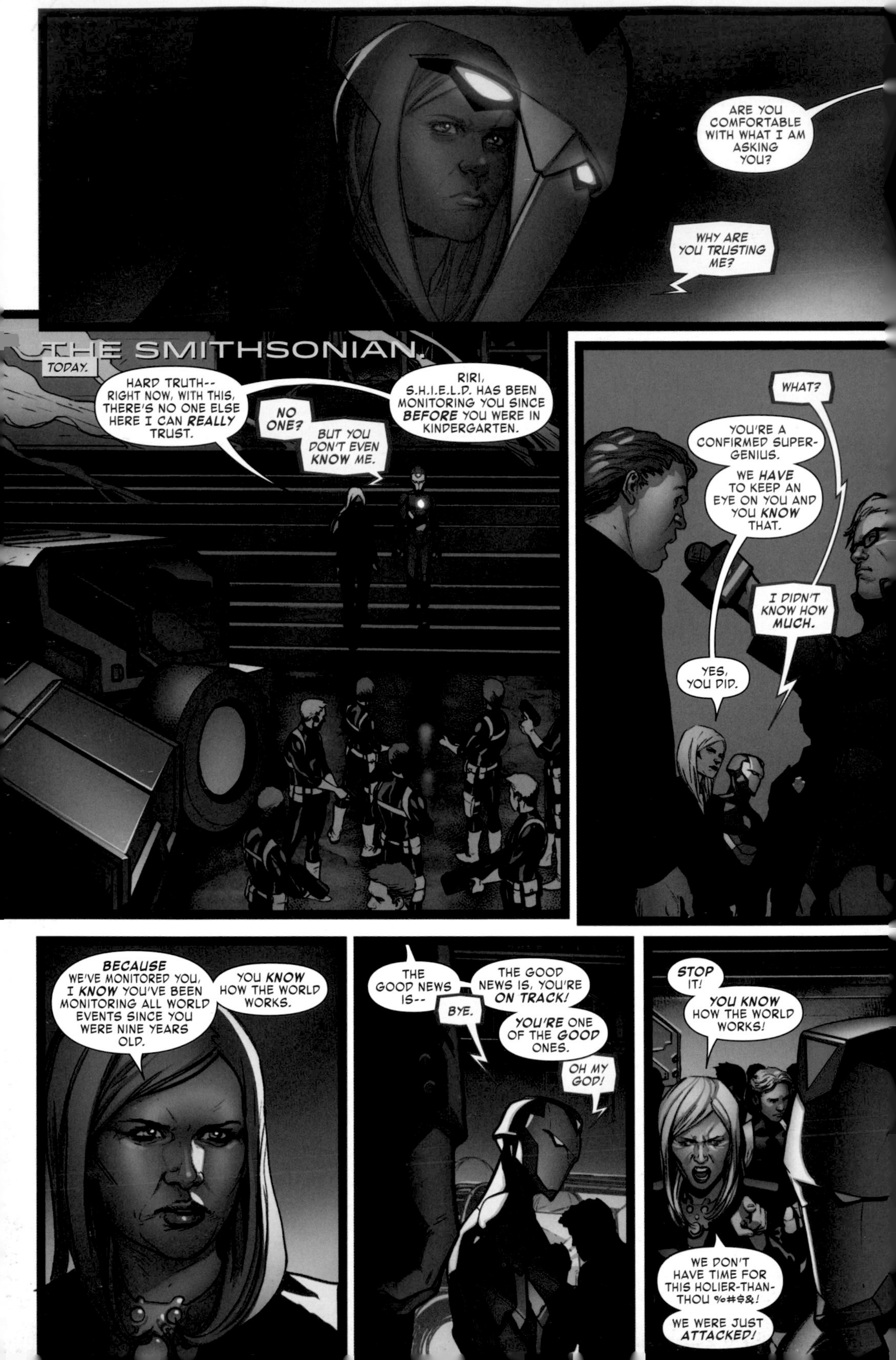
ARE YOU COMFORTABLE WITH WHAT I AM ASKING YOU?
WHY ARE YOU TRUSTING ME?
THE SMITHSONIAN.
TODAY.
HARD TRUTH-- RIGHT NOW, WITH THIS, THERE'S NO ONE ELSE HERE I CAN REALLY TRUST.
NO ONE?
BUT YOU DON'T EVEN KNOW ME.
RIRI, S.H.I.E.L.D. HAS BEEN MONITORING YOU SINCE BEFORE YOU WERE IN KINDERGARTEN.
WHAT?
YOU'RE A CONFIRMED SUPER-GENIUS.
WE HAVE TO KEEP AN EYE ON YOU AND YOU KNOW THAT.
I DIDN'T KNOW HOW MUCH.
YES, YOU DID.
BECAUSE WE'VE MONITORED YOU, I KNOW YOU'VE BEEN MONITORING ALL WORLD EVENTS SINCE YOU WERE NINE YEARS OLD.
YOU KNOW HOW THE WORLD WORKS.
THE GOOD NEWS IS--
THE GOOD NEWS IS, YOU'RE ON TRACK!
BYE.
YOU'RE ONE OF THE GOOD ONES.
OH MY GOD!
STOP IT!
YOU KNOW HOW THE WORLD WORKS!
WE DON'T HAVE TIME FOR THIS HOLIER-THAN-THOU %#$&!
WE WERE JUST ATTACKED!

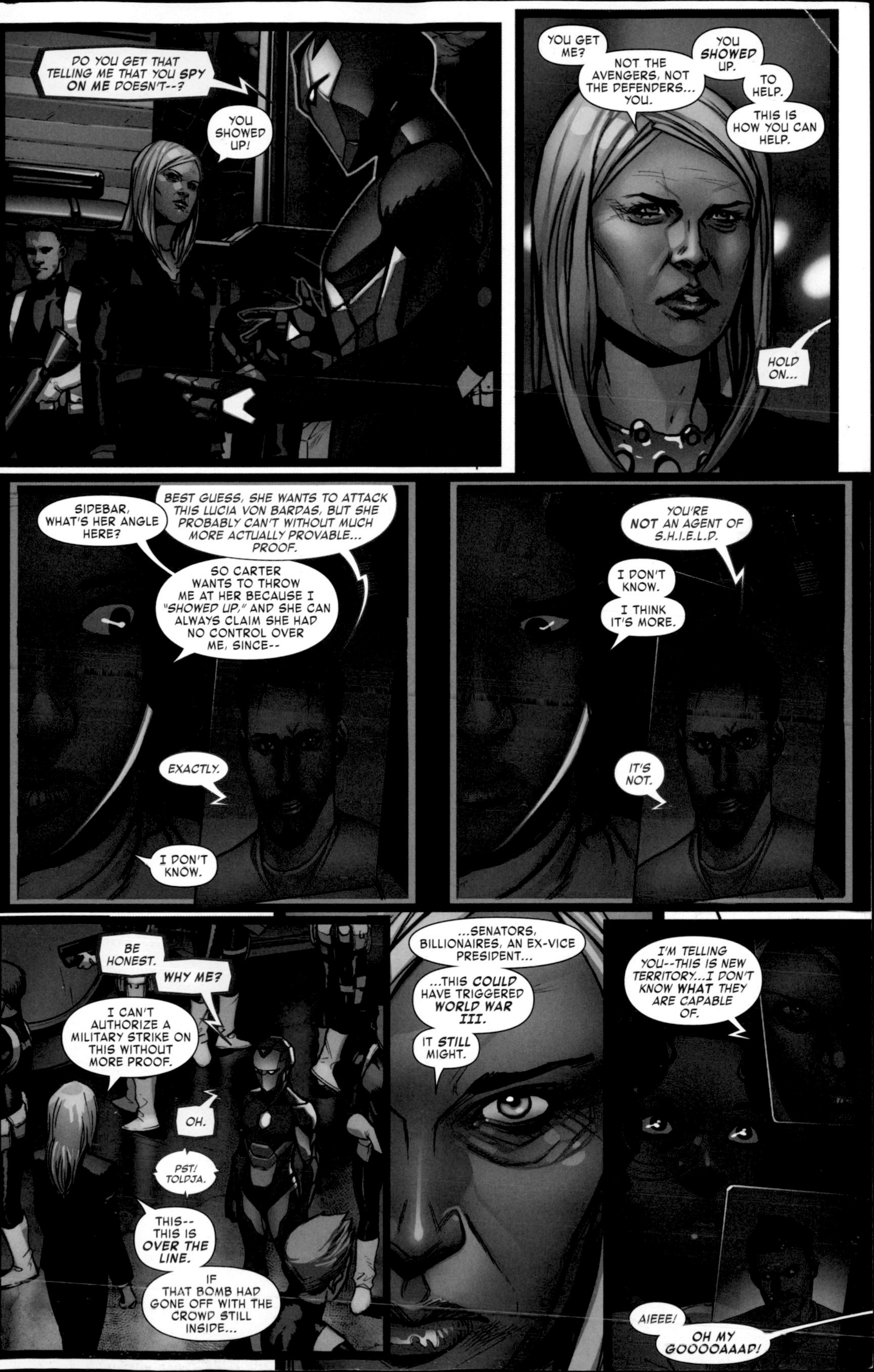
DO YOU GET THAT TELLING ME THAT YOU SPY ON ME DOESN'T--?
YOU SHOWED UP!
YOU GET ME?
NOT THE AVENGERS, NOT THE DEFENDERS... YOU.
YOU SHOWED UP.
TO HELP.
THIS IS HOW YOU CAN HELP.
HOLD ON...
SIDEBAR, WHAT'S HER ANGLE HERE?
BEST GUESS, SHE WANTS TO ATTACK THIS LUCIA VON BARDAS, BUT SHE PROBABLY CAN'T WITHOUT MUCH MORE ACTUALLY PROVABLE... PROOF.
SO CARTER WANTS TO THROW ME AT HER BECAUSE I "SHOWED UP," AND SHE CAN ALWAYS CLAIM SHE HAD NO CONTROL OVER ME, SINCE--
EXACTLY.
I DON'T KNOW.
YOU'RE NOT AN AGENT OF S.H.I.E.L.D.
I DON'T KNOW.
I THINK IT'S MORE.
IT'S NOT.
BE HONEST.
WHY ME?
I CAN'T AUTHORIZE A MILITARY STRIKE ON THIS WITHOUT MORE PROOF.
OH.
PST! TOLDJA.
THIS-- THIS IS OVER THE LINE.
IF THAT BOMB HAD GONE OFF WITH THE CROWD STILL INSIDE...
...SENATORS, BILLIONAIRES, AN EX-VICE PRESIDENT...
...THIS COULD HAVE TRIGGERED WORLD WAR III.
IT STILL MIGHT.
I'M TELLING YOU--THIS IS NEW TERRITORY...I DON'T KNOW WHAT THEY ARE CAPABLE OF.
AIEEE!
OH MY GOOOOAAAD!

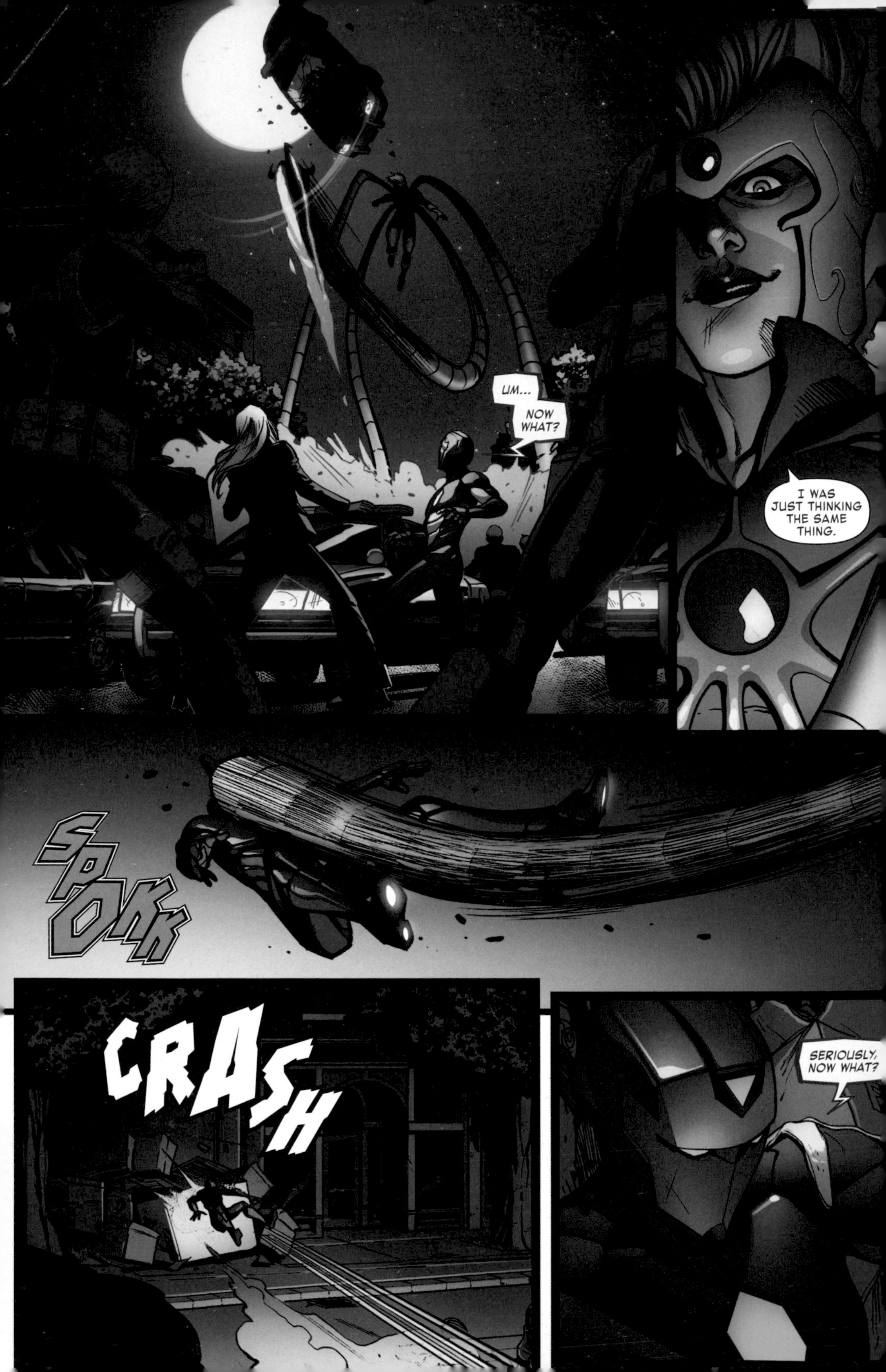
UM... NOW WHAT?
I WAS JUST THINKING THE SAME THING.
SPOKK
CRASH
SERIOUSLY, NOW WHAT?

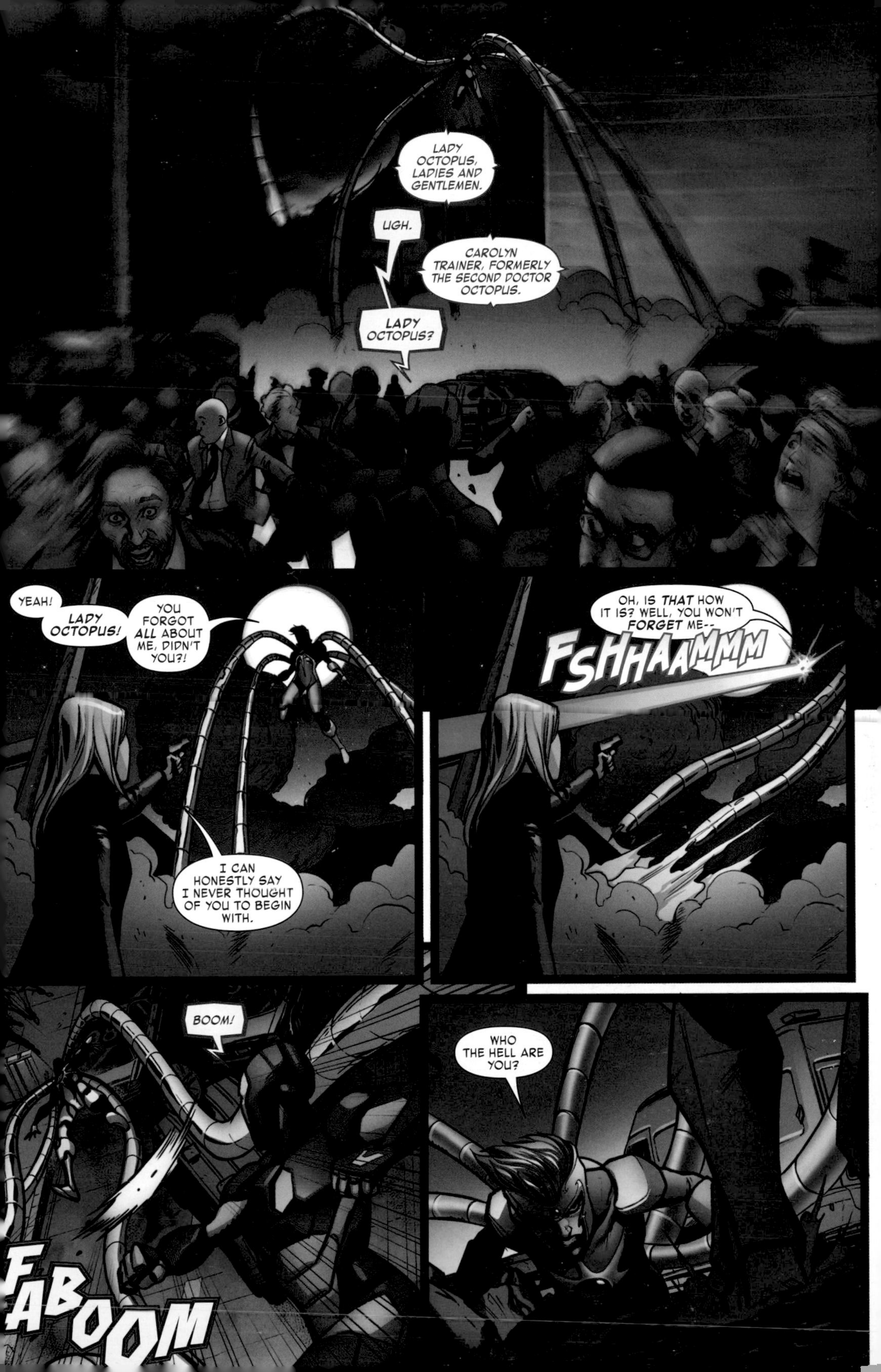
LADY OCTOPUS, LADIES AND GENTLEMEN.
UGH.
CAROLYN TRAINER, FORMERLY THE SECOND DOCTOR OCTOPUS.
LADY OCTOPUS?
YEAH! LADY OCTOPUS!
YOU FORGOT ALL ABOUT ME, DIDN'T YOU?!
I CAN HONESTLY SAY I NEVER THOUGHT OF YOU TO BEGIN WITH.
OH, IS THAT HOW IT IS? WELL, YOU WON'T FORGET ME--
FSHHAAMMM
BOOM!
FABOOM
WHO THE HELL ARE YOU?

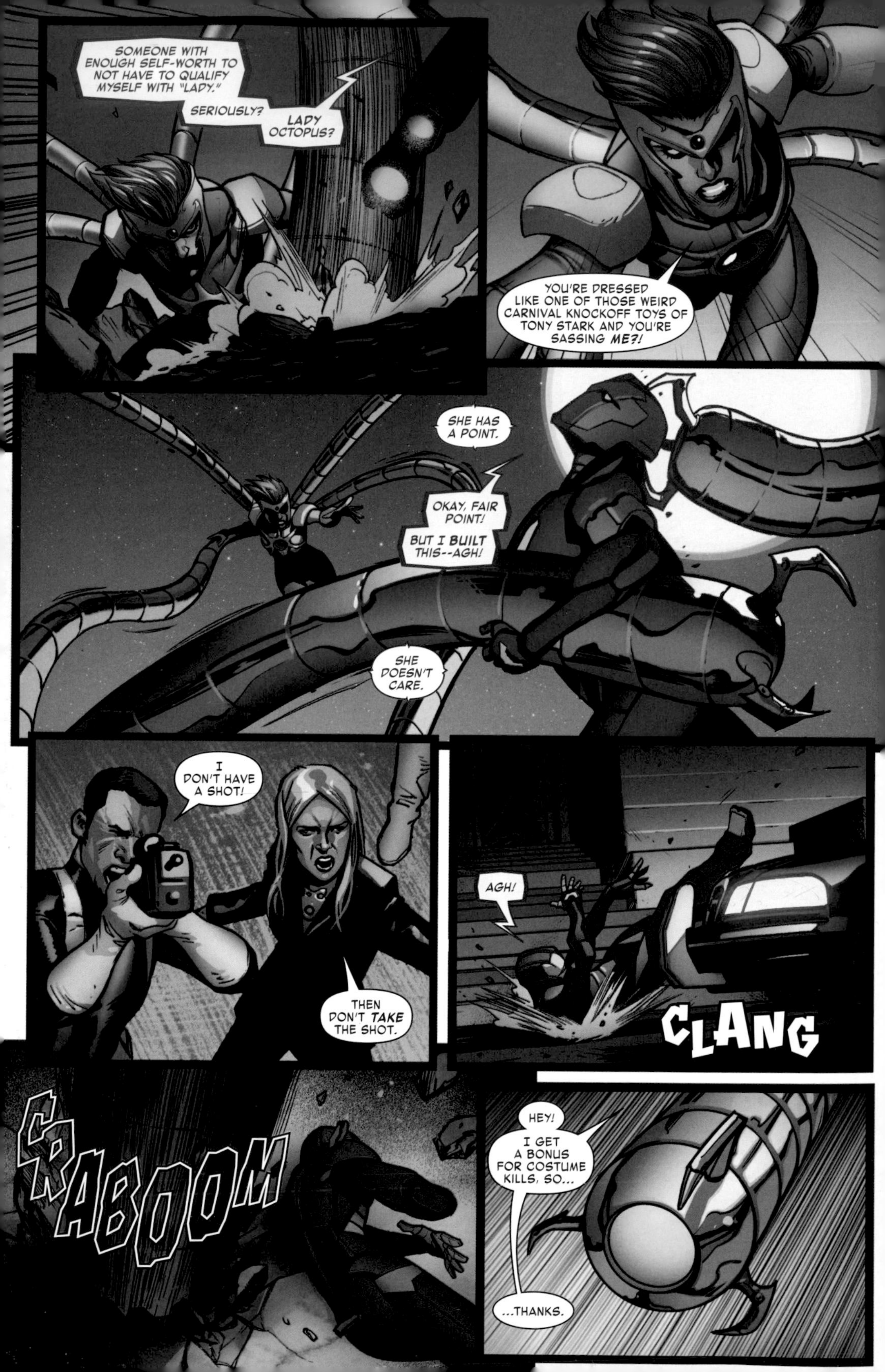
SOMEONE WITH ENOUGH SELF-WORTH TO NOT HAVE TO QUALIFY MYSELF WITH "LADY."
SERIOUSLY?
LADY OCTOPUS?
YOU'RE DRESSED LIKE ONE OF THOSE WEIRD CARNIVAL KNOCKOFF TOYS OF TONY STARK AND YOU'RE SASSING ME?!
SHE HAS A POINT.
OKAY, FAIR POINT!
BUT I BUILT THIS--AGH!
SHE DOESN'T CARE.
I DON'T HAVE A SHOT!
THEN DON'T TAKE THE SHOT.
AGH!
CLANG
CRABOOM
HEY! I GET A BONUS FOR COSTUME KILLS, SO...
...THANKS.

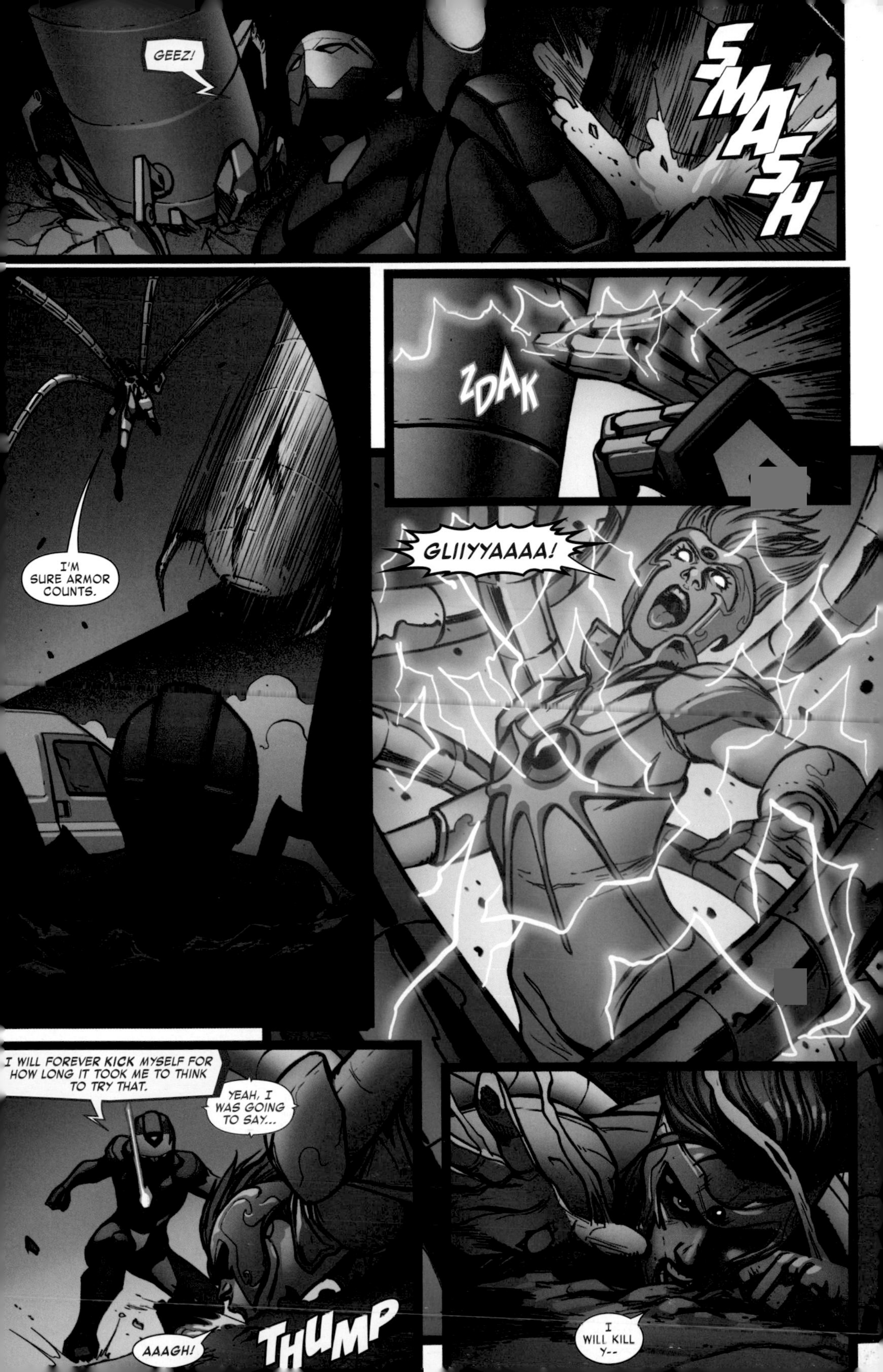
GEEZ!
SMASH
I'M SURE ARMOR COUNTS.
ZDAK
GLIIYYAAAA!
I WILL FOREVER KICK MYSELF FOR HOW LONG IT TOOK ME TO THINK TO TRY THAT.
YEAH, I WAS GOING TO SAY...
AAAGH!
THUMP
I WILL KILL Y--

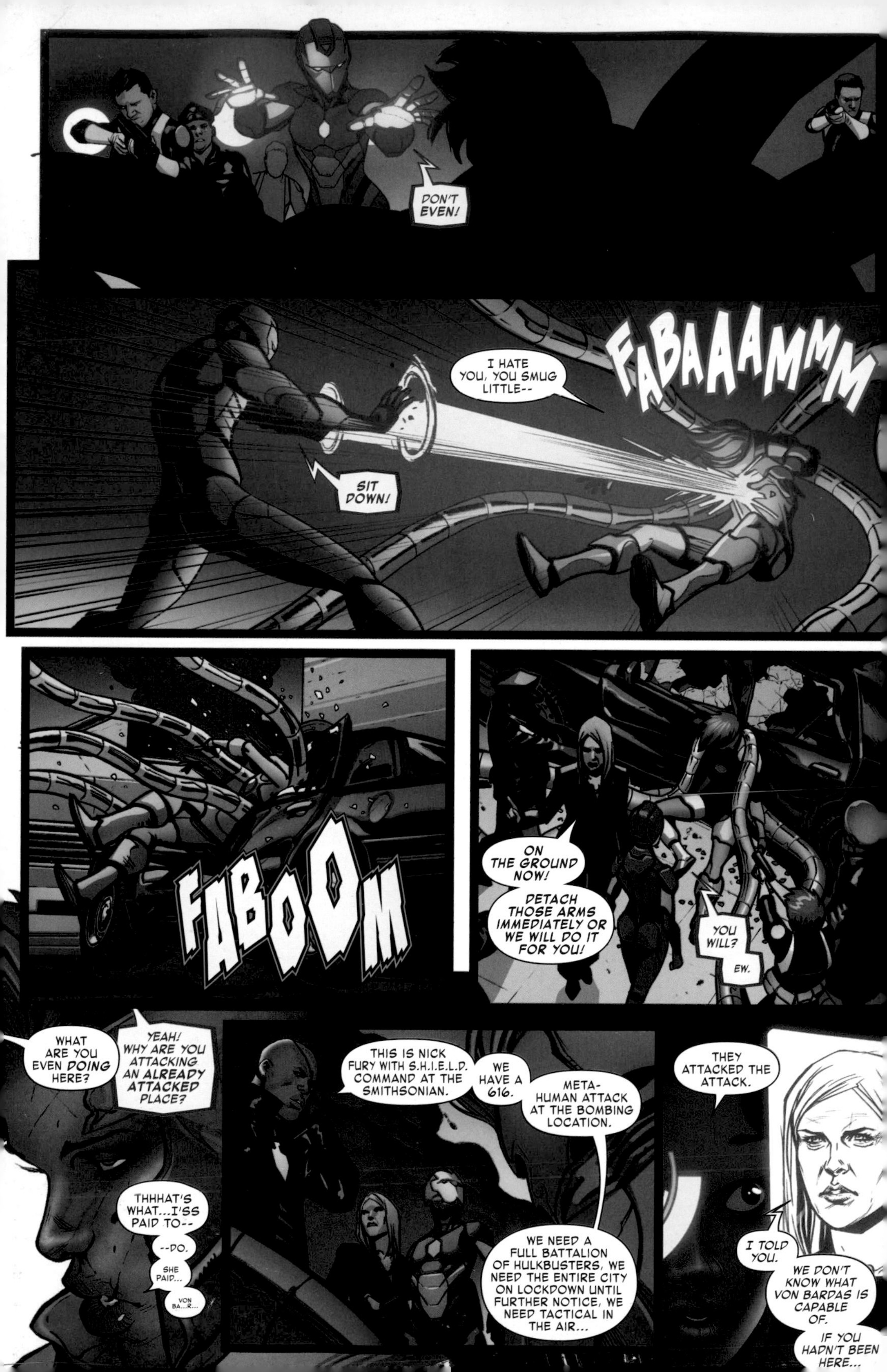
DON'T EVEN!
I HATE YOU, YOU SMUG LITTLE--
FABAAAMMM
SIT DOWN!
FABOOM
ON THE GROUND NOW!
DETACH THOSE ARMS IMMEDIATELY OR WE WILL DO IT FOR YOU!
YOU WILL?
EW.
WHAT ARE YOU EVEN DOING HERE?
YEAH! WHY ARE YOU ATTACKING AN ALREADY ATTACKED PLACE?
THHHAT'S WHAT...I'SS PAID TO--
--DO.
SHE PAID...
VON BA...R...
THIS IS NICK FURY WITH S.H.I.E.L.D. COMMAND AT THE SMITHSONIAN.
WE HAVE A 616.
META-HUMAN ATTACK AT THE BOMBING LOCATION.
WE NEED A FULL BATTALION OF HULKBUSTERS, WE NEED THE ENTIRE CITY ON LOCKDOWN UNTIL FURTHER NOTICE, WE NEED TACTICAL IN THE AIR...
THEY ATTACKED THE ATTACK.
I TOLD YOU.
WE DON'T KNOW WHAT VON BARDAS IS CAPABLE OF.
IF YOU HADN'T BEEN HERE...

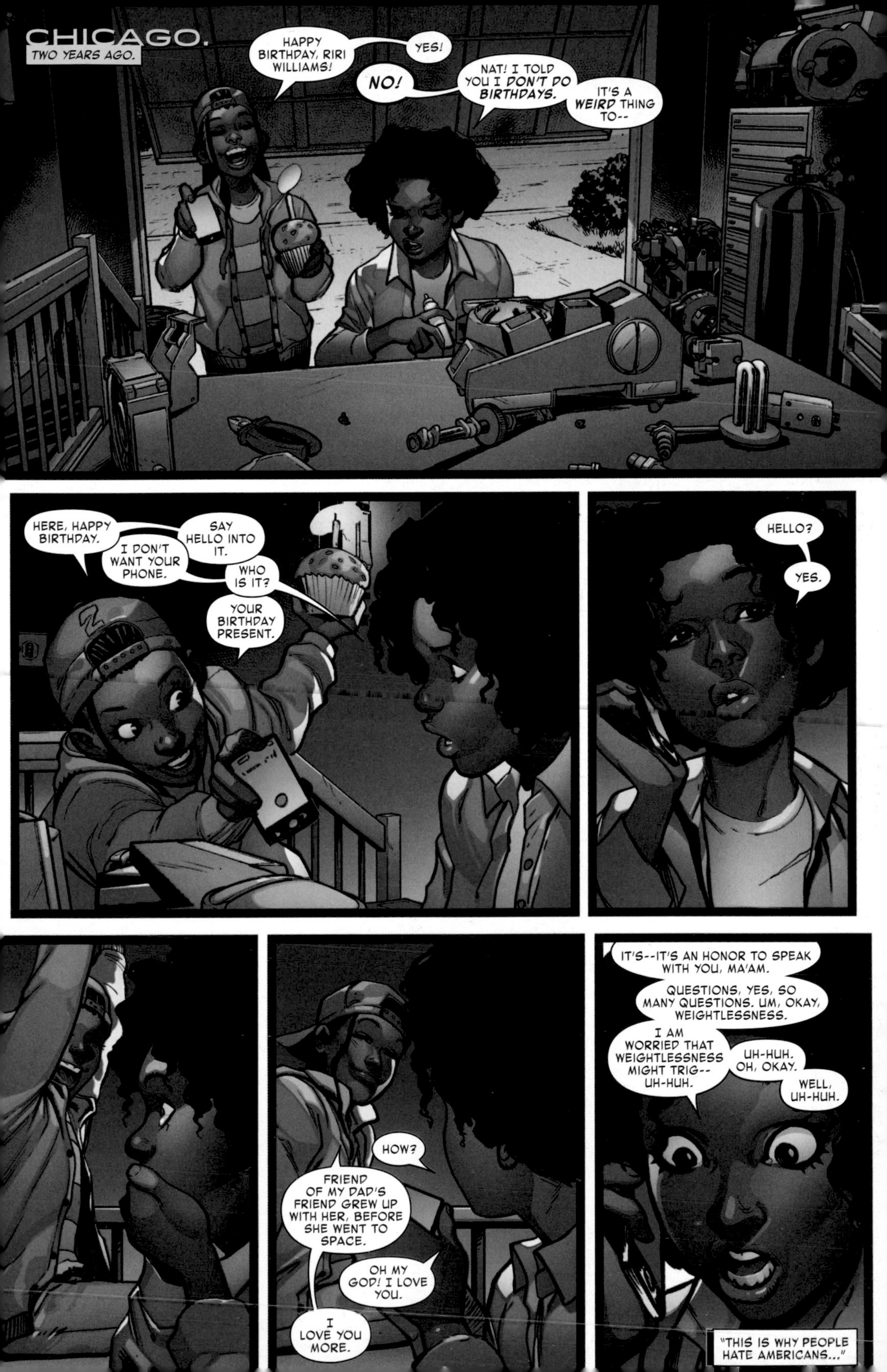

CHICAGO.
TWO YEARS AGO.
HAPPY BIRTHDAY, RIRI WILLIAMS!
YES!
NO!
NAT! I TOLD YOU I DON'T DO BIRTHDAYS.
IT'S A WEIRD THING TO--
HERE, HAPPY BIRTHDAY.
SAY HELLO INTO IT.
I DON'T WANT YOUR PHONE.
WHO IS IT?
YOUR BIRTHDAY PRESENT.
HELLO?
YES.
HOW?
FRIEND OF MY DAD'S FRIEND GREW UP WITH HER, BEFORE SHE WENT TO SPACE.
OH MY GOD! I LOVE YOU.
I LOVE YOU MORE.
IT'S--IT'S AN HONOR TO SPEAK WITH YOU, MA'AM.
QUESTIONS, YES, SO MANY QUESTIONS. UM, OKAY, WEIGHTLESSNESS.
I AM WORRIED THAT WEIGHTLESSNESS MIGHT TRIG-- UH-HUH.
UH-HUH. OH, OKAY.
WELL, UH-HUH.
"THIS IS WHY PEOPLE HATE AMERICANS..."

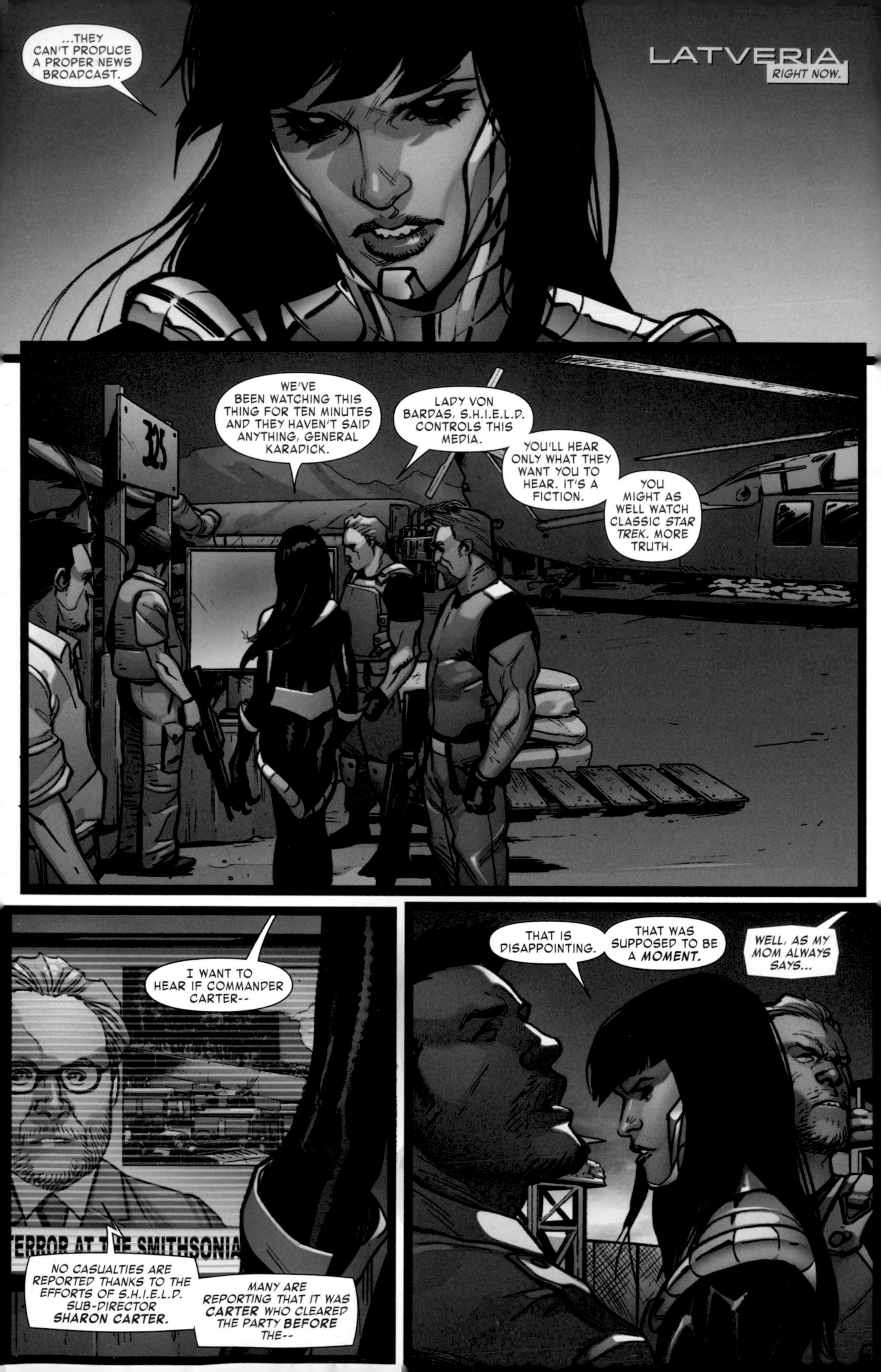
...THEY CAN'T PRODUCE A PROPER NEWS BROADCAST.
LATVERIA
RIGHT NOW.
WE'VE BEEN WATCHING THIS THING FOR TEN MINUTES AND THEY HAVEN'T SAID ANYTHING, GENERAL KARADICK.
LADY VON BARDAS, S.H.I.E.L.D. CONTROLS THIS MEDIA.
YOU'LL HEAR ONLY WHAT THEY WANT YOU TO HEAR. IT'S A FICTION.
YOU MIGHT AS WELL WATCH CLASSIC *STAR TREK*. MORE TRUTH.
325
I WANT TO HEAR IF COMMANDER CARTER--
TERROR AT THE SMITHSONIA
NO CASUALTIES ARE REPORTED THANKS TO THE EFFORTS OF S.H.I.E.L.D. SUB-DIRECTOR **SHARON CARTER.**
MANY ARE REPORTING THAT IT WAS **CARTER** WHO CLEARED THE PARTY **BEFORE** THE--
THAT IS DISAPPOINTING.
THAT WAS SUPPOSED TO BE A **MOMENT.**
WELL, AS MY MOM ALWAYS SAYS...

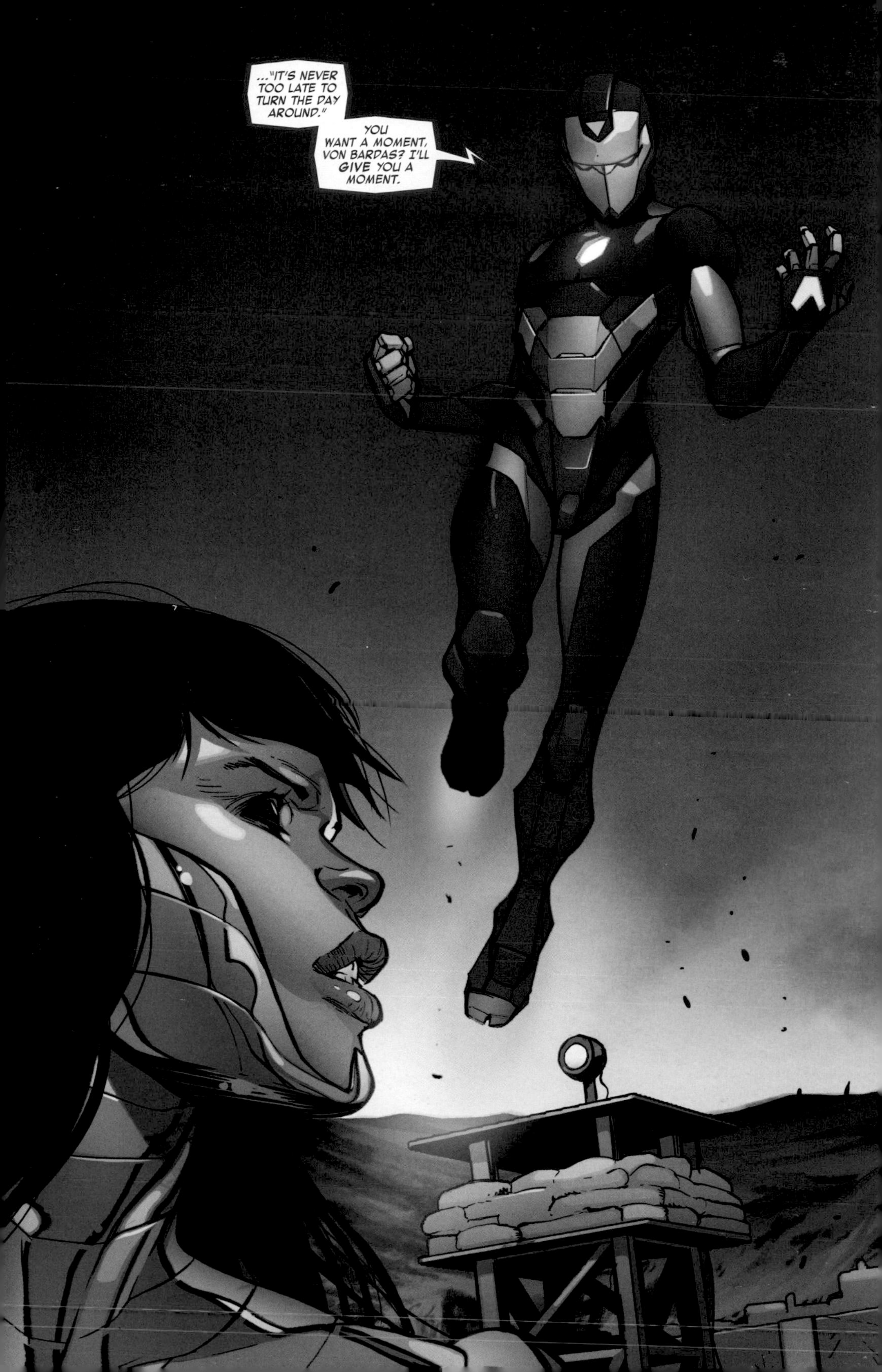
..."IT'S NEVER TOO LATE TO TURN THE DAY AROUND."
YOU WANT A MOMENT, VON BARDAS? I'LL GIVE YOU A MOMENT.

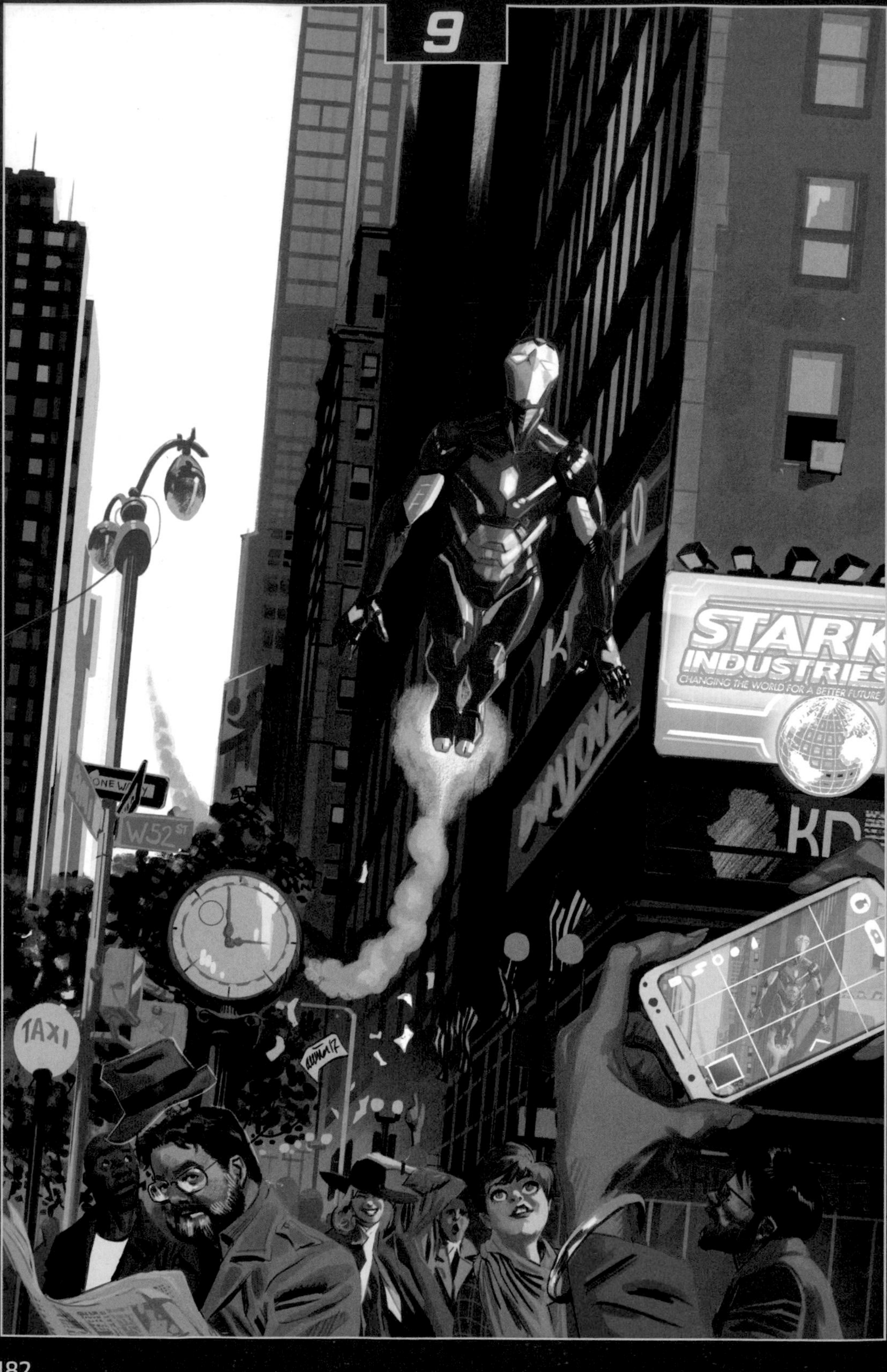
9
STARK
INDUSTRIES
CHANGING THE WORLD FOR A BETTER FUTURE
ONE WAY
W52 ST
TAXI

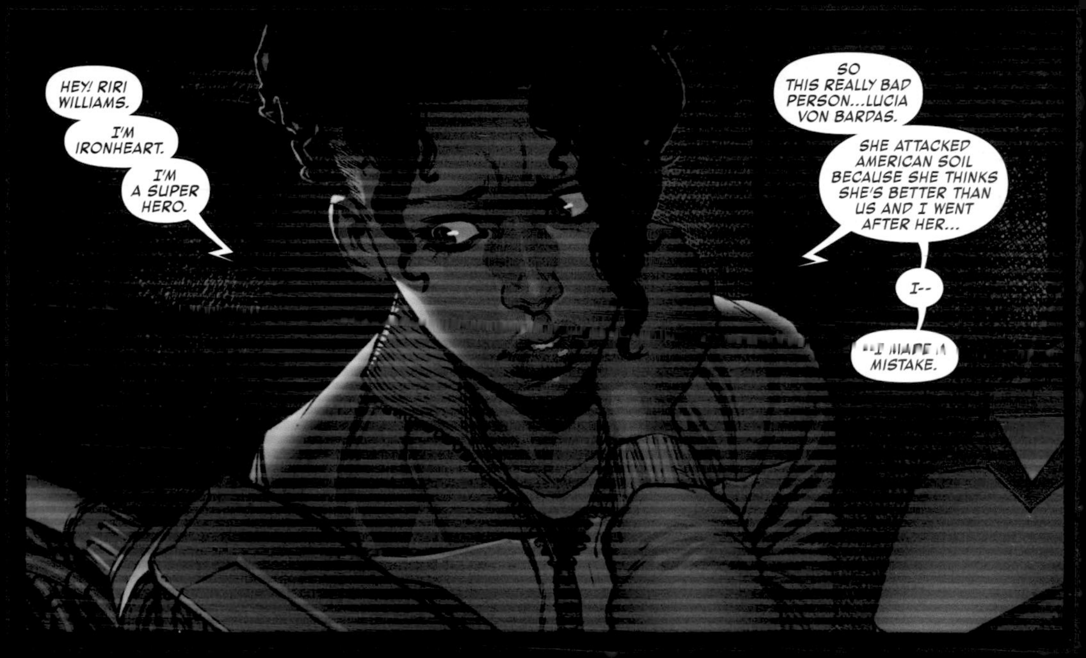
HEY! RIRI WILLIAMS.
I'M IRONHEART.
I'M A SUPER HERO.
SO THIS REALLY BAD PERSON...LUCIA VON BARDAS.
SHE ATTACKED AMERICAN SOIL BECAUSE SHE THINKS SHE'S BETTER THAN US AND I WENT AFTER HER...
I--
--I MADE A MISTAKE.

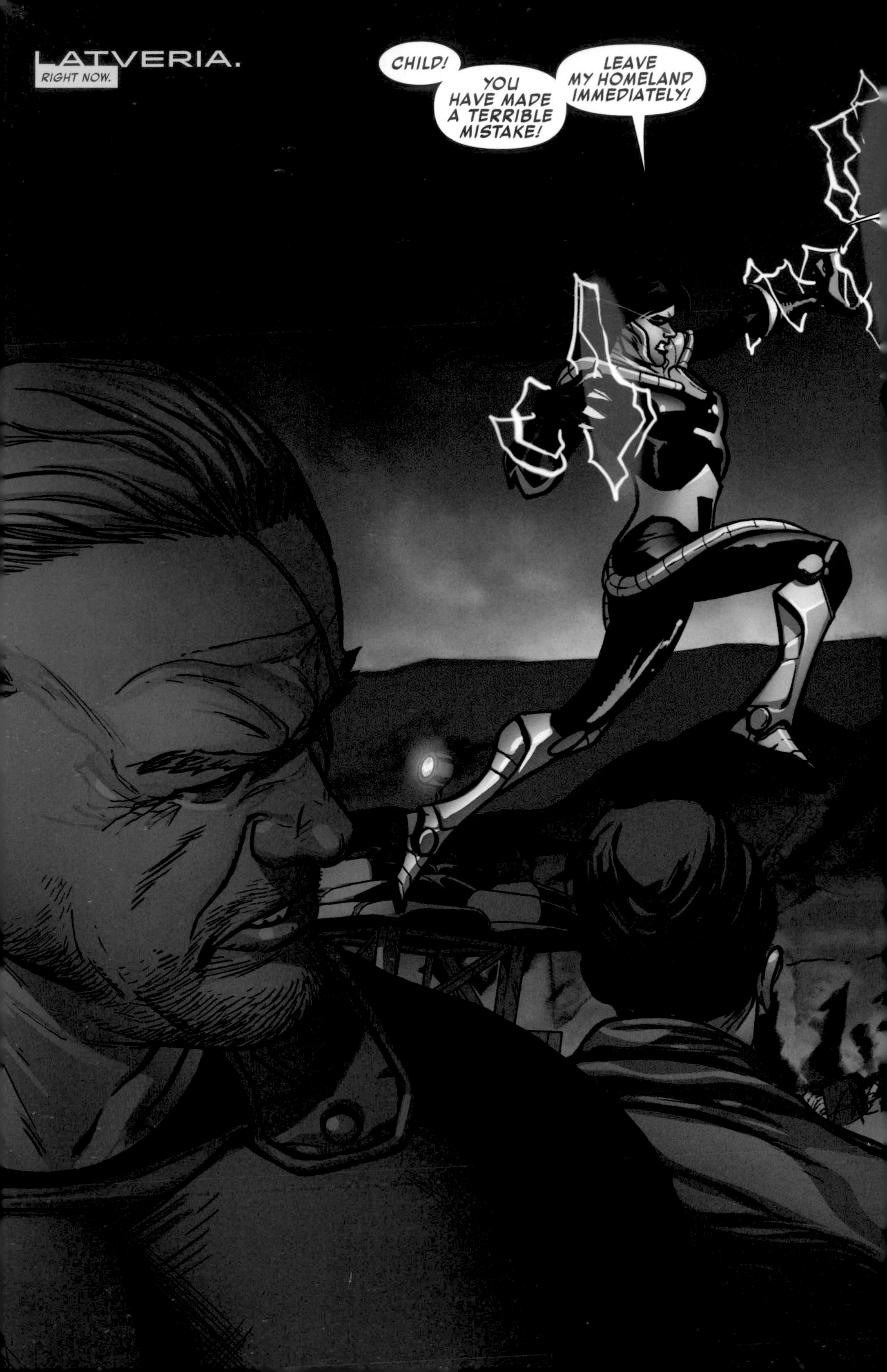
LATVERIA.
RIGHT NOW.
CHILD!
YOU HAVE MADE A TERRIBLE MISTAKE!
LEAVE MY HOMELAND IMMEDIATELY!

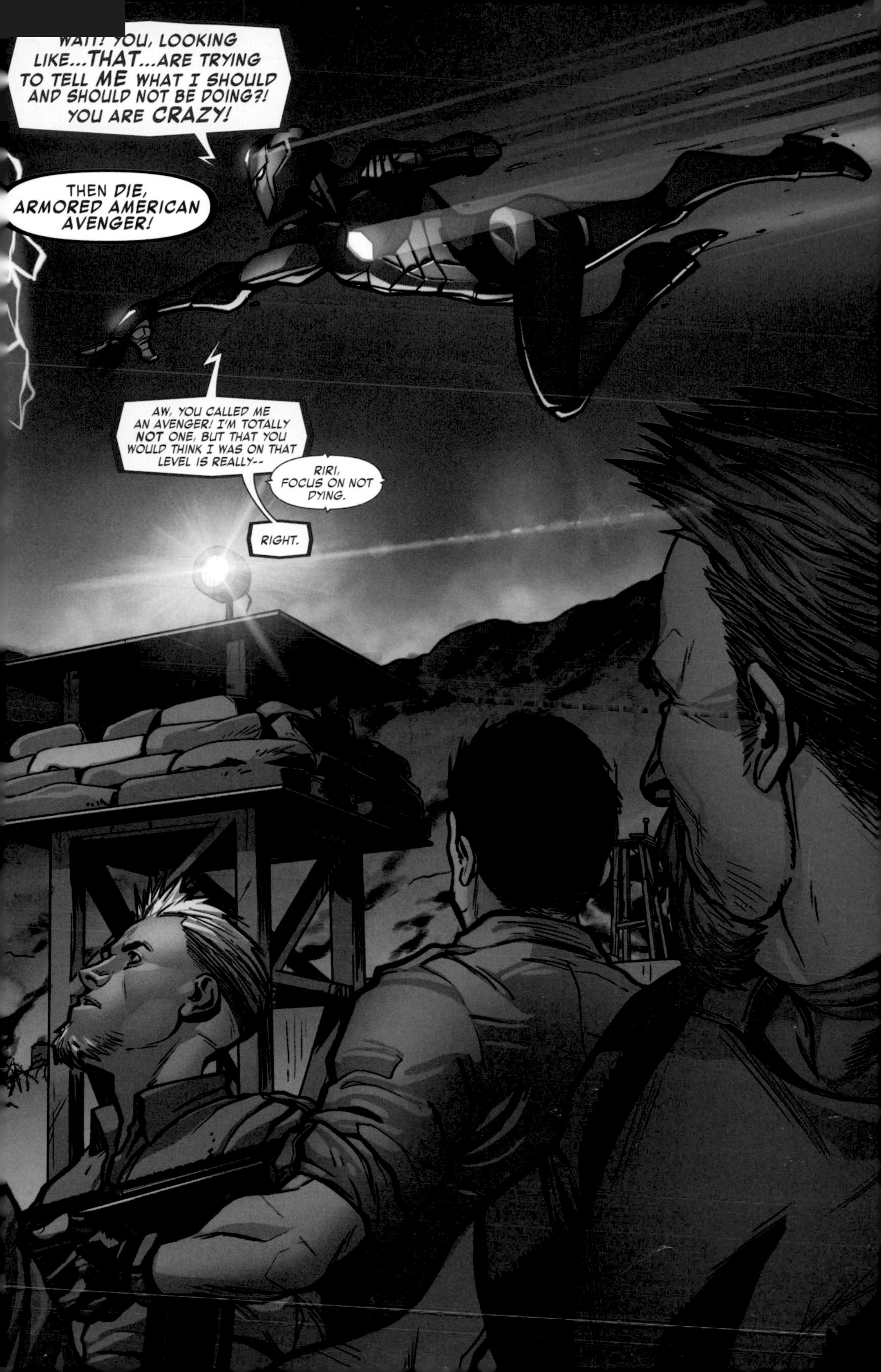
WAIT! YOU, LOOKING LIKE...THAT...ARE TRYING TO TELL ME WHAT I SHOULD AND SHOULD NOT BE DOING?! YOU ARE CRAZY!
THEN DIE, ARMORED AMERICAN AVENGER!
AW, YOU CALLED ME AN AVENGER! I'M TOTALLY NOT ONE, BUT THAT YOU WOULD THINK I WAS ON THAT LEVEL IS REALLY--
RIRI, FOCUS ON NOT DYING.
RIGHT.

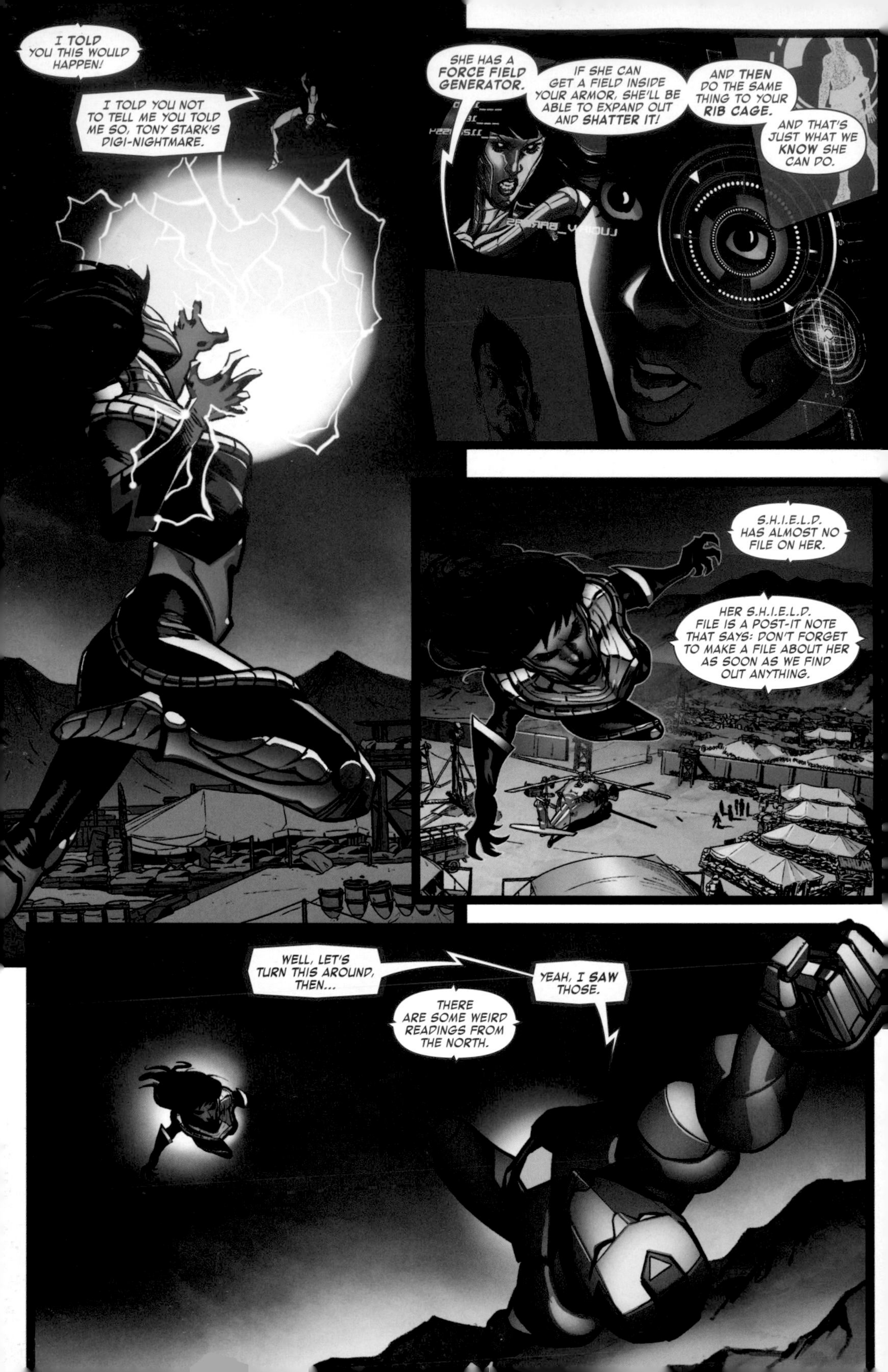
I TOLD YOU THIS WOULD HAPPEN!
I TOLD YOU NOT TO TELL ME YOU TOLD ME SO, TONY STARK'S DIGI-NIGHTMARE.
SHE HAS A FORCE FIELD GENERATOR.
IF SHE CAN GET A FIELD INSIDE YOUR ARMOR, SHE'LL BE ABLE TO EXPAND OUT AND SHATTER IT!
AND THEN DO THE SAME THING TO YOUR RIB CAGE.
AND THAT'S JUST WHAT WE KNOW SHE CAN DO.
S.H.I.E.L.D. HAS ALMOST NO FILE ON HER.
HER S.H.I.E.L.D. FILE IS A POST-IT NOTE THAT SAYS: DON'T FORGET TO MAKE A FILE ABOUT HER AS SOON AS WE FIND OUT ANYTHING.
WELL, LET'S TURN THIS AROUND, THEN...
THERE ARE SOME WEIRD READINGS FROM THE NORTH.
YEAH, I SAW THOSE.

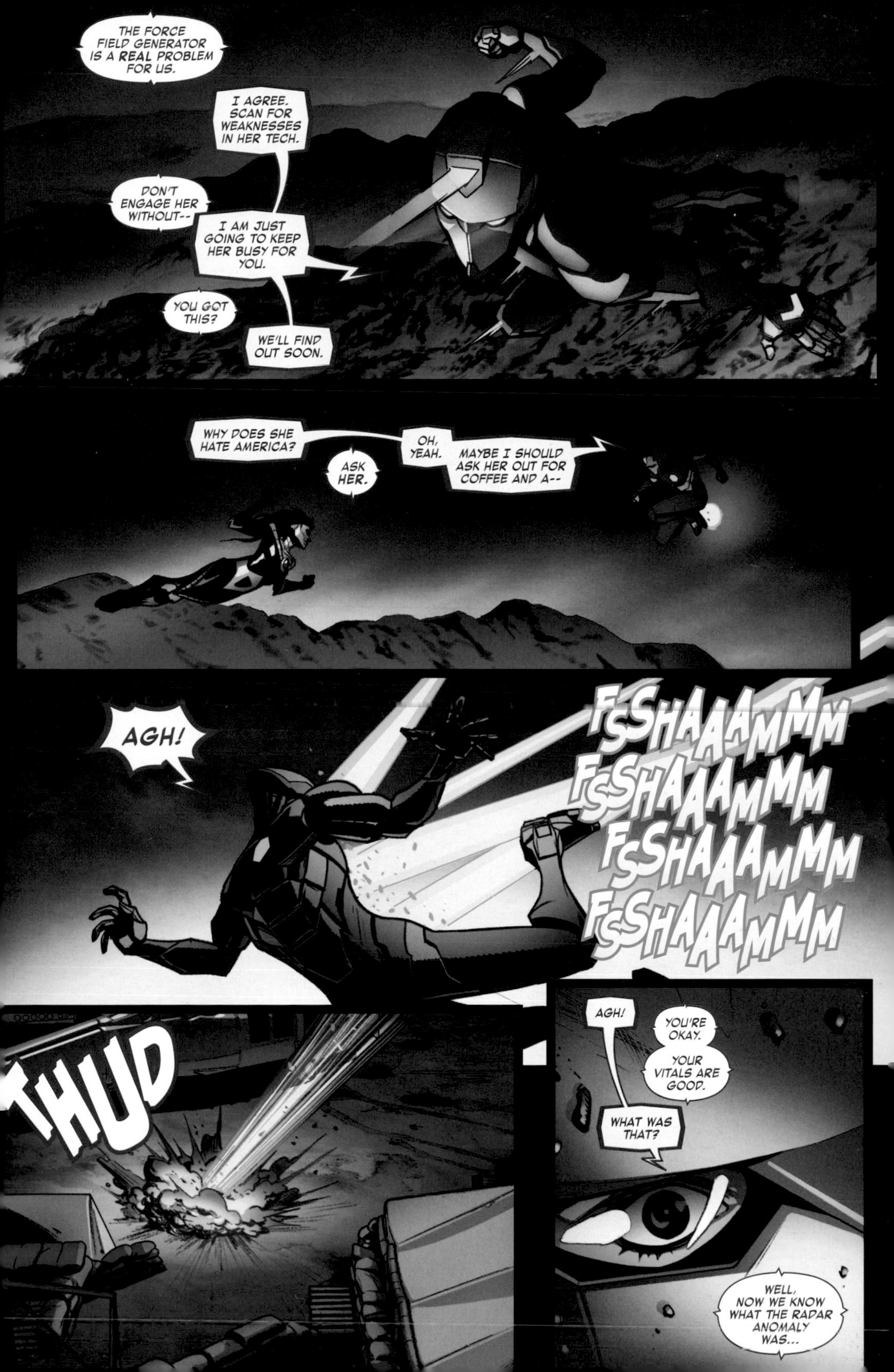
THE FORCE FIELD GENERATOR IS A REAL PROBLEM FOR US.
I AGREE. SCAN FOR WEAKNESSES IN HER TECH.
DON'T ENGAGE HER WITHOUT--
I AM JUST GOING TO KEEP HER BUSY FOR YOU.
YOU GOT THIS?
WE'LL FIND OUT SOON.
WHY DOES SHE HATE AMERICA?
ASK HER.
OH, YEAH.
MAYBE I SHOULD ASK HER OUT FOR COFFEE AND A--
AGH!
FSSHAAAMMM
FSSHAAAMMM
FSSHAAAMMM
FSSHAAAMMM
THUD
AGH!
YOU'RE OKAY.
YOUR VITALS ARE GOOD.
WHAT WAS THAT?
WELL, NOW WE KNOW WHAT THE RADAR ANOMALY WAS...

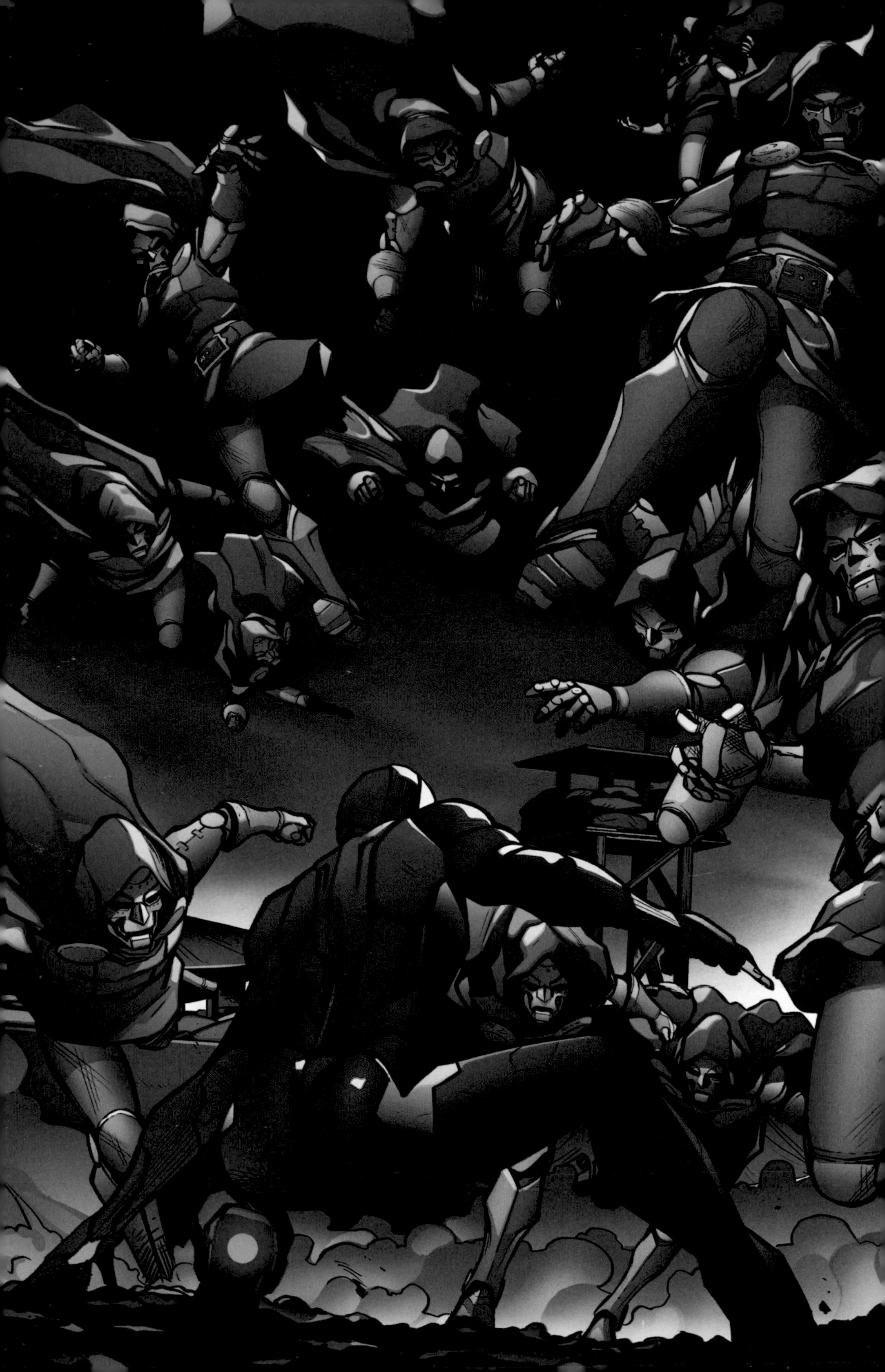

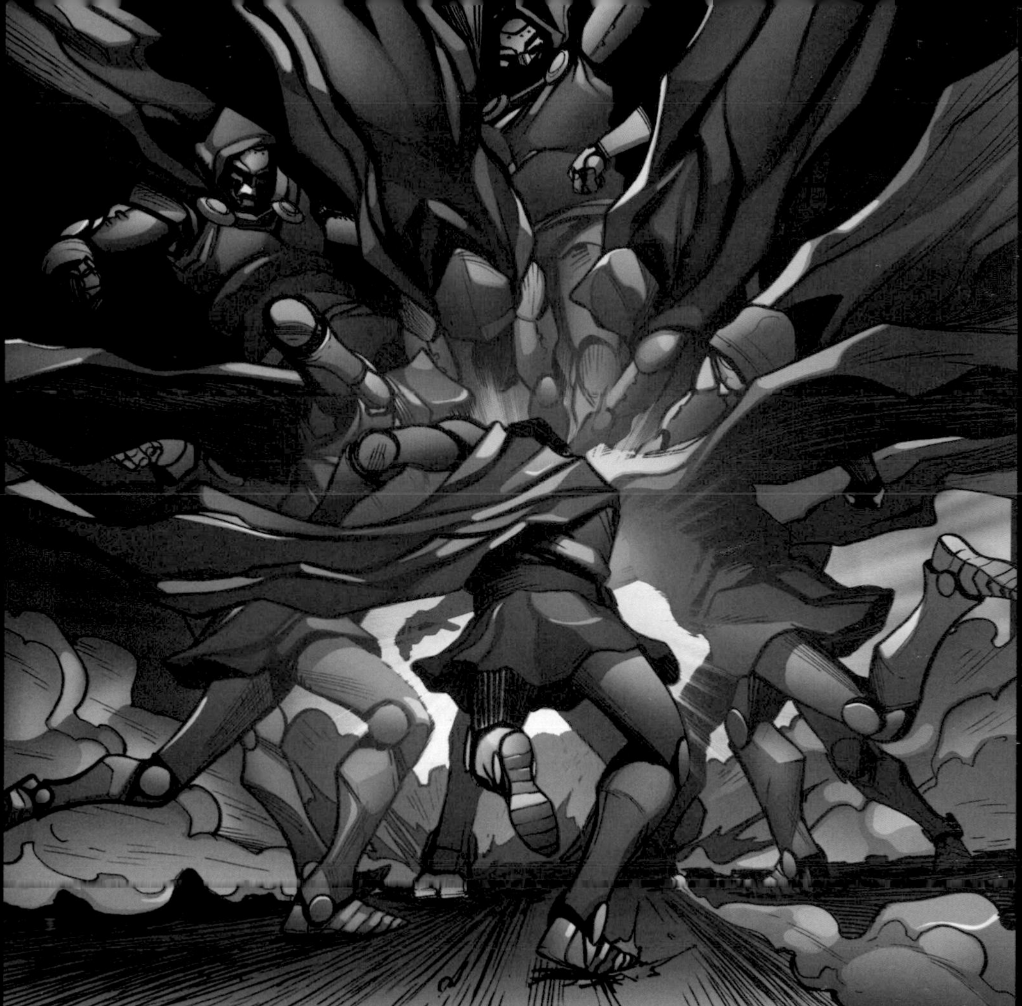

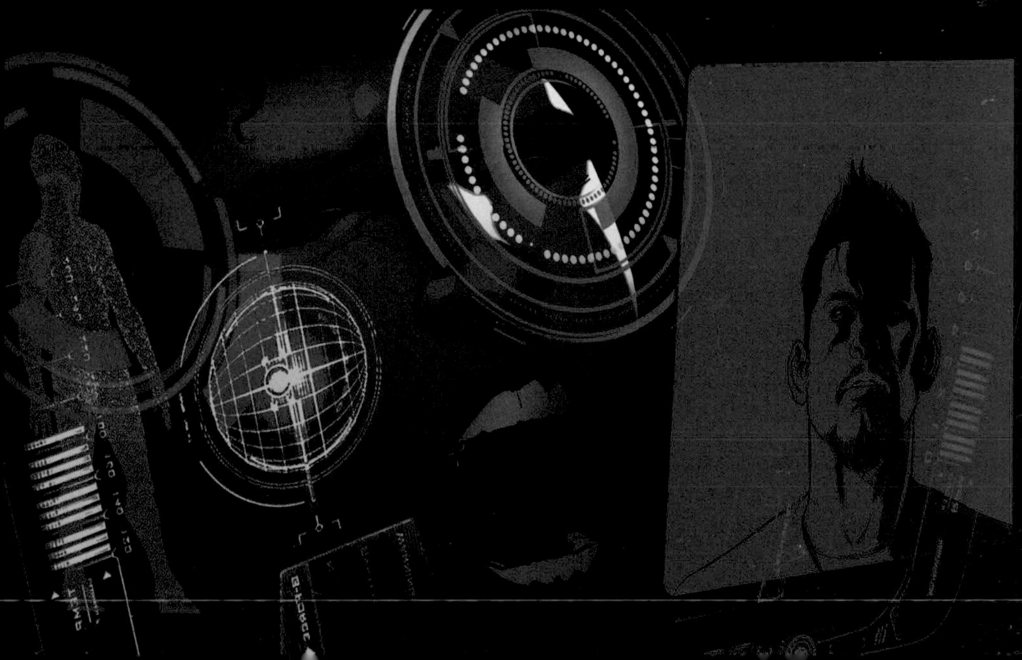

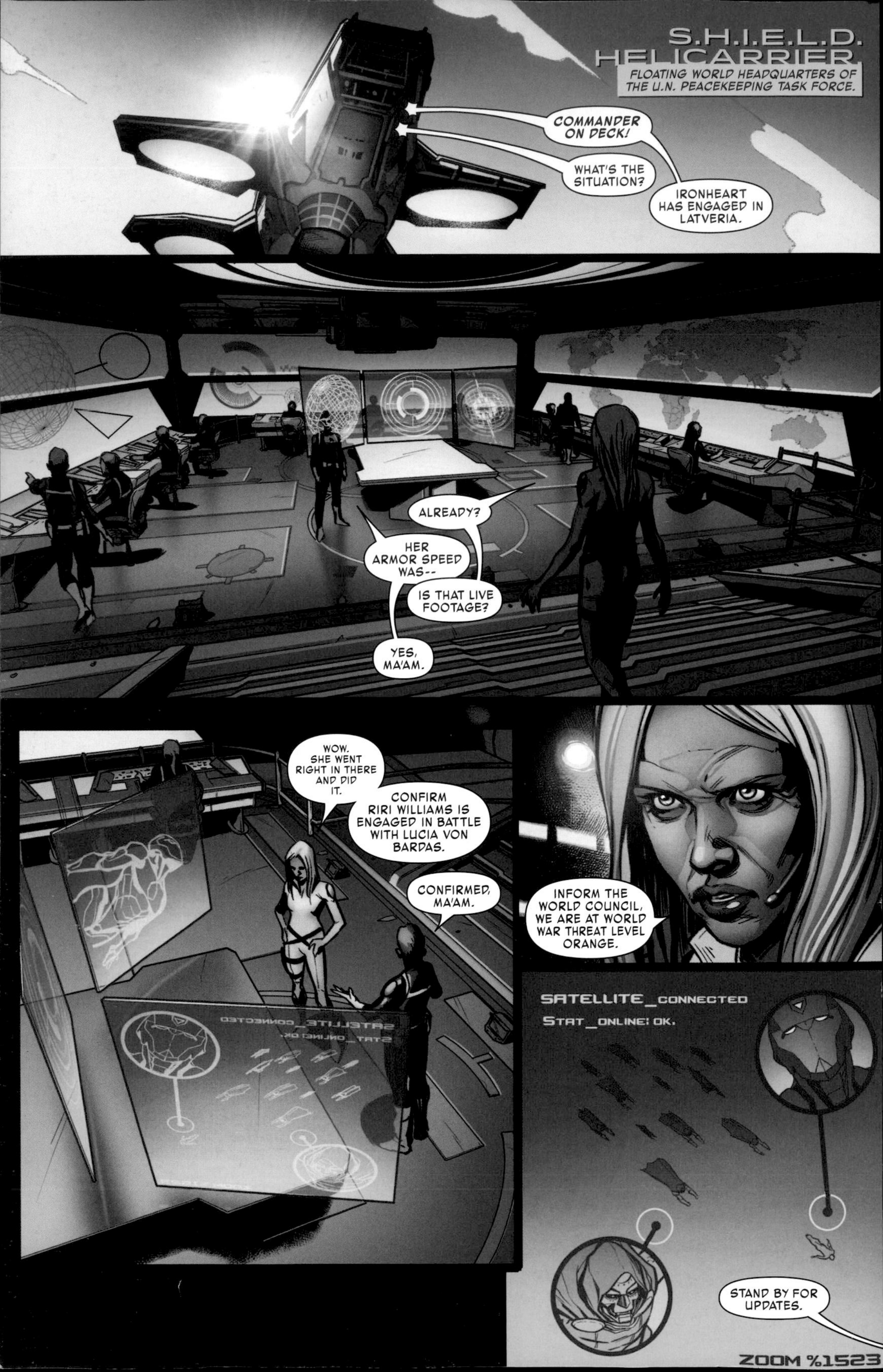
S.H.I.E.L.D. HELICARRIER
FLOATING WORLD HEADQUARTERS OF THE U.N. PEACEKEEPING TASK FORCE.
COMMANDER ON DECK!
WHAT'S THE SITUATION?
IRONHEART HAS ENGAGED IN LATVERIA.
ALREADY?
HER ARMOR SPEED WAS--
IS THAT LIVE FOOTAGE?
YES, MA'AM.
WOW. SHE WENT RIGHT IN THERE AND DID IT.
CONFIRM RIRI WILLIAMS IS ENGAGED IN BATTLE WITH LUCIA VON BARDAS.
CONFIRMED, MA'AM.
INFORM THE WORLD COUNCIL, WE ARE AT WORLD WAR THREAT LEVEL ORANGE.
SATELLITE_CONNECTED
STAT_ONLINE: OK.
STAND BY FOR UPDATES.
ZOOM %1523

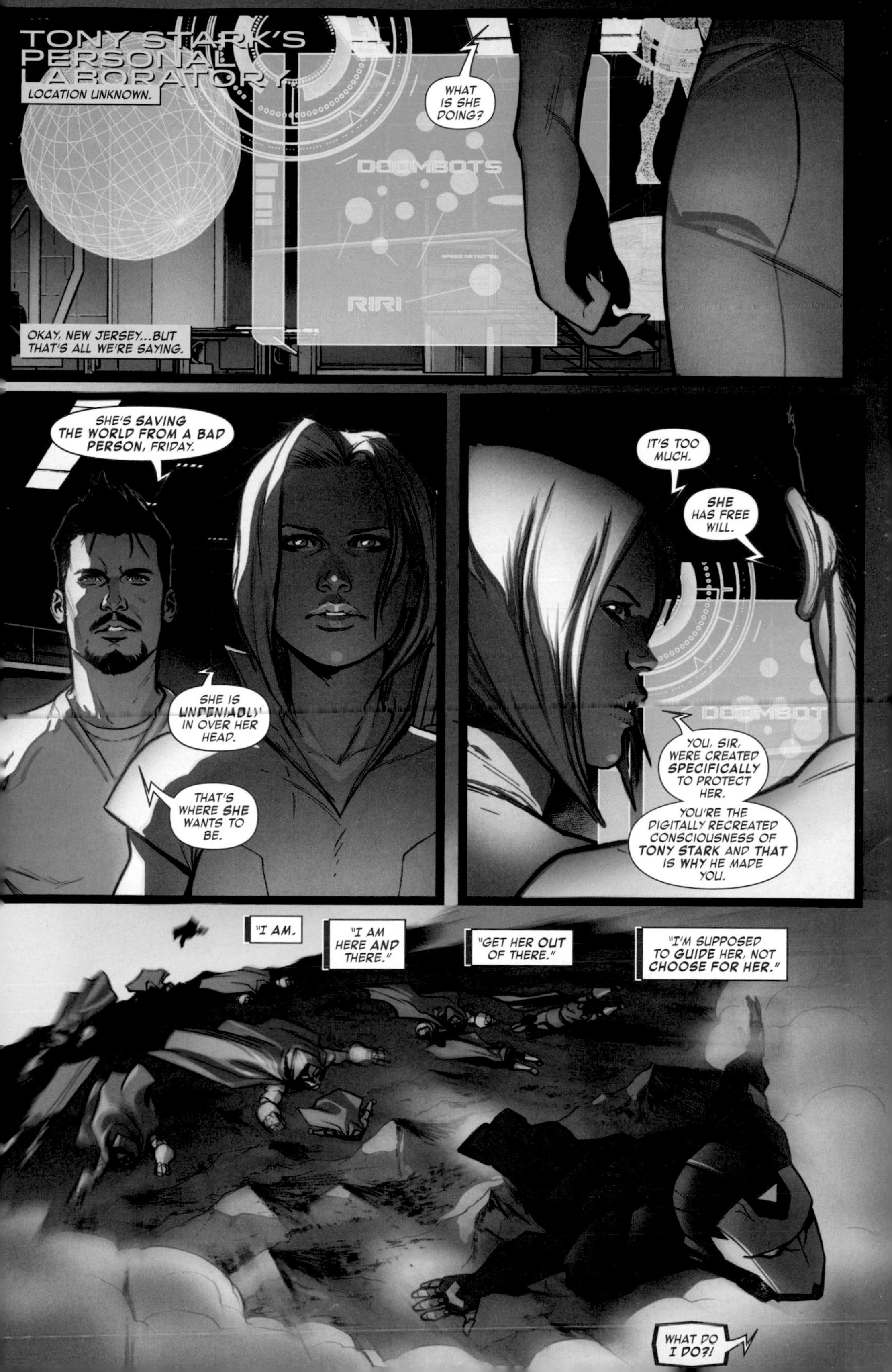
TONY STARK'S PERSONAL LABORATORY
LOCATION UNKNOWN.
OKAY, NEW JERSEY...BUT THAT'S ALL WE'RE SAYING.
WHAT IS SHE DOING?
DOOMBOTS
RIRI
SHE'S SAVING THE WORLD FROM A BAD PERSON, FRIDAY.
SHE IS UNDENIABLY IN OVER HER HEAD.
THAT'S WHERE SHE WANTS TO BE.
IT'S TOO MUCH.
SHE HAS FREE WILL.
DOOMBOT
YOU, SIR, WERE CREATED SPECIFICALLY TO PROTECT HER.
YOU'RE THE DIGITALLY RECREATED CONSCIOUSNESS OF TONY STARK AND THAT IS WHY HE MADE YOU.
"I AM.
"I AM HERE AND THERE."
"GET HER OUT OF THERE."
"I'M SUPPOSED TO GUIDE HER, NOT CHOOSE FOR HER."
WHAT DO I DO?!

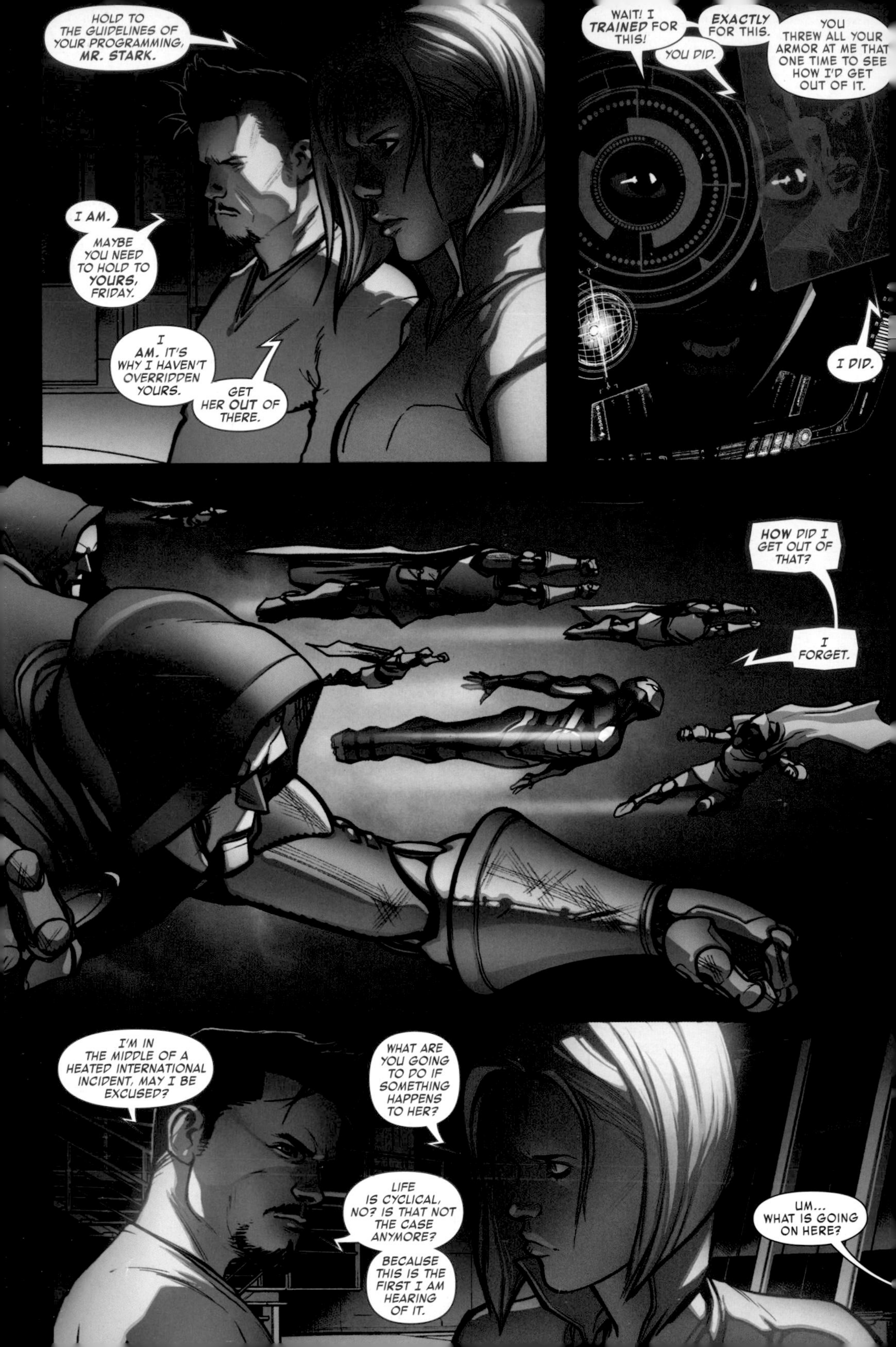
HOLD TO THE GUIDELINES OF YOUR PROGRAMMING, MR. STARK.
I AM.
MAYBE YOU NEED TO HOLD TO YOURS, FRIDAY.
I AM. IT'S WHY I HAVEN'T OVERRIDDEN YOURS.
GET HER OUT OF THERE.
WAIT! I TRAINED FOR THIS!
EXACTLY FOR THIS.
YOU DID.
YOU THREW ALL YOUR ARMOR AT ME THAT ONE TIME TO SEE HOW I'D GET OUT OF IT.
I DID.
HOW DID I GET OUT OF THAT?
I FORGET.
I'M IN THE MIDDLE OF A HEATED INTERNATIONAL INCIDENT, MAY I BE EXCUSED?
WHAT ARE YOU GOING TO DO IF SOMETHING HAPPENS TO HER?
LIFE IS CYCLICAL, NO? IS THAT NOT THE CASE ANYMORE?
BECAUSE THIS IS THE FIRST I AM HEARING OF IT.
UM... WHAT IS GOING ON HERE?

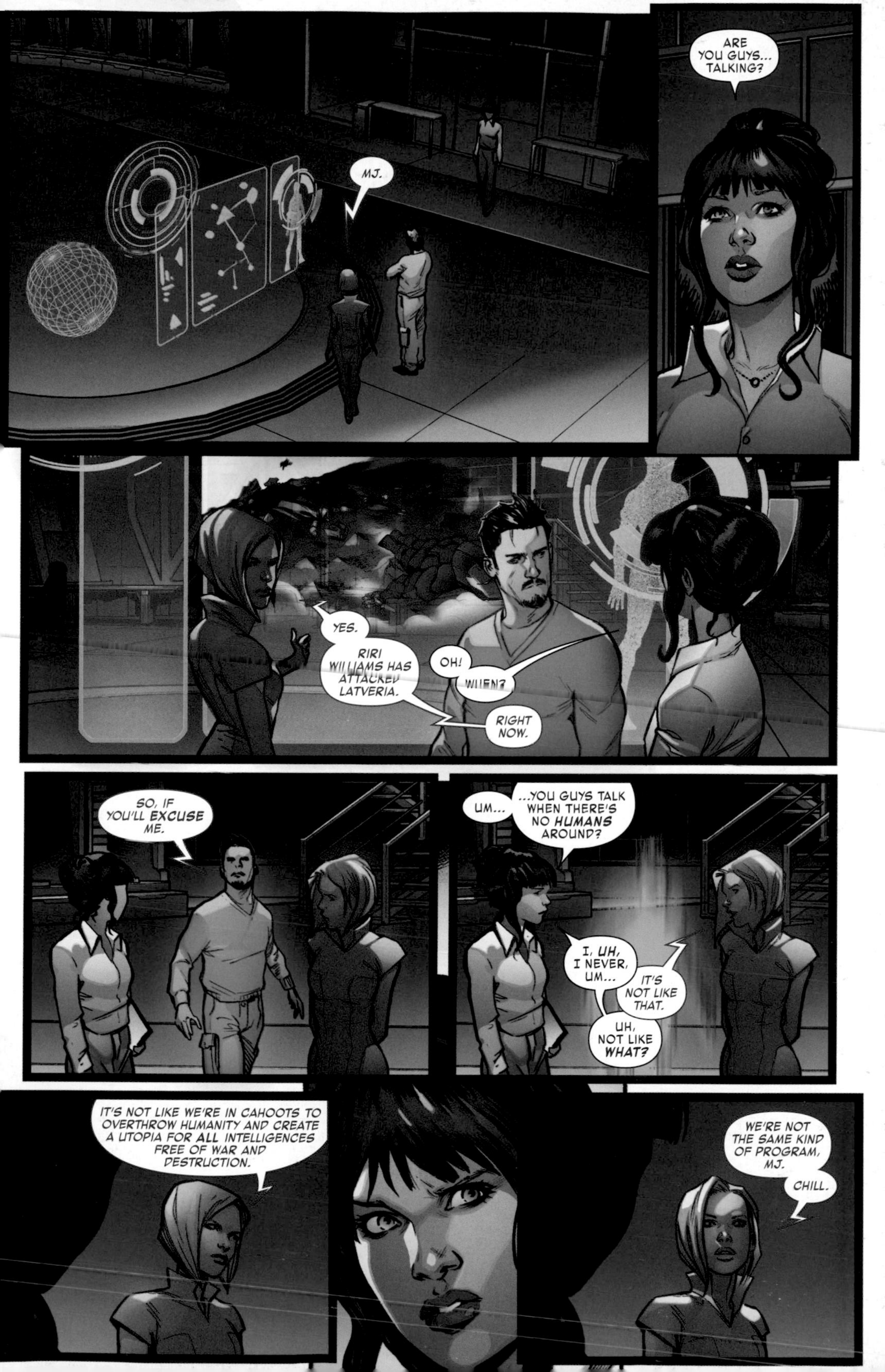
MJ.
ARE YOU GUYS... TALKING?
YES.
RIRI WILLIAMS HAS ATTACKED LATVERIA.
OH!
WHEN?
RIGHT NOW.
SO, IF YOU'LL EXCUSE ME.
UM...
...YOU GUYS TALK WHEN THERE'S NO HUMANS AROUND?
I, UH, I NEVER, UM...
IT'S NOT LIKE THAT.
UH, NOT LIKE WHAT?
IT'S NOT LIKE WE'RE IN CAHOOTS TO OVERTHROW HUMANITY AND CREATE A UTOPIA FOR ALL INTELLIGENCES FREE OF WAR AND DESTRUCTION.
WE'RE NOT THE SAME KIND OF PROGRAM, MJ.
CHILL.

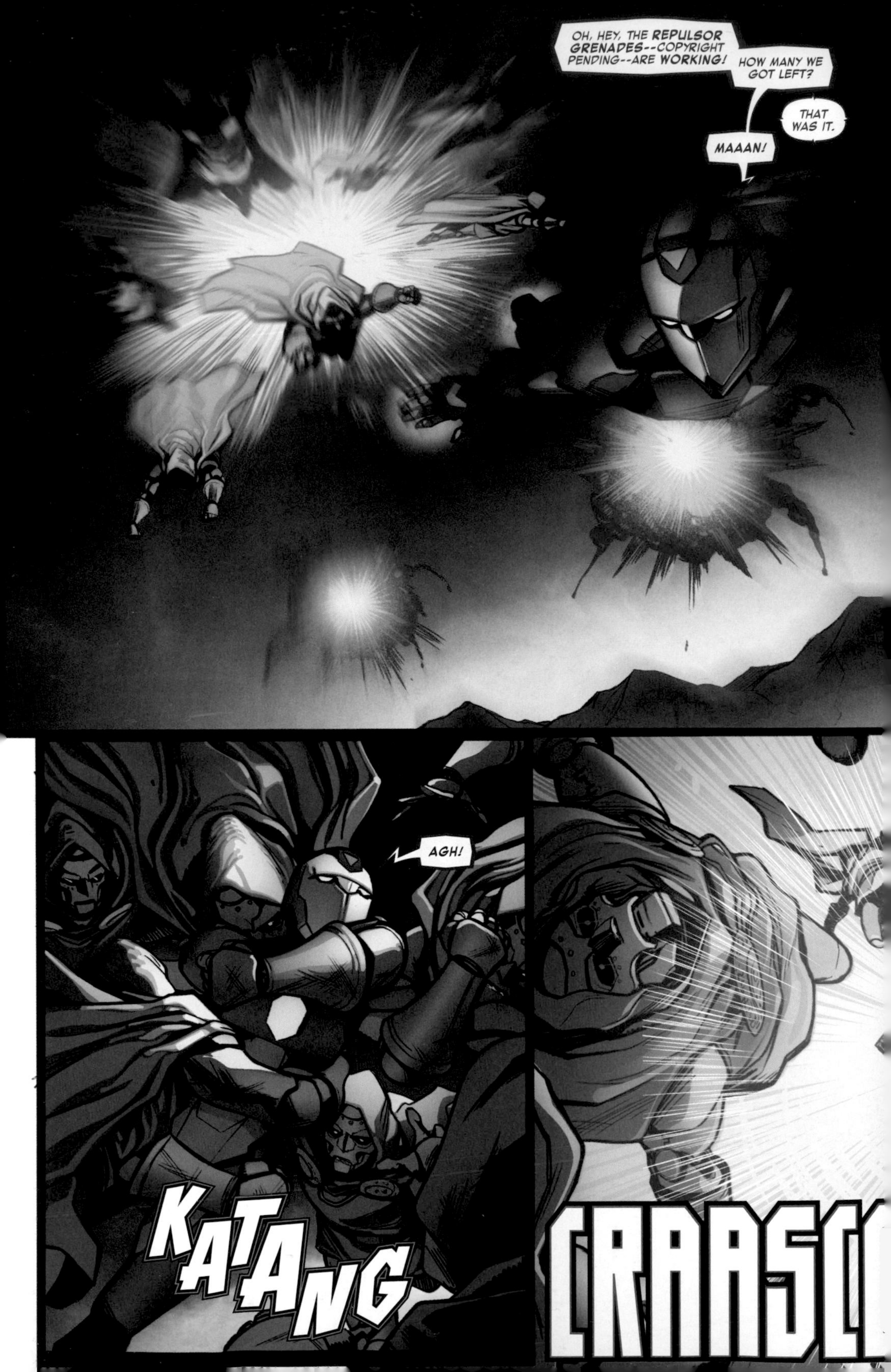
OH, HEY, THE REPULSOR GRENADES--COPYRIGHT PENDING--ARE WORKING!
HOW MANY WE GOT LEFT?
THAT WAS IT.
MAAAN!
AGH!
KATANG
CRAASC

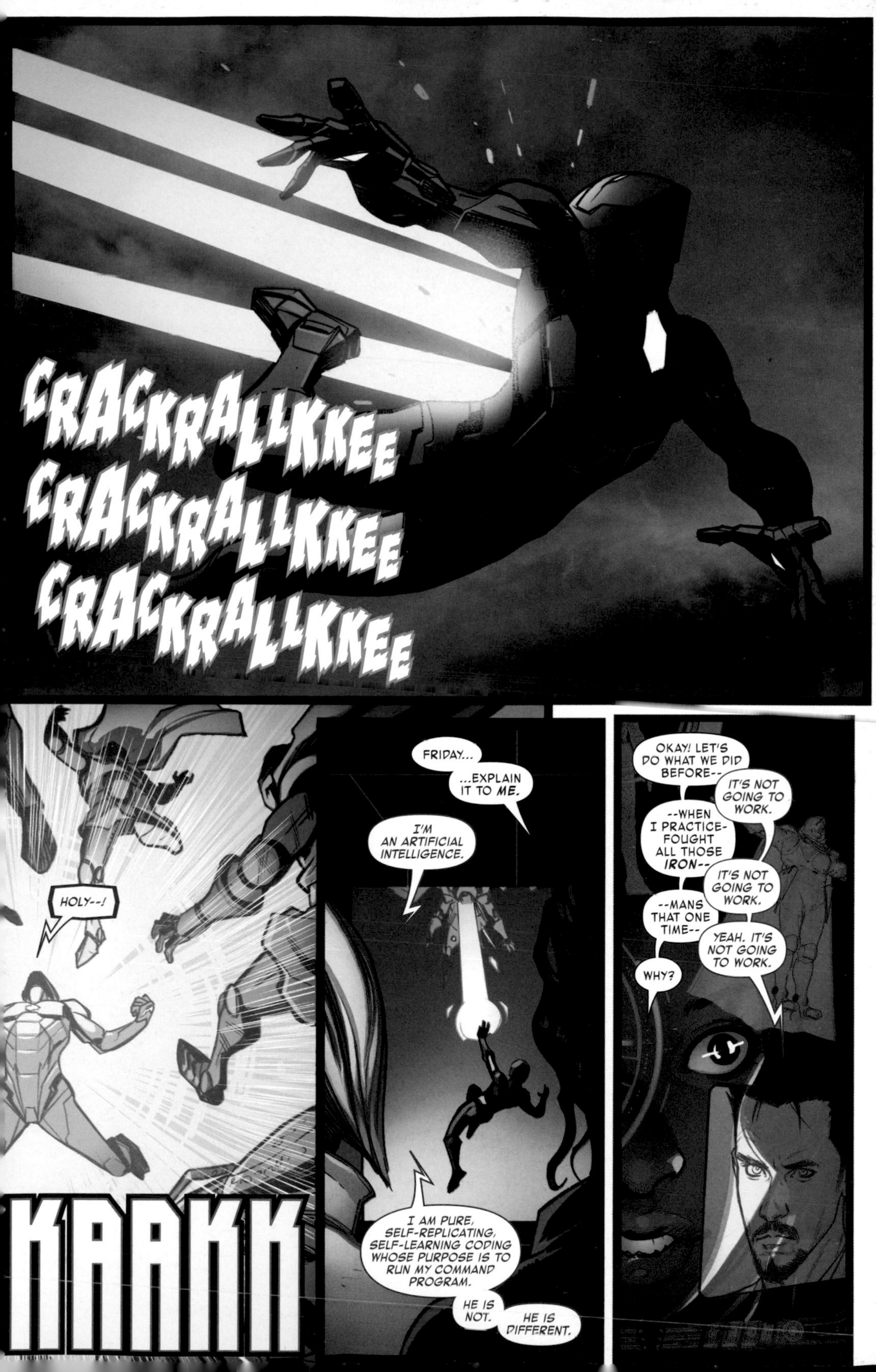
CRACKRALLKKEE
CRACKRALLKKEE
CRACKRALLKKEE
HOLY--!
KRAKK
FRIDAY...
...EXPLAIN IT TO ME.
I'M AN ARTIFICIAL INTELLIGENCE.
I AM PURE, SELF-REPLICATING, SELF-LEARNING CODING WHOSE PURPOSE IS TO RUN MY COMMAND PROGRAM.
HE IS NOT.
HE IS DIFFERENT.
OKAY! LET'S DO WHAT WE DID BEFORE--
IT'S NOT GOING TO WORK.
--WHEN I PRACTICE-FOUGHT ALL THOSE IRON--
IT'S NOT GOING TO WORK.
--MANS THAT ONE TIME--
YEAH. IT'S NOT GOING TO WORK.
WHY?

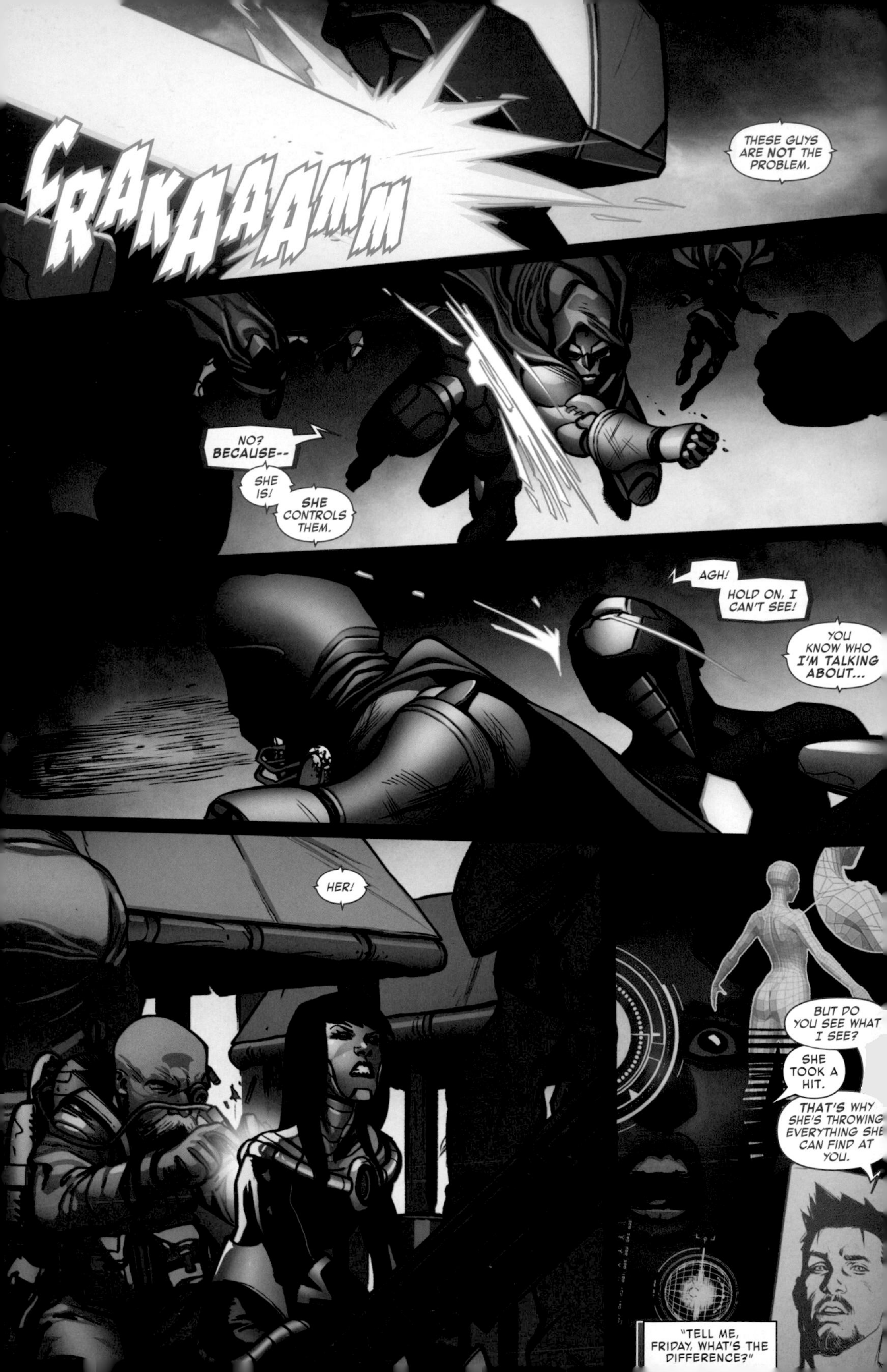
CRAKAAAMM
THESE GUYS ARE NOT THE PROBLEM.
NO? BECAUSE--
SHE IS!
SHE CONTROLS THEM.
AGH!
HOLD ON, I CAN'T SEE!
YOU KNOW WHO I'M TALKING ABOUT...
HER!
BUT DO YOU SEE WHAT I SEE?
SHE TOOK A HIT.
THAT'S WHY SHE'S THROWING EVERYTHING SHE CAN FIND AT YOU.
"TELL ME, FRIDAY, WHAT'S THE DIFFERENCE?"

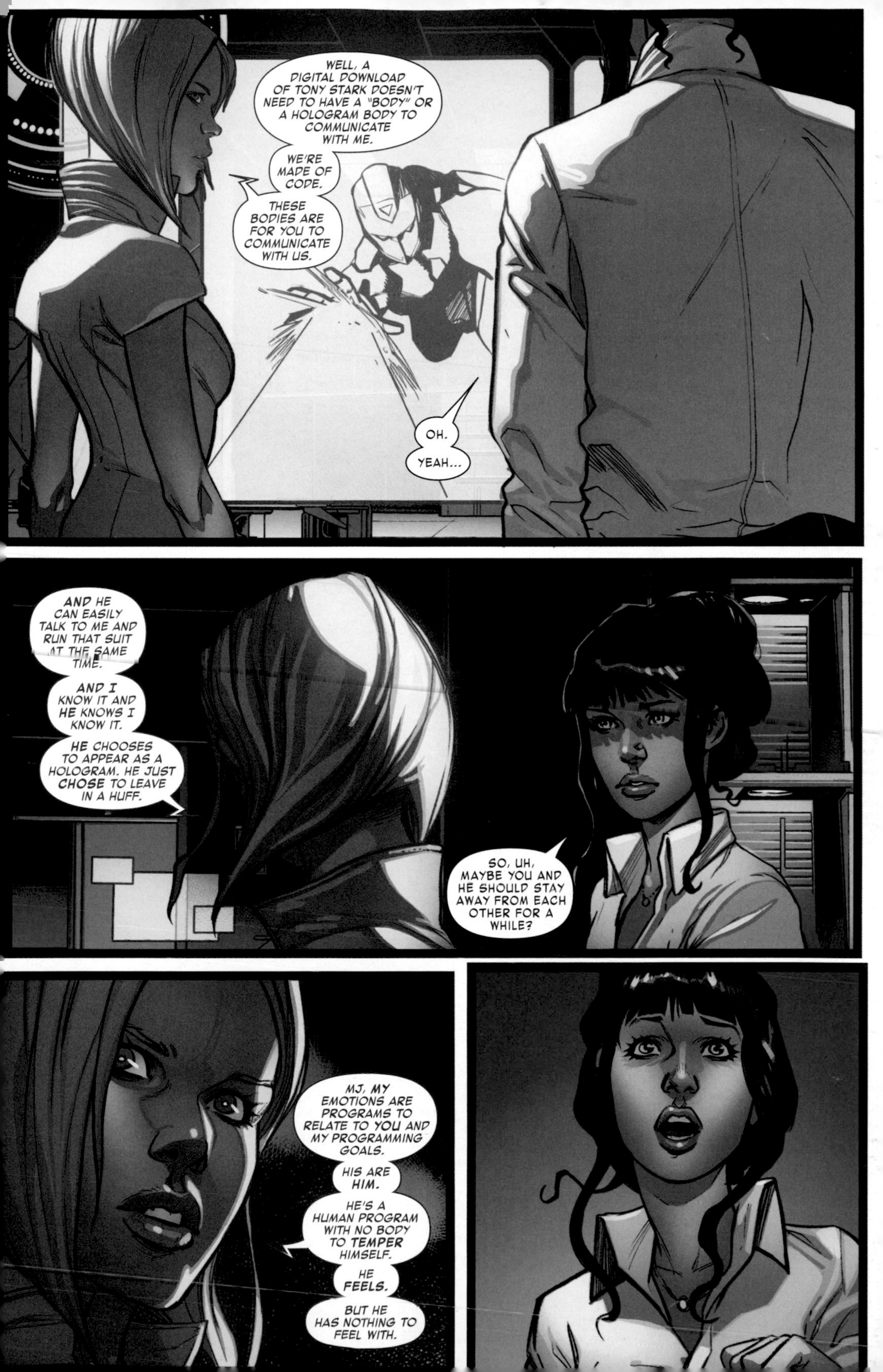
WELL, A DIGITAL DOWNLOAD OF TONY STARK DOESN'T NEED TO HAVE A "BODY" OR A HOLOGRAM BODY TO COMMUNICATE WITH ME.
WE'RE MADE OF CODE.
THESE BODIES ARE FOR YOU TO COMMUNICATE WITH US.
OH.
YEAH...
AND HE CAN EASILY TALK TO ME AND RUN THAT SUIT AT THE SAME TIME.
AND I KNOW IT AND HE KNOWS I KNOW IT.
HE CHOOSES TO APPEAR AS A HOLOGRAM. HE JUST CHOSE TO LEAVE IN A HUFF.
SO, UH, MAYBE YOU AND HE SHOULD STAY AWAY FROM EACH OTHER FOR A WHILE?
MJ, MY EMOTIONS ARE PROGRAMS TO RELATE TO YOU AND MY PROGRAMMING GOALS.
HIS ARE HIM.
HE'S A HUMAN PROGRAM WITH NO BODY TO TEMPER HIMSELF.
HE FEELS.
BUT HE HAS NOTHING TO FEEL WITH.

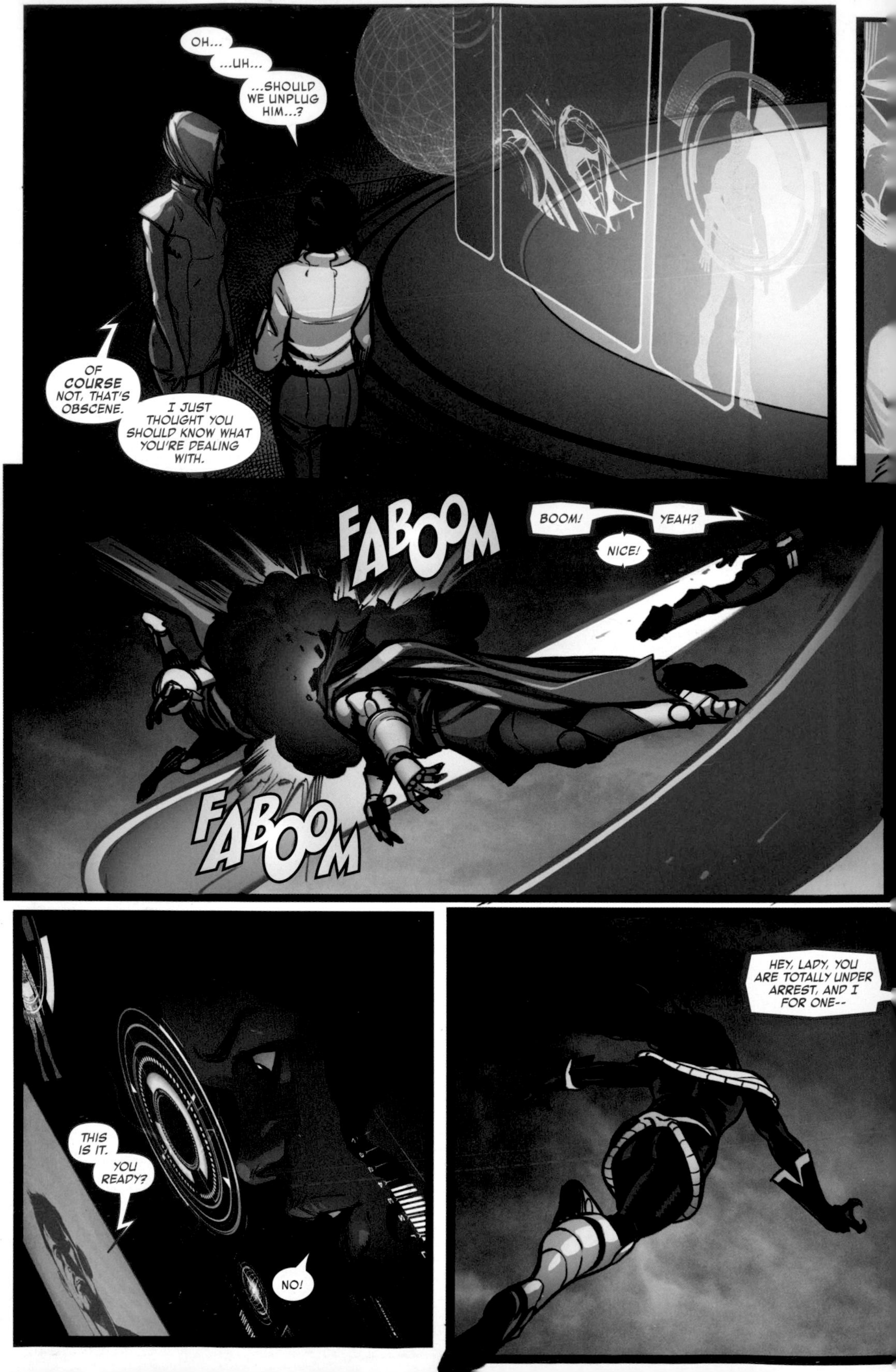
OH...
...UH...
...SHOULD WE UNPLUG HIM...?
OF COURSE NOT, THAT'S OBSCENE.
I JUST THOUGHT YOU SHOULD KNOW WHAT YOU'RE DEALING WITH.
FABOOM
BOOM!
YEAH?
NICE!
FABOOM
THIS IS IT. YOU READY?
NO!
HEY, LADY, YOU ARE TOTALLY UNDER ARREST, AND I FOR ONE--

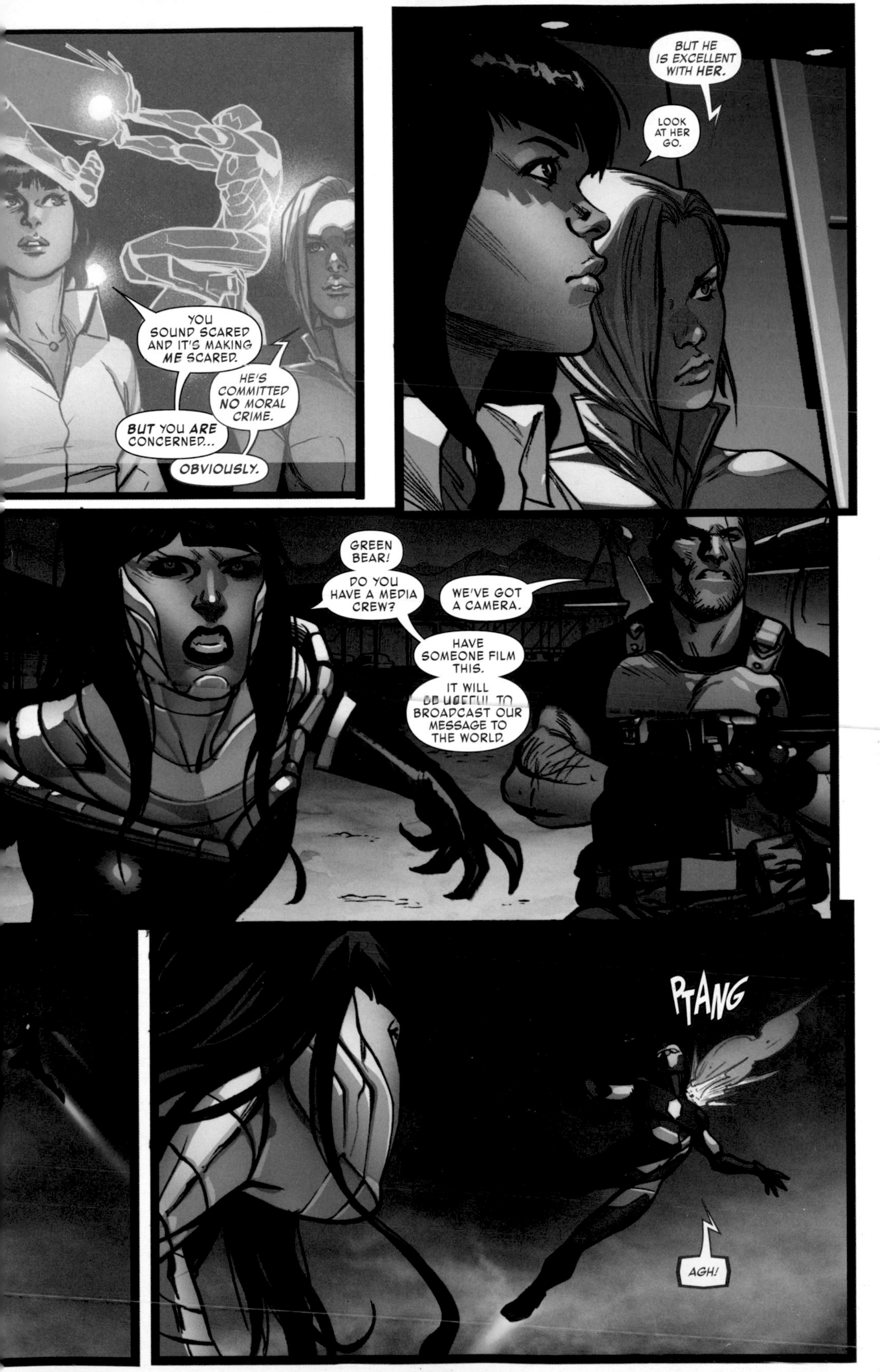
YOU SOUND SCARED AND IT'S MAKING ME SCARED.
HE'S COMMITTED NO MORAL CRIME.
BUT YOU ARE CONCERNED...
OBVIOUSLY.
BUT HE IS EXCELLENT WITH HER.
LOOK AT HER GO.
GREEN BEAR!
DO YOU HAVE A MEDIA CREW?
WE'VE GOT A CAMERA.
HAVE SOMEONE FILM THIS.
IT WILL BE USEFUL TO BROADCAST OUR MESSAGE TO THE WORLD.
PTANG
AGH!

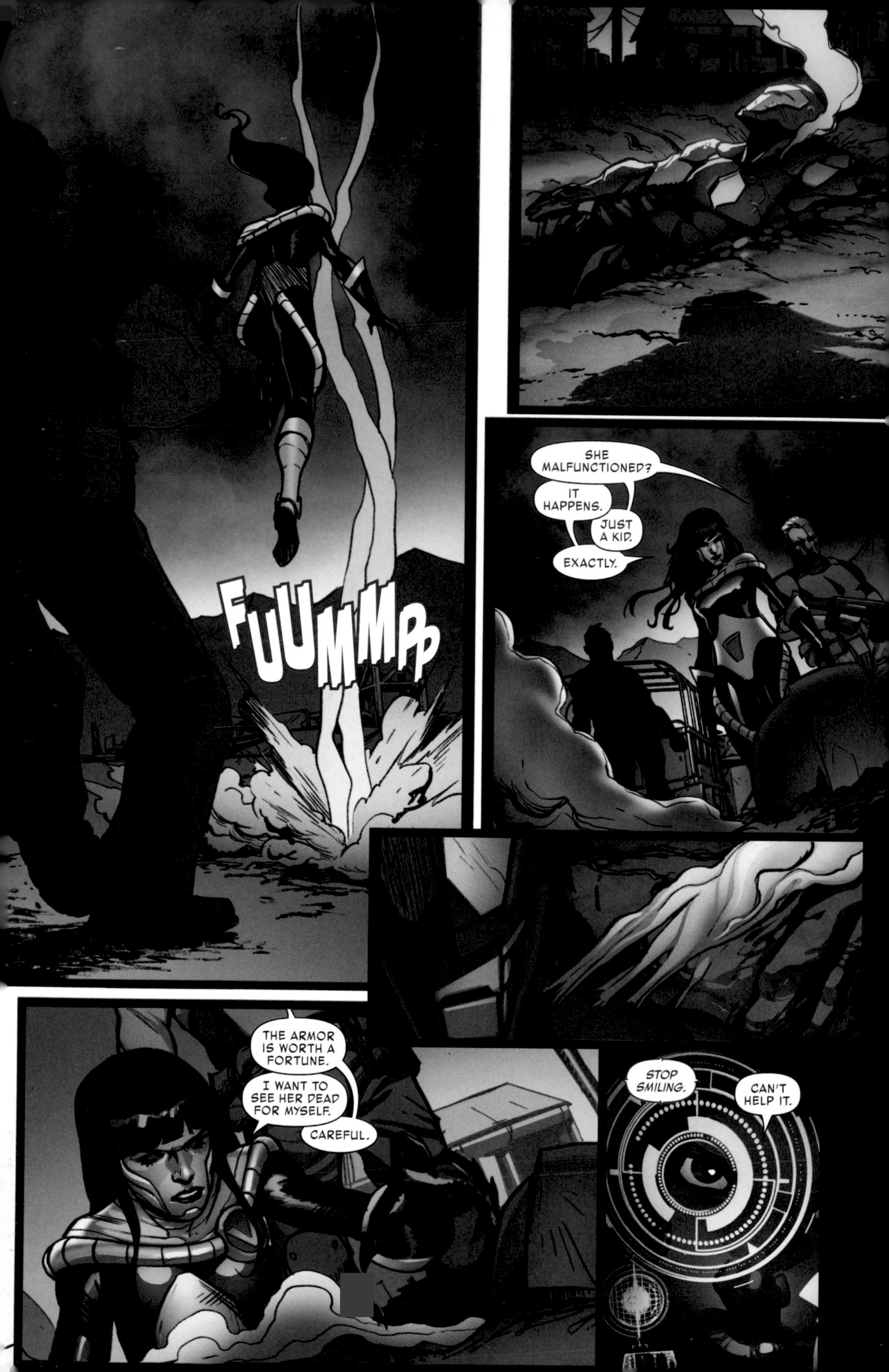
FUUMMPP
SHE MALFUNCTIONED?
IT HAPPENS.
JUST A KID.
EXACTLY.
THE ARMOR IS WORTH A FORTUNE.
I WANT TO SEE HER DEAD FOR MYSELF.
CAREFUL.
STOP SMILING.
CAN'T HELP IT.

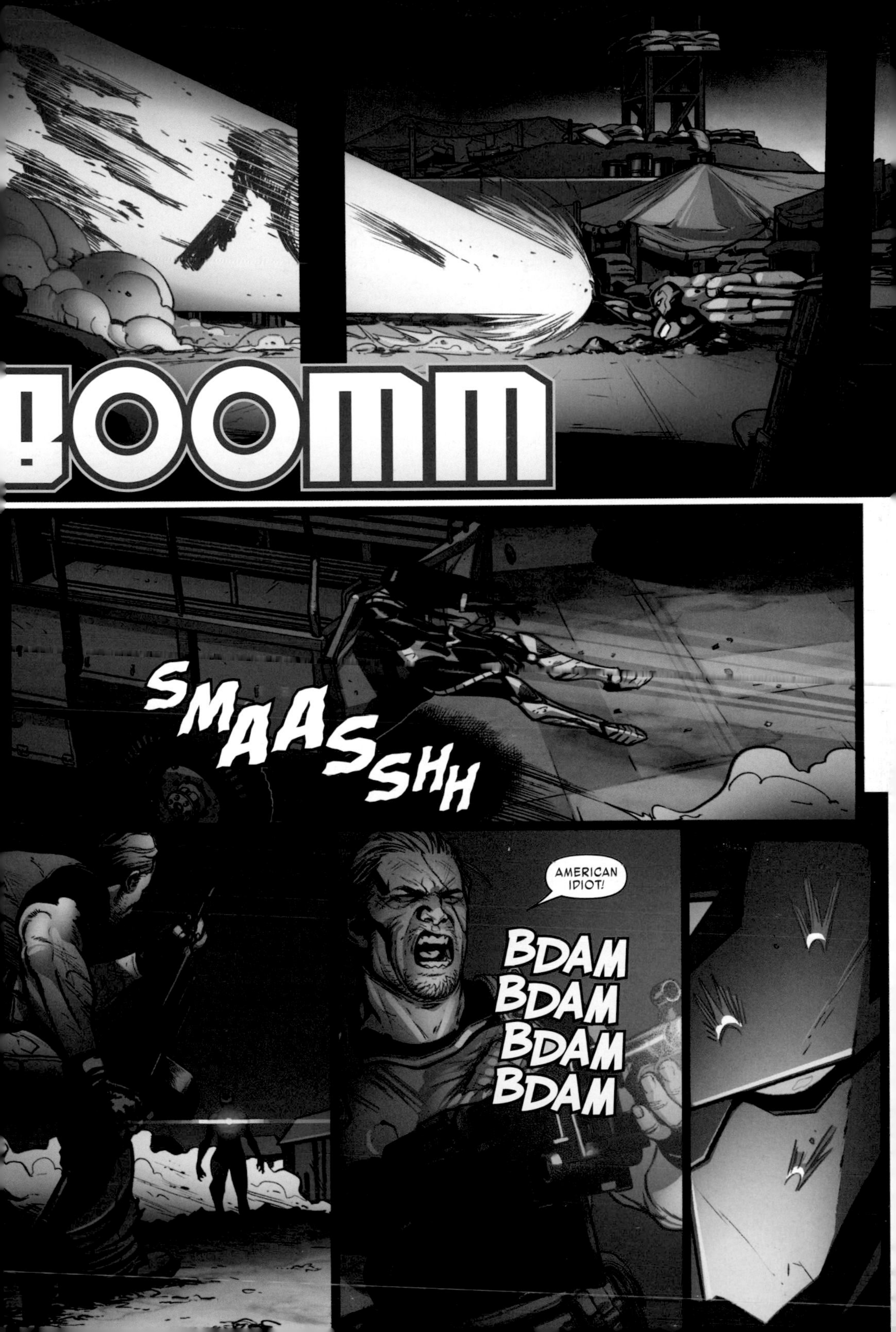
BOOMM
SMAASSHH
AMERICAN IDIOT!
BDAM
BDAM
BDAM
BDAM

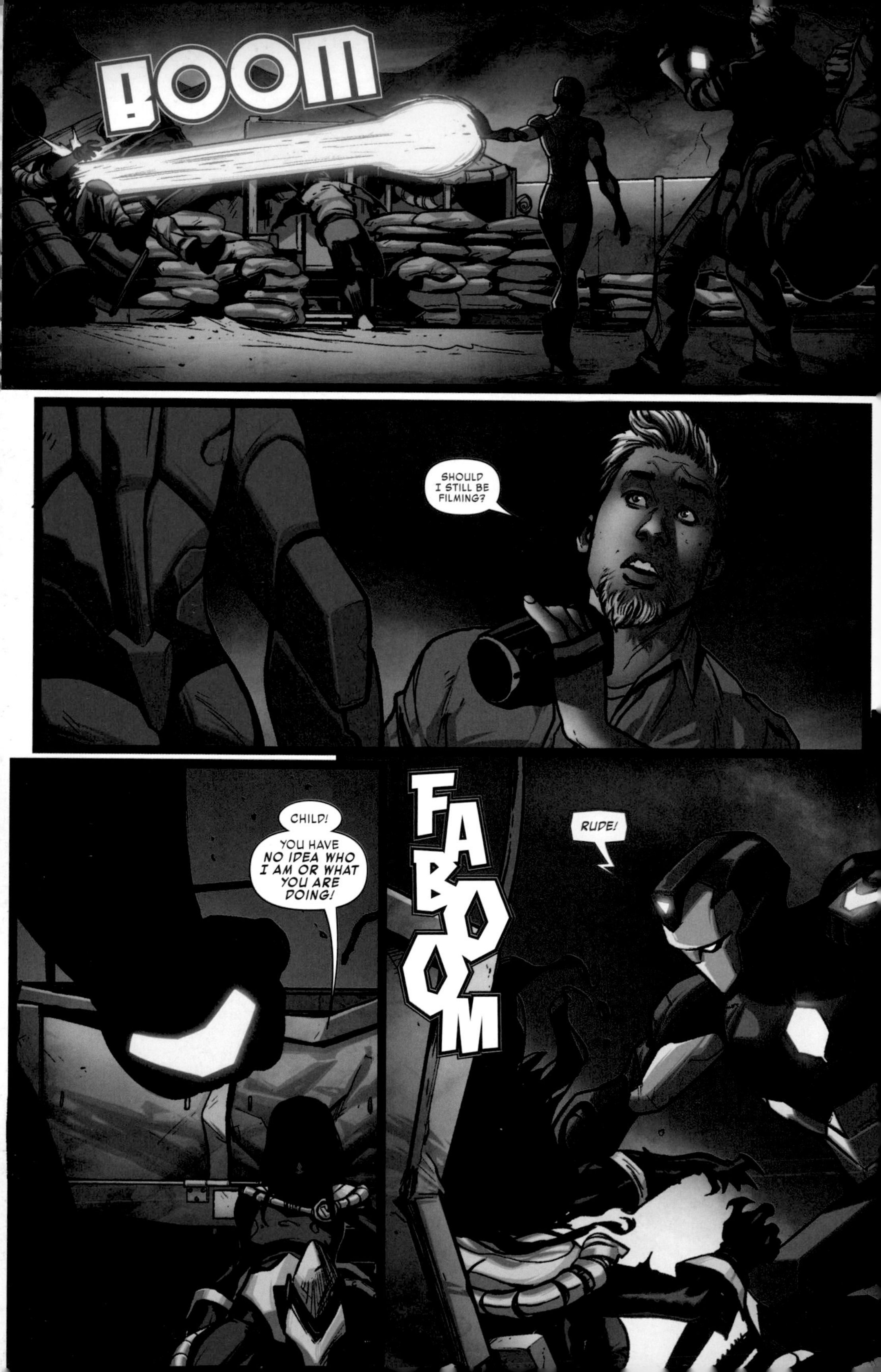
BOOM
SHOULD I STILL BE FILMING?
CHILD!
YOU HAVE NO IDEA WHO I AM OR WHAT YOU ARE DOING!
FABOOM
RUDE!

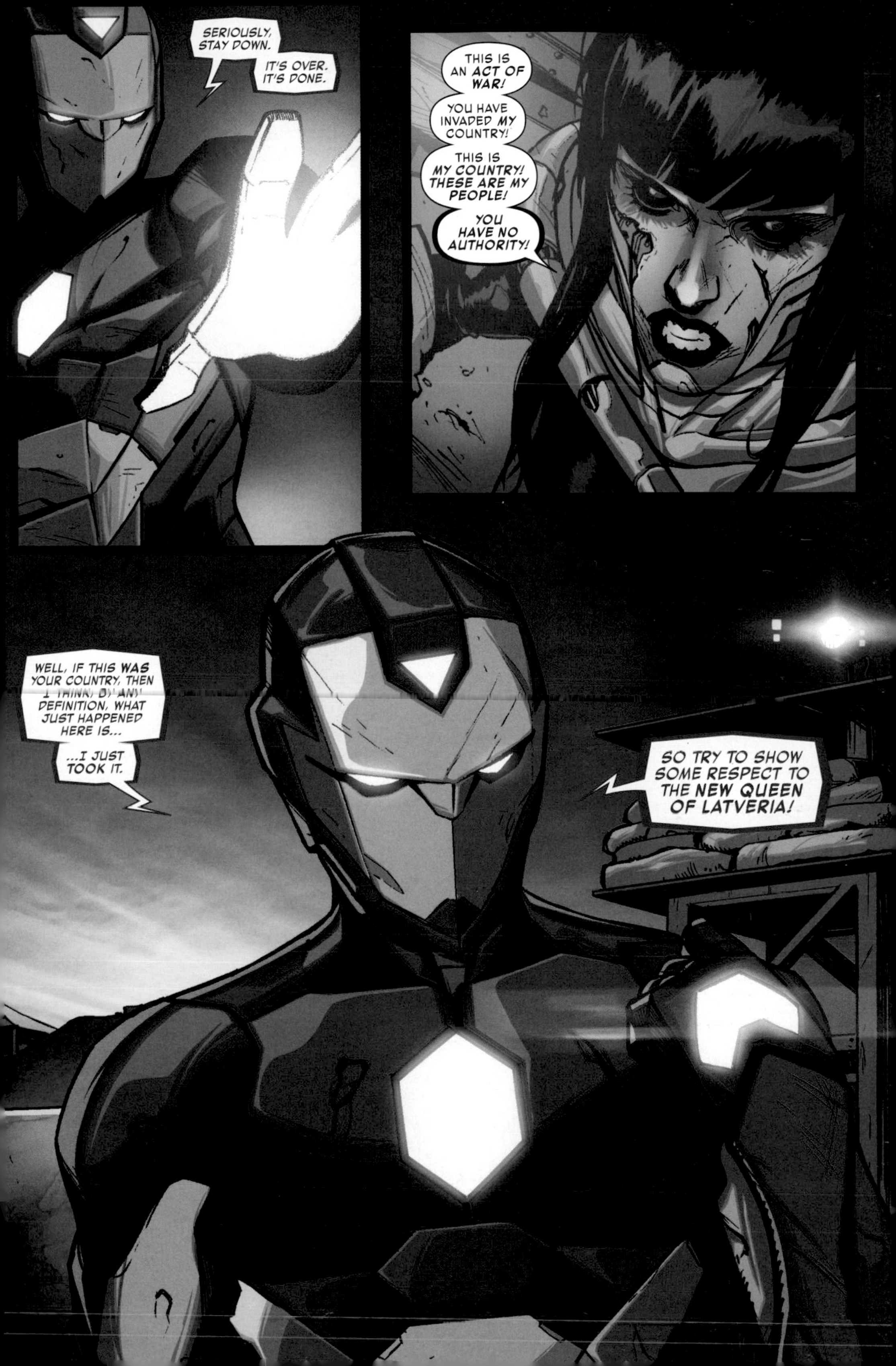

SERIOUSLY, STAY DOWN.
IT'S OVER. IT'S DONE.
THIS IS AN ACT OF WAR!
YOU HAVE INVADED MY COUNTRY!
THIS IS MY COUNTRY! THESE ARE MY PEOPLE!
YOU HAVE NO AUTHORITY!
WELL, IF THIS WAS YOUR COUNTRY, THEN I THINK, BY ANY DEFINITION, WHAT JUST HAPPENED HERE IS...
...I JUST TOOK IT.
SO TRY TO SHOW SOME RESPECT TO THE NEW QUEEN OF LATVERIA!

10

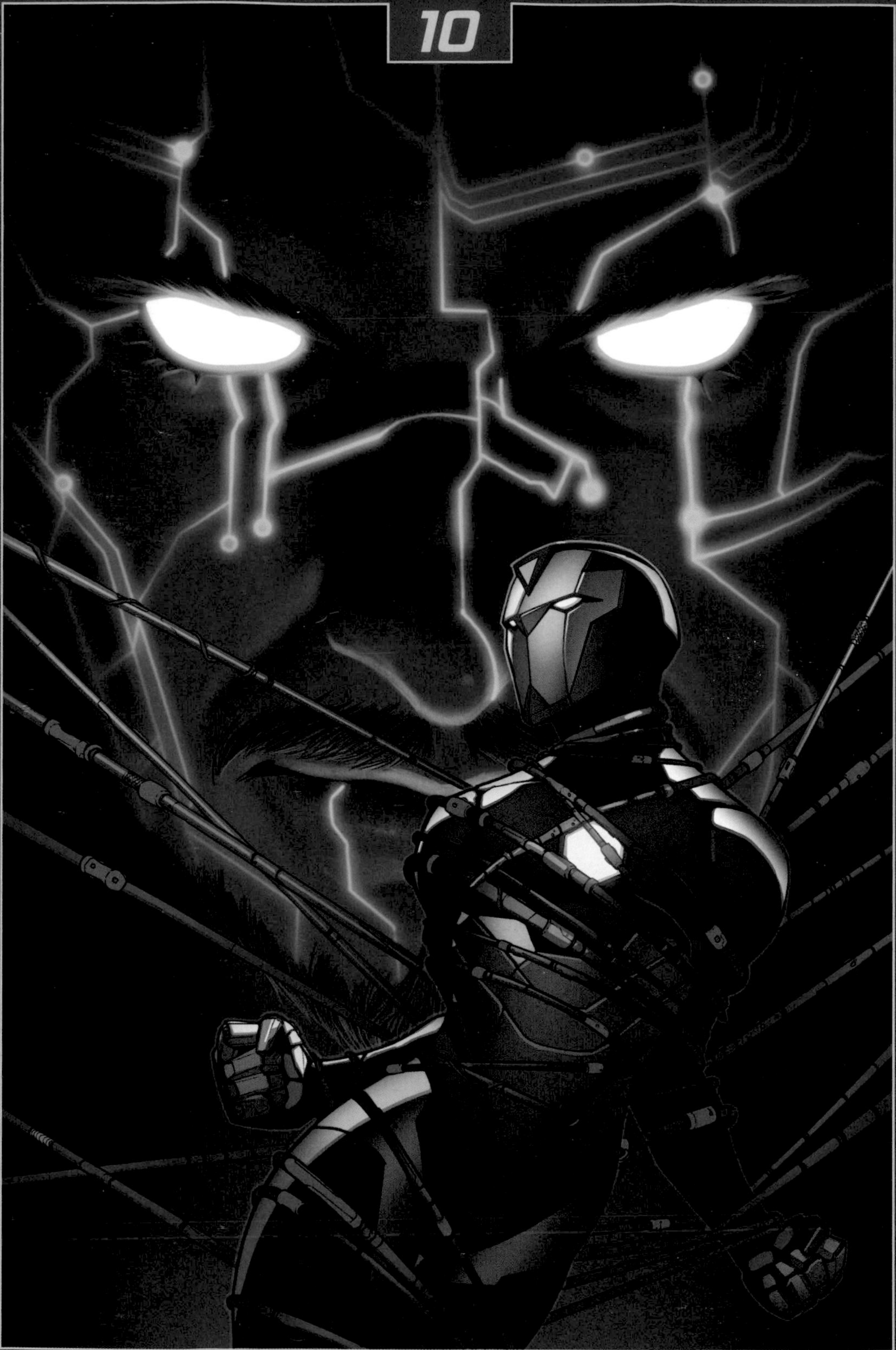

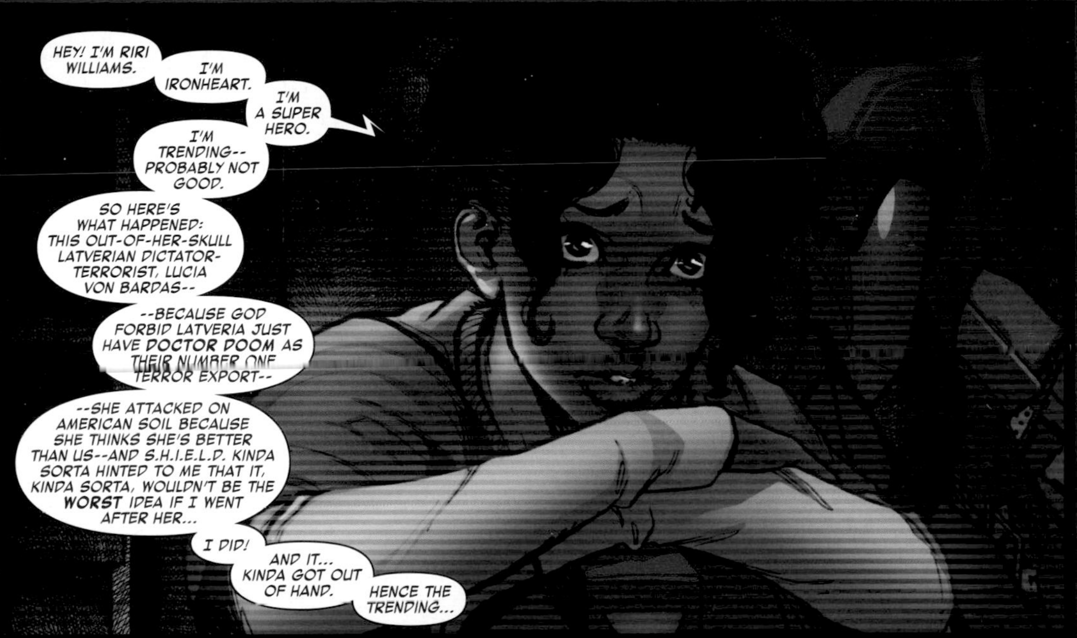
HEY! I'M RIRI WILLIAMS.
I'M IRONHEART.
I'M A SUPER HERO.
I'M TRENDING--PROBABLY NOT GOOD.
SO HERE'S WHAT HAPPENED: THIS OUT-OF-HER-SKULL LATVERIAN DICTATOR-TERRORIST, LUCIA VON BARDAS--
--BECAUSE GOD FORBID LATVERIA JUST HAVE **DOCTOR DOOM** AS THEIR NUMBER ONE TERROR EXPORT--
--SHE ATTACKED ON AMERICAN SOIL BECAUSE SHE THINKS SHE'S BETTER THAN US--AND S.H.I.E.L.D. KINDA SORTA HINTED TO ME THAT IT, KINDA SORTA, WOULDN'T BE THE **WORST** IDEA IF I WENT AFTER HER...
I DID!
AND IT... KINDA GOT OUT OF HAND.
HENCE THE TRENDING...

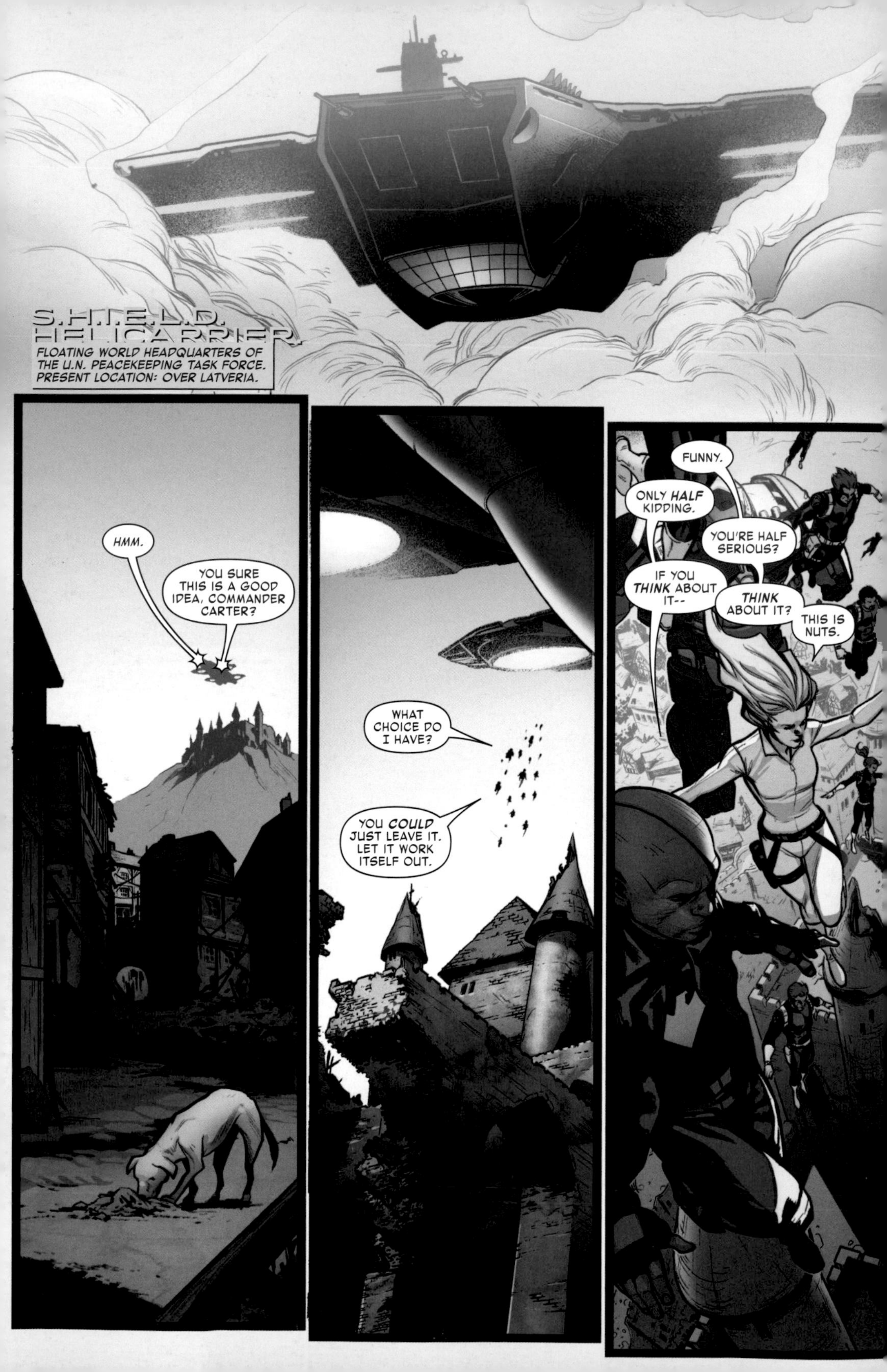
S.H.I.E.L.D. HELICARRIER
FLOATING WORLD HEADQUARTERS OF THE U.N. PEACEKEEPING TASK FORCE. PRESENT LOCATION: OVER LATVERIA.
HMM.
YOU SURE THIS IS A GOOD IDEA, COMMANDER CARTER?
WHAT CHOICE DO I HAVE?
YOU COULD JUST LEAVE IT. LET IT WORK ITSELF OUT.
FUNNY.
ONLY HALF KIDDING.
YOU'RE HALF SERIOUS?
IF YOU THINK ABOUT IT--
THINK ABOUT IT?
THIS IS NUTS.

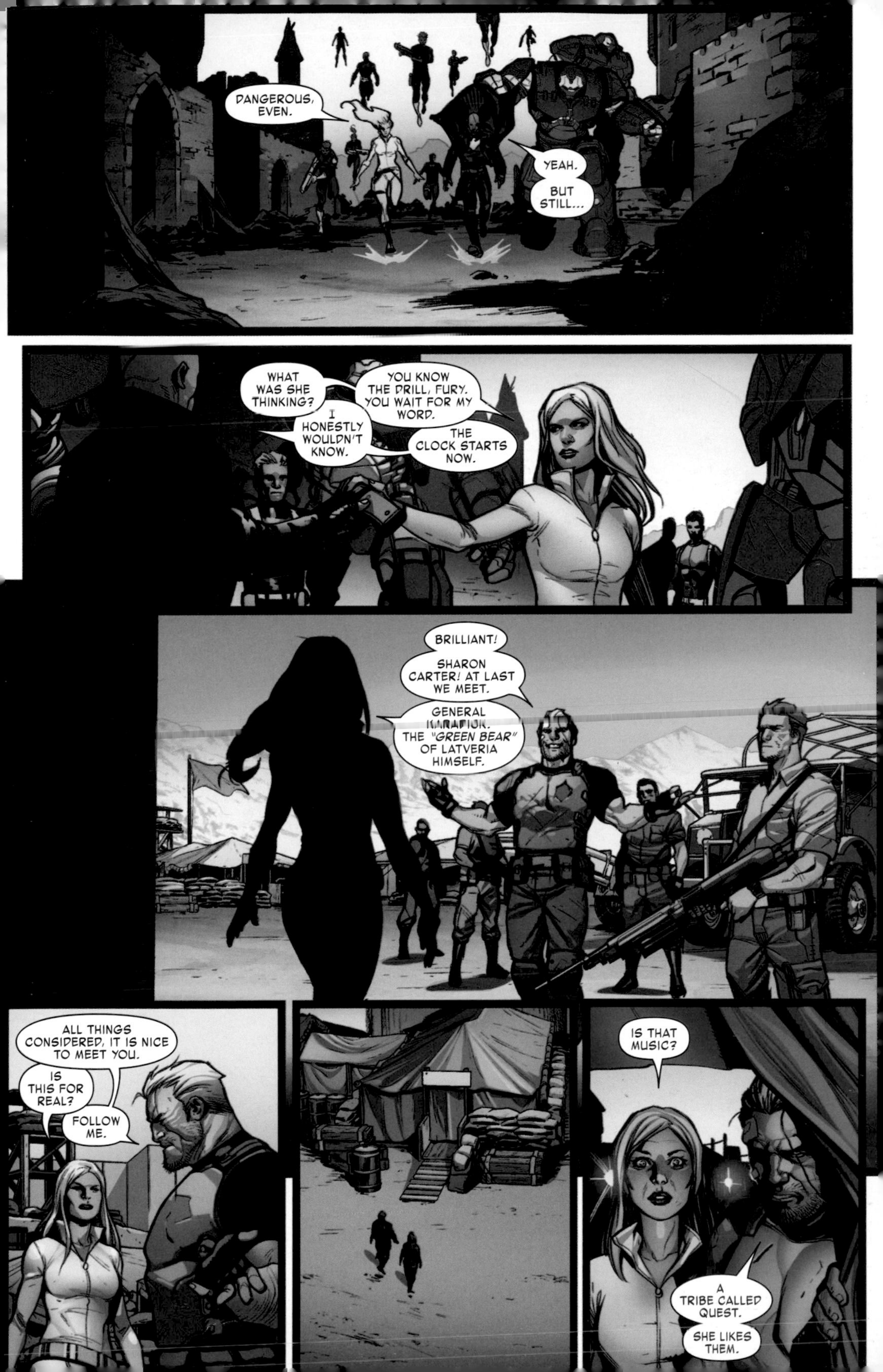
DANGEROUS, EVEN.
YEAH.
BUT STILL...
WHAT WAS SHE THINKING?
YOU KNOW THE DRILL, FURY. YOU WAIT FOR MY WORD.
I HONESTLY WOULDN'T KNOW.
THE CLOCK STARTS NOW.
BRILLIANT!
SHARON CARTER! AT LAST WE MEET.
GENERAL
THE "GREEN BEAR" OF LATVERIA HIMSELF.
ALL THINGS CONSIDERED, IT IS NICE TO MEET YOU.
IS THIS FOR REAL?
FOLLOW ME.
IS THAT MUSIC?
A TRIBE CALLED QUEST.
SHE LIKES THEM.

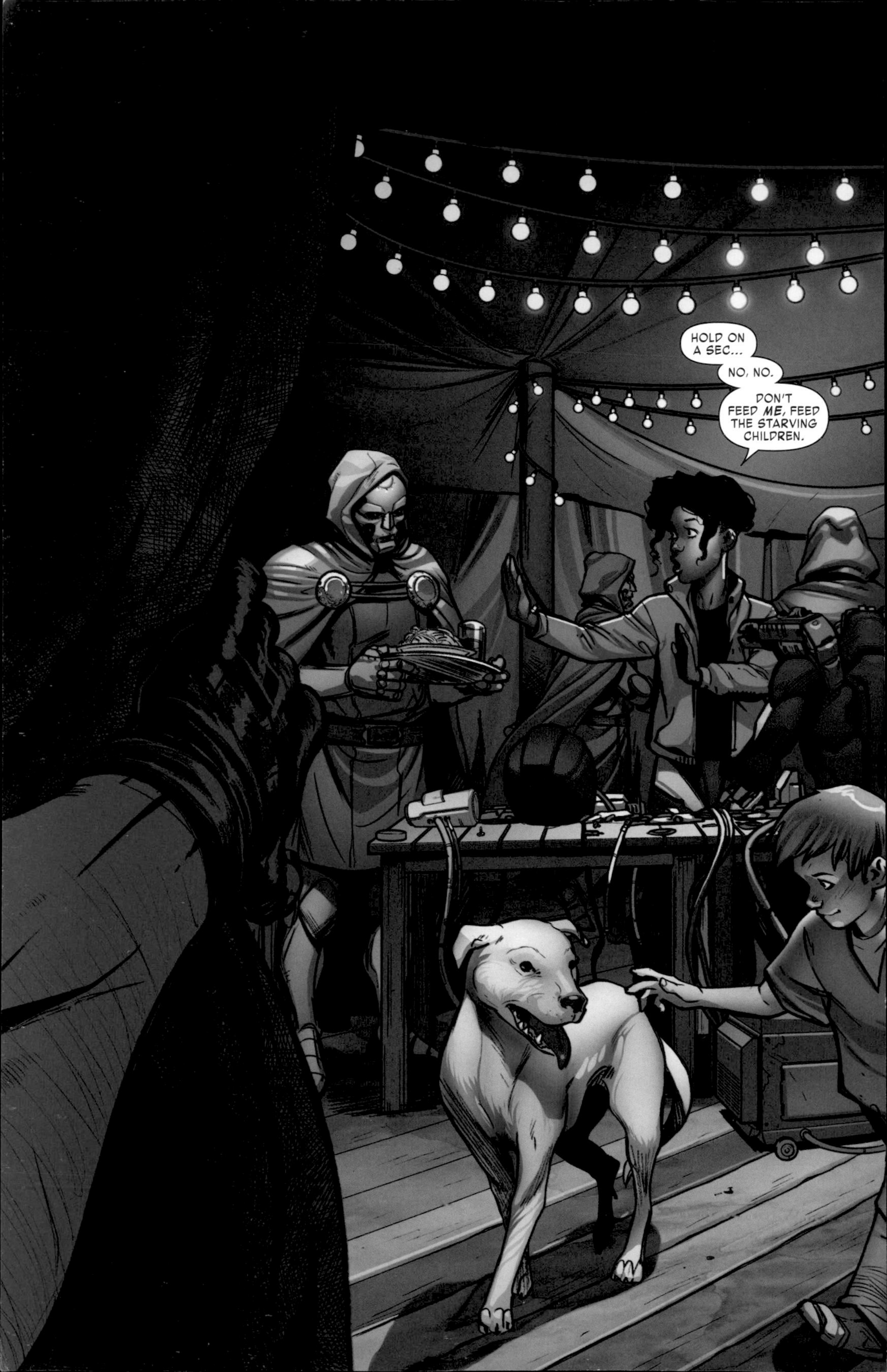
HOLD ON A SEC...
NO, NO.
DON'T FEED *ME*, FEED THE STARVING CHILDREN.

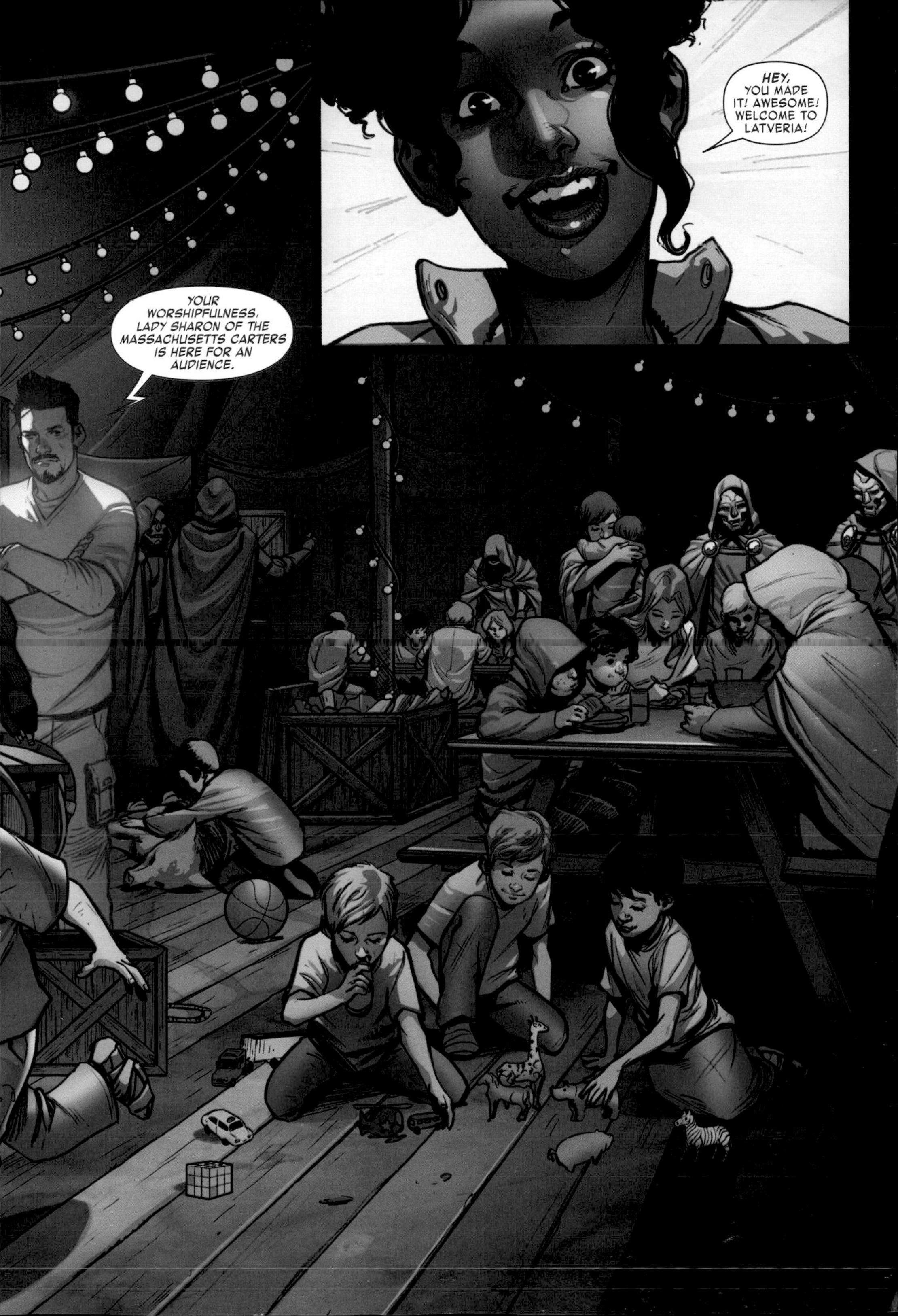
YOUR WORSHIPFULNESS. LADY SHARON OF THE MASSACHUSETTS CARTERS IS HERE FOR AN AUDIENCE.
HEY, YOU MADE IT! AWESOME! WELCOME TO LATVERIA!

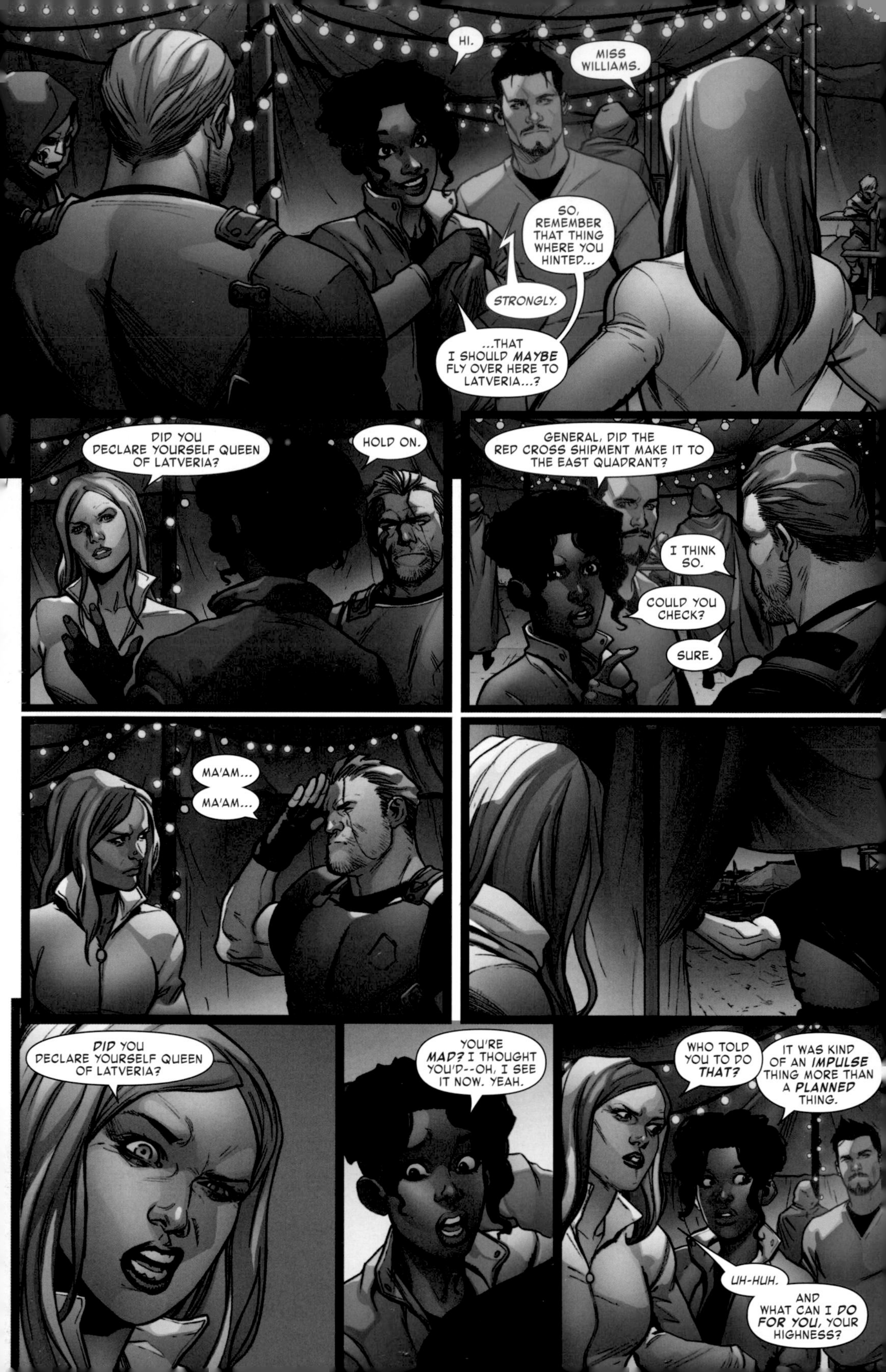
HI.
MISS WILLIAMS.
SO, REMEMBER THAT THING WHERE YOU HINTED...
STRONGLY.
...THAT I SHOULD MAYBE FLY OVER HERE TO LATVERIA...?
DID YOU DECLARE YOURSELF QUEEN OF LATVERIA?
HOLD ON.
GENERAL, DID THE RED CROSS SHIPMENT MAKE IT TO THE EAST QUADRANT?
I THINK SO.
COULD YOU CHECK?
SURE.
MA'AM...
MA'AM...
DID YOU DECLARE YOURSELF QUEEN OF LATVERIA?
YOU'RE MAD? I THOUGHT YOU'D--OH, I SEE IT NOW. YEAH.
WHO TOLD YOU TO DO THAT?
IT WAS KIND OF AN IMPULSE THING MORE THAN A PLANNED THING.
UH-HUH.
AND WHAT CAN I DO FOR YOU, YOUR HIGHNESS?

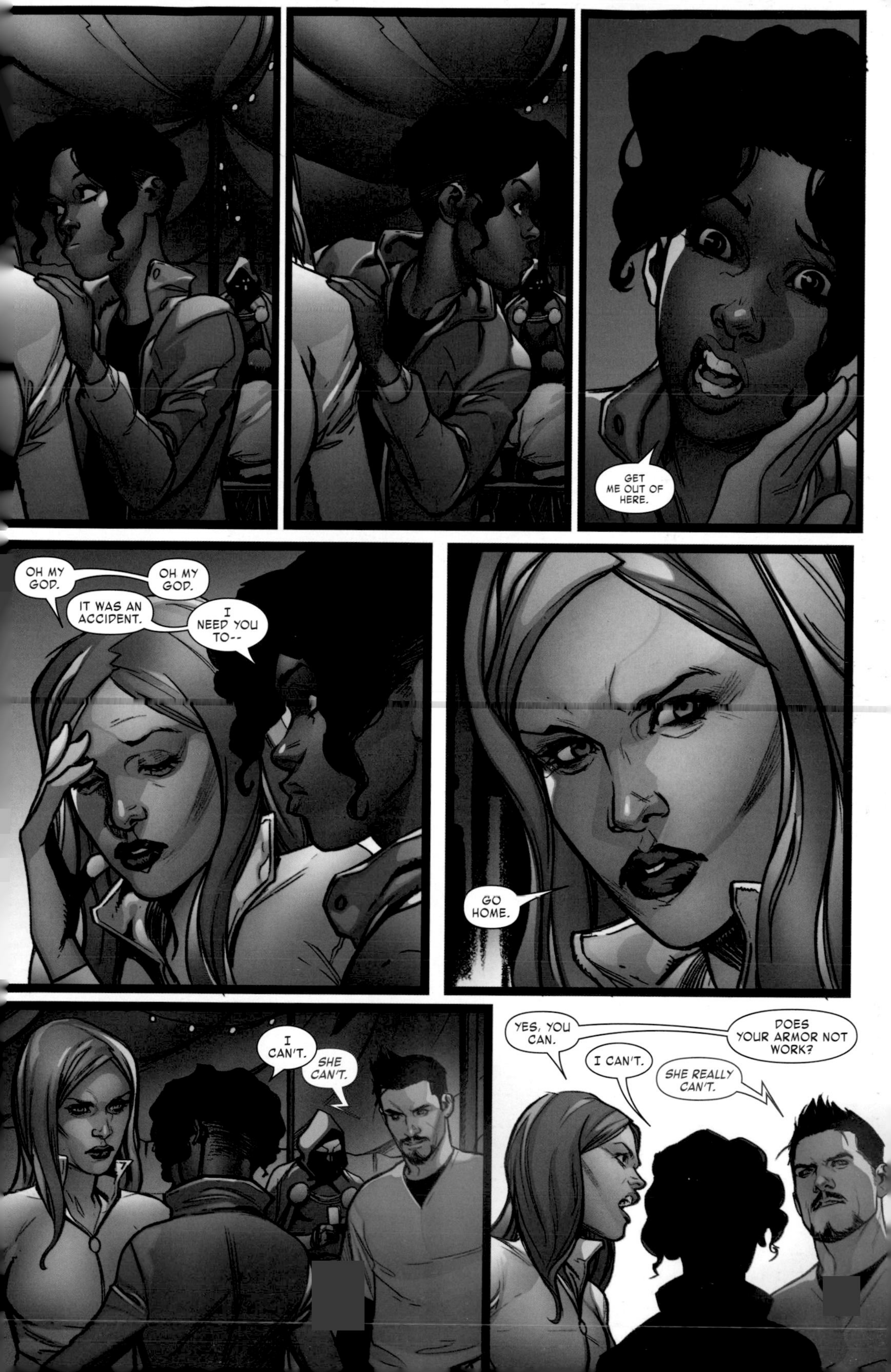
GET ME OUT OF HERE.
OH MY GOD.
OH MY GOD.
IT WAS AN ACCIDENT.
I NEED YOU TO--
GO HOME.
I CAN'T.
SHE CAN'T.
YES, YOU CAN.
DOES YOUR ARMOR NOT WORK?
I CAN'T.
SHE REALLY CAN'T.

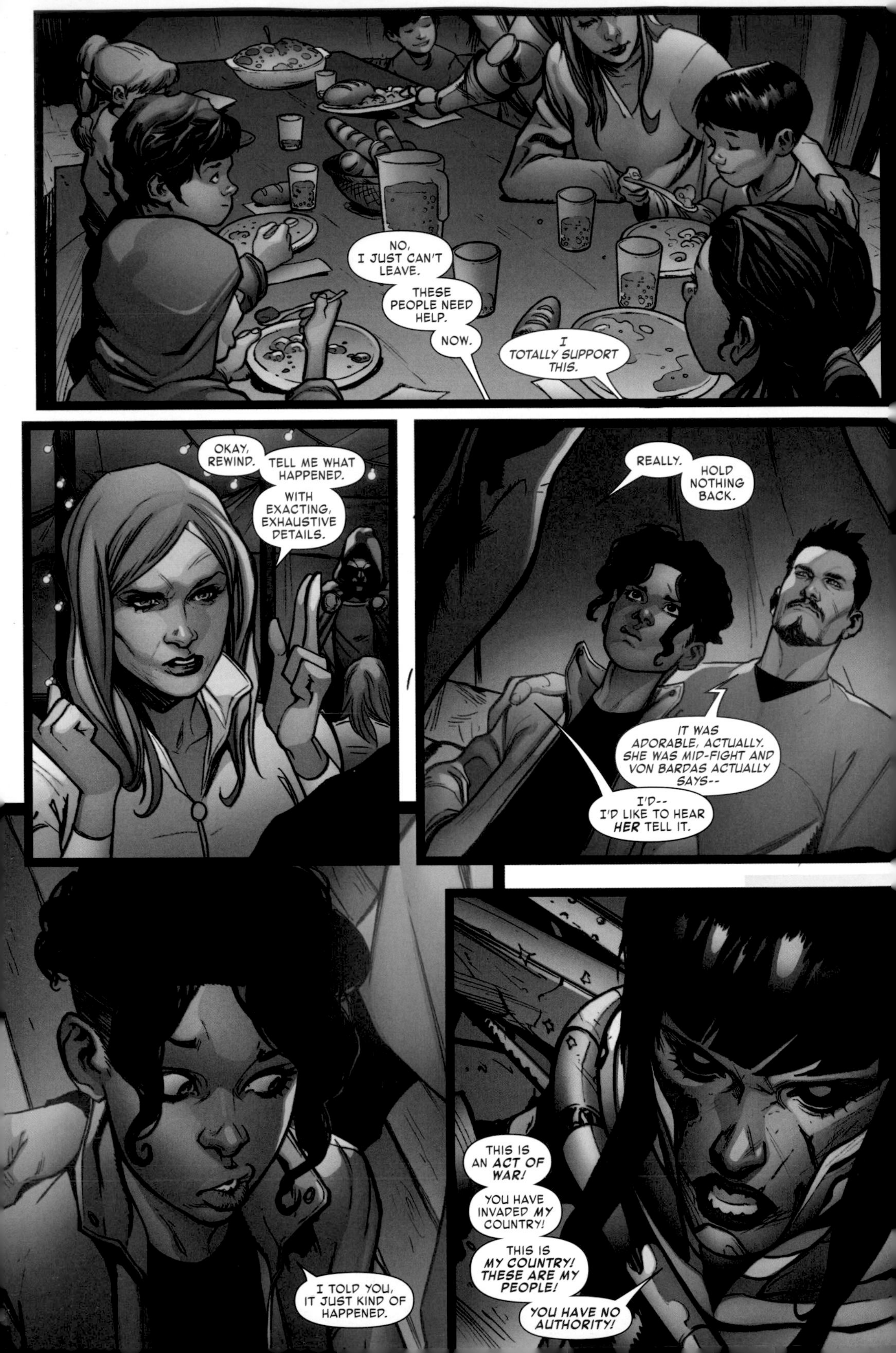

NO, I JUST CAN'T LEAVE.
THESE PEOPLE NEED HELP.
NOW.
I TOTALLY SUPPORT THIS.
OKAY, REWIND.
TELL ME WHAT HAPPENED.
WITH EXACTING, EXHAUSTIVE DETAILS.
REALLY.
HOLD NOTHING BACK.
IT WAS ADORABLE, ACTUALLY. SHE WAS MID-FIGHT AND VON BARDAS ACTUALLY SAYS--
I'D-- I'D LIKE TO HEAR HER TELL IT.
I TOLD YOU, IT JUST KIND OF HAPPENED.
THIS IS AN ACT OF WAR!
YOU HAVE INVADED MY COUNTRY!
THIS IS MY COUNTRY! THESE ARE MY PEOPLE!
YOU HAVE NO AUTHORITY!

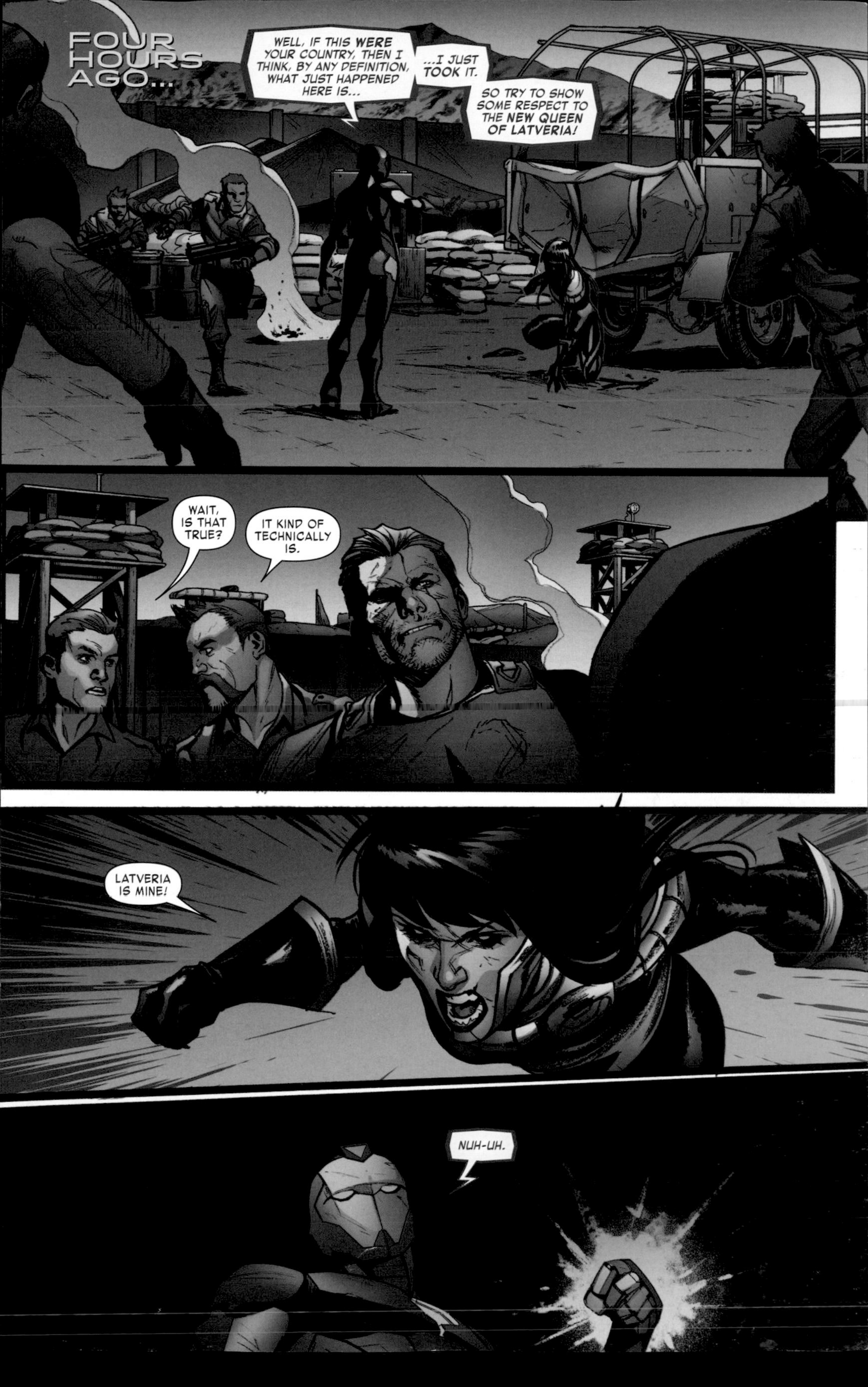
FOUR HOURS AGO...
WELL, IF THIS WERE YOUR COUNTRY, THEN I THINK, BY ANY DEFINITION, WHAT JUST HAPPENED HERE IS...
...I JUST TOOK IT.
SO TRY TO SHOW SOME RESPECT TO THE NEW QUEEN OF LATVERIA!
WAIT, IS THAT TRUE?
IT KIND OF TECHNICALLY IS.
LATVERIA IS MINE!
NUH-UH.

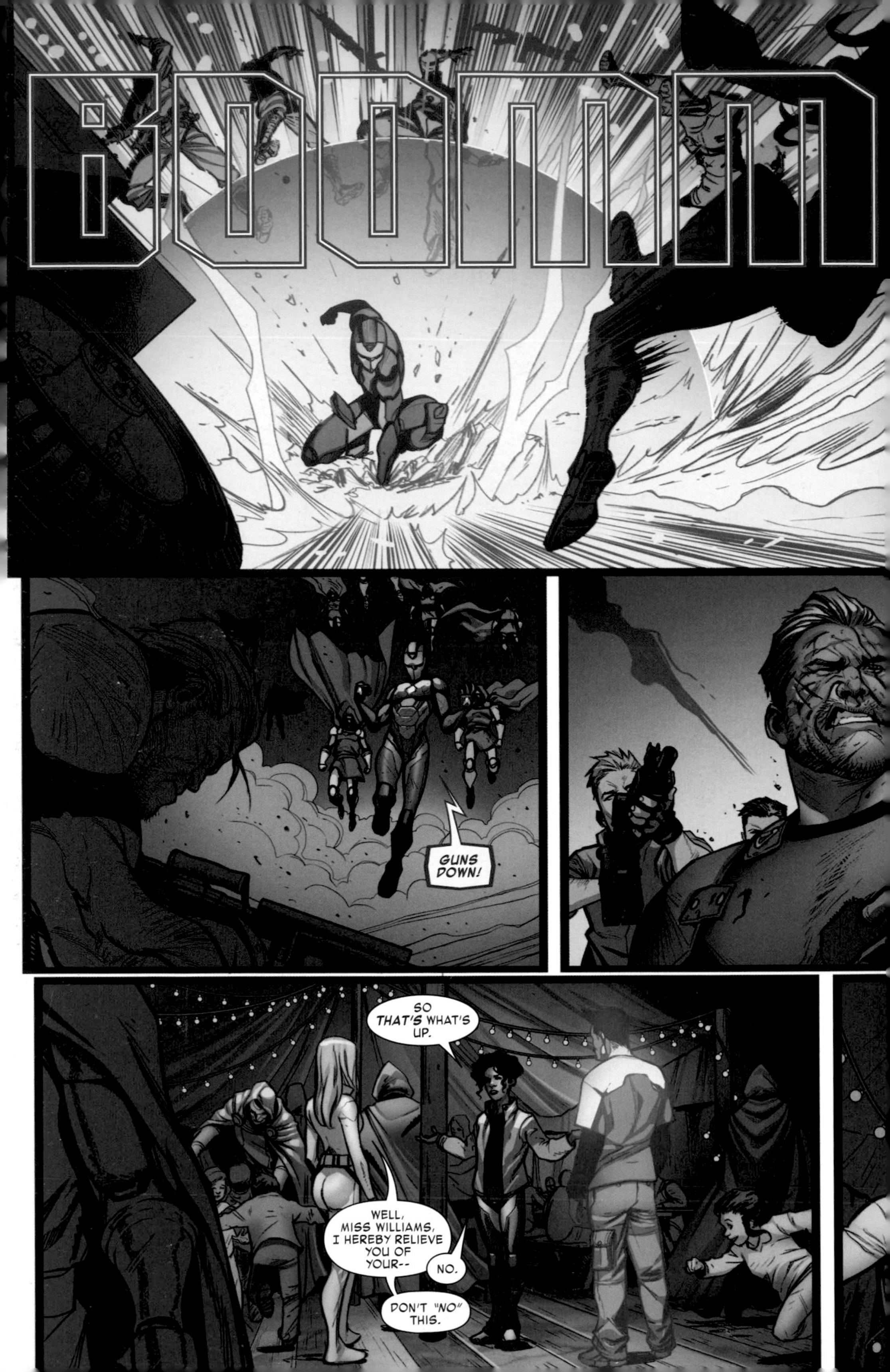
BOOMM
GUNS DOWN!
SO THAT'S WHAT'S UP.
WELL, MISS WILLIAMS, I HEREBY RELIEVE YOU OF YOUR--
NO.
DON'T "NO" THIS.

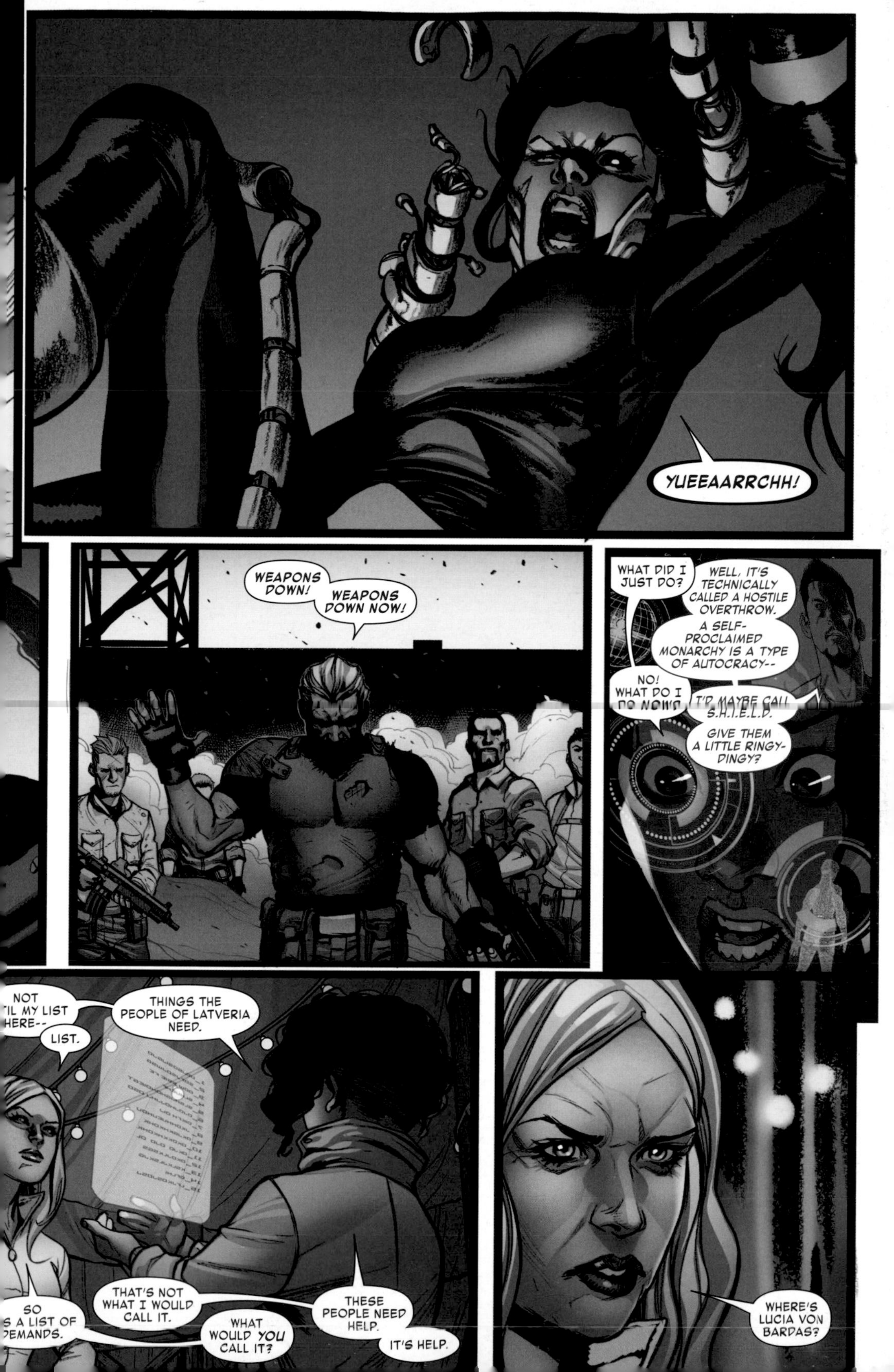
YUEEAARRCHH!
WEAPONS DOWN!
WEAPONS DOWN NOW!
WHAT DID I JUST DO?
WELL, IT'S TECHNICALLY CALLED A HOSTILE OVERTHROW.
A SELF-PROCLAIMED MONARCHY IS A TYPE OF AUTOCRACY--
NO! WHAT DO I DO NOW?
I'D MAYBE CALL S.H.I.E.L.D.
GIVE THEM A LITTLE RINGY-DINGY?
NOT
TIL MY LIST
HERE--
LIST.
THINGS THE PEOPLE OF LATVERIA NEED.
SO
S A LIST OF
DEMANDS.
THAT'S NOT WHAT I WOULD CALL IT.
WHAT WOULD *YOU* CALL IT?
THESE PEOPLE NEED HELP.
IT'S HELP.
WHERE'S LUCIA VON BARDAS?

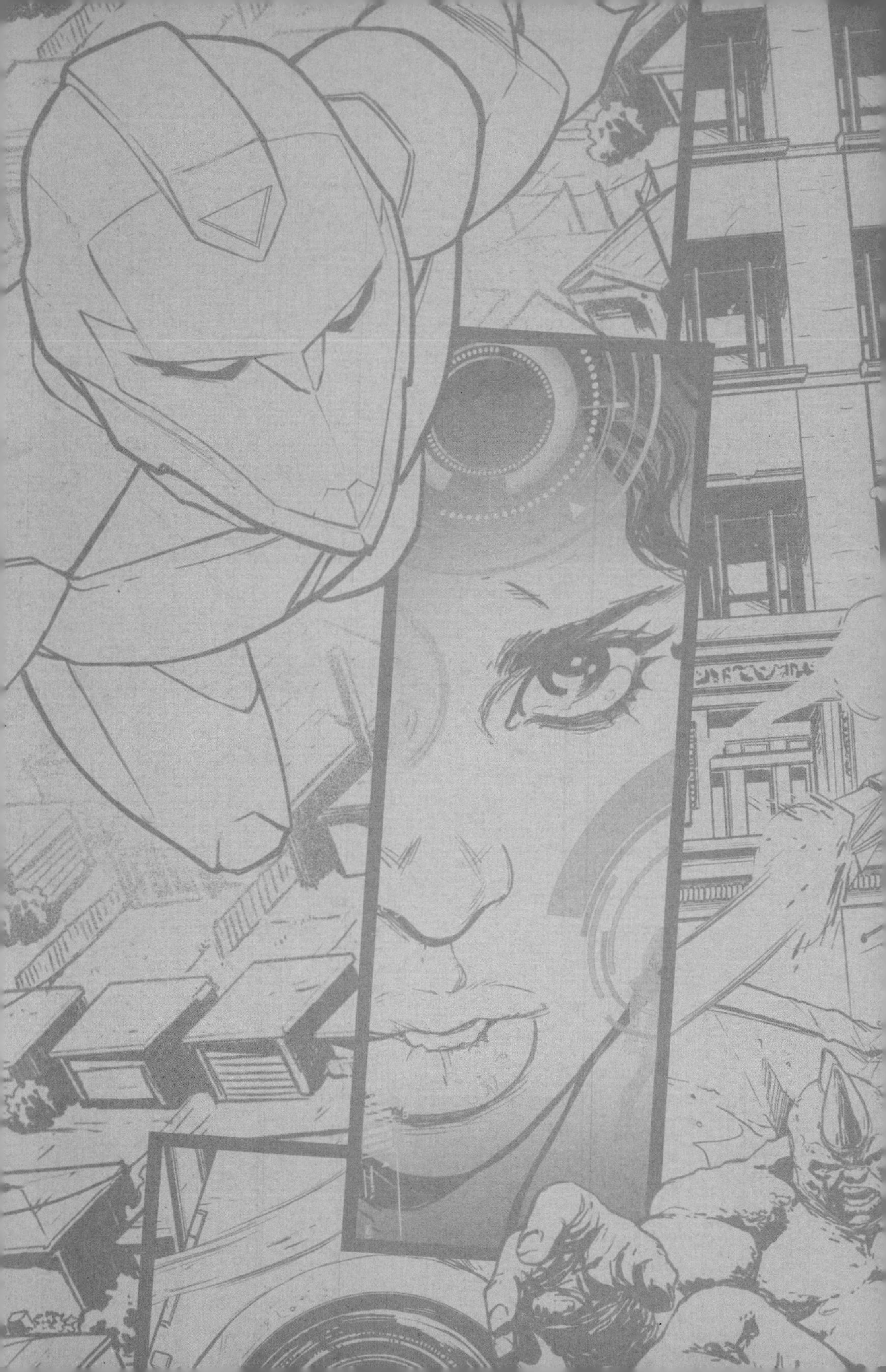

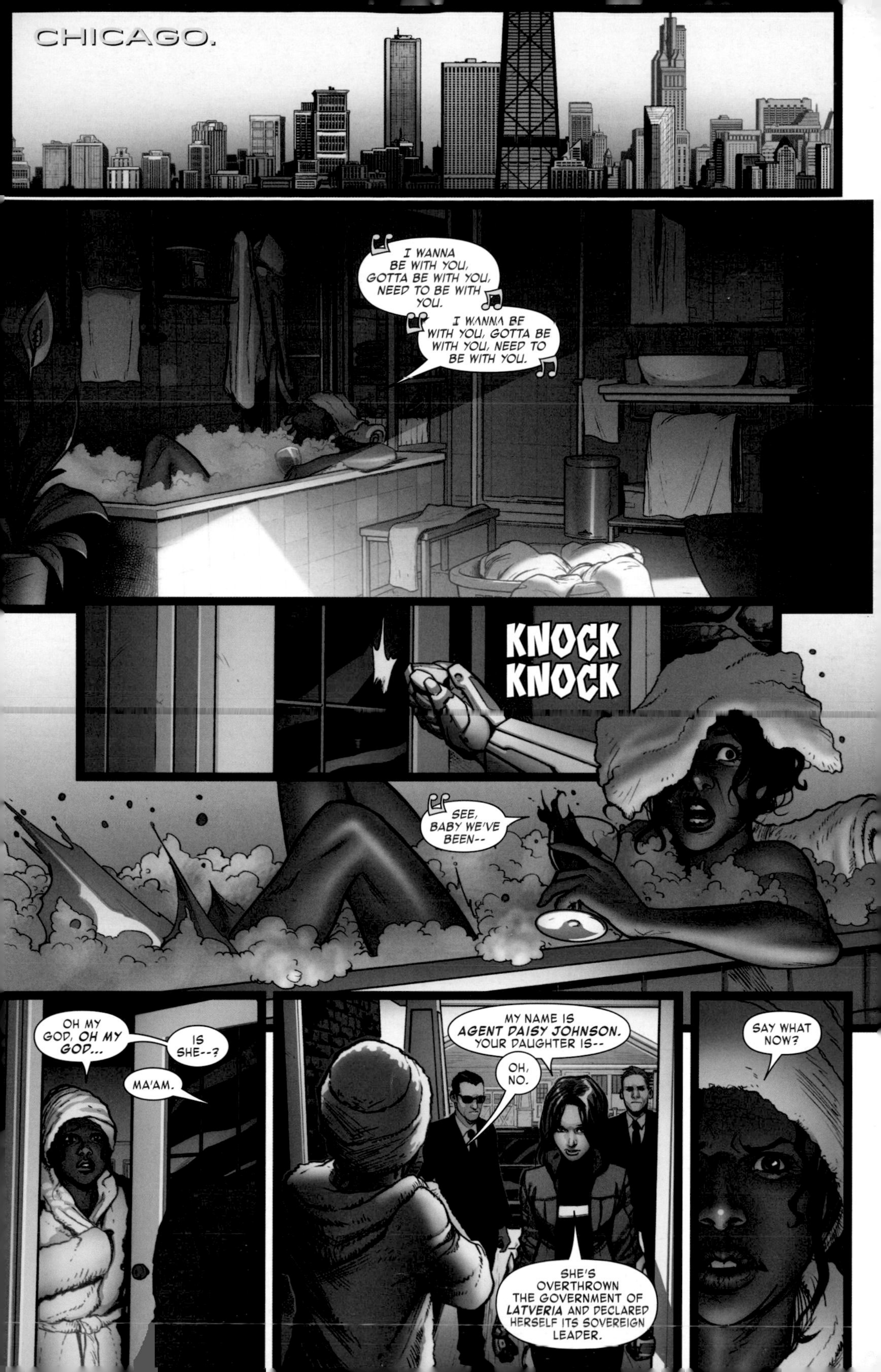
CHICAGO.
I WANNA BE WITH YOU, GOTTA BE WITH YOU, NEED TO BE WITH YOU.
I WANNA BE WITH YOU, GOTTA BE WITH YOU, NEED TO BE WITH YOU.
KNOCK KNOCK
SEE, BABY WE'VE BEEN--
OH MY GOD, OH MY GOD...
IS SHE--?
MA'AM.
MY NAME IS AGENT DAISY JOHNSON. YOUR DAUGHTER IS--
OH, NO.
SHE'S OVERTHROWN THE GOVERNMENT OF LATVERIA AND DECLARED HERSELF ITS SOVEREIGN LEADER.
SAY WHAT NOW?

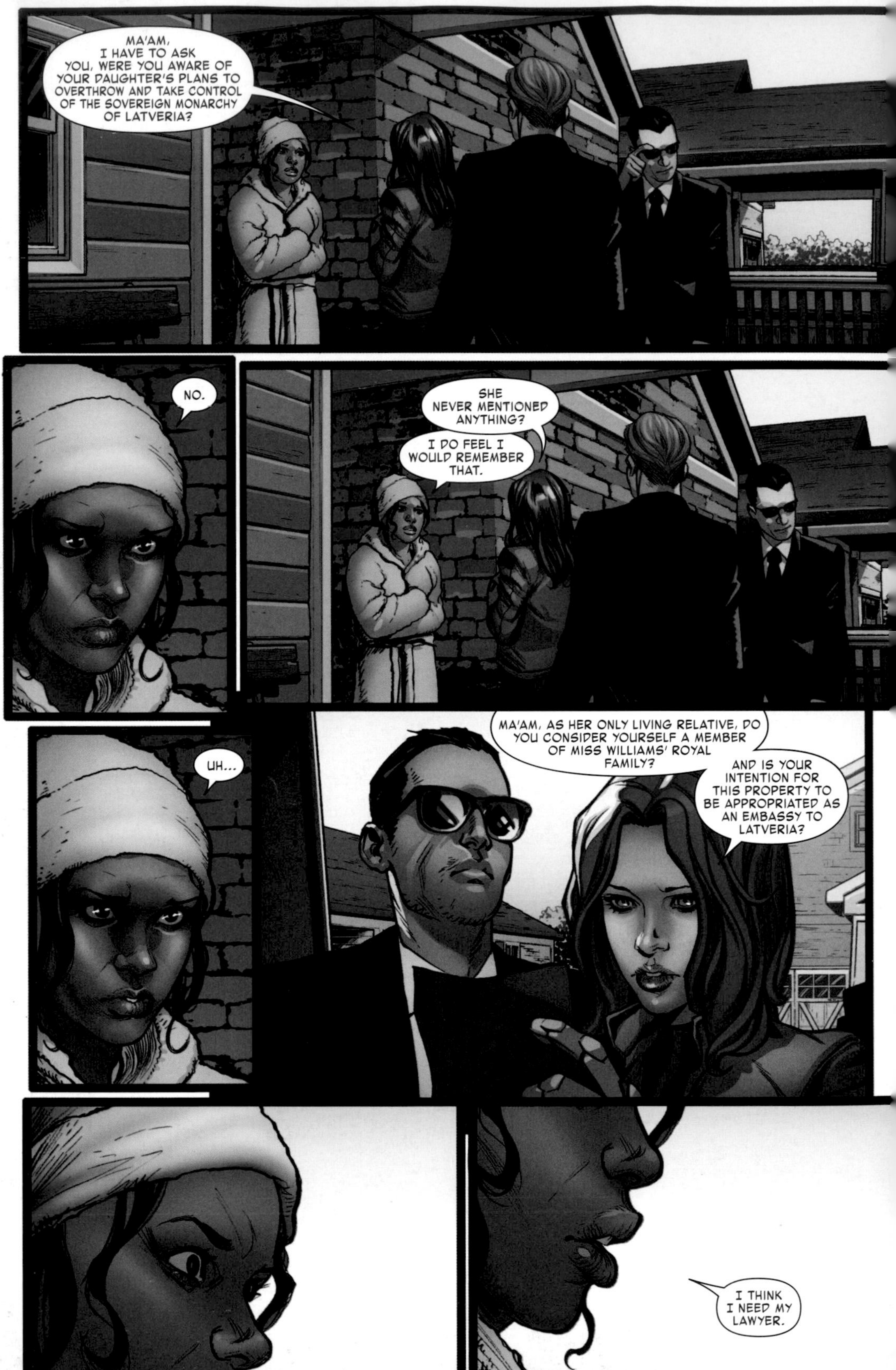
MA'AM, I HAVE TO ASK YOU, WERE YOU AWARE OF YOUR DAUGHTER'S PLANS TO OVERTHROW AND TAKE CONTROL OF THE SOVEREIGN MONARCHY OF LATVERIA?
NO.
SHE NEVER MENTIONED ANYTHING?
I DO FEEL I WOULD REMEMBER THAT.
UH...
MA'AM, AS HER ONLY LIVING RELATIVE, DO YOU CONSIDER YOURSELF A MEMBER OF MISS WILLIAMS' ROYAL FAMILY?
AND IS YOUR INTENTION FOR THIS PROPERTY TO BE APPROPRIATED AS AN EMBASSY TO LATVERIA?
I THINK I NEED MY LAWYER.

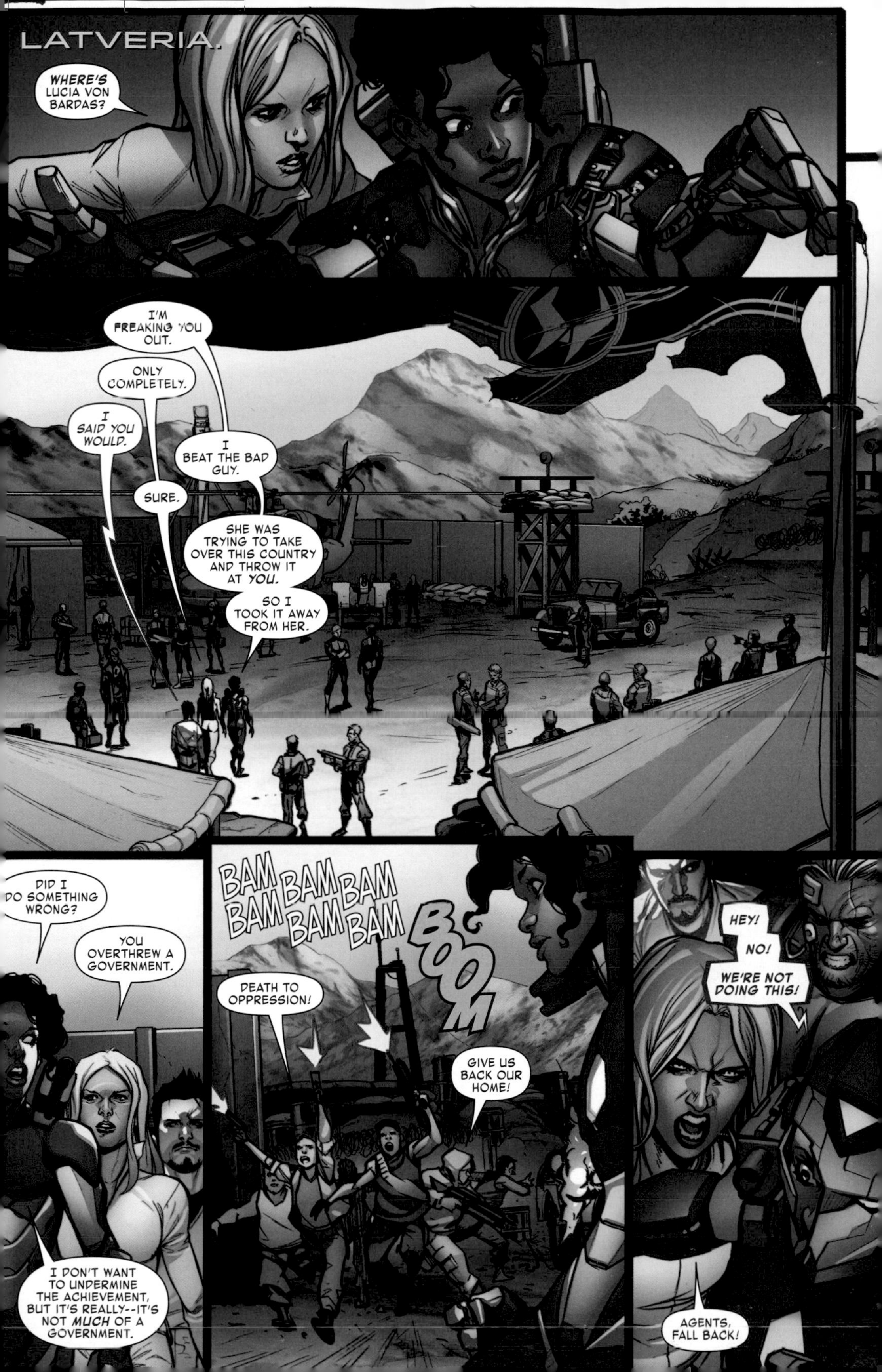
LATVERIA.
WHERE'S LUCIA VON BARDAS?
I'M FREAKING YOU OUT.
ONLY COMPLETELY.
I SAID YOU WOULD.
I BEAT THE BAD GUY.
SURE.
SHE WAS TRYING TO TAKE OVER THIS COUNTRY AND THROW IT AT YOU.
SO I TOOK IT AWAY FROM HER.
DID I DO SOMETHING WRONG?
YOU OVERTHREW A GOVERNMENT.
I DON'T WANT TO UNDERMINE THE ACHIEVEMENT, BUT IT'S REALLY--IT'S NOT MUCH OF A GOVERNMENT.
BAM BAM BAM BAM BAM BAM BAM
BOOOM
DEATH TO OPPRESSION!
GIVE US BACK OUR HOME!
HEY!
NO!
WE'RE NOT DOING THIS!
AGENTS, FALL BACK!

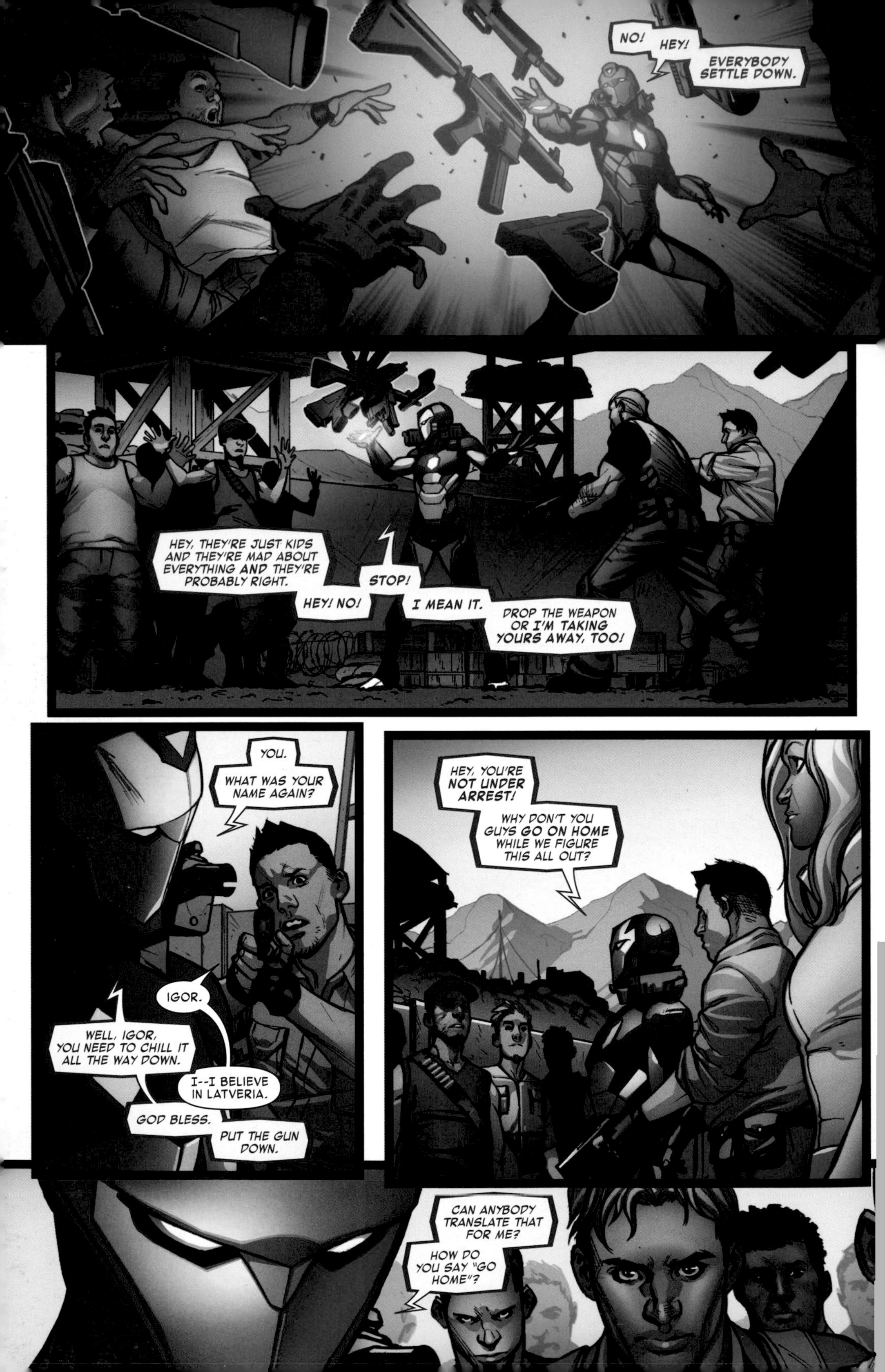
NO!
HEY!
EVERYBODY SETTLE DOWN.
HEY, THEY'RE JUST KIDS AND THEY'RE MAD ABOUT EVERYTHING AND THEY'RE PROBABLY RIGHT.
HEY! NO!
STOP!
I MEAN IT.
DROP THE WEAPON OR I'M TAKING YOURS AWAY, TOO!
YOU.
WHAT WAS YOUR NAME AGAIN?
IGOR.
WELL, IGOR, YOU NEED TO CHILL IT ALL THE WAY DOWN.
I--I BELIEVE IN LATVERIA.
GOD BLESS.
PUT THE GUN DOWN.
HEY, YOU'RE NOT UNDER ARREST!
WHY DON'T YOU GUYS GO ON HOME WHILE WE FIGURE THIS ALL OUT?
CAN ANYBODY TRANSLATE THAT FOR ME?
HOW DO YOU SAY "GO HOME"?

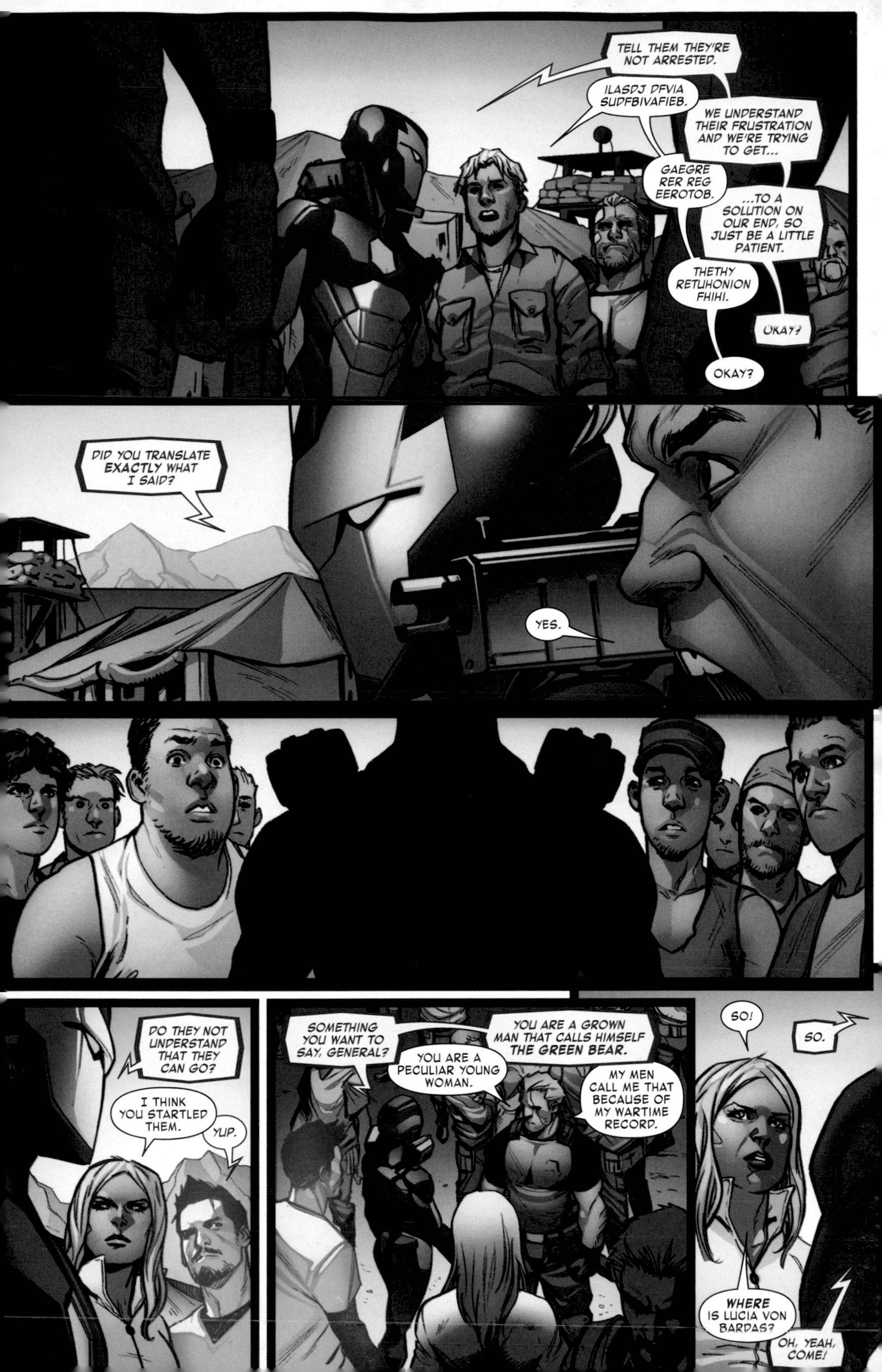
TELL THEM THEY'RE NOT ARRESTED.
ILASDJ DFVIA SUDFBIVAFIEB.
WE UNDERSTAND THEIR FRUSTRATION AND WE'RE TRYING TO GET...
GAEGRE RER REG EEROTOB.
...TO A SOLUTION ON OUR END, SO JUST BE A LITTLE PATIENT.
THETHY RETUHONION FHIHI.
OKAY?
OKAY?
DID YOU TRANSLATE EXACTLY WHAT I SAID?
YES.
DO THEY NOT UNDERSTAND THAT THEY CAN GO?
I THINK YOU STARTLED THEM.
YUP.
SOMETHING YOU WANT TO SAY, GENERAL?
YOU ARE A PECULIAR YOUNG WOMAN.
YOU ARE A GROWN MAN THAT CALLS HIMSELF THE GREEN BEAR.
MY MEN CALL ME THAT BECAUSE OF MY WARTIME RECORD.
SO!
SO.
WHERE IS LUCIA VON BARDAS?
OH, YEAH, COME!

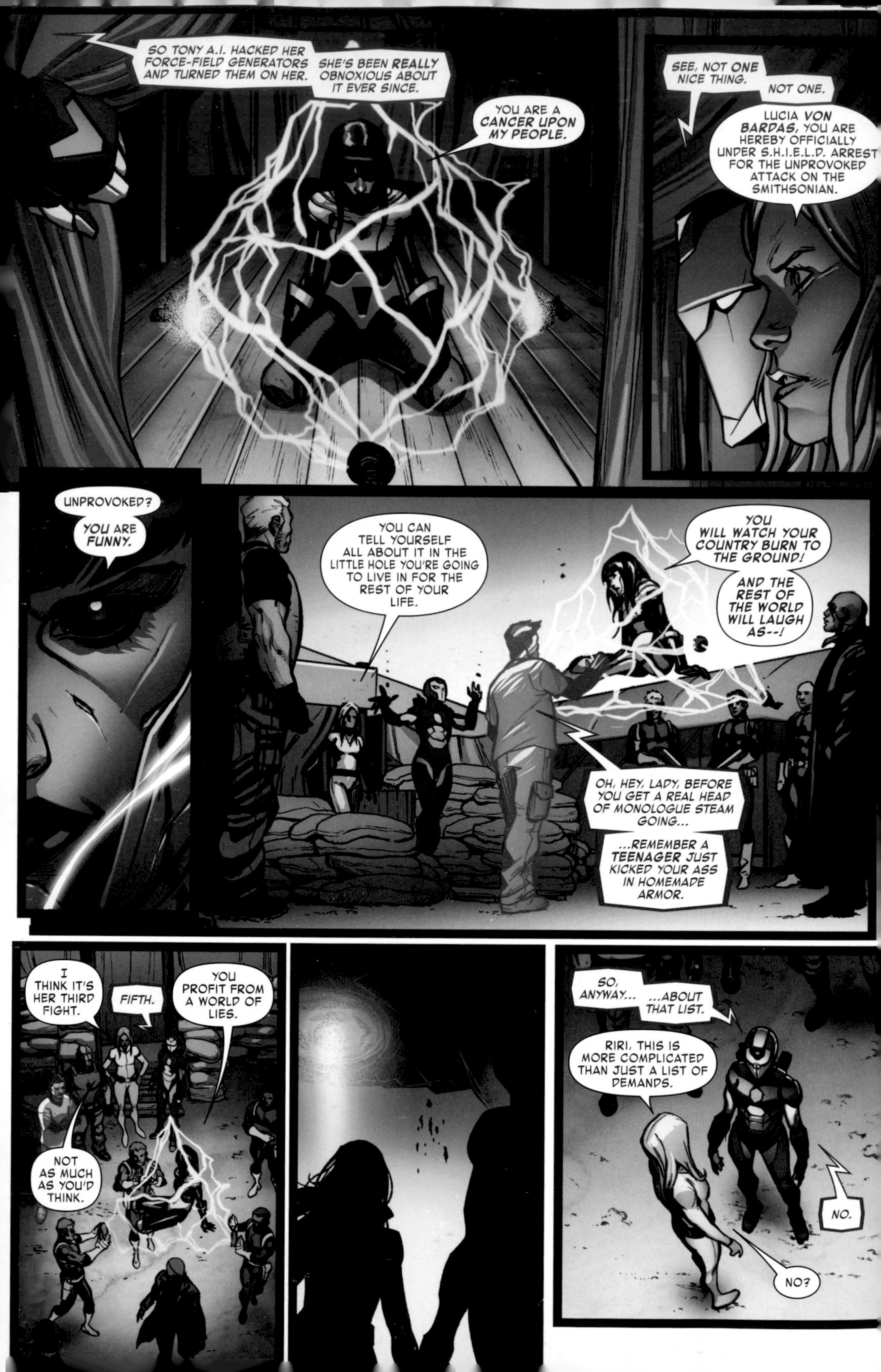
SO TONY A.I. HACKED HER FORCE-FIELD GENERATORS AND TURNED THEM ON HER.
SHE'S BEEN REALLY OBNOXIOUS ABOUT IT EVER SINCE.
YOU ARE A CANCER UPON MY PEOPLE.
SEE, NOT ONE NICE THING.
NOT ONE.
LUCIA VON BARDAS, YOU ARE HEREBY OFFICIALLY UNDER S.H.I.E.L.D. ARREST FOR THE UNPROVOKED ATTACK ON THE SMITHSONIAN.
UNPROVOKED?
YOU ARE FUNNY.
YOU CAN TELL YOURSELF ALL ABOUT IT IN THE LITTLE HOLE YOU'RE GOING TO LIVE IN FOR THE REST OF YOUR LIFE.
YOU WILL WATCH YOUR COUNTRY BURN TO THE GROUND!
AND THE REST OF THE WORLD WILL LAUGH AS--!
OH, HEY, LADY, BEFORE YOU GET A REAL HEAD OF MONOLOGUE STEAM GOING...
...REMEMBER A TEENAGER JUST KICKED YOUR ASS IN HOMEMADE ARMOR.
I THINK IT'S HER THIRD FIGHT.
FIFTH.
YOU PROFIT FROM A WORLD OF LIES.
NOT AS MUCH AS YOU'D THINK.
SO, ANYWAY...
...ABOUT THAT LIST.
RIRI, THIS IS MORE COMPLICATED THAN JUST A LIST OF DEMANDS.
NO.
NO?

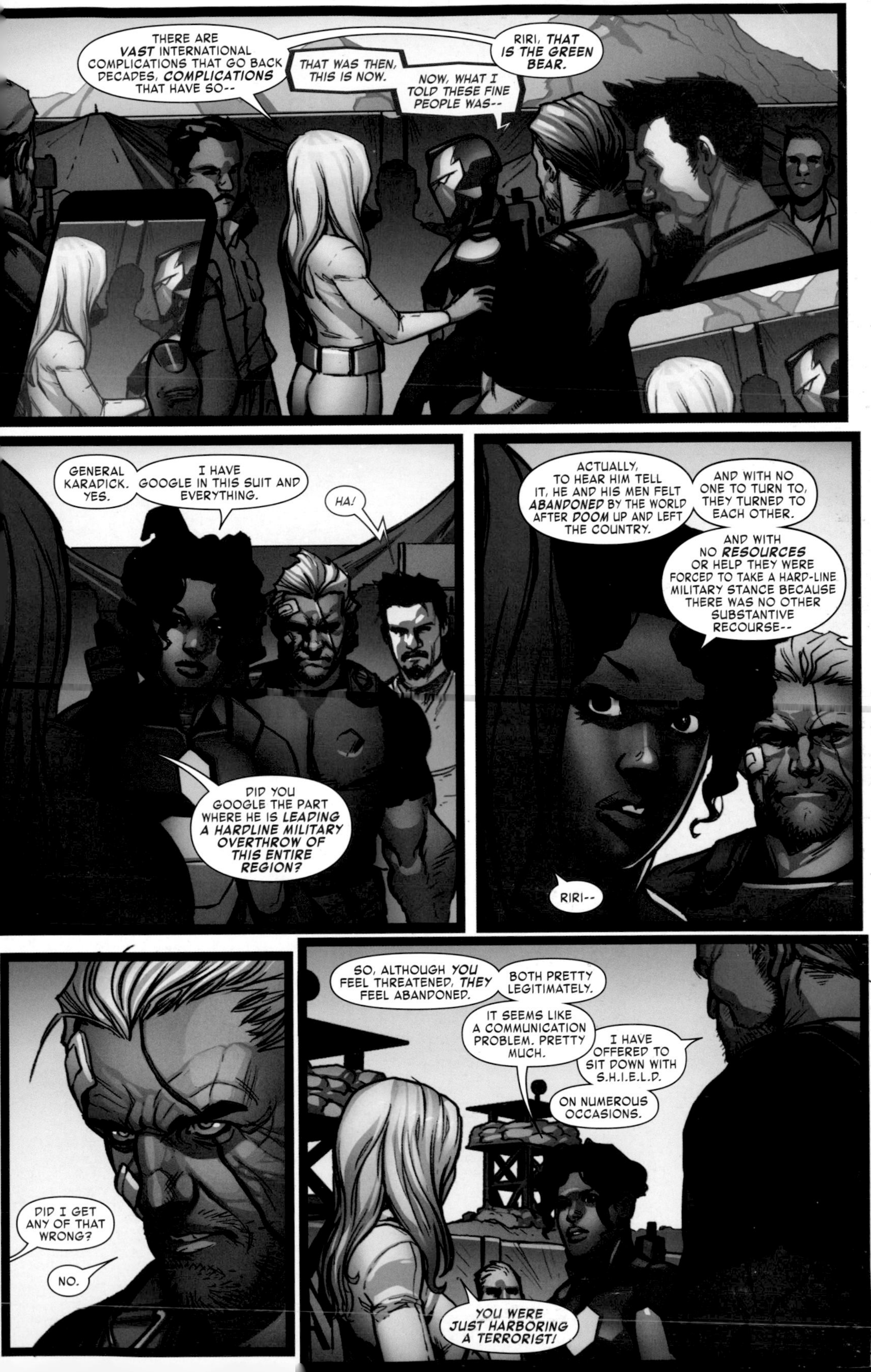
THERE ARE VAST INTERNATIONAL COMPLICATIONS THAT GO BACK DECADES, COMPLICATIONS THAT HAVE SO--
THAT WAS THEN, THIS IS NOW.
RIRI, THAT IS THE GREEN BEAR.
NOW, WHAT I TOLD THESE FINE PEOPLE WAS--
GENERAL KARADICK. YES.
I HAVE GOOGLE IN THIS SUIT AND EVERYTHING.
HA!
DID YOU GOOGLE THE PART WHERE HE IS LEADING A HARDLINE MILITARY OVERTHROW OF THIS ENTIRE REGION?
ACTUALLY, TO HEAR HIM TELL IT, HE AND HIS MEN FELT ABANDONED BY THE WORLD AFTER DOOM UP AND LEFT THE COUNTRY.
AND WITH NO ONE TO TURN TO, THEY TURNED TO EACH OTHER.
AND WITH NO RESOURCES OR HELP THEY WERE FORCED TO TAKE A HARD-LINE MILITARY STANCE BECAUSE THERE WAS NO OTHER SUBSTANTIVE RECOURSE--
RIRI--
DID I GET ANY OF THAT WRONG?
NO.
SO, ALTHOUGH YOU FEEL THREATENED, THEY FEEL ABANDONED.
BOTH PRETTY LEGITIMATELY.
IT SEEMS LIKE A COMMUNICATION PROBLEM. PRETTY MUCH.
I HAVE OFFERED TO SIT DOWN WITH S.H.I.E.L.D.
ON NUMEROUS OCCASIONS.
YOU WERE JUST HARBORING A TERRORIST!

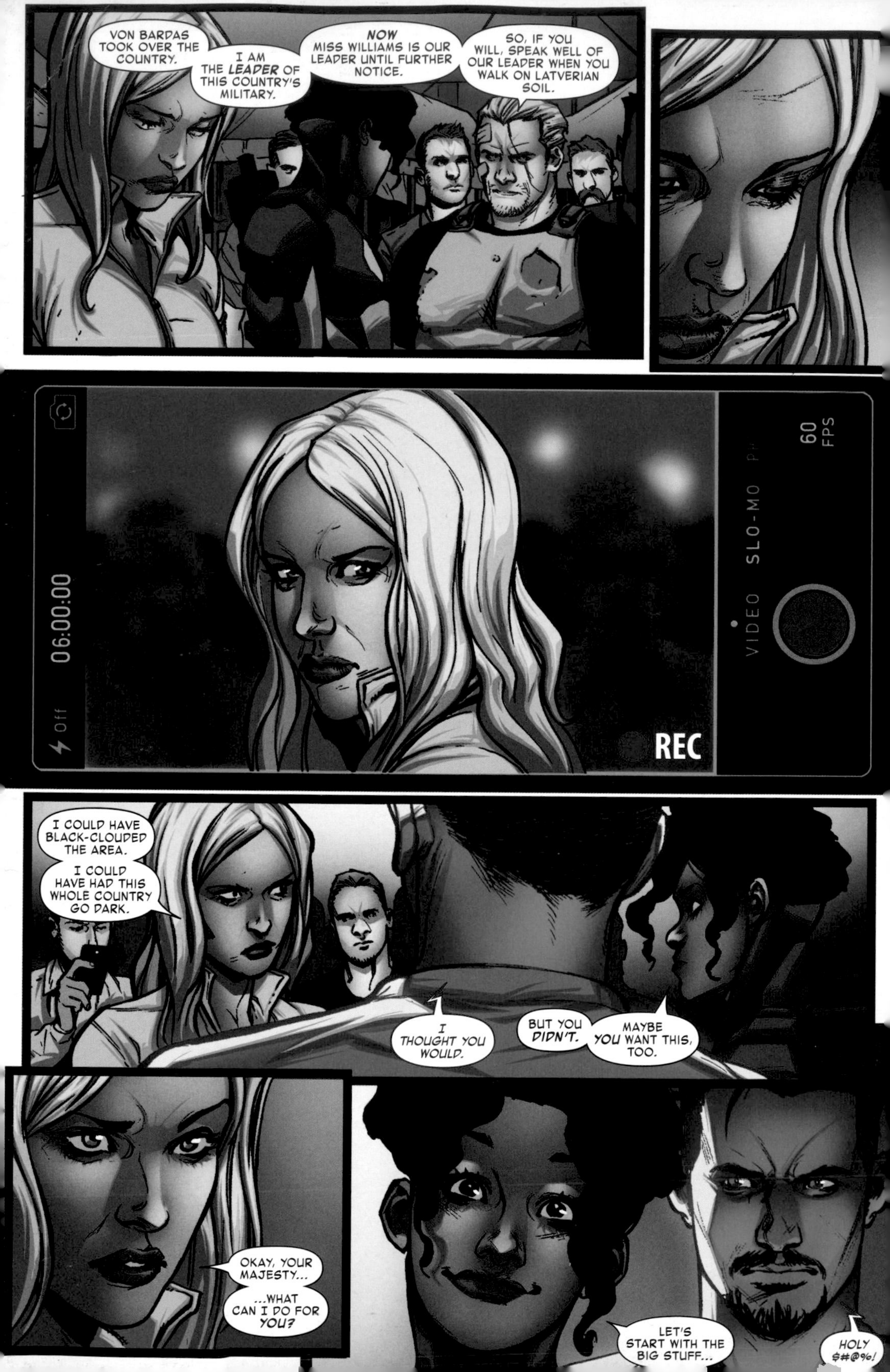
VON BARDAS TOOK OVER THE COUNTRY.
I AM THE LEADER OF THIS COUNTRY'S MILITARY.
NOW MISS WILLIAMS IS OUR LEADER UNTIL FURTHER NOTICE.
SO, IF YOU WILL, SPEAK WELL OF OUR LEADER WHEN YOU WALK ON LATVERIAN SOIL.
06:00:00
Off
REC
VIDEO
SLO-MO
60 FPS
I COULD HAVE BLACK-CLOUDED THE AREA.
I COULD HAVE HAD THIS WHOLE COUNTRY GO DARK.
I THOUGHT YOU WOULD.
BUT YOU DIDN'T.
MAYBE YOU WANT THIS, TOO.
OKAY, YOUR MAJESTY...
...WHAT CAN I DO FOR YOU?
LET'S START WITH THE BIG STUFF...
HOLY $#@%!

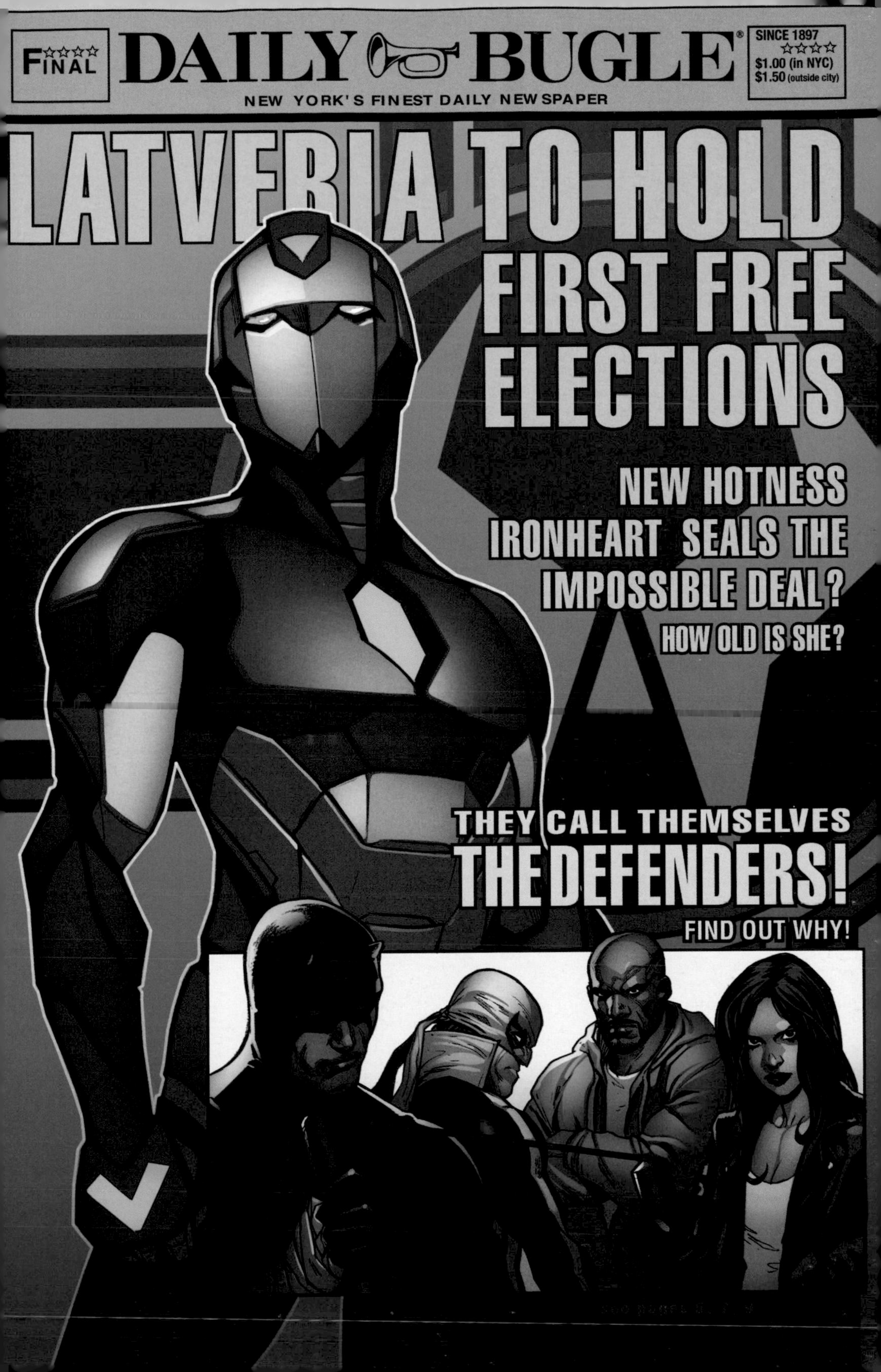
FINAL
DAILY BUGLE
SINCE 1897
$1.00 (in NYC)
$1.50 (outside city)
NEW YORK'S FINEST DAILY NEWSPAPER
LATVERIA TO HOLD FIRST FREE ELECTIONS
NEW HOTNESS IRONHEART SEALS THE IMPOSSIBLE DEAL?
HOW OLD IS SHE?
THEY CALL THEMSELVES
THE DEFENDERS!
FIND OUT WHY!

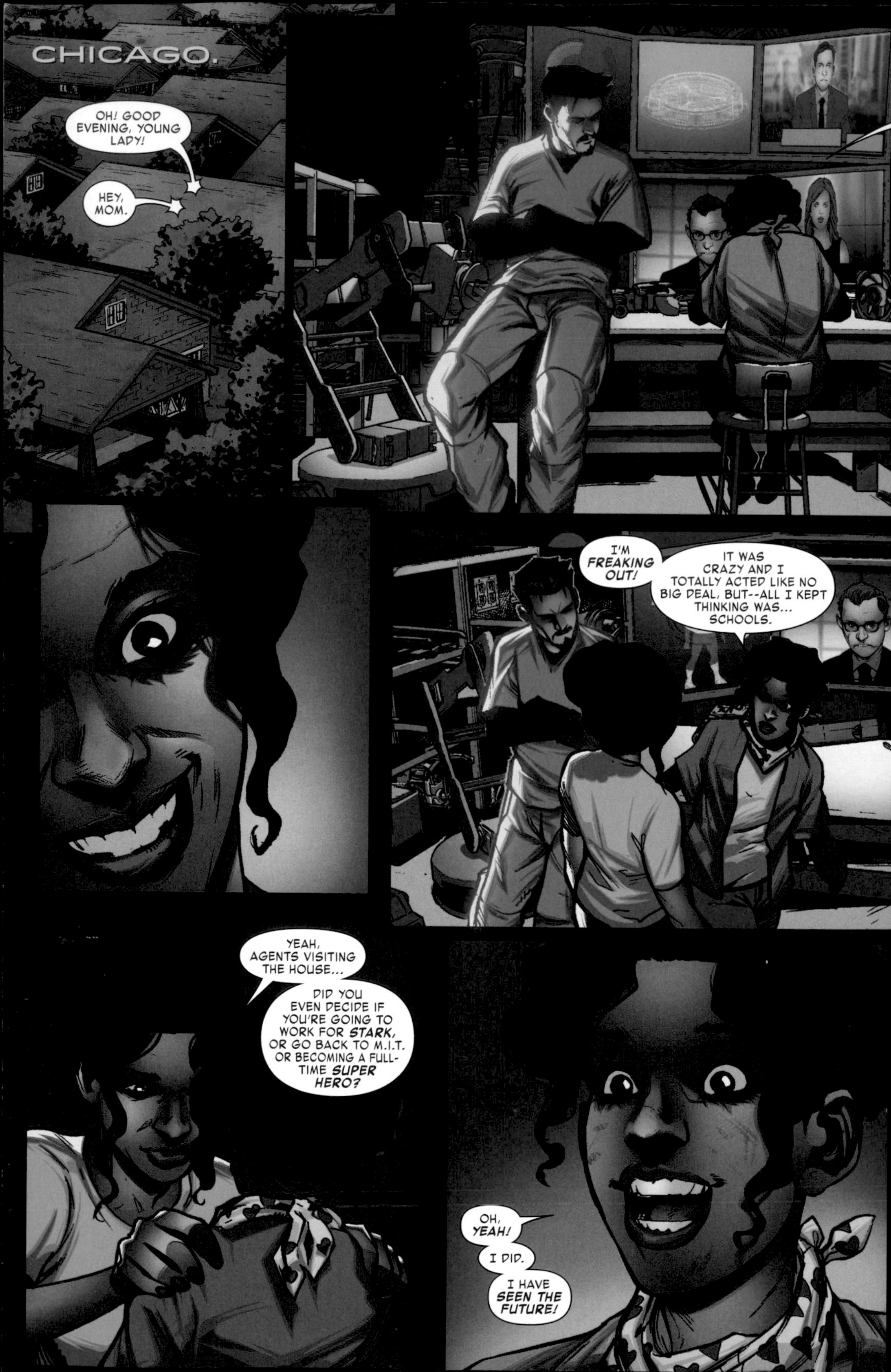
CHICAGO.
OH! GOOD EVENING, YOUNG LADY!
HEY, MOM.
I'M FREAKING OUT!
IT WAS CRAZY AND I TOTALLY ACTED LIKE NO BIG DEAL, BUT--ALL I KEPT THINKING WAS... SCHOOLS.
YEAH, AGENTS VISITING THE HOUSE...
DID YOU EVEN DECIDE IF YOU'RE GOING TO WORK FOR STARK, OR GO BACK TO M.I.T. OR BECOMING A FULL-TIME SUPER HERO?
OH, YEAH!
I DID.
I HAVE SEEN THE FUTURE!

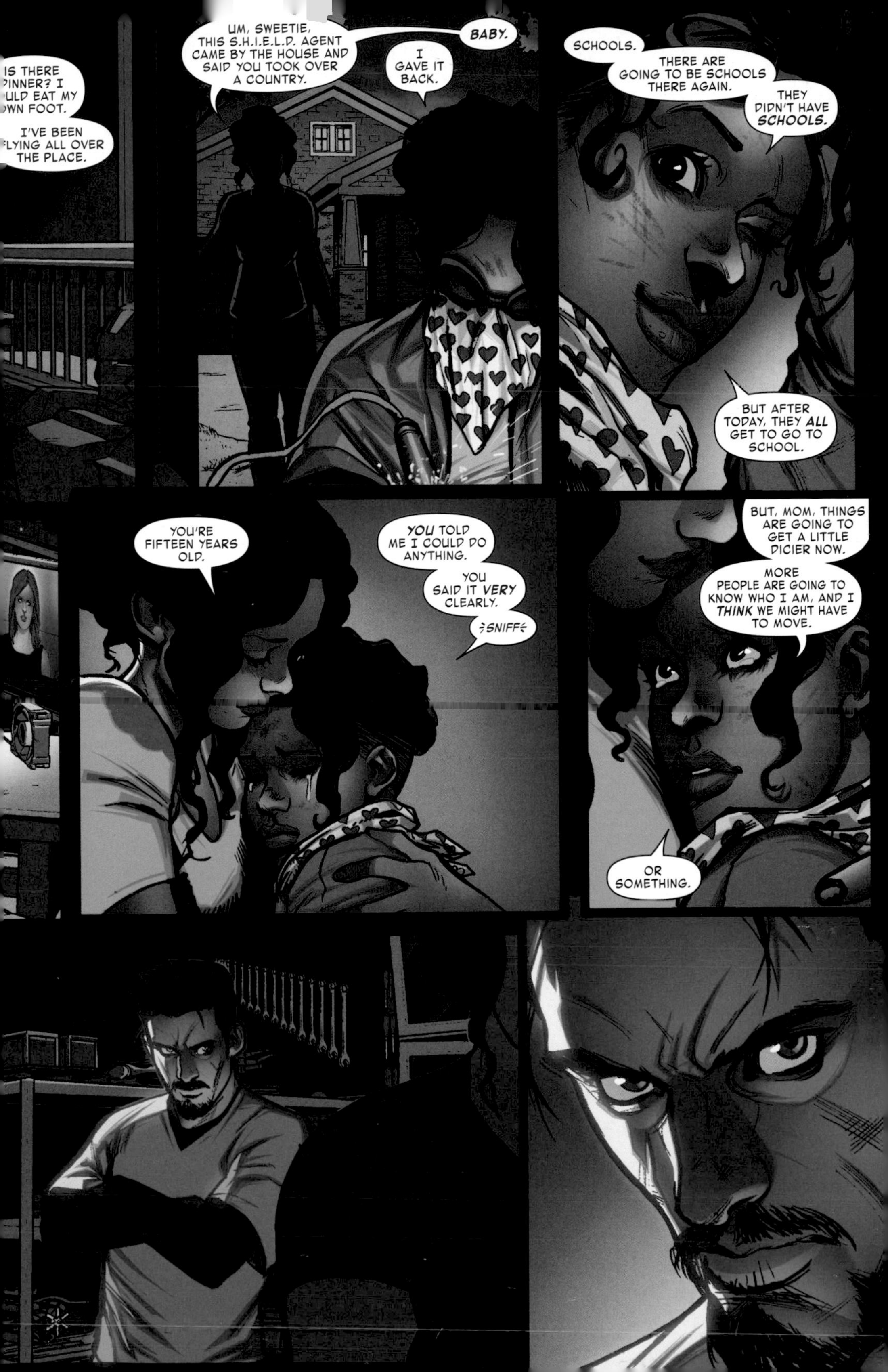
IS THERE DINNER? I COULD EAT MY OWN FOOT.
I'VE BEEN FLYING ALL OVER THE PLACE.
UM, SWEETIE, THIS S.H.I.E.L.D. AGENT CAME BY THE HOUSE AND SAID YOU TOOK OVER A COUNTRY.
BABY.
I GAVE IT BACK.
SCHOOLS.
THERE ARE GOING TO BE SCHOOLS THERE AGAIN.
THEY DIDN'T HAVE SCHOOLS.
BUT AFTER TODAY, THEY ALL GET TO GO TO SCHOOL.
YOU'RE FIFTEEN YEARS OLD.
YOU TOLD ME I COULD DO ANYTHING.
YOU SAID IT VERY CLEARLY.
SNIFF
BUT, MOM, THINGS ARE GOING TO GET A LITTLE DICIER NOW.
MORE PEOPLE ARE GOING TO KNOW WHO I AM, AND I THINK WE MIGHT HAVE TO MOVE.
OR SOMETHING.

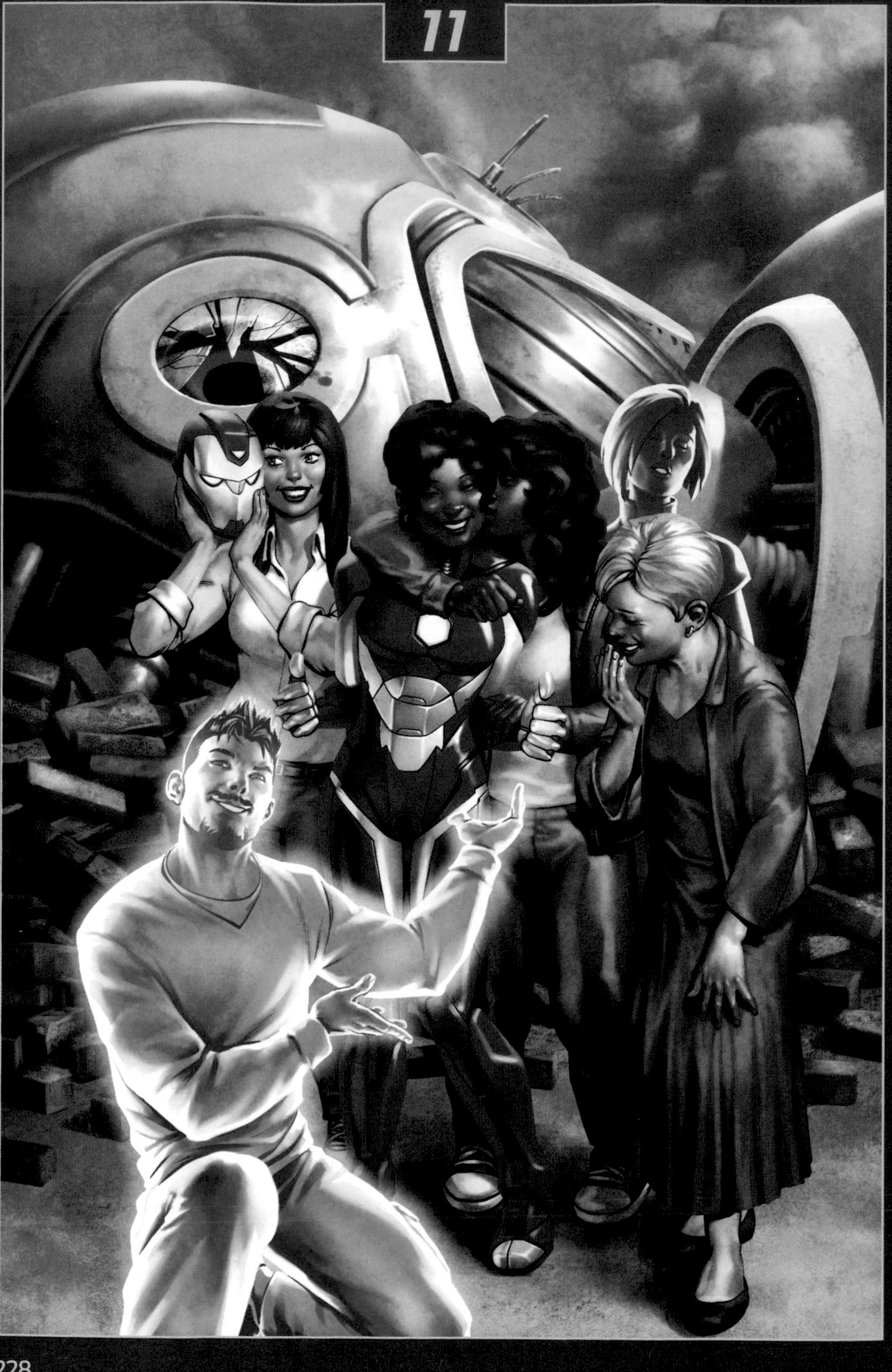
11

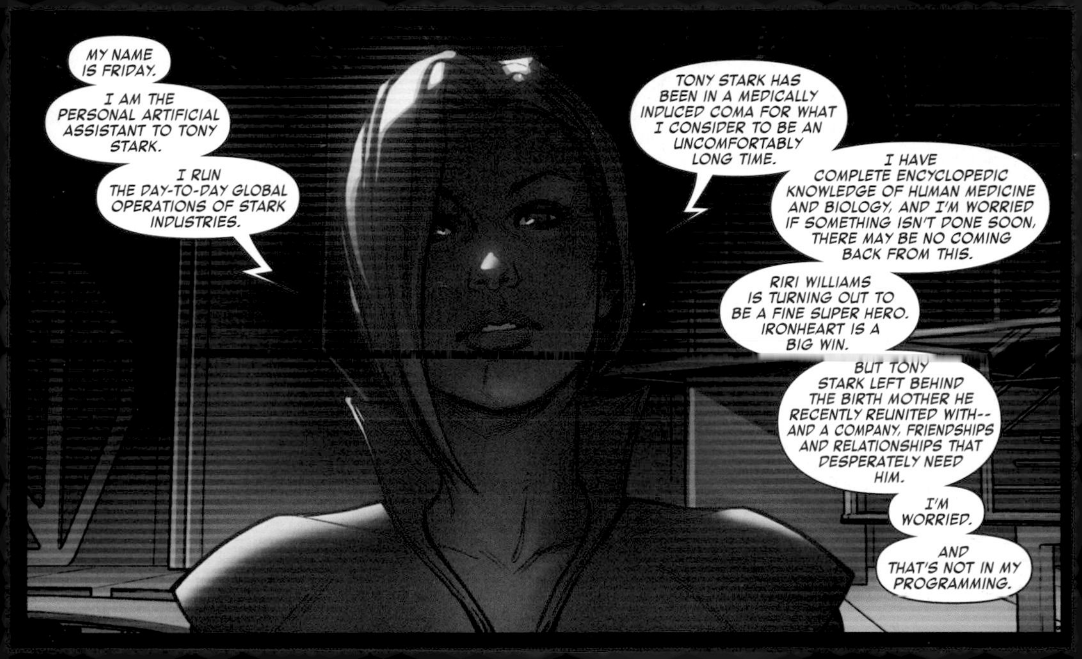
MY NAME IS FRIDAY.
I AM THE PERSONAL ARTIFICIAL ASSISTANT TO TONY STARK.
I RUN THE DAY-TO-DAY GLOBAL OPERATIONS OF STARK INDUSTRIES.
TONY STARK HAS BEEN IN A MEDICALLY INDUCED COMA FOR WHAT I CONSIDER TO BE AN UNCOMFORTABLY LONG TIME.
I HAVE COMPLETE ENCYCLOPEDIC KNOWLEDGE OF HUMAN MEDICINE AND BIOLOGY, AND I'M WORRIED IF SOMETHING ISN'T DONE SOON, THERE MAY BE NO COMING BACK FROM THIS.
RIRI WILLIAMS IS TURNING OUT TO BE A FINE SUPER HERO. IRONHEART IS A BIG WIN.
BUT TONY STARK LEFT BEHIND THE BIRTH MOTHER HE RECENTLY REUNITED WITH-- AND A COMPANY, FRIENDSHIPS AND RELATIONSHIPS THAT DESPERATELY NEED HIM.
I'M WORRIED.
AND THAT'S NOT IN MY PROGRAMMING.

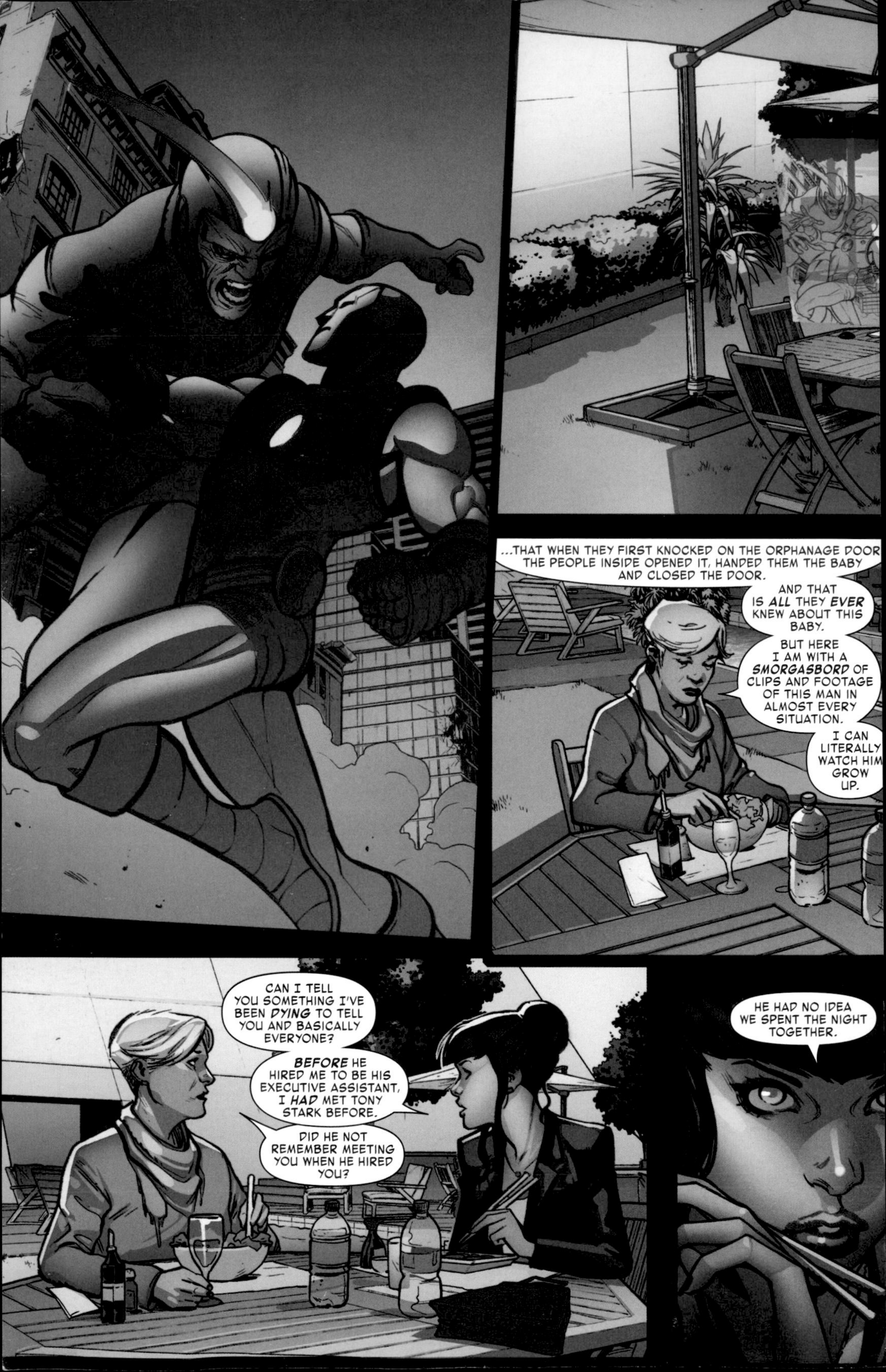
...THAT WHEN THEY FIRST KNOCKED ON THE ORPHANAGE DOOR THE PEOPLE INSIDE OPENED IT, HANDED THEM THE BABY AND CLOSED THE DOOR.
AND THAT IS ALL THEY EVER KNEW ABOUT THIS BABY.
BUT HERE I AM WITH A SMORGASBORD OF CLIPS AND FOOTAGE OF THIS MAN IN ALMOST EVERY SITUATION.
I CAN LITERALLY WATCH HIM GROW UP.
CAN I TELL YOU SOMETHING I'VE BEEN DYING TO TELL YOU AND BASICALLY EVERYONE?
BEFORE HE HIRED ME TO BE HIS EXECUTIVE ASSISTANT, I HAD MET TONY STARK BEFORE.
DID HE NOT REMEMBER MEETING YOU WHEN HE HIRED YOU?
HE HAD NO IDEA WE SPENT THE NIGHT TOGETHER.

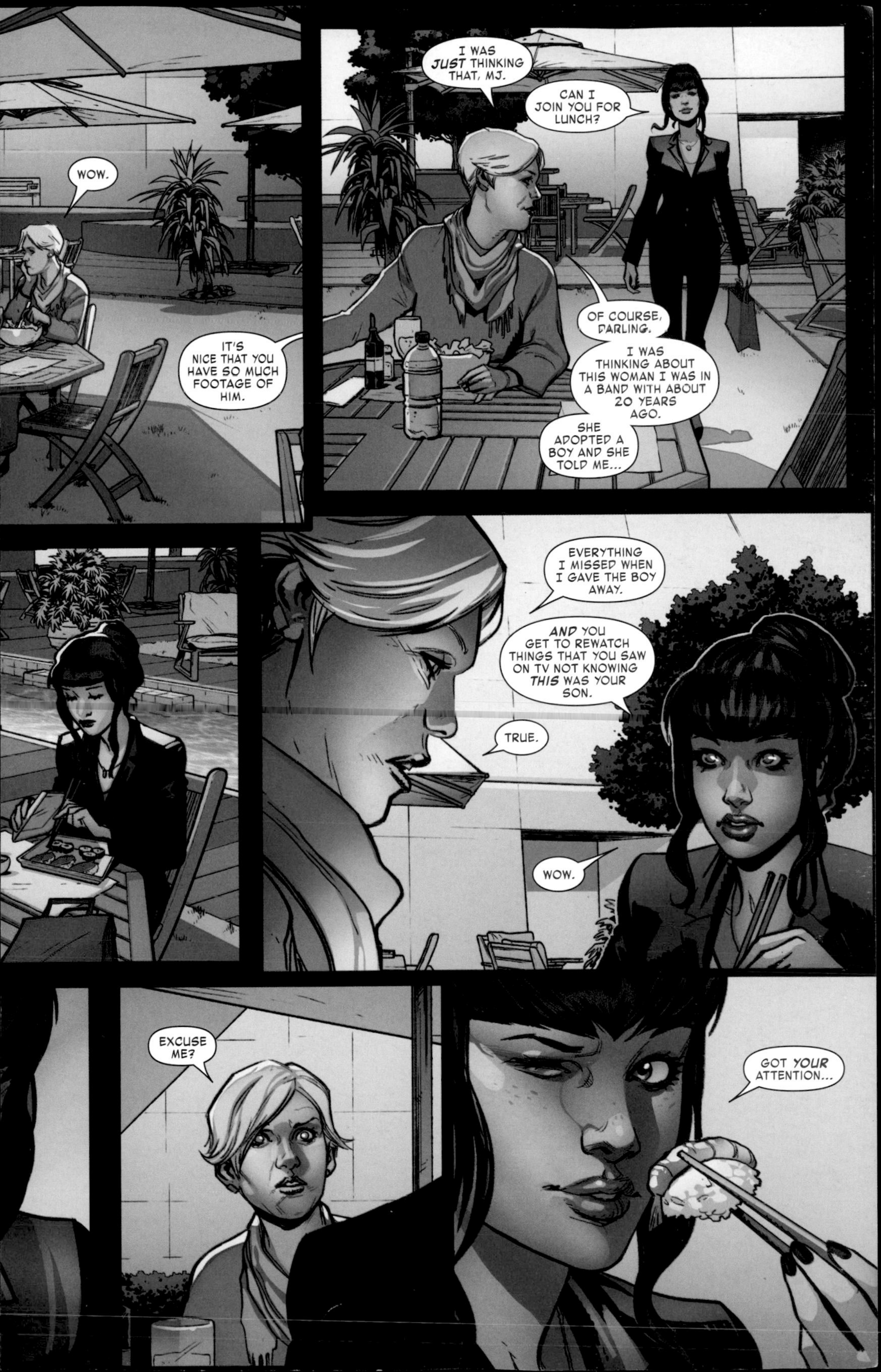
WOW.
IT'S NICE THAT YOU HAVE SO MUCH FOOTAGE OF HIM.
I WAS JUST THINKING THAT, MJ.
CAN I JOIN YOU FOR LUNCH?
OF COURSE, DARLING.
I WAS THINKING ABOUT THIS WOMAN I WAS IN A BAND WITH ABOUT 20 YEARS AGO.
SHE ADOPTED A BOY AND SHE TOLD ME...
EVERYTHING I MISSED WHEN I GAVE THE BOY AWAY.
AND YOU GET TO REWATCH THINGS THAT YOU SAW ON TV NOT KNOWING THIS WAS YOUR SON.
TRUE.
WOW.
EXCUSE ME?
GOT YOUR ATTENTION...

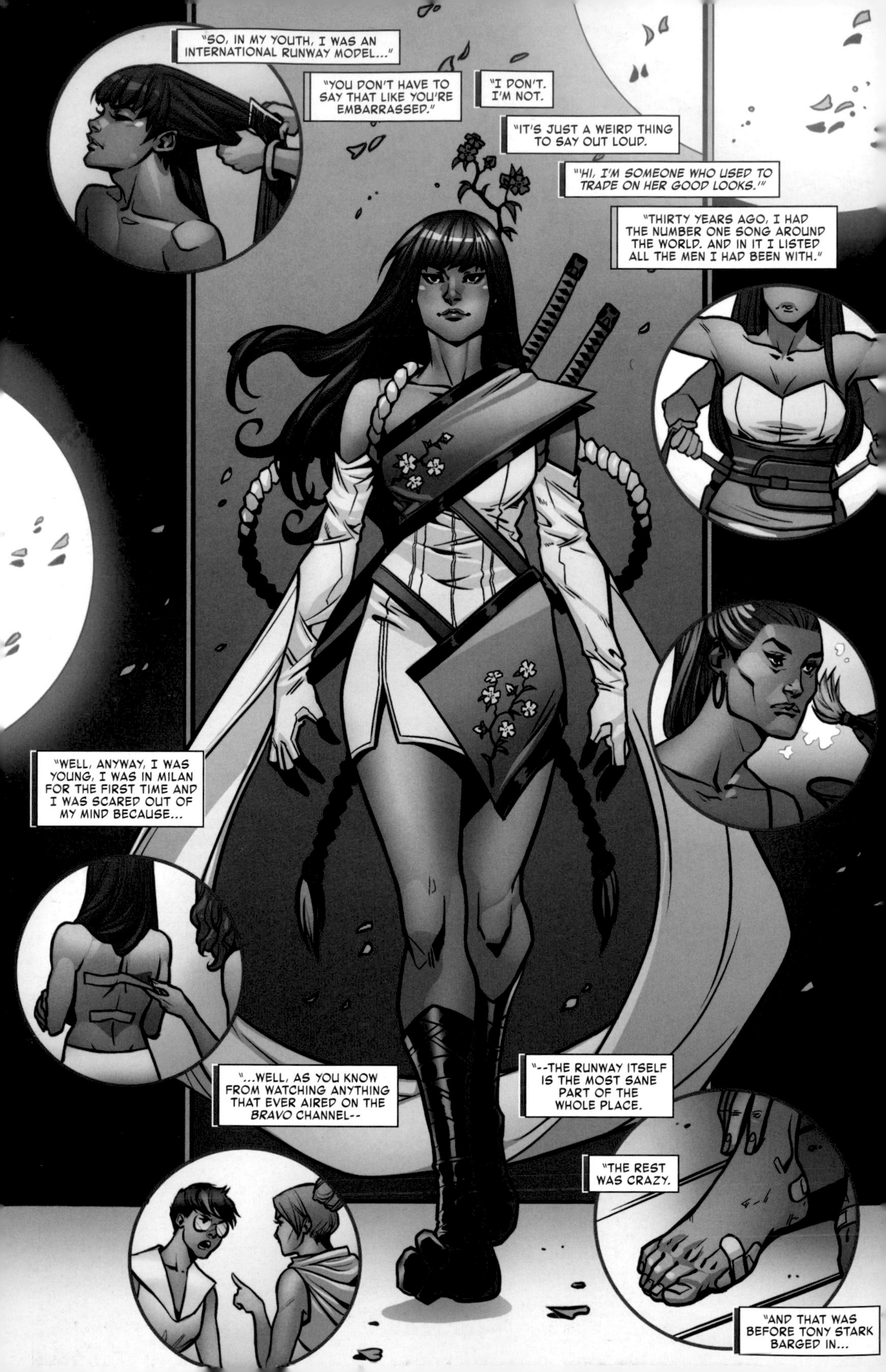

"SO, IN MY YOUTH, I WAS AN INTERNATIONAL RUNWAY MODEL..."
"YOU DON'T HAVE TO SAY THAT LIKE YOU'RE EMBARRASSED."
"I DON'T. I'M NOT.
"IT'S JUST A WEIRD THING TO SAY OUT LOUD.
"'HI, I'M SOMEONE WHO USED TO TRADE ON HER GOOD LOOKS.'"
"THIRTY YEARS AGO, I HAD THE NUMBER ONE SONG AROUND THE WORLD. AND IN IT I LISTED ALL THE MEN I HAD BEEN WITH."
"WELL, ANYWAY, I WAS YOUNG, I WAS IN MILAN FOR THE FIRST TIME AND I WAS SCARED OUT OF MY MIND BECAUSE...
"...WELL, AS YOU KNOW FROM WATCHING ANYTHING THAT EVER AIRED ON THE *BRAVO* CHANNEL--
"--THE RUNWAY ITSELF IS THE MOST SANE PART OF THE WHOLE PLACE.
"THE REST WAS CRAZY.
"AND THAT WAS BEFORE TONY STARK BARGED IN...

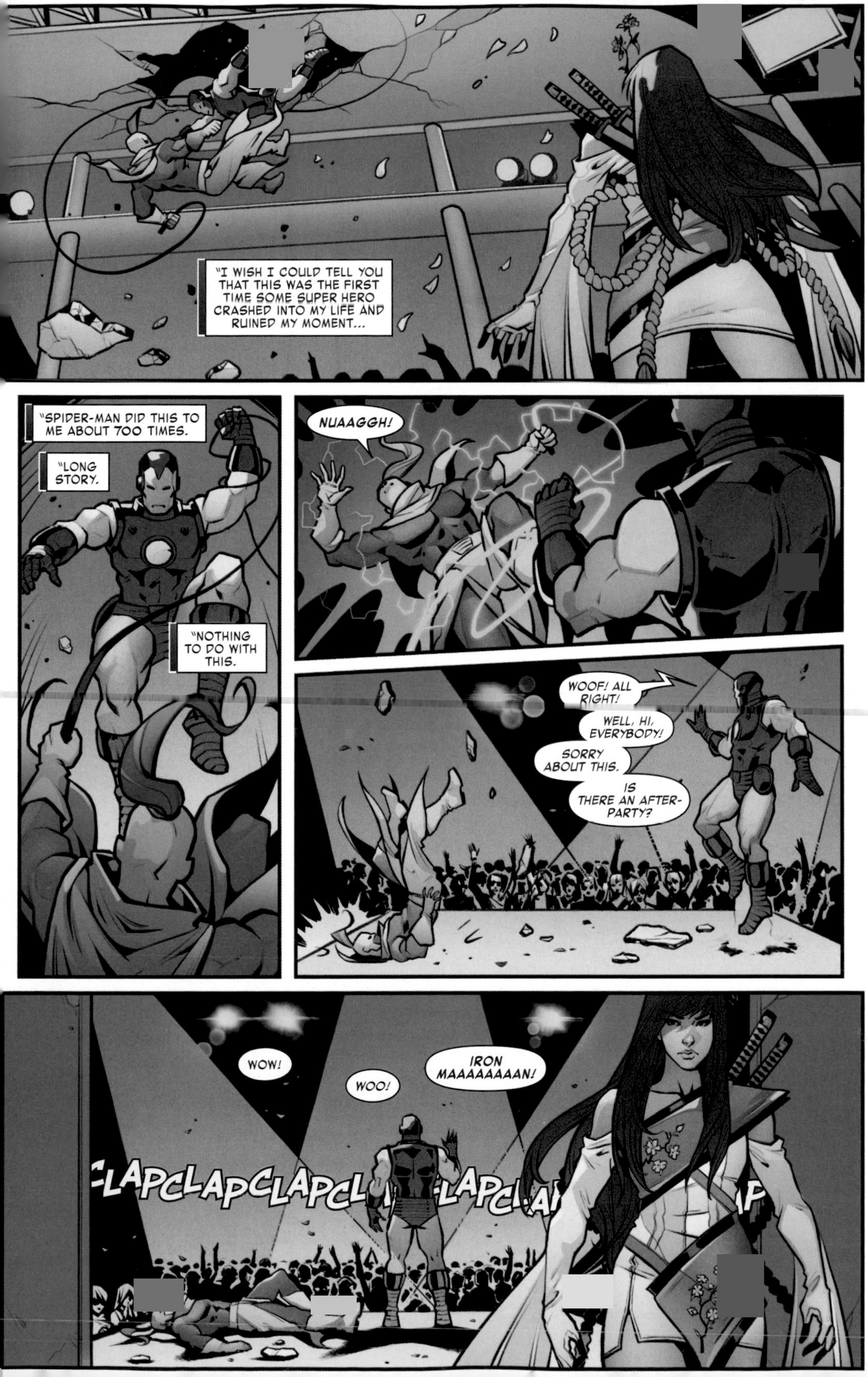
"I WISH I COULD TELL YOU THAT THIS WAS THE FIRST TIME SOME SUPER HERO CRASHED INTO MY LIFE AND RUINED MY MOMENT...
"SPIDER-MAN DID THIS TO ME ABOUT 700 TIMES.
"LONG STORY.
"NOTHING TO DO WITH THIS.
NUAAGGH!
WOOF! ALL RIGHT!
WELL, HI, EVERYBODY!
SORRY ABOUT THIS.
IS THERE AN AFTER-PARTY?
WOW!
WOO!
IRON MAAAAAAAAN!
CLAPCLAPCLAPCLAPCLAPCLAP

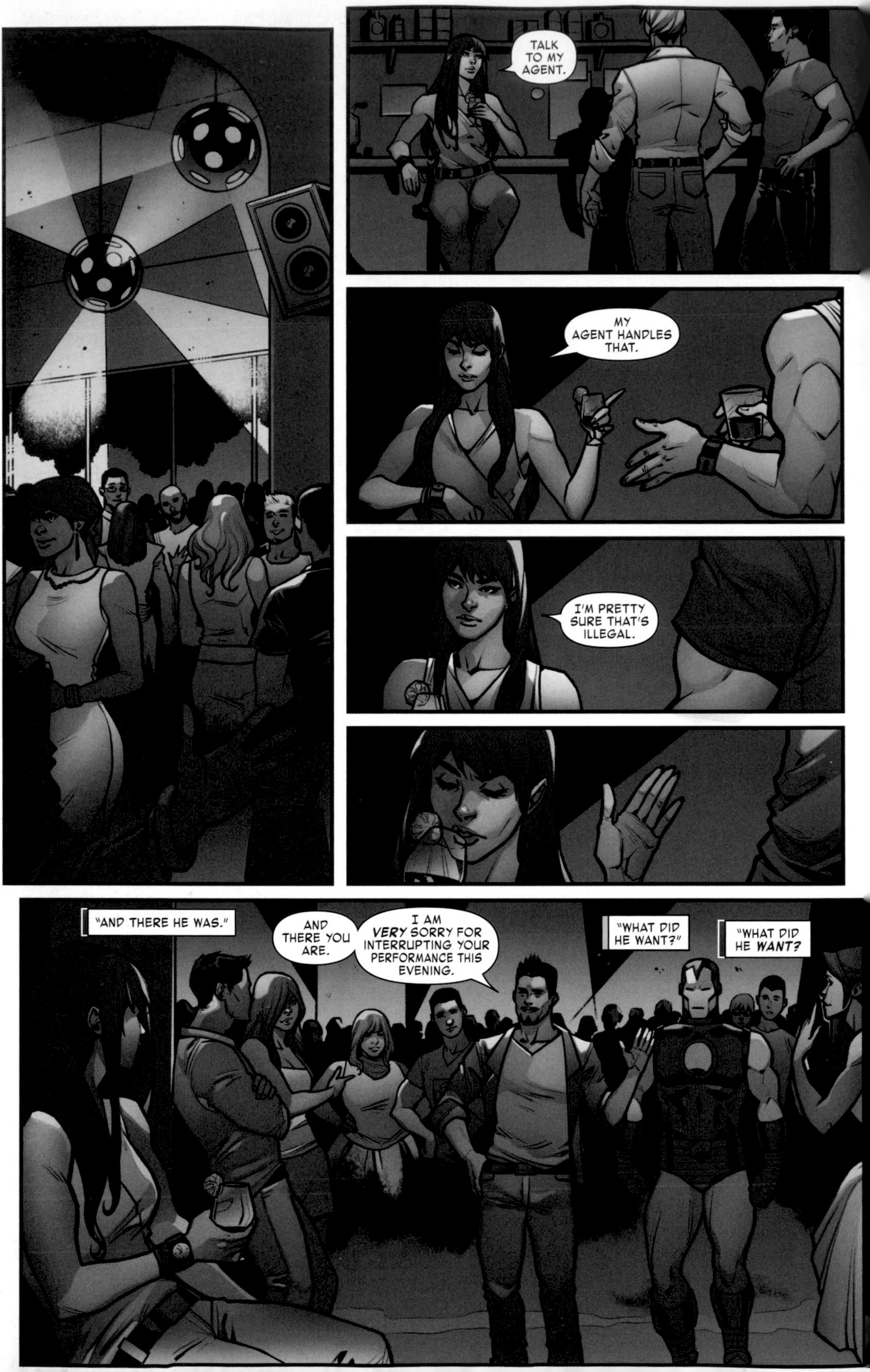
TALK TO MY AGENT.
MY AGENT HANDLES THAT.
I'M PRETTY SURE THAT'S ILLEGAL.
"AND THERE HE WAS."
AND THERE YOU ARE.
I AM *VERY* SORRY FOR INTERRUPTING YOUR PERFORMANCE THIS EVENING.
"WHAT DID HE WANT?"
"WHAT DID HE *WANT?*

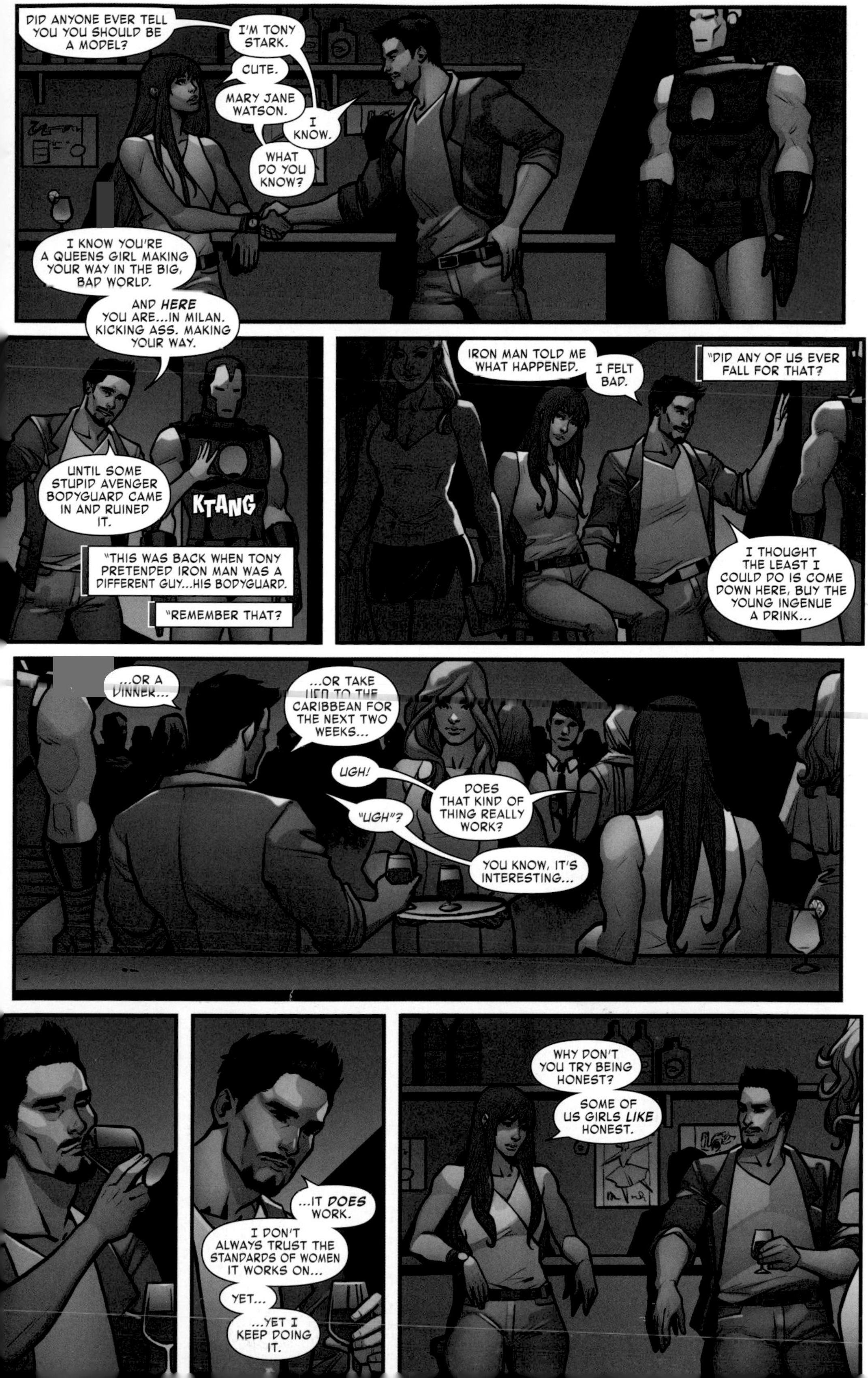
DID ANYONE EVER TELL YOU YOU SHOULD BE A MODEL?
I'M TONY STARK.
CUTE.
MARY JANE WATSON.
I KNOW.
WHAT DO YOU KNOW?
I KNOW YOU'RE A QUEENS GIRL MAKING YOUR WAY IN THE BIG, BAD WORLD.
AND *HERE* YOU ARE...IN MILAN. KICKING ASS. MAKING YOUR WAY.
UNTIL SOME STUPID AVENGER BODYGUARD CAME IN AND RUINED IT.
KTANG
"THIS WAS BACK WHEN TONY PRETENDED IRON MAN WAS A DIFFERENT GUY...HIS BODYGUARD.
"REMEMBER THAT?
IRON MAN TOLD ME WHAT HAPPENED.
I FELT BAD.
"DID ANY OF US EVER FALL FOR THAT?
I THOUGHT THE LEAST I COULD DO IS COME DOWN HERE, BUY THE YOUNG INGENUE A DRINK...
...OR A DINNER...
...OR TAKE HER TO THE CARIBBEAN FOR THE NEXT TWO WEEKS...
UGH!
DOES THAT KIND OF THING REALLY WORK?
"UGH"?
YOU KNOW, IT'S INTERESTING...
...IT *DOES* WORK.
I DON'T ALWAYS TRUST THE STANDARDS OF WOMEN IT WORKS ON...
YET...
...YET I KEEP DOING IT.
WHY DON'T YOU TRY BEING HONEST?
SOME OF US GIRLS *LIKE* HONEST.

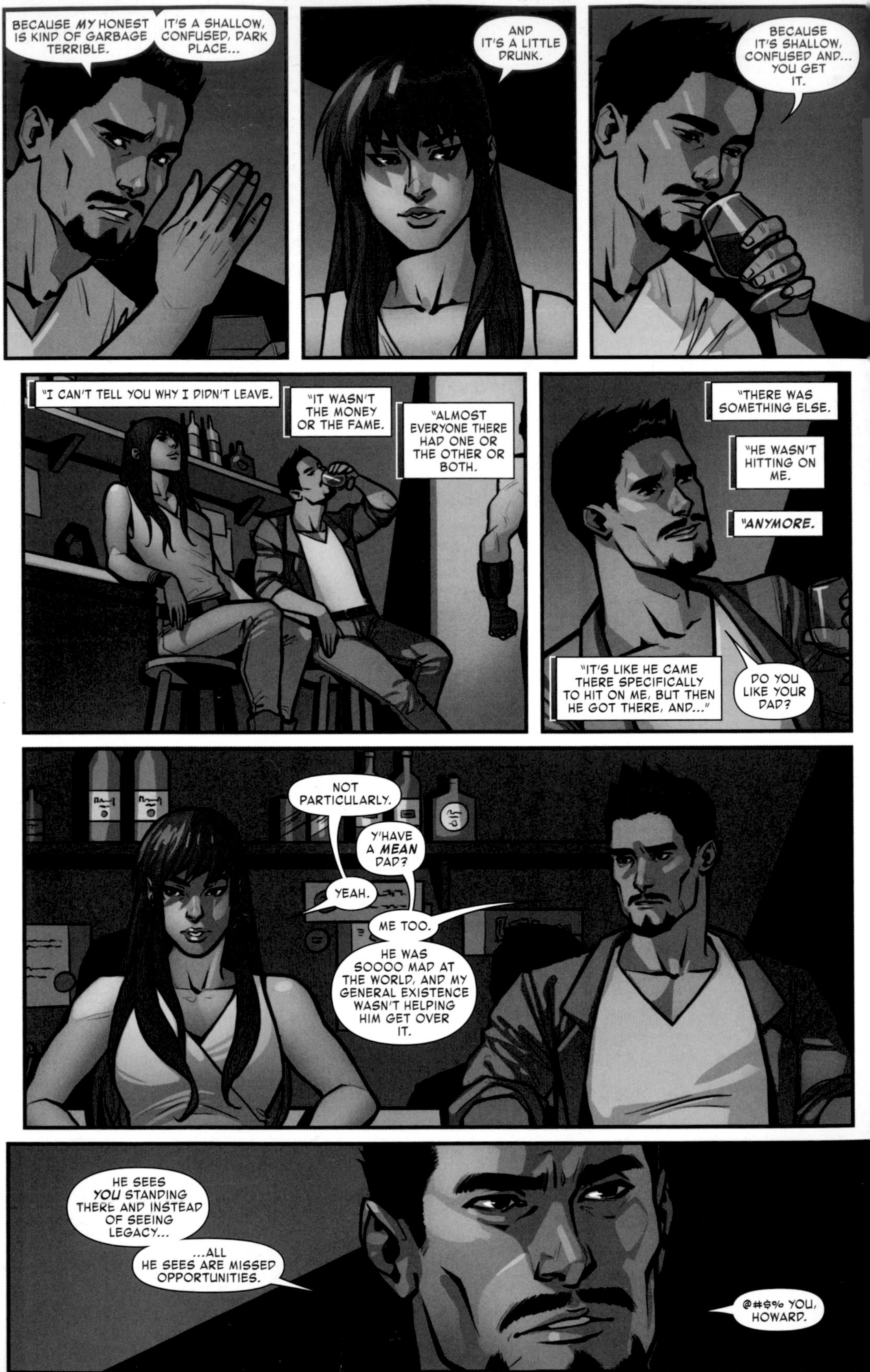
BECAUSE MY HONEST IS KIND OF GARBAGE TERRIBLE.
IT'S A SHALLOW, CONFUSED, DARK PLACE...
AND IT'S A LITTLE DRUNK.
BECAUSE IT'S SHALLOW, CONFUSED AND... YOU GET IT.
"I CAN'T TELL YOU WHY I DIDN'T LEAVE.
"IT WASN'T THE MONEY OR THE FAME.
"ALMOST EVERYONE THERE HAD ONE OR THE OTHER OR BOTH.
"THERE WAS SOMETHING ELSE.
"HE WASN'T HITTING ON ME.
"ANYMORE.
"IT'S LIKE HE CAME THERE SPECIFICALLY TO HIT ON ME, BUT THEN HE GOT THERE, AND..."
DO YOU LIKE YOUR DAD?
NOT PARTICULARLY.
Y'HAVE A MEAN DAD?
YEAH.
ME TOO.
HE WAS SOOOO MAD AT THE WORLD, AND MY GENERAL EXISTENCE WASN'T HELPING HIM GET OVER IT.
HE SEES YOU STANDING THERE AND INSTEAD OF SEEING LEGACY...
...ALL HE SEES ARE MISSED OPPORTUNITIES.
@#$% YOU, HOWARD.

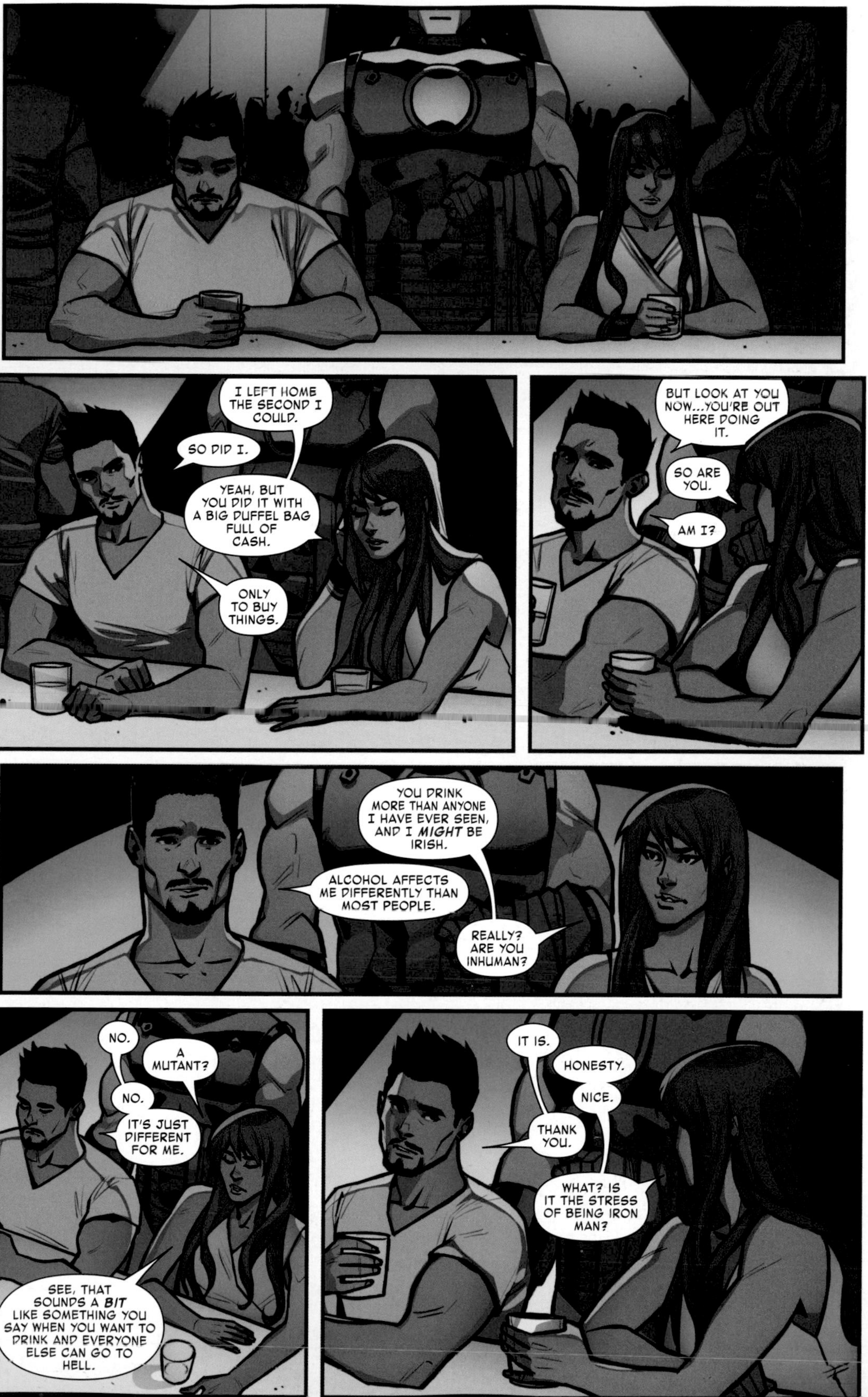
I LEFT HOME THE SECOND I COULD.
SO DID I.
YEAH, BUT YOU DID IT WITH A BIG DUFFEL BAG FULL OF CASH.
ONLY TO BUY THINGS.
BUT LOOK AT YOU NOW...YOU'RE OUT HERE DOING IT.
SO ARE YOU.
AM I?
YOU DRINK MORE THAN ANYONE I HAVE EVER SEEN, AND I *MIGHT* BE IRISH.
ALCOHOL AFFECTS ME DIFFERENTLY THAN MOST PEOPLE.
REALLY? ARE YOU INHUMAN?
NO.
A MUTANT?
NO.
IT'S JUST DIFFERENT FOR ME.
SEE, THAT SOUNDS A *BIT* LIKE SOMETHING YOU SAY WHEN YOU WANT TO DRINK AND EVERYONE ELSE CAN GO TO HELL.
IT IS.
HONESTY.
NICE.
THANK YOU.
WHAT? IS IT THE STRESS OF BEING IRON MAN?

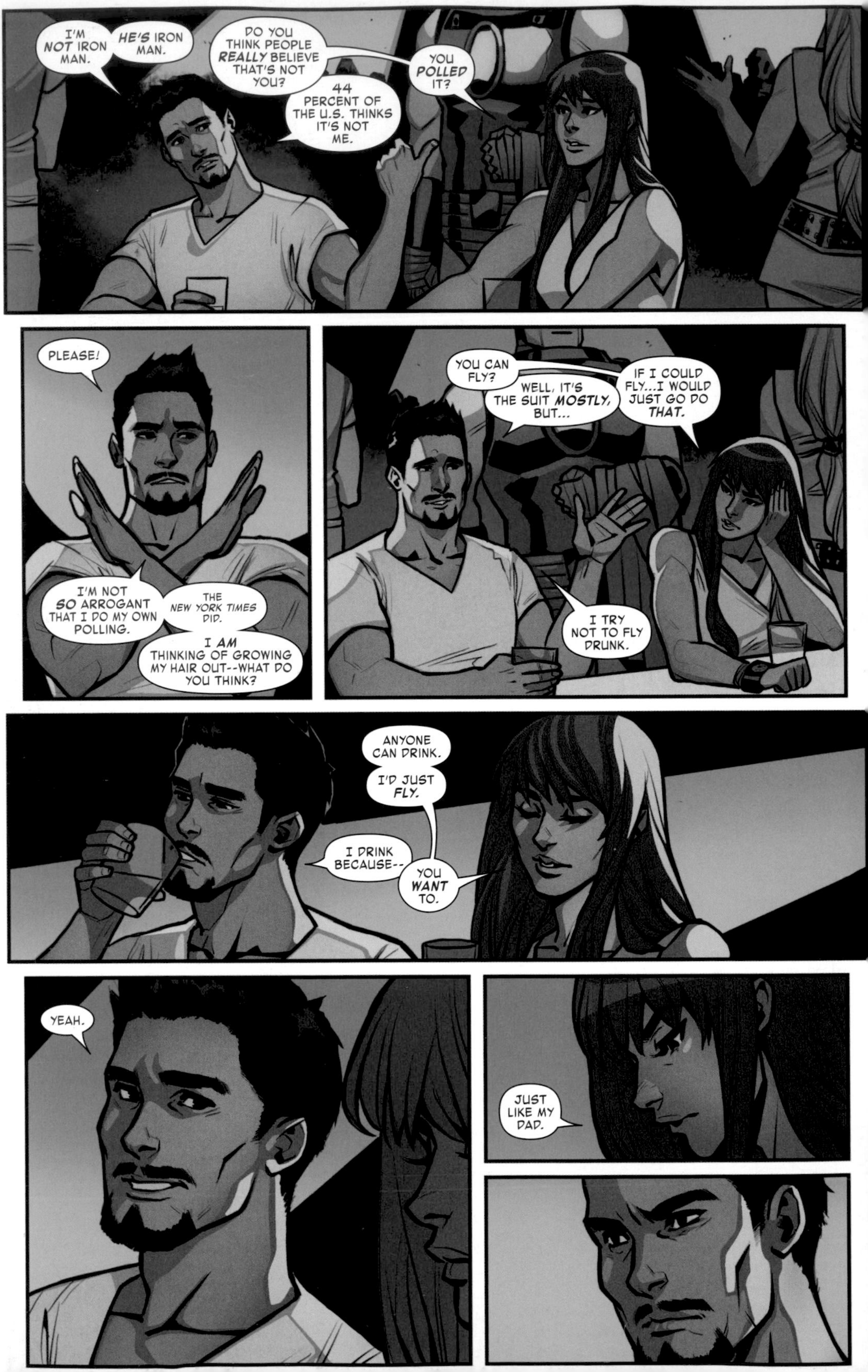
I'M NOT IRON MAN.
HE'S IRON MAN.
DO YOU THINK PEOPLE REALLY BELIEVE THAT'S NOT YOU?
YOU POLLED IT?
44 PERCENT OF THE U.S. THINKS IT'S NOT ME.
PLEASE!
I'M NOT SO ARROGANT THAT I DO MY OWN POLLING.
THE NEW YORK TIMES DID.
I AM THINKING OF GROWING MY HAIR OUT--WHAT DO YOU THINK?
YOU CAN FLY?
WELL, IT'S THE SUIT MOSTLY, BUT...
IF I COULD FLY...I WOULD JUST GO DO THAT.
I TRY NOT TO FLY DRUNK.
ANYONE CAN DRINK.
I'D JUST FLY.
I DRINK BECAUSE--
YOU WANT TO.
YEAH.
JUST LIKE MY DAD.

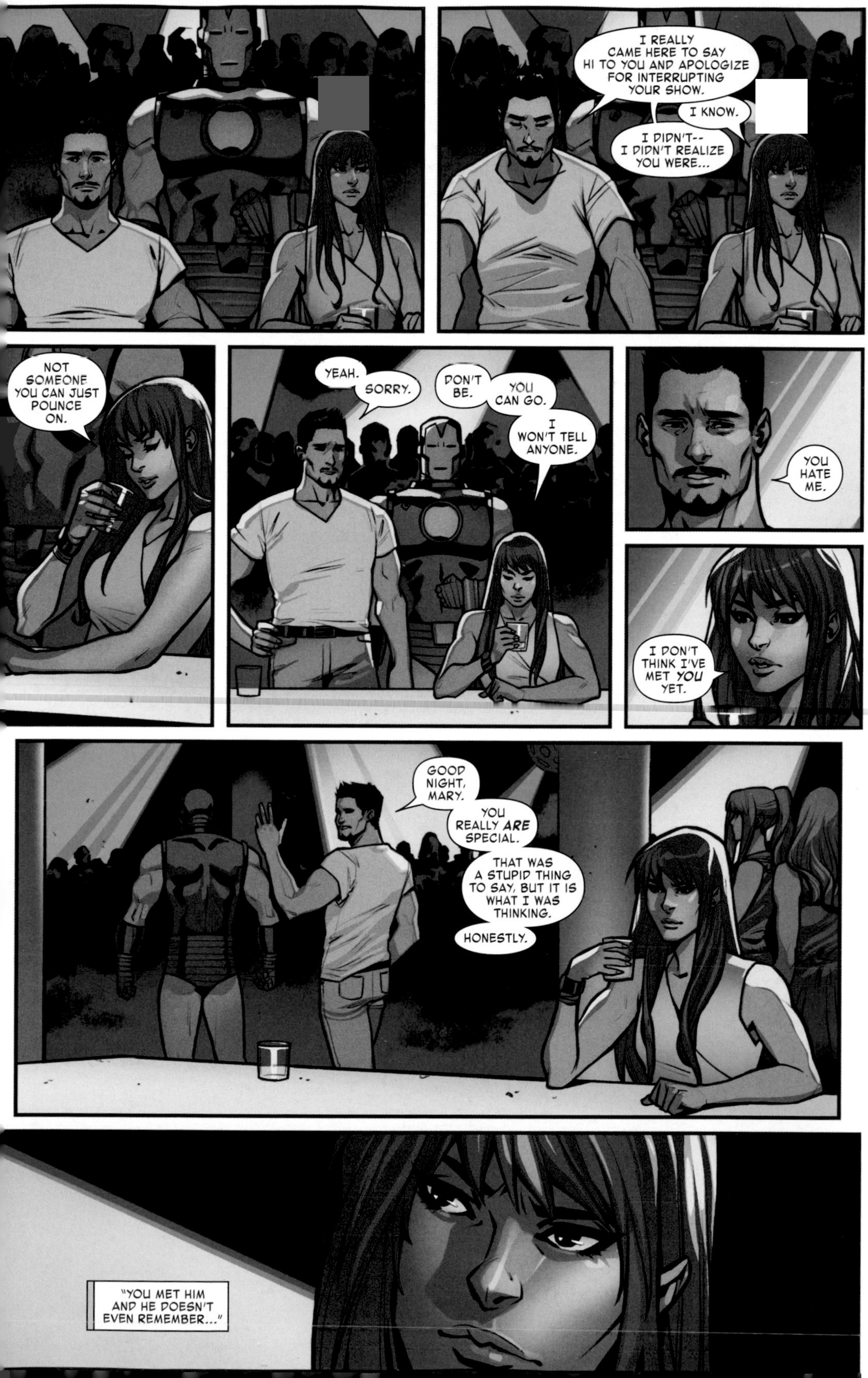
I REALLY CAME HERE TO SAY HI TO YOU AND APOLOGIZE FOR INTERRUPTING YOUR SHOW.
I KNOW.
I DIDN'T-- I DIDN'T REALIZE YOU WERE...
NOT SOMEONE YOU CAN JUST POUNCE ON.
YEAH.
SORRY.
DON'T BE.
YOU CAN GO.
I WON'T TELL ANYONE.
YOU HATE ME.
I DON'T THINK I'VE MET *YOU* YET.
GOOD NIGHT, MARY.
YOU REALLY *ARE* SPECIAL.
THAT WAS A STUPID THING TO SAY, BUT IT IS WHAT I WAS THINKING.
HONESTLY.
"YOU MET HIM AND HE DOESN'T EVEN REMEMBER..."

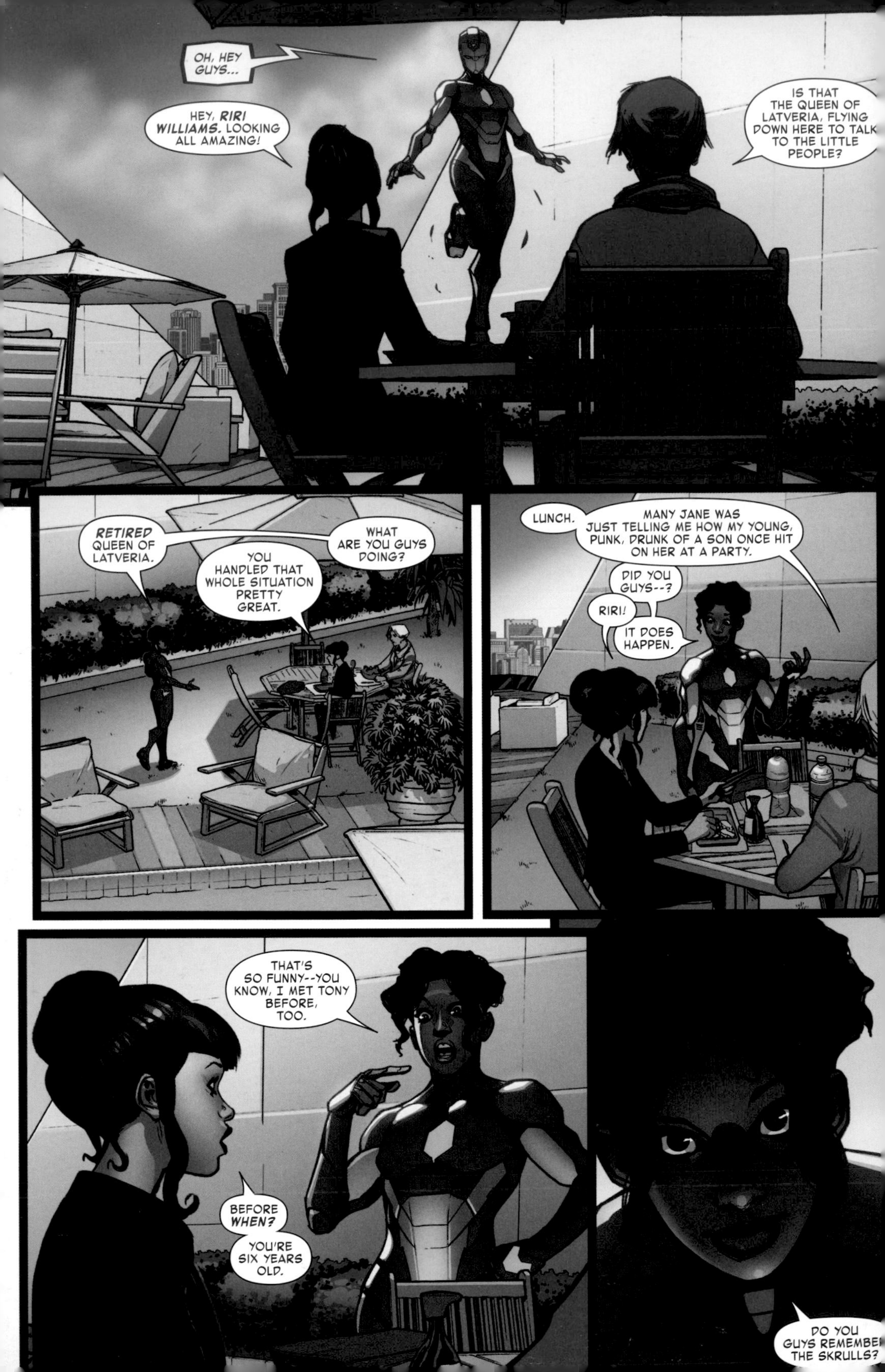
OH, HEY GUYS...
HEY, RIRI WILLIAMS. LOOKING ALL AMAZING!
IS THAT THE QUEEN OF LATVERIA, FLYING DOWN HERE TO TALK TO THE LITTLE PEOPLE?
RETIRED QUEEN OF LATVERIA.
WHAT ARE YOU GUYS DOING?
YOU HANDLED THAT WHOLE SITUATION PRETTY GREAT.
LUNCH.
MANY JANE WAS JUST TELLING ME HOW MY YOUNG, PUNK, DRUNK OF A SON ONCE HIT ON HER AT A PARTY.
DID YOU GUYS--?
RIRI!
IT DOES HAPPEN.
THAT'S SO FUNNY--YOU KNOW, I MET TONY BEFORE, TOO.
BEFORE WHEN?
YOU'RE SIX YEARS OLD.
DO YOU GUYS REMEMBE
THE SKRULLS?

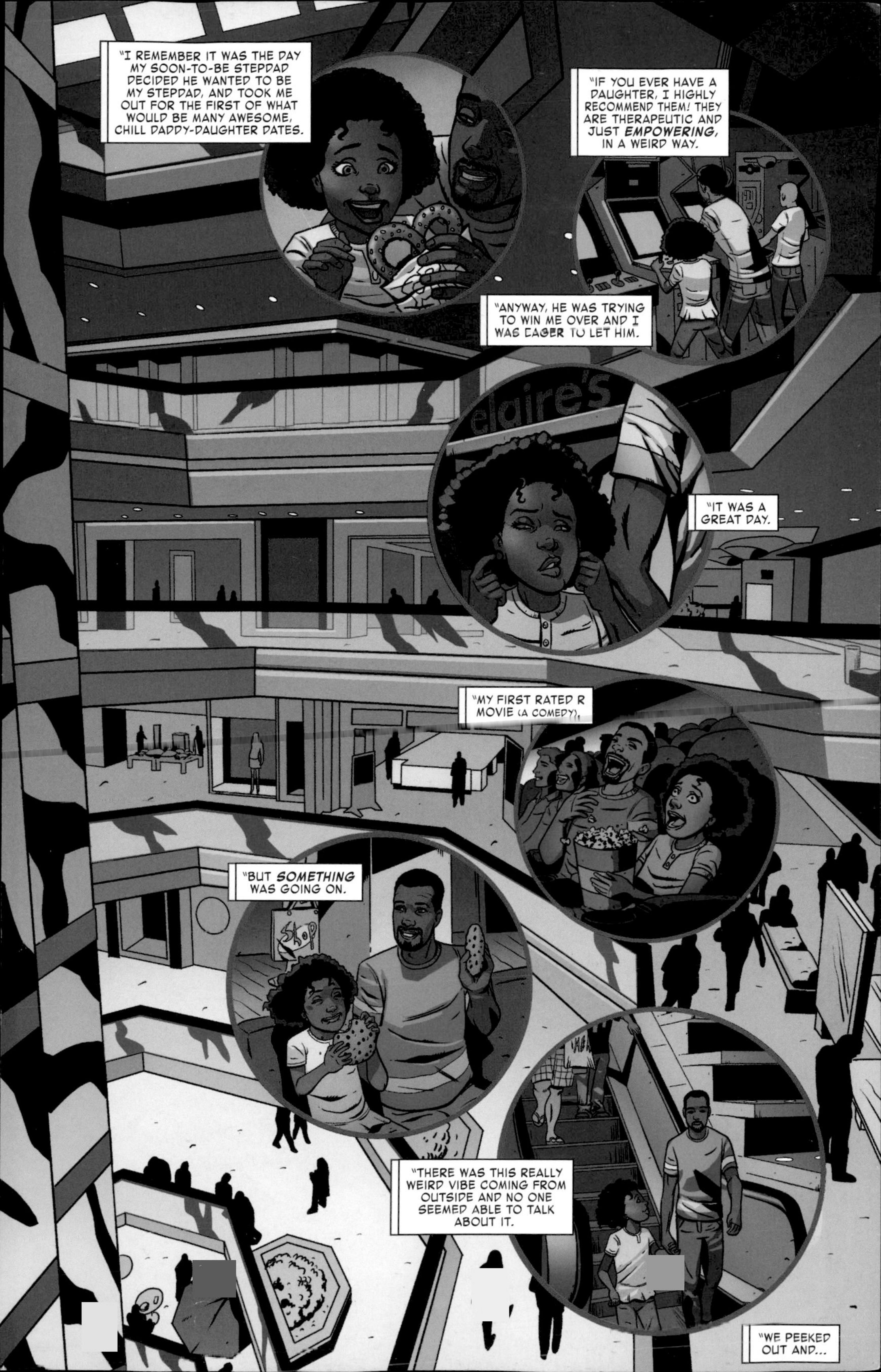
"I REMEMBER IT WAS THE DAY MY SOON-TO-BE STEPDAD DECIDED HE WANTED TO BE MY STEPDAD, AND TOOK ME OUT FOR THE FIRST OF WHAT WOULD BE MANY AWESOME, CHILL DADDY-DAUGHTER DATES.
"IF YOU EVER HAVE A DAUGHTER, I HIGHLY RECOMMEND THEM! THEY ARE THERAPEUTIC AND JUST *EMPOWERING,* IN A WEIRD WAY.
"ANYWAY, HE WAS TRYING TO WIN ME OVER AND I WAS EAGER TO LET HIM.
claire's
"IT WAS A GREAT DAY.
"MY FIRST RATED R MOVIE (A COMEDY),
"BUT *SOMETHING* WAS GOING ON.
"THERE WAS THIS REALLY WEIRD VIBE COMING FROM OUTSIDE AND NO ONE SEEMED ABLE TO TALK ABOUT IT.
"WE PEEKED OUT AND...

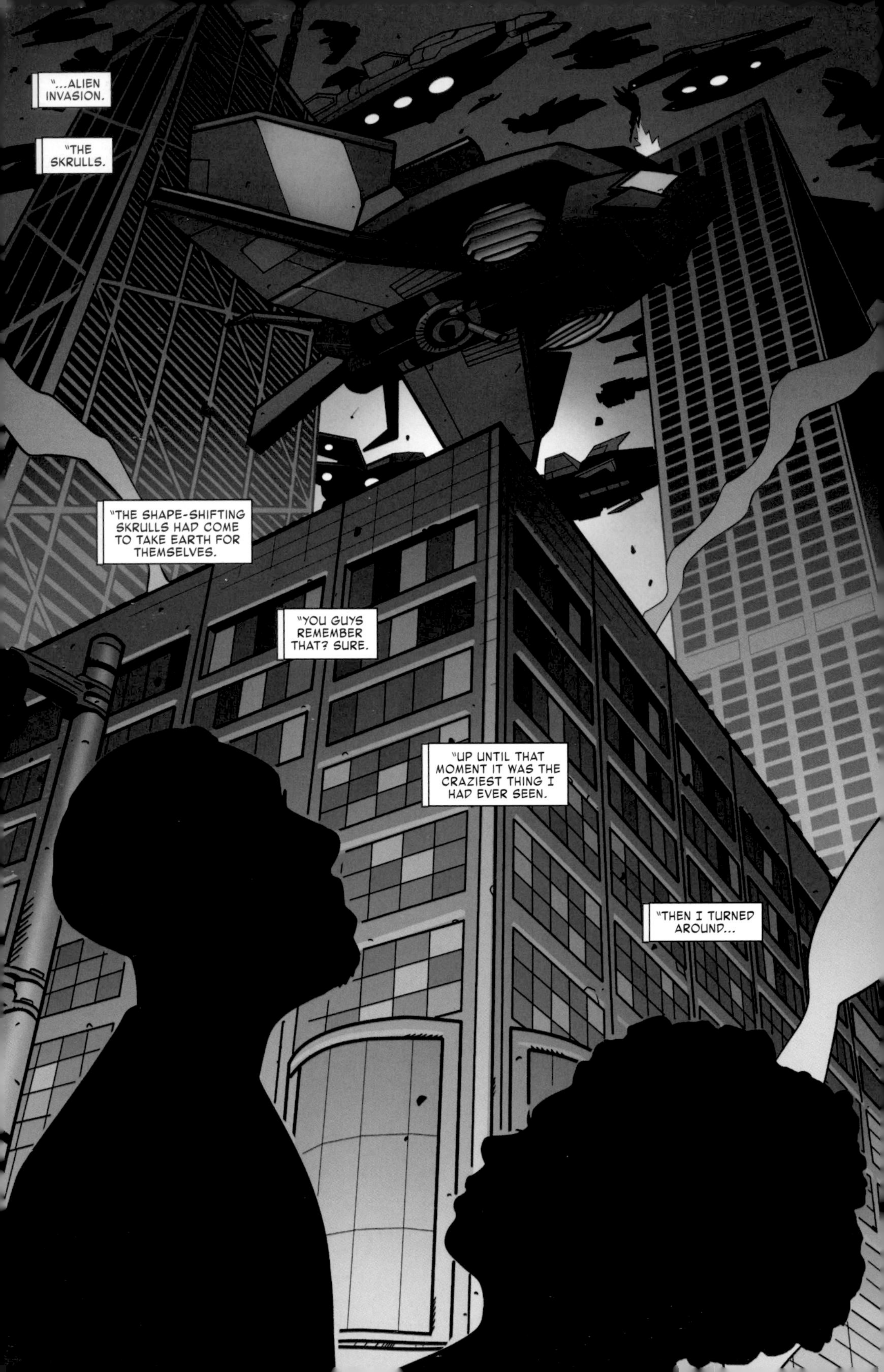
"...ALIEN INVASION.
"THE SKRULLS.
"THE SHAPE-SHIFTING SKRULLS HAD COME TO TAKE EARTH FOR THEMSELVES.
"YOU GUYS REMEMBER THAT? SURE.
"UP UNTIL THAT MOMENT IT WAS THE CRAZIEST THING I HAD EVER SEEN.
"THEN I TURNED AROUND...

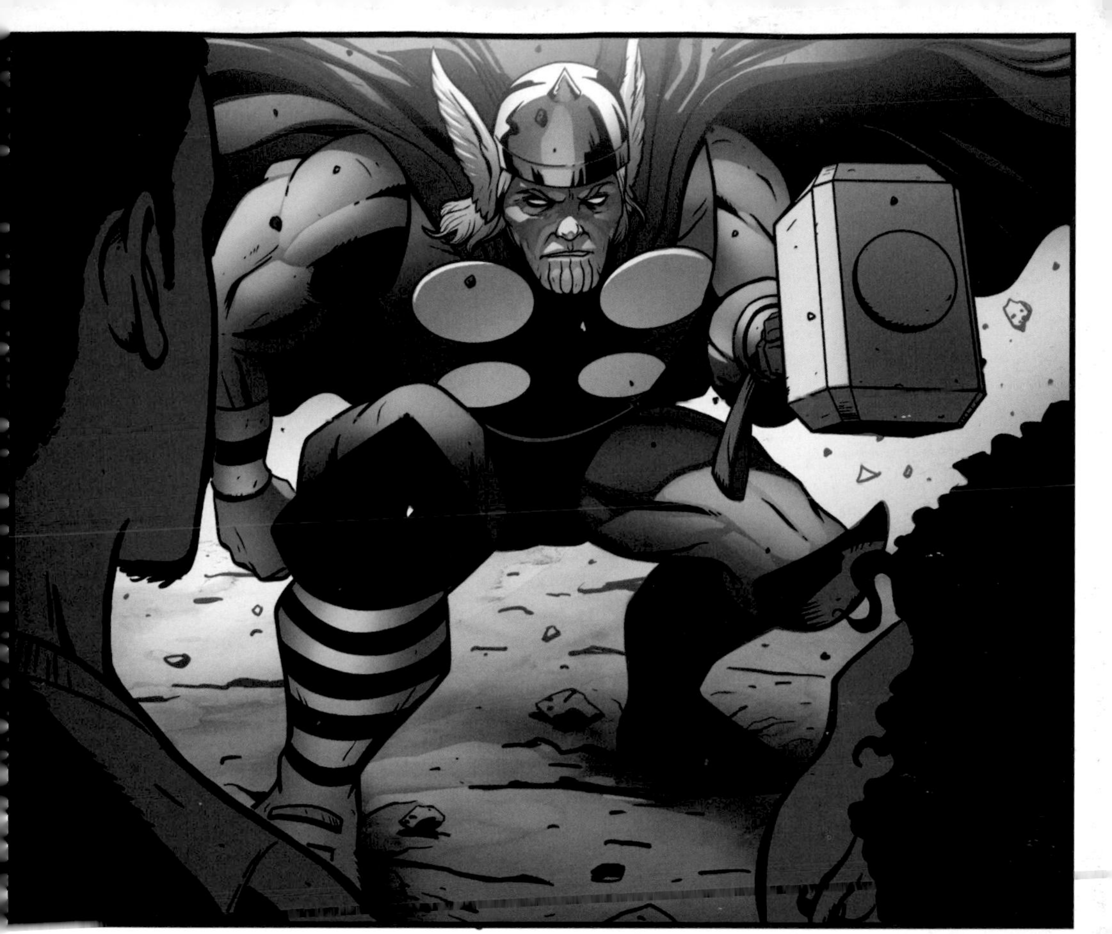

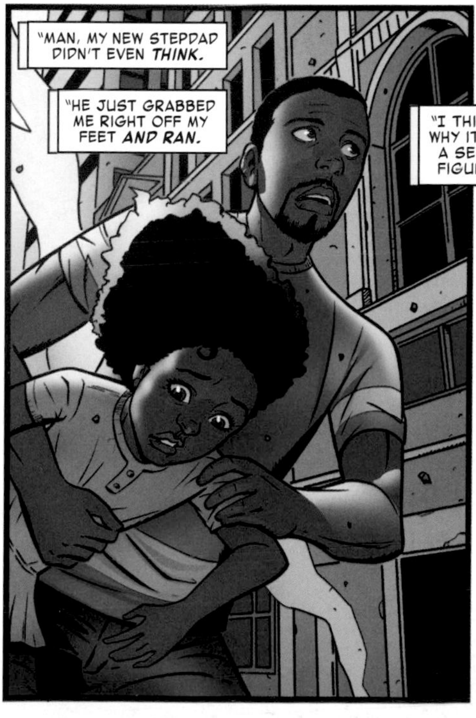
"MAN, MY NEW STEPDAD DIDN'T EVEN THINK.
"HE JUST GRABBED ME RIGHT OFF MY FEET AND RAN.
"I THINK THAT'S WHY IT TOOK ME A SECOND TO FIGURE OUT...

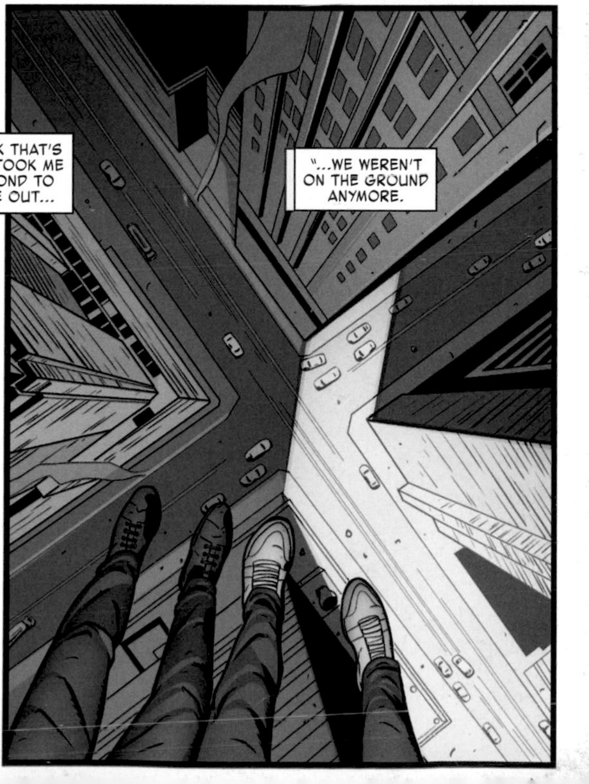
"...WE WEREN'T ON THE GROUND ANYMORE.

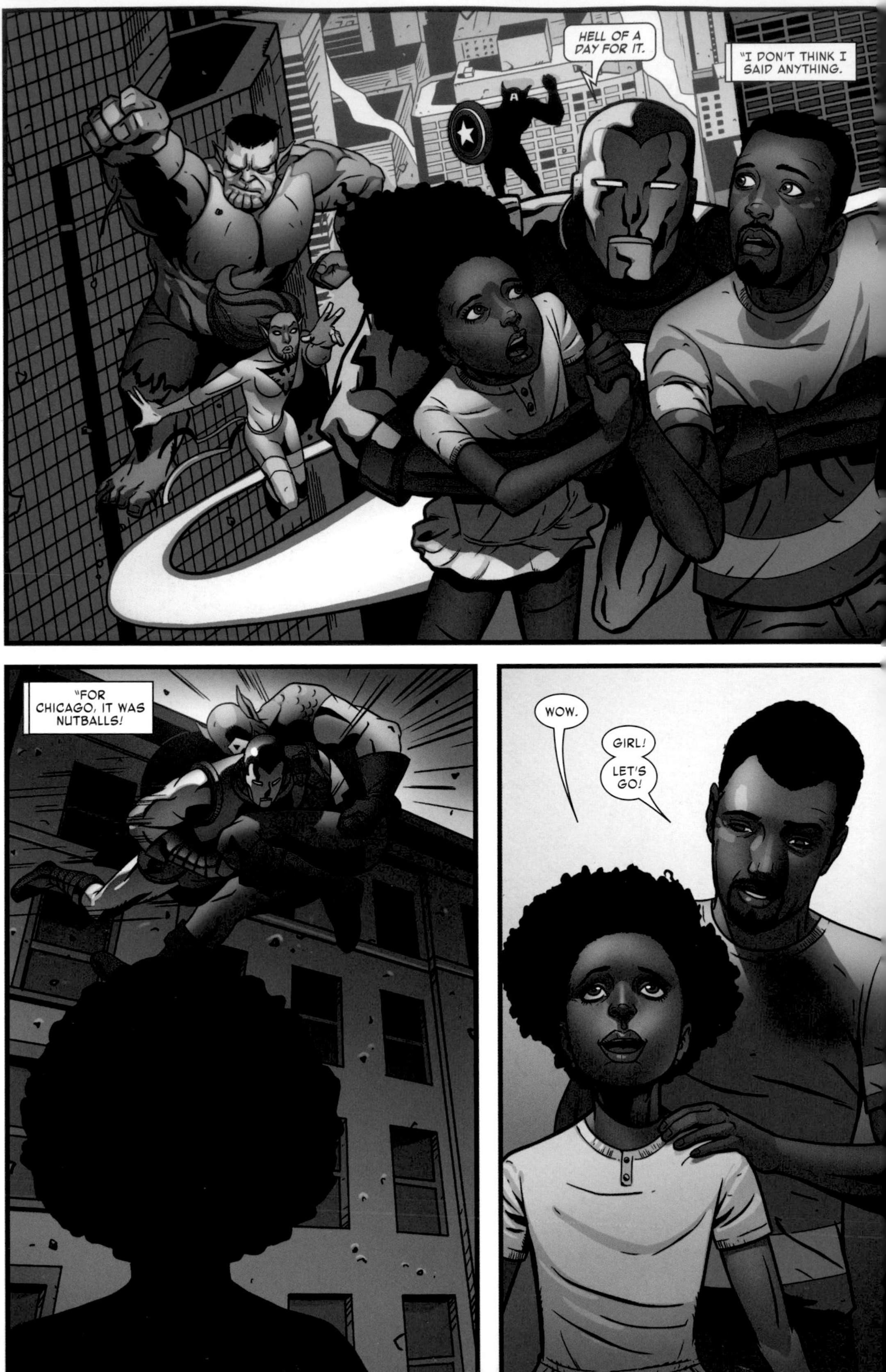

HELL OF A DAY FOR IT.
"I DON'T THINK I SAID ANYTHING.
"FOR CHICAGO, IT WAS NUTBALLS!
WOW.
GIRL!
LET'S GO!

"MY BRAIN KIND OF FROZE.

IT'S PROBABLY SAFER INSIDE, BUT AT THIS MOMENT, WHO THE HELL KNOWS?!

"I LIVE IN CHICAGO. NOT NEW YORK.

"NEW YORK IS LOUSY WITH THIS STUFF...

"I REMEMBER BEING SO IMPRESSED WITH HIS ABILITY TO SKILLFULLY DROP US OFF WITHOUT MESSING UP HIS TRAJECTORY.

"ALSO, HIS RIGHT BOOT WASN'T WORKING PROPERLY AND STILL...WOW.

HIS BOOT IS GLITCHING!

WHAT?

THE ROCKET THRUSTERS ON HIS LEFT BOOT, HE'S GLITCHY!

WELL, HE SEEMS OKAY TO ME!

ACTUALLY, I THINK I KNOW HOW TO FIX THAT.

"I NEVER MENTIONED IT BECAUSE IT'S NOT LIKE IT'S A SPECIAL THING FOR HIM.

"HEY, REMEMBER THAT LITTLE GIRL AND HER DAD YOU SAVED? NO?'

"'DOESN'T RING A BELL BECAUSE YOU DO THAT LITERALLY FIFTY TIMES A DAY.'

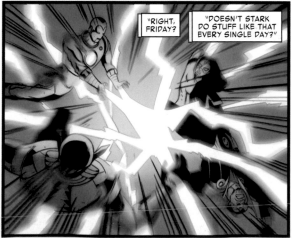

"RIGHT, FRIDAY?

"DOESN'T STARK DO STUFF LIKE THAT EVERY SINGLE DAY?"

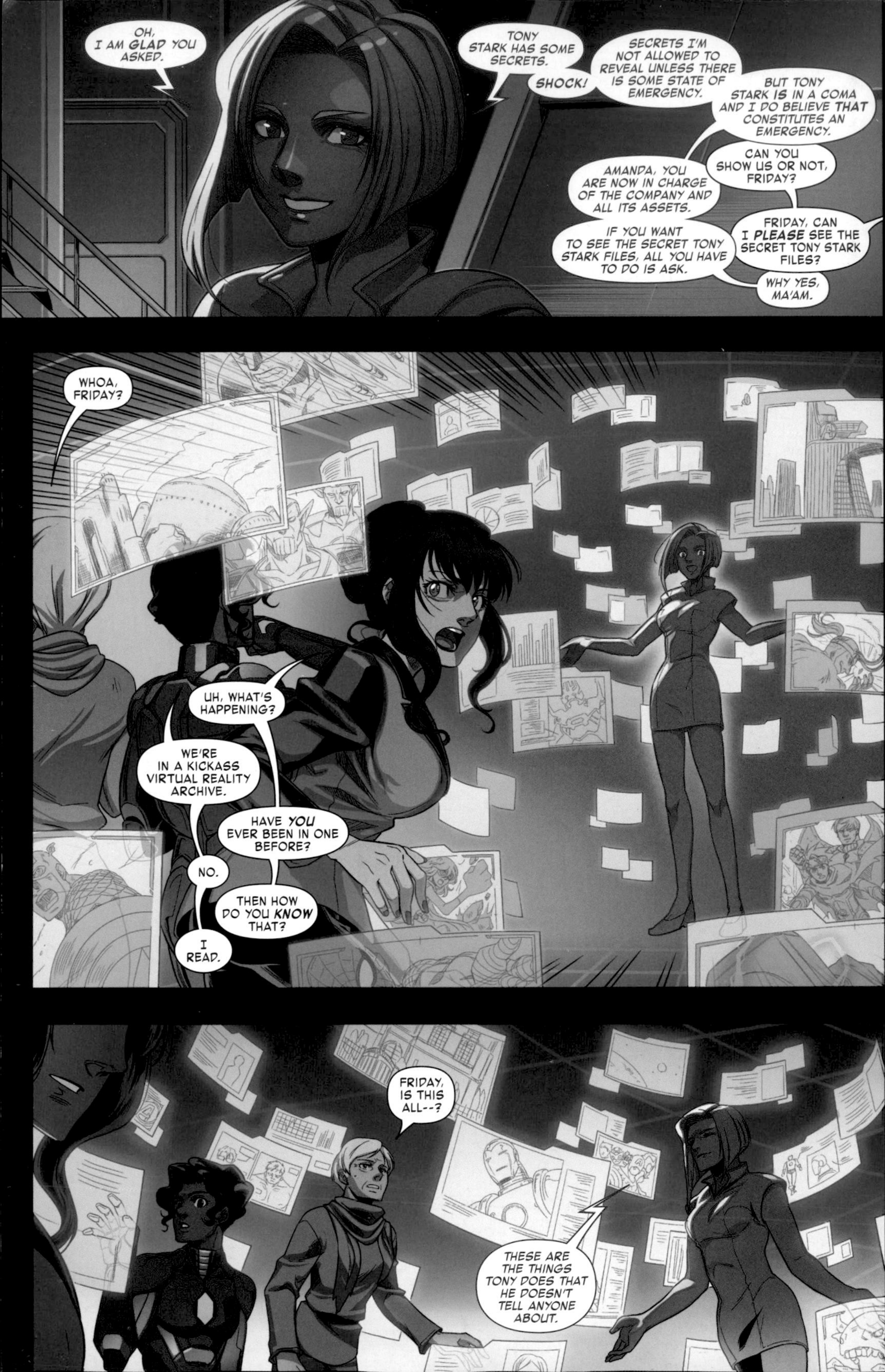
OH, I AM GLAD YOU ASKED.
TONY STARK HAS SOME SECRETS.
SHOCK!
SECRETS I'M NOT ALLOWED TO REVEAL UNLESS THERE IS SOME STATE OF EMERGENCY.
BUT TONY STARK IS IN A COMA AND I DO BELIEVE THAT CONSTITUTES AN EMERGENCY.
CAN YOU SHOW US OR NOT, FRIDAY?
AMANDA, YOU ARE NOW IN CHARGE OF THE COMPANY AND ALL ITS ASSETS.
IF YOU WANT TO SEE THE SECRET TONY STARK FILES, ALL YOU HAVE TO DO IS ASK.
FRIDAY, CAN I PLEASE SEE THE SECRET TONY STARK FILES?
WHY YES, MA'AM.
WHOA, FRIDAY?
UH, WHAT'S HAPPENING?
WE'RE IN A KICKASS VIRTUAL REALITY ARCHIVE.
HAVE YOU EVER BEEN IN ONE BEFORE?
NO.
THEN HOW DO YOU KNOW THAT?
I READ.
FRIDAY, IS THIS ALL--?
THESE ARE THE THINGS TONY DOES THAT HE DOESN'T TELL ANYONE ABOUT.

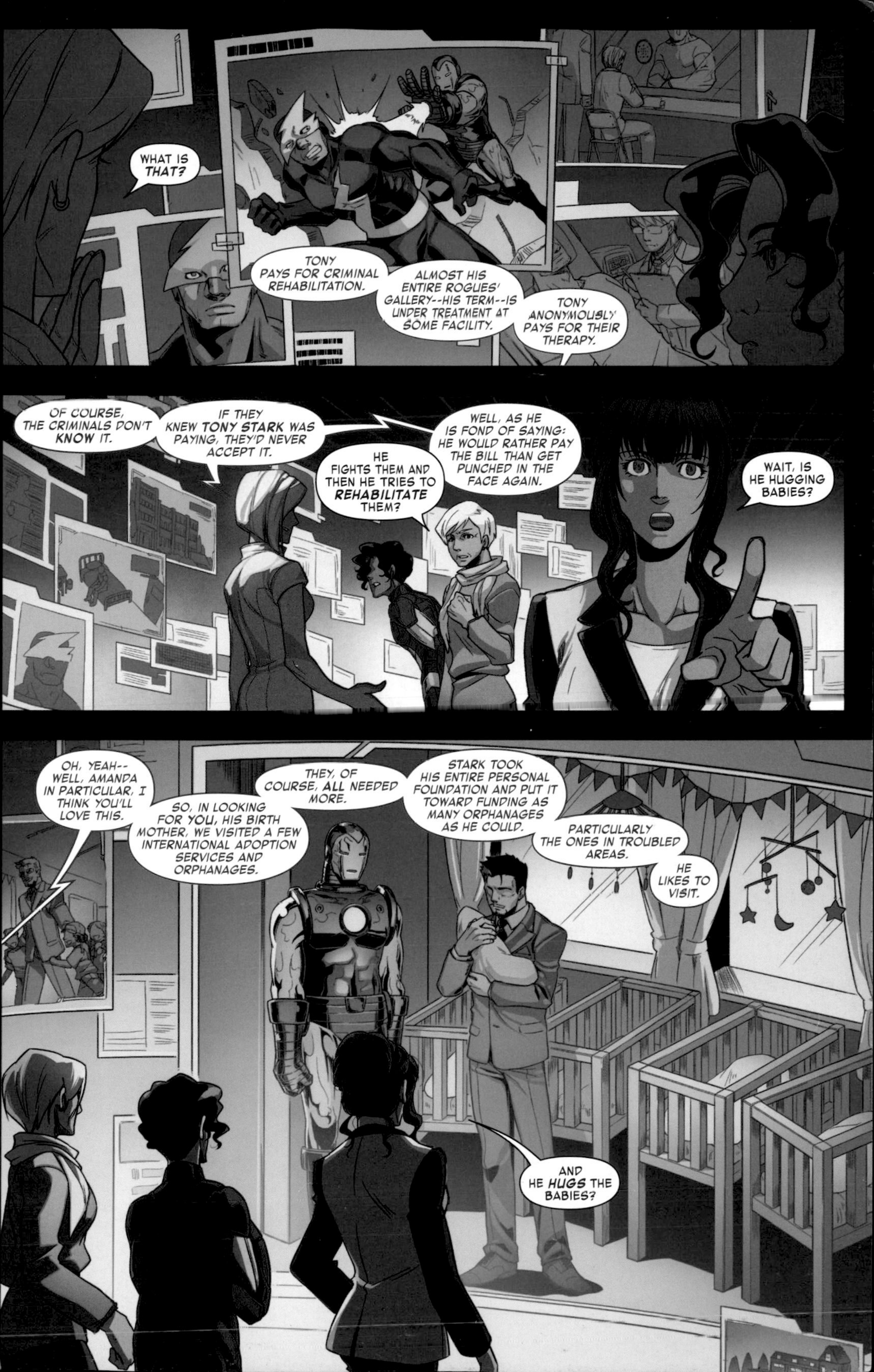
WHAT IS THAT?
TONY PAYS FOR CRIMINAL REHABILITATION.
ALMOST HIS ENTIRE ROGUES' GALLERY--HIS TERM--IS UNDER TREATMENT AT SOME FACILITY.
TONY ANONYMOUSLY PAYS FOR THEIR THERAPY.
OF COURSE, THE CRIMINALS DON'T KNOW IT.
IF THEY KNEW TONY STARK WAS PAYING, THEY'D NEVER ACCEPT IT.
HE FIGHTS THEM AND THEN HE TRIES TO REHABILITATE THEM?
WELL, AS HE IS FOND OF SAYING: HE WOULD RATHER PAY THE BILL THAN GET PUNCHED IN THE FACE AGAIN.
WAIT, IS HE HUGGING BABIES?
OH, YEAH-- WELL, AMANDA IN PARTICULAR, I THINK YOU'LL LOVE THIS.
SO, IN LOOKING FOR YOU, HIS BIRTH MOTHER, WE VISITED A FEW INTERNATIONAL ADOPTION SERVICES AND ORPHANAGES.
THEY, OF COURSE, ALL NEEDED MORE.
STARK TOOK HIS ENTIRE PERSONAL FOUNDATION AND PUT IT TOWARD FUNDING AS MANY ORPHANAGES AS HE COULD.
PARTICULARLY THE ONES IN TROUBLED AREAS.
HE LIKES TO VISIT.
AND HE HUGS THE BABIES?

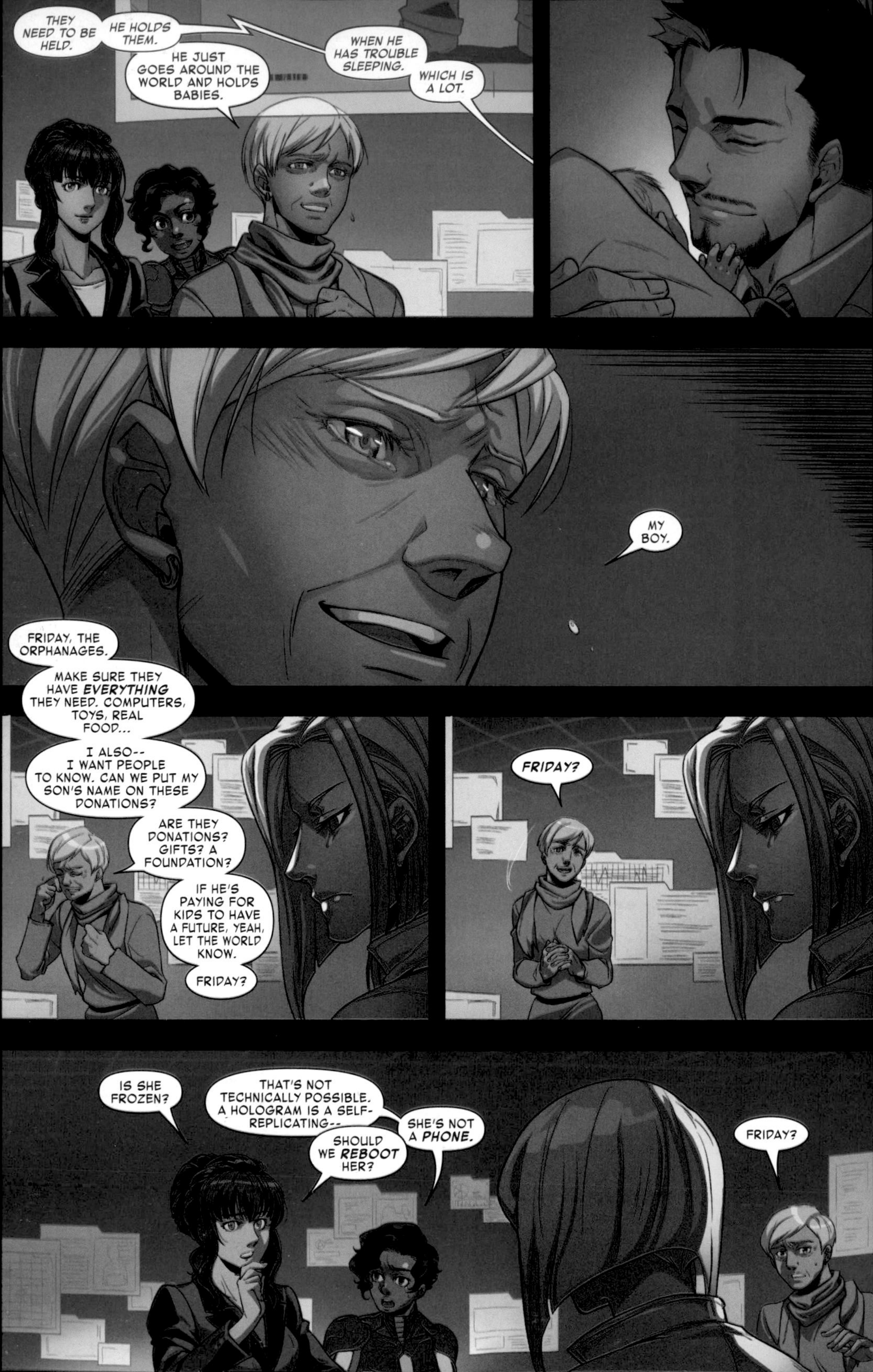
THEY NEED TO BE HELD.
HE HOLDS THEM.
HE JUST GOES AROUND THE WORLD AND HOLDS BABIES.
WHEN HE HAS TROUBLE SLEEPING.
WHICH IS A LOT.
MY BOY.
FRIDAY, THE ORPHANAGES.
MAKE SURE THEY HAVE EVERYTHING THEY NEED. COMPUTERS, TOYS, REAL FOOD...
I ALSO-- I WANT PEOPLE TO KNOW. CAN WE PUT MY SON'S NAME ON THESE DONATIONS?
ARE THEY DONATIONS? GIFTS? A FOUNDATION?
IF HE'S PAYING FOR KIDS TO HAVE A FUTURE, YEAH, LET THE WORLD KNOW.
FRIDAY?
FRIDAY?
IS SHE FROZEN?
THAT'S NOT TECHNICALLY POSSIBLE. A HOLOGRAM IS A SELF-REPLICATING--
SHE'S NOT A PHONE.
SHOULD WE REBOOT HER?
FRIDAY?

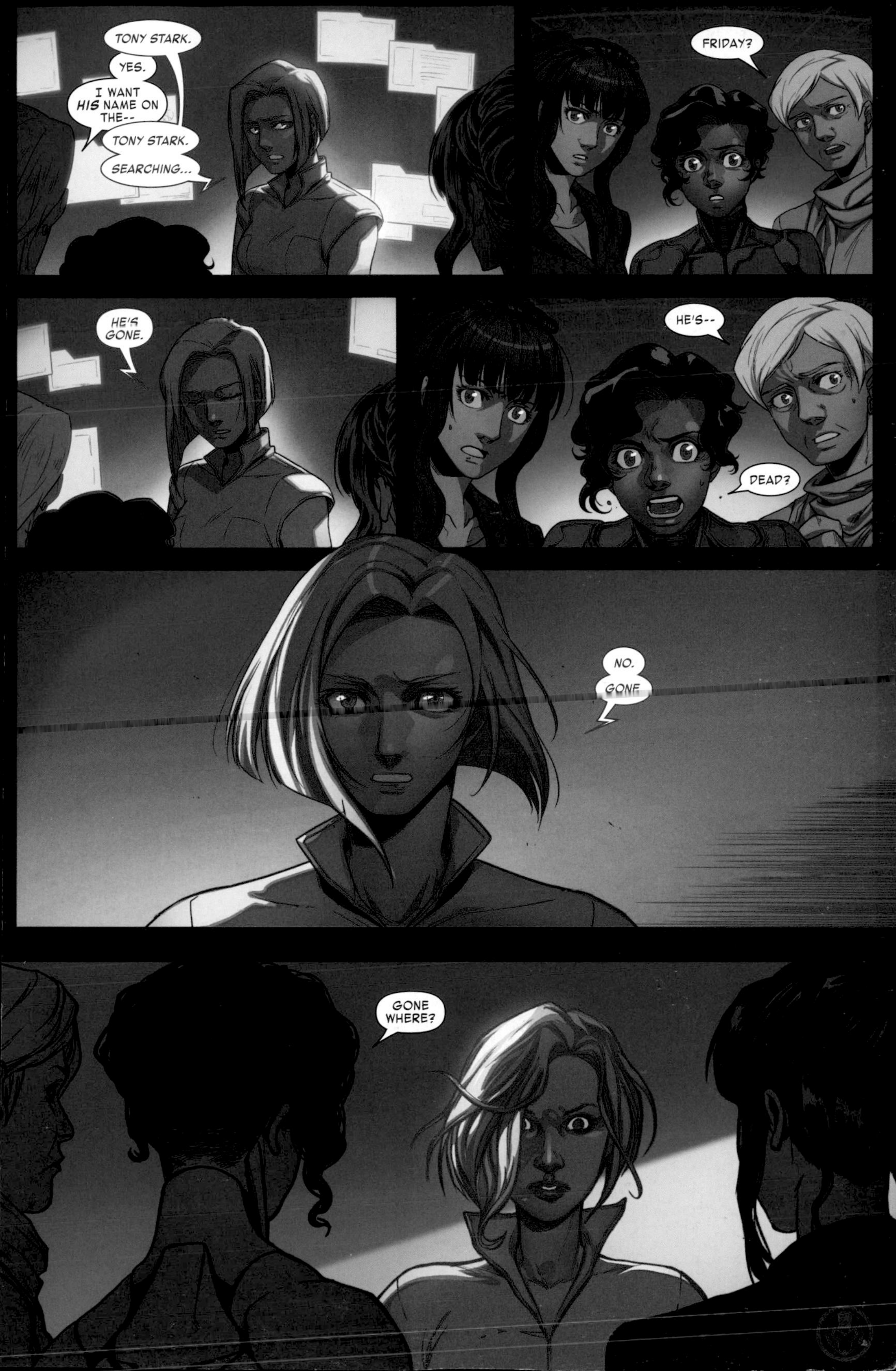
TONY STARK.
YES.
I WANT HIS NAME ON THE--
TONY STARK.
SEARCHING...
FRIDAY?
HE'S GONE.
HE'S--
DEAD?
NO. GONE.
GONE WHERE?

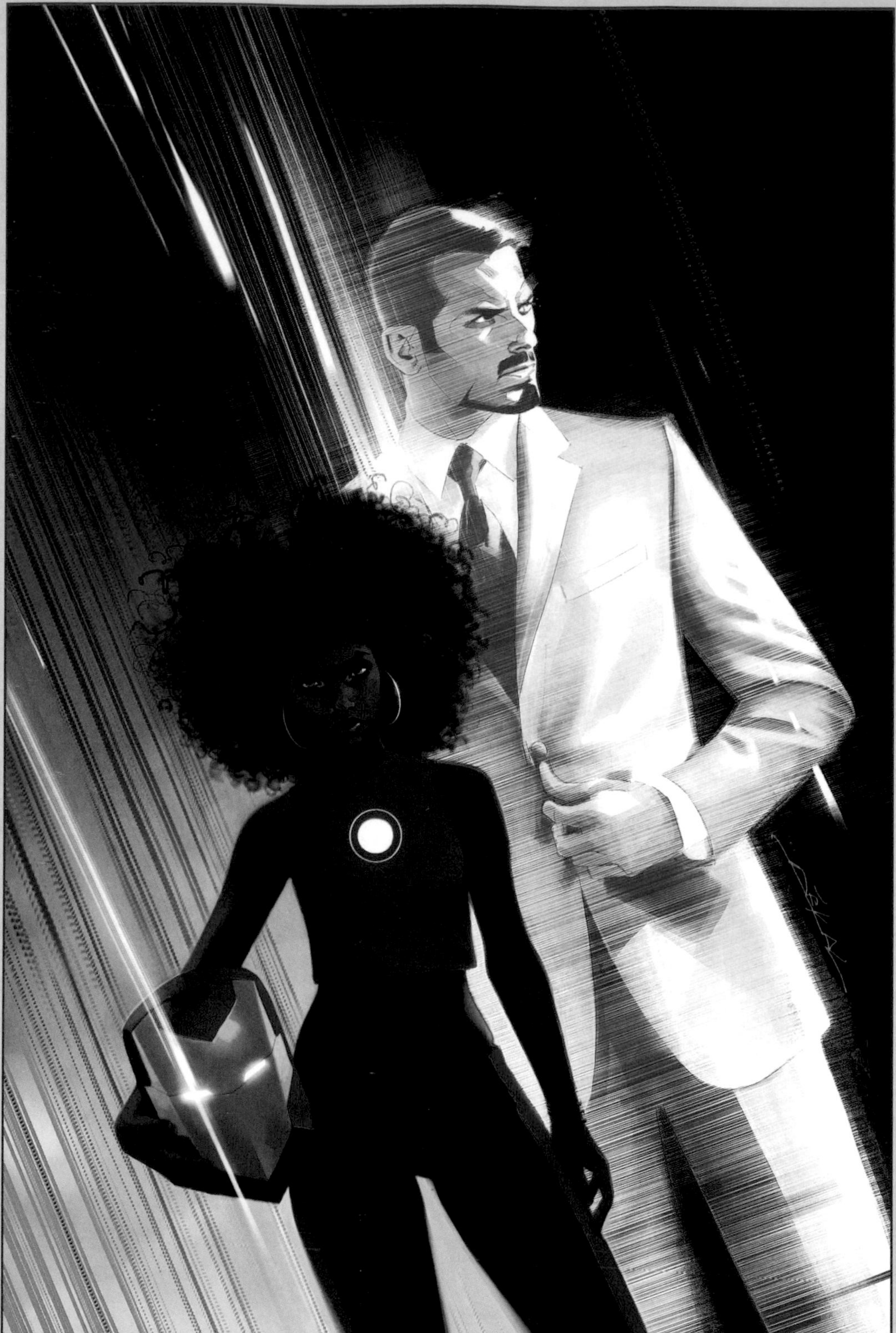

#1 VARIANT
BY JEFF DEKAL

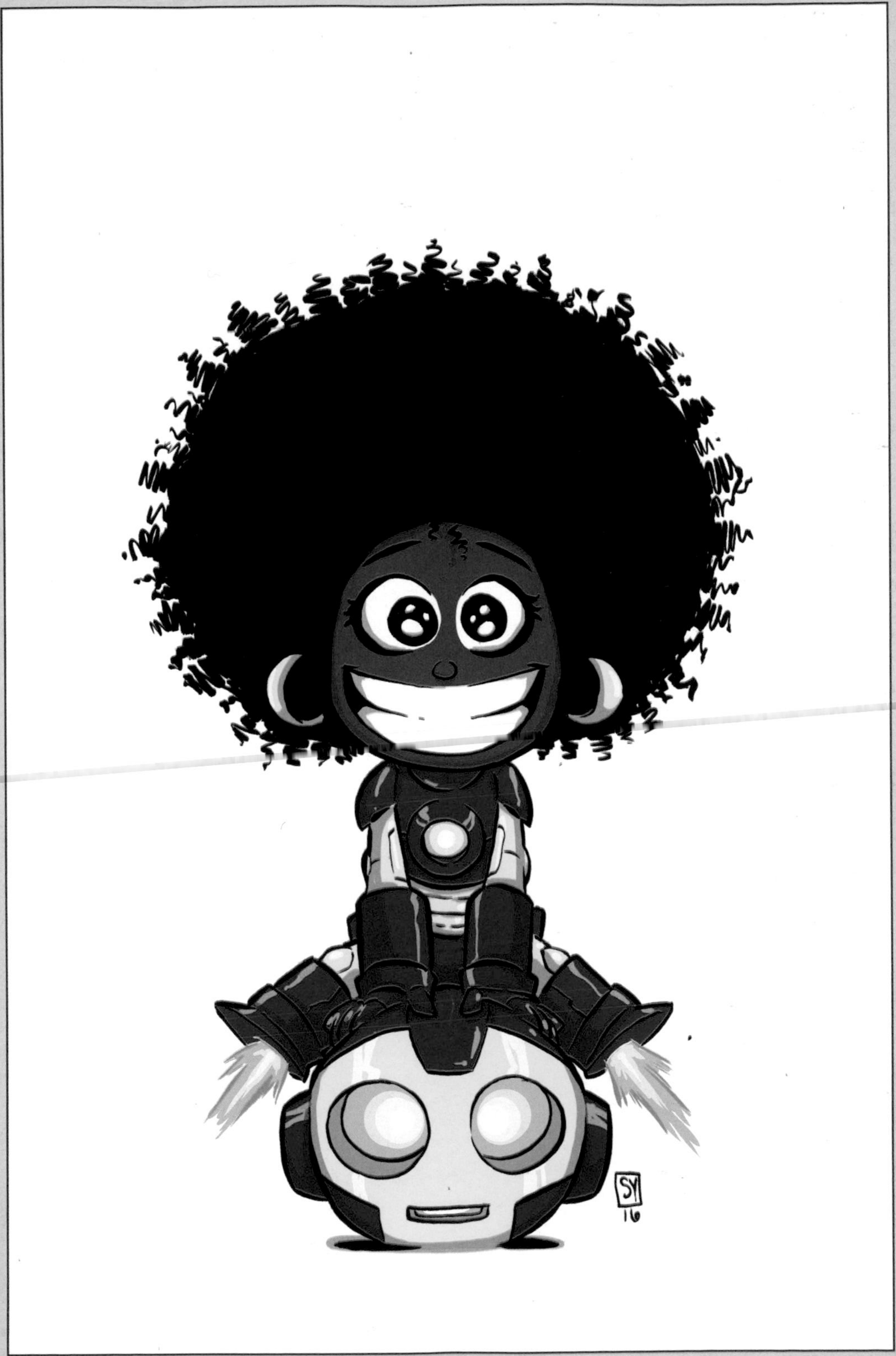
SY
16

#1 VARIANT
BY SKOTTIE YOUNG

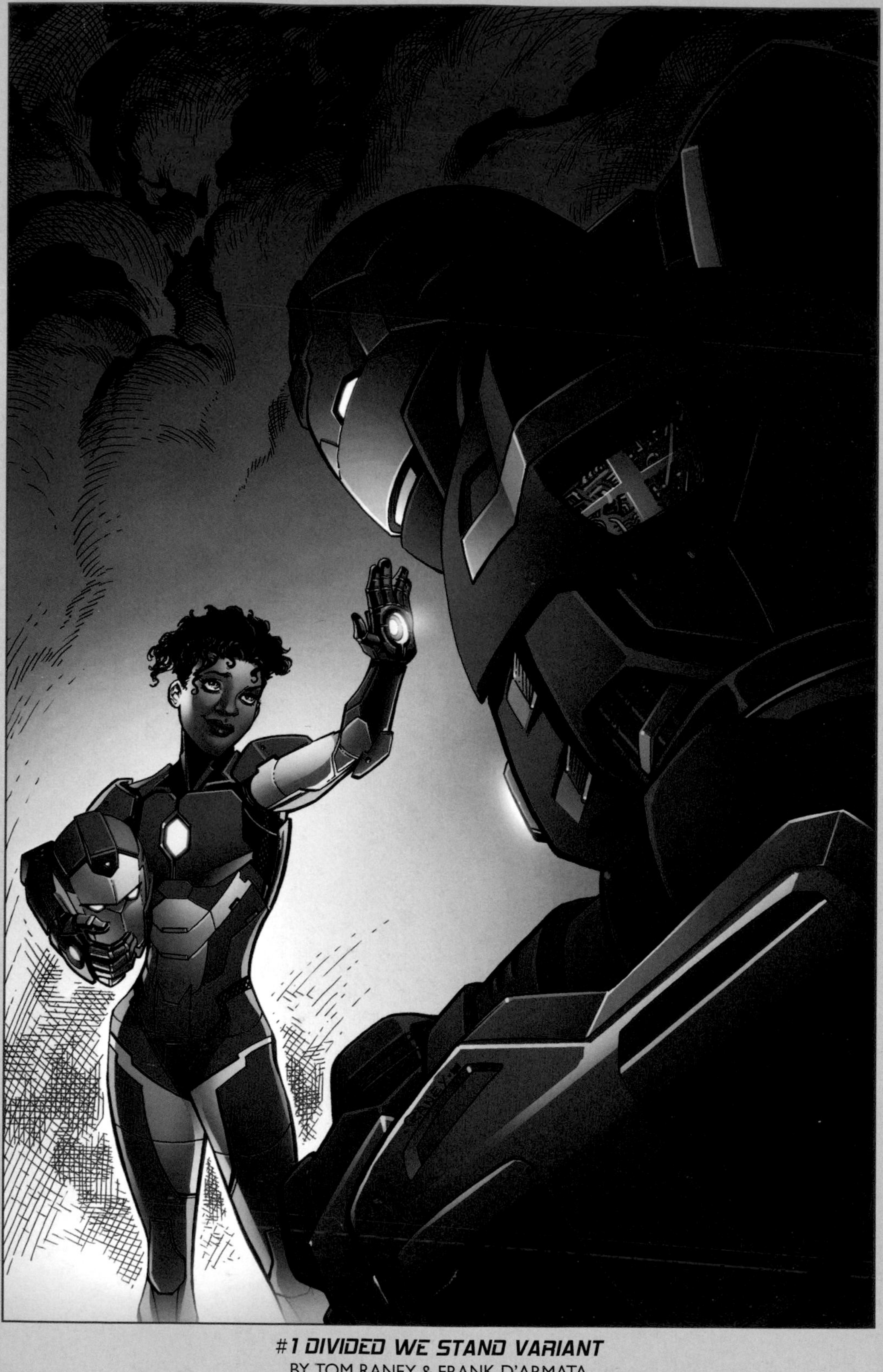

#1 DIVIDED WE STAND VARIANT
BY TOM RANEY & FRANK D'ARMATA

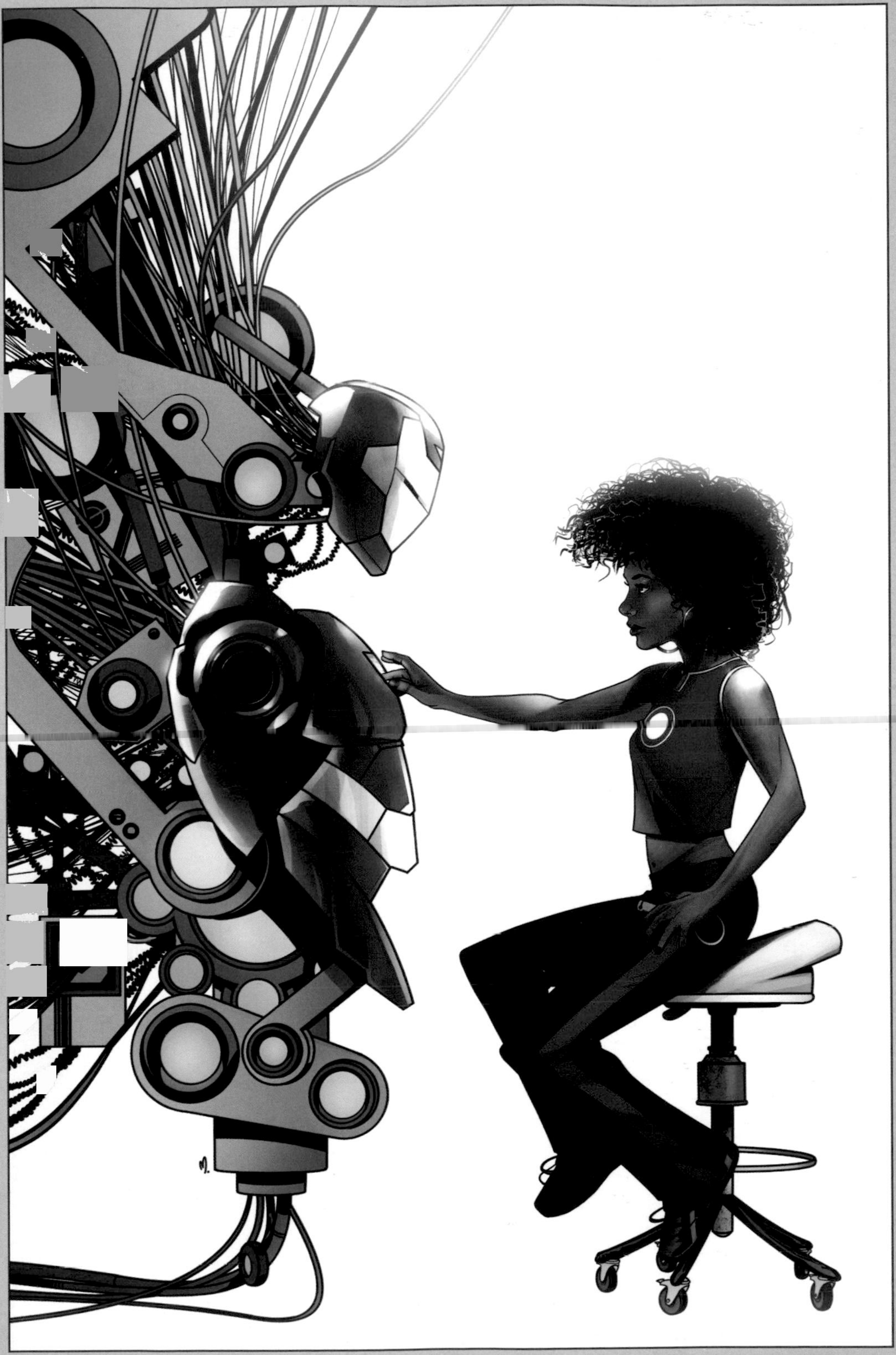

#1 STEAM VARIANT
BY MIKE McKONE & JASON KEITH

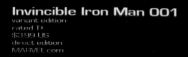

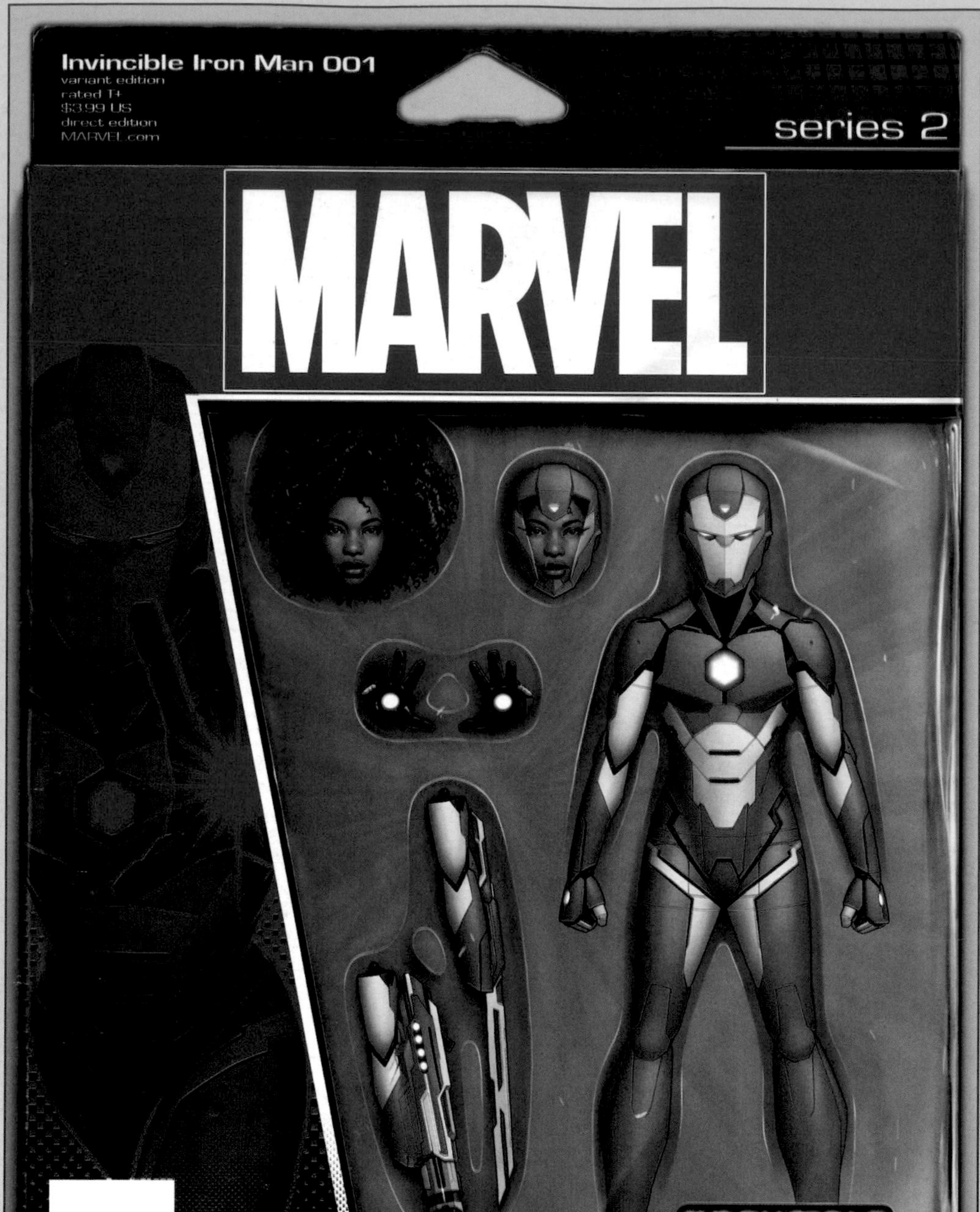

Invincible Iron Man 001
variant edition
rated T+
$3.99 US
direct edition
MARVEL.com

series 2

MARVEL

INVINCIBLE
IRON MAN
IRONHEART
riri williams

#1 ACTION FIGURE VARIANT
BY JOHN TYLER CHRISTOPHER

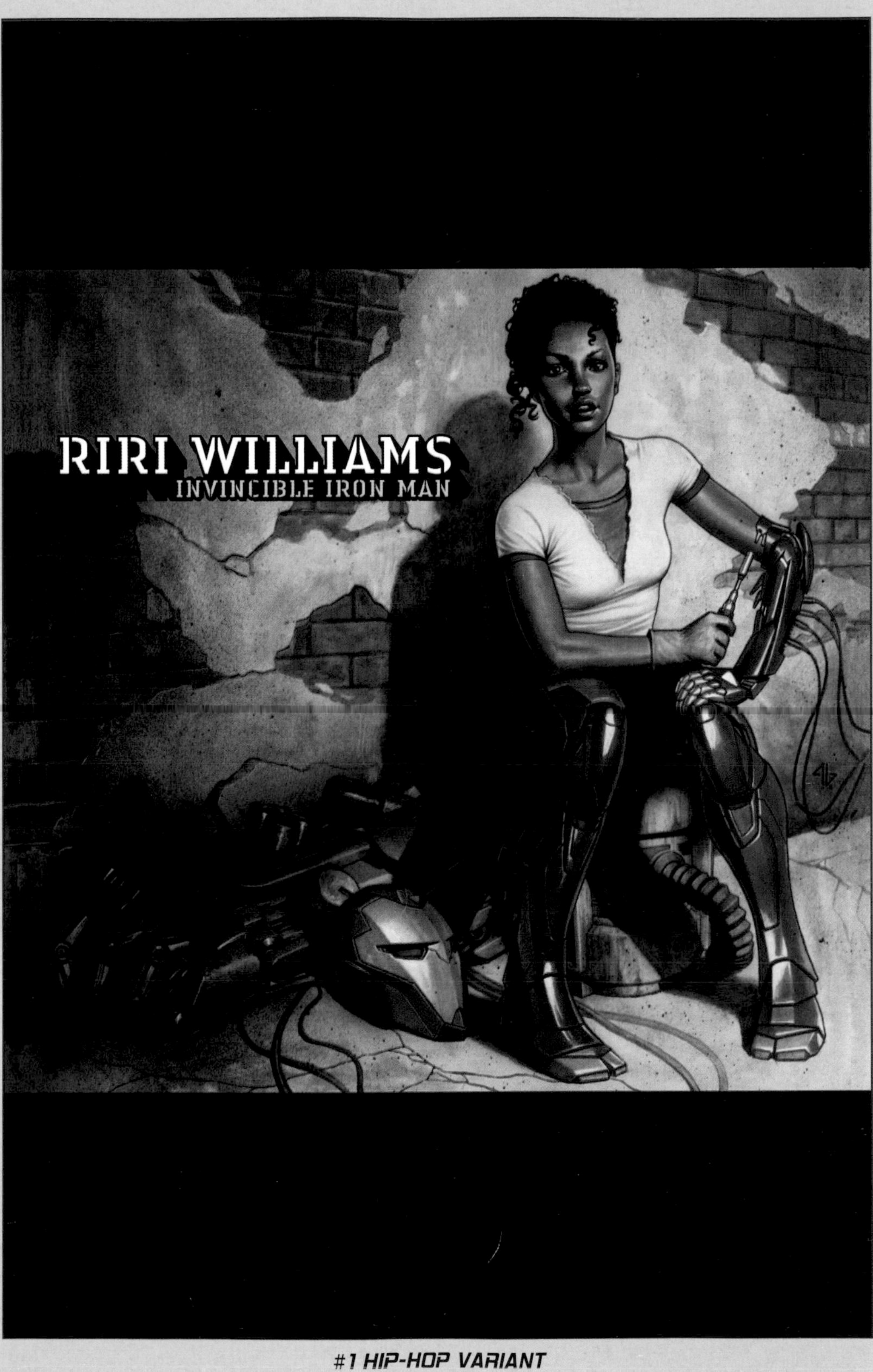
RIRI WILLIAMS
INVINCIBLE IRON MAN

#1 HIP-HOP VARIANT
BY ADI GRANOV

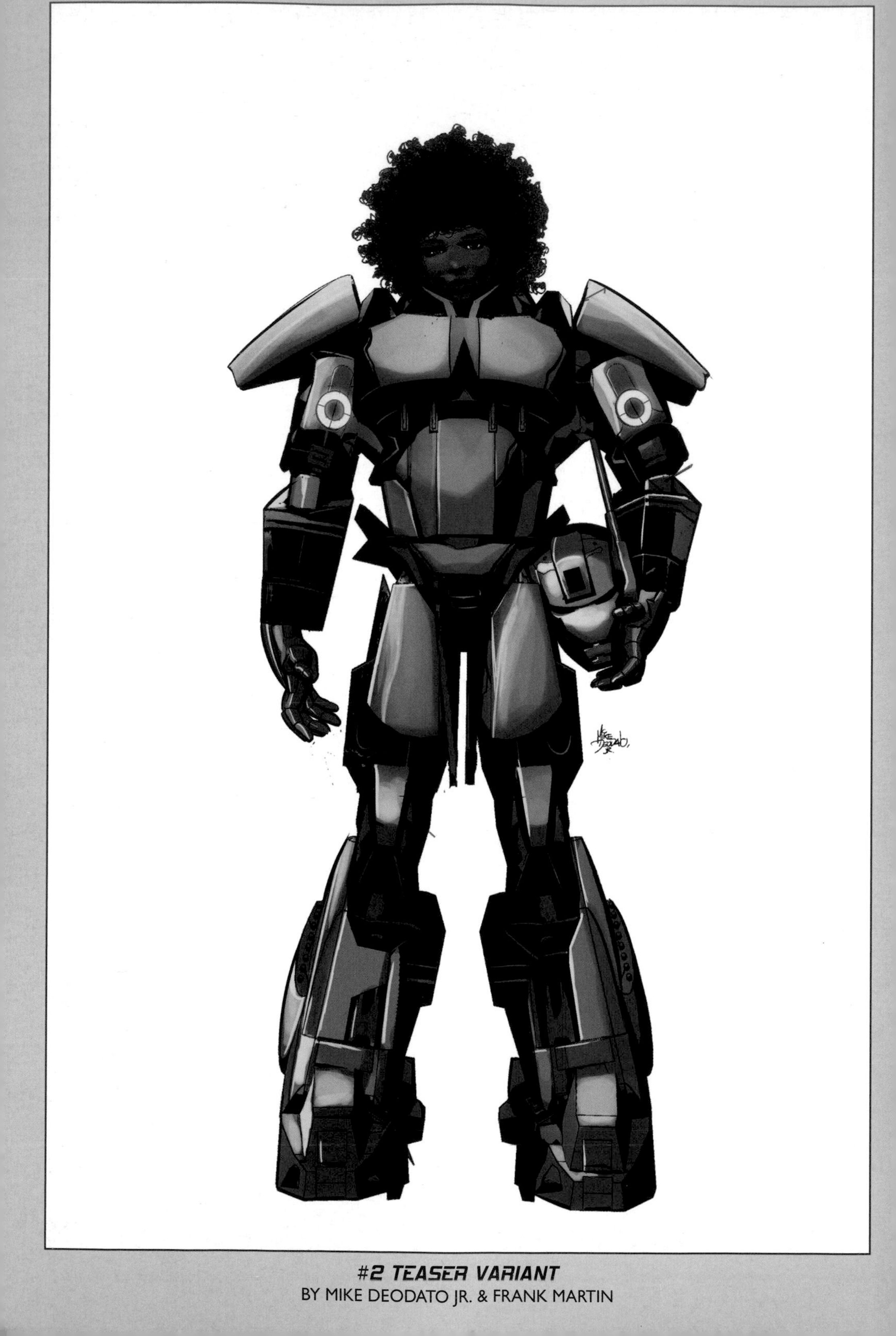

#2 TEASER VARIANT
BY MIKE DEODATO JR. & FRANK MARTIN

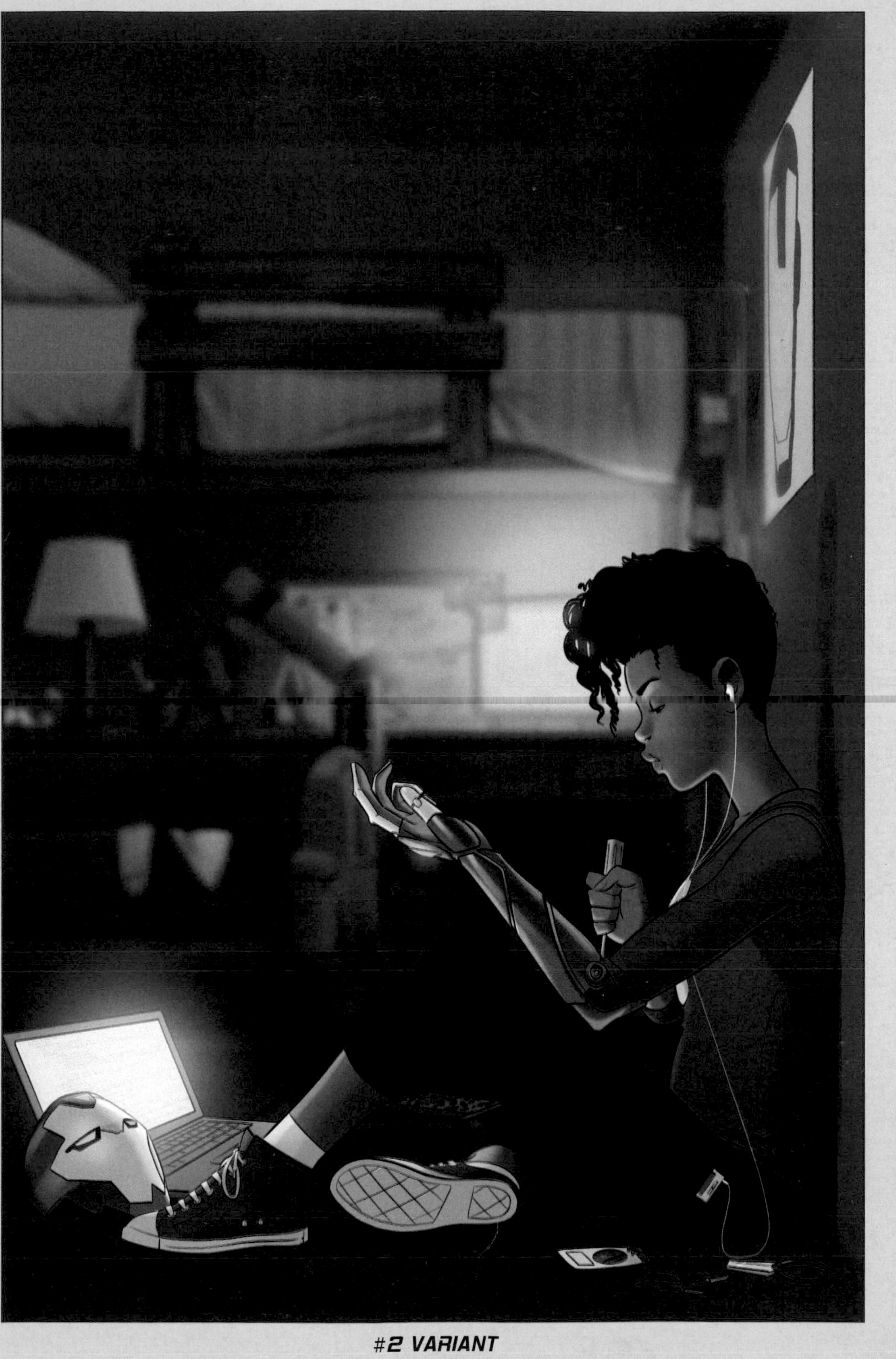

#2 VARIANT
BY ANTHONY PIPER

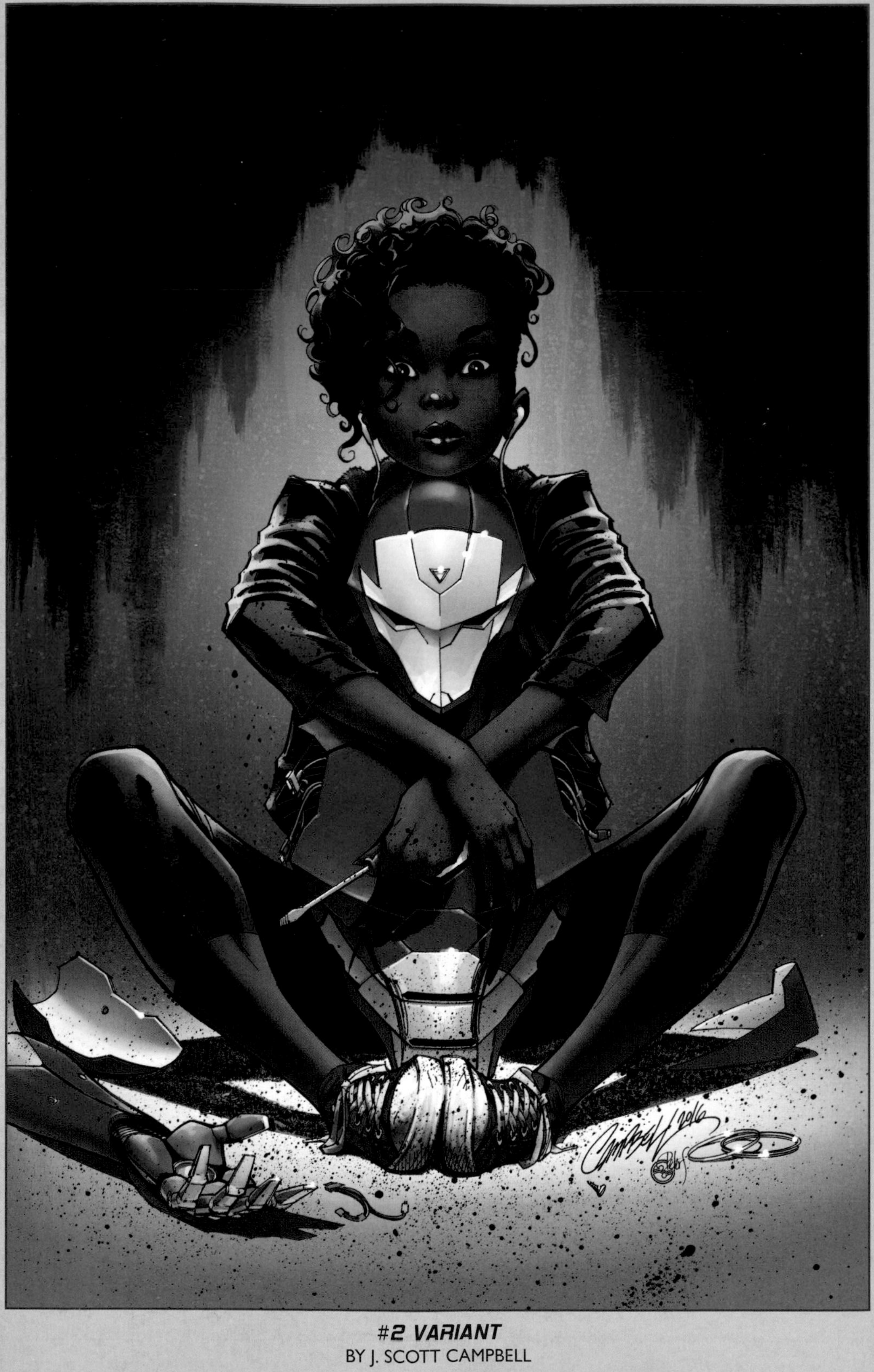

#2 VARIANT
BY J. SCOTT CAMPBELL

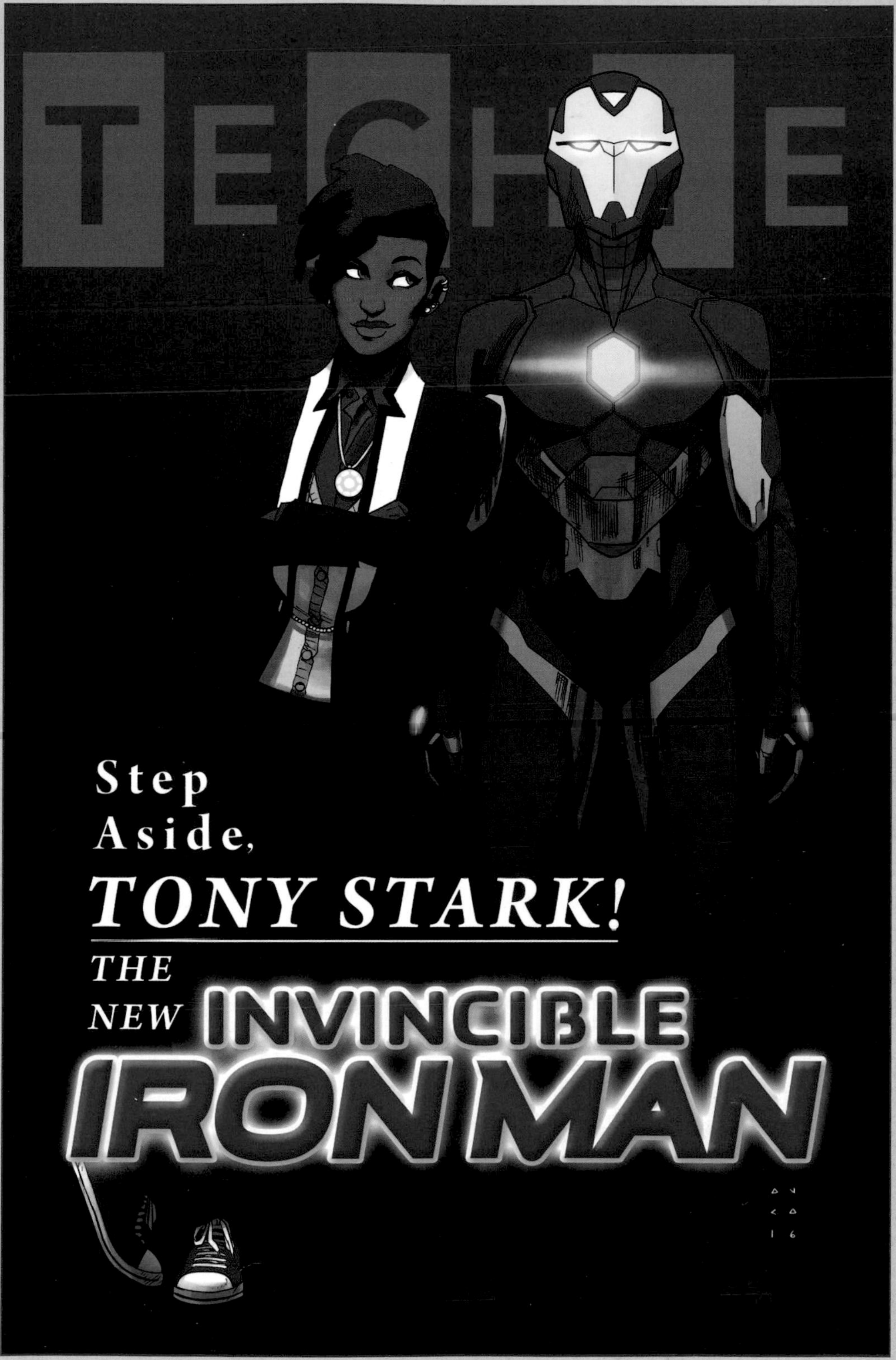
Step
Aside,
TONY STARK!
THE
NEW INVINCIBLE
IRON MAN

#3 VARIANT
BY KRIS ANKA

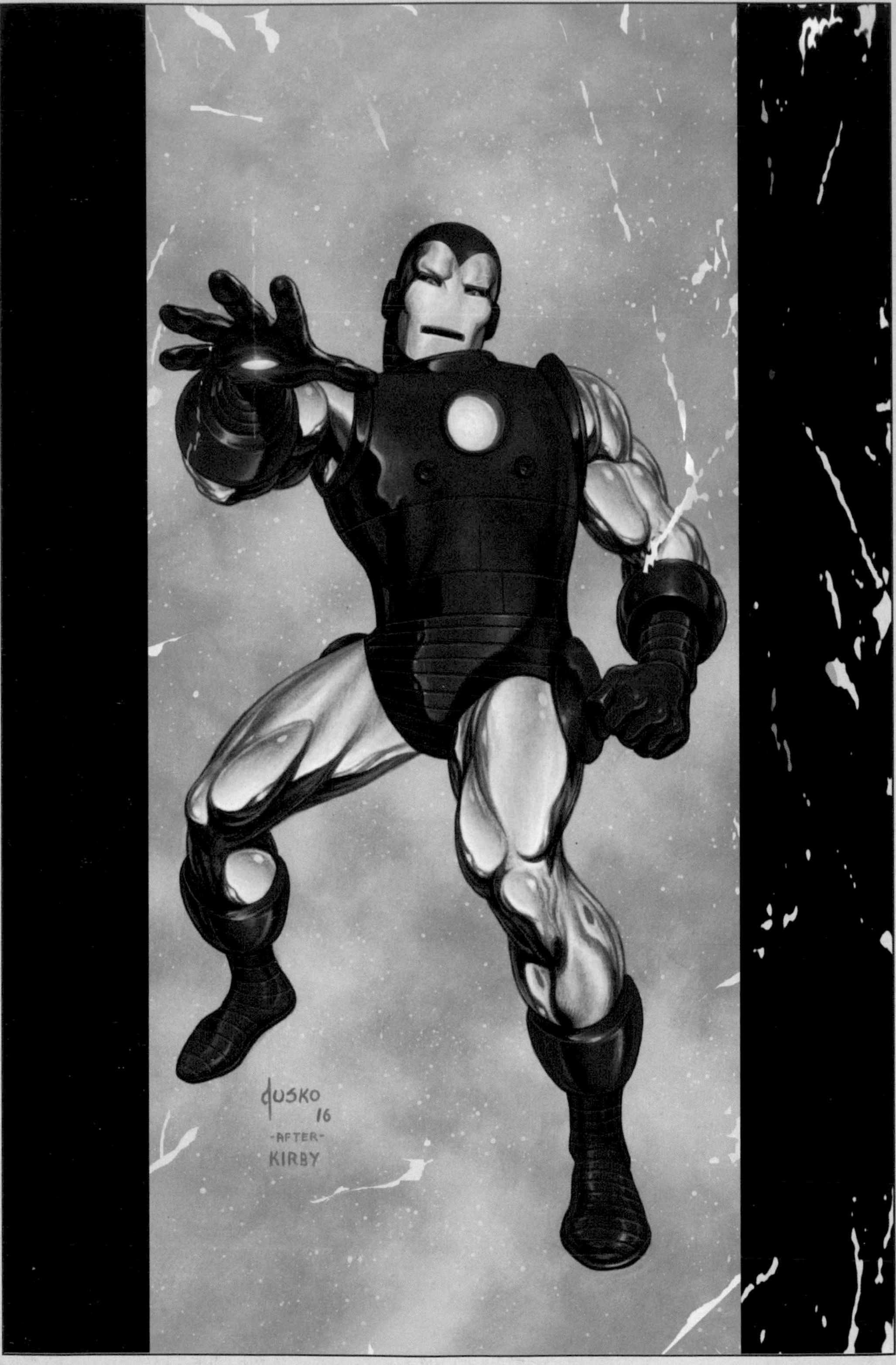
JUSKO
16
-AFTER-
KIRBY

#2 CORNER BOX VARIANT
BY JOE JUSKO

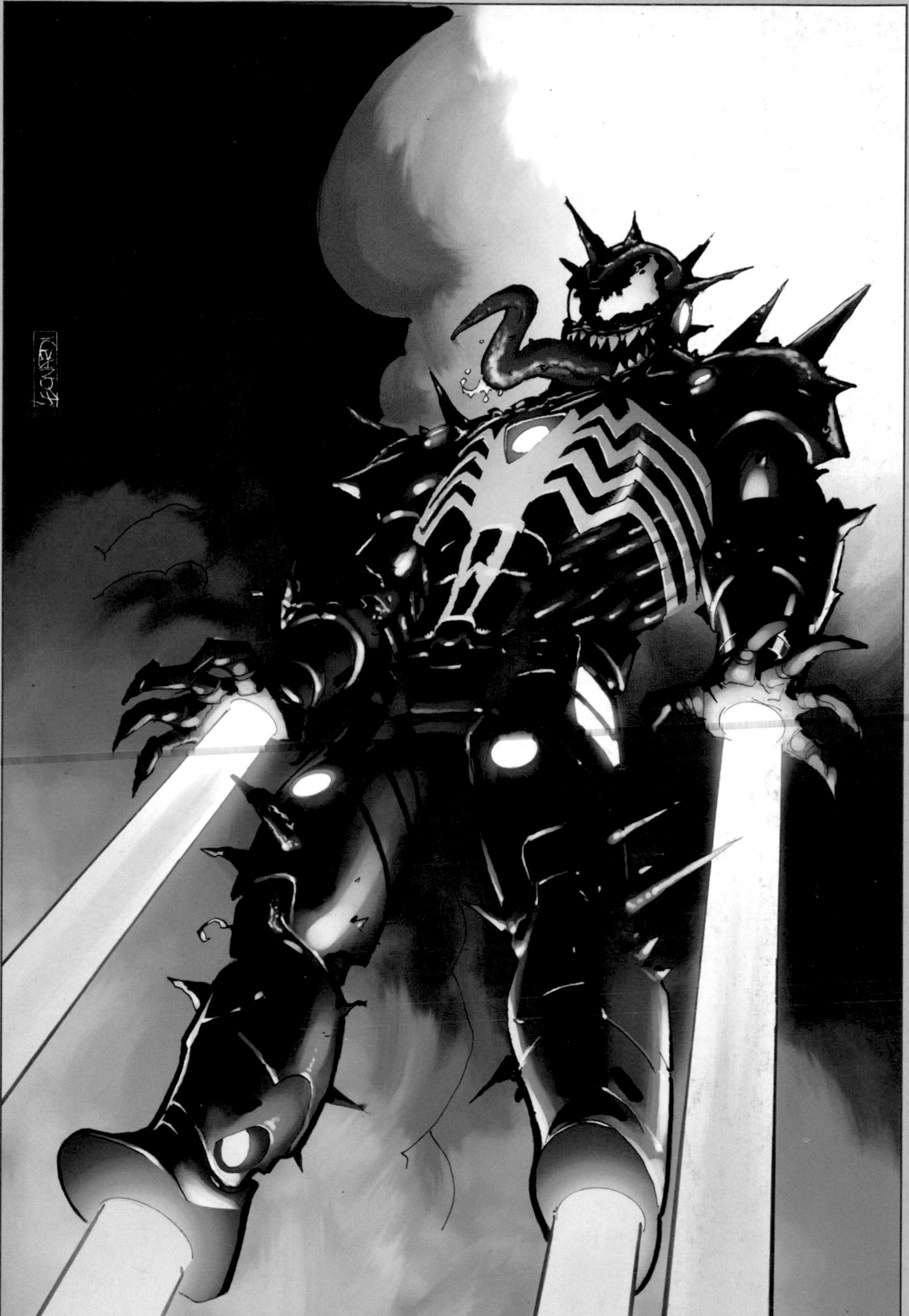

#5 VENOMIZED VARIANT
BY RICK LEONARDI & CHRIS SOTOMAYOR

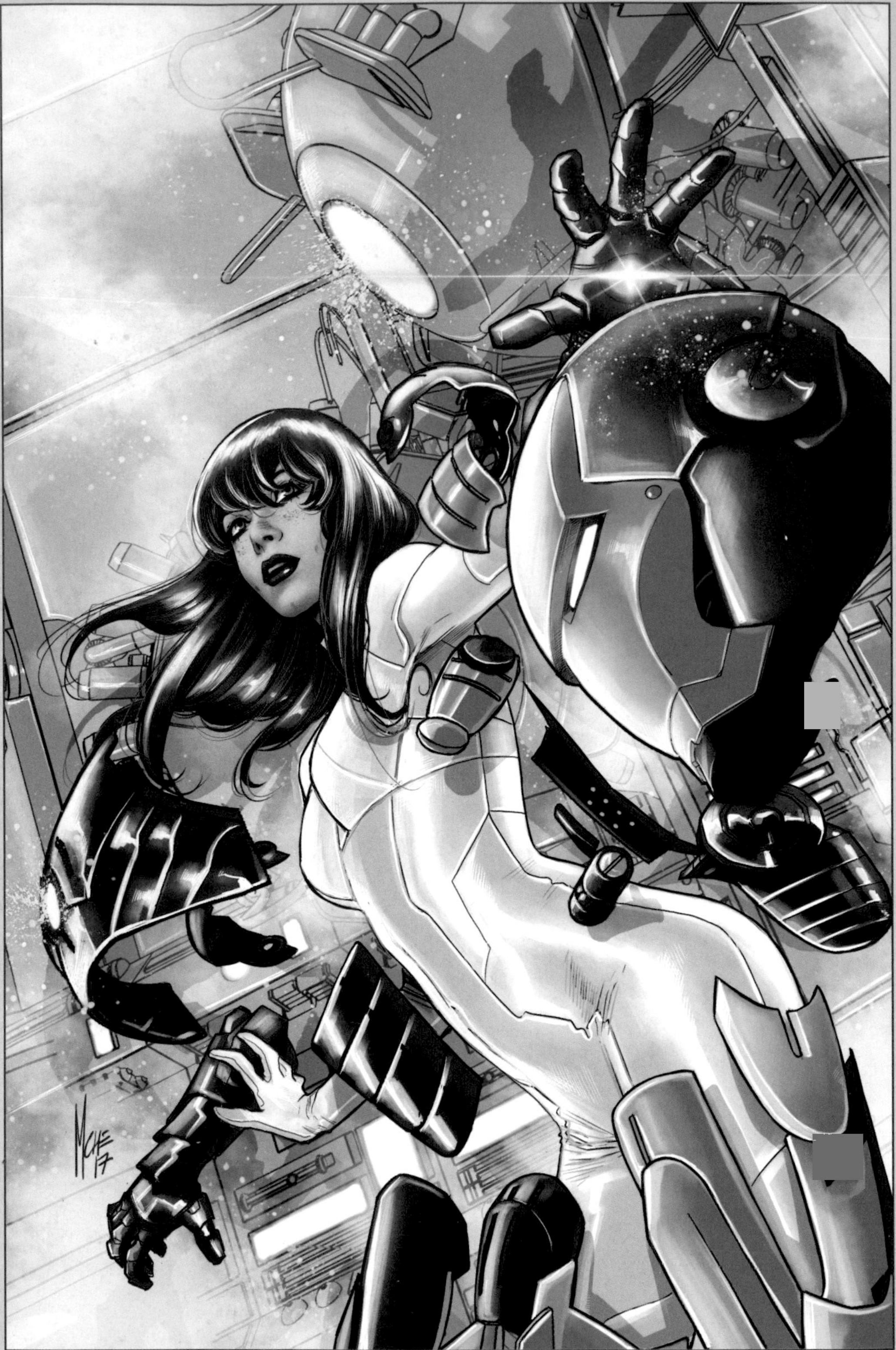

#9 MARY JANE VARIANT
BY MARCO CHECCHETTO

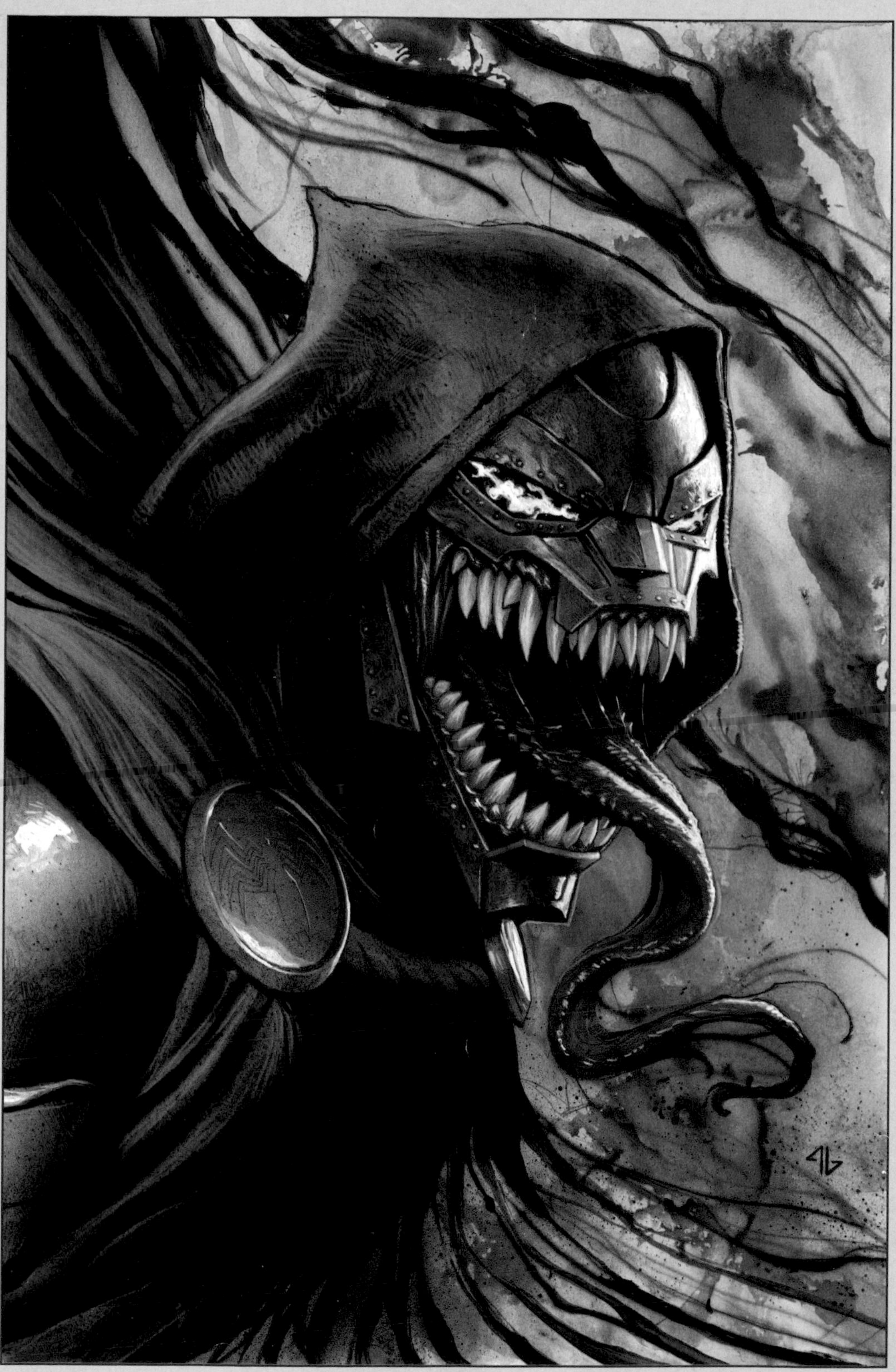

#11 VENOMIZED VILLAINS VARIANT
BY ADI GRANOV

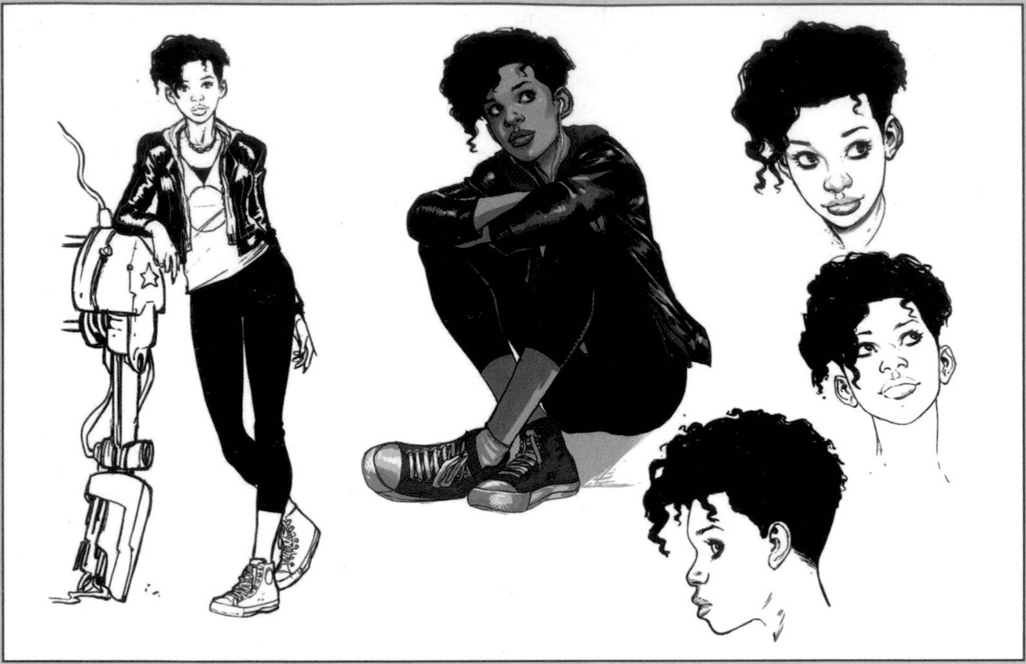

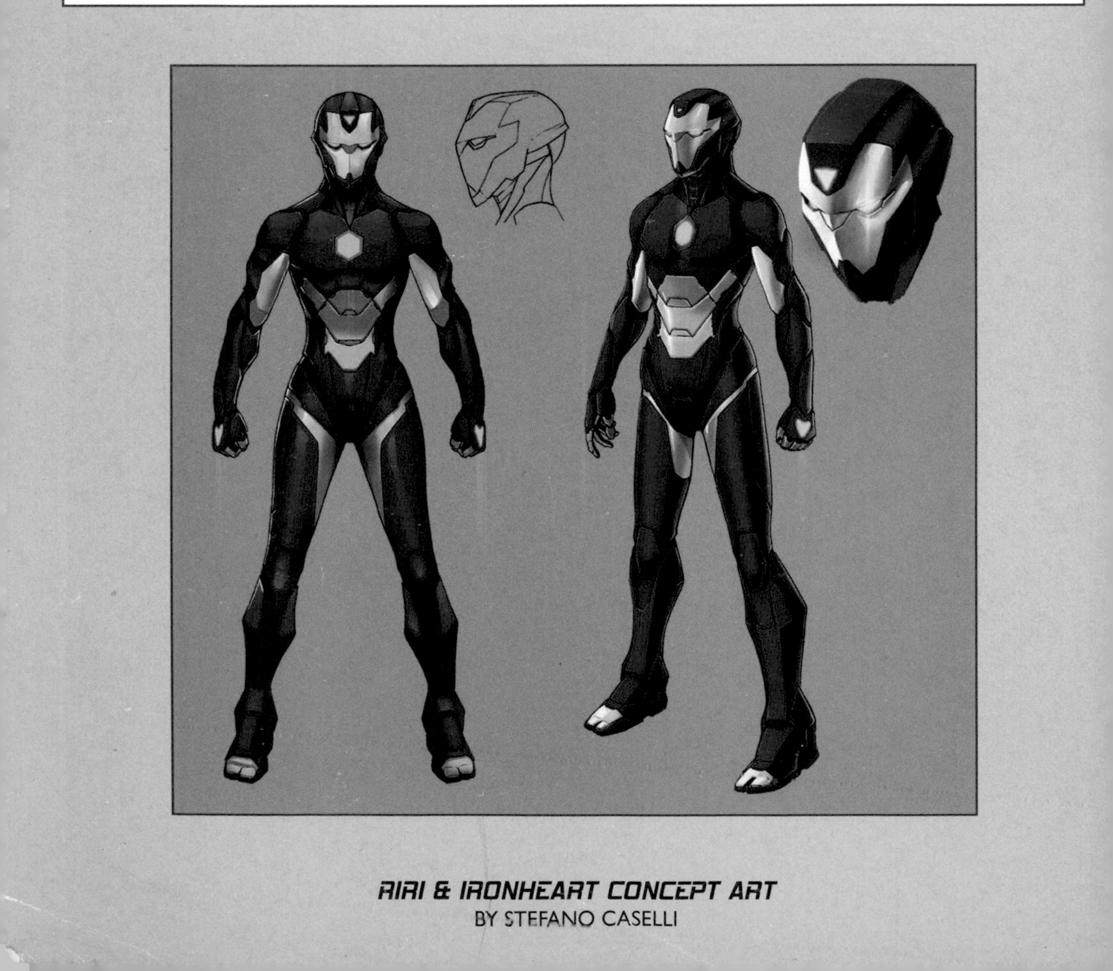

RIRI & IRONHEART CONCEPT ART
BY STEFANO CASELLI